This was serious.

Jeremy didn't hear her protest, or if he did, he didn't understand it. All he knew was that finally, after five long years, he had Maggie exactly where he'd always wanted her—beneath him. And this time, there'd be no interruptions. He'd made sure of that. No menacing uncles, no prying butlers, no self-righteous fiancés. Just Jeremy and Maggie, as it always should have been, WOULD have been, were it not for five years of stubbornness on both their parts. Well, that would never happen again, not while he had breath in his body. She was his, at last . . .

EXTRAORDINARY ACCLAIM FOR PATRICIA CABOT'S *WHERE ROSES GROW WILD*:

"A charming and delightful read from beginning to end."
—*Rendezvous*

"Passion, wit, warmth—thoroughly charming."
—Stella Cameron, author of *Wait For Me*

St. Martin's Paperbacks titles
by Patricia Cabot

WHERE ROSES GROW WILD
PORTRAIT OF MY HEART

Portrait of My Heart

PATRICIA CABOT

St. Martin's Paperbacks

PORTRAIT OF MY HEART

ISBN: 0-312-96814-0

Printed in the United States of America

St. Martin's Paperbacks edition / January 1999

St. Martin's Paperbacks are published by St. Martin's Press, 175 Fifth Avenue, New York, NY 10010.

10 9 8 7 6 5 4 3 2 1

This book is for my husband, Benjamin

Many, many thanks to Shehira Davezac of Indiana University's School of Fine Arts, who supplied much of the art-historical information contained in this book; to my friend Jennifer Brown, for reading every word; to Jennifer Weis, my editor at St. Martin's Press; and especially to my agent, Laura Langlie.

Part One

Chapter 1

"Tell me you didn't," Lord Edward Rawlings groaned, dropping his face into his hands. "Not *Oxford*, Jeremy."

Jeremy regarded his uncle worriedly from across the tavern table. He wondered if he ought to call over the barmaid and order a cup of something stronger than ale. Edward looked as if he could have used a whisky or two. It was still early yet, however, and this was the Goat and Anvil, an alehouse located just a few miles down the road from Rawlings Manor. The staff might look a little askance at the Duke of Rawlings and his uncle tossing back whiskies before noon.

"It's really not as bad as all that, you know, Uncle Edward," Jeremy said lightly. "And you can't say you didn't expect something of the kind. After all, I've already had the distinction of being sent down from Eton and Harrow. I didn't want to deprive your alma mater of the privilege, as well."

Edward didn't laugh. Jeremy hadn't really expected him to, and he studied his uncle's bent head reflectively. In the six months since Christmas, when Jeremy had last seen him, more gray than ever had seeped into the dark hair at Edward's temples. Jeremy didn't flatter himself that *he* was the cause of the discoloration. After all, his uncle was currently one of the most influential men in the House of Lords, in a position of such authority that a bit of gray was not only expected, but necessary to lend authority to a man who, at only a little over forty years of age, might otherwise be perceived as too young by his more conservative peers. But the knowledge that he was adding to his uncle's already burdensome worries didn't exactly sit well with the duke.

"Sent down from Oxford," Edward groaned again, into the foam topping his tankard of beer.

He'd been stating the phrase over and over, ever since Jeremy had casually let drop the reason for his sudden reappearance in Yorkshire. Jeremy was beginning to regret having said anything at all. He ought, he realized belatedly, to have waited until dinner at the manor house, when his aunt Pegeen would have been present, before making the announcement. While there was no one on earth whom Jeremy was more loath to disappoint than his aunt, at least she, unlike her husband, was capable of putting her nephew's many and varied misadventures into perspective. The fact that Jeremy had been sent down from Oxford wouldn't cause Pegeen so much as to raise an eyebrow. Of course, if she'd known the *reason* he'd been sent down . . . now *that* would have made her unhappy, and it was for that reason that Jeremy had chosen to meet his uncle alone before making his way to the manor house.

"Bloody hell," Edward swore, finally looking up to meet his nephew's eye, as clear gray as his own. "Did you have to *kill* the man, Jerry? Couldn't you have simply winged 'im?"

"When a man has stated that he intends to fight you unto death, Uncle," Jeremy said, with some acerbity, "it is generally considered wisest to dispatch him permanently, if at all possible. Had I winged him, he'd only recover and come after me again. And I can't spend the whole of my life looking over my shoulder for crazed assassins."

Edward shook his head. "And yet you say you never touched the girl?"

For the first time, Jeremy looked uncomfortable. Having grown up to be every bit as large as his uncle, who towered over most other men at a few inches over six feet tall, Jeremy had trouble fitting into the narrow settles at the Goat and Anvil, and had to place his elbows on the table in order to give himself breathing room. This was not, however, the reason for his current discomfort.

"Well," he said slowly. "I didn't say I never touched her—"

"Jeremy," rumbled his uncle warningly.

"—but I sure as hell didn't want to marry her! And there's the rub."

"Jeremy," Edward said again, in the deep voice Jeremy knew he reserved for Parliament and the disciplining of children. "Haven't I explained to you that there are women with whom a man may . . . er . . . dally, without exciting the expectation of marriage, and other women, with whom he'd best not associate at all unless his intentions are—"

"I know," Jeremy said, quickly cutting off a lecture he knew by heart, having heard it at least twice a month since he'd been old enough to shave. "I know, Uncle Edward. And I've certainly learned the difference over the years. But this particular young lady was introduced to me—purposely, I know now, and by her own brother, if you can imagine anything so sordid—in such a manner as would have led any man to believe she was nothing more than a charming bit of fluff to be had for the asking. She took my money readily enough, I assure you. It was only after the damage was done that Pierce came forward baying about how I'd sullied his sister's honor." Jeremy shuddered a little at the memory. "He kept insisting that I marry the hussy or meet the business end of his rapier. Is it any wonder, then, that I chose the rapier?" Jeremy lifted his tankard and sipped the yeasty brew within it. "Bad luck for Pierce he chose blades," he remarked bemusedly. "He'd have done better with pistols, I expect."

"Jeremy." Edward's face, which in the eleven years since Jeremy had first met him had grown leaner and better looking as his uncle's way of life became less dissipated, looked very stern. "You *are* aware that you've committed murder, aren't you?"

"Oh, come now, Uncle Edward," Jeremy chided. "It was a fair fight. His own second called it. And I'll admit, I lunged for his arm, not his heart. But the bloody fool tried to feint, and the next thing I knew——''

''I don't condone dueling,'' Lord Edward interrupted imperiously. ''I attempted to make that clear to you the last time this happened. And I clearly remember pointing out to you at that time that if you have to fight, do it on the Continent, for God's sake. You may be titled, but you're not above the law, you know. Now you've got no choice but to leave the country.''

''I know,'' Jeremy said, rolling his eyes. He'd heard this lecture a few dozen times, as well.

Edward didn't notice his nephew's ennui. ''I suppose the villa in Portofino would probably be best, though the apartment in Paris is currently unoccupied, I think. It's up to you. Six months ought to be enough. It's damned lucky for you, Jerry, that the college doesn't have enough evidence against you to prosecute, or——''

''Right,'' Jeremy interrupted with a sly wink. ''Or I'd be behind bars right now, instead of enjoying a tankard with my good old uncle Ed.''

''I'll thank you not to joke about it,'' Edward said severely. ''You are a duke, Jerry, and as such are vested with both privileges and responsibilities, one of which is to refrain from killing your peers.''

It was Jeremy's turn to get angry. After lowering the tankard with a thump, he banged a white-knuckled fist squarely in the center of the table and exploded. ''You think I don't know that?'' He kept his voice just low enough so as not to attract the notice of the other patrons of the alehouse. ''Do you think you haven't successfully drilled that sentiment into my head over the past decade? Since that day you showed up on our doorstep in Applesby and told Pegeen that I was the heir to the Rawlings duchy, I've heard nothing but 'You're a duke, Jerry, you can't do that,' and 'You're a duke, Jerry, you must do this.' Good God, do you have any idea how sick I am of constantly hearing what I must and must not do?''

Edward, looking a little surprised at this sudden outburst,

blinked. "No . . . But I have a feeling you're going to tell me."

"I never wanted to go away to school," Jeremy went on bitterly. "I would have been far happier at the village school here in Rawlingsgate. Yet you shipped me off to Eton, and when I got myself expelled from there, you bribed the people at Harrow and then at Winchester, and on and on until I was instructed that I was to spend the next few years of my life at college. I hadn't any interest in going to Oxford—you know I hadn't—and yet you insisted, even though it was very clear that I'm far more capable with a sword than with a pencil. And now, crime of crimes, I'm sent down from Oxford upon suspicion of dueling with a schoolmate—"

"Whom you freely admit you killed," Edward pointed out.

"Of course I killed him!" Jeremy held out both hands, palms up, in a gesture of helplessness. "Pierce was a cad and a hanger-on, and I'm not the only person who's glad he's dead, though I took no more pleasure in dispatching him than in crushing a mosquito. And you have the audacity to accuse me of joking about it. Well, what else am I to do? My entire life up till now has been a joke, hasn't it?" Jeremy glared across the table at his uncle. "Well? Hasn't it?"

Edward's features, every bit as finely chiseled and handsome as his nephew's, twisted cynically. "Oh, yes," he said, in a voice fairly dripping with sarcasm. "Your existence has been tragic, indeed. You've been unloved and unappreciated. Your aunt Pegeen sacrificed nothing for you all those years she cared for you without the slightest notion that you'd ever inherit a duchy. She didn't go without food herself in order to insure that you'd had a good breakfast—"

"Leave Pegeen out of this," Jeremy cut his uncle off quickly. "I'm not talking about Pegeen. I'm talking about how after you brought us to Rawlings, and married her, you—"

For the first time since Jeremy had told him of his expulsion, Edward looked amused. "If you're upset about the fact that I married your aunt, Jerry, I might point out that it's a bit late to change that. After all, we've already provided you with four cousins. It would be hard work to talk the archbishop into an annulment at this juncture."

Jeremy didn't laugh. "Look, Uncle Edward," he said. "Let me put it to you this way. Why did you spend all that time and money trying to find me eleven years ago, when you could easily have told people your older brother never had a child, and taken over the title yourself?"

Edward looked perplexed. "Because that would have been dishonorable. I knew that John had fathered a child before he died, and it was only right that the child should inherit his father's title."

"That's not what Sir Arthur told me," Jeremy said with a quick shake of his head. "He told me you didn't want the responsibility of being duke, and would have done anything to keep from inheriting the title."

"Well," Edward said, shrugging his shoulders uncomfortably beneath the impeccable cut of his jacket. "That isn't *strictly* true, but not far from the mark. . . ."

"Well, how do you think *I* feel?" Jeremy demanded. "*I* don't want it, either!"

"Why in God's name not?" Edward's voice was just a little too hearty. "Haven't you one of the tidiest fortunes in England? Haven't you the finest horseflesh money can buy? Haven't you a town house in London, one of the grandest manor houses in Yorkshire, an apartment in Paris as well as an Italian villa? You've got over a hundred servants, the best tailor in Europe, a seat in the House of Lords which, now that you've come of age, I will gladly relinquish to you. You've been given every privilege, every reward, that someone of your rank deserves—"

"Except the freedom to do what I want," Jeremy interrupted quietly.

"Oh, well, yes." Again, Edward's face twisted sarcastically. "That is a heavy price, indeed. But what, precisely, is it that you want to do, Jerry? Besides go about whoring and murdering people, I mean?"

It was fortunate for Jeremy that the barmaid chose that moment to approach their table. Otherwise, he might have been guilty of yet another murder.

"Is there anythin' I kin get for Yer Grace?" Rosalinde, a girl who lived up to her name by having extraordinarily pink cheeks and a rosebud mouth, smiled at the two men prettily as she bent to swipe a damp rag over the tabletop, affording Jeremy a healthy view of the valley between her plentiful breasts as she did so. "Another pot of ale, p'raps?"

"Thank you, no, Rosalinde," Jeremy said, lifting his gaze from her bosom to her face with an effort. "You, Uncle?"

"No, I'm quite all right," Edward said. *He* didn't seem to have noticed the way Rosalinde's bodice gaped in the front, Jeremy noticed with disgust. But then, Jeremy had never known his uncle to notice any woman except Pegeen.

"How's your father, Rosalinde?" Edward asked kindly. "I heard he was feeling poorly."

"Oh, 'e's doin' better, thank ye, m'lord. After 'e drunk up that tonic your lady sent over, 'e was right as rain again." Rosalinde managed to convey this message to Edward without taking her eyes off Jeremy, who had given up trying not to look at her cleavage, and was now staring steadfastly out the lead-paned window instead. "Will ye be stayin' at the manor 'ouse for a spell, Yer Grace, or are ye 'eadin' straight back to school, then?"

"I'm not at all sure," Jeremy replied stiffly. "It's likely I'll stay put for a few days, at least. . . ."

With his gaze so carefully averted, Jeremy didn't see Rosalinde's smile, or how her blue eyes shone when she gushed, "Oh, I *am* glad. An' Miss Maggie'll be glad, too. Why, just t'other day I arst 'er outside the mercantile when she might be seein' Yer Grace again, an' she said she din't rightly know, only it'd been so long she liked as if ye wouldn't recognize each other noways!"

This bit of information Jeremy responded to only with a polite nod, but that was apparently enough for Rosalinde, who drifted away from their table as if she'd suddenly grown wings. As soon as she was out of earshot, Jeremy ripped his gaze from the cart horse to which it had been riveted the entire time Rosalinde had been speaking to him and fastened it instead upon his uncle. "See?" he demanded. "See what I mean? I'm not even safe in the local pub! I have to be watching out for mercenaries everywhere I go!''

''Rosalinde Murphy is hardly a mercenary, Jerry,'' Edward replied mildly. ''I believe she has a genuine interest in your welfare.''

''Not my welfare,'' Jeremy corrected him. ''My *purse*.''

''Your per*son*,'' Edward said, with a laugh. ''The young lady's taken with you. What's so wrong with that?''

Jeremy exhaled impatiently.''Because it's not *me* she wants!'' he insisted. ''It's my money, and that damned title! Every woman I meet, the minute she learns I'm a duke, it's *Your Gracé* this and *Your Grace* that. All a woman who meets me can think about is the day when she might begin signing her name Duchess of Rawlings. I can see it in their eyes. They're already picturing themselves with a tiara on their head and ermine round their shoulders.''

''What you're seeing in their eyes, Jerry, is lust, and it's not for your title.'' Edward attempted, unsuccessfully, to stifle a chuckle. ''Look at yourself, Jerry. You might still consider yourself the scrawny little scamp you were when you were ten, but Rosalinde sees someone entirely different. She sees a tall, robust young man, with dark hair and light eyes and a good set of teeth—''

''I hardly think Rosalinde Murphy has ever noticed my teeth,'' Jeremy muttered, to cover the embarrassment he felt at his uncle's assurances.

''Perhaps not,'' Edward laughed. ''But you're still a fine figure of a man, Jerry, and you can't expect women not to respond to that. And when they do, don't automatically dismiss that interest as purely pecuniary in nature.''

Jeremy, thoroughly embarrassed now, muttered into his beer, ''Well, being a duke certainly doesn't make that kind of thing any easier. I mean, my God, I can't even marry whom I choose! I have to marry a woman who'd make a decent duchess.''

''True,'' Edward said. ''But that doesn't necessarily follow that it's impossible for one to find marital bliss with the kind of woman who'd make a decent duchess.'' Thoughtfully, he lifted his tankard. ''I managed to do it, after all.''

''Too bad my father wasn't as discriminating,'' Jeremy

commented bitterly. "Of a pair of sisters, he managed to pick the one who'd eventually end up getting him killed."

Edward cleared his throat uncomfortably as he set the tankard down again. "Yes, well. Pegeen was only ten years old, I believe, when John first came calling on your mother, so I don't believe she was much in the running." Then, as if remembering something, Edward leaned forward and said, in a completely different tone of voice, "You're not to tell your aunt why it was you were sent down this time, Jerry."

"As if I would," Jeremy said bitterly. "The last thing I'd want is for Aunt Pegeen to know. But she's bound to find out anyway. It will probably make the papers."

"Certainly it will make the papers," Edward said with a curt nod. "That's different, however, than you coming straight out and admitting it. That's the only way Pegeen'd ever believe *you* were capable of murder."

"Right," Jeremy agreed, with a smile every bit as cynical as his uncle's had been earlier. "Me, the boy who cried for hours after his first hunt, because he felt so sorry for the fox."

"You didn't cry for all that long," Edward said, shifting in his seat, a little uncomfortable at the memory of that fateful day. "But you're right. It's hard to reconcile what you were then to what you are now."

Jeremy's gaze was still sarcastic. "And what am I now, Uncle?"

"That's up to you, isn't it?" Edward took another sip of his beer, then asked, "What sort of man do you want to be?"

"One who isn't a duke," Jeremy responded promptly.

"But that," Edward said, "isn't possible."

Jeremy nodded as if this were the response he'd expected. Without another word, he started to slide from the settle. Edward looked up at him, surprised. "Where are you going?" he asked.

"To the devil," Jeremy informed him casually.

"Ah," Edward said with a nod. He settled more deeply into his seat, and lifted his tankard in a solemn toast to his nephew's departing back. "Be home in time for dinner, then."

Chapter 2

*O*h, Maggie!'' Lady Edward Rawlings cried, as she brushed aside the tissue paper surrounding the small canvas. ''Oh! Oh, it's lovely!''

Maggie Herbert, her freckled nose wrinkled skeptically, looked down at the painting from where she stood behind Pegeen's chair. Too much green, she thought. Yes, entirely too much green in the background. As she scrutinized the painting, a white blossom spiraled down from the branches stretched overhead, and settled upon the freshly dried canvas. Maggie thought the petal an improvement, but Pegeen impatiently swept it away.

''Oh, I can't wait to show it to Edward,'' Pegeen declared, her gaze still locked upon the painting. ''He simply won't believe it. I don't think any of the other portraits we've had done of the children captures them quite as accurately as this one—''

''Really?'' Maggie's tone was mildly incredulous. She narrowed her eyes until the image on the canvas blurred, but she could still see only a series of shapes and colors she'd laid down the day before, and not the whole of the painting that Pegeen was raving over. And too much green.

''Oh, yes,'' Pegeen assured her. ''Why, it's as if you were able to capture their little souls!''

Maggie laughed. ''Oh, hardly! If I'd done that, Lizzie would look completely different. As it is, she looks too sweet by far—''

"What do you mean, too sweet?" Pegeen lifted the canvas, which was only six inches by another six, and held it out at arm's length, still so entranced by it that she could not look away. "Lizzie looks perfectly adorable. John, too. Oh, and look at Mary's little pout! And Alistair's chin. You've captured it exactly! I've overheard *some* people calling Alistair's chin stubborn, you know, but it's just firm, that's all."

Maggie lifted her gaze and fastened it upon the face of her mother, who sat in a wrought-iron lawn chair opposite Pegeen's. The smile Lady Herbert returned was every bit as knowing as Maggie's. All of the Rawlings children's chins were inevitably thrust out stubbornly in unconscious imitation of their mother's expression when she was at her most intractable, and the fact that Pegeen refused to recognize this was the source of some amusement among her friends and neighbors.

"Oh, Maggie," Pegeen sighed, still unable to take her eyes off the portrait. "It's just beautiful. I don't know how you do it."

"I don't know how she does it, either." Lady Herbert leaned forward to pour out another cup of tea from the silver service on the small folding table that had been set up between the lawn chairs. Since Pegeen was expecting—though not as soon as Maggie's elder sister, Anne, who sat opposite Lady Herbert, her teacup and saucer balanced on the generous swell of her stomach—the older woman had automatically taken on the duties of hostess, though in fact both she and her daughters were Pegeen's guests at the manor house where Sir Arthur, Maggie's father, worked as solicitor to the young duke's estate. The Herberts spent so much time at Rawlings Manor that Maggie had long come to consider it her second home, and tended to treat it as such, a fact that did not sit particularly well with the very ladylike Anne, particularly when she found her youngest sister sliding down banisters, which up until a year or two ago had occurred all too frequently.

"She certainly didn't inherit the talent from me," Maggie's mother declared, stirring sugar into her tea. "It must come from her father's side of the family."

"Papa?" Anne looked uncomfortable, as she always did whenever her youngest sister's talent with a paintbrush was mentioned. "Certainly not! No, one on Papa's side of the family ever took up *painting*. Goodness, Mamma. How could you make such a suggestion?"

Maggie, turning her gaze back down to the little portrait she'd rendered, shook her head. "No, Lizzie's smile isn't right," she murmured to herself. "Not nearly wicked enough."

Unfortunately, Lizzie's mother overheard.

"Wicked!" Pegeen cried, snatching the painting to her chest, as if she feared Maggie might try to take it away to make adjustments. "Nonsense. There isn't a wicked bone in my daughter's body. She's a little angel. They're *all* little angels." Seeing that Maggie had no intention of retrieving her gift, Pegeen snuck another peek, and immediately launched into further raptures. "Oh, Anne, look at the way she's done John's eyes. Have you ever seen anything so uncanny?"

Maggie, still unconvinced, looked away from the painting and toward the rest of the garden, where Pegeen's "little angels" were currently engaged in tearing up one of the rose beds. They were joined in their efforts by Anne's children, though Maggie's well-behaved nieces and nephew were considerably less boisterous than the Rawlings brood, and by approximately fifteen orphans from the Rawlings Foundling Home, whom Lady Pegeen was entertaining to a May Day picnic on the manor house grounds. A single glance at Pegeen and Edward's eldest child told Maggie that she had, indeed, erred on the side of sweetness. Elizabeth Rawlings was a pretty girl, but obviously as headstrong as both of her parents. This was illustrated by the clod of dirt she promptly launched in her brother John's direction when he failed effectively to carry out her orders.

"And have you managed to talk your father into letting you attend that Parisian art school you were telling me about, Maggie?" Pegeen wanted to know.

"No," Maggie said. She couldn't keep a note of sullenness from creeping into her voice. "He's terrified that the moment I set foot off English soil unescorted, I shall allow myself to be seduced and whisked off to Morocco and sold as chattel to some Arab prince."

"Maggie!" Anne's teacup went crashing back into its saucer.

Lady Herbert echoed her eldest daughter's astonishment, though in a considerably milder tone of voice: "Really, Maggie. What in heaven's name are you talking about? Your father thinks no such thing."

"He does, though," Maggie said, leaning back against the trunk of the cherry tree with a sigh. "Papa's quite aware of my peculiarly carnal inclinations."

"Maggie!" Anne's cheeks had gone crimson with mortification. "How many times do I have to beg you not to use words like . . . like"—her voice dropped to a whisper—"*carnal* in public conversation?" Turning toward Pegeen, she pleaded, "Oh, do stop laughing, Lady Edward. You'll only encourage her."

"Oh!" Pegeen wiped tears of laughter from the corners of her green eyes. "Oh, dear! Maggie, my dear, you mustn't, you really mustn't say things like that. You'll end up getting a reputation—"

"With whom?" Maggie asked disgustedly. "The local tenant farmers? I hardly think *they* care whether or not I use the word *carnal*."

"Not the tenant farmers, Maggie dear," Lady Herbert said gently. "Young men."

"What young men?" Maggie reached behind her and began scraping bark away from the cherry-tree trunk with a sharp stick she'd found in the fresh spring grass. "The only young men around here are the ones herding sheep, and I'll wager there's not much *they* don't know about carnality."

"Maggie!" Anne looked as if she would have very much liked to pinch her little sister. Unfortunately, the size of her swollen belly forbade quick movements, and she knew from past experience that she'd have had to be very quick indeed if she wanted to pinch Maggie and escape a reciprocal slap. "For heaven's sake!"

Maggie shrugged. "Well," she said. "It's the truth."

"Yes, but you're nearly seventeen, now, dear." Anne spoke with obviously forced patience. "You'll be coming out next year. The young men you'll meet during your first season in London won't care to hear about your, er, inclinations—"

"Actually," Pegeen interrupted thoughtfully, "I'm quite certain they'd *love* hearing about it, but I'm not sure it's something Maggie ought to go about advertising. . . ."

"There," Anne declared. "You hear that, Maggie? Listen to Lady Edward. It's what I've been trying to tell you all along. If you're going to find yourself a husband in London, you're going to have to start acting more like a lady—"

"I don't *want* to act like a lady," Maggie muttered, the full of her concentration on the hole she was gouging in the trunk of the tree. "If acting like a lady means doing nothing all day but attend dress fittings—" She grunted as a good chunk of bark gave way beneath the point of her stick. "And nothing all night but listen to the insipid conversation of idiotic baronets—"

"What are you doing to that tree?" Lady Herbert demanded. "Come sit down and put away that dirty stick."

Maggie dropped the stick, but she did not sit down. Instead, she pressed her back against the hole she'd made in the tree trunk. She didn't know why she'd felt compelled to take out her aggression upon an innocent tree, but she felt that, overall, the tree was a better choice than her elder sister.

"If you don't want to act like a lady, Margaret," Maggie's mother inquired, with some amusement, "what *do* you want to do?"

"I *told* you, Mamma." Maggie sighed. "I want to paint. That's *all* I want to do. And I want to go to Madame Bonheur's to learn to do it right."

Lady Herbert lifted her gaze heavenward, but it was Anne who burst out, "But Madame Bonheur's art academy is out of the question! Mamma, you *must* tell her, and be *firm* this time. Maggie *must* not be allowed to—"

"But why?"

Pegeen sounded impatient. Maggie couldn't help smiling. It seemed as if Lady Edward Rawlings was forever finding some new cause for which to campaign, and today she'd chosen Maggie.

"Why is it out of the question? It's perfectly ridiculous to waste talent like your sister's, Anne. Why, Maggie's a thousand times more skilled than that silly little painter Edward hired to do my portrait last year. Look at the colors in this painting she's done of the children." Pegeen held the canvas out for the other women to see. "The way she's mixed them so that each one looks like a separate jewel. And the way she's captured the children's expressions—why, it's more accurate than any daguerreotype!"

"I perfectly agree with you, Pegeen," Lady Herbert said a bit tiredly. "But—"

"Sir Arthur doesn't have some silly old-fashioned notion about not wasting money educating a girl, has he?" Pegeen demanded. "Because if he has, I will gladly march right over to Herbert Park and enlighten him—"

"It isn't just that, Pegeen," Anne said, solemnly. "Papa doesn't approve of women pursuing occupations outside the home, and an occupation in the arts—Heavens! The very mention of it sends him into apoplexies. But I must say, I can't help but agree with him. It's quite scandalous, really, the number of girls going to London to pursue livings as nurses and clerks and teachers, and, oh, I don't know what all! But I suppose they can't help it—they *need* the work, you know, to survive. But Maggie? She doesn't *need* to work at all. She simply *wants* to, which is, of course, perfectly ridiculous. Everyone knows the only avocation for which women are suited is motherhood—"

"Yes, dear," Lady Herbert interrupted. Her smile was tolerant. "We're all quite aware of your feelings on the importance of motherhood. But I believe your father's primary objection to Maggie's going away is just that she's the youngest of you girls. She's the only one still at home." Lady Herbert smiled fondly at Maggie, who was squinting up at the cherry blossoms overhead. "We none of us are quite prepared to let her grow up just yet."

"Well, you're going to have to let her go eventually," Pegeen said. "I mean, if she's to come out next season."

Lady Herbert made a suffering noise as she lifted a piece of cake to her lips. "And if I know Maggie," she sighed, after she'd brought the fork back down to the plate in her lap, "she'll hate every minute of *that*."

Pegeen did not laugh. "Of course she'll hate it. A girl like Maggie—"

"A girl like Maggie won't last a minute in London," Maggie mimicked, annoyed that everyone was talking *about* her, while no one talked *to* her. "The *haut monde* will rip her apart. The other girls will snicker at her, because she's too tall and too loud and has paint under her fingernails, and the men, if they pay her any mind at all, will be disgusted by the fact that she uses words like *carnal* in public conversation."

"Oh, no," Pegeen cried. "Surely not, Maggie! Why, you're so very pretty, with all of that dark hair, and those big brown eyes. You're far prettier than the eldest Smythe girl, and look how well *she* married. . . ."

"What does it matter what she looks like?" Anne asked pointedly. "The minute Maggie opens her mouth, the room has a tendency to empty. She's far too outspoken—"

"She's not," Pegeen protested. "She merely states her mind. She always has." She turned her head to smile back at Maggie. "That's why I like her so."

Anne, however, was doing anything *but* smiling at her youngest sister. "She says the first thing that pops into her head, without a thought to the consequences, and generally when no one has asked her opinion in the first place."

"She's refreshingly honest," Lady Herbert said, coming to Maggie's defense.

"Mother, she hasn't any sort of sense of decency! The other day I caught her with the hem of her gown tucked up inside the waistband of her unmentionables, climbing a tree!"

The faces of all three women swung accusingly in Maggie's direction. Straightening, she said, with as much dignity as she could muster, "I needed blossoms. For a still life I was doing."

"Margaret," her mother chided. "*Really*. You *do* go a little too far sometimes. You could have asked the gardener to bring you a bough of blossoms."

"I think," Maggie said, swallowing, "I shall go and see what the children are up to."

"I think you should do that, dear," Lady Herbert agreed, so readily that it was obvious to Maggie that her mother had every intention of talking about her as soon as she was out of earshot.

Sighing, Maggie pushed herself away from the tree, and began wandering in the direction from which she could hear the children shouting. It was an unnaturally hot day for May, the first really warm weather of the spring thus far, and Maggie had been feeling somewhat lethargic since morning. Part of her lethargy, she knew, was due to boredom. Since finishing the portrait of the Rawlings children, she really hadn't had anything to do, no new projects on the horizon. Oh, there was the portrait old Dame Ashforth wanted done, but it was of two cats, and Maggie hadn't much interest in painting cats. Painting people was so much more challenging, getting their expression exactly right, rendering an accurate likeness without actually insulting them . . . now *that* was interesting. Cats were just too easy.

As she approached the children, Maggie saw that Elizabeth, whose smile she'd rendered too sweetly, had her brother's head locked beneath her arm. Their nurse and the orphanage attendants were nowhere to be seen. Knowing the children as well as she did, Maggie wouldn't have been surprised to learn that they'd left the poor young women gagged and tied in the shrubbery maze. Sighing, she lifted the hem of her white muslin gown and hurried forward to rescue the shrieking little boy from his sister's tyranny.

"But he keeps saying *he*'s the prime minister," Lizzie declared when Maggie remonstrated her. "But *I'm* supposed to be the prime minister today. Mamma said I might!"

"But girls can't be prime ministers," John insisted. "Papa said so!"

Maggie, recalling similar arguments between herself and the Duke of Rawlings, many years earlier, looked down at John and said, "Why don't we play something else instead of Parliament today? What would you think about playing a game your cousin Jerry and I used to play, back when he and I were little?"

Lizzie, who had to crane her neck to see Maggie's face, looked curious. "You mean *you* were little once?" she asked in disbelief. "But you're so tall!"

Maggie, trying to hide her annoyance, muttered, "I'm not all that tall."

"Yes, you are," John declared. "You're taller than Papa."

"I am *not* taller than your father," Maggie said, her irritation mounting. "Your mother, maybe. But not your father."

"You are," John said staunchly. "Isn't she, Lizzie?"

Elizabeth looked Maggie up and down and finally said, "No, she isn't. But she's still *very* tall. For a girl, that is."

Maggie felt herself flush, and then was angry with herself for letting the innocent prattle of children irritate her. She knew she was far too sensitive about her height. So what if she had always been the tallest girl in her school? At least she'd stopped growing. At five feet eight—a height she'd achieved at the age of ten—she was taller than her mother and all of her sisters, and only a little shorter than her father.

But there were undoubtedly advantages in being so tall. She knew she looked very nice indeed in the new half-crinolines that had come into style, the ones that were straight in front but ballooned out in back, a fashion that suited her curvaceous figure very well. And she could always be counted on to reach items on the highest shelves at the mercantile, a plus while shopping.

"Listen," Maggie said to the Rawlings children. "When your cousin Jerry and I were young, we used to play a game called Maharajah, and it was a good deal of fun. One of you can be the Indian prince or princess. Someone else can be the intrepid English explorer whom the maharajah captures and ties to a stake to be burned alive in tribute to a pagan god. And the rest of you can be British soldiers who try to rescue him, or savages who dance around the burning pyre and try to shoot the soldiers with poisoned darts. Doesn't that sound like fun?''

"*I* shall be the maharajah,'' Lizzie announced.

"No,'' John shouted. "*I* shall!''

"You,'' Lizzie said, calmly, "can be the intrepid explorer.''

John promptly became as infuriated as Jeremy used to become when Maggie had insisted that he be the explorer. Feeling that she'd done her duty, Maggie turned and started back toward the group of women seated beneath the shade of the cherry tree, but not before their lilting voices arrested her mid-step.

"There's nothing the least bit improper about lady portrait painters, Anne,'' she heard Pegeen say in her distinctive, throaty voice, her soft Scottish accent slightly blurring her vowels. "There've been any number of them, you know, throughout history—''

Anne interrupted, indignantly, "And how many of them ever married, I'd like to know? Very few, I'll wager. A woman can't have a marriage as well as an occupation.''

"Perhaps not,'' was Pegeen's thoughtful reply. "Unless she marries very wisely, that is. To a man who understands. . . .'' Then, in a more cheerful voice, she added, "But the nice thing is that, talented as she is, Maggie need never marry at all. I mean, unless she wants to. She could support herself quite nicely doing portraits of society children.''

Aware that they really were talking about her, Maggie felt her cheeks begin to burn once more. She knew she ought to announce herself, but the temptation to eavesdrop was just too great. Feigning a sudden interest in a stalk of irises, Maggie strained her ears to overhear what was being said.

"But that's exactly what I'm most afraid of, Pegeen,'' Anne exclaimed. "You know how unconventional Maggie can be. Supposing she falls in love with some starving French poet, and has to live in a nasty garret near Montmartre with a lot of other artistic types? None of them believe in the institution of marriage, you know. They think it bourgeois. Maggie will be a fallen woman. And what will people say about us then, I'd like to know?''

Pegeen inhaled to reply, but Lady Herbert said quickly, ''Really, Anne, you're being too hard on your sister. She isn't a silly girl. I think it entirely unlikely that she'd do anything as stupid as fall in love with a Frenchman.''

Anne did not share her mother's opinion. ''She'll do far stupider things than that, Mamma. On that you may count. You and Papa have let her run completely wild. Kindly don't try denying it, I've seen it with my own eyes! You've spoiled her, Mamma. How else can you explain it? None of us, not Elizabeth nor I nor Fanny nor Claire are anywhere near as stubborn and headstrong as Maggie is.''

''Well,'' Lady Herbert said thoughtfully. ''None of you had quite the same *influence* Maggie had, either. . . .''

Lady Herbert's voice trailed off, but Maggie wasn't the only one who caught her meaning. Pegeen was quick to rush to her nephew's defense. ''Oh, you mean Jerry, I suppose,'' she said airily. ''Well, it's true the two of them were thick as thieves at one time. But I do have to say that despite the fact Jerry was so much older, it always seemed to me that *Maggie* was the one running things. She was so much bigger than he was for so long. You know, I once caught her rubbing his face quite forcibly in some dirt. Jerry was perfectly helpless to stop her. He was twelve at the time, I believe, which would have made Maggie only about seven, but even so, she was taller than he was, I do think it was rather humiliating to him, at the time. . . .''

''I suppose we won't be seeing His Grace anytime soon,'' Anne ventured, in a deceptively casual voice. Maggie knew perfectly well how much her sister disliked the duke. ''He's still at Oxford, is he?''

''As a matter of fact,'' Pegeen said calmly, ''we received a wire from him just last night, saying he was coming home today. According to Lucy, who heard it from Cook, whose nephew has been acting as Jerry's valet this term, there was some sort of secret assignation between Jerry and his uncle just this morning, which necessitated that Edward sneak down to the village to meet the carriage an hour ago, ostensibly so I would not learn the reason for Jerry's sudden return. It shall be interesting to see how long the two of them think they can keep it a secret from me this time.''

Maggie didn't hear the rest of the conversation. She didn't stop to listen to it. The moment she heard Jeremy's name, and the fact that he was on his way back to Rawlings, a slow smile spread across her face, and her feet, as if of their own accord, began moving briskly toward the front of the house. She was well aware that if Jeremy were coming home today, he would have to ride through the allée of oak trees that lined the drive. Which meant he'd have to pass under one of the oldest oaks on the estate, the one that leaned so closely to the drive—despite the best efforts of the gardeners, who for years had tried to prop up the trunk with metal supports—that its branches hung like a canopy only seven or eight feet from the paved road. Wouldn't it be fun, she thought, to ambush him, the way they'd used to attack the traffic approaching the manor house when they were children? With any luck, she'd be able to knock him flat off his horse. No more than he deserved, for getting himself thrown out of yet another school, if what Pegeen had said was correct.

Forgetting all of her sister's exhortations to act like a lady, Maggie hiked up her skirts and began running across the front lawn of Rawlings Manor, perfectly heedless of the fact that her long, shapely calves were showing above the tops of her flat-heeled boots. It had been so long since she'd last seen Jeremy—years, in fact, since their school holidays had generally never coincided, or when they had, one or the other of them had nearly always been in the city or abroad—that she wasn't even sure she'd recognize him. If one could believe his aunt and uncle's proud reports, Jeremy had turned into everything a young gentleman ought to be: a skilled equestrian, superb fencer, excellent boxer, strong swimmer. She'd heard rumors from her elder sisters, who had occasionally run into him at society balls in London, that the Duke of Rawlings had matured into an extraordinarily good-looking man, a fact Maggie found hard to believe. Even more laughably, they insisted that he had actually grown tall, which she believed not at all. Jerry, taller than she? Impossible!

After she'd shimmied up the oak's trunk, a feat Maggie performed easily, despite ripping one stocking, tearing her crinoline, and popping a pearl button from the front of her bodice, all of which she ignored, it was the work of a moment to settle herself in the leafy shelter of its branches. From this perch, some eight feet off the ground, Maggie had a fairly unimpeded view of the driveway, down which a lone horseman was cantering, even as she watched. But it couldn't, she saw with disappointment, be Jeremy, since the rider was far too broad shouldered, and too tall in the saddle, besides. It looked a good deal like Lord Edward, only Lord Edward's horse was a bay, and the horse this man was riding was black as pitch . . . not unlike Jeremy's mount, King.

Leaning forward until she lay fully stretched out along the sturdy branch, Maggie squinted past the green foliage and saw, to her utter astonishment, that the horse really *was* none other than King, the first horse Jeremy had ever owned, and his admitted favorite. But no one was allowed to ride King except Jeremy, and that meant . . .

But no! It couldn't be. No one could change that much, not in only—Maggie looked down at her fingers, counting swiftly—five years. Lord, had it really been *five years* since she'd last seen the duke? Looking up again, Maggie saw that the horse and rider were very nearly beneath her now, and there was no mistaking it, it *was* Jeremy.

And her sisters hadn't been lying, he *was* good-looking . . . if one liked those kind of Byronic, brooding types, which Maggie did not, preferring fair-complexioned men. His dark hair curled raffishly out from under an expensive-looking top hat, beneath the brim of which his piercing gray-eyed gaze stared derisively. His expression was one she recognized instantly. Jeremy was angry, his determined jaw set, his clefted chin held high above a frilled cravat, his long, gloved fingers curled easily round the reins of his mount, which he rode as naturally as if King were an extension of his own body. A body which, Maggie observed with interest, looked every bit as lean and as hard as those belonging to the men who worked at the local blacksmith, men whose naked chests Maggie had often observed surreptitiously while they hammered out shoes for her father's horses. . . .

Lord, there went another one of those carnal thoughts!

But this was *Jerry*! She shook herself. What was she *thinking*? She couldn't possibly be thinking of *Jeremy* that way! She had pounded that body down there with snowballs more times than she could count, and rubbed that face in the dirt just as often. And now he was riding directly beneath her, so close she could easily have knocked the hat from his head. In another second, he'd shoot right past her, and the surprise would be utterly ruined.

Without further hesitation, Maggie swept down an arm, intending to seize his hat and have a good laugh at his reaction. Unfortunately, at the same moment she leaned down, she lost her balance, and felt herself slipping from the branch. Frantically, she tried to cling to the limb, but to no avail. A second later, she was sailing through the air. . . .

Chapter 3

Jeremy's first thought, when he heard the shriek and then felt the impact of a body against his, was that, somehow, Pierce had come back from the dead and was finally getting even with him for both the defloration of his sister and his own subsequent murder. Accordingly, Jeremy twisted about in the saddle and attempted to sling his adversary away. His progress in doing so, however, was hampered by the fact that his assailant had wrapped a pair of smooth, sun-kissed arms tightly about his neck, and was doing an excellent job of dragging them both down to the ground.

At what point Jeremy became aware that his attacker had both waist-length hair and quite sizable breasts, he was never afterward exactly certain, but it was probably at about the point both of their bodies hit the driveway and rolled a few feet into the grass in a tangle of crinoline, skirts, and coat-tails. The wind partially knocked out of him, it took Jeremy a moment before he became aware that he was lying on top of a body that, unless Pierce had sprouted a bosom in the afterlife, was quite obviously female. In fact, his face, before he lifted it, had been resting between two cantaloupe-sized breasts that seemed to have sprung loose from the bodice that had been confining them and, despite the fact that their owner was lying in a prone position, still reached quite perkily for the sun.

Although this was, to say the least, a pleasant sensation, Jeremy knew that if he had had the wind knocked out of him, the woman beneath him had probably been knocked unconscious by the force of their landing, and so he did the gentlemanly thing, and lifted his head to see whether or not he could render her some aid . . .

. . . and found himself staring straight into a pair of laughing, and strangely familiar, brown eyes.

"You great sow!" a lilting voice, oddly sweet for the taunts it was uttering, mocked him. "You bellowed like a stuck pig. I've never heard anything like it."

For a moment, Jeremy truly did believe he was looking at a ghost. Only a supernatural being could so closely resemble someone he thought he knew, and yet not look like her at all. For the woman lying beneath him was undoubtedly Maggie Herbert—Maggie Herbert was the only female he knew who'd not hesitate to call him a great sow—and yet not Maggie Herbert, not the Maggie Herbert who'd spent the whole of her childhood tormenting him. *That* Maggie Herbert, the last time he'd seen her, had been gap-toothed and rail thin, with pigtails on either side of her head and legs so long and gangling that she'd hardly known what to do with them, causing her to resemble a newborn foal taking her first steps every time she walked.

But *this* Maggie Herbert had a body as lush and as full as any high-priced courtesan—and Jeremy had been with more than a few of them, and so knew whereof he spoke. There was no longer any hint of coltishness about her, and Jeremy would be the first to testify that the legs he lay so snugly between were anything but gangling. In fact, the thighs that had parted beneath the weight of his body were very much in keeping with every other part of her against which he was pressed—supple, strong, but ultimately very, very feminine. Maggie Herbert had blossomed, he realized, into what one might call a bosomy girl, but having been graced with slim wrists and ankles, and an infinitesimally small waist, she carried off the look better than a lot of other women Jeremy had known, not seeming the least self-conscious about her new womanly curves . . . but also seemingly unaware of the devastating effect those curves could have on a man.

It was only when he glanced at her face that Jeremy realized that this Maggie and the one he remembered were one and the same. Gone were the braids, it was true, replaced by a curtain of chestnut hair so deep brown as to look almost black against the new green grass, and as for her teeth, they were even and white now, without a gap to be seen. But there was a glint in those dark eyes that he recognized: a flash of something too good-natured to be malice, but too mischievous to be purely ingenuous. And there was a twist to those lips, which at one time he'd thought too wide by half, but which, upon more recent inspection, he found quite temptingly plump, that harkened back to the Maggie of old, the one who'd teased and tortured him unmercifully and against whom, because she was a girl, he'd been told he could not retaliate.

And now it appeared that merely by growing up, Maggie Herbert had won yet again, because he had never in his life seen a woman who struck him as quite so handsome . . . and yet remained quite so oblivious to his own charms.

"Oh!" Maggie exclaimed, laughing breathlessly. "The look on your face! It was priceless, simply priceless!"

Rising up onto his elbows, his face still only a few inches from her remarkable new bosom, Jeremy inquired, quite seriously, "Have you gone mad?"

When her only response was to laugh harder, he remarked, "You might have killed yourself, you know."

"It would have been worth it," Maggie replied with relish. She was laughing so hard that Jeremy, still sprawled on top of her, could feel her stomach muscles spasming beneath her corset stays. Maggie Herbert, in a corset! He never thought he'd live to see the day.

"Nevertheless," he said severely. "You can't go bashing about like that. You could have seriously injured yourself."

"Oh, la. You never could take a joke. I see all that fancy schooling hasn't changed *that*, anyway." After brushing some tangles of dark hair off her heart-shaped face, Maggie struggled up to her own elbows, which caused the bodice of her dress to gap open even more dramatically, affording Jeremy a splendid view of what lay in the lace cups of her camisole. Unlike earlier in the day, he was perfectly incapable of looking away this time, and instead of climbing off her, as he undoubtedly should have, he lay exactly where he was and admired the twin curves of soft white flesh.

It only took Maggie a second or two to notice that Jeremy's eyes, which she had always considered a somewhat bland shade of gray, were actually not quite as colorless as she'd remembered. They were really a very subtle shade of light blue, with small dashes of silver within them—and they were not focused anywhere near her face. They appeared, in fact, to be glued to her chest. When Maggie followed the direction of their gaze, she saw that the button she'd lost climbing the oak had actually been a rather integral one, and that her considerable cleavage was spilling out from beneath the front of her white dress.

Instantly, Maggie found herself drowning in a flood of conflicting emotions. On the one hand, there was a comic element to the situation that even in the throes of the excruciating embarrassment which immediately consumed her, Maggie could not fail to recognize. Bare-breasted in front of the Duke of Rawlings! What would Lady Herbert say? On the other hand, there wasn't anything comical about the way the Duke of Rawlings was looking at her. If she'd harbored any doubts before as to whether or not Jeremy'd changed since she'd last seen him, the look on his face just then abolished them. She had never seen him wear a look like *that* before. . . .

At least, not directed at *her*.

This was exactly the sort of look she'd been attracting lately, however. She'd seen it on the faces of strangers as she walked past them in the village; an admiring look, to be sure, and yet there was also something more there than simple admiration, something she could only describe as . . . well, lust.

Lust?

From *Jeremy?*

And it was then that Maggie realized that this was no longer any children's game. This was a man, over twenty years of age, not a boy, lying on top of her. And she was a woman—well, just about—and he had better get the hell off, before anyone happened to stroll by, or look out one of the manor house windows. . . .

"Get off me," Maggie grunted, unpropping her elbows, though doing so lowered her head and shoulders back onto the ground and increased the overall impropriety of the situation. It allowed her, however, to grapple with the opening at the front of her dress.

Jeremy, enjoying Maggie's discomfort as much as he was enjoying the view, remarked, almost offhandedly, "You appear to be missing a button, Mags."

"You think I don't know that, you smarmy git?" Maggie could not look him in the face. His eyes, like the rest of him, had changed, and now they seemed to have some kind of strange effect on her, an effect that was as much the reason for her crimson cheeks as her missing button. Observing her struggles with a single raised eyebrow, Jeremy said, "You look as if you could use some assistance. May I?"

Maggie, her embarrassment quickly turning to outrage, slapped at his hands—big brown hands, she saw with alarm, heavily calloused and considerably larger than her own—while clutching the front of her dress closed with her other fingers. "No, you may not," she said, emphasizing each word with a swat at him. "Get off me this instant!"

"Given the fact you that *you* jumped *me*, Mags," Jeremy pointed out, "your current indignation is heartily misplaced."

"Get off!" Maggie glanced around. "My God, someone might see us!"

"Again, you might have thought of that, young lady, before you so violently unseated me from my horse." Jeremy, noting with disappointment that she had finally managed to close her dress, looked down at her clenched fingers with a frown. "Why are you fussing so much, anyway? I've seen you in your altogether before, you know. Though not, I'll admit, since you developed such a smashing figure—"

"*Get off!*" Thoroughly mortified, Maggie rammed the side of his head with the elbow of her free arm. Though the blow could not have hurt—much—Jeremy did look very sur-

prised. It couldn't be all that often, Maggie supposed, that
the Duke of Rawlings got it upside the head. What kind of
girl would want to offend a duke, particularly an eligible
one? But then, Maggie wasn't all that concerned about what
the Duke of Rawlings—or any other duke, for that matter—
thought.

Perhaps that was just as well. Because what the Duke of
Rawlings was thinking was that he'd been a fool to stay away
from home so long. What he said, however, was, "I say, that
wasn't very sporting." Rubbing his ear, he tried to look displeased. "You haven't turned into one of those silly slapping
sort of girls, have you?"

"Oh, for God's sake," Maggie snapped. "Get off me.
My *father* might be watching."

"That," Jeremy said emphatically, "is the only sensible
reason I can think of for ending this highly enjoyable interlude."

And he slowly disengaged himself, being careful to observe, as he did so, the way her skirt had hiked up, revealing
a pair of calves so superbly rounded, they'd have been the
envy of any chorus girl. And that wasn't all he noticed. After
he'd climbed to his feet, he extended a hand to help her to
her own, and managed, while doing so, to catch a glimpse
of the spot where her stockings ended and her garters began,
just inside the curve of a smooth white thigh.

Maggie, on the ground, didn't miss Jeremy's swift glance
between her legs, and in a tizzy of confusion, she shoved her
skirt down before looking up, suspiciously, at the hand he
held down toward her.

"What?" Jeremy exclaimed, noticing her narrowed eyes.
"I'm offering you a helping hand, that's all, you silly girl.
You needn't look at me as if I were going to bite you."

Maggie swallowed. That's precisely what he looked like
he was about to do . . . bite her, or something worse. Handsome as he'd turned out, it seemed pretty likely that there
were a lot of girls to whom Jeremy had offered a bit more
than a helping hand . . . and done a lot more than bite.

Misunderstanding the reason for her hesitation, Jeremy
rolled his eyes. "I'm not going to dunk you in the reflecting

pool again, if that's what you're thinking," he informed her. "I think we're both old enough now to forgo those kinds of childish pranks, your recent ambush aside."

Knowing she was being ridiculous, Maggie lifted a hand, careful to keep the front of her dress anchored with the other. The moment Jeremy's strong fingers closed over hers, she knew she was in trouble. His was not the kind of grip that was easily broken. He was going to hang on exactly as long as he wanted to, and there wasn't a blessed thing she could do about it.

But despite the strength in those long fingers, he was surprisingly gentle, not yanking her at all as he might have done when they were younger. It was a good thing he hung on to her a little longer than necessary, too, because as soon as she was fully upright, Maggie suffered the biggest shock of all.

Jeremy was taller than she was.

Not just taller than she was. A *lot* taller than she was. Her head only reached to his shoulder. Her nose would have smacked right into the middle of his chest if he hadn't tightened his grip on her hand when she stumbled in shock.

"Maggie?" Jeremy peered down at her, a quizzical expression on his face. "Are you all right? You didn't break anything after all, did you?"

Dazed, Maggie shook her head. *Jeremy Rawlings, taller than she was?* And not just a little taller, either, but at least *six inches* taller than she was! When had this happened? The last time she'd seen him, she'd towered over him by half a foot at least. He had grown twelve inches in five years. Good God, he was as tall as Lord Edward!

"I never would have thought it," Jeremy said wonderingly. "Maggie Herbert, a fainter *and* a slapper! How times have changed. I never thought *you'd* turn out to be such a delicate flower."

That was all it took to bring Maggie out of her stupor. Lifting her head—she couldn't believe she actually had to *lift her head* to look him in the eye—she snapped, "I'm no fainter. And I didn't slap you, I elbowed you, and you deserved it. Now let go of my hand."

Jeremy smiled, and she quickly looked away. His smile seemed to have the same devastating effect on her heart as his eyes. They both made it do some kind of flip inside her chest. "Same old Mags," he said, lifting her fingers to his lips in hearty tribute. "Despite the fresh new curves."

Maggie, horrified at both the casual reference to her bosom and the way his eyes so carefully gauged her reaction as his lips caressed her knuckles, immediately and ineffectually tried to pull her hand away. But Jeremy, a knowing smirk spreading across his face, kept hold of her fingers, and even flipped them over, to study her nails.

"Ah," he said. "Vermilion, magenta, and a bit of . . . what's that, now? Oh, yes, flake white. I see we're still painting. And how *are* Dame Ashforth's cats? She must have enough portraits of them by now to fill the Great Hall—"

"Let go of my hand." Maggie tried to keep her voice steady, but it wasn't easy, since she was a few seconds away from panicking. "I mean it, Jerry. Let go!"

" 'Let go of my hand,' " Jeremy mimicked. " 'Get off me.' What sort of way is that to greet an old friend, one you haven't seen in half a decade?"

That distracted her, and she quit pulling so frantically on her fingers. "Friend?" Maggie echoed. Then she gave a snort. "Since when were *we* ever friends? Enemies would be more like it."

"You were the one who harbored all the adversarial feelings," Jeremy said, mockly hurt. "I never understood why. You lived to make my life a misery, when all I ever wanted to do was—"

"All you ever wanted to do was lord it over everybody," she interrupted. It was her turn to mimic. " '*You* can't be the pirate captain, Maggie. I'm the duke, *I* get to be the pirate captain. *You* can't have the last cherry popover, Maggie. I'm the duke, *I* get the last cherry popover. You have to do as I say, Maggie, because I'm the—' "

"So what?" Jeremy cut her off, managing to look supremely unconcerned. "It's not as if you ever did what I told you anyway."

"Good thing *somebody* wouldn't let you browbeat

them," Maggie pointed out. "Or you might have grown up to be a nasty sort of man who wouldn't let go of girls' hands when they asked you to."

"Nasty? So I'm nasty, am I?" He grinned, seeming to like the sound of that, though Maggie had hardly meant it as a compliment. But he dropped her hand anyway, and stood looking down at her, a bit speculatively, Maggie thought. She wondered what he was thinking, and then defensively folded her arms across her chest. So he liked her new figure, did he? And had the audacity to admit it, to her face! Lord, how her sister Anne would have fainted if she'd overheard *that* conversation!

Maggie's sister would have done more than faint if she could have been privy to Jeremy's thoughts just then. He was mentally kicking himself for not having attempted to seduce Sir Arthur Herbert's youngest daughter years before. How could he not have seen it? he asked himself. How could he not have known she'd turn into such a delectable morsel? True, none of her sisters had been anything much, so he hadn't had a lot of warning, but Maggie . . . What a find! He'd never had this much fun with a girl he hadn't paid for. There was something about her, something in that uninhibited impertinence of hers, that hinted that though the girl might only just be out of the schoolroom, there wasn't a bit of schoolroom in the girl. It looked as though his visit home might just turn out not to be such a bore after all. . . .

For Maggie's part, she was not liking this turn of events. Not liking it at all. There weren't a lot of people Maggie saw on a day-to-day basis who were bigger than she was, and so she wasn't used to being made to feel small, but Jeremy, whom she'd pretty much bullied for years, now had the advantage of being able to make her feel so. Worse, he was *so* much bigger that he actually made her feel a little afraid. And the last thing Maggie liked to feel was afraid. She considered herself fearless, having—unlike her elder sisters—aversions to neither heights nor water, mice nor insects, enclosed spaces nor the dark. How she could possibly be afraid of Jeremy Rawlings, she wasn't certain, but the trepidation was there, all right, and she was going to have to do something about it, or admit to herself that there was one thing she feared . . . but whether that thing was Jeremy Rawlings, or how he made her feel, she wasn't sure.

Risking a glance toward Jeremy's face, she saw that he was still looking down at her, and still wearing the same thoughtful expression. Lord, he was attractive! How could she not have noticed that before? Not that she liked good-looking men . . . well, except for Lord Edward, and Alistair Cartwright, her brother-in-law. But in general, Maggie thought handsome men tended to think entirely too well of themselves. She supposed Jeremy had a reason to feel superior, since he'd turned out to be good-looking, and had more money than the queen, as well. But in his case, both his looks and his money were gifts of fortune. Only a fool took pride in gifts from God. . . .

Then Maggie's gaze strayed past his broad shoulders. "Uh, Jeremy," she said.

"Yes?" Both of his eyebrows lifted expectantly.

"You might want to catch your horse. He's running away."

Startled, Jeremy turned around to see King trotting off toward the south pasture, where the fillies were grazing.

"Hell," Jeremy swore. He turned quickly back to Maggie. "Stay here," he said, making a gesture rather like Yorkshire shepherds made to their collies when they wanted them to stay in one place. "All right? I'll be right back."

"Oh," Maggie said, nodding seriously. "Of course."

The minute his back was turned, however, she started heading toward the house . . . not running, exactly, because that was hard to do while holding the bodice of one's dress closed—and besides, she didn't want him to think she was running *away*—but walking very briskly. Retreat seemed the best strategy at that point. She needed to make repairs to more than just her dress . . . her mind was in a veritable whirl, after having been bombarded with so many new sensations at once. Jeremy Rawlings, looking just as manly and strong as the local blacksmith's sons, whom she'd been admiring from afar for well over a year now? Jeremy Rawlings, looking down at her with lust in his eyes, eyes she'd once thought dull, but which now shone as brightly as her mother's silver tea service? Jeremy Rawlings, *taller than she was*?

What was her world coming to?

It was too much for a girl like Maggie to assimilate all at once. Used to quiet country living, she wasn't at all sure how to react to this new turn of events. She needed time for reflection, time to pull herself together—both literally and figuratively—time to figure out how best to beat this new and disturbing discovery: She was afraid of Jeremy Rawlings.

She never had a chance. She'd hardly made it past the turnaround in front of the rambling, three-storied manor house, before she heard a deep voice—Lord, even his *voice* had changed!—call her name. Damn! Maggie stopped dead in her tracks, looked heavenward for strength, then slowly pivoted toward him.

"Where do you think you're going?" Jeremy's voice, though deep, had a note of amusement in it that Maggie recognized. It was the same tone in which he'd often addressed her, shortly after suffering through one of her innumerable pranks.

"Uh," Maggie said. "Nowhere. Inside. To find a button." Mentally, she kicked herself. Oh, brilliant conversation, Maggie!

"Come with me," Jeremy said. He had caught King, and now stood panting from the exertion and looking, in Maggie's opinion, far too handsome, with the sun bringing out blue highlights in his jet-black hair—he'd apparently lost his hat in their tumble—and his cravat untied just enough to reveal a few dark curls of chest hair at the base of his throat.

"Uh," Maggie said. Again, she was having trouble with her tongue. Normally, she couldn't keep it still, but today, it was as heavy as a brick inside her mouth. "No. I can't. I've really got to—"

"Just come with me while I get this beast safely stabled away." He was grinning down at her as if her reluctance were one of the funniest things he'd ever seen. "Then we'll go inside and find you a button. Come on."

"I really can't, Jeremy. My mother—"

"Oh, dash your mother." The silver eyes flashed challengingly, as the grin on his face grew wider. "What are you afraid of?"

Maggie froze. "Nothing," she said, too quickly. Nothing wrong with her tongue anymore.

The silver eyes glinted. "You wouldn't be afraid of me, now would you, Mags?"

"Certainly not!"

"Are you lying to me, Mags?"

"No . . ."

The grin turned into a smile so wide that she could see all of his white, even teeth. "No, of course not. I didn't think so. So come on." He turned to present her with the crook of his free arm. "Walk with me. I want to hear all about how you've been keeping yourself these past five years. You're still painting, obviously. But what else have you been doing?"

Maggie cast one last, longing glance at the large double doors of the manor house. Beyond them lay safety, sanity, and a maid with a sewing kit. But Maggie had never been able to abide cowardice, least of all in herself. So, sighing, she crossed the drive and slipped a hand through the crook of Jeremy's elbow.

"Oh," she said, breezily. "Not much."

Chapter 4

$\mathcal{I}$t had been too easy. All it had taken was a goad at her pride, and she was his. Well, not really his . . . not yet, anyway. But he'd managed to discover her weakness—or rather, rediscover it, since he remembered now, quite clearly, that Maggie could always be coerced into doing just about anything by one simple sentence: You're not afraid, are you, Mags?

She was doing a very good job of looking unafraid, supremely unafraid, at the moment, perched on a bale of hay just outside of King's stall, her feet swinging above the floor as she leaned back against a wooden post. Unfortunately, she still kept one hand clenched around the front of her bodice, depriving him of another glimpse of the curves of those pale beauties. He didn't think it would be long, however, before he got to do more than just look at them. Now that he knew what to say to get a rise out of her, he had no doubt that soon, very soon, he'd finally be getting revenge on Maggie Herbert for all those tricks she'd played on him in their childhood. . . .

But in the meantime he was content to just look at her, since she looked very nice indeed, sitting amidst all the slanting rays of sunshine that spilled through the open stall doors, her long hair loose and soft-looking, shimmering down her back. It was good luck he'd managed to coordinate his homecoming with teatime. All of the grooms and stablehands were indoors, enjoying some of Cook's famous seed cake. He and

Maggie were alone in the stables, except for the horses, and
a few birds that had built nests in the rafters, and twittered
irritatedly at them for invading their privacy.

Maggie, for her part, was feeling more at ease. Jeremy
had toned down the lusty glances to such a degree that she
was beginning to think perhaps she'd been mistaken about
them. After all, the Duke of Rawlings could have any woman
in the world. Why would he want *her*? She was just the
daughter of his solicitor, a knight who lived a few estates
away. Her sister had happened to marry his uncle's best
friend, and her mother was very fond of his aunt, and so
they'd been thrown together quite a bit as children, but that
was all. Surely all of this marked friendliness of his was just
for old time's sake. He couldn't possibly see her as anything
else but an old friend. This reminder went a long way toward
soothing her somewhat jumbled nerves.

"So," she was saying, as he went about the business of
unsaddling King, "Evers senior is still here at Rawlings
Manor, while his son is at the town house in London, and
his son, if I understand correctly, is attending some kind of
butlery school, in hopes that his grandfather will retire someday soon, and he can take over the post. Only according to
your aunt, Evers senior says he'll retire when he's dead, and
he still insists upon doing all the decanting himself, even
though his hands shake terribly whenever he picks up anything heavier than a fingerbowl."

Jeremy, who'd removed his coat while he brushed out his
horse, now thought he might as well take off his cravat, and
he tried to do so casually, laying the simple piece of linen
over the coat he'd thrown across the stall door.

"Really," he said, bending down to give King's forelocks
a good rub.

"Yes. And your aunt's maid Lucy had another baby girl,
and that makes four, but she says she won't be happy until
she has a boy, though you'd think four girls would be
enough, for God's sake."

"I see," Jeremy said. He straightened, and threw the
brush aside, fixing Maggie with a stare she couldn't see,

since the sun was full on her face, and his back was to the light.

"And Mrs. Praehurst is turning sixty-five next fall," she went on, happily filling him in on the details of the private lives of his servants, "and your aunt and uncle are sending her on a trip to Italy, but Mrs. Praehurst hates Italians, and says that cuisine that depends so heavily on the tomato can't be good for the digestion, so somebody ought to warn them—"

"Maggie," Jeremy said. Something in his voice warned her that he wasn't interrupting her because he had a question about his housekeeper's attitude toward Mediterranean cooking. He had opened the stall door and then shut it again behind him, and now stood just a few feet away from the hay bale upon which she sat. She couldn't read his expression at all, but she supposed, from the way his voice had sounded, that it wasn't particularly composed.

"Ye-es?" she said slowly.

But when he stepped close enough for his shadow to fall over her face, she was able—though she had to crane her neck to do so—to see that he didn't look nervous or upset at all. In fact, he looked downright teasing.

"You've told me everything about everybody remotely connected to Rawlings Manor," he said, sitting down beside her on the hay bale, without so much as a by-your-leave. "But you haven't said a word about yourself."

Maggie, because he'd sat so close to her that their shoulders brushed—well, her shoulder brushed up against his upper arm—moved over a little, to give him more room. "Well, there isn't much to tell," she said dryly. "I've been at school."

"Yes, of course," he said. Was it her imagination, or had he moved closer the second she scooted away? "But what now?"

"Well," she said, moving away again. "I don't know. I wanted to study painting in Paris, but my father won't let me."

"Oh?" Did he have to sound so pleased about that? And how had she ended up on the very edge of the hay bale all of a sudden, with nowhere else to go but the floor?

"So what will you do instead?"

"I don't know," Maggie said, glancing down at the floor. It wasn't that she was nervous, exactly, because he was sitting so close; it was just that she couldn't figure out why he was doing it. The floor looked preferable, she thought, to his lap, which was where she was going to end up if he moved much closer. Maybe if she kept on talking, she could keep him distracted. "I suppose I'll just have to go to London, you know, for my coming out—"

"Oh, your coming out," Jeremy echoed. He lifted an arm and draped it across her shoulders. Maggie stared at his hand as it dangled off to her left, and saw, with some alarm, that there were black hairs, not unlike the ones at the opening of his shirt, all over his arm where it jutted out from the shirt cuff he'd rolled up. There was something so distinctly masculine about the coarseness of those hairs that Maggie felt a spurt of anxiety simply by looking at them.

"And are you looking forward to coming out, Mags?" he asked.

"Not particularly," Maggie replied. She turned her head until she was looking into his eyes, which wasn't difficult, since his face hung just inches from hers. But that turned out to be something of a mistake, since his eyes still seemed to have a strange sort of effect on her—only now, instead of her heart flipping over, gooseflesh sprung up on her bare arms, even though she was sitting in direct sunlight and was actually feeling quite warm. "The whole thing seems rather stupid to me," she managed to say. Her tongue had gone curiously dead again. "I hate parties, and I don't like to dance—" She saw his gaze drop. "Jeremy," she said, a spurt of anxiety once again shooting through her. "Why are you staring at my mouth?"

He smiled, and the hand that had been hanging over her left shoulder curled around it, enfolding her in a sort of half-embrace. "Because I'm going to kiss you, Mags," he said, in a voice so soft it was a caress in itself. "Don't you want me to?"

Now Maggie's heart began some strenuous activity, turning over sickeningly inside her chest. "Not particularly," she said, quickly leaning back—right into his waiting arm. Realizing she'd been caught as surely as a rabbit in a snare, she flung up both hands defensively, forgetting all about her missing button. "No—"

But it was too late. This wasn't the Jeremy of five years earlier, whom she'd been able to bully at will. This was the new Jeremy, a full-grown man, a good deal bigger and stronger than she was, and who didn't seem the least bit concerned about how she felt in the matter. Even as she protested, he lowered his mouth over hers. . . .

And then she could only wonder what all her fussing had been about. Because while it was strange—*exceedingly* strange—to be kissed by Jeremy, it was also actually quite pleasant.

Maggie had never been kissed by a man before. She'd never been held in a man's arms, or even stood near enough to a man to know that everything about them—*everything*— was different. They didn't feel the way women did—there was no hint of softness about them. They were hard all over. Every place Maggie laid her hands, she felt only hard muscle constricting. Even their skin wasn't soft—Maggie felt the abrasion of Jeremy's day-old growth of beard against her mouth. His whiskers were as sharp as nettles. And men didn't even *smell* the way women did. Jeremy smelled of leather and horse and, faintly, of tobacco, all scents that, had they clung to Maggie, she'd have taken great pains to scrub away. But somehow, they seemed right coming from a man. *Everything* seemed right: The arm that he slid around her waist to pull her closer to him seemed right. The lips he moved over hers, in dozens of small, eager kisses, seemed right. Even the slow, seductive exploration of the inside of her mouth that his tongue embarked upon . . . even *that* seemed right.

What didn't seem right, however, was the way these things were making Maggie *feel*. She ought, she knew, to be wildly angry with Jeremy for being so forward. She ought, she was certain, to be trying to push him away. But she couldn't. She couldn't summon up an ounce of indignation, because the moment he'd started kissing her, a delicious lethargy stole over her. With his body pressing hers back until she was supported only by his strong arms, and his mouth moving so hungrily over hers, she suddenly felt like the fragile, dainty kind of girl she'd always wanted to be. The kind of girl who really did need smelling salts, who wasn't too tall for a man to lift easily and carry up a staircase. . . .

But that wasn't all she felt. No, there was something entirely different going on beneath her underthings. Because while the rest of her body felt languorous and lovely, there was a distinct tightening sensation between her legs, and a sudden rush of moisture for which there was no conceivable explanation, except that, as Maggie had always feared would happen, her carnal inclinations had completely taken over. *Something* was certainly making her feel as purry as a cat in heat, and there was no denying the fact that as insistently as Jeremy was pressing his body against hers, she was pressing right back, to the point where certain parts of her actually *ached* because she longed for him to touch them. . . .

But when his free hand, which had been caressing the smooth bare skin of her upper arm as they kissed, dipped into the place where her bodice gaped open to fondle one of her heavy round breasts, she stiffened with surprise. That, she knew immediately, was *not* right. Not because it didn't feel good—she didn't think she'd ever felt anything quite as nice as his callused fingers moving almost worshipfully over her bare skin—but because it felt *too* good, so good, in fact, that Maggie had a pretty good idea that she might not be able to stop him at all if she didn't stop him just then.

"Jerry," she breathed, when his lips moved from hers to burn a path of kisses down the side of her throat.

"Mmmm." The fingers he'd slipped beneath the bodice of her dress found the lace edging to her camisole, and slid beneath it to glide across her satiny skin. Maggie inhaled sharply.

"Jerry," she said again, more urgently this time. "Stop—"

"Why?" He sounded genuinely curious, but he didn't pause in his exploration of her breast. Discovering a hardened nipple, he flattened his palm against it, and gently began to squeeze with his fingers, while pushing with his palm. This caused a sound to leave Maggie's throat, a sound that, more than ever, reminded her of a cat in heat, as she arched her back instinctively against his fingers. She could feel the gusset of her drawers growing even slicker with moisture.

"Jeremy!" This time, there was no breathiness to her voice.

Jeremy's voice in reply, however, was as lethargic as if he were drunk.

"What is it, Mags?" he asked, right before he pressed his lips to the top of the swollen curve of her breast.

Maggie's hands went to his hair as she tried to prevent his head from dipping lower. She was surprised by how silky the ink-black curls felt against her fingers. "Jeremy," she said. It was almost causing her physical pain to fight against the impulse to fling herself at him. "You've got to stop. . . ."

"I can't," he replied, into the cleft between her breasts. He was already raining kisses closer and closer to the nipple he'd palmed. "Oh, God, Maggie. When did all this happen?"

She blinked down at his dark head. "When did all what happen?" she asked confusedly.

"All this," he said wonderingly, and moved his hand from one breast to the other, leaving the nipple he'd been massaging stiffly erect in the open air. Before Maggie had a chance to cover herself, however, Jeremy's mouth performed that service for her, his lips closing over the hardened peak. A wave of heat coursed through her, and again a sound escaped Maggie, a helpless mew of desire.

This was awful, much worse than she'd orginally thought! Now she not only did not want him to stop, she had a physical *need* for him to continue . . . and yet what was going to happen if he did continue? If she was practically writhing beneath him when all he'd done was touch her nipple with his tongue, what was going to happen, God forbid, if he should lift up her skirts and . . .

No. Maggie's heart was pounding so hard, she could feel every beat in her temples. No, the thought of that was much, much too frightening. The thought of this man, who for all intents and purposes she hardly knew, disrobing in front of her—the thought of him touching her even more intimately than he was now—the thought of how she'd react to both the sight of his nakedness and those touches—was simply too much for Maggie. He'd accused her of being afraid: Damned right she was afraid. More afraid than she'd ever been in her whole life. More *alive* than she'd ever been in her whole life . . . and because of that, afraid.

Fear won out over desire. And with the fear came the indignation, at last. How dare he? How *dare* he? *He* might be used to rolling about in the hay whenever the fancy seized him, but he was a man. Not just a man, but a duke. He could rut on whomever he pleased and never have a thought for the consequences.

She, on the other hand, had never even been kissed before today. How dare he try to take advantage of her inexperience, of her relative naïveté about the ways of the world?

Having channeled the sexual feelings he'd stirred up within her into a fine, solid rage, Maggie hefted twin handfuls of Jeremy's hair and tried with all her might to strain his head away. "Get . . . off . . . me," she hissed between gritted teeth.

To her utter astonishment, Jeremy lifted his head, looked her right in the eye, and said, unsteadily, "Oh, no. You had your fun while we were growing up. It's my turn now, Mags." Then he lunged once more for her lips.

Maggie didn't have to think twice. She reacted as instinctively as she had before, when she'd let her mouth fall open beneath his. Only this time, her action was fueled by anger, not passion. Releasing the handfuls of hair she held, Maggie drew back her right fist and sent it, with all the force she could muster, in the direction of his nose, which, he'd explained to her once, five years or so before, was the ideal place to strike a man, since nasal cartilage was very fine, and breaking it wouldn't cause undue bruising to the knuckles.

Unfortunately, due to the constrictive embrace in which he held her, she misaimed, and nearly lacerated her fist on his teeth. Nevertheless, the blow had the desired effect: His grip on her loosened at once, and Maggie leapt to her feet, dancing out of his reach and waving her sore knuckles in the air.

"What the—" Jeremy reached up to dab at his throbbing mouth. When he brought his hand down again, he saw a drop of blood on it from where her fist had driven his upper lip into his teeth. The blow hadn't hurt—much—but it had certainly surprised him quite a bit. He lifted his incredulous gaze to her face. "Maggie!" he cried, perfectly astonished. "What did you do *that* for?"

Maggie, wondering if she hadn't dislocated one of her fingers, said testily, "I *told* you to let me go." She glared down at her already swelling knuckles. What was she going to do now? She'd broken her hand on the Duke of Rawlings's teeth. How was she going to explain *that* to her mother?

"Yes, but . . ." Jeremy gazed down at the blood on his own knuckles, his expression still one of utter disbelief. "You *hit* me, Mags."

She shot him an aggravated glance from where she stood in a puddle of bright sunlight. "Oh, what?" she demanded, managing to sound more saucy than she actually felt. "You think just because you're a duke, you can get away with mauling anyone you choose? Well, think again, you conceited git. I told you to stop, and I meant it." She noticed the trickle of blood at the side of his mouth with no small satisfaction. Her heart had finally begun to beat at something like its normal pace, and she was relieved to find that the mysterious yearnings which he'd stirred up inside of her had receded—at least for the moment.

"I wasn't trying to hurt you, Mags," Jeremy pointed out gently. He had, Maggie saw, a strange expression on his face, one she'd never seen him wear before in all the years she had known him. What she didn't know was that this was an expression *no one* had ever seen the Duke of Rawlings wear before: This was the first time Jeremy had ever had occasion to wear it. This was the first time, after all, he'd ever been rebuffed by a woman.

"I know," Maggie said, her anger still hot as a fire iron, "*precisely* what you were trying to do. And you had just better think twice about ever trying it again, Jeremy Rawlings, or I promise you, you'll get more of the same.''

Jeremy could not quite believe what he was hearing. Here was the finest piece of womanhood he'd seen in a good long while—never mind that she happened to be someone he'd known for nearly half his life—and she *wouldn't have him*. Nothing like this had ever occurred in the whole of Jeremy's long and inarguably varied sexual experience. No woman had ever rejected him before. Never. It simply had never happened.

He didn't know what to think. It couldn't possibly be because she wasn't attracted to him. There'd been desire in her kiss. He couldn't have mistaken that. So why had she stopped him?

Well, there was the fact that she'd been brought up, he supposed, to believe that one had to be married, or at least engaged, before one allowed a man to do the kinds of things Jeremy had been doing to her quite without the benefit of matrimony. But that hadn't stopped any number of young society misses from quite happily allowing him to do those things last season, when he'd been in London. Why had it stopped Maggie?

He looked at her as she stood in the sunlight, a hectic flush on her cheeks, her chest rising and falling rapidly as she attempted to catch her breath—further proof that she was not indifferent toward him. He admired the way the gap in the bodice of her dress widened each time she inhaled. . . .

Which was the first thing his uncle Edward noticed too when he strode into the stables a second later.

"Jeremy!" Edward thundered. The starlings in the rafters let out startled cries and took flight almost as one as his voice boomed through the quiet, sun-dappled building. And they weren't the only things Jeremy's uncle startled. Maggie yelped and, blushing scarlet, folded her arms quickly over her half-exposed breasts.

"What," Edward demanded furiously, "in hell is going on in here?"

"Good God, Uncle Edward," Jeremy drawled from the hay bale upon which he still lounged. "Must you always time your entrances so ill? Maggie and I were just getting to know one another again.''

''Margaret.'' She jumped at the balefulness in Lord Edward's voice. He sounded angrier than Maggie had ever heard him, including the time that he'd caught her and Jeremy tying firecrackers to the back of the vicar's brougham. ''Get back to your mother. *Now*.''

''Yes, my lord.'' Maggie needed no more urging. Without another word, she spun round and fled—or tried to. She was stopped dead in her tracks when someone reached out and seized one of the metal hoops of her crinoline through the material at the back of her skirt. Letting out a soft *oof* as the ribbons that kept her crinoline tied around her waist cut into her midriff, she flicked an accusing gaze over her shoulder. But Jeremy wasn't looking at her. He was looking at his uncle.

''There's no need to send Maggie scampering back to her mother,'' the duke—for that's exactly what the imperiousness of Jeremy's voice put Maggie in mind of—said. ''*She* wasn't doing anything wrong. If you're going to be angry with someone, be angry with me, but Maggie's completely innocent—''

''Oh, I'm perfectly aware of Maggie's innocence,'' Lord Edward said. Maggie's trepidation grew as the older man began shrugging out of his coat—Lord Edward, whom she'd never seen with so much as a hair out of place, was disrobing in a stable! ''It's *you* I'm preparing to thrash until there isn't a shred of flesh left on your body. But if you'd like Maggie to watch while I do so, she's perfectly welcome to . . .''

Maggie let out a squeak of alarm and, yanking her crinoline hoop out of Jeremy's grasp, turned and ran for all she was worth.

Chapter 5

$\mathcal{W}$atching Maggie's booted feet fly as she disappeared into the sunshine outside the stable doors, Jeremy frowned. "You needn't have frightened her witless, you know," he said, irritably, to his uncle.

"Oh, no," Edward said, concentrating on the shirt cuffs he was carefully rolling up. "You were doing that admirably yourself."

"*Me*?" Jeremy looked offended. "*I* wasn't frightening her."

"Weren't you?" Edward, his shirtsleeves pushed up over his elbows, loosened his cravat. "Then why are you bleeding at the mouth?"

Jeremy lifted a hand to his lip, having long since forgotten the cut there. "Oh, that." He chuckled. "Can you believe that? I taught her that right cross, you know. I can't say I ever expected her to use it on *me*."

"Didn't you?" Edward glared at him. "What did you think she was going to do, Jerry? Swoon in your arms?"

"Well," he said. "They usually do. In fact, this is the first time one didn't. Haven't quite figured out why yet, but—"

Edward looked grim. "Haven't you? Try this one: You may have reached the age of majority, Jerry, but Maggie Herbert is still a child."

"Oh, please," Jeremy said disgustedly. "She's nearly seventeen. My mother gave birth to me at seventeen."

Edward, though he looked a little surprised at Jeremy's reference to his mother, of whom he spoke rarely, if at all, said only, "Maggie Herbert is the daughter of a knight. Her father is your financial advisor and my friend—" Jeremy rolled his eyes at that, since he'd often overheard his uncle complaining about Sir Arthur's somewhat trying personality, but Edward continued, "She is here as a guest of my wife, which means she is visiting Rawlings Manor under *your* protection, and you had the gall—no, excuse me, the *stupidity*— to attempt to seduce her, in a stable, no less, as if she were some barmaid you happened to meet one night while you were out carousing with your friends—"

"That isn't true," Jeremy said, with wounded dignity. "I would never attempt to seduce a barmaid in a stable. At the very least, I would demand that she take me to a room with a bed before I so much as laid a hand on her—"

He saw the fist coming. He had to have seen it coming. But to Edward's amazement, his nephew didn't duck, or in any way try to avoid the blow. His knuckles met Jeremy's jaw with a solid *thunk*, and Jeremy went down, falling back upon the pile of hay bales.

Shaking his hand, which throbbed from the force of the blow—it had been a while since Edward last participated in a brawl; members of the House of Lords were generally discouraged from fisticuffs—he said, with a good deal of indignation, "I'm sorry I had to do that. But, by God, Jerry—"

"I know." Jeremy, hay sticking up from his mop of unruly black hair, sat up, carefully stroking his twice-bruised jawbone. "I know. I deserved it."

"That and more," Edward said severely. "You'll ride over to Herbert Park tonight and apologize, to both Maggie— if she'll see you, which I doubt—and to her parents. You'll leave for the Continent first thing tomorrow morning." Crossing over to where Jeremy sat, Edward held out a hand to help the younger man to his feet. "The sooner you're out of the country," he said, grunting as he lifted Jeremy's considerable weight, "the sooner we'll all be able to put this wretched incident behind us."

On his feet again, Jeremy began swatting at the pieces of straw that clung to his trousers. "And then when will the wedding be? Six months? Do you think I'll still have to wait six months before coming back, to be on the safe side? Because of Pierce, I mean?"

Edward, who was flexing his throbbing hand experimentally, as if uncertain whether or not he might have broken a knuckle, grew still, and cast his nephew a sharp glance. "What wedding?" he asked suspiciously.

"The wedding," Jeremy said, pulling a piece of straw from his hair. "You know. Mine and Maggie's."

Edward stared. "You asked Maggie Herbert to marry you?"

"Well, no," Jeremy said. He let out an uncomfortable laugh. "Of course not! No man *wants* to marry, does he?" The laughter died as abruptly as it had begun, and Jeremy asked nervously, "But aren't you going to *make* me marry her? You know, since you caught us, uh, how shall I put it? In *flagrante delicto*?"

"Pleased as I am to learn that you acquired some Latin, anyway, during your sojourn at Oxford," Edward said carefully, "I must confess that no, I never had any intention of forcing you to marry Maggie Herbert."

To Edward's utter astonishment, his nephew actually looked disappointed. "But Uncle," he said. "I've seriously compromised her. I would think—"

"All I saw was that the front of her dress was undone," Edward interrupted. He raised his still-throbbing fist meaningfully. "Are you telling me that you really did seduce her?"

Jeremy eyed the fist. "Well," he said. "No. But I would have, if she hadn't tried to knock my head off. And you hadn't walked in, of course."

"All the more reason to send you off to France," Edward said complacently. He lowered his arm. "You can seduce all the French girls you like. Just stay away from the English ones, especially Maggie Herbert. Now go and get yourself cleaned up. Your aunt was asking about you. That's why I came looking for you in the first place."

Edward went to the stall door across which he'd laid his coat and cravat. When he turned around again, he found Jeremy standing before him, his jaw looking red and swollen, his gray eyes stormy with anger.

"Why not?" he demanded, in a low, gravelly voice his uncle didn't recognize.

Taken aback, Edward said, "I beg your pardon?"

"Why not Maggie?" Both of Jeremy's hands, his uncle noted cautiously, were curled into fists at his sides. "You don't think she'd make a good duchess? You don't think she's good enough for me?"

Calmly, Edward began shrugging into his coat. "On the contrary," he said, his kindly tone in direct contrast with the harsh words he uttered. "Maggie would make a splendid duchess. It's *you*, my boy, who isn't good enough for *her*."

A muscle in Jeremy's cheek leapt, just once. "Because of who my mother was?" he demanded sharply.

Edward let out a bark of humorless laughter. "Good God, no. This hasn't a thing to do with the fact that your mother was a whore." When Jeremy didn't flinch at the word, Edward went on, feeling slightly more respect for the younger man. "No, you don't deserve Maggie—or any other decent sort of woman—because you're nothing but a ne'er-do-well."

Jeremy blinked at him. "A *what*?"

"Jerry, I'm surprised at you." Edward shook his head as if greatly disappointed in his nephew . . . but inwardly, he was smiling. "Haven't you ever noticed how dedicated your aunt Pegeen is to all those charities and foundations she donates to in your name? Why, there are a dozen orphans tearing up the rose beds in the garden this very instant, because Pegeen is hosting some kind of picnic for them." When Jeremy looked blank, Edward rolled his eyes. "She raised you from a baby, Jerry. Hasn't *anything* she taught you sunk in? Your aunt has devoted her life to making this world a better place, for children, for women, for the poor. That's what you ought to be doing."

"Philanthropic works?" Jeremy asked, the distaste he felt

at the thought of involving himself in such activities evident in his expression.

"Not necessarily," Edward said impatiently. "But you've got to *make* something out of the life you've been given."

"Why should I have to?" Jeremy inquired belligerently. "I'm a duke."

"It's because you're a duke that it's even more essential that you make something of yourself. You've got to show that you're worthy of the title. You can't simply spend your entire life fighting duels and seducing young women—"

"Why not?" Jeremy demanded. "When you were my age, that's all you did."

"Yes," Edward said. He raised an index finger. He didn't mean to look pedantic. He simply couldn't help it. "Yes, you're right, I did. I was like you. I thought my only obligation in life was to enjoy myself. But you see, Jeremy, when I met your aunt, I learned how very wrong I'd been. Because if winning a particular woman is important to you, you can't simply try to seduce her in a stable and expect her parents to force her to marry you—"

"That isn't *precisely* what I set out to do," Jeremy grumbled, flushing a little.

"—and you can't expect any woman worth winning to be impressed with you simply because you're in possession of a title. No, you've got to make yourself at least appear to be worth her while . . . and quite frankly, the man I was when I met your aunt wasn't worth anything, except a few hundred pounds a month in tailoring bills, which she quickly pointed out to me. But I changed, you see, Jerry. I made something of myself. I found something I did and did well—arguing— and I turned it into an occupation. Now I argue, quite effectively, for the betterment—I believe, anyway—of the people of England. That's what you've got to do, Jerry. You've got to find out what you do well, and then do it. *That's* when you'll find a girl like Maggie and—"

"I don't want a girl *like* Maggie," Jeremy snapped. "I want *her*."

Edward raised his eyebrows. It wasn't that he was surprised, particularly. After all, Maggie Herbert was one of the only women in Jeremy's acquaintance who hadn't the slightest interest in becoming a duchess. It was just that Edward wasn't sure that Jeremy was aware that that might be exactly where his attraction to her lay. "Well," Edward said. "Regardless. You've got to find something—"

"The only thing I can do," Jeremy said firmly, "is fight."

Edward nodded. "Well, yes, you've certainly shown a certain aptitude for that. Certainly a scholar's life hasn't held any appeal for you, and I doubt politics is exactly your cup of—"

"I can fight," Jeremy said, again. He didn't seem to be listening to his uncle anymore. In fact, he turned his back on him, and quickly paced a few yards through the straw. "I'm best at fencing, but I can shoot, as well. Also, I'm good on a horse."

"Right," Edward said slowly. "And those are admirable qualities. But—"

Jeremy stopped pacing a few feet away from the door to King's stall. Edward saw his shoulders go back, and his head come up. "That's it," Jeremy said, apparently to his horse, since his back was to his uncle. "I shall go into the cavalry."

It was a statement, not a question. Edward said, "Well, now, let's see if we can examine—"

"There's nothing to examine," Jeremy interrupted matter-of-factly. He turned to face his uncle. "I need an occupation. The army's as good as any. It isn't possible to purchase commissions anymore, so I shall have to earn the rank of officer. That's just as well. It's more impressive to earn something than to buy it."

Edward began to experience a growing sense of unease. "Yes, but Jeremy, the army is really more for, er, second sons, young men who don't expect to inherit a title or property and don't care to go into the church. Dukes generally don't—"

"I shall join the Horse Guards," Jeremy said. Edward wasn't certain if he hadn't heard him, or was simply ignoring him. Jeremy began pacing again, excitedly this time. "I shall ask to be stationed in India. That's the most dangerous place we have armies stationed right now, isn't it? Too bad there isn't a war on. I should have quite liked a war. Well, perhaps I can start one." He headed, without another word, for the stable doors.

"Jeremy," Edward called after him.

Jeremy turned, as if surprised his uncle was still there. "Yes?"

"You aren't—you aren't serious, are you?" Edward cleared his throat. "You can't really mean that you intend to join Her Majesty's army, can you?"

"Well, Uncle," Jeremy said with a grin. "I'm a duke, am I not? I can do anything I like."

Chapter 6

"*What?*" Pegeen cried, nearly dropping the silver-backed hairbrush she held.

"The cavalry," Edward said. He sat on the edge of their bed, a few feet away from his wife's dressing table, his elbows on his knees. His expression was one of abject misery. "At least, that's what he said."

"But Edward . . ." Pegeen stood up, the hairbrush hanging limply from her fingers. "But Edward, the *army*? He told you he's joining the *army*?"

"The cavalry," Edward said again. He watched helplessly as his wife, whom he'd interrupted while she was dressing for dinner, began to pace the length of their bedroom, wearing only a camisole and a new pair of French-cut pantaloons. In her hands, she clutched the hairbrush, as if it were some kind of link to the orderly existence she'd led up until he'd come in, a few moments ago, and delivered this unexpected piece of news.

"The cavalry?" Pegeen's husky voice rose, a note of panic creeping into it. "The cavalry? My God, Edward, he'll be killed. He won't last a minute in the cavalry. He's much too sensitive—"

Edward wondered if he ought to reveal to his wife the fact that her sensitive nephew had, in fact, fatally wounded a man in a duel just the day before. He thought perhaps he'd wait until she calmed down a little before doing so, however.

"What's a boy like Jerry going to do in the cavalry?"

she demanded, storming past the bed and then doing an about-face, her long, dark hair swinging out behind her in a smooth arc, before storming off in the opposite direction. "He'll be shot the first day—"

"He won't be shot," Edward said. "The Horse Guards employ swords, not pistols."

"It doesn't matter what kind of weapon he employs. He won't be able to defend himself," Pegeen cried. "He can't even bring himself to shoot a pheasant. He'll never actually be able to kill a live person!"

"Well," Edward said, slowly. "Actually—"

"And India! My God, Edward! India! He'll catch malaria and die, alone in a strange, hot country—"

"Pegeen," Edward said, watching her as she paced back and forth across the rose-patterned carpet.

"You've got to stop him," she said. "That's all there is to it. You've got to forbid it, Edward."

"I can't forbid it, Pegeen," Edward said tiredly. "He's a grown man. He can make his own decisions."

"A grown man!" Pegeen whirled on him, pointing the hairbrush accusingly at his chest. "A grown man! He's a boy, Edward. He's barely twenty-one. And if you don't stop him, he'll never see twenty-two!"

"Legally," Edward said, "he's a man now, Pegeen." Edward reached out and gently pried the hairbrush out of her fingers, so she could no longer brandish it like a weapon. "We can't stop him from doing anything he wants to do. And I don't think the army is such a bad choice, really. It will teach him some discipline. And it will keep him away from Maggie—"

"Maggie!" Pegeen's hands went to her burning cheeks. "Oh, Lord! I'll never be able to forgive myself for that. Poor Maggie!"

"Forgive yourself?" Snaking out a long arm, Edward took hold of his wife's hips and pulled her onto his lap. "What did *you* have to do with it? I don't recall seeing *you* in that stable."

"Oh, God!" Mortified, Pegeen hid her face against her husband's neck. "How will I ever be able to face Anne—

not to mention her mother—again? How could he, Edward?'' She banged Edward's chest with a small, impotent fist. ''How *could* he?''

Edward shook his head, although he understood perfectly well how his nephew could have done something so reprehensible . . . and tempting. Edward, who had actually been around to witness the process, had still been as surprised as his nephew at how well Sir Arthur's youngest daughter had turned out. Had he been twenty-one and single, he'd have acted exactly as Jeremy had. He wouldn't, however, have been so amenable to marrying the girl. That was the curious part of the matter, as far as Edward was concerned.

''Do you suppose,'' Edward said, his chin resting on the top of his wife's head, ''that he's in love with her?''

Pegeen's voice was slightly muffled by the fabric of Edward's shirt. ''With Maggie? Oh, I don't see how. She's never been anything but nasty to him.''

''If I recall correctly, you were fairly nasty to me, too, upon first making my acquaintance.''

Pegeen lifted her head. ''I wasn't!''

''You were. You tried to hack one of my fingers off with a bread knife.''

''Oh.'' Pegeen laid her head back down upon his chest. ''Well, you deserved it.''

Edward raised his eyebrows, but wisely said nothing.

''You don't suppose,'' Pegeen said thoughtfully, a moment later, ''that's it, do you?''

''Suppose what's it?''

''Well, you said she'd hit him. . . .''

Edward nodded. ''Yes. Every bit as forcefully as I did, I think. Though she misaimed, and got him in the mouth. I wouldn't be surprised to see Miss Maggie Herbert with her hand in a splint upon the morrow.''

Pegeen winced. ''Oh, Edward, really, I wish you hadn't. It was hardly necessary for *both* of you to punch him.''

''If you'd heard him, Pegeen, you'd have hit him, too, I'm quite sure,'' Edward assured her grimly.

''Well, in any case,'' Pegeen said, managing to sound somehow dignified, even though she was perched on her husband's lap in nothing but her underwear, "I imagine that Maggie's resistance to his, er, charms might be what attracted him to her in the first place. I can't imagine any woman has ever resisted Jeremy before, let alone *struck* him. It must have been quite novel for him."

Edward grunted. "Novel enough to make him want to *marry* her?"

"People have married for far stupider reasons. Why shouldn't Jeremy want to marry someone who treats him as an equal, and not like some kind of god, like all of those girls he met last season in London, who did nothing but fawn over him just because he's got a title and some wealth?"

"I highly doubt," Edward said, "that Maggie's punching Jerry in the face was what induced him to suggest they marry. I believe it had more to do with her suddenly comely appearance. You'd be surprised, my dear, what a long way a pretty face can go in making a man forget all his firmest resolutions." Edward lowered his head to nuzzle his wife's neck. "For instance, I merely came in here to tell you that our nephew's joining the army, but now that I find you so fetchingly garbed"—Pegeen, giggling, didn't protest as Edward lowered her onto the wide canopied bed—"I'm quite certain you and I are going to be late for supper again."

Chapter 7

A few miles away, Maggie Herbert was doing anything but giggling. She was trying to brave the wrath of her parents, which, since Jeremy had only left her father's library approximately twenty minutes earlier, was still palpable.

"I am not," Maggie's father began, from behind his massive mahogany desk, "going to ask you, Margaret, if what His Grace just came in here and told me was true. I am going to trust that a man like the Duke of Rawlings has no reason to be going about making up tales about his neighbor's daughters."

Maggie, standing before her father's desk with her hands behind her back—she didn't dare let him catch a glimpse of her newly bandaged finger—glanced nervously at her mother, who had sunk into a green leather armchair a few feet away, looking a bit pale but nonetheless more composed than Maggie would have expected, under the circumstances.

"And there's no use looking to your mother for support in this, young lady," Sir Arthur said, as gruffly as he was able, which, since Maggie's father had never been much of a disciplinarian, was not considerable. "She and I stand united in our mutual shame for you. You have disgraced this family, and, I must add, heartily embarrassed the house of Rawlings. I have no doubt that Lord Edward shares my disappointment in the behavior of both you and the duke . . . though I must say I feel the burden of the blame lies primarily with you, Margaret."

Maggie opened her mouth to protest this unfair accusation, then noticed her mother's small headshake. With an effort, she kept her tongue. .

"You have always proven something of a trial to the young duke," her father went on, "though you've been asked repeatedly to refrain from teasing him. His Grace's childhood was not the happiest, due to his father's unfortunate choice of a bride—"

Maggie rolled her eyes. She had heard this particular story too many times to pay attention to it. On and on her father went, about how Lord Edward's elder brother, John, had married a vicar's daughter, Lady Pegeen's elder sister, Katherine, a mistake for which he'd eventually paid with his life. No mention was ever made of where Jeremy's mother was now, but snippets of conversation that Maggie had overheard as a child led her to believe that Katherine was not only alive, but living in London, forbidden by Lord Edward from ever seeing her son. The reason for this seemed to stem from Lord John having been murdered in a duel over her.

"I've no doubt that this incident today," Sir Arthur continued phlegmatically, "like similar incidents in the past, is a result of your tricking His Grace into behaving with impropriety—"

Again, Maggie drew a swift breath to defend herself, and again, her mother shook her head. Gritting her teeth, Maggie lowered her flashing eyes to the floor, so her father would not notice their mutinous expression.

"I have therefore given His Grace my sincerest apologies for your behavior, though he, tactful young man that he is, insists it is entirely his fault, and that you are blameless. Tomorrow, I shall extend a similar apology to Lord and Lady Edward, as well." Sir Arthur, a portly man, placed both of his plump hands on his green leather desktop blotter and sighed. "And now, Margaret, your mother and I feel that the question of your future is at stake. I hardly need point out to you that the kind of behavior exhibited by you today would be quite out of place in the ballrooms of London. I have also heard you admit in the past, Margaret, that you are a young lady governed by your, um, impulses. If this is any evidence of where your impulses guide you, then I can only say, a season in London would be a highly questionable undertaking. The introduction of any young woman into society is a significant financial commitment. There is lodging to be considered—we can hardly, after this, count on the kindness of Lord and Lady Edward for the use of the duke's town house, as we did for your sisters—and all manner of gowns and hats and such fripperies to be purchased. This is a considerable expense for a young woman who will most likely embarrass us by throwing herself into the arms of the first man who asks her to dance—"

Maggie lifted her gaze then, to pierce her father with a furious glare. But he did not appear to notice the poisoned darts her eyes were sending in his direction. Instead, he said, "And so, after careful consideration, your mother and I have decided that you are *not* to have a season in London next winter."

Since Maggie knew her father meant this as a punishment, she did not shout hurray, although that was her first impulse. Instead, she lowered her gaze once again, and tried not to smile too widely. "Yes, sir," was all she said, and that sounded suitably humble.

"Now we come to an impasse, your mother and I. For while I feel—and I might add, your sister Anne agrees with me—that a few months in a convent might be just the thing for someone of your, er, temperament—"

Maggie lifted startled eyes toward her mother, who gave a barely perceptible shrug.

"—your mother disagrees. She seems to feel that part of your problem, young lady, is that you have the restless soul of an artist"—He made a face as he said the word *artist*, as if its pronunciation made a bad taste in his mouth—"and that it is our obligation as parents to try to rein in that restlessness as best we can. While I think the convent would be eminently suited to this, your mother feels someone of your talent might be stifled in so stringent an environment. Accordingly, she has suggested that the art school in Paris you mentioned last month is the best solution—"

Maggie could not contain her feelings this time. She

whirled around to face her mother. "No!" she cried incredulously. "Really? Do you really mean it?"

Lady Herbert was a little better at disguising her emotions. "Yes, dear," she said calmly, though her face was beaming with pleasure. "You're to start in the fall—"

Maggie fell upon her mother's neck in a rain of grateful tears. Her father, still seated behind his desk, cleared his throat several times before he again captured the attention of both women. "This is not meant as a reward, Margaret," he reminded her severely. "You are to study hard, and any reports I hear from Madame Bonheur about any more, er, skittish behavior will result in your immediate removal. . . ."

"Oh, yes, Papa," Maggie sniffled happily, wiping her eyes with a handkerchief her mother had extracted from her sleeve. "You shan't regret allowing me this opportunity. I swear you won't hear a peep from Madame Bonheur, except in praise."

"I sincerely hope so. We shall be sending Hill with you, young lady, to keep an eye on you. Don't think we'd ever allow you out of England without a chaperon."

"Of course not," Maggie said, from her perch on the arm of her mother's chair. "Oh, Papa, you don't know what this means to me—"

"No, you're right," Sir Arthur interrupted a bit testily. "I don't. In my day, young women didn't follow young men into stables . . . particularly not unmarried dukes! And they certainly didn't go to art school, either. I don't pretend to understand what's happening to this generation, and I don't expect I ever will. A woman's place is in the home, keeping her husband happy and providing him with heirs. Your sisters all seem to have grasped that concept. It is my hope, Margaret, that when you've gotten this infernal interest in doodling out of your system, you will return home and settle down with a suitable fellow, like your sister Anne has. I don't understand why you can't be more like Anne. Anne never insisted upon attending school in France. English schools were fine enough for your sisters. And when they were through with their education, they married, exactly as ladies should. This unfortunate new propensity women seem to have to want to pursue an occupation outside the home will be the ruin of all—''

"Yes, Arthur," Lady Herbert said, reaching up to tuck a lock of her daughter's hair behind her ear. "I know. But Maggie isn't like our other girls. She's special."

"Especially troublesome," Sir Arthur grunted, "is all I can tell that's special about her. Now, if you two are done weeping, I'd like my supper. And what's that you've got on your finger, Margaret? Some kind of bandage? What have you done to yourself *now*?"

After supper, Maggie repaired to her room with Hill, her mother's maid, to start making a list of things they'd both need for Paris. True, she wasn't leaving for another four months, but Maggie felt it was never too early to start planning for an extended trip abroad. Besides, she needed something to keep her mind off what had happened earlier in the day, and constant activity had a way, she'd noted, of keeping one from brooding.

Not that Maggie was brooding over the Duke of Rawlings. Not at all. She understood perfectly what had happened between them, and felt nothing but the most excruciating embarrassment—and occasional burst of anger—because of it. It was all perfectly obvious. Jeremy, bored, had chosen to pass a little of his spare time attempting to seduce a girl with whom he'd been childhood friends. It was certainly nothing more than that, or wouldn't have been, if Lord Edward hadn't caught them.

Of course, there was the fact that Maggie had allowed it to happen at all to be taken into account, but that was fairly easily explained. She had always been a highly excitable sort of girl, and she had simply gotten carried away by the moment. Fortunately, she had been saved from ruin—this time— and had learned a valuable lesson in the meantime, which was that men were not to be trusted, and, more importantly, she was not to trust herself around men, either. Prevention of future, similar incidents would be all too easy. She'd simply never allow herself to be alone with a man again. That was all.

Problem solved.

Her first chance to put her new prevention plan into practice came a little sooner than anticipated, however. As she and Hill were cataloguing the contents of the wardrobe in her dressing room, Maggie heard a tap on the French doors to the terrace just off her bedroom, and when she went to open them, thinking it was her cat asking to be let in, she was startled to find the Duke of Rawlings standing in the moonlight, a warning finger to his lips.

"I've got to talk to you," he whispered.

Maggie, one hand still on the door latch, the other on the frame, said, through suddenly bloodless lips, "Have you lost your mind? My father is downstairs. If he finds you up here, he'll kill you."

"He will not," Jeremy said, looking perfectly unimpressed. "I'm his employer, remember?"

"Acting as your solicitor is his hobby," Maggie said, with an imperious toss of her head. "He certainly doesn't need the work. He is a man of independent means. Now go away."

She tried to close the door, but to her fury, Jeremy insinuated a booted foot between the door and the frame, and no matter how hard she tried, she could not shut him out.

"Do you mind?" she demanded at last. "I never want to speak to you again."

The moonlight was strong enough for Maggie to see the corners of Jeremy's lips curl up. "That sounded very convincing, Mags. Maybe if you actually kept your mouth shut, the threat would carry some weight."

Furious, Maggie hissed through clenched teeth, "I mean it, Jerry. You got me in a lot of trouble today—"

"*I* got *you* in trouble?" Jeremy interrupted with a humorless laugh. "Oh, I like that! *I'm* not the one going about, looking like that. . . ." He nodded at her meaningfully.

"Looking like what?" Maggie demanded defensively.

"Like every man's idea of perfection," he finished, though he clearly hadn't wanted to admit it. "Now, are you going to let me in, or am I going to have to rush the door?"

"Don't you dare!" Maggie's cheeks were on fire. Over her dead body was there going to be a repeat performance of what had happened that afternoon. "I nearly got sent to a convent because of you!"

Jeremy took a deep breath, as if fighting for patience. "Look, Mags," he said at last. "I've come to apologize. Will you let me in? Or am I going to have to stand out here and shout until your father comes along and puts a bullet in my brain?"

Maggie's heart began its unsteady rattle inside her chest once more. "I—" She glanced nervously over her shoulder, but it wasn't Hill she was worried about. It was her bed, a very large, comfortable four-poster, looming just a few yards away. "It's just that . . ."

Jeremy held out both of his hands. Even in the moonlight, they still looked menacingly large and masculine to Maggie. "If it's these you're afraid of," he said amiably, "they'll stay in my trouser pockets. I swear it."

Maggie stuck out her chin. "I'm not afraid of you," she lied contemptuously.

"Oh, I know," Jeremy said with a smug smile. "I've got the bruises to show it. So if that's the case, why not let me in?"

It was a challenge. Maggie could not back down from it, and still retain what little honor she had left. So, eyeing him distrustfully, Maggie called, over her shoulder, "Hill?"

From the depths of her dressing room came a muffled, "Yes, miss?"

Keeping a careful eye on the man on her terrace, Maggie asked, "Hill, would you be so good as to leave the rest until tomorrow? I'm afraid I've developed a headache. I want to go to bed now."

Behind her, the middle-aged maid popped her head out from the dressing room. "A headache, miss?"

Belatedly, Maggie realized her excuse had not been a good one. Miss Margaret Herbert had never been ill a day in her life, and the entire staff at Herbert Park knew it.

"Do you want me to fetch your mother? Or the surgeon, Mr. Parks?"

"Oh," Maggie said, turning swiftly so that her back was

to the French doors. "No, that isn't necessary. I just need a little sleep, that's all."

"P'raps I should fetch a tonic fer you, miss. Wouldn't be no trouble a'tall—"

"No, no," Maggie said, waving away the older woman's concern. "Just run along, and thank you so much. We'll finish tomorrow."

The maid bobbed a slightly disapproving curtsy. "Very well, miss. But if you be needin' a tonic later, be sure to ring fer me."

"Yes, Hill, I will." Maggie smiled gratefully. "Thank you."

No sooner had the woman closed the bedroom door behind her than Jeremy came barreling in through the French doors, nearly knocking Maggie over in his haste to get inside.

"So," he said, after taking a long and careful look about the white, femininely furnished room. "I've finally been granted admittance into Miss Margaret Herbert's boudoir. I must say, I feel honored. I've never seen anything quite so virginal in all my life."

"Oh, do be quiet." Blushing furiously, Maggie went to the terrace doors, which he'd left standing wide open, and closed them. "It's no thanks to you that my virginity's still intact, thank you very much."

Jeremy raised his eyebrows at this piece of information, but decided that he'd best not pursue that particular topic. "Yes," he said. To be on the safe side, he put his fingers in his pockets, as promised. "Well. I'm sorry about all that. Were they really going to stick you in a convent?"

"Yes." Maggie had never let a member of the opposite sex into her bedroom before, and it was only after she'd already admitted one that she realized what a dreadfully inappropriate place it was to entertain a man. Undergarments lay in untidy piles all about the room, including her torn crinoline, looking like a deflated birdcage on the floor, and various pairs of stockings, camisoles, and corsets draped over the back of a pink satin chair. Jeremy, after his initial comment, tactfully ignored these things, however, and strolled—

his hands in his pockets, as promised—over to the easel she'd set up by the bay window.

"Say," he said, after examining the small canvas resting there. "This is really good. I didn't know you'd started doing landscapes, too."

"Well," Maggie said uncomfortably. "Around here, I sometimes run out of people to paint."

"I saw that portrait you did of my cousins. Very impressive. It could easily have passed for the work of a professional. You certainly haven't been wasting your time, whatever else you've been up to, these past five years."

Maggie didn't know what to say. She had never received a compliment from the Duke of Rawlings before—unless one counted the ones he'd delivered earlier in the day, about her new figure, which she didn't, because her new figure was something that had occurred independent of any effort on her part. The compliment on her painting, however, meant something, and she found herself blushing even more furiously than before. Because she was so uneasy, what she did say came out sounding less gracious than she'd intended: "Look, Jerry, I'm very flattered, but why don't you just say what you came to say and get out? You really did get me into a lot of trouble, you know."

"I know." Jeremy stood in the center of her room, his hands still in his pockets, and looked at her. In the lamplight, Maggie looked just as beautiful as she had in bright sunshine. The darkness of her hair and eyes, contrasted with the ivory tone of her skin, was more startling at night, and lent her a more exotic air. In another simple muslin gown, this one of the palest pink, she appeared almost otherworldly, like a sylph, or even a Gypsy princess. She certainly held herself with all the regality of royalty. Jeremy didn't have the slightest trouble picturing her with a tiara on her head or ermine about her shoulders.

Except, of course, that she had a very ungainly white handkerchief tied around the middle finger of her right hand.

He nodded toward it. "Does it hurt much?"

She glanced down. "Only when I paint. You?"

He grinned. "Only when I smile."

Maggie took a few steps forward until she stood only a foot away from him. It was a little unnerving, the fact that he was now so much taller than she was, but she reached up anyway. Taking hold of his chin, she turned his head so she could get a better look at his swollen lip. She saw him wince a little at her touch, but he didn't try to stop her. It was then that she noticed the purpling bruise on his jaw.

"Hmmm," she said, with admirable calm. "Lord Edward really *did* thrash you, didn't he?"

"Oh," Jeremy said lightly, with a short laugh. "That. Yes, he popped my cork, all right. Between the two of you, I'm not sure who's got the better punch. No more than I deserved, though." He gazed down at her, observing that she still worried her lower lip with her teeth when she looked at something closely. "I really am sorry, Maggie, about what happened today."

To his disappointment, Maggie dropped her hand from his face, so quickly it was almost as if she'd been singed. "Yes," she said, lowering her eyes. Two deep red stains began to grow in her otherwise pale cheeks. "Well...."

"I would have called on you like a normal person, at the front door, if I'd had any confidence that you'd see me," Jeremy went on quickly. "But I knew you'd only say you were indisposed, or some such nonsense, and I wouldn't have been able to stand it. I'd have probably struck your butler, or something, in a rage. That's why I climbed up the back way. I had to see you, Mags...." He reached out and seized her uninjured hand. It felt vibrant and warm in his fingers, the way the rest of her had felt, back in the stables. "There's something I've got to ask you."

Maggie looked pointedly down at their hands. "What happened to your promise?" she demanded.

He followed her gaze, but saw nothing but his large brown hand engulfing her small white one. "What promise?"

"To keep your hands in your pockets, you miserable sot."

Jeremy glared at her. "Do you have any idea how exceedingly difficult it is," he inquired, through clenched teeth, "to propose to a young woman who's just called you a miserable sot?"

Chapter 8

"Propose?" Maggie's big brown eyes went even larger still, until they seemed to consume half her face. Then, to Jeremy's chagrin, she burst out laughing. "Oh, I like that!" she cried cheerfully. "And do you propose to every girl you kiss, Jerry, or am I just lucky somehow?"

Jeremy, though he had never been in a similar situation before, was fairly certain that proposals of marriage were not generally received with gales of laughter. He found Maggie's reaction disheartening. Still holding on to her hand, he said stiffly, "I'm not joking, Maggie, and I'd appreciate it if you quit laughing."

She seemed perfectly incapable of obliging him, however, and so he just kept speaking, in a quiet voice. "I've given this a lot of thought, and I feel that, all things considered, you and I are eminently suited for one another. I have to go abroad for a while, but I think it would be good fun if you'd come with me. We could stop in Gretna Green along the way—"

Maggie, during the course of this speech, seemed to recover herself. Straightening, she rubbed at the corners of her eyes with the back of her free hand while looking up at him suspiciously. "Good God," she said, her voice slightly hoarse now from all the guffawing she'd been doing. "You're serious!"

"Of course I'm serious," Jeremy said irritably. "I hardly make a habit of going about tossing off marriage proposals right and left, you know." Reaching into his waistcoat, he drew out a gold pocket watch and, after examining the time, said, "If we leave now, we could be at Gretna Green by morning. Are you going to need help packing your things? Because it would probably be best if we didn't alert the mater and pater by asking your maid for help. . . ."

Maggie wrenched her fingers from his and took a few hasty steps backward, until her backside met up with the far wall. "You've gone mad!" she cried, her dark eyes wide and incredulous. "You can't be serious!"

"You keep saying that," Jeremy said, calmly putting his watch away. "Clearly I'm not mad. I'm speaking to you in a perfectly rational manner. It's you who keeps laughing like some kind of demented hyena—"

Maggie barely heard him. She was trying to make sense of the fact that the Duke of Rawlings had actually asked her to marry him. Funny, he didn't *look* like a madman. But of course he *was* one. Only a madman would want to marry a sixteen-year-old girl who'd just a few hours earlier split her knuckles on his front teeth.

Taking advantage of her bemusement, Jeremy crossed the few feet of floor that separated them. He saw Maggie's eyes flare even wider at his approach. She cast her gaze about the room in search of something . . . probably a weapon, he thought wryly, with which to defend herself against him. He placed both hands against the wall on either side of her, so that escape was impossible. Then, leaning so close to her that his chest skimmed the peaks of her breasts, Jeremy said, in his deepest, most persuasive voice, the one that never failed to get him what he wanted, "Maggie. I mean it. I want you to marry me. Now. Tonight."

Maggie, desperately attempting to shrink as far back into the wall as possible, swallowed. She was trying not to breathe too deeply, because every time she inhaled, her senses were assailed with the manly smell of him . . . and the swell of her breasts swept the front of his satin waistcoat. This couldn't be happening, she thought. Not to her. This was the sort of thing that happened to girls in books, not to Maggie Herbert. Never to Maggie Herbert.

Jeremy, reading the uncertainty in her face, sighed. He hadn't wanted to have to resort to this. He had wanted her to agree to marry him without having to try to sway her using his more physical charms. But his pride had been tweaked by her initial laughter at his proposal; her subsequent behavior had left him feeling a little desperate. He'd expected *some* resistance to the idea . . . that was only natural. After all, she had hit him earlier in the day, and forcefully, too. But he certainly hadn't expected *this*.

Nor could he understand it. Maggie Herbert wasn't a simpleton. He was one of the wealthiest men in England, and had the land and the title to prove it. And for once, he didn't care if this particular woman wanted him for his money, so long as he got her, somehow. Besides, despite what he'd told his uncle that morning, he knew perfectly well that women found him attractive for his person, and not always his purse. That could only work in his favor, where Maggie was concerned.

But Maggie seemed unswayed by all of these things. She was actually looking up at him with anxiety in her eyes—even fear—and seemed about as ready to agree to marry him as to strip naked and dash through her father's library singing "God Save the Queen" at the top of her lungs.

He was going to get to the root of that fear, even if it took all night.

Lowering his head, Jeremy pressed his mouth against hers, cutting off whatever it was she'd drawn breath to say, most likely the word *no*, which seemed to tumble from her lips with disturbing regularity.

Maggie struggled for only a second or two this time. She seemed to know she was caught and, with a sigh of resignation, finally relaxed against him. And though she kept her hands thrust out defensively against his chest, and did not circle his neck with her arms, or in any other way invite him closer, her lips did part again beneath his. And that was invitation enough, as far as Jeremy was concerned. Slipping his hands around her narrow waist, he drew her to him until she was standing on her toes, her weight supported almost completely by his arms, and ravaged her mouth with his.

Maggie, her heart thudding dully in her ears, could not quite believe she was in the exact same position she'd been in only a few hours ago . . . only worse, because this time, there would be no one to interrupt them, and there was a bed just a few feet away. God, what was wrong with her? Why hadn't she even *tried* to fight him off? There was something seriously wrong with her. She yearned for this man's embrace, and yet when she found herself in his arms, all she could think about was how frightened she was of what might come next!

And he had asked her to *marry* him! He didn't even appear to be intoxicated, but he had *asked her to marry him*. Oh, he hadn't exactly professed his undying love for her, or anything like that. In fact, as far as proposals went, his had been remarkably unromantic.

But, oh God, when he kissed her, how nice she felt! Well, not nice, exactly—in fact, the opposite of nice. His kisses made her feel positively wicked . . . which was actually a lovely feeling, she was discovering. But surely this couldn't last. At some point, kissing gave way to other things, things Maggie had only witnessed in the sheep meadow, and which she wanted absolutely no part of, thank you very much. It seemed all right for the rams, but the ewes had never seemed to be enjoying themselves very much . . . and then, a few months later, they looked astonished when a lamb popped out their backside! Maggie wasn't about to spend the rest of her life popping out lambs. Not when she'd finally convinced her parents to let her go to Paris. . . .

But *marriage*? To the Duke of Rawlings?

No. Maggie's blood went cold at the thought. Maggie Herbert, the duchess of Rawlings? Why, that would be like having to endure a season in London every day *for the rest of her life*. What could he possibly be thinking? Was he mad? She would make the worst duchess in the history of England! What kind of duchess had paint under her fingernails and spent all of her time falling out of trees? Why, no amount of kisses, no matter how wicked, could ever compensate for that!

It was right about then that Maggie felt something stiff

prodding at her through the whalebone stays of her corset. She wasn't certain, but it seemed to be coming from the front of Jeremy's trousers. Without thinking, Maggie dropped one of her hands from his chest and laid it, curiously, on the hard thing, thinking that she was going to find a knife hilt, or more amusedly, the butt of a derringer, and that she'd then be able to tease Jeremy about why he'd felt the need to come to Herbert Park armed.

But what she felt beneath her fingers was neither a knife hilt nor a derringer. It was pure, unadulterated Jeremy.

To say that Jeremy felt *surprised* when Maggie suddenly placed her hand on his burgeoning erection would be something of an understatement. The truth was that he was suddenly filled with hope—among other things—that he'd managed to change her mind after all. He hadn't expected her to be quite so daring, however. After all, she *was* only sixteen, and he was fairly certain that the kiss they'd shared that afternoon had been her first. Still, if Maggie Herbert wanted to fondle his erection, he wasn't going to try to stop her. . . .

And so when she abruptly pulled her hand away, as if it had been pressed upon a red-hot coal and not a simple piece of flesh, Jeremy realized that Maggie hadn't had the slightest notion what she'd been doing. She went stiff in his arms. He felt it, and instinctively knew what was coming: His kiss, like his words, had failed to persuade her. Damn, what was wrong with the girl? What more could she possibly want? Did he have to fall to his knees and pledge unrequited love to her?

Apparently so. Because suddenly, Maggie pushed him away, with so much unexpected force that he staggered backward. Quick as a cat, she darted behind the pink satin chair, as if an armchair could afford her some sort of protection against the force of his will.

When she spoke, she only uttered one word, but her voice still broke heart-wrenchingly on it. "*Why?*"

Taken aback, Jeremy lowered his eyebrows into a glower. "Why what?"

"*Why* do you want to marry me?" Maggie asked, her anxiety readily apparent in her eyes.

Why? The girl had to ask *why*? He nearly burst out laughing. Wasn't it perfectly obvious? No other girl he'd ever known had leapt at him from tree branches, kissed him with such fervent abandon, punched him in the mouth, then seized hold of his erect penis as if it were a badminton racket. What man *wouldn't* want to marry a girl like that?

"What do you mean *why*?" he asked, unable to stifle a grin.

"Just that," Maggie said, appearing to be perfectly serious. "I mean, Jeremy, you hardly even *know* me. . . ."

"Hardly even know you?" Jeremy echoed with a laugh. "I know you better than anyone, Mags. I know the way your eyes shine when you laugh. I know the way you squint when you're trying to see something far away. I know the way you chew your bottom lip when you look at something up close. I know the way your nostrils flare when you tell a lie." Maggie drew swift breath to deny this, but even as she did so, he chuckled. "Like they're doing now. Maggie, there isn't anything about you that I don't know. I even know how your lips part when you're kissed. . . ."

That statement brought Maggie's eyes instantly to his mouth. Which reminded her of the bruise along his jaw. And suddenly, it all became very clear to her.

Of course. That explained it perfectly.

Her eyes narrowing with suspicion, she said knowingly, "It was Lord Edward, wasn't it?"

He blinked. "I beg your pardon?"

"Lord Edward put you up to this." She was suddenly furious. Really, truly, spitting mad. How *dare* he? How dare he burst into her room like this and demand that she marry him? His uncle had put him up to it, of course! "Well, you can tell your uncle from me that he's really being too old-fashioned for words if he thinks that just because you kissed me, I expect a marriage proposal. I mean, that may have been how things were done when he was our age, but this is eighteen seventy-one! Does he really think—"

"What?" Jeremy looked confused. "Maggie, what are you talking about?"

Maggie shook her head so energetically that all of her loose brown hair fell over her shoulders to frame her face. "You can just march right back to Rawlings Manor and tell him thank you very much for the concern over my reputation, but if he'd found me standing stark naked in your bedroom, I *still* wouldn't marry you, not if you were the last man on earth!"

Though he was more than a little bit taken aback by this last piece of information, Jeremy stood his ground. Even the expression of sheer fury on her face could not dissuade him from the course upon which he'd set himself that afternoon. He knew the fury only masked what she was really feeling just then, which was fear, plain and simple. Maggie, he knew now, was afraid of him. He had a pretty good idea why, too: Maggie only feared what she didn't know.

And he was going to see to it that he, and no other man, was the one who assuaged that fear.

"My uncle Edward," Jeremy said, slowly and deliberately, "did not put me up to anything, Mags. This was all my idea."

But Maggie looked as if she hadn't heard him. "I think," she said unsteadily, "that you ought to leave now, Jerry."

Her cheeks, he noted, were crimson. Not pink. Not just red. But the color of blood.

"I'm not leaving," he said evenly, "until you say yes."

"Then you're going to be here a long time," Maggie informed him tartly. "Because I'm not marrying you, Jeremy."

He didn't even flinch. "Why not?"

Behind the chair, Maggie stamped an impatient foot. "What do you mean, why not?" she demanded. "Why do I have to give you a reason? Just get out!"

"No," he said, calmly folding his arms across his chest. "Not until you've told me why you won't marry me."

"Because," Maggie said with another stamp. "It's perfectly ridiculous! We're too young to marry."

"Granted," Jeremy said. "I'm willing to wait for you. Will you wait for me?"

"I—"

How could she tell him that he could wait until he was one hundred years old, and she'd still be too afraid of him to marry him? Maggie had never been able to admit to weakness of any kind. Better that he think she didn't like him than that she was frightened of him.

"No," she said firmly. "I won't wait. My parents have agreed to let me go to school in Paris. I shall probably be there for a long time."

"So?" Jeremy shrugged. "I'm joining the army. I shall probably be gone some time, too."

Maggie nearly came out from behind the protection offered by her chair, she was so surprised. "Really, Jeremy?" she cried, delighted for him. "The army? How exciting! I'm sure you'll look very dashing in uniform. Do you think you'll get to go to India, and meet a maharajah, like in our game?"

"Yes," Jeremy said impatiently. "So, will you wait for me, Mags?"

The smile left her face. "Oh, Jerry, no. Really, we'd better not. Who can tell what might happen, given a few years' time? It's possible I shall never marry at all, if I'm able to make a living selling my portraits. Your aunt thinks I might be able to—"

"Never marry at all?" Jeremy echoed disbelievingly. Blast Pegeen for putting such a wretched idea in the girl's head! While the thought of Maggie never marrying at all was at least preferable to the thought of her marrying someone other than himself, he nevertheless couldn't imagine her going through her whole life as celibate as a nun. No woman who looked as she did *could*. It simply went against nature. "Don't be ridiculous," he said. "Of course you'll marry. Say it won't be anyone but me, and I'll go."

"Jerry, really, think about it." Maggie realized that somebody had to say it. If he wouldn't, she would. "I wouldn't make a very good duchess. I certainly don't *look* like one, and all I'm interested in doing, ever, is painting. I wouldn't be any good at duchessy sorts of things. You know, going

to balls and opening harvest festivals down at the vicarage
and things like that. I can't make small talk, and I always
end up saying the wrong thing.'' She saw Jeremy inhale, as
if to refute this, but she hurried on, not letting him interrupt.
''And I'm not in the least domestic! I don't know what's the
right kind of wine to serve with duck, and I always end up
using the fish fork with the vegetables. Why, I can't even
stand wearing my hair up! The pins always feel like they're
jabbing into my scalp. I just wouldn't do, Jerry. You're better
off finding someone else.''

But even as she said it, Maggie realized that the thought
of Jeremy with any woman at all filled her with a sort of
sickening feeling, as if she'd been kicked in the stomach by
a horse.

''No,'' Jeremy said. ''That isn't it.'' He crossed the room
until he was standing before the chair, and leaned forward
to peer at Maggie's face. ''You're lying again. Your nostrils
are flared. What's the real reason you won't marry me?''
Maggie started backing away the minute he placed a knee
on the seat cushion, but Jeremy reached across the chair back
and snatched her by the wrist, to keep her from retreating
farther. ''Christ,'' he said wonderingly, as he felt her pulse
leap beneath his fingers. ''You really *are* afraid of me!
Why?''

Maggie shook her head. ''I'm not afraid of you,'' she said
with a shaky laugh. ''Don't be ridiculous.''

''You are. And you'll be telling me why, my fine girl, or
I'll still be here in the morning when Hill comes back. We'll
see how Sir Arthur feels about sending you to Paris then.''

Maggie inhaled sharply. ''That's . . . that's blackmail!''

''It isn't,'' Jeremy said. ''It's coercion, but the two are
fairly similar, so the error's understandable. Now, are you
going to tell me, or am I going to have to make myself
comfortable in this lovely chair for the rest of the evening?''

Maggie took a deep, steadying breath. ''It's just that . . .''
Lord, how was she going to be able to explain this, without
sounding a fool? Maybe if she didn't look at him. Lowering
her eyes to the floor, Maggie said haltingly, ''It's just that
when you . . . touch me, like you do, all I can think about is

how much I want you to touch me . . . in other places. And I know those aren't proper thoughts for a lady to have! And then I start feeling frightened that I'm not a lady at all, and that I won't be able to say no, and things will go too far, and I'll end up in a convent, just like my sister Anne always said, because I'm entirely too carnal by nature. . . .''

This was so far from what Jeremy had been expecting her to say that for a moment he was silent, absolutely staggered by her confession. Then he grasped her uninjured hand and, bringing it to his lips, said eagerly, between kisses, ''Darling, don't you see? That just proves that you *do* like me a little. Now you've simply *got* to marry me—''

''No!'' Maggie wrenched her hand from his fingers. ''It doesn't prove anything of the kind! All it proves is that I go all melty inside when a man kisses me. I don't know if it's just you, or any man, because—''

''Because I'm the only man who's ever kissed you,'' Jeremy finished for her, bitterly.

''Well,'' Maggie said, her shoulders slumping in defeat. ''Yes. I'm sorry. But yes.''

It wasn't that he blamed her, really. It wasn't her fault. But he couldn't help feeling bitter about a lot of things—the difference in their ages, for one; her sheltered upbringing, for another. Not that he *wanted* her to go about kissing other men, to find out if there was anything special about her reaction to him. But it looked like such an experiment was going to be necessary. And he sure as hell wasn't going to be able to stick around to watch it. Not without wanting to throttle the neck of each and every man with whom she came into contact.

Sinking back into the armchair with a sigh, Jeremy raised a hand to his head. The headache Maggie had lied to her maid about seemed suddenly to be plaguing him.

Maggie, watching him from the end of her bed, where she'd perched a little warily, said, ''I'm sorry, Jerry.''

''You said that already.''

''Well, it's the truth. I *am* sorry. But you asked—''

''I know I asked,'' Jeremy interrupted. ''I am only too well aware of the fact that I asked.'' Suddenly very much craving whisky, Jeremy gripped the arms of the pink satin chair and pushed himself up. "Well, Mags, you win. I'm going now."

"Oh." Maggie stood up, feeling a little disappointed. She didn't know what it was she'd said that had depressed Jeremy so thoroughly. Now it looked as if there wouldn't be any more marriage proposals—or kisses—forthcoming. While part of her was relieved, another part was sad.

Heading toward the French doors through which he'd come, Jeremy turned just once in her direction. "Promise me one thing, though, will you, Mags?"

She crossed the room to stand beside him, rather like a hostess showing a guest to the door after afternoon tea. "Certainly. If I can."

"I think you can. It's just a little thing. I'll be going away for a while, but Aunt Pegeen will always know where to find me. If you should happen to . . . find out whether or not it's just me, or men in general, would you send me a line? Nothing elaborate. Just a simple 'Yes, it's you,' or 'No, it's not' will suffice. Do you think you could promise to do that for me? For old times' sake?"

Maggie nodded hesitantly. "All right, Jerry."

"Good girl." He leaned down and gave her a brotherly kiss on the cheek before stepping out onto the terrace. "Good-bye, then."

It was a warm night. Maggie stood in the open doorway and watched as Jeremy swung a leg over the terrace wall and started to climb down the ivy to the lawn below. "Jerry?" she called after him.

He looked at her. "Yes?"

"Where are you going?" she asked.

He smiled, a bit lopsidedly. "I don't know. To the devil, I suppose."

"Oh," Maggie said. "Well, give him my regards."

The smile vanished. "I will," Jeremy said, and then he was gone.

Part Two

Chapter 9

A butler in a household like that belonging to the Duke of Rawlings could expect to perform many duties. There were the common tasks associated with butlering, of course, including the hiring, firing, and supervision of the lesser household staff. There was the wine cellar to keep stocked and well tended, the silver to lock up at night, the announcement of callers, and even the newspapers to iron in the morning, if they arrived with the ink still tacky. When the master of the house was at home—in this case the duke's uncle, Lord Edward—there were always peculiar duties in addition to the normal ones, such as the tracking down of a dozen perfect roses in the dead of winter to be laid at Lady Edward's place at the breakfast table, or, as occasionally happened while Parliament was in session, the random death threat to be reported to the local magistrate.

But it was extremely rare, despite the odd hours kept by Lord and Lady Edward during the height of the season, for the household butler to be wakened from a dead sleep at five o'clock in the morning by the ringing of the front doorbell. Usually, a footman could be counted on to stumble downstairs and answer the summons. But as Lord and Lady Edward had not yet arrived from the country—though they were expected any day—and the footmen had gone out with their mates for the night to celebrate an impending nuptial, the only male within the Rawlings town house that night was Evers. And the last thing Evers wanted to do was haul his fifty-odd-year-old carcass out of his cozy bed, pad down four flights of stairs, and open the door to what could only, at this hour of the night, be bad news.

For a while Evers lay with a pillow over his head, hoping the strange caller would go away, thinking no one home. But whoever was ringing the bell evidently knew someone would answer eventually, because he went right on ringing it. Knowing that if he allowed this sort of behavior to go on much longer, the bell would wake the females staying in the house, who undoubtedly would react with typical feminine hysteria to this nocturnal visitation, Evers finally threw back his warm covers and, shivering, donned his dressing gown, slippers, and nightcap, and, with all the speed that his age and infirmity allowed, he started the long journey down from the fourth floor of the five-story house.

It took him approximately ten minutes to reach the door. During that time, the caller, whoever he was, continued to ring the bell, but made a sort of game out of it, ringing it twice, and then stopping, ringing it once again, and then four times, quickly. The pattern varied, but the message was clear: *Answer the door. It's cold out here.*

"Coming," Evers called, in a creaky, sleep-roughened voice, when he finally shuffled into the marble foyer. If it was cold outside, it was just as cold inside that unheated entranceway. Evers thought longingly of his hot-water bottle, which had undoubtedly gone tepid by now. "I'm coming. Blessed Jesus, stop ringing that bell. I'm coming!"

But when Evers finally managed to work all the locks on the door and fling it open, the man standing on the front stoop was neither the night watchman, as he'd expected, nor the dairy man, mistaking the front door for the one marked Staff. The man who stood out in the thick yellow fog that inevitably enveloped London in winter was a stranger to Evers, but a gentleman, one could see at a glance. Swathed in greatcoat, fur hat, woolen muffler, and leather gloves, the man might not have been recognizable to his own mother. As it was, Evers saw only a long nose, which might once have been aquiline but had apparently been broken and badly reset, and a pair of rather startlingly light eyes, set back in a tanned, slightly yellowish face.

"Yes?" Evers inquired. He was already starting to shiver in the frigid morning air. "Can I help you, sir?"

"Evers?" The man's voice was muffled by all the scarves he wore, but the voice was cultured and deep, the voice of an Englishman, despite the yellow skin.

"Yes. I'm Evers," the butler said. "Who might you be?"

"But you're not Samuel Evers," the man said.

"Of course not. I'm his grandson, Jacob. Samuel Evers has been dead these past four years. He worked at the manor house, in Yorkshire, where my father, John Evers, buttles now. Who might you be, sir, that you knew my grandfather?"

"Don't you recognize me, Evers?" the gentleman inquired, a hint of amusement in his deep voice.

Evers squinted out into the fog. The bitter cold had already sent his knees knocking, and was starting to seep through the brocade of his dressing gown. The gentleman on the doorstep, however, did not look in the least bit cold.

"I can't rightly say," Evers said, his teeth beginning to chatter. "It's a bit cold out for guessing games, though, sir."

"Quite right, Evers," the stranger said. "And you never were very good at them, anyway." Lifting a long arm, the man plucked the fur cap from his head, revealing a scalp covered with a riot of longish black curls. The hair, coupled with the silver eyes, caused Evers to inhale, sharply.

"God bless me," he cried. "Is it really you, Your Grace?"

The Duke of Rawlings threw back his head and laughed. It was a rich sound on the quiet street, a bit startling in its wild abandon. It wasn't the kind of laughter one typically heard on Park Lane, London. At least, not at five in the morning on a wintry February Wednesday.

"Yes, Evers," Jeremy said at last, when his laughter had died down a little. "It's me. Fresh from the Far East, and full of malarial promise. My valet will follow shortly with my trunks, so be on the lookout. Now, have you got a drink for a poor wandering duke? I fear I've lost any resistance I might once have possessed against this damned English cold, and I need a whisky so badly, it hurts."

"Of course, Your Grace." Evers moved hastily out of the way, so that the duke could enter his own house. "I beg your pardon. But we weren't expecting you. We received no communication that Your Grace had left India. . . ."

"No, and nor were you to," Jeremy said. He had crossed the foyer and thrown open the double doors to the drawing room, where he unceremoniously began shedding his many outer layers, letting wrap after wrap fall upon one of the green velvet chaise longues. "I left New Delhi rather suddenly. I doubt the hospital had time for any sort of communiqués with the family. . . ."

Evers had already begun lighting the gas lamps. In a matter of seconds, he had a fairly decent fire going in the ornately carved marble fireplace, as well. "Hospital, Your Grace?"

"Yes," Jeremy said shortly. "Army hospital. Good as it gets in New Delhi, but then, it doesn't get that good there. Food wasn't bad, I suppose, but there's a deplorable lack of drinkable liquor in India. I wish someone had warned me." Eschewing the pair of chaise longues for a green leather armchair closer to the fire, the duke collapsed with a sigh, and stretched his long legs out before him. "God, Evers," he said, closing his eyes. "It's good to be home."

"It's good to have Your Grace back. Though if I might say so, I shall regret no longer being able to read the newspaper accounts of Your Grace's heroics overseas. We were all very proud of your bravery, especially the part you played in squelching the rebellion in Jaipur."

"Oh," Jeremy said uninterestedly, his eyes still closed. "You heard about that, did you?"

"Heard about it, Your Grace? Why, it was all anybody talked of for weeks. To have been awarded the Medal of Honor by the queen . . ." Evers's voice trailed off reverently. Then, seeing that the duke intended to make no reply, the butler cleared his throat and added, "And to have been honored so by the maharajah himself! The Star of Jaipur, from what I understand, is truly one of the wonders of the world. . . .''

''Hmph,'' was all Jeremy had to say about that.

Seeing that he was to get no more information out of the duke along that line, Evers turned to pour the whisky. He had noted with approval that underneath the greatcoat, the duke was dressed in the height of European fashion, despite the fact that he hadn't set foot in Europe in nearly five years. A charcoal-colored morning coat covered a white shirt and matching waistcoat, while tight-fitting black breeches tapered down into a highly polished pair of Hessian boots. Evers further noted that His Grace's cravat had the requisite number of knots to it. His valet had not gotten lazy in that hot, barbarous country, anyway.

But there the butler's approval ended. For the duke was not looking well. Not looking well at all. The yellowish skin tone which Evers had noticed had not been a result of either the gaslit street lamp or the fog. The duke was clearly malarial. He had either recently gotten over a bout of the illness, or was still in the throes of it. Since surely no man would risk his life traveling with such a deadly disease, Evers assumed the former. But a visit from the surgeon, Mr. Wallace, might be in order. Evers would see to it as soon as the rest of the household woke, and he could send one of the maids out with a missive.

''Ah,'' Jeremy said, opening his eyes when Evers cleared his throat and presented him with a piece of cut crystal containing about two fingers of familiar amber liquid. ''Evers, my good man, you, like your grandfather before you, are a saint.''

''Hardly, Your Grace,'' Evers said, with his family's customary modesty. ''Shall you be staying in London long?''

''As long as it takes,'' Jeremy muttered enigmatically into his glass. Tossing back the whisky in one practiced motion, the duke heaved an involuntary shudder, then passed the glass back to the butler, who moved to refill it. Realizing, apparently for the first time, that Evers was dressed in slippers and a robe, Jeremy drawled, ''Lord, Evers, what time is it? I didn't wake you, did I?''

"Indeed, Your Grace did catch me somewhat unawares," Evers said pleasantly. "And the time is twenty past five."

"In the morning?" Jeremy was so shocked he nearly dropped the glass the butler passed to him. "Good God, man! Why didn't you say so before? And there I was, ringing that blasted bell. It's a wonder I didn't wake everyone in the house."

"It's quite all right, Your Grace. At present there is no one staying in the house, with the exception of—"

"What?" Jeremy looked up at the butler in wonder. "Where's my uncle?"

"Lord and Lady Edward were called back to Yorkshire just this weekend to attend a funeral." After Jeremy had made an appropriate grimace, the butler continued. "Yes, tragic. The infant child of one of Your Grace's tenant farmers. But," he added, on a more cheerful note, "they are expected back any day now. Would it suit Your Grace to stay in the chambers normally occupied by his lordship, or would you prefer one of the guest bedrooms?" Evers tried again, less subtly this time, to address the subject of the Star of Jaipur. "Is it only yourself and your valet, Your Grace? Or shall I prepare more rooms?"

"More rooms?" Jeremy echoed. "Why in the devil would you need to prepare more rooms?"

"Well, in the event that Your Grace had brought, er, the Star of Jaipur home with him. . . ."

"Of course I brought it home with me," Jeremy said impatiently. "What sort of fool would leave something like that behind? But I hardly think it needs a room all to itself. It isn't *that* big."

Evers coughed. "Er, no. Of course not." Evers thought it prudent to change the subject. "Might I suggest the Green Room, then? The White Room is, I'm afraid, currently occupied by Miss Margaret, but I can have the fire in the Green Room lit at once if Your Grace prefers—"

Jeremy choked on his whisky. Concerned, Evers stepped forward and only just managed to restrain himself from patting the Duke of Rawlings on the back. "Your Grace?" he asked worriedly. "Are you unwell?"

Still coughing from the whisky that had gone down the wrong way, Jeremy managed to sputter, "*Maggie*? What the devil is *she* doing here?"

"Why, Miss Margaret accompanied Lady Edward to London this season, and has been with us since just after the New Year, Your Grace." Calmly taking the glass from the duke's limp fingers before—as it appeared he would—Jeremy allowed it to drop to the floor, Evers retraced his steps to the sideboard to fill it a third time. "My understanding was that Miss Margaret was only to stay a short while here at Park Lane while she looked for a flat of her own. But it appears that she has yet to find suitable housing. I would imagine it can't be easy for a young lady to establish herself in a large city like London, particularly a young lady striving to make a living in a very competitive field—" Turning away from the sideboard only to find that the duke had risen, not very steadily, to his feet, Evers could not help inquiring, perhaps more solicitously than his station required, "Forgive me, Your Grace, but are you well? You look exceedingly ill. . . ."

But Jeremy waved aside the butler's concern. "And what of this fiancé my aunt wrote to me about? He isn't staying here, too, is he?"

"Mister de Veygoux?" Evers looked genuinely shocked. "A Frenchman, under this roof? Certainly not!"

Jeremy nodded grimly. "I thought not, but I've been away a while. One never knows how things might have changed in one's absence, does one?" Giving the ends of his morning coat a resolute tug, Jeremy asked, "In the White Room then, is she, Evers?"

"Yes, Your Grace," the butler said. Then, as the duke began moving determinedly toward the doorway, Evers cried out, before he could stop himself, "Your Grace!"

Pausing at the threshold, Jeremy turned, his dark eyebrows raised questioningly. "Evers?"

"You aren't . . . Your Grace can't be thinking of going to Miss Margaret's room. . . ." Evers smiled nervously. "You know that your aunt would not approve." Though he nearly choked on the words—an Evers never presumed to correct a Rawlings, no matter how wildly he might be behaving—the butler said gently, "Gentlemen do not call on young ladies in their boudoirs, Your Grace. I'm sure Lady Edward would be very shocked indeed were she to discover that you had even entered the *house* without an appropriate chaperon while Miss Margaret was staying here—"

The duke smiled, and Evers took an involuntary step backward. It was ridiculous, the butler knew, but for a moment, with his ink-black hair and eyebrows, his silver eyes, and that strange, yellowish skin surrounding them, the Duke of Rawlings bore an uncanny resemblance to . . . well, to the devil.

"Your concern for Miss Maggie's reputation is touching, Evers," Jeremy said with a smirk. "It really is. But last time I checked, this house belonged to me. Which makes everything in it mine, as well."

Without another word, Jeremy turned and headed up the marble staircase leading to the second floor. Behind him, Evers, standing in the foyer in his nightcap and dressing gown, lifted the glass of whisky to his lips and hastily drained it. He had enjoyed his all-too-brief employment with the Rawlings family, and had hoped to remain in it as long as his grandfather had. It appeared, however, that his career was about to come to an abrupt end. Because if the Lady Edward didn't terminate him for allowing the duke and Miss Margaret to remain unchaperoned under the same roof, then the duke would surely do so, for objecting to that very thing.

Evers decided that a short letter to his father was in order. He needed, he was afraid, some advice. Some advice and, he was sorry to say, another drink.

Chapter 10

*J*eremy had not spent as much of his childhood in the house on Park Lane as he had at the manor house in Yorkshire, but he remembered it well enough to know why Maggie had chosen to stay in the White Room. Unlike the other rooms in the house, it alone was not papered in one muted color, carpeted in another, and furnished with yet a third, a decorative practice that his aunt Pegeen had espoused, being convinced that the more color in a room, the less likely that the finger smudges would show—and since a large number of children had frequented the town house, including Jeremy himself, this scheme had not proven unwise.

But the White Room was just that, white-walled, with a rich white rug upon the parquet floor, gauzy white curtains over the windows, and entirely white furniture. It was the only room in the house in which children, with their dirty hands and propensity to track mud, had been traditionally forbidden to enter. And it was the kind of room that only a painter, mixing colors all day long, would find restful.

Which, Jeremy knew, was precisely why Maggie had chosen it above the other ten bedrooms in the house. Jeremy could see quite clearly, even in the orange glow from the dying fire in the white marble fireplace, that Maggie had already stamped the room with her own unique personality. There was a collapsible easel leaning against a far wall, along with a wooden case that Jeremy remembered contained brushes and tubes of paint. Beside these loomed a very large, very heavy-looking black leather portfolio, which held either works in progress or copies of Maggie's canvases, undoubtedly to show prospective sitters. On a low table beside a matched set of ivory-backed chairs lay a few less obvious tricks of Maggie's trade, a large stuffed bird on a stick, some sort of mechanical horse, a *papier-mâché* sailboat, and a number of different-sized, colorfully garbed dolls. Jeremy had no idea what possible use these toys might serve, unless at twenty-one, Maggie was still more of a child than she ought to be.

Of more interest to Jeremy, however, were the items thrown over the backs of the chairs scattered about the room, including a corset and a pair of frilled pantaloons. These things were almost as distracting as their owner, who lay in the middle of the large white canopied bed, a few yards from the dying fire. Maggie, Jeremy observed, was as untidy sleeping as she was awake. She had kicked off most of her covers until she lay only half-under a single linen sheet, despite the distinct chill in the room. Unfortunately, she was probably kept quite warm by the very thick cotton nightdress she wore, which covered her, from what Jeremy could tell, from the neck to the ankles.

Still, when Jeremy moved closer to the bed to get a better look at its occupant, he saw plenty to interest him. For one thing, the nightdress had hiked up a little, revealing one bare calf and the slim curve of an ankle. For another, Maggie slept with one arm flung up over her head, which stretched the material of her nightdress taut over one of her breasts—still quite surprisingly large, Jeremy noted with delight, especially for a girl who'd completely lacked a bosom for so many years—and revealed the soft indentation of an unawakened nipple. Her long hair, unbraided, lay in a thick dark tangle beneath her head. Maggie's face, turned toward the glow of what remained of the fire, had lost its childish roundness, and Jeremy was startled to see how the planes of her high cheekbones stood out, lending her winsome looks an air of haughtiness they'd completely lacked before.

My God, Jeremy thought, stooping to examine the sleeping girl at close range. She's gone and turned into a society beauty behind my back.

The thought nettled him almost as much as the fact that she had a fiancé.

Well, what had he expected? Had he thought her parents would be able to shield her from the attentions of other men forever? That he was the only man capable of appreciating her natural, country-bred beauty? That a girl like Maggie, whose mouth, as he knew only too well, had a tendency to fall open when she was kissed, would wait around for him forever?

Suddenly tired, Jeremy sat down on the edge of the bed, raising a hand to his brow. His skin felt hot. He was probably feverish again. But what else was new? He'd been fighting off secondary attacks of the disease for weeks now. The doctors in New Delhi had assured him that this was normal. One of them had even explained that Jeremy would continue to suffer malarial bouts three, even four years after his initial contraction of the disease. Jeremy had nearly struck the physician upon being told this, but had been too weak with fever to raise his fist.

Taking his hand away from his eyes, Jeremy looked down at Maggie. She was still sleeping soundly, her breathing deep and even. She had always, he remembered with some amusement, been a heavy and untroubled sleeper, never stirring even when she'd had to be carried to bed after falling asleep in her chair at the dinner table as a child. This time she had slept, he realized, right through his ringing of the doorbell, and now was perfectly unconscious of his presence at her bedside. He could, he realized, have violated her ten different ways already, and she'd undoubtedly have slept right through it.

The thought was a tempting one. Looking down at the peacefully slumbering body, hidden as it was inside the voluminous nightgown, Jeremy recalled a certain afternoon, five years earlier. As if of its own volition, his hand began creeping toward the hem of the nightdress, toward that bare white calf. . . .

What stopped him, Jeremy had no idea. One minute, his

hand was so close, he could feel the heat of her skin beneath his fingertips. The next, he was drawing back. What, he wondered, could be the matter with him? He had every right, every right in the world, to touch this girl. When he left England five years earlier, it had been with the conviction that upon his return, he would marry Maggie Herbert.

Granted, he hadn't exactly refrained from seeking comfort in the arms of others in the meantime. Jeremy had considered it wise to at least *attempt* to rid himself of the memory of Maggie Herbert's kiss. He wasn't, after all, a eunuch. Lieutenant Colonel Rawlings's sexual misadventures had been greatly admired by the men serving beneath him, and became the subject of numerous jokes by Jeremy's fellow—mostly married—officers. For the most part, Jeremy had ignored the ribbing, only resorting to fisticuffs when he was drunk or in a foul mood . . . which had been frequently enough, for he had found India to be an unbearably hot country, a cesspool of poverty and disease, and hardly the magical place he and Maggie had imagined in their games of childhood.

But though Jeremy, for almost half a decade, dallied with dozens of women, he never encountered a single one who caused his heart to race the way it had that day in the stable with Maggie. He never met any other woman who so fully captivated him, emotionally and intellectually—not to mention physically—the way Maggie Herbert had. While this discovery had proven occasionally awkward—case in point, that incident concerning the Star of Jaipur—it had also been extremely motivating. Jeremy, remembering his uncle's advice, concentrated the full of his considerable powers of intellect upon proving himself worthy of a girl of Maggie's caliber. Rather to his own surprise, this resulted in a quick rise through the ranks of Her Majesty's cavalry. Jeremy made quick work of every task assigned him, from escorting important ambassadors through the jungle to subjugating the occasional peasant uprising, tasks in which he took pleasure, since they, at least, kept him from brooding, as he tended to do when left otherwise unoccupied.

Though it was the last thing he'd had any intention of doing, Jeremy ended up impressing his superiors with his intelligence and apparent lack of fear. Having purposely dropped his title upon joining up, few knew that the young man who began his army career as Jeremy Rawlings was actually one of the richest men in England, a titled peer whose uncle was an extremely powerful force in the House of Lords. To his fellow officers, Jeremy was only Captain Rawlings, though he remained a captain only a short time before receiving a promotion to major—as well as that Medal of Honor from the queen, for his quick snuffing out of the Jaipur rebellion. By the time he was finally felled—and by disease, not an enemy bullet—Jeremy was perceived by all as one of the bravest men in the queen's service, a fearless hero whose skill with a sword was unrivaled. His rank, accordingly, had been elevated to that of Lieutenant Colonel, and another gold star added to the high collar of his red coat.

And yet, to Jeremy, the promotions, the medals, the honors—even the bequeathal of the Star of Jaipur—meant nothing. He was conscious only of the fact that, for the first time in his life, he was doing something he was not only good at, but that he actually enjoyed. And through it all, he waited for only one thing: a letter from Maggie, asking him to come home.

He thought it might come the fourth year, during which his aunt Pegeen wrote to tell him that Lady Herbert, Maggie's mother, had succumbed to a long illness, and died in the spring. His condolence letter, however—the only communication he sent to anyone during his long absence, having a distinct abhorrence of letter-writing—went unanswered. It wasn't until twelve months after that, when Jeremy received the information about Maggie's engagement, that he realized his long years of waiting had been for nothing: The girl he'd intended to marry was marrying someone else; had apparently never taken his proposal seriously in the first place; and had forgotten him as easily as another woman might forget to purchase eggs at the market.

He had been duped. He had been made to feel a fool. He had suffered in a hot and barbarous country for five years for nothing.

And now he was coming home to take his revenge.

Since he'd learned of her treachery, Jeremy had thought of little else save the vengeance he would wreak upon Maggie at the first opportunity. In fact, it was the thought of revenge that had kept him alive those weeks when he'd been half delirious with fever. His thirst for revenge had, he was convinced, saved his life. Dead, he could not make Maggie Herbert sorry for giving herself to another. In the end, revenge had been what drove him from his sickbed, insisting upon leaving for England even though the physicians urged him to remain in the hospital until he was stronger.

And yet now that he had the object of his torment close at hand, he found he could not bring himself to punish her. Not yet.

Yes, that was it. Not quite yet. He would play with her first, the way he'd seen tigers play with their prey before devouring it. How much more satisfying to torture her a little, before moving in for the kill.

Accordingly, Jeremy brought a hand to his face and, stroking his chin, watched Maggie for a few moments as she slept. And then, lowering that same large, deeply tanned hand, he brought it down with considerable force, and a good deal of noise, upon her heart-shaped backside, unprotected except for the cotton of her nightdress.

Chapter 11

$\mathcal{M}$aggie shrieked with as much volume as if someone had lit her hair on fire, and sat bolt upright in her bed, her eyes, wide with indignation, searching out the offender who'd so rudely wakened her. When her startled gaze focused on the man sitting upon the edge of her bed, she let out another shriek, this one of outraged modesty, and dove for the sheet tangled at her feet. It lay, unfortunately, beneath the laughing man, and no matter how hard she tugged at it, Maggie could not pull it out from under him. At last, breathing hard, Maggie clutched one of her pillows to her chest and, using its plump shape to hide what the nightdress didn't, demanded, the words spilling over one another in her haste to get them out, "W-who are you? Get out of my room at once! I shall call for the Bow Street runners!"

Jeremy couldn't stop laughing. The look on her face had been well worth five years of hellish climate. In fact, he'd have crossed the Sahara on foot if he could have been assured of another glimpse of her expression upon opening her eyes to find him in her room.

"Ah, Mags," he said, still laughing, though not quite as hard now. "If only you could have seen your face. . . . Priceless. Absolutely priceless!"

Instantly, recognition flooded her pretty features. It was hard to tell in the dim light cast by the embers on the hearth, but the person sitting on the end of her bed appeared to be . . . was the right size and shape for . . .

"Jeremy?" she ventured cautiously, her dark eyebrows slanting down over her even darker eyes. "Is that you?"

"One and the same," Jeremy said. He found that his eyes had begun watering, he had laughed so hard, and he raised an arm to wipe them with his coat sleeve. "God, what a shriek. You sounded like Praehurst, that day we dangled the snake down from the balustrade in the Great Hall."

"What in the world . . ." Maggie was still staring at him, round-eyed. "What are you doing here?"

He grinned at her. "I live here. This is my house, remember?" He nodded toward her nightdress. "Do you always wear such boring nightclothes? Haven't you anything with bits of lace stuck in it?"

Maggie was sure her cheeks were scarlet. Good God, Jeremy! Jeremy, back from India. Jeremy, in her bedroom! It was a dream, it had to be. Lord knew she'd dreamed of his homecoming often enough. And yet . . . and yet, none of her dreams had been like this. The Jeremys she'd dreamt of had never whacked her on the behind.

Then again, the Jeremys of her dreams had never gone and gotten themselves betrothed to an Indian princess. . . .

"W-what are you doing back in England?" she stammered. "I thought . . . It was my understanding that . . ."

"That what? That I was going to stay in India until I rotted? Well, you thought wrong."

Maggie glanced toward her bedroom door. It was closed. Where was the princess? Waiting in the hallway outside? "Are you . . . did you come back . . . alone?"

"Do you see anyone else in here? Of course I'm alone, Maggie. What's gotten into you? You've gotten absolutely dense since I went away."

He expected her to take umbrage to that statement. Instead, she continued to stare at him, chewing on her lower lip, her dark eyes troubled. Jeremy wondered, briefly, what ailed her. Guilt, perhaps. Yes, that was it. She was tortured, riddled with guilt over the wrong she'd done him. He sat there, quite pleased with himself, until she said flatly, "You look like hell."

He did, too. Maggie studied the man on her bed. He certainly *looked* like Jeremy . . . or at least like Jeremy as she'd last seen him, climbing down from the terrace outside her bedroom in Herbert Park, five years ago. And by smacking her on the behind, the way he'd done, he had certainly *acted* like Jeremy. Jeremy would have seized any opportunity to fondle her buttocks, Maggie was quite sure.

And yet this couldn't be Jeremy Rawlings. Because Jeremy Rawlings, she knew all too well, was thousands of miles away, cutting a wide swath with an imperial sword through Her Majesty's colonies in India . . .

. . . while somewhere, the Star of Jaipur, the *prize* Jeremy had been awarded for saving the city from ruin, waited for him.

Unless, Maggie thought, with something akin to horror, that prize was *here*, right here in London.

She swallowed down whatever it was that inevitably rose in her throat every time she thought of the Star of Jaipur. Maybe, she said to herself, this isn't Jeremy Rawlings at all. Jeremy Rawlings had been handsome—heart-stoppingly so—and this man, with his pallor of poor health, would not have turned a single head along the Ladies' Mile, even had he been wearing his uniform.

Jeremy had lifted a hand defensively to his face. This was not the sort of greeting he'd been expecting. Some feminine consternation would have been nice, maybe even a few tears. But Maggie exhibited none of these emotions. She looked genuinely concerned—or perhaps disgusted was the better word—about his appearance.

"What do you mean?" Jeremy heard himself demanding defensively. "What do you mean, I look like hell?"

"What happened to your nose?" Maggie asked.

Jeremy lowered his hand from his face and glared at her. "I broke it, all right?"

"Several times, from the looks of it." Maggie loosened her hold on the pillow. This clearly *was* Jeremy, in any case. Only he would answer her rude inquiries with matching in-civility. "What, they don't use pistols in India? Everybody throws punches instead?"

"Not everybody," Jeremy replied calmly. "But when the

other officers and I had a disagreement, we tended to resort to—''

"You'd strike one another?" Maggie reached up and flicked a long strand of dark hair back over her shoulder. "How very barbaric. You must have lost quite often, judging from the look of that nose."

"That isn't true," Jeremy began testily. "As a matter of fact, I—"

"Why is your skin such a funny color?" she wanted to know.

Jeremy stared at her. "I'd forgotten," he said, as if to himself, "what a joy you can be in the morning."

"If you hadn't wakened me the way you did," Maggie pointed out, "I might have welcomed you home more obligingly. As it is, I don't think you deserve civility. If it's flattery you're looking for, you've come to quite the wrong place."

"Yes," Jeremy said, a little taken aback. He hadn't exactly expected her to throw her arms around him—well, all right, he *had*—but this hostility of hers was ridiculous. Was it possible she had never really been in love with him, after all? "I can see that."

"What time is it, anyway?" Maggie reached down to the foot of her bed and attempted to drag one of the feather-stuffed comforters up toward her. "It's cold as death in here. Lay another log on the fire, would you?"

Jeremy would not have gotten up if she hadn't been tugging so adamantly at the duvet upon which he sat. And she was right, it *was* cold. Colder to him, even, than it could possibly have seemed to her, since she hadn't spent the past five years under an equatorial sun, and hadn't contracted any malarial fevers.

So he rose, and when the duvet came loose quite suddenly in her hands, it caused her to lose her balance and fall back across the pillows, dislodging a fuzzy white thing that yapped indignantly at her before shaking its ears back and forth, causing a flapping noise not unlike the ones the swans at Rawlings Manor used to make when they shook water off their wings.

"Good God," Jeremy said, pausing beside the hearth with a piece of firewood in his hand. "What is *that*?"

Maggie had already flung the comforter around her shoulders, and now sat cocooned in its fluffy confines, only her head and neck sticking out. Jeremy mentally kicked himself. He ought to have yanked the nightdress off when he'd had the chance.

"That?" She looked down at the bundle of fur that sat between her pillows. "That's my dog."

Jeremy blinked at the small, beady-eyed animal. "It doesn't look like a dog," he said. "It looks like a mop."

Maggie didn't seem the least bit offended by his accusing her dog of being a mop. She shrugged beneath the comforter and said, "He's a bichon frise."

"What the devil is a bichon frise? French for *mop*?"

"No. It's a breed of dog, you fool. You haven't answered my question."

Jeremy looked away from the dog, who was glaring rather accusingly at him, and continued building up the fire. "Yes?" he said, employing the blower with rather more force than necessary. "Which question?"

"The one about your skin." Maggie, rather like a dog herself, he noted, wouldn't let this bone alone. "You look quite ill, you know."

"That," Jeremy said, straightening now that he'd got the fire going, "would be because I *was* ill."

"Were you?" Maggie observed him through narrowed eyes as he laid aside the bellows. Still every bit as tall as she remembered, Jeremy was also just as broad-shouldered, while still being narrow about the waist and hips. She supposed that whatever illness he'd had, it hadn't been a wasting one. With the exception of his skin tone, he looked as vigorous as he had the last time she'd seen him. . . .

And God knew the memory of *that* day was still as clear and as vivid as if it had been yesterday, and not half a decade ago. In fact, it was a memory Maggie hardly ever allowed herself to think about, since doing so invariably awoke fires she'd rather let lie dormant.

"Your aunt never told me you were ill," Maggie said,

inadvertently revealing something else she'd rather not have let him know.

He was on it in a second, though, like a hawk on a field mouse. Moving back toward the bed, Jeremy sat down, feeling quite pleased with himself. "Oh? You and Aunt Pegeen often discuss me, Mags?"

Maggie, to her humiliation, felt herself flush. Lord, it had been ages since she'd blushed! Why did she have to start doing so *now*? "Certainly not," she said with a sniff. "But when Lady Edward starts bragging about you, it's hard to escape, you know. She does go on and on, when it comes to her darling nephew."

"Oh." Feeling slightly let down, Jeremy said, "Well, I didn't let Uncle Edward and Aunt Pegeen know about this particular illness."

Maggie sniffed. "No, I would imagine not. You never wrote to them, did you? Every bit of information we heard about you had to come from either the newspapers or White-hall—"

Jeremy shrugged. "I'm no good at writing letters. They know that. How are they, anyway, Mags? Aunt Pegeen and Uncle Edward, I mean."

"They're fine." Maggie poked a hand out from beneath the comforter and laid it upon her dog's head. He panted appreciatively, his pink tongue lolling. "They're more than fine, actually. You'll be able to see for yourself. They ought to be back in town today. Unless . . ."

"Unless?" Jeremy raised his eyebrows.

"Didn't she tell you in her last letter?"

He raised his eyebrows expectantly. So, he thought. She's going to admit the truth about the fiancé at last. "No. Tell me what?"

"Your aunt's in the last few weeks of her confinement. You'll probably have another cousin next month."

"Good God," Jeremy cried, collapsing back against the mattress. He put both hands behind his head, and stared up at the canopy. "Don't tell me they're still at it! Like a couple of rabbits, are Aunt Pegeen and Uncle Ed, don't you think? And at their age, too. It's disgusting."

"Really, Jeremy," Maggie chastised mildly.

"What is this? Number eight?"

"Seven," Maggie corrected him. "*Really*, Jerry. They're your *family*."

"I suppose."

Jeremy rolled over onto his stomach and looked at her. She rather wished he wouldn't. It was exceedingly strange, having a man in her bedroom . . . even stranger having one in her bed. The last thing she wanted to do, however, was convey how strange she thought it to him. Five years had passed since that last . . . incident . . . and Maggie was a thousand times more sophisticated now than she'd been back then. After all, she'd lived in Paris. She'd seen something of the world outside of Yorkshire. She'd sketched and painted naked men. She'd been extremely alarmed about doing so, at first, but there was no need for Jeremy to know that. All he needed to know was that Maggie Herbert knew her way around the male body. Granted, only with a pencil or paintbrush, but that was beside the point. She'd overcome her shyness and most of her unease with the society of those outside her own family. She'd conversed with intelligent and witty people, and had been acknowledged as intelligent and witty in her own right.

And, most importantly of all, she'd gotten over her attachment to Jeremy Rawlings.

Oh, it hadn't been easy. It had taken a long, long time. But she'd done it. She was cured. There was nothing he could do or say that would affect her. Nothing at all.

"I was sorry to hear about your mother, Mags," Jeremy said, in a voice so gentle that Maggie nearly jumped out of her skin with surprise.

Trying to appear as nonchalant as he evidently felt, sprawled as he was at the end of her bed, Maggie said airily, "Oh, you heard about that? I suppose your aunt wrote you."

Abruptly, Jeremy sat up on his elbows, his gray eyes very bright on her face. "Of course I heard about it," he said, in the same deep voice. "Didn't you get my letter?"

"Letter?" Maggie blinked a few times. "I never received a letter from you, Jeremy." She tried not to sound as pathetic as she suddenly felt. No, she had never gotten a letter from him. Not when her mother died. Not when the newspapers had announced his victory in Jaipur. Not when word of the nature of his reward for having done so began to circulate. . . .

"Well, I wrote to you," Jeremy said. His voice wasn't gentle anymore. Now he sounded outraged. "It was a good letter, too. Where the hell could it have got to? I sent it to Herbert Park."

Maggie, a little alarmed at his vehemence, said, "Well, it likely went astray. Letters do, sometimes. I wouldn't worry about it. It was kind of you to think of me—"

The gray eyes glowed silver now as Jeremy stared at her in the rosy light from the fire. "Christ, Maggie. Of course I thought of you."

Maggie looked quickly away. It wasn't so much his eyes—though God knew, his eyes were troubling enough, glowing the way they did, like an animal's eyes, caught at night in lantern light. No, she was over that now. He couldn't affect her that way. But mention of her mother's death did, every time, too. Dead almost a year, and Maggie still couldn't think of her, or of the way her father's face had looked upon hearing Mr. Parks's solemn announcement that Lady Herbert had passed, without her eyes filling up.

Something warm settled over Maggie's hand. Looking down, thinking it was the dog, Maggie was surprised to see Jeremy's large brown fingers close reassuringly around her own slim white ones.

"Mags?" He was sitting just a few inches away from her, his head and shoulders taking up all of the space in her field of vision. His face wore an expression of concern. "Maggie? Are you all right?"

She nodded, not trusting her voice to speak.

"Are you sure?"

When she nodded again, he lifted her hand and casually, the way he had when they'd been children, he began inspecting her fingers.

"Ah," he said happily. "I see we've been working in umber lately. And what's this? What's this? Some black!

How bold of you, young lady. You didn't used to be partial to black. What else? Ah, some sky-blue—"

"Azure," Maggie said, a laugh escaping, in spite of the fact that she knew she ought to draw her hand away. Supposing her maid walked in? How shocked would Hill be, finding a man in her mistress's bedroom? Never mind that the man was master of the house. Hill would surely scold her in the morning for even having spent the night in the same *house* as an unmarried man, let alone having entertained that man in her bedroom. . . .

"Azure?" Jeremy shot her a suspicious look. "A fancy art-school term, I suppose. What's wrong with sky-blue?"

"Nothing," Maggie said, more warmly, perhaps, than she ought to have. So warmly, in fact, that Jeremy cast her a startled look over her fingertips.

Oh, Lord, she thought, he's going to kiss me. Suddenly, her heart began that same uneven tattoo from five years earlier. . . . They were alone in her bedroom, and this time, there wouldn't be anyone to stop them. Maggie didn't know what time it was, but she suspected, due to the darkness outside her bedroom windows, that it was early, too early for even Hill to be up yet. If he were to kiss her, and she was once again too caught up in his embrace to stop him, what would happen?

Chapter 12

Jeremy didn't kiss her. The thought crossed his mind, as it had a hundred times since she'd opened those big, luminous brown eyes. But something held him back, some inner voice told him the time wasn't yet right. . . .

And of course, there was the fiancé to consider, as well. Not that Jeremy cared a jot about *him*. He did want a glimpse at the bloody ass, though. He wanted to avoid having to kill him, if at all possible. In the past five years, Jeremy had grown rather tired of killing, and sometimes found it less messy, overall, to allow someone to live, instead of dispatching him. Not that Jeremy would *mind* killing the fiancé. Not at all. It would, however, complicate matters if it turned out Maggie was genuinely fond of the bastard.

So instead of kissing her, Jeremy tossed her hand away.

"So," he said, as if continuing a conversation begun previously. "You're a famous artist now. At least, that's what Pegeen said in her last letter."

Maggie, her relief at having escaped his embrace palpable, was nevertheless a little disappointed that he hadn't kissed her after all. Her heart was still pounding rather sickeningly inside her chest. But she had to remember that his kisses were forbidden to her now. They belonged, as she knew only too well, to someone else.

"I don't know about famous," she said cautiously. Yes, it was all right. Her voice wasn't obviously shaking. "But I'm an artist, anyway. At least, I suppose so."

"Yes?" Jeremy climbed to his feet, and instantly regretted doing so. The room swam a little before him. Still, he couldn't show weakness in front of Maggie, so he rallied his strength, and took a few steps until he could sink onto one of the brocade-covered chairs by the fire. "So what you're telling me, Mags, is that people actually *pay* you for your doodlings now?"

"They aren't doodlings," Maggie said, her back suddenly stiff as a rake. "They're portraits, and people pay me quite a lot for them, actually."

"Really?" Jeremy leaned forward and lifted the stuffed bird from the ivory-topped table. "And is this how they pay you? In children's toys?"

"Certainly not," Maggie said. "They pay me in the queen's sterling. The toys are to entertain the children while I endeavor to sketch them. I specialize in children's portraits."

"Children?" Jeremy echoed, curling his upper lip in distaste. "What about pets? Do you still do pets, too?"

"Sometimes," Maggie said. What cheek! She couldn't believe it, the way he was strutting about her bedroom as if he owned it. Which, in fact, he did. But that didn't give him the right to toss about her things. The army had certainly failed to teach Jeremy Rawlings anything about gentlemanly behavior. She longed to get out of bed and snatch the bird away from him, but dreaded parading around in only her nightdress, with no corset underneath to keep her bosom from bouncing. She knew only too well how much she had to hide, and how ill-equipped mere cotton was at hiding it. "When I must, occasionally, to pay the bills."

"Bills?" Jeremy laid the bird down, and picked up the mechanical horse. "What bills could you possibly have? Surely you aren't paying Uncle Edward and Aunt Pegeen to let you stay here!"

"Of course not," Maggie said. "But I rent a little studio down in Chelsea, so I don't stink up your house with the smell of turpentine. And there's canvas to buy, not to mention stretchers and paints, and I pay for my own transportation to and from the homes of my sitters, and my meals when

I can't make it back here in time for them, and then there's Hill—''

Jeremy, in the act of winding up the mechanical horse, stopped and stared at her as if she'd suggested she liked to eat dirt. ''What on earth,'' he said, with genuine shock, ''are you doing, paying for all of that yourself? Don't tell me Sir Arthur's put you on some kind of allowance. Surely your mother left you something. . . .''

Damn it, she was blushing again. She could feel the heat spreading across her face. Looking down at her dog, she said, as evenly and as unconcernedly as she could, ''Papa doesn't exactly approve of my painting. The only money I have is what I've earned these past few months. That's why it's taking me so long to find a flat of my own. Your aunt and uncle have very kindly offered me the use of your town house for as long as they're in town—''

Jeremy was up and out of the chair before the words were completely out of her mouth. ''*What*?'' he shouted, so loudly that the dog's floppy little ears pricked forward. ''Old Herbert's cut you off?''

She raised her chin defensively. ''You needn't sound so astonished. I earn quite enough to support myself. Or at least I will, after the exhibition—''

''Exhibition?'' Jeremy had set the mechanical horse down, and now it stalked, stiff-legged, across the table, making a rather irritating humming sound. ''What exhibition?''

''An exhibition of paintings,'' Maggie explained tiredly. ''Of my work up till now, what's not already sold, I mean. It's on Saturday. It's quite a big to-do, actually. The more commissions I can get, the more—Jeremy, don't let that fall. It will break, and I can't afford a new one.''

Jeremy leaned down and caught the toy as it walked over the edge of the table. ''I can't believe it,'' he said, shaking his head. ''Herbert cut you off because he doesn't approve of your painting! The old scalawag.'' Now Jeremy understood a little more of what lay behind Maggie's tears for her mother. With Lady Herbert had died any hope she might have had of parental approval for the only thing she loved to do, and did well. How Jeremy understood that!

Then he remembered something. "What about all of those sisters of yours?" he wanted to know. "They're all married now, and quite well off, too, if I remember correctly. Why don't you beg for a few scraps from them now and then?"

"Goodness," Maggie exclaimed mildly, "as attractive as you make that sound, I'm not about to stoop to it. You see, they all agree with Papa."

Though she tried, she wasn't able to keep a hint of pathos from creeping into her voice. Her sisters' disapproval stung the most. It was one thing to be a disappointment to one's father. It was quite another to be a disappointment to all five of one's sisters, especially the eldest, whom the others unquestioningly followed. Anne had never approved of any of Maggie's choices, from her relationship with the Duke of Rawlings to her decision to go to art school, but since their mother's death, her patience with her youngest sister had worn especially thin. Anne could not forgive her sister for choosing painting over motherhood, the only occupation, according to Anne's way of thinking, that was suitable for a woman.

Maggie thought she understood why her sister felt the way she did. Anne, always the most delicate of the Herbert girls, had suffered a recent miscarriage, the third she'd endured during the course of her ten-year marriage. Her four living children were all the more precious to her because of the babies she'd lost, strengthening her conviction that the only worthwhile occupation for any woman was motherhood. Maggie's decision to be an artist—and the fact that their mother's death had in no way altered that decision—had shocked her sister to the core, while her recent engagement only seemed to infuriate the rest of the family: Apparently, no husband was preferable to a French one.

Seeing Maggie's distress, Jeremy balled his fingers into fists, and jammed them, impotently, into his trouser pockets. "Well, never you mind, Mags," he said, with forced heartiness. "They were all of them a pretty pallid lot, I always thought. Except for you, of course."

She managed a ghost of a smile. "Thanks, but I think this

time they're right. Honor thy father and thy mother, remember? It's in the Bible.''

"True, true,'' Jeremy said dismissively. ''But isn't there also something in there about whosoever amongst us has not sinned, let him cast the first stone? Your sisters might do well to keep their fingers in their own pies—''

Maggie couldn't help laughing at that. ''Oh, Jerry! I think you're mixing Scripture with Mrs. Praehurst's Yorkshire-isms.''

"Probably am,'' Jeremy agreed, relieved to see that she could still laugh, anyway. ''I'll have a word with the old man when I get back home, though, don't you worry.''

"Home? You mean . . . this isn't just a visit?'' She felt something very much like panic begin to creep into her voice. ''You're out of the Horse Guards for good, then?''

"Well,'' Jeremy said, suddenly uncomfortable. He didn't want to reveal too much, in case she caught on to the reason behind his sudden return. ''Not exactly.''

"Oh,'' Maggie said. ''They transferred you back because of your illness, did they? It was that serious? What did you have, anyway, Jeremy?'' With another bright laugh, she said, ''Not malaria, I hope! Your aunt would *die* of worry!''

"No, it wasn't that,'' Jeremy said thoughtfully. ''I just decided, all things considered, a trip back home was called for. There appear to be some . . . loose ends that need tying up.''

His voice trailed off, and Maggie, who'd been waiting for him to make some reference to what had happened in Jaipur, had to be satisfied with that one. While it wasn't very flattering to be called a loose end, she didn't suppose he was referring to *her*. Certainly not! It was quite clear he'd forgotten all about Maggie Herbert, except perhaps as an old friend. The loose end he spoke of could only be his aunt Pegeen, who, Maggie knew only too well, had been livid over the announcement of the reward he'd received for the part he'd played in liberating the Palace of the Winds. Well, and who wouldn't be? The whole thing had been shocking, completely shocking. And yet they'd never heard a word about it from Jeremy. Not a single word.

Jeremy watched Maggie closely, wondering how kindly she'd take to being referred to as a loose end. But if he'd hoped for a flash of guilt, or even a sigh, he was disappointed. Maggie's face did not change one bit. She only said, "Oh," and looked back down at her ridiculous, curly-headed mop of a dog. No mention, he noticed grimly, of the fiancé. No mention of *that* change in her life at all. Had she simply forgotten—the bloke was obviously not worth remembering—or was she purposely avoiding the issue?

Clearing his throat, Jeremy glanced at the frost-tinged windows. He saw that the sky outside was lightening over Hyde Park. Barely perceptibly, but lightening just a bit. He said, "Well, I suppose I ought to go and see if Peters has got in yet. He was following me from the docks with my things."

Things. Maggie felt a little sick. Even though she knew it made her sound a jealous fishwife, she couldn't help asking, cattily, "Do those *things* include the Star of Jaipur?"

As soon as the words were out of her mouth, she regretted them. But as much as she might have wished them unsaid, it was a topic that simply had to be broached. A part of her— a very small part of her—was still hoping against hope that the reports they'd received via *The Times* were incorrect, that there was no Star of Jaipur, that the maharajah, in his gratitude to Jeremy for saving the Palace of the Winds, had given Jeremy a horse, or something.

But she was disappointed.

Jeremy looked at her in surprise. "Well, of course! You don't think I'd leave it behind, do you? You and Evers, you're two of a pair, both asking the same thing like that."

Maggie simply stared at him. She could not, simply could not, believe he could be so cold. How could he have changed so much? Granted, it had been five years. And yes, he'd spent those five years fighting, killing people, destroying things. Still, it seemed impossible that a human being could become that cold, that unfeeling.

But then, five years was a long time. Things changed. She knew that only too well.

Feeling more sick to her stomach than ever, Maggie said,

"Well, you'd better hurry, then, hadn't you? You wouldn't want to keep something as precious as the *Star of Jaipur* waiting, now would you?"

Jeremy glanced at her curiously, but finally rose, and said, "I suppose not. I'll see you at breakfast, then?"

"I hardly think we'll be able to avoid one another," Maggie said, more miserably than sarcastically, which was how she'd meant to say it.

Jeremy raised his eyebrows at this, but decided not to comment. She was clearly upset about something, though for the life of him, he couldn't imagine what that could be. If anyone had reason to be upset, it was *he*. *He* was the jilted party, after all.

Still, he tried to keep his tone light as he reached out to ruffle the fur on her dog's head. "Good night, then, Fido."

To Maggie's astonishment, her little dog actually growled at that approach of Jeremy's hand. "Jerry!" she cried, remonstrating her pet before she stopped to think what she was saying. "Stop that! Shame on you!"

She didn't realize what she'd done until she looked up and saw the bewilderment sketched across Jeremy's face. She looked away just as quickly, but it was too late. Heat began to pour into her cheeks.

"Good God," Jeremy said in a strangled voice. He had never, not once in his life, actually felt emasculated, but he did just then. "You named *your dog* after me, Mags?"

Maggie was blushing crimson now. There was nothing to be done about it, though, since he would have found out anyway. She said, indignantly, "Jerry's a nice name."

"Yes," Jeremy choked. "Well. Good morning, Mags." Turning stiffly, Jeremy stalked, with all the grace of the mechanical horse, from the room, closing the door quite firmly behind him.

Chapter 13

$\mathcal{W}$ell, she told herself, as soon as he was gone. That hadn't been so awful, had it? As far as first interviews went, it had gone quite smoothly. She'd behaved with a modicum of composure. She certainly hadn't swooned or done anything else foolish. She hadn't, she thought, with a feeling of self-satisfaction, done or said anything at all that might make him think she still had feelings for him.

Except for the dog.

But that was all right. She'd see him at breakfast, and explain.

The whole thing was really rather silly. The truth was, when she'd first arrived in Paris, Maggie had felt . . . well . . . lonely. Wretchedly so. Madame Bonheur, though a celebrated artist, honored with a medal from Queen Victoria, no less, turned out to be a bit alarming: She dressed in waistcoat and trousers, and smoked little cigarillos. Maggie had been rather shocked by her appearance, and was quite glad neither her parents nor her sister Anne had met Madame Bonheur beforehand . . . she surely wouldn't have been allowed to attend her school!

Her fellow pupils hadn't made things any easier. Few of Madame Bonheur's students had any actual talent, and even fewer of those had any desire to improve upon that talent. The others appeared to be there because their parents hadn't known what else to do with them. Too old, too unattractive, or too poor to expect any marriage proposals, they had been sent to art school either in the hopes that they might learn a marketable trade, or simply to get them out of the house a few days a week.

Therefore, the girls with real talent ruled the school. They led the critiques, they set the tone of each class, they received the bulk of the praise and precious little criticism. Their leader, Maggie observed her very first day, was a wealthy, attractive young Frenchwoman named Berangère Jacquard, exactly Maggie's age, but her opposite in every other way. Berangère was light where Maggie was dark, dainty where Maggie was large, and cruel where Maggie was kind. The only thing—besides age and social status—that the two girls had in common was their talent. Berangère was an excellent draftswoman. She could render anything in startlingly lifelike detail, so that the results might almost pass for a daguerreotype, they were that accurate. Only in Maggie's dreams could she have hoped to draw so well.

And so Maggie was miserable. She was alone—well, except for Hill—in a foreign country. She missed her family. She had no friends. She was often the object of ridicule by her fellow classmates, for her accent and odd English habits. She was, for the first time in her life, not even the best artist in her class.

And then one day she arrived at the painting studio early and was sitting at her easel, waiting for Madame Bonheur's assistant to set up the still life they were to paint, and trying to decide whether she ought not to simply pack it all in and return to England, when Madame Bonheur herself entered the studio. After looking around to make sure everyone was paying attention, Madame plopped a tiny white thing on the pedestal before them.

"From the latest litter of my niece's bitch," Madame Bonheur explained in her gruff voice, lighting one of the brown cigars she habitually smoked.

Maggie looked down at the squirming ball of fur in the center of a still life of fruit and harvest vegetables and quite totally lost her heart.

"But you cannot expect us to paint *that*, Madame," Berangère Jacquard said laughingly, from behind her easel.

Madame Bonheur exhaled a thin stream of blue smoke. "Why not?"

"Why, because it's . . . moving!"

Madame Bonheur looked at the puppy. "Yes, it is moving. What do you want me to do, Mademoiselle Jacquard? Kill it?"

Maggie let out an exclamation that caused the painting instructress to swivel her head to look at her. "Never fear, Mademoiselle Herbert," Madame Bonheur said with a faint smile. "We French love our pets quite as much as you English do. Now, girls, stop squabbling, and *paint*."

Maggie needed no further urging. Though the puppy did squirm—and even walked about, eyeing the edge of the pedestal trepidatiously, and whining because it was too high for him to jump down from—she managed to produce a lovely portrait of him. So lovely, in fact, that at the end of the class four hours later, Madame Bonheur approached, stared, and then wordlessly removed it from its easel.

Placing the painting on the edge of the windowsill, so that it leaned up against the glass, Madame Bonheur then went to Berangère's easel, removed her painting, and leaned it side by side with Maggie's. And that was when Maggie made an amazing discovery.

Her painting was better than Berangère's. A lot better.

Oh, it wasn't perfect. The grapes were a little too green, and the background needed work, and she'd muffed the peaches, making them a little too large in the foreground. But that, as Madame Bonheur was quick to point out, didn't make any difference. What was important in this painting was the dog. The dog that Mademoiselle Herbert had managed to render not so much as he actually *looked*, but as he actually *was*. Maggie had captured the dog's soul. One could tell, Madame Bonheur explained, simply by glancing at this painting, that its object was a slightly silly, highly excitable, but very good-natured little dog. A dog quite unlike anybody else's dog, with his own personality, his own likes and dislikes, his own doglike qualities.

Moving to Berangère's painting, Madame Bonheur pointed at the cleanly executed animal featured on the large canvas. This dog, she explained to the class, could be any dog. He had no personality. His eyes could have been made of glass. There was nothing behind them. He was painted without emotion, without joy. A stranger, Madame explained, would pay money for this painting, and hang it above his fireplace, and be pleased to own it, for it was a thing of beauty. But anyone who *knew* this dog would prefer to own Maggie's painting. And in the world of portrait painting, where the public commissioned an artist to render a family member, animal or human, it was the *personality* of that pet or person they wanted captured, not just his or her looks.

And that was why, Madame Bonheur went on to say, Mademoiselle Herbert was going to be a great portrait painter, while Mademoiselle Jacquard was only going to be an average one.

Berangère, outraged, exclaimed that if the dog hadn't been moving around so much, she might have been able to capture it better, to which Madame Bonheur replied that it was unfortunate that not many people commissioned works of the dead.

And then, without another word, Madame Bonheur went to the still-life pedestal, scooped up the puppy, deposited it in Maggie's lap, and left the room. It wasn't until four years later, when Maggie had established herself as the school's star pupil, and had become one of Madame Bonheur's closest confidantes, that she finally asked the illustrious painter how she had known that Maggie had wanted that dog. Madame Bonheur only smiled and said, "My dear, anyone who looked at that painting could tell that you were already in love with him. I only gave you what, in your heart, you already owned."

That reply had struck Maggie as ironic considering that, almost upon her first moment of owning the dog, she'd started referring to him as Jerry. Not that Jeremy Rawlings in any way reminded her of a small, fluffy white dog. God, no. It was just that, those first few months away from home, hardly a moment seemed to go by when she was *not* thinking about Jeremy. She found herself constantly wondering what he was doing, how he was feeling, what he was thinking.

She worried about him. India was a long way away. His family never heard from him at all. Only Lord Edward's connections in the Horse Guard kept him informed of his nephew's well-being, and since Maggie was not at Herbert Park, just a short way away from Rawlings Manor, but all the way across the Channel, very little of this information trickled her way. Certainly her mother and father went out of their way never to mention the Duke of Rawlings to her, considering the subject something of a taboo.

And so she was left to wonder about the dangers Jeremy must necessarily be facing in that far-off land, dangers like exotic foreign princesses, with jewels in their navels; the attractive wives of his fellow officers; even a passing Hindu peasant girl, bearing a water pitcher upon her head. Whenever she entertained thoughts of this kind, sleep, which to Maggie had always come easily, evaded her for the night, and she was left bleary-eyed and testy the following day.

She knew she was being ridiculous. She had no right to feel jealous. She had turned down his proposal, thereby cutting off any right she might have to feel possessive toward him.

And it was ridiculous to suppose that, in spite of her rejection, he might remain faithful to her. Ridiculous and unrealistic. The Duke of Rawlings was a virile man . . . more than virile; an almost *unearthly* specimen of the human male. He had, like all males, needs. These needs, since she'd given up her right to cater to them, would necessarily be met by someone.

And so it was childish of her to suppose that he was not seeing someone else . . . perhaps even making love to someone else. Perhaps even proposing to someone else, and getting accepted this time. There was every possibility he'd return from India with a bride in tow, a submissive little bride who'd make an excellent duchess because she was interested in the kind of things that interested duchesses, like clothing and jewels and who was married to whom and who was sleeping with whom. Whereas the only knowledge that Maggie could have brought to the marriage would have been a love of art and a particularly detailed familiarity with the habits of bichon frises.

But sometimes—not very often—Maggie allowed herself to fantasize about what might have been: What if she'd accepted Jeremy's marriage proposal? What if she'd gone with him to Gretna Green? What if she'd thrown caution to the wind and allowed him to make love to her that night in her bedroom?

These were thoughts Maggie hardly dared let herself entertain . . . primarily because they made her feel a little short of breath. The thought of Jeremy Rawlings's naked body pressing against hers filled her with a longing so intense she generally had to put Jerry the dog on his leash and take him outside for a brisk walk.

Something, Maggie knew, was very wrong with her for even thinking thoughts of this kind.

And instead of getting better over the years, it only got worse. Because as Maggie's painting skills increased, her classes became more advanced, until she was placed in private tutorials with actual live models, all of whom were unclothed, and some of whom were male. Given, for the first time in her life, a good long look at the male physique only increased the frequency of Maggie's fantasies about Jeremy. Did he, she often caught herself wondering, have as broad a chest as Philippe, their gesture model? Was he as muscular all over as Etienne, the model in her anatomy class? Did Jeremy's inguinal ligaments have as much definition as Gérard's? And of course, she was often horrified to find herself wondering about Jeremy's genitalia, comparing them with that of models she'd painted, and wondering if they were as large, as dark, as thickly haired. . . .

She supposed she was obsessed. Other girls in the school were obsessed with men—their lovers, their fiancés, the man who delivered their milk in the morning, the waiter at the café on the corner—and talked of them incessantly. Berangère Jacquard, who, after her set down by Madame Bonheur, actually became rather friendly toward Maggie, talked of nothing *but* men. In fact, Maggie was just about the only girl at Madame's studio who *didn't* talk about men. Jeremy's

name never once left her lips, not in five years. What was
the point in talking about him? She had lost him, in a moment of childish fear, fear of the unknown, fear of losing
control. A girl as cowardly as Maggie considered herself to
be didn't deserve a second chance, and so she didn't expect
one. Never, in five years, did it occur to Maggie that Jeremy
had been serious when he'd asked her to contact him if she
changed her mind about marrying him. No man, once rejected, would consider risking his heart a second time on the
same object. Maggie didn't know much about men, but she
at least knew *that*.

But just because she never spoke of him didn't mean she
never thought of him. On the contrary. She never *stopped*
thinking of him. It was a rare day, in fact, that round about
mid-morning, she didn't lay down her paintbrush and think
to herself, Lord, it's nearly eleven o'clock, and I've thought
of nothing all day but Jeremy! And that thought was always
accompanied by so much pain and regret that she continued
to think of little else until sleep overtook her at bedtime.

So when she woke that morning to find Jeremy sitting on
the edge of her bed, Maggie had been more than just a little
surprised. Her initial shock hadn't been so much over Jeremy's altered looks. Those had been startling, it was true.
But the fact that he was there *at all* had been what jarred her
most. *Why* was Jeremy Rawlings sitting on her bed? He had
forgotten all about her, hadn't he? He hadn't spared her a
passing thought in five years. Why now, when there could
be nothing between them, had he chosen to reappear in her
life?

To give credit where credit was due, she supposed Jeremy
could have had no way of knowing she'd taken up residency
in his home. Surely, had he known, he'd have had the tact
to avoid her . . . especially considering the fact that he had
brought the Star of Jaipur home with him. But perhaps he'd
been carried away with the excitement of being among
friends again. Yes, that was it. They were old friends, that
was all. Very old friends.

It was for that reason, she was prepared to explain, that
she had named her dog after him. Because he was a good,

old friend. It certainly hadn't been because thoughts of him rarely, if ever, left her. It certainly wasn't because he had, that day five years earlier, seared an image into her memory that she'd been unable to shake ever since. It wasn't because Jeremy Rawlings had become her definition of the ideal man, and no man, not even her own fiancé, could ever match—

It was at that moment, sitting at the breakfast table, waiting for Jeremy to put in an appearance, that Maggie remembered Augustin.

Good God! Her fiancé! She had forgotten her fiancé!

Well, that cinched it. Maggie was deranged. Reserve a room in Bedlam, because Maggie was on her way. She had sat in the wee hours of the morning, chatting with a man who had once proposed to her, and she had completely forgotten the fact that she was engaged to someone else. Not just forgotten the fact that she was engaged, but forgotten all about the man himself! Oh, Lord. She was the most ungrateful, unappreciative girl in the entire world. What could she have been thinking, sitting there with Jeremy in her nightdress while Augustin, the man to whom she was engaged, was sleeping just a few city blocks away?

But the fact that she was undeserving of Augustin's attentions wasn't quite as important as the fact that she had completely forgotten to mention his existence to Jeremy. Not that she fancied Jeremy would care. Certainly not! Why, he had the Star of Jaipur! But she ought to have said *something.* . . .

Well, it was a dilemma easily remedied. She'd simply casually announce it over breakfast, along with her explanation of her dog's name. Yes, that was it. Jeremy, I named my dog after you because you're a dear old friend, and by the way, did you know I'm engaged to be married? Pass the butter, will you?

But when Jeremy did not appear at the breakfast table by ten o'clock, a half hour before Maggie's first appointment of the day, she became irritated. She wanted to tell him about Augustin while her courage was still high. Where *was* he? A consultation with Evers proved highly unsatisfactory. According to the butler, His Grace was still sleeping. Subtle questioning as to the whereabouts of the Star of Jaipur were equally unsatisfactory. According to Evers, only one bedroom besides her own was currently being utilized. Since she felt sure Jeremy wouldn't put the Star of Jaipur up in a hotel, she could only assume he was sharing his own bedroom with her. Well, that might explain, she supposed, why Jeremy was sleeping so late. Had he gone straight from her room to . . .

She felt nauseous just thinking about it.

So instead of thinking about it, she gathered her things and took the omnibus to her first appointment, a consultation with Lord and Lady Chettenhouse, who wanted to commission a portrait of their eldest daughter, a rather spoiled little society miss. A gown, pose, and sum were agreed upon within an hour, and Maggie was back at the house on Park Lane by noon . . . only to learn that the duke was still sleeping.

Biting back a resentful remark, Maggie had a long lunch, dallied as long as she could in her room before finally admitting she was acting like a fool, then took another omnibus to her studio. There she put in five solid hours of painting, hardly once thinking about her nocturnal visitor. It was only after she laid down her paintbrush and flexed her sore arm that she wondered if Jeremy was finally awake. Shutting up her studio for the night, Maggie returned to the house on Park Lane, preparing herself the entire way for an unpleasant interview with its owner. She was wearing a blue tartan day dress, with a long ruffled train and a tight bodice that ended in a point just over her abdomen. She didn't, she knew, look particularly smart, but then, she didn't look dowdy, either. At least her hair was up. It would be the first time Jeremy had ever seen her with her hair up. If it would just *stay* up during the course of their interview, all would be well.

What she hadn't thought to prepare herself for was an interview with the duke's mistress. But that's exactly who she found standing in the foyer when she threw open the front door.

Chapter 14

The Star of Jaipur, Maggie saw at once, was everything that she had most feared: petite, exotic, and beautiful. In fact, standing next to her, Maggie felt like an ungainly cow.

It wasn't just that the Indian princess had the largest, darkest eyes Maggie had ever seen. It wasn't just that, even swathed in a cloak of ermine and velvet, she looked dainty enough to sit in the palm of Maggie's hand. It wasn't just that her feet, peeping out from beneath the hem of her pink silk sari, were shod in jeweled slippers, or that the fingers she slipped out of her furred muff were heavy with rubies and emeralds.

Oh, no, the Star of Jaipur had to *smile* at her as she came blowing in from outside. A sweet, gentle smile that caused Maggie to stumble over her own train and nearly upset a vase of half-blown roses that rested on a tiny marble-topped table just inside the door.

Lord, Maggie thought miserably, as she held on to the table for support. Did she have to be beautiful and *nice*, too?

"Excuse me," said a soft, masculine voice from behind her. The English was accented, but quite good, nonetheless. "But are you unwell?"

Maggie took a deep breath. She was going to live through this, she told herself. This was not going to kill her. All she needed to do was utter a few pleasantries, go up those stairs, and then . . .

Start packing. Because she could not live in this house a second longer.

Maggie turned, slowly, and found herself looking up at a slim, but very tall, brown-skinned man, who wore on his head a scarlet little hat with a tassel in the crown. He was smooth-shaven, with an intelligent face, that, though not handsome, was nevertheless pleasing. Though Maggie could not have begun to guess his age, she suspected he was younger than he seemed.

Somehow, Maggie managed to smile at him. "I'm quite well," she said. "You merely startled me."

"Ah!" The man smiled and nodded, then turned to say something incomprehensible to the Star of Jaipur. The language he spoke was lilting and melodic, with no guttural sounds whatsoever. Hearing it put Maggie in mind of the games she and Jeremy had played as children, of the way the wind had sounded in summertime, as it rustled through the treetops on the Rawlings estate.

When the Star of Jaipur responded in the same language, something in her soft, fluty voice caused the hairs on Maggie's arms to stand up beneath her sleeves. When she was through speaking, the Indian man turned to Maggie and said kindly, "Allow me to make introductions, please. This is the Princess Usha Rajput of Rajasthan. I am her interpreter, Sanjay. The princess wishes you to know that you are welcome in her home. She wonders if you have come to see herself, or the colonel."

"In her . . ." Maggie's voice trailed off. Good God. This was worse than she'd ever imagined. Jeremy actually intended to *marry* this . . . this . . . *woman.* It had been one thing when they'd all assumed he'd merely keep her, like a pet. But evidently, he intended to marry her. Or at least that was the impression the princess herself seemed to be under. Unless . . . unless they were married already!

"Um," Maggie stammered. "Actually, neither. You see, I've been staying here—"

"Ah," the little man cried. "You are a servant? Very good! We need someone to take our wraps." He indicated the princess's heavy, ermine-trimmed cloak, and his own cape, of the same scarlet as his cap. "The man who opened the door to us was very rude. He told us, wait here, and then he disappeared. We have not seen him for some minutes. The princess grows tired of waiting and wishes to sit down."

Maggie nodded, feeling as if there were a bee buzzing inside of her skull, trying to get out. She could not, in her wildest imaginings, have ever envisioned quite so awkward a situation. She supposed that Evers, opening the door to this couple, had felt the same. Otherwise, why would he have simply left them there in the foyer? A well-trained butler simply did not leave guests waiting in the foyer. He saw them either comfortably seated, or he turned them away. He did not, however, leave them standing in the hallway.

But Maggie could not blame Evers. She quite understood his feelings. It was all simply too much for an ordinary Englishman—or woman—to bear. For the maharajah of Rajasthan, the supreme power of that province—outside of Her Majesty, of course—to have presented his own niece as a reward for heroism—And for Jeremy to have accepted that reward!—was beyond all comprehension.

Maggie was glad it had been so long since luncheon. Otherwise, she might have lost what she'd eaten right then and there.

Instead, however, she did what any decent British citizen ought to have done: She swallowed the sour taste in her mouth and said, as graciously as possible, "If you will follow me, I'll show you to the drawing room. And of course, I'll be happy to take your wraps."

The Indian man beamed at her. "Thank you," Sanjay said. "Thank you very much. We have traveled a long way, and are very tired. And I am afraid the cold here is not what we are used to. It is quite wearing."

Maggie smiled—though she feared that smile was terribly sickly. "I'll see that someone brings you some tea straightaway, then."

And then she turned, and threw open the doors to the drawing room.

It took her only a few minutes to see that the princess and her translator were settled comfortably. When it appeared that all their needs—save the tea, which Maggie rang for—had been attended to, she took her leave. It was only as Maggie was leaving that the princess reached out and seized her hand.

Looking down at the lovely, upturned face, Maggie could see, with perfect clarity, why Jeremy had not said no to the maharajah's offer. The Star of Jaipur was aptly named. Besides her large, hypnotic eyes, the princess had been blessed with a perfectly bow-shaped mouth, skin the color of hazelnuts, long ebony hair, and a figure as lithe and as fine-boned as a dancer's. Two of her would have fit easily into Maggie's corset. Though his aunt would object, of course—Pegeen had been very vocal in her disapproval of the maharajah's beneficence, calling him, perhaps not incorrectly, a peddler of human flesh—Jeremy had surely found a perfect duchess for Rawlings, one who would not shame the heavy diamond tiara that came with the title.

The princess hung on to Maggie's gloved hand for a few moments, while she spoke rapidly in what Maggie assumed was Hindustani. When she finished her little speech, Sanjay translated: "The Princess Usha wishes you to know that your kindness will not go unrewarded. For the generosity you have shown us this evening, you will always be a valued member of Her Highness's personal staff. She wishes to know the extent of your experience as a lady's maid, and whether or not you can read."

It took Maggie a full minute before she could summon up a reply. When she did, she was pleased she managed to do so without laughing . . . or vomiting.

"I'm extremely flattered," Maggie said slowly, "however, I am not a servant, merely a guest in this house. I do hope you have a pleasant evening, but now I really must retire to my own room."

Without waiting for the princess's reply, she turned and hurried away. All she wanted was to flee to the sanctuary of her own room. But of course, no sooner had she reached it, than her maid, Hill, bustled out from the dressing room, a white satin evening gown in her hands.

"There you are," she said, just as Maggie threw herself

dramatically across the bed, preparing to burst into a storm of tears. "You're late. You've only a few minutes to get changed."

"Changed?" Maggie echoed dejectedly. "Changed for what?"

"Lord and Lady Althorpe's cotillion." Hill shook her head. "Really, Miss Margaret. Is that skull of yours forever in the clouds?"

Maggie gasped. "Oh, Lord, no! I'd completely forgotten!"

The cotillion! What an idiot she was! She had fussed at Augustin for weeks, fearful that Lady Althorpe would forget to issue her an invitation to this all-important society event. Every matron in town would be in attendance, along with their unmarried daughters, and they'd all of them get a glance at the portrait Maggie had just completed of Cordelia Althorpe, in whose honor her parents were hosting the cotillion. Maggie would never have a better chance to gain introductions to the sort of people who'd be most likely to commission portraits from a painter like herself. If she could win over Lord and Lady Althorpe's rich, influential friends, she might never want for money again!

"Oh!" she cried, rolling over, and heading straight for her dressing table. How in the world was she going to cry out her troubles when she had to prepare for a ball? "Oh, Hill," she cried, to her maid's reflection in the large gilt-framed mirror that hung above the dressing table. "I'd completely forgotten!"

"Well, fortunately, Mr. de Veygoux didn't. He'll be here in half an hour to pick you up. Least, that's the message he left earlier this afternoon. Come on, now, and get out of those things. We've got a lot of work to do, if we're to make you presentable by the time he gets here."

Heaving a sigh, Maggie slumped forward, burying her head in her arms. "Oh, Hill," she said. "You can't even begin to imagine the day I've had."

"The day *you've* had!" Hill tugged on her mistress's hat. "I like that! Well, prepare yourself, miss. I'm about to make it a good deal worse."

"Oh, no," Maggie exclaimed, looking up. A sudden tightness appeared in her chest. "You haven't received bad news from Herbert Park, have you, Hill?"

"Oh, Lord, no, miss," Hill said, plucking pins out of Maggie's hair. "No, nothing like that. It's only just . . . Well, it's just that—"

The only other time Maggie had ever seen Hill look so perturbed was the night Maggie had tried to dismiss her, shortly after her father had cut her off, and Maggie had finally had to confess to her maid that she didn't have the money to pay her salary. Hill had only lifted her nose at this information, and said gravely, "Your good mother put me in charge of you when you was sixteen, miss. She'd be rollin' over in her grave if she heard I was leavin' you now, when you're needin' me most. You never mind about my wages. We'll muddle through somehow. We always have."

Maggie, curious over what could possibly have upset the usually phlegmatic Hill so much, asked, "Whatever can be the matter, Hill? Has Evers done something to upset you? I know he's a bit of a trial, but do try to get along with him. We are guests here, you know."

"No, miss, it isn't Mr. Evers what's botherin' me this time." Hill picked up the hairbrush from the dressing table and began raking it through Maggie's thick, tangled tresses. "It's *him*."

Maggie knit her dark eyebrows, both in confusion and pain from her maid's brutal brushing technique. "*Him?* Him who?"

"Miss Margaret—" The maid paused for dramatic effect. "He's back. The duke, I mean. From India."

"Oh," Maggie said.

Seeing that her mistress had not fainted from the news, Hill stooped to look her in the eye. "You knew!" she exclaimed, after she'd studied the younger woman's reflection for a few seconds. "You knew all along he was back!"

"Well," Maggie began slowly.

Hill straightened up, and launched another vicious attack on Maggie's hair. "I can't believe you knew he was back, miss, an' you din't have the goodness to tell me!"

"Ow!" Maggie cried, as Hill twisted her hair so tightly, she flinched. "Hill, I swear to you, I only just found out myself."

Hill was not showing any mercy, however. She jerked Maggie's head this way and that as she attacked the snarls in her hair. "Shame on you, Miss Margaret! What would your good mother say, if she knew you were staying in a house alone with an unmarried gentleman? And not just any unmarried gentleman, but the Duke of Rawlings! She wouldn't like it, and you know it!"

Maggie sighed. "Yes," she said. "Yes, I know, Hill. You're right."

"I'm more'n right," Hill declared. "I'm *dead* right." Hill stopped brushing, and started braiding. "We can't stay here, Miss Margaret. Not with a man who consorts with a *heathen.*"

Maggie, startled, glanced at her maid's reflection in the large mirror over her dressing table. "Heathen? Whatever do you mean?"

"You know what I mean," Hill said darkly. "That so-called star. Star!" Hill snorted. "I'll show *her* a star or two!"

"Oh," Maggie said, in a small voice. "I see. Only, Hill . . ."

"Only what?" Hill had hairpins in her mouth, so her next sentence came out sounding garbled. "There ain't no only about it. It's a good thing Lord and Lady Edward are expected back this evening. Because if they weren't, well, I'd make you clear out this instant. We can't stay here with *him* in the house."

"Yes, only where would we go?" Maggie looked up at her maid. "You know I haven't the money yet to rent a flat . . . a *decent* flat, anyway, in a neighborhood where we needn't be afraid to walk Jerry at night. I suppose I could ask Berangère—"

Hill looked horrified. "That Frenchwoman who rents the paintin' studio across the hall from yours?" she cried.

Maggie glanced up at her maid apprehensively. "Really, Hill. She's a good friend. I'm sure if she has the room, she'll let us stay with her for as long as—"

"I'll not be livin' with that Frenchwoman," Hill declared crisply. "Nor will you. That Mam'selle Jacquard, she's no sort of lady, if you ask me, in spite of all her money, and you'll not be sharing any flat with her. I know all about women like her, those *artistic* types. . . ."

"Hill," Maggie said gently. "*I'm* the artistic type. Remember?"

Hill stamped her foot furiously. "Don't you be comparin' yourself to that little miss. I seen women like her. I know their ways. No better than that heathen the duke's marryin'. You know, don't you, that if the duke was any sort of gentleman, he wouldn't't've put you in this situation. You know that, don't you, miss? The two of you ain't children no more. Things can't be the way they was between you. He's a man now, and you, Miss Margaret, are a lady, in spite of what *some* people in your family might think." Hill, loyal to the last, disapproved highly of the way Maggie's father and sisters had been treating her of late. "We'll just see what Lady Edward says about all this, when she gets back. I imagine she'll have a proper word or two to give that nephew of hers, for all he's a duke and a war hero! I only hope I'm about to hear it, I do."

Maggie stared glumly at her reflection. She sincerely hoped she *wasn't* around to hear Lady Edward light into her nephew. She had seen Pegeen lose her temper before, and it was not a pretty sight.

Lord, Maggie thought with a sigh. What a mess her life was turning out to be. . . .

And all because of that blasted Jeremy!

Chapter 15

For as long as Jacob Evers could remember, his family had served the Duke of Rawlings. His father, his father's father, even his grandfather's father had all buttled in a Rawlings household, either the town house in London or the manor house in Yorkshire. And in all that time, only one piece of advice had been handed down. Just a single axiom, passed from one generation to the next, that had never, so far as Jacob Evers knew, ever been broken. . . .

Until now.

Standing in front of the door to the duke's bedroom, the one normally occupied by Lord and Lady Edward when they were in town, Evers hesitated. He knew that the punishment for what he was about to do would be swift. He needn't worry that he'd suffer long. Still, he couldn't help wondering if the current duke would merely give him the sack, or accompany the sacking with a physical beating. From what Evers understood, the former duke, Jeremy's grandfather, had been famous for beating his servants. Though Evers had heard no such horror stories about Lord John's son, he nevertheless steeled himself for some kind of abuse. After all, he was about to do the unthinkable:

Wake a Rawlings.

The butler lowered his fist to the door and thumped, several times. Then he quickly leapt back, as if the portal might itself reach out and strike him.

It took a minute or two, but eventually the door opened,

revealing a large room, the windows of which, though curtained now, overlooked Hyde Park. The walls were painted in a pleasant hunter-green motif coupled with a maroon so pale it might almost have passed for mauve.

There was nothing pleasant, however, about the person who'd opened the door. It was, Evers saw, with a sinking heart, Peters, His Grace's valet, a young man who'd apparently fought under the duke's command, and had, as far as Evers could tell, not a single bit of formal training as a gentleman's valet. Even worse, he had only one complete leg, having lost most of what had existed beneath the knee of his right leg in some sort of battle abroad. The young man had already unstrapped the wooden peg he wore once when he'd been belowstairs, disgusting Cook and terrifying the scullery maids with the sight of his stump. Peters was not a particular favorite among the household staff at Twenty-two Park Lane.

"What," the valet whispered, his expression one of complete disbelief, "do you want, mate? The colonel's *asleep*, you know. . . ."

Before Evers could open his mouth to voice his indignation at being referred to as *mate,* a wooden voice sounded from somewhere in the room. "Correction," Jeremy said flatly. "The colonel *was* asleep."

Peters turned a grim face toward the butler. "Jesus," he breathed. "You're in for it now. Don't you know no one's s'posed to wake the colonel? 'Ave you got a death wish?"

"What is it, Evers?" demanded the duke imperiously. In the doorway, his valet muttered, "'E's not *well*, you know, mate. 'E needs 'is sleep. . . ."

Evers cleared his throat. "I would not deign to disturb His Grace's sleep were it not for the direst of circumstances."

"Dire circumstances, eh?"

Evers was relieved to hear a note of amusement in His Grace's voice. For the first time since opening the front door a half hour earlier, he allowed himself to feel hope that perhaps, just perhaps, he might manage to retain his employment after delivering this terrible news.

"If the circumstances are dire enough that Evers felt it

necessary to wake me, then you had better let him come in, Peters.''

Pursing his lips with disapproval, Peters removed his wooden leg from where he'd thrust it, directly in Evers's path, and limped backward in order to allow the butler to enter. Evers did so, his chin held high—until his eyes met with the figure that lay in the great curtained bed just a few yards away. It was only years of careful training that kept his jaw from dropping. He could not, however, keep from exclaiming, in surprise, ''Good God!''

''Oh, come, Evers,'' Jeremy said with a mocking smile. ''You've seen worse, surely.''

Evers recovered himself. Blinking rapidly, he crossed the dimly lit room, careful not to trip on any of the many items that had been strewn across the floor in Peters's efforts to unpack His Grace's trunks.

''Not quite, Your Grace,'' the butler said stiffly. ''I hope you'll forgive me if I suggest that you allow me to send for a physician. There is an excellent man just down the street, a Mr. Wallace, who could no doubt be here momentarily.''

Jeremy looked shocked . . . or as shocked as a man who was laid up in bed with a high fever could look. ''Bite your tongue, Evers,'' he said. ''There's nothing the doctors can do for me now. I've just got to sweat it out. I'll be right as rain in half an hour.''

'''E's right, Mr. Evers.'' Peters had closed the bedroom door, and now limped over to a trunk he'd apparently been unpacking. ''These fevers take the colonel, and leave 'im just as quick. I wouldn't be surprised if he was up and around by suppertime.''

''Speaking of which . . .'' Jeremy, shirtless, was leaning back against a multitude of pillows, many of which looked as if they'd been twisted by a pair of strong, fevered hands. ''. . . what's Maggie doing tonight?''

Evers, taken completely by surprise by the question, stammered, ''Miss Margaret, Your Grace? Why, I believe her maidservant told me that Miss Margaret and Monsieur de Veygoux are attending a cotillion given by the Earl of Althorpe.''

A look of utter horror crossed Jeremy's face. "*What*?" he cried, bolting upright in the vast bed. "You mean that frog-eater is escorting her?"

"Yes, of course, Your Grace," Evers said. "He is, after all, her fiancé. Your Grace, might I recommend that you put on a shirt? When one is suffering from a very high fever, it is usually advisable to—"

"Damned right," Jeremy said, throwing back the sheets entirely, and making it clear that beneath the butter-soft linen bedclothes, the duke wore precisely, well, nothing. "Peters," he said in a commanding voice. "My uniform, if you will."

Horrified, Evers looked quickly away. "Your Grace!" the butler cried. "I really think—"

"Dress uniform, Colonel?" Peters asked. He hobbled up to the edge of the bed and seized one of the muscular arms thrust at him, helping to pull the duke toward the side of the large bed.

"Dress uniform, Peters," Jeremy grunted, as he started climbing down the set of stairs that led from the steep bed frame. "I'll need my sword, white gloves, decorations—"

Peters looked happily surprised. "Really, Colonel? Your *decorations*? *All* of them?"

"All of them, Peters." Naked, Jeremy pulled himself up to his full height and happened to glance in his butler's direction. Evers was staring with something akin to horror at him. "Thank you, Evers," Jeremy said mildly. "That will be all."

Evers shook himself. "B-but . . . Your Grace can't be thinking of *going out*."

"Of course I'm going out, Evers," Jeremy said with a smile. "I've got a sudden desire to pay a call on the Earl of Althorpe."

"But . . ." Evers shook his head, like a dog trying to rid his ears of water. "Your Grace, I really must protest. You are obviously not a well man. It is sheer lunacy for you to venture outdoors, in this cold weather, running a high fever."

"For God's sake, old man," Peters hissed disgustedly, as he threw a clean white shirt over his master's broad shoulders. "Pull yourself together. Don't you know who you're speaking to?"

Evers looked offended. "I most certainly do. I am speaking to the seventeenth Duke of Rawlings."

"No you ain't," Peters whispered. "You're speakin' to Lieutenant Colonel Jeremy Rawlings. And the lieutenant colonel ain't afraid of anything or anyone, as his many medals and honors prove."

"Are my boots polished, Peters?" Jeremy inquired, as he tugged on the billowy-sleeved white shirt.

"With a cold biscuit, Colonel," the valet said, quickly unfolding a pair of fawn-colored breeches. "Just the way you like them."

"Very good." Though he'd managed to don his underwear without assistance, Jeremy was forced to lay a hand upon his valet's shoulder to support himself as he stepped into his tight-fitting trousers. "Evers, order my carriage to be brought round directly after Maggie's has left." Then, looking up, Jeremy inquired, "Do we still have that pair of grays my uncle won from the Prince of Wales?"

"Yes, Your Grace. But—"

"Excellent." Jeremy shrugged into the handsomely cut, deep scarlet coat, the tails of which brushed the backs of his knees. The heavy gold epaulets upon his shoulders caught the candlelight, and Peters hurried to comb out their sweeping fringe. The duke turned to examine his reflection in the full-length mirror standing in the far corner of the room. Critically, he pulled at some tangles of black curl that fell over his broad forehead. "Peters, you'll drive me."

"Of course, Colonel," the valet replied cheerfully. "I think I remember me way through the streets of London, though it's been a while, o' course."

Evers could contain himself no longer. "Your Grace!" he cried. "You are not well. I must insist that you allow me to send for a physician. At the very least, stay home tonight and rest. You look dreadful, my lord. Very dreadful, indeed!"

This caused Jeremy to stare at his reflection even more critically. "Do I?" he asked, surprised. "Well, only because

Peters hasn't pinned on my decorations yet. Wait until you see them, Evers. I glitter quite like a dowager.''

Undaunted, Evers continued. ''It would be absolutely disgraceful, Your Grace, were you to simply show up at the Althorpe cotillion without having been issued an invitation—''

''You think the Earl of Althorpe would begrudge a cup of punch to the seventeenth Duke of Rawlings?'' Jeremy smiled cynically at his reflection. ''I think not. Peters, can't anything be done about this hair of mine?''

''Certainly, Colonel.'' Peters brandished a pair of scissors. ''You're only needing a trim. Let me throw a towel round your neck, to protect your coat—''

''Madness,'' Evers muttered. ''Absolute madness.'' Then, more loudly, he declared, ''I am afraid, Your Grace, that you have left me no choice. Your neglect of your own health has forced me to come to the conclusion that I must notify Lord and Lady Edward as soon as they arrive—''

Before the words were fully out of the butler's mouth, Jeremy had whirled around and, in a single motion, seized both of Evers's lapels and hauled him six inches off the floor. Speechless for once, the butler looked down at the floor, over which he hovered, then back at the enraged face of his master, who was not, apparently, as weak with illness as Evers had thought.

''At your peril, little man,'' the duke hissed, in a voice that sent chills up the butler's spine. ''At your peril do you utter a word to them about my illness. Not a word. Do you hear what I'm telling you?''

Evers, petrified, and more than ever convinced that his master had become bedeviled in the Far East, stammered, ''B-but, Your Grace, they—they're bound to notice as soon as they see you. Surely—''

''I'll tell them myself,'' the duke informed him coolly. ''In my own way. I don't need anyone running to my aunt and uncle every time I come down with a touch of something. You're to keep quiet about it. Understand?''

Evers couldn't speak, he was trembling so badly. The duke's valet sauntered over and said cordially, ''Don't you worry about 'im, Colonel. I'll take care of 'im for you, if'n 'e lets anything slip. I'll do 'im the way we did those Bengals back in Jaipur—'' To illustrate, he drew a finger across his own throat, making a hideous hissing noise as he did so.

"I won't," Evers gasped. "I won't say a word, Your Grace! I swear it!"

Jeremy studied the older man's face, unaware of the fact that his own face had taken on an expression of such desperation that it would not have been recognized by any who'd known him in his youth. The Duke of Rawlings had never wanted for anything, had never known deprivation.

Not until recently, anyway.

"See that you don't," Jeremy grumbled, and he set the butler down, quite gently, considering his rage just seconds before.

Evers, his relief immense at having escaped a pummeling from the massive fists that had held him, sagged against a bedpost. His heart was hammering inside his chest, and his mouth had gone dry as cinder. Good God. What was he to do? He was in the employ of a madman. Never in the history of his family had any Evers been treated so by a Rawlings.

Well, what had he expected? It might very well be true, what they said about the latest duke's parentage. One certainly would expect such behavior from the progeny of a whore. . . .

"Now," Jeremy said evenly, as his valet threw a towel about his shoulders, and began to trim his hair. "What was this dire message you needed to convey to me, Evers?"

Good Lord. He had almost completely forgotten. Clearing his throat, Evers straightened and said, "I'm so sorry, my lord. It is only that the Star of Jaipur is downstairs in the foyer."

The duke glanced curiously at his butler's reflection in the standing mirror. "No, it isn't," he said.

"I beg your pardon, Your Grace," Evers said, with some indignation. "Do you think I would have disturbed your rest had I not been absolutely sure—"

"The Star of Jaipur is right here," Jeremy said, turning away from the mirror and looking, a bit confusedly, at all the trunks piled on the floor. ''Well, somewhere around here. Peters, where is it?''

''Right 'ere, Colonel.'' The valet bent and, after rooting about in the bottom of one of the trunks for a few seconds, straightened, and held out a small velvet sack.

''Right,'' Jeremy said. ''Toss it here, would you, old mate?'' The valet obliged, and Jeremy caught the bag on the fly, one-handed. Then, overturning the sack so its contents fell out into his palm, Jeremy extended his hand toward Evers, revealing a gem the size of a baby's fist, and the color of a Mediterranean sea. ''Here it is, Evers. The Star of Jaipur. Quite safe and sound.''

Evers stared at the sapphire in confusion. ''But . . . forgive me, Your Grace. . . . If *that* is the Star of Jaipur, then who is the young Indian lady standing downstairs in the foyer?''

If Evers had feared for his life before, it was nothing compared to how he felt when he caught a glimpse of the duke's face as these words registered.

Chapter 16

$\mathcal{T}$he Earl of Althorpe's eldest daughter was not what anyone would consider a handsome girl. In fact, with her buck
teeth, complete lack of chin, and figure running to fat, due
to the amount of sweets she consumed, one could safely call
her ugly . . . though Maggie hadn't the slightest intention of
doing so. After all, she'd been lucky—very lucky, indeed—
to have been the artist commissioned to paint the Honorable
Miss Althorpe's portrait. Other artists had vied for the
honor—and the several hundred pounds that accompanied
that honor—but Maggie had been chosen, and chosen over
portrait painters of considerably more renown.

But though they might have been more well-known, none
of them managed, in their initial sample sketches, to capture
Cordelia Althorpe's single beauty—her jewellike, almost ir-
idescent green eyes. None of them, that is, with the exception
of Maggie, who, staring at the unfortunate Cordelia with
something akin to despair, desperately seeking to find *something* attractive about the girl, finally noticed the eyes, almost
hidden between folds of fat.

And, Maggie thought, with a feeling of satisfaction, as
she stood sipping a glass of champagne beneath the finished
portrait, if the bright-eyed, smiling girl in the painting bore
little resemblance to the rather dour Cordelia, at least her
parents were happy, and had come through with the handsome—and much-needed—check right on schedule, just as

Maggie had completed the portrait in time for the cotillion given in the sitter's honor.

"That," an amused voice intoned, just right of Maggie's ear, "is nothing short of a miracle."

Turning her head, Maggie smiled up at her fiancé. "I couldn't agree more," she said, with mock solemnity. "The fact that anyone would pay so much money for a piece of canvas with paint splattered on it is simply shocking."

"Not *that*, Mademoiselle Herbert." Augustin de Veygoux chuckled. "I'm talking about the clever way in which you managed to make Cordelia Althorpe, a remarkably unattractive young woman, pass for pretty, without committing an absolute act of perjury."

Maggie looked quickly away, but did not manage to suppress her smile. "You insult me, monsieur. I am a portrait painter. I do not embellish. I paint exactly what I see."

"Then would that I saw the world through your eyes, mademoiselle," her fiancé laughed. "For they are surely the most benevolent lenses imaginable. They see beauty everywhere, especially where there is none at all to be seen."

"*Vous êtes un homme horrible*," Maggie chastised, raising her fan to tap it playfully against his chest. "The Honorable Miss Althorpe is an accomplished young woman. She sings and plays most admirably. What she lacks in beauty, she makes up for with talent."

"With money, you mean." Augustin looked across the vast ballroom, at the opposite end of which the young lady in question was consuming a large puff pastry, ignoring everyone and everything else around her. "The only reason any man would condescend to marry that creature is for her money."

Maggie opened her fan and began to employ it. Though it was February, the ballroom was not particularly large, and had grown a trifle warm from all the bodies crowded into it. "What a dreadful thing to say. Really, Augustin. There's no need to be cruel."

"It is not I who is cruel, *ma chérie*, but the world," Augustin de Veygoux said lightly. "Unattractive, uninteresting women like Cordelia Althorpe have no hope of marrying for

love. Unless they find themselves attracted to an equally uninteresting, unattractive man. But how often does something
like that happen? No, I'm sorry to pain you, mademoiselle,
but the Honorable Miss Cordelia's appeal lies only in her
papa's purse.''

Maggie glared at him. ''That may very well be true, but
you needn't say so out loud. You can't know how thankful
I am that I need never worry about overhearing someone say
the same of me.''

Augustin smiled. ''Now, you, *ma chérie*, a man would
marry if you were as poor as a church mouse—''

''But I am,'' Maggie reminded him. ''I *am* poor as a
church mouse! That's what I meant. No one would marry
me for my money, because I haven't any.''

''Yes,'' Augustin agreed. ''But you have something considerably more appealing than money.''

''Do I?'' Maggie looked dubious. ''What is that?''

Augustin smiled wickedly down at her. ''*Votre silhouette,
naturellement*,'' he said, and watched with delight as a blush
suffused her cheeks, as he'd known it would.

Maggie, very much aware that her face had grown hot at
his reference to her figure, glanced around anxiously to see
if he had been overheard. As sophisticated as she told herself
she was, remarks about her looks still tended to embarrass
her. She would have thought that after five years in Paris,
she'd be used to flattery, bored with it, even. After all, French
men, unlike English ones, were quite vocal in their admiration of a pretty girl, even in such civilized settings as salons
and private balls, and Maggie had been admired everywhere
she went. Unfortunately, statements like Augustin's only
served to make her uncomfortable. Despite what the mirror
told her every time she glanced into it, Maggie still thought
of herself as the awkward, gangling girl she'd been in her
childhood, and vaguely distrusted anyone who claimed to see
her as otherwise.

That was not to say that she didn't trust her fiancé. Far
from it! Maggie glanced at him over the lace edging of her
fan. Augustin de Veygoux, despite his tendency to compliment her too much, was one of the kindest, most trustworthy

people Maggie had ever known. A tall, charismatic man a little over a decade Maggie's senior, Augustin had been a frequent visitor to Madame Bonheur's studio, and not just because of Madame's generosity with her fine cigars. The de Veygoux family was highly respected in the art community. They owned galleries in as many as seven European cities, and one in America, and had a collection of Renaissance paintings rumored to be one of the most valuable in the world. Augustin himself was always searching for new talent to promote in his Parisian salon, and Madame Bonheur, as gifted a businesswoman as she was an artist, saw to it that several of Maggie's paintings fell his way. It was Augustin who purchased the portrait of Jerry, before ever even having met the painter who rendered it. How soon after finally having met the artist Monsieur de Veygoux's plans for promoting her work took on a more personal significance, Maggie was never certain, but for the final two years of her stay in Paris, she was rarely without his company of an evening.

She was not in love with him. There had never been any question of that. When Augustin first declared himself, some two or three weeks into their acquaintance, Maggie had only laughed, thinking he was teasing her. When he persisted, however, in pressing his suit, she finally, and very awkwardly, informed him that his feelings for her were in no way returned.

When Augustin walked into a room, her heart did not skip a beat. When he kissed her hand, she felt nothing. Maggie knew what love felt like . . . knew it only too well. She knew she was not in love with him, and frequently pointed out to him that he deserved better. He certainly could have gotten any other woman he set his mind to, since he was both rich and relatively good-looking, if one was willing to overlook the rather thick shock of red hair that grew in waves from his head.

But Augustin apparently preferred the challenge of wooing the only woman in the world who was hopelessly, irrevocably, in love with another—though whether or not Augustin ever guessed this was the case, she never knew.

The closest she ever came to admitting to the existence of such a person was the day her mother died.

Augustin, who'd insisted upon escorting Maggie back to England upon learning the gravity of Lady Herbert's illness, had been there when Mr. Parks, the surgeon, made his solemn announcement. He had been witness to Sir Arthur's horrible reaction to the news. It was Augustin who consulted with the vicar about the funeral arrangements, Augustin who sent the messenger to Maggie's eldest sister, Anne, trapped in London in the ninth month of her fourth pregnancy, Augustin who consoled the servants as they draped black cloths over the mirrored panels in the dining room.

And it had been Augustin who found Maggie weeping on the terrace outside her bedroom, despite the autumnal chill in the air. Though he was good with words, the Frenchman chose not to use any at that moment, simply draping his coat over Maggie's shuddering shoulders and sitting beside her, for all the world as if they were sitting in his box seats at the Paris opera house. When he finally did speak, it was to remind Maggie that *his* mother was still alive, and that if she would consent to marry him, she would have a living mother still. Granted, she would only be a mother-in-law, but that was better than no mother at all, was it not?

While the inappropriateness of this remark might have made Maggie laugh despite her tears at any other time, at that particular moment, she felt nothing but shame. Because for the first time that day, she hadn't been crying for her mother at all, but for herself. Despite her sisters' efforts to hide it from her, she had seen that morning's *Times*, with the story of Jeremy's amazing victory in Jaipur—he had almost single-handedly deflected a rebellious faction's attempt to burn down the Palace of the Winds—as well as the highly unusual reward he'd subsequently been granted by the maharajah. *The Times* had added the latter almost as an afterthought, the exciting story's quaint epilogue, which had most of London snickering. Imagine, in this day and age, proffering a human being as a reward for bravery! Why, the abolitionists were certainly going to be up in arms about this one!

But to Maggie, that small detail—that Jeremy had been offered, and had apparently accepted, since there was no mention in the paper that the maharajah's reward had been turned down, an Indian princess for his very own—was hardly quaint, and definitely not amusing. It quite literally devastated her. It had been nearly five years since she'd last seen him, and in all that time, she'd never received a single communication from him to indicate that he even remembered her existence. And why should he? She was only a girl with whom he'd once dallied in a stable, that was all. Why, when he could have an Indian princess, would he ever want Maggie Herbert?

Shameful as it was to be crying over something so ridiculous on the day of her mother's death, that's exactly what Maggie had been doing when Augustin proposed to her, for what turned out to be the final time. Final because, when she had collected herself enough to speak, she said yes.

She was not so grief-stricken as to be unaware of how much Augustin had done for her family during her mother's dreadful last days. What had Jeremy Rawlings ever done for her? Nothing! In the whole of the time he'd been away, he had never once written. He had not even sent any messages through his family. He had not, as far as she knew, ever wasted a passing thought on Maggie since that day in the stables. What was she doing, giving up a perfectly good marriage proposal, from a perfectly good man, for someone who hadn't bothered to send her so much as a line in years, and who had gone and gotten himself saddled with an Indian princess in the bargain?

And Augustin had done so much for her! The very least she could do was try to make him happy. Maggie knew good and well she would never love any man but the Duke of Rawlings, but she and Augustin were quite good friends, and she was genuinely fond of him. That was more than many married couples had, friendship and affection, wasn't it?

And so rather than turning Augustin down yet again, as she might have, had she not happened to see the newspaper that day, Maggie agreed to marry him instead. What else could she do?

Still fanning herself, Maggie looked up at Augustin as he turned to greet some acquaintances of his. True, his shock of red hair was unfortunate. On a woman, it might have been flamboyant, but on a man, it looked . . . well, as Berangère put it, distracting. And his mother! There was no doubt that Augustin's mother was a trial. But he would make a good husband, Maggie knew.

And she needed a good husband. She couldn't go the whole of her life pining away after a man who hadn't spared a thought for her in five years. Five years! Oh, there was that letter he'd said he'd written. Perhaps he *had* written. But what did a single letter mean? Nothing. She obviously meant nothing to him. She had only been one woman in a whole string of them with whom he'd once passed a pleasant afternoon. It was only because she'd been so naïve, so inexperienced, that she'd fallen in love with him. Well, she was going to fall *out* of love with him. She didn't care how long it took. She would *not* go the rest of her life loving Jeremy Rawlings. She would *not*.

So intently was she meditating on this particular resolve that she didn't, at first, hear the sudden lull in the conversation around her. Despite her assertions, half a decade before, that a ballroom was the last place on earth in which she'd ever feel at ease, Maggie had gotten well-used to the noise and the heat and the jostling. Consequently, there was nothing that caught her attention faster in a ballroom than a voice lowered to a whisper. Folding her fan, Maggie glanced interestedly at Augustin's companions. She recognized them immediately as Lord and Lady Mitchell, whose collection of Flemish paintings rivaled the de Veygoux family's, and with whom Augustin was frequently in friendly competition at auctions. Both the Mitchells and Augustin were peering at someone on the dance floor, their backs to Maggie.

''I haven't the slightest idea who he is,'' Lord Mitchell said in a loud voice. He, clearly, did not mind whether or not he was overheard. ''And I don't care, either. I can't think why you dragged me here, Leticia. You know I can't abide crushes like this.''

''But he's got to be *someone*,'' his wife insisted. ''The

Althorpes wouldn't invite just *anyone* to their only daughter's coming out.''

Ah, Maggie thought, unfolding her fan again. They've only spotted a face in the crowd that they can't identify, that's all. She smiled to herself. Really, Augustin was so funny about that sort of thing! Like a woman, almost, in his fascination with the mechanics of the *haut monde*.

Poor Augustin. He had never been any good at hiding his feelings, particularly enthusiasm, with which he fairly bubbled over at times. It had been difficult for Maggie to convince him to conceal his glee upon her acceptance of his proposal, since he had claimed himself the happiest of men. But their engagement had had to be kept secret until a suitable period of mourning for her mother had passed. It had been a difficult year for Augustin, made no easier by the fact that Maggie's father had expressed no more approval for the engagement than he had over Maggie's decision to pursue a professional painting career. According to Sir Arthur's way of thinking, his youngest child's duty was to himself. He expected Maggie to return home to Herbert Park to tend him, despite the fact that he had two daughters already living within an easy distance of his home.

Thinking of her father, Maggie fanned herself with more energy than was necessary. What was Sir Arthur going to say, she wondered, when he learned that the Duke of Rawlings had returned home from India . . . and with a royal bride in tow? He would not be pleased. Sir Arthur had an inherent distrust of anything foreign. It wouldn't be easy for him to supplicate himself in front of a duchess who didn't speak the queen's English. And Jeremy's aunt and uncle! Pegeen had nearly suffered an apoplexy, Maggie remembered, when she'd first heard of the existence of the Star of Jaipur. Seeing the Princess Usha serve tea in the Gold Drawing Room back at Rawlings Manor might just finish off Lady Edward entirely.

Maggie closed her eyes. Hill was right. She was going to have to find a flat of her own, and at once. She couldn't possibly continue living there, not knowing she was sharing the same roof as that . . . that *woman*.

Not to mention that *man*.

"*Zut*," Augustin was saying, admiringly. "Look at the way all the women are eyeing him! He has even caught the Honorable Miss Althorpe's eyes, and I never thought *she'd* forsake that pastry of hers for a pretty face. . . ."

Lady Mitchell laughed shortly. "He's hardly *pretty*, Monsieur de Veygoux. But what girl could resist a man in uniform? You know how they react on the Ladies' Mile, whenever the Horse Guards ride by. There's just *something* about a cavalryman. . . ."

Her husband made a rude noise. "I'll say. The stench of horse manure, which follows 'em everywhere."

"Really, James. Just because you're too awkward in the saddle to ride with a sword at your side doesn't mean you have the right to be rude about those who can." Lady Mitchell was squinting now. "La, but this one is tall. And so many medals! He must have been very brave in some battle somewhere."

"India, it looks like," Augustin said. "Where else could he have picked up such an extraordinary tan? He's dark as a Gypsy."

It was at that point that Maggie, who'd been listening with only half an ear, took a quick step forward. It was impossible. It was *quite* impossible, since Jeremy didn't even *know* the Earl of Althorpe. Certainly his uncle might, but Jeremy? How would *he* know Lord and Lady Althorpe?

Because the backs of both Lord Mitchell and Augustin were blocking Maggie from seeing the dance floor, she darted behind a pillar until she found an unimpeded view. . . .

And then her heart, quite simply, stopped.

The orchestra didn't stop playing the waltz it had launched into. Certainly a hush did not fall over the room. The dancers did not part, like the Red Sea, to allow her a path across the parquet floor. But it seemed to Maggie as if all of these things happened. Because suddenly, she could hear nothing but the sound of her own swift intake of breath as she caught sight of the tall, uniformed cavalryman on the other side of the room.

Good God. It was Jeremy.

Granted, last time she'd seen him had been in her dimly lit bedroom. It had been at the crack of dawn, and she hadn't exactly been at her sharpest, having been frightened senseless first by the presence of a man in her room, and then by the identity of that man. But there was no mistaking the fact that Jeremy was standing not fifty feet away from her, a champagne flute raised to his lips as his silver-eyed gaze casually raked the dancing couples between them.

She had thought Jeremy's looks ruined by his sallow complexion and broken nose, but she'd been wrong. True, he was no longer breathtakingly handsome, as he'd been five years ago. But now there was something so much more masculine about him—and therefore so much more innately appealing—that Maggie wondered why every woman in the room wasn't falling down into a swoon at his feet, as she was very much afraid *she* might. In his immaculately cut coat, the epaulets of which emphasized the swell of his broad shoulders, he stood proudly as an admiral, as if the ballroom floor were the deck of one of Her Majesty's great warships, and he was about to give the order to fire all cannons.

And yet there was also a hint of something dangerous in his stance, something only just barely kept in restraint, that lent him the air of a brigand or highway robber. Maybe it was Jeremy's riotous crown of black curls, the curls no one had ever been able to keep under control, and which, no matter how recently cut, had a tendency to fall across his forehead. Or maybe it was the derisiveness in his glance, the utter contempt in which he seemed to hold everyone around him. In any case, had she seen a glint of gold at his earlobe, Maggie would not have been surprised.

He was dictatorial in his self-assurance. Maggie had never seen any man fill a room with his mere presence the way Jeremy was doing just then, and for the life of her, she couldn't figure out how, exactly, he was managing it. Certainly *she* was incapable of placing her eyes anywhere else than on his tall, elegant form.

But then she, of course, was in love with him.

It was that thought which, like a slap, brought Maggie round. Good Lord! What was she doing, standing there gaping at him like a simpleminded chambermaid? Jeremy was clearly looking for someone. . . . *Me?* her heart whispered hopefully. Hardly. Why on earth would he be looking for *her* when there was a woman like the Star of Jaipur in existence? Where *was* his little consort? Straining her eyes, Maggie could see no sign of Princess Usha. But that didn't mean she wasn't in the ballroom somewhere. And Maggie would be damned before she'd stand there and watch the two of them find one another. She hadn't eaten that much that evening, but a sight like that would definitely bring it back up.

She moved just a second too late. Not even a second. A *fraction* of a second too late. But that fraction of a second was enough. Jeremy's restless gaze was attracted by the movement, despite all the other motion in the room, and suddenly, his eyes were locked on hers. She froze, watching helplessly as he took in her upswept hairstyle, the bare curves of her neck and shoulders. His eyes widened a little at her décolletage, which was considerable, then narrowed as they followed the sweep of her long white skirt as it fishtailed into a three-foot-long train behind her.

There was a loop upon that train that could be attached to Maggie's wrist when she wanted to dance or move without a tangle of satin about her feet. With all the dignity she could muster under that insulting gaze, Maggie bent, lifted the train, slung it over her arm, and coldly turned her back on the Duke of Rawlings.

Chapter 17

*J*eremy nearly burst out laughing. She certainly was something, his Maggie. Just where, he wondered, did she think she was going? There was nowhere, nowhere on earth, she could go to escape him. He'd follow her into the bowels of hell if he had to.

Not that he imagined such extremes were going to be necessary.

No. She was obviously put out with him. What woman wouldn't be? If she'd been under the same impression as the rest of London seemed to be—that the Star of Jaipur was of the animal, and not mineral, variety—then he perfectly understood her animosity. Well, maybe not perfectly. After all, she was the one who'd gone and gotten herself engaged to a frog-eater. And *she* was put out with *him*! Little hypocrite.

He wondered if she'd have been as angry had she been privy to his thoughts upon finally spotting her across the ballroom. The sight of Maggie Herbert as he'd never seen her before, coolly elegant in a snow-white off-the-shoulder evening gown, from which crystal beads dripped like icicles, had staggered him. Certainly there were women in that ballroom who were more beautiful than Maggie Herbert. But none of them made his pulse beat quicker.

And when she bent to lift her train, that pulse had stuttered and nearly stopped. Bending over in a dress like that, with a figure like Maggie's, ought to have been a capital offense. Her breasts, full to the point of nearly overflowing from the tight constriction of the corset she wore, all but toppled out of the neckline of her gown. Jeremy's gaze had torn around the room, jealously seeking to know if any other man had glimpsed what he considered his own rightful property. Where was this fiancé of hers? How dare he let her go about in such a dress? Why, the man deserved a thrashing simply because of *that*.

Quick as a snake, Jeremy crossed the dance floor, dodging whirling couples and feeling the occasional sweep of a woman's train across his legs. Maggie, he saw, had ducked behind a massive pillar, but when he too rounded it, he found only a tall, redheaded man and a rather pompous-looking couple blinking at him astonishedly.

"What's the matter, then?" Jeremy demanded of them. "Never seen a member of the queen's Horse Guards in the flesh before?"

He didn't wait around to hear their response. Instead, he hurried off in the only possible direction Maggie could have gone, through a door paneled to look like part of the wall. Beyond it, he found himself in a dark, masculinely furnished room, a library, he thought, though it was hard to tell, since there wasn't any fire. The only light was that which spilled through a pair of tall windows at the far side of the room, and that was moonlight, and there wasn't much of it, since the moon was only half-full.

Still, there was enough to see by, enough to reflect against the beading on Maggie's dress. Standing by the window, her gloved hands clenched into fists at her sides, Maggie stamped her foot and cried exasperatedly, "Oh, Jerry, really! What do you want? Why are you following me?" He might have been mistaken, but he thought her voice caught on a sob. "Why can't you go away and leave me be?"

Jeremy didn't feel like laughing anymore. There was nothing, he suddenly realized, even remotely amusing about this situation.

"I did that already," he said, closing the door behind him with a soft click. The music from the orchestra and the laughter of the revelers outside was suddenly cut off. There wasn't a sound in the library, not even the crackling of a fire on the hearth. It was damnably cold.

Maggie, however, didn't seem to notice the chill, in spite of the indecent cut of her gown.

She had turned her back on him again . . . only this time, she was cornered. She seemed to know it, too, if the defensive way she'd folded her arms across her chest was any indication. Her breath, he saw, fogged the glass of the windowpane before her as she spoke. "What do you mean?" she demanded hoarsely. "What do you mean, you did that already?"

"What I said." Jeremy was aware that, though she was pretending not to, she was looking at him out of the corner of her eye. He slid his hands into his trouser pockets, in an effort to appear less threatening. He remembered her fear of him as well as if it had been yesterday. "You wanted to be left alone. I left you alone. For five years, to be precise."

"Well," Maggie said, swallowing quite audibly. "Apparently, five years wasn't long enough."

"Apparently not," Jeremy observed. "You know, Maggie, you are a bit trying. You're lucky I'm so forgiving. A lesser man than myself might have begun to feel a bit unwanted by now. I mean, after waiting five long years for you." He slowly circled the far end of a leather sofa, his gaze locked on her slender form.

"You seemed to manage to keep yourself busy in the interim," Maggie remarked to the window.

"Oh?" Jeremy navigated his way around an ivory-topped end table.

"Yes," Maggie said. "We were all kept highly entertained by the newspaper accounts of your heroic activities in the Far East."

Jeremy was close enough now to touch her, but he kept his hands planted firmly in his pockets. He had not come this far just to have his face slapped. Though Maggie, if he recalled correctly, had never been much of a slapper—more of a puncher. Instead he said nonchalantly, "Yes, I understand *The Times* was quite faithful in reporting my every move. There might have been one or two rather important points, however, that they got wrong.''

"I highly doubt that," Maggie said coldly. "*The Times* is, after all, the most widely read newspaper in the world. I'm quite sure the journalists who write for it exercise great care in researching their stories."

"There's one particular story, however," Jeremy said gently, "that I know for a fact they got wrong."

That got her attention. She whirled away from the window and, obviously taken aback by the fact that he'd managed, without her noticing, to get so close, took a quick step backward, until her shoulder blades obliterated the foggy patch her breath had made. "Stop it," she said, in a voice that wasn't exactly steady.

"Stop what?" Jeremy stayed where he was, lest another step forward send her backing out the window.

"You know what I mean," Maggie snapped. With her back to the window, he couldn't see her eyes, but he imagined they were as tear-filled as her voice. "Jeremy, I *know* they didn't get the story wrong. You admitted last night that you had the Star of Jaipur with you, and I saw her myself, in the foyer, not two hours ago!"

Jeremy raised an eyebrow. That was the only muscle in his body that moved as he said, "You saw the Princess Usha in the foyer two hours ago. You didn't see the Star of Jaipur."

Maggie thought she might burst a blood vessel, she was so angry. She lifted her folded fan and held it, as another woman would have held a knife, to his chest. "Jeremy," she said, from between gritted teeth. "The Princess Usha *is* the Star of Jaipur!"

"In her opinion, maybe," he said, with a slight shrug. "She's certainly been called that by a number of people, including her doting uncle. Sort of like a nickname. But the real Star of Jaipur isn't a woman. It's a stone."

The fan stayed exactly where it was, pointed threateningly at his heart. "Jeremy," Maggie said. "The newspaper said you'd been awarded the Star of Jaipur for your valor at the

Palace of the Winds. According to *The Times*, the Star of Jaipur is the maharajah's niece. . . .''

"Right." Jeremy nodded briskly. "That much is true. He did try to foist his niece off on me. It was a bit of a sticky situation, you understand, because in India, you know, giving a man your niece or daughter is supposed to be a very great honor. Especially a woman like the princess, who many of the natives believe is too beautiful to look upon directly—"

Maggie couldn't help snorting at this. Jeremy ignored her.

"What I'm trying to say," he went on, as if she hadn't interrupted, "is that I couldn't very well stand there and say, Well, thanks, but no thanks, to a maharajah. It would have been a terrific insult. We aren't too popular over there, and something like that would have completely ruined whatever chances we might have had at eventually coming to an amicable relationship with the local government of the province—"

Maggie looked as if she were going to plunge her fan into his eye at any moment. "Is there an end to this story?" she demanded.

Jeremy grinned. There wasn't any other woman on earth, with the possible exception of his aunt, who was so routinely rude to him as Maggie Herbert. He supposed that was why he loved her. "Yes, there is, Mags. What *The Times* obviously failed to report, most likely because it didn't make a very good story, is that later, I went back and explained to His High Exaltedness that while I was very appreciative of the honor he'd bestowed upon me by giving me his niece, I already had a girl back home." Jeremy began to dig around in his pocket. "He was a jolly good sport about it. He gave me this instead."

Pulling his hand from his pocket, he opened his fist. There, dazzling even in the weak moonlight, was the Star of Jaipur. It had collected a bit of lint from having been in his pocket so long, but otherwise, it was as perfect a gem as had ever existed.

Maggie, however, did not lower the fan. He saw at once that she was completely unimpressed by both the stone's beauty and obvious worth, a typically Maggie-like reaction.

"If what you just told me is true," she inquired coolly, "then why was the Princess Usha in your foyer this afternoon?"

"Now, that," Jeremy said, closing his fist with a sigh, and dropping the stone back into his pocket, "is a bit of a mystery to me, too. Near as I can get out of her translator—Usha doesn't speak much English, you know—she's madly in love with me, and is determined to marry me, despite all of my protestations."

Maggie threw the fan at him with all the force she could muster. Fortunately, he anticipated the move, and ducked. The fan struck the arm of the leather couch and fell, with a clatter, to the parquet floor. Jeremy, stunned, looked up at her from where he was crouched.

"I *knew* it," Maggie shouted. "I just knew it! Jerry, how could you? How *could* you?"

"What?" Jeremy held up his arms in order to shield himself from her flailing hands. Apparently, in his absence, Maggie had become something of a slapper after all. "What did *I* do?"

"What did you do?" Maggie echoed, her voice breaking hoarsely. "What did you do? I'll tell you what you did, you stupid, stupid man! *You made her fall in love with you . . .*"

. . . the same as you did me, she finished. But to herself, only to herself. The thought was so enraging that she felt an overwhelming need to strike something, and since Jeremy was just standing there, blinking at her in confusion, he seemed like the perfect outlet for her pent-up rage. Unfortunately, her fist connected only with his upper arm, which he'd flung up instinctively to ward off the blow he saw coming.

Even padded as that arm was with muscle, Jeremy couldn't help wincing. The girl still threw a very wicked right. Considering that he was the one who'd taught her to punch, the blow was all the more humiliating.

Loath as he was to hurt her, Jeremy was even more loath to see her hurt herself, and from the way she was hopping about—a rather interesting sight, considering the depth of her décolletage—cradling her right hand, which she'd apparently bruised once again by hitting him, he saw that she'd already done so. Jeremy decided to put an end to these antics, and like any good military man, he determined to do so as quickly and decisively as possible.

Perhaps seizing Maggie about the waist and throwing her, rear end first, onto the leather couch wasn't the most tactful way to handle the situation. And Jeremy didn't suppose it really helped things along when he flung himself after her, effectively pinning her where she lay with his body weight, then, when she struggled to get up, anchoring both her wrists to the sides of her head with his hands. It did, however, cheer him up excessively, despite her livid expression.

"Get," Maggie panted, "off me!"

"I don't think so," Jeremy said, admiring the way her breasts had swelled up over the edge of her gown. He could see both rosy nipples peeping out from beneath the satin fabric. What with Maggie being so out of breath, and her chest heaving up and down, he didn't suppose it would be too long before more of her came spilling out. He knew he'd be a fool not to stick around and watch. "That last time I got off you, if you'll recall, five years went by before I got the chance to get on you again. One thing I learned in the cavalry, my dear, is that opportunity is everything, and retreat gets one exactly nowhere."

"Jer—" Maggie started to yell, but Jeremy found that crushing her mouth under his worked quite effectively at keeping her quiet.

Chapter 18

"Jeremy," Maggie said when he finally let her come up for air.

"What?" He bent his head and began to kiss her long throat, starting where her pulse was beating as rapidly as his own, and moving inexorably toward the back of her right ear.

"What if someone comes in?" she asked breathlessly, even as she turned her head so that he could reach his target more easily.

"I'll ask them"—he nuzzled her ear—"to leave."

Maggie gasped at the sensations he was evoking. She wasn't sure what had happened. One minute, she'd been furiously angry with him. She had, in fact, wanted to kill him. She had prepared herself mentally for his eventual homecoming—for she knew he'd return. He *had* to. He was the Duke of Rawlings, after all. She had rehearsed what she'd say to him, how she'd behave. . . .

But never, in all of her imaginings, had she supposed that, within twenty-four hours of his return, she'd be lying in his arms, letting him kiss her behind her ear.

And that wasn't all he was doing, either. He'd released her wrists, and now both of his hands were on her breasts, eagerly canvassing territory only he had ever touched before. She couldn't help the fact that the feel of his callused fingers on her petal-soft skin was causing her back to arch. She couldn't help the fact that her arms had risen to circle his neck, and that she'd moved her head to intercept his lips once more. It wasn't her fault that once his mouth was on hers, her lips fell open. Could she help it if she let out a little moan as his tongue met hers? And so what if that little moan caused him, in his excitement, to press down on her nipples, which had gone hard as stones, both from desire and the chill in the air, with his palms?

This is *Jeremy*, was all she could think. *This is Jeremy*. And somehow, that made it all right.

It wasn't like it had been before. It wasn't like that at all. Before, she'd been a girl. She hadn't understood what was happening to her. She understood it only a little better now— she was, after all, still completely inexperienced—but at least she knew, from what Berangère had told her, that the tightening sensation she felt between her legs was perfectly normal. When Jeremy bent his head to taste one of her firm nipples, she knew the purpose of the corresponding rush of wetness she felt at the jointure of her thighs. And she was no longer so ignorant as to think that the very firm object pressing so insistently against her abdomen was a knife handle. She knew precisely what it was, and even felt a thrill at knowing that *she* had caused it, *she* had made it that way. So intoxicating was the idea that she couldn't help reaching down, tentatively, to brush his erection with her fingertips, just to reassure herself that it was there . . . and that it was hers.

Imagine her surprise when Jeremy, who'd caught his breath raggedly at the first pass she made with her hand, followed suit, touching her between her own legs!

Maggie hadn't the slightest idea how he'd done it, but he managed to insinuate his hand under the hem of her gown and over the waistband of her pantaloons. For the first time ever, she appreciated his vast prior experience with women. Never in her life had she ever felt anything quite as nice as Jeremy's fingers as they gently opened, and then caressed, her. She didn't even blush when he lifted his head to watch her face as he slipped a finger along the rim of her tight, wet sheath. She gasped maybe, a little—it was such an odd sensation!—but she didn't blush. Not even when he pressed his hand—now slick with her own moisture—against her pubic bone, and began to gently massage her there, causing her back to arch even more as she pressed hungrily against him.

She didn't know it, but she'd answered a question that had been plaguing Jeremy since he'd received Pegeen's letter informing him of Maggie's engagement. For months, he'd been torturing himself with the thought that someone else might actually have chartered this territory that he had claimed for himself all those years before. But Maggie's gasp when he first touched the hot furrow between her legs settled that question definitively: She was a virgin still. He'd have staked his life on it. And yet she was more eager, more giving than any of the more experienced women he'd been with. . . .

It was then that he whispered, in an unsteady voice, "Touch me, too."

She knew what he meant. She knew exactly what he meant. And she didn't hesitate. Instead, she reached for the front of his trousers. They unbuttoned easily beneath her trembling fingers. And then all at once, she was holding his thick manhood in her hand, wondering at its alien hardness, feeling it throb against her palm, as he pressed his hand, more urgently now, against her core, causing an ache to grow within her, a feeling of emptiness that she suddenly knew only he could fill. . . .

It was at that moment that the door to the library was thrown open, and above the strains of the orchestra and shrill, feminine laughter, a man's voice called, "*Marguerethe? Est-ce que êtes vous ici?*"

Maggie moved so fast, all Jeremy saw was a sparkling white blur. One second, it seemed, she was trembling on the brink of orgasm beneath him, her sweet hand closed tightly around him, and the next, she was standing a few feet away, fully dressed, but her breasts rising and falling as quickly as if she'd run to get there.

"Oh, hello, Augustin," she said, her voice betraying no emotion whatsoever. "Yes, I'm here. I'm sorry, were you looking for me?"

Jeremy, on the couch, began to button his trousers slowly,

feeling something hot beginning to burn somewhere deep within his chest. It was, unfortunately, a familiar sensation. It was how he generally felt right before he killed someone.

He stared over the back of the couch at the man standing in the open doorway, silhouetted against the bright light from the ballroom. All Jeremy could tell about the Frenchman was that he was tall. And that he didn't pronounce Maggie's name correctly.

"But why are you hiding in here, *ma chérie*, in the cold and dark?" de Veygoux inquired in a gently chastising manner. "I have the Marchioness of Lynne out here. She wants to speak to you about doing a portrait of her grandchildren. ..." His voice trailed off as Jeremy stood up. The Frenchman had noticed him at last. "Ah, but who is that with you, *chérie*?"

Maggie threw a hasty glance over her bare shoulder, as if becoming aware of Jeremy's presence for the first time. "Him?" she asked. She was stalling for time, fervently hoping this was a bad dream from which she was going to awaken at any moment. "Um, well, he's . . ."

Sensing that Maggie was going to muff the introduction, or simply prevaricate, Jeremy said, "The name is Rawlings." Carefully, knowing what he was going to have to do, Jeremy circled the couch. "Lieutenant Colonel Rawlings, Her Majesty's Horse Guard."

"Really?" The Frenchman slipped into the room, closing the door a little behind him, to shut out some of the light and noise. "How curious! *Marguerethe*, doesn't your father serve as the Duke of Rawlings's solicitor?"

Maggie could only nod mutely. All ability to speak had apparently been lost to her.

"Tell me, Colonel," Augustin went on. "Are you one of the duke's relations? I have met his aunt and uncle, but haven't yet had the pleasure of meeting the duke himself—"

"Well, we'll have to rectify that situation, won't we?" Now that de Veygoux had closed the door, Jeremy could see that Maggie's fiancé was nearly his own height, and close to his own age. He had, however, red hair. *Very* red hair. He was, in fact, the red-haired man who'd been staring so at him, back on the dance floor. Yet another reason to dislike him. "I could most likely secure an introduction for you."

"Ah, well, how wonderful!" de Veygoux exclaimed. He strode forward, his right hand extended toward Jeremy. "Allow me to introduce myself, Colonel. I am Augustin de Veygoux, Mademoiselle Herbert's fiancé—"

Things couldn't have turned out more to Jeremy's liking than if he'd actually succeeded in deflowering her on Althorpe's leather couch. Whirling toward her as if thunderstruck, Jeremy cried, "*What*? You're *engaged*, Maggie?"

Maggie closed her eyes, hoping that when she opened them again, she'd wake up in her own bed back in Herbert Park, far, far away from London. No such luck, however. When she opened her eyes again, Augustin and Jeremy were both still staring at her, one confused, and the other, apparently, outraged.

"Jerry," she sighed. "I meant to tell you. Only I—"

But Augustin interrupted.

"*Jerry*," he echoed, casting a suspicious look in Jeremy's direction. "But isn't that the name of your little dog, *ma*—"

"She is *not*," Jeremy cut him off tersely, "your *chérie*, you French bastard."

Without another word, Jeremy pulled back a fist and then thrust it, with all of his strength, into Augustin de Veygoux's face.

Chapter 19

"*D*at, I take it," Augustin said, his voice muffled beneath the blood-soaked linen of Maggie's handkerchief, "was de Duke of Rawlings?"

Maggie, hardly able to stay in her seat in the brougham, she was still so angry, said, exasperatedly, "Well, of course it was! Who *else* would have the gall to walk up to my fiancé and punch him in the face?"

Augustin blinked sadly at what he could see of the gaslit, fog-shrouded street through the glass of the brougham's window. "I wasn't aware dat de nature of your relationship wid de Duke of Rawlings was such dat he might feel compelled to punch your fiancé in de face," he observed, his broken nose making correct pronunciation of *th*, always problematic for a Frenchman, impossible. "I feel dat dere is someding, perhaps, you have neglected to tell me, *chérie*."

Maggie just shook her head impatiently, the diamond ear bobs that her mother had left her swaying pendulously. It wasn't that she didn't feel sorry for Augustin—the poor man had had his nose broken, after all, and it was all her fault!— but she was simply too furious to speak. She wanted to see Augustin safely home, and then return home herself . . . where she intended to have a confrontation with Jeremy of such unpleasantness that he just might find himself with a broken nose of his own before she was through with him.

Good God, he had *mortified* her at the cotillion! Mortified her, first by very nearly seducing her in Lord Althorpe's library, and then by striking her escort. His violent display had been completely unprovoked. Augustin had been far too surprised even to attempt to defend himself. Not that Jeremy had followed his first blow with any others. No, one had been enough to send Augustin reeling back into the sideboard, where he'd upset a number of bell jars that had been resting over some stuffed birds and dried flower arrangements. The resulting crash had, of course, brought everyone running, including Lord Althorpe. And even though Jeremy had been standing there, goading Augustin into standing up and fighting like a man—Lord, Maggie blushed to remember it!—no one had a said a word of rebuke to him, *no one*.

Because, after all, he *was* a duke.

Well, duke or not, Maggie had a few choice words for him, but unfortunately, not a one of them could be said within the hearing of Lord and Lady Althorpe's other guests—guests from whom Maggie had fostered hopes of gaining a few commissions. Well, no use hoping for that now. Oh, no. Who wanted a portrait painter who might engender a fight and consequently smash up a sideboard? All her hard work that night, all the socializing, all the smiling . . . and for what? For *nothing*, because Jeremy Rawlings, that scoundrel, that popinjay, that damned son of a bitch—yes, that's what he was, a son of a *bitch*—had ruined it for her!

And why? Why? Because of his stupid, abominable pride. Jeremy Rawlings didn't want her. Oh, he *wanted* her, but only because he hadn't had her yet. How dare he, how dare he feign indignation over the fact that after *five years* of not having heard from him, she'd gotten engaged to someone else? Had she been supposed to wait around indefinitely for him? For what? To become his mistress? Because Maggie had certainly never heard that attempting to seduce one's future wife on the divan in a complete stranger's house was an accepted courtship ritual of modern-day England. . . .

He'd rue the day, though. Oh, Maggie would see that he would. Lord Althorpe might slap him on the shoulder and offer him a cigar and say placatingly, ''Oh, well, boys will be boys,'' while his servants mopped up the blood and swept away the broken glass, but Maggie was not about to let him off that easy. She wasn't about to let him off at all. When he got home, she was going to light into him like nothing he'd ever seen before. He thought the tigers in India were bad? He'd never seen Maggie when she was in a temper as fine as this one.

"Dere was someding between you two, once, I dink."

Augustin's soft voice broke into Maggie's dark meditations. She turned, startled, to look at him in the misty light from the brougham's oil lamp.

"Yes," Augustin said studying her face in the fine spray of ermine that framed it. "Yes, dere was. Don't deny it, chérie."

"There . . ." Maggie's voice was rough, and she cleared her throat. "There wasn't, Augustin," she said quietly, and as she said it, she firmly believed it. "I was sixteen. He was . . . older. It was just one foolish afternoon." Noticing Augustin's expression, she added hastily, "Nothing happened. He went away, and so did I. That was all." She turned her head to look out the window. She knew her eyes could betray her just as surely as the gusset of her pantaloons, which was still damp with the evidence of her arousal earlier in the evening.

Despite her efforts at hiding the truth, however, Augustin seemed to sense she was lying. "Dat was not all," he said, in the same gentle voice he used when he advised her that she was employing too much gesso on her canvas. "Maybe to you, dat was all, but not to him, Marguerethe. I do not dink a man breaks de nose of your fiancé if dat is all."

Inside her fur muff, Maggie balled her fingers into fists. "You're wrong, Augustin. He doesn't feel anything for me. I was just a way to pass a spring afternoon. That's all. Besides, he has someone else now." Her voice didn't even throb as she said it. "Surely you've read about it. A princess. An Indian princess."

"Den why did he hit me?"

"Because," Maggie said disgustedly. "Hitting is all he knows. He used to hit people all the time, when he was younger. The only difference is that apparently, in India, people started hitting back.''

"Should I hit him back, *chérie*, next time I see him?''

Maggie swiveled her head around to stare at him in horror. "Good God, no! He'd kill you, Augustin!''

Augustin smiled bitterly, but she could not see it, since the bloody handkerchief covered the lower half of his face. "You have so little faid in my pugilistic abilities, *chérie*?''

Maggie, realizing her mistake, said quickly, "No, it isn't that. It's just that—''

But just then the brougham lurched to a halt, and one of Augustin's footmen pulled open the door, anxious to get his master indoors, where a physician already waited, Maggie having sent word of Augustin's "accident'' ahead to the de Veygoux household. There was only one thing about which she could be grateful, and that was that Augustin's mother was still in Paris. God only knew what Madame de Veygoux would have said had she known the sorry fate that had befallen her most beloved child.

"Make sure he does what the doctor tells him,'' Maggie admonished the footmen, as they helped their master down. "Augustin, you do what the doctor tells you.''

"I don't like dis,'' Augustin said from the street. He struck a rather sad figure there, in the lightly falling snow, a tall man in a top hat, with a bloody kerchief to his nose. "I don't like your going home alone. What if *he's* dere, waiting for you?''

Maggie didn't have to ask who *he* was. "Don't you worry about me,'' she said heartily. "Lord and Lady Edward should be back from Yorkshire by now, so you see, I shan't be alone at all. Besides, I'm quite capable of taking care of myself, Augustin.''

Without waiting for the footmen to do it for her, Maggie slammed the brougham door shut and sank back upon the leather seat. Lord, what a night! And it was only going to get worse. Well, for one person, anyway.

But when Maggie returned to the house on Park Lane, she was informed by Evers that His Grace had not yet returned. Maggie wasn't particularly surprised. He was probably still enjoying some of Lord Althorpe's excellent cigars. Undoubtedly the two men were playing at billiards. Jeremy had always been a fine billiard player. What kind of country was it, Maggie fumed to herself as she undid the ribbons to her cloak, where a man could strike a party guest and smash up a sideboard and be instantly forgiven for it, just because he was the seventeenth Duke of Rawlings? Disgusting, Maggie told herself. It was in every way disgusting.

"I want to be informed when His Grace returns," Maggie said tersely to the butler as he took her wrap. "The *minute* he returns, Evers, no matter how late."

"Yes, miss," Evers said. "Of course, miss."

"Only you needn't," Maggie added casually, "let Lord and Lady Edward know. About my asking to see His Grace so late at night, I mean."

"Lord and Lady Edward have not yet returned from Yorkshire," the butler replied mildly.

Maggie whirled to face him, her eyes wide. "*What?* But I thought they were expected back tonight!"

"Indeed they were. I suppose they have been delayed." Evers shook out her cloak before draping it over his arm. "A blizzard, I wouldn't doubt. Or perhaps Lady Edward's time has come—"

"Oh, dear!" Maggie brought both hands to her face, unable to hide her dismay. "Oh, Evers, if they don't—I mean, I can hardly stay here alone with—"

Evers said—rather kindly, for him, Maggie thought—"I shouldn't worry, Miss Margaret. It is most likely foul weather that has delayed them. Often, this time of year, trains from Yorkshire don't arrive at the station until well after midnight. If you'd like, I'll rouse you upon their return."

Maggie bit her lip. Good Lord, what was she to do? If it were to get out that she'd spent the night unchaperoned in the Duke of Rawlings's town house . . .

Then again, after that scene at Lord Althorpe's, her reputation could hardly be more ruined than it already was.

Her glance falling upon the doors to the drawing room, Maggie was suddenly struck by an even worse thought. "Evers," she gasped, then bit her lip.

"Yes, miss?"

She wasn't certain how to broach the subject. "The, um, callers we had earlier this evening . . ."

Evers shuddered, very subtly. "You mean the, ahem, princess, miss?"

"Yes," Maggie said. "The, um, princess. Where . . ."

"The princess and Mr. Sanjay returned to the Dorchester, where, I understand, the princess has taken a suite of rooms."

Maggie hoped her relief didn't show. "Oh," she said. "Thank you, Evers."

"Of course, miss."

Despite that comforting information, a long, hot bath, and a soothing toddy supplied by Hill, Maggie still lay awake a long time, idly scratching Jerry's ears and listening for the sound of a carriage. As the minutes crept into hours, and the church bell struck midnight, and then one, Maggie's anxiety escalated. No sign of either the duke or his family. Where *were* they? She could understand Jeremy's lateness, she supposed. He was no doubt afraid to come home, too ashamed to face her. The coward.

Then again, he *was* a decorated military hero. Would a decorated military hero really shy from a confrontation, any confrontation? Supposing he wasn't avoiding her at all? Supposing he was merely having too good a time somewhere out there to come home. Supposing . . . supposing he was with the princess at her hotel! Maggie sat up, sleep completely evading her now, and squinted at her bedside clock in the dying light from the fire. Two o'clock in the morning. Where else could he have gone? Even in London, there were few places open this late, even to dukes. He *had* to be with the princess. Where else *could* he be?

And why not? The *princess* hadn't thrown any fans at him, or punched him in the arm, or gotten herself engaged to another man. The *princess* hadn't screamed at him like a fishwife, or sneered at him sarcastically, or in general comported herself as disagreeably as Maggie had since his return. What man *wouldn't* have preferred the company of another woman, any other woman, to that of Maggie's, unpleasant as she'd made herself recently?

Oh, God! That *had* to be where he was! With Usha. The beautiful, almond-eyed Usha, with her jeweled slippers and pert little breasts and clever brown fingers. . . .

The subtle knock at her door did not wake her. She had decided long ago that sleep that night would be impossible. She was tearing open her bedroom door and blinking at the light from a candle flame, before she realized that that candle was held by *Evers*, of all people, Evers not looking at all as he did during the day, in his starched white cravat and black suit, but in a nightdress and robe, a bright red nightcap dangling down from his head.

"I'm sorry to wake you, Miss Margaret," the butler whispered, an undertow of urgency beneath his polite apology. "But I'm simply at my wit's end. Someone has got to reason with him. . . ."

Maggie blinked at the butler. "Reason with whom?" she asked, her voice hoarse from disuse. "What time is it?"

"Half three. With the duke, miss. I'm afraid he's—"

"The duke?" Maggie shook her head bewilderedly. "He's home?"

"Yes, miss. Only—"

Maggie was already reaching for her dressing gown. "Only what?" she asked, as she thrust her arms through the woolen sleeves of her robe. Then she froze, turning her face toward the butler's. "Oh, my God. He isn't sick, is he?"

"No, not sick, miss." Evers swallowed before continuing. "Stabbed, I'm afraid."

"*Stabbed?*"

Without waiting for further explanations, Maggie darted past the butler and out into the hall.

Chapter 20

*J*eremy had muffed it.

He knew it. He didn't mind admitting it. It took a big man to admit he'd been wrong, and Jeremy was as big as they came. He'd been wrong. He'd muffed it. Ruined it. Made a mess of things.

The only question now was, how was he going to fix it?

Hitting the frog-eater, he was prepared to admit, had not been the smartest move he'd ever made—though he didn't think he could necessarily be held accountable for his actions just then. After all, he'd been just minutes—maybe even seconds—away from achieving what, to him, had become a seemingly lifelong goal.

Some men dreamed of building bridges. Others, of winning wars. Still others dreamed of curing famine and disease, while others wished only for wealth. Jeremy understood those dreams, and was prepared to tolerate the men who harbored them. But to him, there had only been one goal worthy of his time and energy; one goal, one single goal, that had propelled him for five long years. And that goal was, simply: Maggie Herbert.

He had been so close. So close. Only to have his hopes dashed to dust by a gangling, red-haired Frenchman.

Althorpe struck him on the back, drawing Jeremy out of his reverie. "Come now, Your Grace. It's not as bad as all that. Those bell jars weren't worth more'n ten, twenty pounds. And the stuff beneath 'em . . . just a lot of silly stuffed birds. Don't listen to my wife. S'far as I'm concerned, we're well rid of 'em. Have another brandy.''

Jeremy, sitting on the same couch upon which, a few hours earlier, he might well have found the bliss he'd sought for five long years, held out his glass for a refill. ''I've muffed it,'' he said, as Althorpe poured. He knew he was becoming morbidly sentimental, but he couldn't help it. After all, he'd been so close . . . so very close. . . .

''Bah,'' Althorpe said, straightening to examine the contents of the crystal decanter in his hand. ''You haven't muffed anything. Buy 'er a bracelet. She'll forgive you. They always do.''

''No,'' Jeremy said with a sigh. ''Not her.''

''Nonsense. Of course, her. She's a woman, isn't she?''

''Yes . . .''

''Then she'll forgive you.'' Althorpe sighed as he collapsed into an armchair. Now that there was a fire going in the hearth which had previously stood empty, the library was overbright as well as overwarm, but Lord Althorpe didn't seem to notice. He was foxed, Jeremy knew, the more so since the Duke of Rawlings's indiscretion had given him an excuse to drink long after the other party guests had gone home.

It wasn't much comfort, discussing his love life with a forty-something earl who was completely in his cups. At the moment, however, Jeremy didn't have too many options. He could, he supposed, have gone home, but that would inevitably result only in further anguish. Oh, certainly, Maggie was there. But he couldn't touch her, couldn't even go near her, not when she was so angry with him for hitting her fiancé. He'd seen her face the moment after he'd had the satisfaction of breaking the frog-eater's nose. Her expression had not been forgiving. And her cold ''I will see you at home'' had sounded more like a threat than a promise of a continuation of what de Veygoux had interrupted.

No, there was nothing for it: Jeremy had muffed it, but good.

''All right, all right,'' Althorpe said suddenly, his words slurred with drink. ''Maybe not a bracelet. How 'bout a town house? A town house of 'er very own. No woman can resist a town house. She can fix it up, put lace curtains in the windows, that sort of thing. Women love that. Town house is the way to go, my boy. Try Cardington Crescent, why don't you? My sister lives there. Loves it. Just loves it.''

Jeremy looked woefully at his host. This help, he felt, was not quite better than no help at all. Well, it was entertaining, he supposed. But Lord Althorpe seemed incapable of grasping the magnitude of Jeremy's blunder. Because it didn't start with flattening the frog-eater's beak. No, it had all begun months and months before, back in India, when he'd first heard that ridiculous rumor that he was about to be given the hand of the maharajah's niece in return for his derring-do in Jaipur. Jeremy had laughed the rumors off, not believing a word of them—more fool he—until the very night the maharajah actually made the offer.

And even then Jeremy had only laughed, treating the entire situation as one magnificent joke. He ought to have known better, especially when the princess herself began hanging about, casting him looks heated enough to cause his men to elbow one another knowingly at public functions. At the private functions Jeremy was forced to attend, Usha had seemed a nice enough girl—though the only words they'd ever exchanged had been through her translator—but Jeremy had never been more than distantly polite to her. It was only when a bloke from the embassy took him aside and impressed upon him the possible consequences of breaking the heart of a member of Rajasthan's royal family that Jeremy realized what he'd thought a quaint gesture on the part of the maharajah had actually been deadly serious. The princess considered herself engaged. And the embassy considered Jeremy a diplomatic risk. . . .

A few private words with the girl's uncle were all that had been required to straighten out the mess . . . at least as far as Jeremy was concerned. The Princess Usha, however, had feathers that were ruffled beyond Jeremy's straightening abilities, as her little stunt earlier that evening had illustrated only too well. He had been livid upon finding her in his drawing room . . . livid and, for the first time, aware that what he had thought a rather diverting episode in his adventures abroad had actually been blown out of all proportion by the English press. It was clear that while to him, the Star of Jaipur meant one thing, to the rest of the population of London—and most particularly, to Maggie—it meant something else altogether.

It hadn't been until that moment that Jeremy began to understand, with a sort of growing horror, that there might possibly be a reason behind Maggie's sudden engagement that he hadn't yet considered, that reason being that *she* considered *him* engaged. While this certainly didn't excuse her faithlessness—she ought to have known him well enough to realize that he could never love anyone but her, princess or not—it made it a good deal easier to understand. Now, of course, he had the monumental task of proving to her that Usha didn't mean anything to him . . . a task made all the more difficult by Usha herself, who had flung herself into his arms upon his stalking into the drawing room earlier that evening. Thank God Maggie hadn't been there to witness that!

"Colonel-Duke," Usha had cried, as she'd pressed her lithesome body against him. "Hallo!"

Rolling his eyes, Jeremy had gently disentangled himself, saying to the princess's interpreter, a decent fellow who'd graduated from the very university that had sent Jeremy down five years earlier, "Sweet Christ, Sanjay. What is she doing here? Does her uncle know where she is?"

Sanjay shook his head mournfully, the tassel on his silk hat swaying from side to side. "No, Your Grace. She insisted we travel here under assumed names. I believe that was part of the excitement of—how do you say it?—oh, yes, running away from home."

"Well, you can't stay here," Jeremy said. "You'd best write the maharajah, and make it fast. The last thing I need is for him to think I've abducted the Star of Jaipur."

"Already done, Your Grace," Sanjay said. "I left a letter for His Excellency when Her Highness's back was turned."

"Good." Jeremy looked down at Princess Usha, who was gazing up at him with every appearance of adoration in her dark eyes. There was something slightly calculating in the curl of her lips, however, and Jeremy quickly looked away, feeling more than a little uncomfortable. "Uh, listen, Sanjay, this is damned awkward. You can't stay here, you know."

"You needn't worry about our accommodations, Your Grace. I've secured the princess a suite of rooms at the Dorchester." Sanjay cast a quick look at the princess, who still hadn't taken her eyes off Jeremy. "Much to the princess's disapproval, of course. She was convinced you'd want her to stay with you."

"But we've been through this before," Jeremy began tiredly. "I thought we—"

"I tried to explain to her, Your Grace," Sanjay interrupted somberly, "what you'd meant back in Jaipur, when you told her there was someone else. But you have to understand that if the princess does not marry you, her only alternative is to return to Jaipur and marry the man to whom she's been betrothed since birth, a maharajah of a province some distance from Rajasthan."

Jeremy said, "Well, that doesn't sound so bad."

"Indeed it *is* bad, Your Grace. The princess will not, you see, be the maharajah's first wife, which is the honor she feels she deserves, but his third, which means she will be forced to wait upon the other two. Marriage to you is the princess's only hope of maintaining the same quality of life to which she has become accustomed, living in the Palace of the Winds. That is why your rejection comes as such a blow." Sanjay's voice contained no hint of rebuke. He was simply stating a fact. "Well, that and the fact that the princess is, obviously, unused to any sort of rejection at all. The Rajputs are well-known in my country for their inability to take no for an answer. They are a warring tribe, producing many of India's finest military leaders, as well as their most famous beauties."

Jeremy wasn't falling for this sad story. "Why can't the princess simply refuse to marry this man her uncle has picked out for her?"

Sanjay looked grave. "Such a refusal would only bring dishonor upon the Rajput family. The princess would be banished from the palace and cut off from all the comforts that she has ever known. The only wealth she possesses is that which her uncle deigns to give her. Should she displease him, she would soon be penniless—''

Sanjay broke off as the princess, who had sunk down onto a chaise longue, her sari a bright pool around her, made a short little speech, accompanied by many sidelong glances in Jeremy's direction. When she was finished, Sanjay sighed, and said, with obvious reluctance, ''The princess wishes you to know that she's given the matter considerable thought, and she'd be willing to allow you to marry this other woman, providing you make it very clear that she, Usha, is First Wife, and that this second wife must necessarily wait upon her. . . .''

Jeremy rolled his eyes again. ''Christ. Did you mention to her that bigamy is illegal in this country?''

Sanjay looked offended. ''Of course I did, Your Grace. But I'm afraid the princess is incapable of understanding why a man who is a military hero as well as a member of the ruling class can't have two wives.''

Jeremy, completely frustrated, made a sound very like a growl. ''Look, Sanjay,'' he said. ''This has gone far enough. I don't care how you do it, but you have got to make it clear to your mistress that under no circumstances am I ever going to marry her. Ever. It's nothing personal. But I'm simply not interested. And now, if you'll both excuse me, I've got an important engagement just now, so I really must go—''

But even as he'd turned to go, the princess sprang from her seat and tried to detain him, wrapping those sun-kissed arms around his neck and refusing to allow her ''colonel-duke'' to leave. It had taken all of Sanjay's powers of persuasion—and a good deal of cursing on Jeremy's part—to convince her to let him go, and even then, Jeremy escaped with the feeling that he had not seen the last of the Princess Usha. He had to admire the girl's tenacity. Once the Star of Jaipur knew what she wanted, she'd apparently stop at nothing to get it. Not unlike, Jeremy couldn't help thinking, himself. The only difference was that while Usha was deceiving herself if she thought Jeremy would ever grow to love her, Jeremy *knew* Maggie loved him.

The problem was getting *her* to admit it.

It was as Jeremy was entertaining these gloomy thoughts that he happened to glance over at his host and saw that he had finally succumbed to Morpheus; Lord Althorpe was asleep in his chair, his chin resting in the silky folds of his cravat, a gentle snore issuing from his lips every few seconds. Sighing, Jeremy set aside his own glass and stood up. The room spun dizzyingly for a moment or two before righting itself. Lingering symptoms of his malarial fever, he wondered, or simple drunkenness? Whichever the reason, it was time, he decided, to head for home.

This was easier said than done. Peters, while an excellent valet, was not the world's best driver, and it took him some time to find Park Lane. When he finally pulled up in front of number Twenty-two, it was close to three o'clock in the morning, and Jeremy was feeling the cold as he never had before. February is a cruel month, which might explain why it was also the shortest; who could stand that bone-chilling cold for a full thirty days? Not the Duke of Rawlings. So debilitated was he by the freezing wind that he could not easily lower himself from the carriage, and called for his valet's assistance. Peters hurried round, and offered his master a strong shoulder to lean upon. The wooden leg, however, did not offer much support on the icy walk, and the two men were soon stumbling about as if they'd both been in their cups.

Perhaps it was for that reason that they were staked out as prey for the malicious attack that followed. Or perhaps it was the fact that the street lamp had gone out, leaving the snowy road cloaked in darkness. Had the lamplighter, discouraged by the extreme cold, failed to make the rounds? Or had someone purposely doused the flame? Whatever the reason, Park Lane was darker and colder than at any time in Jeremy's memory, but since he was concentrating so hard on remaining upright, he did not stop to wonder at the fact. Later, he chided himself for this: He ought to have recognized that two ostensibly drunk men, on a darkened but exclusive street such as Park Lane, in the early hours of the morning, made a tempting target for thieves.

When the attack came, however, Jeremy was far from expecting it. It was disgraceful, really, that two military men should have been taken so unawares. Peters was just helping him up the first step to the door of number Twenty-two, when a tall figure, cloaked all in black, came swooping out from the shadows by the servants' entrance, where he'd apparently been lying in wait. Jeremy had only time to lift his head and say, "What the—" before he was struck quite forcefully in the shoulder with a glittering object the specter held in his right hand.

Beside him, Peters cried out hoarsely, and moved to protect his employer, but their attacker was quicker, and surer of foot. Circling behind the duke, he raised his arm again . . . only this time, Jeremy was ready for him. Although the first blow had not hurt, Jeremy was going to be damned before he let the bastard get in another one, and this time when he saw the arm coming down, he swung at it with his fist, apparently taking his assailant by surprise and causing him some degree of pain, since he let out a harsh cry.

And then, before Jeremy could get in another punch, the figure in black had scuttled away, like a spider retreating after losing a leg, leaving the duke and his valet panting and incredulous at the bottom of the steps.

"Good God, sir," Peters cried, the first to recover his voice. "Are you all right?"

Jeremy, having leaned forward in order to keep from falling down, his hands on his knees, nodded. "I believe so," he said. "Did he get your purse, Peters?"

"No, sir. Yours?"

"No." Jeremy felt wonderingly at his waistcoat pocket. "He didn't even reach for it."

"Curious be'avior," Peters observed, "fer a footpad, sir."

"Yes," Jeremy agreed. "If that's what he was. . . ."

"What else could 'e 'ave wanted, sir, if not our money?"

Jeremy strained his eyes looking after his assailant. "I

couldn't begin to guess. London's gotten quite out of hand since I saw it last, Peters.''

"Yes, sir. You want I should fetch someone, sir? One of the footmen? We could send 'im for the Bow Street runners—'' Peters broke off, choking. "Sir! Why, you're bleedin', sir!''

"What?'' Jeremy looked up at his valet from where he leaned. "What are you talking about? I'm not hurt. . . .''

And then he saw the snow beneath him, and the red drops, like rose petals, that were spreading out across it. They seemed to be coming from his chest.

"Damn,'' Jeremy said crossly.

Chapter 21

*W*ould you stop fussing at me? I'm all right, I tell you."

Those were the first words Maggie heard upon crossing the threshold into the duke's bedroom. Uttered as they were in the most irritable of tones, she felt instantly relieved. If Jeremy could complain so, he was surely not seriously injured.

He did look a fright, however. Lying shirtless—and for all Maggie could tell, pantless as well, though a sheet covered him from the waist down—against a wall of pillows, his skin looked as sallow as candle wax . . . except for where a glaring white bandage had been applied to his right shoulder.

"I just want to see whether the bleedin' 'as stopped," a man Maggie had never seen before was saying truculently. Apparently Jeremy's manservant, the fellow had climbed the ladder attached to the side of Jeremy's enormous bed, and was trying to peer beneath the bandage. But he was having a hard time of it, hampered both by the duke's resistance and what appeared to be a wooden peg that was strapped to his right leg, just below the knee. It was hard, Maggie supposed, to stay balanced on a ladder rung with just one leg.

Unfortunately for the manservant, it became even harder to remain upright a moment later, when Jeremy looked up and happened to notice Maggie in the doorway. The shock was apparently so great that Jeremy sat bolt upright—even though the movement made him wince—causing the one-legged man to lose his balance completely. Only a well-timed lunge for the curtains hanging from one of the four bedposts caught his fall.

"You!" Jeremy bellowed. He shifted a glass of what appeared to be whisky from one hand to another, then pointed at Evers, who'd meekly followed Maggie into the room. "You're dismissed. Pack your bags and be out by tomorrow morning."

"Oh, dear," Evers quavered.

Maggie glared at the figure in the bed. "Oh, Jerry, do shut up. You can't dismiss Evers. He only fetched me because he said you'd been stabbed, and wouldn't allow anyone to send for a doctor."

"Or Scotland Yard," Evers put in querulously.

"I also forbade him to wake you," Jeremy said with a glower. "A direct order that he disobeyed. Evers, you can pick up your pay next week. Now get out."

"No, Evers," Maggie said to the hastily departing butler's back. "Stay where you are."

Evers froze mid-step, but looked back over his shoulder. "I believe I had better do as His Grace suggests," he said miserably to Maggie.

"Nonsense," was Maggie's terse reply. She turned back toward the bed. "How bad is it?" she asked the manservant, who'd been staring at her, openmouthed, since she'd entered the room.

"Er . . ." The young man glanced down at his employer.

"The truth, please," Maggie said, folding her arms across her chest.

"'E'll be right enough. Knife blade glanced off 'is collarbone. Just worried the flesh a little, is all. 'Course, woulda killed a lesser man. But the colonel 'ere, 'e's strong as an ox, for all 'e's got—"

"Peters," Jeremy hissed, angrily.

The young man—Peters—grinned down at the duke. "What?" he said, sounding amused. "You goin' to sack me, too, Colonel?"

"Nobody," Maggie said, imperiously, "is getting sacked this evening. What has the colonel got, Peters?"

"Why, malaria, o' course," Peters said with a shrug.

This was just too much. To have been told first that Jeremy had been stabbed, then that he had malaria, was simply more than Maggie could be expected to bear. Fortunately, there was a trunk on the floor quite near her. She slumped down onto it, her knees seeming to have given way completely beneath her.

"Malaria," she murmured. "Why didn't you tell me? Jeremy, why didn't you say anything?"

"Maggie," Jeremy said, waving the glass of whisky. "It's not what you think."

"No," Maggie said mournfully, shaking her head. "It never is with you, is it?"

Jeremy was staring at her, his gray eyes hooded by shadow. The only light in the room came from the lamp beside his bed, and the fire in the hearth. Maggie could not read his expression, but she could hear the concern in his voice. "Peters," he said to his valet, "pour Miss Maggie a drink. She looks as if she could use one."

"No, no," Maggie said, raising a hand limply. "I'm all right."

But she wasn't all right. Stabbed? Malaria? *Stabbed?*

Before she could ask another question, however, Peters appeared at her side, a small glass of amber liquid in his hands. " 'Ere you go, miss," he said kindly, as he slipped the glass into her hand. "Drink this down, now. And don't you worry about the colonel. Why, 'e's the strongest man I ever met! I seen 'im keep swingin' 'is sword arm, even though his elbow was broke. When the doctors in New Delhi told 'im the voyage back 'ere would kill 'im, 'e only laughed."

Blinking, Maggie looked back at Jeremy. All of her earlier, murderous intentions toward him faded in a wave of adoration. Stubborn, stupid man! What could he have been thinking, returning to England while still in the throes of a life-threatening illness? Why, the voyage alone might have killed him, let alone the sudden change in climate. No wonder he had spent all day in bed! He hadn't, as Maggie had thought, been dozing lackadaisically. He'd been fighting off fever.

But stabbed?

She lifted the glass to her lips. Even though the whisky burned her eyes, she deliberately closed them, and tipped the glass back until every drop was gone. When she swallowed, she felt the fiery liquid course down her throat. . . .

She gagged, and began to cough. Peters very sweetly banged her a few times between the shoulder blades, thinking she was choking.

"No, no," she finally managed to say. "I'm all right." And she did feel better. The whisky warmed her, sending strength flowing back down to her knees. Maybe things weren't quite as bad as she'd thought. . . .

"*Stabbed?*" she echoed incredulously.

"Now, Maggie," Jeremy said from the bed. "It was nothing. Peters and I just ran into a little trouble—"

Maggie snorted. "I shouldn't wonder. Where were you, out so late? The Vauxhall? You know it isn't safe—"

"Oh, we weren't at the Vauxhall," Peters informed her cheerfully. "The bloke what jumped the colonel got 'im just outside the door downstairs—"

"Peters," Jeremy barked warningly, but it was too late. Maggie was up and striding toward the bed, the whisky glass left abandoned on top of the trunk.

"*What?*" she cried hoarsely. "Someone stabbed you right here on Park Lane?"

"You see, miss?" Evers still stood, all but forgotten, in the doorway. "I told you. I said we ought to send for Scotland Yard, but His Grace—"

"Evers," Maggie said, controlling herself with an effort. "*Please*. Do go on, Jerry."

Jeremy, however, was squinting at her dressing gown. "Why is it," he wondered, "that women spend so much money on the clothes they wear outside the house, and a mere pittance on the things they wear inside, when it's the clothes they wear inside that a man sees most often?"

Maggie, standing at the foot of his bed, looked down at

herself. True, the plaid robe was a bit on the plain side, but . . .

"Don't try to change the subject," Maggie said furiously. "I want to know how you got stabbed."

"Oh, Maggie," Jeremy said, throwing himself back against the pillows—but carefully, so as not to jar his shoulder. "I don't know. Do we have to discuss it now? I'm certain there are more important things—"

"If you ask me," Peters chimed in, "it was the Frenchman."

Maggie's jaw dropped. "*What?*"

Jeremy, in the bed, sent his valet an aggrieved look. "Thank you," he said. "Thank you, Peters. That will be all."

"Well," Peters said. "You said it yourself, not ten minutes ago. . . ."

Maggie, horrified, exclaimed, "Augustin would *never*—"

"Yes, yes, Maggie," Jeremy said soothingly. "We know. It was probably just a bungled attempt to pick my pocket, that's all."

Unconvinced, Maggie clutched one of the bedposts, looking down at him wide-eyed. The bandage was not a large one, but it had already soaked through with blood. Not *a lot* of blood, but enough. Someone had certainly tried to injure Jeremy, injure him seriously. Just a few inches lower, and the knife would have plunged into his heart. *Could* Augustin be capable of inflicting such a wound? Maggie wondered. He had certainly been angry enough, she supposed. Angry enough to want to hit Jeremy back . . .

But Augustin wasn't the type to sneak about in the dark, wielding a knife. Far from it! He was too decent, too even-tempered . . . too, she had to admit, dull. The thought was ludicrous.

But who else had a grudge against Jeremy—besides herself, that is?

Jeremy couldn't help squirming a little uncomfortably beneath Maggie's troubled gaze. He couldn't tell what she was thinking, but he didn't like it. Didn't like it one bit. She could protest all she wanted, but he'd see to it Evers got the sack, and Peters, too. Imagine, the two of them, teaming up like this to humiliate him in front of her. He'd see them both in the workhouse, that he would. It was getting so that a man couldn't find decent help these days. . . .

Well, he'd better, he decided, try to make the best out of a bad situation. Accordingly, he closed his eyes, and groaned.

"Jerry?"

He cracked an eyelid and saw that Maggie was staring down at him, worriedly chewing her lower lip. Perfect. He closed his eye again, and moaned, this time thrashing his head a little upon the pillows.

"Colonel?" Peters's voice was tinged with suspicion, not concern. "Are you all right?"

Jeremy pretended both of his eyelids were too heavy to lift. He blinked a few times, groggily. "Yes," he sighed. "I just want to be left alone."

Peters, damn his eyes, couldn't seem to control a grin. "Oh, I see," he said. "Yes. Well, then I guess I'll see you in the morning, sir." And he turned to retire to the billet he'd made up in the adjoining dressing room.

"What?" Maggie cried, flabbergasted. "You're just . . . going to bed?"

Peters looked at her in surprise. "Well, yes, miss. The colonel wants to be left alone. So I'm goin' to bed."

"But he's . . . he's ill!"

Peters ran a critical gaze over the figure in the bed. "Yes, miss. But 'e don't want no coddlin' from me."

"But . . . but somebody's got to look after him!" Maggie exclaimed.

"Right," Peters said with a sharp nod. "But it won't be me. *'E* may not mind gettin' the sack"—the valet jerked his head toward the nightcapped butler—"but I ain't takin' no chances. G'night."

Peters limped off, leaving Maggie and the butler staring at one another. Evers cleared his throat. "For as long as I can remember," the butler said, with some dignity, "there has been an Evers in service to the house of Rawlings—"

"Of course there has," Maggie said encouragingly.

"That's why the idea of Jeremy dismissing you is so ludicrous—"

Jeremy, alarmed at hearing this, lifted his head and shot the butler a look so full of venom that Evers staggered backward. Maggie, whose back was turned toward the duke, had no idea what had transpired, and so could only watch in confusion as Evers fumbled for the doorknob.

"Far be it for me," Evers stammered, "to break with family tradition. If you need me, Your Grace, you may simply ring for me."

With a hasty bow, he tore open the door, and just as quickly scuttled through it. It was only when the portal had clicked shut, and Maggie and Jeremy were alone at last, that she looked down and noticed that his eyes were only half-lidded.

"Jeremy," Maggie began suspiciously, but it was too late. Jeremy snaked an arm out from beneath the sheet, seized her by the wrist, and pulled her bodily forward, until she was sprawled, in a very undignified manner, across his lap.

It was then that she discovered, in no uncertain terms, that he wore nothing beneath the bedsheet.

Chapter 22

"Jeremy," Maggie cried indignantly, although it was difficult to speak clearly with her face to the mattress. "What do you think you're doing?"

Jeremy had lifted the hem of her dressing gown up over her hips, and was noting with interest that he could observe the heart shape of her bottom quite clearly through the cotton of her nightdress. "Me?" he queried innocently. "Just continuing where we left off earlier. . . ."

"My God!" She tried to roll over, but Jeremy held quite firmly onto her hips. "Jeremy, really!" Maggie chastised him over her shoulder. "Somebody just tried to kill you! How can you think about making love at a time like this?"

"My dear Mags," he said dryly. "If I can think about making love with you with hundreds of Bengalese bullets flying over my head, I can certainly think about making love with you at a time like this." Leaning over to place a kiss on her backside, he added, when she opened her mouth to speak again, "And don't ask me about my shoulder. It doesn't hurt, and I don't foresee our lovemaking reopening the wound. . . ."

Maggie sucked in her breath. "You conceited pig," she cried, this time managing to wriggle out of his arms. "As if I would even *consider* making love with you, after what you did!"

"What'd *I* do?" Jeremy asked, raising a black eyebrow.

Maggie was dismayed by the fact that she couldn't help

but notice that his bare chest, besides being scarred, was also quite thickly haired. The dark curls formed a rich mat that fanned out over his flat nipples, narrowing as it trailed down his lean, muscular stomach, and then disappeared beneath the sheet in a provocative arrow. Maggie, however, wasn't about to investigate what lay in the direction that arrow pointed.

Or so she told herself.

"You know very well what you did," she said, tossing her long hair loftily. "You—"

And the next thing she knew, Jeremy was upon her. Though she hastily flung out a pair of hands to brace her body from the impact of his, she found them immediately seized in grips of iron, and pinned to the mattress, as if Jeremy suspected she might try to strike at him again, as she had in the Althorpes' library—not to mention that day in the Rawlings Manor stables, five years earlier. With the full weight of his body pressing down upon her, however, she could barely move, let alone launch any sort of counterattack. Blinking up at his face, which hovered mere inches from hers, she grunted, "Get off me, you fool."

Jeremy, delighting in the feel of her luscious body beneath his, felt a little short of breath. He was more than aware that Maggie felt the same, since her breasts, crushed beneath him, were rising and falling rapidly. He could even see her heart rattle hard against her chest, making the soft flesh above it quiver with each pulsation. Was she as impassioned as he, or merely frightened? There was only one way to be sure.

Lifting a single eyebrow, he inquired casually, "Scared, Mags?"

Her lips parted indignantly. "Not on your life, you—"

His mouth, colliding with hers, didn't allow her to finish that sentence.

For a moment, she panicked, her fingers balling into fists against the pillows as she murmured an unintelligible protest against his mouth. It wasn't that she didn't like it. It was just that *this* . . .

This was *serious*.

Jeremy didn't hear her protest, or if he did, he didn't understand it. All he knew was that finally, after five long years, he had Maggie exactly where he'd always wanted her—beneath him. And this time, there'd be no interruptions. He'd made damned sure of that. No menacing uncles, no prying butlers, no self-righteous fiancés. Just Jeremy and Maggie, as it always should have been, *would* have been, were it not for five years of stubbornness on both their parts. Well, that would never happen again, not while he had breath in his body. She was his, at last. . . .

And what a prize she was, already well worth all of the trouble and misery he'd gone through on her behalf. Jeremy had been with scores of women in the past, but never before had he held one that felt so completely right in his arms, whose body offered such a perfect complement to his own. With her generous bosom and slender waist and limbs, Maggie was everything that was feminine, while he, broad shouldered and narrow hipped, with muscles hardened to stone from long hours of riding and fencing, was the epitome of masculinity. Of *course* they belonged together.

And if she didn't see it that way yet, well, he'd make damn sure she would by morning.

But she seemed to be getting the message already, if her reaction to his kiss was any indication. At the first touch of his lips on hers, she'd seemed to melt beneath him, all the tension leaving the arms that, up until that moment, he'd kept pinned to the mattress. Her mouth opened to his as naturally as it had that afternoon in the stables, as willingly as that evening in the library, and she returned his kiss with just as much innocent enthusiasm. Only this time, to Jeremy's lascivious delight, she was wearing far less clothing. When he released one of her wrists in order to place his hand over the place where her heart was drumming, he didn't have to push away layer upon layer of gown and camisole. He only had to undo a single mother-of-pearl button. Wherever he laid his fingers, he felt only bare skin, skin that was smooth as satin, and radiated a fiery warmth, despite the chill in the room and her state of relative undress, a heat that staggered him.

Maggie let out a whimper as his fingers scorched the delicate skin of her chest. When those fingers dipped lower, greedily pushing back the collar of her nightdress to expose one of her ripe, heavy breasts, Maggie tore her lips away from his, lifting her eyelids to stare up at him in the half-light, shocked by the myriad sensations he'd managed to arouse within her. Because suddenly, she felt more alive than she had at any time in the past five years. What she'd felt in the library, a few hours earlier, was nothing to it. It was as if her body, into which he'd breathed life in the stables that day so long ago, had gone into hibernation until this very moment. And now, all of the emotions and sensations she'd felt that day came flooding back, with a vengeance.

For Jeremy, the look of absolute wonder on Maggie's face had a shattering effect. He had meant to go about this business slowly, carefully. After all, Maggie was a virgin—though by her own admission, a highly sensual one. He didn't want to frighten her, wanted to take things slowly, wanted to allow her to set the pace.

But one glimpse of her wide, astonished brown eyes and moistly parted lips, and he was lost. Self-control vanished. Suddenly, the hands over which he'd thought he had complete mastery were doing things he hadn't directed them to, fumbling for the tie to her dressing gown, reaching to pull up the hem of her nightdress. If he wasn't mindless in his lust, then he was the closest thing to it.

But fortunately for Jeremy, Maggie seemed to feel the same way. Instead of shrinking from him and his unbridled passion, as any other innocent might have, she matched him, heated kiss for heated kiss. Suddenly, it became vital for her to feel his bare flesh against hers. Even as Jeremy was tearing at the rest of the buttons to her nightdress, she reached up and began wrenching off her dressing gown, gasping when he suddenly reared up and, heedless of his wounded shoulder, flung the offending garment away himself. For one moment, his darkly tanned torso glowed bronze in the firelight, and Maggie was able to admire, with an artist's eye, his physique, which was every bit as manly as Michelangelo's David. . . .

Only this work of art was made of hot flesh, not cool marble.

And then, with a cry of triumph, Jeremy managed to undo the last button that had held her nightdress closed, liberating what he seemed to have waited for so long to see. Maggie's breasts spilled from the cotton material, the firelight playing over the creamy expanses of flesh like sunlight on snow. Lifting her gaze at Jeremy's sharp intake of breath, Maggie was bemused to see him smile—a slow, self-congratulatory smile that, more than his kisses, more than the stiff urgency of his need, which she could feel pressing against her, convinced her that this man wanted her. That he not only wanted, but *needed* her. And that realization caused what had begun as a tender throb at the jointure of her legs to become an all-out ache, an ache she knew could only be relieved in one way. . . .

And then he lowered himself over her once more, moving to catch the rounded globes of her breasts in his hands. Maggie writhed as his hard palms ground against the sensitive skin of her nipples, but that was only the beginning of that particular sweet torture: A second later, his palm was replaced by his mouth. Maggie gasped at the unfamiliar sensation of hot wetness surrounding the hardened peak of her breast. At the first flick of his tongue, her fingers, which she'd already buried instinctively in his hair, tightened in the curly mass, and her hips, as if of their own accord, began to undulate. She could feel the stiff length of his masculinity pulsing against her now, and she began to move against that stiffness, hardly aware that she was doing so.

Jeremy, however, was very much aware that she was doing so, and it was only with effort that he kept himself from exploding right then and there. With gritted teeth, he lifted his face from her breasts and looked at her. Maggie's head was thrown back against the pillows, her long dark hair a thick curtain over the satin bed-covers, her eyes half-lidded and her breath coming in short little gasps. When she noticed his gaze on her, she did not try to hide her nakedness, as other women might have. She was clearly more comfortable nude than clothed, which was unusual, in Jeremy's experience, for a large-breasted woman. The discovery delighted him, however . . . though not as much as the sight of her long, pale legs, flat belly, and, most of all, the fluff of black hair that lay between them.

That silky triangle attracted him as no other he'd ever encountered. Jeremy found himself as drawn toward it as water is drawn toward the moon. Moving until his body was once again covering Maggie's, his mouth sought hers . . . while his fingers delved into that dark patch at the jointure of her thighs.

Maggie's knowledge of the sexual act had become significantly more sophisticated since her schooldays, thanks primarily to her life drawing classes and Berangère's informative gossip. She had seen naked men before—though, to Jeremy's credit, she'd never seen one quite *that* large—and she knew what went where, but nobody had warned her about what it *felt* like. Maggie had thought she would die of shock when his mouth closed over her nipple, but when Jeremy inserted first one finger, and then another, inside of her, she was completely unprepared for the sensations that shot through her. Suddenly, it was all she could do not to seize hold of that velvet rod she'd touched so hesitantly in Lord Althorpe's library—and which Jeremy had looked so surprised to see her holding—and guide it into her. But if he had looked that shocked when all she'd done was touch it, what would he think of her if she tried to—

Maggie needn't have worried. Jeremy was not surprised at the willingness with which she opened her legs to receive him. Nor was he surprised at the slick moisture his fingers encountered there. When her hips instinctively rose so that the heel of his hand brushed against the core of her womanhood, eliciting from her a soft moan, he knew, with joyous certainty, that she was ready for him.

For a single heartbeat, they lay like that, breathing hard, Jeremy's fingers pressed hotly inside of her, Maggie's hard nipples tangled in his chest hair. He looked down into the depthless pools that were her eyes, while she blinked under the intensity of his silver gaze.

And then Jeremy lowered his mouth, tasting the sweetness of her lips at the same time that he removed his fingers, and replaced them with that part of him that most longed for Maggie's touch.

Maggie gasped against his mouth as he started to enter into her. This was a *very* different sensation from the fingers he'd slipped so easily in and out. In fact, from the very first moment the tip of his hard shaft prodded her, she became convinced that this was not going to work, that she was abnormally small, that *he* was abnormally large, that their joining was a physical impossibility best left untested. Suddenly, all the fear she had so ingenuously admitted that night so long ago in her bedroom came back, with a vengeance. . . .

She was on the verge of protesting, of shouting at him to stop—despite what she knew would follow, an accusation of cowardice, at the very least—when something inside of her broke. Maggie's fingers, which she'd flung up against his wide chest in a last-minute effort at self-preservation, sank into his bare flesh, her nails raking him—until that impossible length sank all the way into her, and the pain miraculously disappeared.

Jeremy froze, buried inside of her, aware not just from the way she'd clawed him, but from the way her hips had stilled, that he'd hurt her. For one moment, he felt nothing but panic. What could he do? The last thing in the world he'd wanted to do was hurt Maggie. He'd thought she was ready for him! She'd certainly been wet enough. Oh, God, why had it been his misfortune to fall in love with a virgin? Why couldn't he have fallen in love with a prostitute, like his father had?

"Maggie," he gasped. "I'm so—"

But she wasn't listening to him, and a second later, he saw why. Her hips began to move again, tentatively at first, and then, discovering that the pain was well and truly over, with more confidence. Jeremy sucked in his breath as the hot skin that encased his shaft pulled it more deeply inside of her. Then Maggie lowered her hips, releasing him . . . only to pull him inside again a second later when she undulated once more against him. Jeremy, stunned, met her hips with an answering thrust of his own. Maggie, beneath him, murmured with pleasure, her head thrashing against the pillows beneath it.

Jeremy needed no more encouragement. Besides the fact that this woman happened to be *Maggie*, hers was the hottest, tightest sheath he had ever been inside. He could feel her pulsating all around him, her ivory thighs clenching his sides, her fingers tangled in his hair, bringing his lips down to meet hers again. Seizing hold of her soft breasts, Jeremy drove himself into her as deeply as he could, with his tongue as well as his shaft.

And Maggie, his Maggie, met him, thrust for thrust.

It wasn't very long before the ache Maggie had been experiencing—centered between her thighs—became an urgent pull, driving her to press closer and closer to Jeremy's hardness. Still, she was completely unprepared when, after one particularly hard thrust of his, one that she was sure was going to lance her to the mattress, she seemed to leave her body—though physically, she clung to him, harder than ever. Emotionally, however, she was suddenly drowning in a sea of color—of golds and sapphires and vermilions, more colors than she'd ever been able to mix in her paint box, more colors, she knew with a painter's certainty, than existed. They flashed beneath her eyelids in an explosion of liquid light, pulsating all around her like a shower of jeweled paint drops, and Maggie, with a feeling of consummate joy, threw out her arms to catch as many as she could.

When Jeremy felt Maggie begin to climax beneath him, his first thought was one of elation—he had never, in all of his experience with women, been so sure that his partner was genuinely climaxing, and not performing for the sake of satisfying him—or his purse. With Maggie, however, there was no doubt, no doubt at all. He had satisfied her, more than satisfied her, if the look of beatific bliss on her face was any indication. . . .

And then, at the sight of that face, of Maggie's long throat, her head thrown back in ecstasy, Jeremy himself climaxed, with such intensity that Maggie, only just recovering from her own release, thought for a panicky second or two that he might split her in half. He exploded within her, pounding her body back against the mattress, letting loose as he did so a shout of such boastful joy that she was certain the entire household would be raised.

Then he collapsed against her, his damp brow resting in the hollow between her neck and shoulder. He was breathing heavily, his heart hammering so hard against her that she found herself wondering, vaguely, if he'd suffered an apoplexy. And she couldn't help thinking smugly, *I caused that. Me. I did it.*

That feeling was almost as gratifying as her release had been.

It wasn't until a little while later, when he started to slide from her, that Jeremy saw her wince. A glimpse at the sheets beneath them revealed the reason why.

"My God," he cried, rearing up onto the heels of his hands, heedless of the pain that shot through his shoulder at the movement. "Are you all right, Mags?"

Maggie, not sure what he was talking about, followed the direction of his gaze. "Oh, no," she said, when she saw the crimson stain that had spread over the white linen sheets. "However are we going to explain *that*?"

Jeremy frowned at her. "Never mind that. *Are you all right*?"

Maggie glanced at him, bemused. "Yes, of course. A little sore, is all. Maybe if we soak them overnight—"

"Never mind the damned sheets," Jeremy said through gritted teeth. "I'll buy new ones tomorrow."

Maggie brightened. "Oh, I'd forgotten! How nice it must be to be rich."

Jeremy thought about pointing out to her that once she married him, she'd be rich, too, but at the last minute, he decided now was not the best time to bring up the subject. Yes, he'd got her into his bed. Now, he had to make certain he got into her heart.

But in the meantime, he intended to take full advantage of the time he had her in his bed.

Maggie must have recognized the glint in his eye, because

suddenly she said, "Oh, no. Not again. Jeremy, I've got to get back to my own room before Hill—"

But he didn't let her finish. He didn't think he would have much liked what she had to say on the subject anyway.

Chapter 23

*J*eremy was convinced he was dreaming. He'd had this dream before, and it always turned out the same: He woke, and the delectable figure in his arms, the one with all the very nice padding up front, vanished, as all her dream-sisters had, into nothingness.

But this time, Jeremy had figured out a way to keep that from happening. He simply wouldn't wake up. That's right. He'd keep his eyes closed, forever, if he had to, but it would be worth it, because he'd have all this cozy warmth to curl up against, and that was all he needed. Who needed food or drink when there was this bounty of female flesh to wrap one's arms around? Jeremy could never remember feeling quite so comfortable in the whole of his life. Damn if he was going to ruin it all by waking up.

Then something happened that had never occurred in any of his dreams. The figure in his arms rolled over. Rolled over and nuzzled her face into the hollow between Jeremy's neck and shoulder.

Waves of pain shot through him. *That* had never happened in any dream, either. Jeremy opened his eyes.

Good God! It was a dream come true! Jeremy had actually awakened to find Maggie Herbert in his arms!

True, he was in pain. Agonies of it. The place where he'd been stabbed the night before felt as if it were on fire. Still, when Maggie came into focus in the soft morning light, all of her, from the thick tangle of inky hair across his pillows to the full weight of her naked breasts against his chest, he could easily forget his pain. It had been a while since he'd wakened in the company of a woman. Fraternization with the locals had been frowned upon by his fellow Horse Guards, so Jeremy had been forced to frequent houses of pleasure, where staying the night was generally discouraged.

But if memory served, the truly passionate woman—which Maggie, as he knew only too well, clearly was—was most effectively aroused by the application of a pair of lips placed directly beneath and a little behind the earlobe. . . .

Moving aside some of Maggie's long, thick hair, Jeremy leaned forward to press his mouth to her neck. As he kissed her, he felt the steady beat of her pulse beneath his lips. Maggie stirred, hitching up a shoulder in response to the sensation below her ear. Her lips, however, curved into a slight smile, as if she were dreaming of something vaguely pleasant. Encouraged, Jeremy transferred his next kiss to that smiling mouth, and was even more pleased when Maggie seemed to kiss him back, sweetly, with the perfect innocence of a child.

But it wasn't a child he was interested in. It was the woman that child had become.

Still, he was willing to be patient. The innocence of her unconscious kiss pleased him. She still kissed, even in her sleep, like someone who wasn't used to it, but was very eager to learn. That was good. That was very good. Jeremy leaned down to taste her lips again.

This time when he kissed her, she surprised him by letting out a sigh. This was a highly encouraging sign, especially since the sigh parted her lips enough to allow him to deepen the kiss. Slipping his tongue inside her mouth, Jeremy found himself marveling once again at Maggie's responsiveness, which was more genuinely sensual than any other woman he had ever known. The minute his tongue touched hers, Maggie let out a throaty little noise. . . .

And rolled over, effectively breaking the kiss. She did, however, move to press herself more closely against him—only, since her back was to him, all she succeeded in doing was capturing his stiffening erection between the sweet curves of her backside.

His heart pounding unsteadily, Jeremy began to feel that all-too-familiar ache in his loins.

Suddenly, what had started out simply as a lusty alternative to spanking Maggie awake turned into something else altogether, something Jeremy no longer felt he was going to be able to suspend should she wake with different feelings toward him than she evidently felt while sleeping.

All the more reason, Jeremy decided, to enjoy her good will while it lasted, even if she was only bestowing it upon him because she was unconscious. God only knew when he'd be allowed to hold her in his arms like this again.

Jeremy raised a hand and ran it along the length of her body, pausing as his fingers encountered the swell of one of her breasts. He palmed that soft, heavy globe, feeling her nipple swell the same way he was swelling against her. Was it possible, he wondered, that even in her sleep, she wanted him?

He curved an arm around her narrow waist until his questing fingers found the soft down between her thighs. Separating the velvet folds gently, he was able to confirm his suspicions: She was wet. His fingers were suddenly awash with her essence. That discovery excited him to a point from which, he knew, there was no going back. He was rock hard against the tender valley between her buttocks. The moist heat from her womb seemed to beckon him. To enter her, all he'd need do was move the slightest bit, and . . .

He was amazed at how easily he was able to slide into her slick sheath; and then, once inside, further amazed at how tightly she closed around him, like an eager, fevered hand. Keeping one arm around her hips, his hand pressed against the hard little knot of flesh just below her pubic bone, and the other to one of her full ripe breasts, he began to move slowly in and out of her, his chest pressed hotly to her back, his eyes, like hers, closed, as he relished the bounty in his arms.

So it hadn't been a dream. It hadn't been a dream at all. The two of them had made love long through the night, until, exhausted, they'd sunk into dreamless slumber. But Jeremy was full aware that often, that which was constructed by candlelight lost its luster when exposed to the harsh light of the day. He wasn't about to let that happen with Maggie. He intended his mastery over her to be total. He would not let her plead that the moonlight had caused her to lose her head. He would not allow midnight to excuse what dawn brought with it.

It wasn't until he heard her breathing quicken that he increased the pressure of his fingers between her legs. The movement of her own hips, as he entered and then retreated from behind, caused her to press against his callused fingers. His face buried in the fragrant curtain of her hair, he heard her moan softly in her sleep, felt her body opening, yielding to the demands of his. He plunged deeper and deeper into her, glorying in her eager acceptance of him, the dew that drenched his fingers, her ragged gasps for breath as he drove himself at her very core. . . .

And then he felt her stiffen all around him, her back arching while she thrust her pelvis greedily against his palm. The hot hand that had been clutching him so tightly, trying to hang on every time he pulled away, clenched convulsively, and then spasmed. And this time, Jeremy couldn't pull away. He was caught in a trap of his own making, with no desire to escape. Instead, he gripped Maggie's hips and erupted within her, filling her with liquid fire. She cried out hoarsely, her body shimmering with her own climax.

It wasn't until he'd exhausted himself within her that Maggie's eyelids began to flutter. Suddenly, he found himself gazing down into those dark brown depths that he knew so well.

"Good morning," Jeremy said pleasantly, but because of the force of the orgasm he'd just experienced, his voice came out sounding raw and unsteady, not like his own voice at all.

Maggie blinked up at him. Her mouth, where he'd ravaged it with his own, was reddened from his whiskers, and her breasts were still rising and falling rapidly as she tried to catch her breath. "That," she said huskily "was unfair."

Jeremy lifted an eyebrow. Though he was still buried inside of her, he leaned up on one elbow, resting his head in his hand, and feigned innocence. "What was unfair?" he asked.

"You know exactly what I'm talking about." But Maggie didn't seem at all perturbed. She moved away from him, rolling over onto her back, before stretching languidly, like a cat. It was in doing so that she happened to brush her fingers against the bandage that was still tied around Jeremy's shoulder. Suddenly, her eyes flared wide, and memory came flooding into them like tears. Jeremy, lying a foot away, watched in fascination as her irises went from brown to black.

"*Jeremy,*" she said, as she clutched at the sheets, dragging them up to her chin. Her expression was one of horror. "What have we *done*?"

Jeremy shrugged, though the movement caused a twinge in his wounded shoulder.

"*I* haven't done a blessed thing," he replied in mock indignation. "Here I was, sleeping peacefully, when I woke to find myself under lascivious attack. I defended myself as best I could, but you were simply too ardent, Mags. I'm afraid, in the end, I simply gave in to your lustful demands."

"Oh, God, Jerry! How can you joke about it?" Maggie sat up, her long hair spilling about her creamy shoulders. "Someone tried to *murder* you last night, and we . . . we . . ."

"We made wild, abandoned love?" He nodded. "Yes, I'd noticed that. I had no idea you were so bloodthirsty, my dear. If I'd known all I had to do to get you into my bed was bleed profusely, I'd have tried to get murdered more often."

"Oh, Jerry!" Maggie covered her cheeks, which had been growing steadily more and more crimson, with her hands. The enormity of what had occurred was only just sinking in. She had made love with the Duke of Rawlings. Not just once, but several times. Her body was still tingling from his touch. As if that wasn't proof enough, the sheets below her were stained with her blood. Good Lord, she'd lost her virginity last night, *to a man who was not even her fiancé*!

What had she been thinking? What had she *done*?

Jeremy, completely oblivious to the private torture Maggie was putting herself through, folded his hands beneath his head—his shoulder protested, but now that his limbs had been loosened up from their lovemaking, the wound did not feel quite so bad—and happily studied the canopy over his bed. "So," he said. "What shall we do today, eh, Mags? Hop a train and head on up to Yorkshire, pay a call on the family? Or would you rather stay here in London, maybe do some shopping, catch a show? I haven't been to the theater in five years. I wouldn't mind seeing something with some nice musical numbers. . . ." He happened to glance in Maggie's direction in time to see her struggling into the nightdress he'd stripped off her the night before. "Say, Mags," he said, with only a very little suspiciousness. "Where are you going?"

"Back to my room, of course," was the pert response. "Have you seen my robe?"

Jeremy raised an eyebrow. "Isn't that it?" he asked, lifting the garment with his foot. "You know, Mags, I really think you ought to invest in something a little more daring than plaid. Maybe something diaphanous, with feathers. . . ."

Maggie snatched the dressing gown from him. "Oh, do shut up," she said, through tightly gritted teeth. "*You* aren't the one who has to go sneaking back down the hallway like a criminal—"

"What," he asked, trying very hard not to laugh at her adorable indignation, "are you talking about?"

She shot him an irritated look. "Hill, of course!"

Jeremy raised an eyebrow. "Your maid?"

"Yes, of course. Oh!" Maggie hurried to thrust her arms through the plaid sleeves of her dressing gown. "I just hope she hasn't noticed I'm missing yet."

"What do you care what your maid thinks, Mags? Follow my example. If she gives you any guff, just dismiss her."

"Dismiss her?" Maggie turned to glare at him, her normally gentle brown eyes crackling. "Jeremy, I'll have you know that Hill is the only member of my family—well, of Herbert Park, anyway—who's stuck by me these past few months. I can't dismiss her.'' She gave the sash to her robe a savage yank. ''Though she'll probably give her notice this morning, anyway. . . .''

''Why?'' Jeremy asked curiously.

''Because no respectable lady's maid would stay in the employ of someone like me,'' Maggie replied, a bit exasperately. ''It's bad enough that I consort with artists and Bohemians, and that my own family has cut me off. Now I've completely ruined what little reputation I might have had left by spending the night alone in the Duke of Rawlings's town house—''

''What do you mean, alone? We weren't a bit alone. I had to go to a lot of trouble to get rid of all the people who were hanging about, as a matter of fact—''

''Oh, Jerry,'' Maggie said. ''Surely you can't think servants count! We were *unchaperoned*. Your aunt and uncle were supposed to return from Yorkshire, but something must have delayed them—''

''Thank God,'' Jeremy muttered.

''—and now if it gets out that you and I were in the house alone—''

A nasty thought struck Jeremy, one that caused him to actually sit up. ''What if it does? What would it matter? You're not worried about what that *frog-eater* will think, are you?''

''I'm worried about what *everyone* will think, particularly your aunt and uncle, who will probably be here at any minute.'' Maggie primly tied the sash to her robe. ''And kindly refrain from referring to Augustin de Veygoux as a frog-eater. He does not, to my knowledge, eat frogs.''

Jeremy opened his lips to refute this, though based on what knowledge, he wasn't sure, when a low tap sounded on the door. Maggie turned wide and startled eyes toward him, but he raised a finger to his lips. ''Shh,'' he said with a chuckle. ''No need to panic. It's only Peters. He's the only member of this household who'd dare disturb a Rawlings while he slept.''

Maggie, far from heeding his advice not to panic, dove for the ladder that led down from Jeremy's massive bed.

Scrambling down it, she nearly tripped over the hem of her nightdress, but she recovered herself, and shot Jeremy an outraged look as he smirked at her near-hysteria.

"Oh, it's all very well for you," she hissed. "You have no reputation to worry about!"

"I take exception to that," Jeremy said with mock gravity. "I am extremely conscious of your reputation. So conscious, in fact, that I shall ask Peters to act as lookout for Hill while you make your way back to your room—"

"No," Maggie gasped. "Don't—"

But it was too late. Jeremy was already calling for his valet to enter. The one-legged man did so, casting only a single, entirely incurious glance at Maggie. "Good morning, sir," he said politely. "Miss 'Erbert. 'Ow's your shoulder this morning, sir? Is it still troubling you?"

"Not a twinge," Jeremy replied calmly. "Peters, have you seen Miss Herbert's maid up and about this morning?"

"Yes, sir," Peters said. He had gone to the windows, and was throwing open the long velvet curtains. "I took the liberty of creating a diversion belowstairs that Mrs. 'Ill is busy trying to clean up. If Miss 'Erbert wishes to retire to her own room, now would be an ideal time."

Maggie hesitated not a moment. Her feet padding noiselessly on the parquet floor, she hurried to the door. She did turn, however, with her hand on the latch, to look back at Jeremy. He was sitting up in the middle of the great canopied bed, his skin very dark against the whiteness of the sheets. His eyes, however, shone bright as coins.

"Um," Maggie said. Good Lord. This was extremely awkward. She had been sure—quite sure—that he would have mentioned something, *anything* about marriage, or at the very least, about *love*. She had *given* herself to him, after all. She was quite aware that most girls tended to wait to do that until after they were married. He had suggested going to the theater. But he hadn't said a word about taking any trips toward the altar.

Oh, dear. How very presumptuous on her part to have even thought . . .

"Yes, yes," Jeremy said, his lips twisted upward. "Go

on and run, then, little mouse, before the cat gets wind of it.''

Maggie, ducking her head so that her long hair hid her blushing cheeks, slipped from the room without another word. As soon as the door clicked shut behind her, Peters turned from the windows and said mildly, ''Congratulations, sir. I see you finally managed to—''

''Careful, Peters,'' Jeremy said, without the slightest rancor. ''That's my future wife you're talking about.''

''Meanin' no disrespect, sir.''

''None taken.'' Perfectly content, Jeremy sank back against the pillows. Though it was February, he couldn't help thinking that the sun had never shone quite so brightly, nor the birds outside his windows sung quite so well. ''Peters, let this be a lesson to you. Man can achieve *anything*, with a little charm, ingenuity, and patience.''

''You are a model for us all, sir,'' was Peters's dry reply, as he headed straight for the whisky decanter on the sideboard. ''The maid, though. That Mrs. 'Ill. She's goin' to be a problem, sir.''

''Easily rectified, my good man. Easily rectified. In about an hour, you and I will head downtown and secure a special license. By this afternoon, Miss Herbert will become the seventeenth Duchess of Rawlings, and our good Mrs. Hill won't be able to say a word about it.''

Peters shrugged, and splashed a generous slug of whisky into a glass. ''Beggin' your pardon, Colonel, but we might 'ave a slight difficulty securin' that special license today.'' He lifted the glass and headed toward the bed. Jeremy eyed him with a single raised brow.

''Whisky for breakfast, Peters?'' he asked curiously. ''Surely it's not as bad as all that.''

''Yes, sir,'' Peters said. ''I think you'll agree wi' me that it is.'' Shoving the glass into his employer's hand, Peters unfolded the crisp pages of the newspaper he had held tucked under his arm—*The Times*, Jeremy noted—and presented him with the society page, across which blared the headline, *Military Hero Returns to London to Marry Indian Royal.*

Jeremy brought the whisky glass swiftly to his lips.

Chapter 24

"*I* just don't know," declared the Baroness of Lancaster. "The blue is nice, but I think white is more appropriate."

"Oh, Mamma!" sixteen-year-old Fanny Lancaster wailed. "Only babies wear white, and I'm not a baby. I'm wearing the blue."

"I just don't know," fretted Lady Lancaster. "It doesn't seem right. Miss Herbert, what do you recommend?" Glancing over at the portrait painter, Lady Lancaster smiled tolerantly. Daydreaming, of course. Well, what else could you expect from a lady artist? Lavinia Michaels had said the girl had a tendency to drift off. Probably up all night at some Bohemian party or another. But that portrait she'd done of Lavinia's niece! Perfection! One hardly noticed the girl's double chin at all. "Miss Herbert?"

Maggie had been up all night, but not at any party. She still could not quite fathom what had occurred only a few hours before. She had made love with the Duke of Rawlings. Not once. Not twice. But three, possibly four times . . . she'd lost count after a while. It had been the most thrilling, the most exhilarating, night in her life.

Of course, when she'd sat down to her breakfast tray that morning, and opened the paper to the society page, which she habitually perused for potential clients, she found that it had been the most humiliating night in her life, as well.

Well, at least now she knew why he hadn't proposed.

"Miss Herbert?" Lady Lancaster peered through her lorgnettes at the young woman perched on the end of her chaise longue. The girl looked all right—slightly peaked, maybe, from keeping such odd hours—but otherwise quite present-able in a dark wool visiting dress. Her hat was jauntily pinned to a saucy little confection of curls on top of her head—not at all the look for someone of Lady Lancaster's class, but quite appropriate for a pretty Miss Herbert. Still, what ailed the girl? She'd been staring fixedly at the same rose in the carpet for nearly five minutes.

"Miss Herbert," Fanny said, with another petulant stamp of her foot. That got Maggie's attention, especially since Fanny had managed to rattle the Dresden shepherdess on the mantel.

"Yes?" Maggie asked brightly.

Ah, there, Lady Lancaster said to herself. She's back.

It took only a few minutes of effort on Maggie's part to convince Fanny that white was really the only appropriate color for a young girl having her first portrait painted. That done, the women decided on a mutually agreeable time for the sitting—Tuesday next at one o'clock—and then Maggie gathered up her sketchbooks and crayons and bade the bar-oness and her daughter adieu.

Out on Grosvenor Square, the crisp winter wind brought some color to Maggie's otherwise pallid cheeks. She took in a few deep gulps of the icy air, hoping to clear her head before catching the omnibus and returning to her studio. She felt as if she'd had too much to drink the night before. Granted, she'd only had a few hours of sleep, but she'd got-ten by on less in the past and not felt so gloomy. Well, she supposed that finding out that the man to whom one had lost one's virginity was actually engaged to marry someone else had a way of dampening one's spirits. If only, she said to herself, for the thirtieth time at least that day alone, her mother were still alive. Lady Herbert would know exactly what Maggie ought to do.

The truth was, Maggie had no one to whom she could turn for advice. None of her sisters were speaking to her, but even if any of them were, she couldn't possibly have shared her problems with them—they would have been horrified beyond all belief. She knew good and well what Hill, who adored Augustin for all the good deeds he'd done her mistress, would have to say on the matter. Conversely, she knew that if she turned to Jeremy's aunt Pegeen, who had remained Maggie's staunch supporter throughout all of her family trials, she'd find herself being urged not to give up on Jeremy. There wasn't a single impartial person to whom Maggie could turn.

Late that afternoon, back in her studio, Maggie gazed moodily at a portrait she was finishing up for the show on Saturday, a painting of a pair of towheaded toddlers, sweetly smiling while clinging to the neck of a long-suffering greyhound, and didn't notice the door behind her swing open. She jumped when she heard a throaty voice behind her purr, "What is this? The ever-cheerful *Mademoiselle Marguerethe*, looking *triste*? *C'est impossible!*"

Maggie glanced over her shoulder, and managed a small smile when she saw Berangère Jacquard leaning in the doorway, her arms folded across her chest. Dressed as usual in the height of Parisian *chic*, though she was going nowhere more stylish than her own studio across the hall from Maggie's, Berangère made a tsk-tsking noise with her tongue.

"What is this?" she demanded, slinking into the light-filled studio. "I thought you Englishwomen did not allow yourselves the luxury of sulking."

"I'm not sulking," Maggie said with a sigh. "Well . . . not really."

"Aren't you? Then you are doing a very good imitation of it, *princesse*." Berangère curled her lip at the painting Maggie was sitting in front of. "Ugh! *Quelle horreur*! I suppose they are little earls, *non*?"

"A marquis," Maggie said. "And his baby brother."

"But of course. How proud their *papa* and *maman* must be. Little brats. You ought to have painted them with their fingers up their noses, where they undoubtedly are, the majority of the time." Dismissing the painting with a shudder, Berangère strolled over to the windowsill, where Maggie kept a bottle of red wine for just such occasions. Pouring herself a glassful, Berangère went to a low divan, piled high with pillows, and sank down onto it with a delicate sigh. All of Berangère's movements were deliberate and graceful, like a cat's. In fact, that's exactly what she reminded Maggie of: a sleek, sly little cat, not at all unlike the Princess Usha. While Maggie herself was nothing but a great, galumphing dog.

"Now, *princesse*," the older girl said, after taking a sip of wine. "Tell *Tante* Berangère what is making you look so positively *malheureuse*."

"Oh, Berangère," Maggie said miserably. "I wouldn't know where to start."

"Ah," Berangère said. She looked down into her wine glass, noticed a piece of cork floating in it, and delicately removed it with a long index finger. "This would not have something to do with the fact that your precious Augustin got his *nez* bashed in last night?"

Maggie gasped. "How did you hear about that?"

Berangère waved a dismissive hand. "La, who has not heard of it? It is all over the hallways."

Maggie groaned. The building in which their studios were situated was an old one, run-down, and filled with other painters and the odd sculptor or two. Maggie and Berangère, being the only women renting studio space in the building, were sources of constant speculation by the other artists, their activities faithfully reported on by those who traveled in similar social circles.

"Oh, Berangère," Maggie said, dropping her face into her hands. "What am I going to do?"

"Do?" Berangère sipped her wine. "About what, *princesse*?"

"Why, about Jerry, of course!" Maggie lifted her head, smoothing back a tendril of hair that had come loose from her coiffure, and leaving a streak of violet across her smooth white forehead.

Berangère smiled tolerantly. "And what is the problem with Jerry, now, *princesse*? He is making water behind the divan again?"

"*What*?" Then Maggie started to laugh, in spite of her

misery. "Oh, no!" she cried. "No, not *that* Jerry. Not Jerry the dog. I mean Jeremy Rawlings!"

Berangère knit her perfectly plucked eyebrows. "Jeremy Rawlings? This is the soldier who broke the *nez* of Augustin?" At Maggie's nod, a knowing look spread over Berangère's pointed face. "Ah," she said. "Things become clearer to me, now. Jeremy Rawlings. I have heard this name before." Berangère tapped her front teeth thoughtfully with a long, manicured fingernail. "Where have I heard this name?"

"In this morning's paper, I wouldn't doubt," Maggie said with a sigh.

Berangère raised a fine blond eyebrow. "*Pardon?*"

"His engagement to the Princess Usha of Jaipur was announced in today's society page."

"Ah," Berangère said knowingly. "Yes. Now I remember. *That* is the Jerry for whom you have pined all these years I have known you?" At a hesitant nod from Maggie—she didn't like admitting to being in love with Jeremy, let alone having been *pining* for him—Berangère went on. "I see. No wonder you look so *triste*. He has come back from India with a royal bride, broken the *nez* of your fiancé, and you do not know what to do?"

Maggie nodded again.

"*Pfui!*" said Berangère, a curious noise she always made when she was incredulous about something, a small explosion of lips and breath that invariably sent the golden curls of hair upon her forehead flying. "I always thought you were too polite for your own good, *princesse*, but I never thought you were *stupide*."

"I'm not stupid," Maggie said defensively. "I just don't know what to do. I've never been in this situation before."

"Never had two men fighting over you before?" Berangère looked shocked. "*Ma pauvre princesse!* Then, truly, you have not lived. It is the most delightful thing in the world, to be fought over. You must try to prolong it as long as possible."

"Are you insane?" Maggie glared at her friend. "Berangère, this is *serious*. Someone . . . someone tried to stab

Jerry last night, and I think he suspects it was Augustin.''

Berangère sat up, her pretty features alight with excitement. ''Really? *Très romantique!*''

''Romantic?'' Maggie shuddered. ''Berangère, it was awful.''

''Awfully *romantique!* Do you think it was Augustin?'' Berangère looked perplexed. ''I would not have thought Augustin was the murderous type. Duel, yes. But murder? *Non.* Still, with that red hair, one cannot be sure of anything. . . .''

''Berangère!'' Maggie buried her face in her hands. ''It isn't funny, and it isn't romantic. Someone tried to kill Jeremy last night, and I can't help thinking—''

But Berangère interrupted her. ''*Nom de Dieu,*'' she said, and something in her throaty voice caused Maggie to raise her head and eye her uncertainly. Berangère was staring at her, round-eyed with astonishment. ''You and this Jerry. You made love.''

Maggie's jaw dropped. ''Berangère!''

''I cannot believe it. *Ma petite princesse!* No wonder Augustin tried to kill him.'' Berangère applauded enthusiastically. ''How was it? Did you like it very much? Isn't it lovely?''

Maggie stared at her, round-eyed, not even attempting to deny it. ''How did . . . How could you . . . *tell?*''

Berangère shrugged elegantly. ''You glow.''

Horrified, Maggie gasped, ''I don't!''

''You do, *princesse.* I am sorry to tell you so, but you do. Only a fool—or a fiancé—would fail to notice.''

''It just happened,'' Maggie cried, covering her face with her paint-spotted hands. ''Oh, God, Berangère, it just happened! I didn't want it to. I never expected it to. And he told me he wasn't engaged!''

Berangère snorted. ''Don't they all?''

''But Berangère, I believed him! He told me the Star of Jaipur wasn't a woman. He said she was a rock!''

''Now,'' Berangère said incredulously, ''I have heard everything.''

''Oh, I've made such a mess of things!'' Maggie couldn't stifle a sob. ''Oh, I know I brought it all upon myself, and

I don't deserve anyone's sympathy. I was so sure—so very sure—that he meant to marry me! I don't—I just don't know what came over me!"

"I do."

Maggie looked up, blinking back tears. To her surprise, Berangère was standing beside her, a glass of newly poured wine in either hand. She handed one of the glasses to Maggie before gently guiding her over to the divan, and then sitting down beside her—a move that took some maneuvering, due to the size of both their bustles.

"I know exactly what came over you," Berangère said. "*L'amour*. Let us drink to it, shall we?" She clinked the edge of her glass against Maggie's, and then downed a good third of its contents.

Maggie took a hesitant sip from her own glass, though she'd never in her life drunk wine before teatime. But she'd never lost her virginity before, either, so she supposed the occasion warranted it. To her astonishment, the hearty burgundy felt quite nice going down, warm and nourishing. She took another sip.

"Then you . . ." she asked carefully. "Then you don't despise me utterly, Berangère?"

"*Despise* you?" Berangère, thoroughly surprised by the question, came as close to spilling a drink as Maggie had ever seen her. "Why should I despise you?"

Maggie sniffled forlornly. "If my sisters knew—about what Jerry and I did, I mean—they would never speak to me again."

"Your sisters are already not speaking to you," Berangère reminded her, "and your only crime has been that, like a good many women before you, you are trying to make a living on your own, using the talent that God gave you." Berangère shook her head until her blond ringlets swung. "You are an artist! There is no disgrace in being an artist. It is not as if you were a . . . a . . ." Berangère struggled to think of a truly shocking occupation. "A prostitute!"

"No," Maggie admitted reluctantly. "But I suppose, in their minds, painters lead scandalous, sordid lives. And now they've been proven right, you know, Berangère." She heaved a miserable sigh. "I *am* a fallen woman."

Berangère's lips quirked into a wry smile as she leaned back down upon the couch. "*Ma chérie*, if *you* are fallen, I shudder to think what *I* am. I should truly like to meet these sisters of yours, *princesse*. How is it that you grew up in a home so *bourgeois*, yet paint the way you do?"

"I don't think my home was *bourgeois*," Maggie said defensively. "At least, no more than anyone else's. I think I was just cursed with a more ... carnal nature than anyone else in my family. I can't imagine, for instance, that any of my sisters made love with their husbands before they were married. Especially not Anne. She is so very proper. Although, when Mamma was alive, Anne was a good deal more ... tolerant. Now, it is as if, with Mamma gone, Anne seems to feel that it is her duty to bring me to task."

"And you will not be," Berangère said. "Being far too ... how did you say it? *Oui*, carnal. That is a very good word. It is fortunate that you managed to find a man to marry who is equally carnal."

"Augustin?" Maggie finished off her glass of wine. "Augustin isn't a bit carnal."

"Not Augustin, *imbécile*," Berangère snorted. "This Jerry you speak of."

"*Jeremy*?" Maggie blinked at her. "But I can't marry *Jeremy*."

Berangère blinked right back. "And why not?"

"Why not?" Maggie echoed. "Why not? Haven't you heard a word I just said? *He's engaged to someone else!*"

"*Pfui!*" was Berangère's skeptical reply to that.

"Berangère, the Star of Jaipur is a beautiful, exotic woman. You haven't seen her. She's like ..." Maggie stopped herself just short of saying *She's like you*. Instead, she said, "Well, nothing you could ever imagine. . . ."

"*Oui, chérie*. But with whom did this Jerry spend the night last night? This rock—this Star of Jaipur—or you?"

Maggie shook her head. "Oh, Berangère. Don't you see? Even if by some miracle Jerry *did* want to marry me, I couldn't marry him. . . ."

"Why not?"

"Because I'm engaged to Augustin, that's why not! I can't just break off my engagement to him like that—" Maggie snapped her fingers. "It wouldn't be fair, not when he's been so kind. . . ."

"So?" Berangère clasped her hands behind her head and leaned back against the pillows, gazing up at the skylights that revealed a cold and gray winter sky. "You did not *ask* Augustin to be so kind. He was kind of his own volition. You do not have to marry him for it. You can merely thank him and walk away."

"But it would be wrong! I let him believe I returned his feelings, when all the time, I was in love with someone else!"

Berangère rolled her eyes. "You are a stupid, stupid girl. Marry the soldier and be done with it. If you like, *I* will take care of Augustin. Though I cannot abide red hair on a man." She shuddered expressively.

"What do you mean," she inquired suspiciously, "you'll *take care* of Augustin?"

"What I said." Berangère shrugged.

"You mean . . ." Maggie straightened. "You mean you'll—" She broke off, suddenly extremely embarrassed. "Oh, Berangère," she murmured. "You really oughtn't—"

Berangère's laugh rang out through the studio, bouncing off the skylight and crashing back down upon the wooden floor like glass. "*Ma pauvre princesse!*" she cried. "I've shocked you!"

"But that's just it, Berangère," Maggie said sadly. "I'm *not* a princess. I never could be. You're the only one who thinks so. And Jerry—the soldier—isn't just a soldier. He's a duke. Even if he asked me to marry him, I don't think I could, because then I'd have to become a—"

"A *duchesse*?" Berangère sat up and clapped her hands, clearly entranced with the idea. "Oh, *Marguerethe, c'est magnifique*! What a lovely *duchesse* you will make! You will invite me to all your dinner parties and balls, and I will meet many handsome, rich men!" Stars shone in Berangère's eyes. "Oh! How perfect! The *princesse* will be a *duchesse*!"

"No I won't, Berangère," Maggie insisted. "I'm only a

princess in *your* eyes. I'm actually a social disaster by English standards. But this woman—the Star of Jaipur—she really *is* a princess. She'd make a much better duchess than I ever would.''

Berangère, on her divan, narrowed her eyes, much in the way a cat, eyeing her prey, will take aim before a particularly daring pounce. ''I see,'' the French girl said slowly. ''So you are willing to give him up so easily, because you would not make a suitable *duchesse*?''

''I—it's not just that, Berangère. I told you, he hasn't asked me—''

Footsteps sounded in the hall. Berangère had left the door to Maggie's studio wide open. There were only two studios on the top floor of the building, her own and Maggie's, so whoever was approaching had to be coming to visit one of them.

''Well?'' Berangère persisted. ''And if he asked you? Would you?''

But Maggie's reply dried up in her throat. Because just then, Jeremy himself walked through the door of her studio.

Chapter 25

$\mathcal{J}$eremy was not in a particularly good mood. Nearly getting killed did that to a fellow. Well, nearly getting killed as well as having one's engagement announced in *The Times*, by someone to whom one was not engaged.

Not that Jeremy was brooding, or anything. He had completely gotten over the first attempt that had been made to murder him. In fact, what with all the other disasters in his life, he had forgotten all about it. It wasn't until he was storming out of the offices of *The Times*—where he'd gone to demand a retraction—that he was nearly run down by a chaise-and-four.

Now, it was one thing to get stabbed, in the dead of night, in front of one's own home. That could easily be blamed upon the increase in urban crime. It was something else entirely, however, to be nearly trampled to death in front of the offices of *The Times*. Jeremy, getting up from the slush, into which he'd dived to avoid being killed, decided that it was time to take action. He dispatched his valet with instructions to find Augustin de Veygoux, follow him, and determine whether or not he was, in fact, the man responsible for these murder attempts . . . not because Jeremy feared for his life, but because, well, it was getting to be a damned nuisance, this diving about the street, dodging knives and flying hooves. And if de Veygoux was the one trying to kill him, Jeremy would have a perfect excuse to call him out. A duel would kill two birds with one stone: Jeremy would be rid of his annoying assassin, and Maggie would no longer have a fiancé.

"And at your peril," Jeremy warned Peters, "do you let Maggie see you. The only way we're going to convince her that this bloke's the one that stabbed me is if we catch him in the act. But if she sees we're following him, she'll think we're just trying to harass him, and that'll only make her feel sorry for him."

Peters saluted. "Never fear, Colonel. You can count on me. This is one mission I shan't fail."

That done, Jeremy returned to the town house, where he changed out of his ruined clothes, and into something more presentable before heading straight out again. His first stop was the Dorchester, where he found the Princess Usha in deep consultation with a number of dressmakers and milliners. It seemed the Star of Jaipur had decided saris were passé; she was intent on purchasing a Western trousseau. Her efforts at doing so were hampered, however, by the absence of her translator—he had apparently slipped out some time earlier to send another letter to the maharajah. This made it exceedingly difficult for Jeremy to make his feelings concerning the announcement in that morning's *Times* understood . . . at least by the princess. The dressmakers understood him well enough, though, if their nervous looks at one another, as Jeremy was leaving, were any indication. Providing a trousseau for a bride with so reluctant a groom was not good business practice, and everyone in the room, with the exception, perhaps, of the princess, knew it.

Having failed to impress upon Usha his unhappiness with her behavior, Jeremy decided to concentrate instead on the equally difficult job of finding Maggie and repairing whatever wounds the announcement might have inflicted. His fervent hope—that she had not seen that morning's paper—had been dashed shortly after breakfast, when he'd gone to her room to speak with her about it, and her maid had answered the door.

"Good morning, Your Grace," Hill had said icily. "I'm afraid Miss Margaret has already left for her first appointment. But might I wish you joy? I am certain you and the princess will be very happy together. Your aunt and uncle must be *so* pleased. . . .''

Jeremy knew good and well that his aunt and uncle would be anything *but* pleased. Oh, he supposed if he'd really loved Usha, they'd have accepted her willingly enough . . . at least until she managed to alienate them with her complete and utter disregard for anyone's feelings but her own. *That* they might take exception to. . . .

Jeremy's interrogation of Maggie's maid had proven disappointing. The only thing he'd been able to get out of Hill—and he'd nearly had to wring it out of her, stubborn old woman—was the address of her mistress's studio. Still, that was better than nothing.

But when he arrived at the address in which Maggie's studio was housed, he suffered yet another shock. He had never seen a more dilapidated building, with the possible exception of some attempts at European architecture he'd witnessed in Bombay. Was this, he wondered, the best that Maggie could afford? Now he had a new reason to resent Sir Arthur. His pomposity was forcing his daughter to rent in a clearly uninhabitable building. No wonder the flats in this particular structure had all been converted to artists' studios: The only people who could be convinced to inhabit them were painters and sculptors, who lived in worlds of their own making, anyway.

Jeremy had managed to pry the address of Maggie's studio from her maid, but not the exact flat number, so it wasn't surprising that he found himself wandering about the long, dismally lit corridors, fruitlessly searching for her. The smell of turpentine was heavy in the air, as was a very distinct odor of opium, which Jeremy recognized from a brief foray into Burma. As he wandered down the hallways, he glimpsed several men painting naked women, using actual live models, robust but strangely unpleasant-looking women who stood shivering on pedestals or had draped themselves, rather uncouthly, for Jeremy's tastes, across soiled couches. Some of the efforts he thought rather good. Then, as he passed a studio in which a man was painting not a naked woman, but a naked man, an odd thought occurred to Jeremy: Had *Maggie* ever painted any naked men? Was his not the first nude male body she'd ever encountered?

The idea of Maggie being in the company of an unclothed male other than himself made Jeremy feel very uncomfortable, and caused him to hasten his efforts to find her. He leaned into one studio on the third floor and asked a rather harried-looking young man, who was cleaning out his brushes at a slopbucket, "I say, but would you know where I might find Miss Herbert?"

The young man jumped, swiveled his head sharply in Jeremy's direction, then laid aside the opium pipe he'd been drawing upon. "You mean Maggie?" he asked, in a surprisingly high-pitched voice.

"Er, yes," Jeremy said. She was on first-name terms with these men? He'd see that an end was put to *that* after she became Duchess of Rawlings. "Which studio is hers?"

"Sixth floor, door to the left," came the laconic reply. "But it's no use askin' her to pose for you, mate. She and that French bitch won't take off so much as a stitch. Believe me, I've asked." He put the pipe back to his lips, and sucked mournfully. "We've *all* asked."

Jeremy cleared his throat. "I see," he said. "Well. Thank you, then."

"But if it's wine you're lookin' for," the young man added, just as Jeremy was leaving, "she's not stingy with it. That's the thing with these lady portrait painters. Won't take their clothes off, but they're gen'rous with their liquor." He stared moodily at a canvas sitting on an easel in the center of the room. "'Course, *they* can afford to buy plenty of wine. *Everybody* wants their portrait painted. Hardly nobody wants a picture of the doors to Newgate prison."

Jeremy hastily took his eyes off the depressing painting. "Yes," he said. "Well. Good evening." He beat a hasty retreat, before the young painter could show him any more of his masterpieces.

Three rickety flights of stairs later, and Jeremy could hear her sweet voice lilting down the corridor. He couldn't tell precisely what she was saying, nor could he tell to whom it was she was speaking. But the leap of joy he felt in his heart at hearing her told him it hardly mattered. He'd found his Maggie, and that meant he was home.

He strode confidently through the open door to her studio.

Chapter 26

$\mathcal{M}$aggie stared at him incredulously. She'd left Twenty-two Park Lane thinking that if she ever saw Jeremy Rawlings again, it would be too soon. To see him simply stroll into her studio, looking as if butter wouldn't melt in his mouth, was a shock from which she would not soon recover.

Not that he looked bad. Not at all. He had on evening clothes. Not his dress uniform, but actual evening clothes, black beaver-lined cloak over well-tailored black coat and trousers, white shirt and vest, a froth of a cravat at his throat. His shoes had been polished to a high sheen. Even the white evening gloves he wore were without blemish. His held his top hat in his hand, and she could see that an attempt had been made to comb his hair, but no amount of styling could control those curls. Still, to Maggie, Jeremy looked heartbreakingly handsome.

A quick glance at Berangère, who was staring at the duke in the manner of one who'd been put into a trance, revealed that her thoughts were traveling along a similar vein.

"Oh, there you are," he had the nerve to say to Maggie, as nonchalantly as if they'd merely met on the street. "May I come in?"

"H-hullo," Maggie stammered, wrenching her gaze from Berangère and swinging it back round to Jeremy. What was the *matter* with her? She was supposed to be angry with him, furiously angry with him! He had robbed her of her virgin-

ity—well, all right, she had given it to him, but why quibble
over incidentals?—and here she was, scrambling up from the
divan, hastily smoothing her skirt into place. She realized
she was wearing a paint-smeared smock over her dress, and
hurried to untie its strings. And all the time, she was thinking, He tricked you, Maggie. This man knowingly and cold-
heartedly tricked you. You are *not* to be kind to him. You
are *not*.

"Would you . . . um," she stammered, trying desperately
to sound as nonchalant as he had, "care for a glass of something? Wine?"

"Wine would be splendid," Jeremy said, but he wasn't
looking at her. He had stepped into the high-ceilinged studio
and was looking around curiously at the half-finished paintings leaning up against the walls, the wooden racks that contained completed works, the cheerful fire burning in the
wood stove, the slop bucket, the sides of which were caked
with paint, and, most of all, at the blond woman reclining,
felinelike, across a low divan before the window.

"Hello," Jeremy said to Berangère.

Berangère smiled beguilingly. "Hello. You must be
Jerry." Berangère rolled the *r*'s provocatively, in spite of the
warning look Maggie cast at her.

"That's right." Jeremy grinned. "And who might you
be?"

"Her name," Maggie said, more sharply than she meant
to, "is Berangère Jacquard, and she was just leaving." Then,
when both Jeremy and Berangère turned their heads to blink
at her, Maggie had no choice but to make grudging introductions. "Your Grace, may I present Mademoiselle Jacquard? Mademoiselle Jacquard, His Grace, Jeremy, Duke of
Rawlings."

Berangère extended a slim hand toward Jeremy. "*Je suis
enchantée*," she purred.

"The pleasure's mine," Jeremy said, stooping to take that
hand in his own and raising it toward his lips. With gentlemanly gallantry, Jeremy did not actually press his mouth to
her knuckles, Maggie observed, but kissed the air an inch or
so above Berangère's hand. Still, he didn't let go of that hand
right away. Instead, he looked down at it. "And are you

sitting for one of Miss Herbert's portraits, Mademoiselle Jacquard?''

"*Moi?*" Berangère chuckled deep in her throat. "*Non, non—*"

"Berangère attended the same painting school as I did in Paris," Maggie interrupted quickly. "She has come to London, like me, to try her hand at painting portraits. She rents the studio across the hall. As a matter of fact, she was just going back to work, weren't you, Berangère?''

Berangère hadn't taken her eyes off Jeremy's face, any more than Jeremy had straightened up yet, or released her hand. "*Il est superbe, princesse,*" she said to Maggie. "*Un duc diabolique. Vous êtes un vrai imbécile.*"

Maggie closed her eyes in order to utter a quick prayer of thanks that Jeremy, to her knowledge, spoke not a word of French.

"The reason I asked whether you were sitting for a portrait, Mademoiselle Jacquard, is because I don't see any paint on your fingers." Jeremy held up the appendage in question and examined it with a speculative air. "Maggie's are usually covered with the stuff."

"Ah," Berangère said knowingly. "But, unlike *Marguerethe*, I wear gloves when I paint. You see, the substances with which we work—the turpentine, the linseed oil—are very harsh to a woman's delicate skin, and I want to keep my hands as soft as possible."

What kind of idiocy was this? Maggie yanked off her painting smock. The two of them were chatting about *skin*, while her heart was breaking! Well, she'd put a stop to it.

"What brings you down to Chelsea, Your Grace?" Maggie inquired, wadding her painting smock into a tight ball as she spoke, then throwing it unceremoniously into a corner before going to the table where she kept the wine, and pouring Jeremy a glass.

Jeremy straightened, taking the glass of wine from her, his top hat dangling from the fingers of his other hand. "Well, I thought I'd stop by and see what you were doing tonight. I have tickets to the ballet, and I thought we could have dinner—"

"Ballet?" echoed Berangère, sitting up alertly.

Jeremy glanced at her over his shoulder. It was clear he did not know quite what to make of Mademoiselle Jacquard, let alone her friendship with Maggie. "Er, yes," he said, turning his attention upon Maggie once more. "The ballet. And dinner, either before or after."

Behind him, on the couch, Berangère leaned back so that she could see around him, and mouthed, quite unabashedly, at Maggie, *Je l'adore!* Maggie, acutely aware of the fact that compared to Berangère, she must look a mess, what with her paint-streaked hands—she was not aware of the smudge on her forehead—and not very stylish wool dress, decided it was time to stop playing hostess. She said coldly, "I hardly think it appropriate, Your Grace, for you to be escorting a woman other than your fiancée to the theater."

Jeremy took a sip of wine. "Oh," he said, with infuriating matter-of-factness. "You needn't worry about that. That little matter has been taken care of."

"Little matter!" Maggie echoed incredulously. Berangère, watching from the divan, turned her head back and forth between them, as if she were at the theater. "Jeremy, that *little matter* is the future Duchess of Rawlings!"

"No," Jeremy said. "She isn't."

"Oh, isn't she?" Maggie felt ready to explode. How dare he stand there and deny what she—and every other reader of the most widely circulated newspaper in the world—had learned that very morning? "Well, you might want to let *The Times* know. Unlike me, they didn't seem to fall for your ridiculous insistence that the Star of Jaipur is not a woman, but a *rock*."

"I like that part," Berangère commented from the divan. When Jeremy looked at her, she said, "The rock part, I mean. Very creative."

"It's not creative," Jeremy ground out. "It's the truth. And it isn't a rock, it's a sapphire. A twenty-four-carat sapphire, to be exact."

That caused Berangère to rise to her elbows. "Twenty-four carats, did you say? *Twenty-four?*"

"Twenty-four carats, my foot," Maggie said, her hands

going to her hips. "The Star of Jaipur is a five-foot-tall, one-hundred-pound *woman*, with dark eyes and tiny feet and her own personal translator, which is evidently something *I* need, since I've somehow found myself the mistress of the man she's supposed to marry!"

"You're not my mistress," Jeremy growled, obviously making an effort to remain calm. "And I'm not going to marry her."

Maggie rolled her eyes. "Oh, I see. I'm certain that there is so little news in the world that *The Times* has been forced to start making things up to entertain its readers—"

"I didn't say they made it up," Jeremy interrupted. "I'm just saying the story wasn't correct. I have dealt with the party responsible, and a retraction will appear in tomorrow's edition—"

"Oh, certainly it will," Maggie said sarcastically. "And I understand the sky is supposed to hail twenty-four-carat sapphires tomorrow, as well."

Berangère, from the divan, suddenly sat up and said, "Someone is coming."

Jeremy ignored her. "Do you honestly think," he demanded of Maggie, his voice considerably lowered, and filled with unmistakable hurt, "that I would try to make you my mistress?"

Maggie looked away from him, confused. Half an hour earlier, had someone asked her that question, she'd have shouted an unequivocal *yes*. But now, looking at Jeremy's serious face, his almost desperate expression, she remembered the hours they'd spent together, the way he'd held her, and she couldn't help but wonder—

"Augustin!" Berangère cried, in tones of sheer delight as she scrambled off the couch.

Maggie whirled, a sudden roaring sound in her ears. No. It couldn't be. It wasn't possible.

But it was. Augustin stood in the open doorway, his top hat and cane in one hand, and a large bouquet of white roses in the other. During the course of her argument with Jeremy, Maggie had not heard his step in the hallway.

"Good evening," he said, in a slightly wounded tone.

And no wonder, Maggie thought, as her eyes rose from his satin waistcoat—Augustin, like Jeremy, was also dressed in evening clothes—to his face. She was barely able to restrain a gasp as she took in the purple bruises around both his eyes, and the painful swelling of his once aquiline nose. There was blood-encrusted cotton packed into his nostrils, and his breathing, from having climbed the six flights of stairs to the top floor of the building, was a labored wheeze.

And *this* was the man Jeremy suspected of having tried to kill him! This near-invalid, who clearly could not have raised a knife above his head even if he'd wanted to, he was still in that much pain! Oh, Maggie didn't blame Jeremy, exactly, for having thought it, but the idea was simply too ludicrous. *Augustin* hadn't been the one who'd tried to kill him. *Augustin* wasn't capable of such violence. . . .

Poor Augustin! How she had wronged him! Maggie found that she could not look him in the eye. What was she going to do?

Always the gentleman, Augustin stepped into the room, gave a low bow, and presented Maggie with the roses.

"For you, *ma chérie*," he said, and Maggie did not miss the glance he flicked at Jeremy, as if daring him to contradict the endearment. "With my apologies for last night. It was, I'm afraid, cut short by that, er, rather unfortunate incident."

Maggie gathered the beautifully arranged bouquet to her breast, thankful the florist had carefully stripped the blooms of thorns, yet feeling that she deserved more than a few pricks, for her hideous betrayal. Lord, how was she ever going to tell him? How could she hurt him so?

"Well," she said, nearly sick with regret, but hoping it didn't show too obviously. I'll tell him tonight, she said to herself. I'll get him alone, and I'll tell him tonight. "Well, thank you so much, Augustin. But really, you shouldn't have. It's I who should be apologizing—"

"No," Jeremy said, his deep voice calm.

Maggie shot him a quick warning glance, very much afraid they were about to have a repeat performance of last night's debacle. Jeremy, however, went on to say, very civilly, "I should be the one apologizing. I behaved scandalously toward you, Mr. de Veygoux. I wish to offer you my sincerest apologies.'' Jeremy extended his right hand stoically.

Augustin wasn't the only one who stared down at it incredulously. Both Maggie and Berangère, after a quick glance at one another, stared at it, as well. What, Maggie wondered frantically, is Jeremy up to? Has the malaria scrambled his brains? Could he possibly want to be *friends* with this man? *Why?*

Augustin was the first to recover. He reached out and grasped Jeremy's gloved right hand in his own. Neither man flinched at the other's grip, though Maggie suspected a certain amount of steeliness on both their parts.

"Apology accepted, Your Grace," Augustin said goodnaturedly. "And may I say that I appreciate your protectiveness of *Mademoiselle Marguerethe.* She has no family, as I am sure you know, who will stand by her, so it is gratifying to know that someone, at least, cares for her.''

Jeremy, to his credit, flushed at this statement and, releasing the older man's hand, said gruffly, "I suppose I got a little carried away last night. Maggie's always been . . . ahem . . . like a sister to me, and . . . well, I just want her to be happy.''

"So do I, Your Grace," Augustin said with a smile. Reaching out, he put an arm around Maggie's shoulders and squeezed, looking down at her worshipfully. "So do I.''

Maggie managed to smile weakly back up at him. Oh, Lord. This was going to be dreadful.

"So," Augustin said suddenly, his voice far too cheerful for the dour mood that pervaded the room. "What brings you here, Your Grace? Did you come to see the artist at work? She has some lovely things here, some lovely things. It's a good thing you chose to visit now, since tomorrow, they're all being packed away for transport to Bond Street. You know about her exhibition on Saturday, at my gallery? You'll be there for opening day, of course, won't you?''

"Indeed," Jeremy said, his gaze straying toward Maggie's face. She shook her head desperately, but he said, "I wouldn't miss it.''

"Good, good," Augustin cried. "She is going to be a smashing success, a smashing success. I wouldn't be surprised should she be asked to exhibit at the Royal Academy this May. No, not surprised at all. Were she to win a commission from the queen herself, I would not be surprised. She is a rare one, *Marguerethe* is."

"Yes," Jeremy said, never taking his eyes from her. "She is, isn't she?"

Augustin suddenly became aware of the direction of the duke's gaze, and that it was bold enough to have raised the color in his fiancée's cheeks. Looking from Maggie's face to Jeremy's, he asked the duke abruptly, "You *did* come here to see *Marguerethe*'s paintings, did you not, Your Grace?"

Maggie's heart flew into her throat when she saw Jeremy's expression. It was one of almost devilish delight. Oh, God, she thought, panicking. He's going to tell! He's going to tell! She wanted Augustin to know the truth, but not this way!

"Actually," Jeremy began, "I came to see—"

Jeremy was cut off mid-sentence, however, by Berangère, who leapt up from the divan and declared, quite loudly, "His Grace came to see *me*."

When all eyes, including Jeremy's, had turned upon her incredulously, she cried, with a laugh, "La, why do you look so surprised?" She tossed her head so that her many golden ringlets bounced becomingly, then stepped to Jeremy's side and grabbed hold of his arm with both hands. Berangère was petite enough to look doll-like beside the tall, athletically built duke—not unlike, Maggie realized, feeling something very like a knife blade slipping into her heart, how the Princess Usha would have looked beside him. "He is taking me to dinner. Dukes eat, too, you know, just like the rest of us."

Augustin beamed, clearly pleased by this turn of events. "What a coincidence," he cried. "*Marguerethe* and I are going to dinner, as well." At Maggie's sharp glance, he looked a trifle hurt. "You remember, surely, *Marguerethe*? We promised to dine with Lord and Lady Mitchell tonight. And I think, *chérie*, that if we are to be on time, you must go home now to change. My chaise is downstairs. Are you ready to go?''

Maggie, feeling the beginnings of a sharp headache behind her right eye, replied, ''Yes, of course, Augustin.'' She was careful not to meet Jeremy's gaze. ''Only let me get my wrap—''

Please, Maggie found herself praying. Please don't let him say anything to Augustin. Please don't let him say anything like *'I'll see you back home, then, won't I, Maggie?'* I've got to tell Augustin my own way, in my own time.

''Well,'' Jeremy said, straightening enough to let them pass. ''Good night, then.''

''*Bon soir*,'' Augustin said and, steering Maggie by the elbow, he guided her out into the hall.

''Good night,'' she said, so softly that she doubted Jeremy heard her.

They were nearly to the stairs, and Maggie was thinking that they were perfectly safe, when Jeremy's voice rang out down the hall.

''Oh, and Mags,'' he called.

She froze, one hand on the rickety balustrade, her foot poised and ready to sink down onto the first step.

''I'll see you back home, then, won't I?''

Chapter 27

"You are going about this all wrong," Berangère observed, as she peeled and ate yet another shrimp.

Across the table, Jeremy sat slumped with his chin in his hand, an elbow by the bowl into which Berangère was tossing the shells from the shrimp she was devouring with an appetite he envied. He himself had not managed, during the course of their dinner, to get more than a couple of whiskies down his gullet. But Berangère had managed to put away a dozen oysters, a tin of caviar, and a meringue. This was their second bowl of shrimp.

"I'm certainly going about *something* wrong," Jeremy agreed bitterly. "I'm sitting in a restaurant I can't abide with a woman I don't even know. I spent a fortune on ballet tickets I didn't use, while the woman I love is off God knows where with a man who is trying to kill me. Yes, I definitely get the impression I'm doing something wrong."

Berangère chewed elegantly, swallowed, and reached for her champagne flute. "It was a shame you had to waste the tickets," she said, after she'd drained her glass. "After you'd gone to the trouble of procuring them. That particular ballet has been sold out for weeks. However did you manage to get tickets to it?"

Jeremy shrugged carelessly. "Paid a fortune to some bloke on the street."

Berangère, watching him, suddenly burst out good-naturedly, "*Imbécile.*"

Jeremy blinked at her. "I beg your pardon?"

"You heard me. Why did you spend a fortune on tickets to the ballet, when *Marguerethe* does not even care for the ballet?"

"She doesn't?" Jeremy looked skeptical. "I thought all women loved the ballet."

"*Bête*," Berangère accused him. She reached for another shrimp. "Not *Marguerethe*. She says the sight of all those tiny women standing on their toes makes her feel clumsy as an elephant." Slipping her fingers beneath the hard shell, she neatly peeled away the seasoned flesh. "Myself, I have always loved the *pompe* of the ballet. I would have been a very great ballerina, I think. I am very small, and I have very nice feet." She glanced at him flirtatiously. "Would you like to look at my feet, *Jerry*?"

Jeremy blinked at her. Berangère Jacquard was a beautiful woman—more strictly beautiful than Maggie, with her golden hair, porcelain skin, heartbreakingly blue eyes, and pink cupid's-bow mouth, though not as beautiful as Usha— but then, what woman was? Dainty as a child, Berangère had a figure, he'd realized belatedly, when she'd emerged from her boudoir in evening dress, after insisting that they stop at her flat so that she could change before dinner, that was anything but childish: small but pert breasts, a reed-slim waist, and an extremely fetching backside, emphasized by an insouciant bustle of silk roses. Under any other circumstances, Jeremy would have jumped at an invitation to look at the feet of a woman like Berangère Jacquard.

Under the present circumstances, however, he'd have as soon accepted an invitation to look at her feet as he would an invitation to another ballet.

Berangère wasn't the least offended by his disinterest. In fact, it seemed to delight her.

"Ah," she said, popping the shrimp she'd peeled so arduously into her mouth. "I approve."

He looked at her miserably. The orchestra had launched into a polka, and on the stage, the dancing girls kicked up their heels and shook out their skirts, showing anyone who cared to look their black velvet garters.

Something, either the whisky, the noise, or the fact that Maggie was somewhere in London with another man, was giving Jeremy a headache.

"What did you say?" he asked Berangère.

"I approve of you," Berangère said. "For *Marguerethe*."

Jeremy laughed bitterly. "It's all well and good for *you* to approve of me, Miss Jacquárd. The problem is, *Maggie* doesn't approve of me."

"That is not the problem, Jerry."

Jeremy snorted. "No. The frog-eater's the problem."

Berangère frowned at him disapprovingly. "The problem is not Augustin, either."

Jeremy rolled his eyes. "I suppose you're going to tell me the problem is Usha."

"No. The problem is *Marguerethe*."

"Maggie?" He looked at her curiously. "What do you mean?"

It was Berangère's turn to roll her eyes. "*Mon Dieu! Think* a little, Jerry."

"Thinking is not my strong suit," Jeremy told her frankly. "I'm much better at tearing things up with my hands."

Berangère glanced down at those large brown hands as they curled around his whisky glass. She cleared her throat uncomfortably. "Yes," she said. "I can see that. However, we are talking about a love affair right now, not some sort of rebel uprising that needs to be subdued. This wooing of *Marguerethe* . . . it needs *finesse*, not fists."

Jeremy stared at her. "Why," he demanded suspiciously, "would *you* want to help *me* win over Maggie?"

Berangère seemed taken aback by the question. "Why, because *Marguerethe* is my friend," she said indignantly.

"Is she?" Jeremy looked skeptical. "You don't even call her by her real name."

"*Non*," Berangère said confidently. "*You* do not call her by her real name. *Marguerethe* is her real name, not this ugly sound you make, this Mag-gie." Berangère shuddered. "Ugh! I have never understood how you English can take a perfectly good name and ruin it beyond—"

"All right." Jeremy cut her off before she could launch into another lecture about the superiority of the French culture over the English. He'd already received several such lectures during the course of the evening. "All right. So Maggie's your friend."

"And I want my friends to be happy," Berangère said with a graceful shrug. "Especially *Marguerethe*. She is truly the sweetest, most genuine girl I have ever met." Berangère stabbed irritably at the shrimp on her plate. "She has been *most* abominably used by her dreadful family. I have walked into that studio and found her weeping—*weeping!*—at her easel, over the foul way her father and those sisters—bah!— have deserted her, just when she should be happiest, when she is being celebrated for her talent!" Berangère raised her eyes and pierced Jeremy with the intensity of her gaze. "I would like to see *Marguerethe* happy, if I can," she said. "And if, in order for her to be happy, she must have you, then I will do all that I can to see that she has you . . . even if it means I must plot against *Marguerethe* herself to make that happen."

Jeremy found himself blinking at the Frenchwoman once again. In the vehemence with which she expressed herself, she reminded him a little of his aunt . . . only Pegeen, he knew very well, had never offered to show her feet to anyone in a restaurant.

"All right," he said. "What do you suggest?"

Berangère's first suggestion was that he order another bottle of champagne; her glass was empty. Her next suggestion was that he convince Maggie's family to accept her decision to become a professional portrait painter.

Jeremy balked at the very idea. "How am I supposed to do *that*?" he demanded.

Berangère beamed as the waiter poured more champagne into her glass. "How do *I* know?" she said, when the waiter had succeeded in his task. "You're the duke. Cannot you order them to do it?"

"I most certainly cannot," Jeremy replied.

Berangère looked shocked. "Then what good is it, this being a duke, if you cannot make people do what you say?"

"It isn't any good," Jeremy said. "That's what I've been telling people half my life. The whole thing is a joke."

"Hmm." Berangère tapped the side of her champagne flute impatiently. "This is not good. *Marguerethe* needs her family's approval, you see. Unlike myself, *Marguerethe* actually cares what her family thinks about her. This business of theirs of not speaking to her because she has the gall to want to paint for a living . . . it has been very painful for her. It is my feeling that she clings to Augustin because he was the only person who stood by her when her father issued his—how do you say? Oh, yes—ultimatum. That is why, if you were able to change their minds, she would transfer that gratitude from Augustin to you."

"Why?" Jeremy asked.

Berangère lifted her eyes to the ceiling. "*Stupide!* Because in order for *Marguerethe* to stop feeling so indebted to Augustin, she must be made to feel indebted to someone else. Were you to give her back her family, she would realize that you had rendered her a very great service, a service that must be repaid."

Jeremy blinked. "All right," he said. "I'll do it." He didn't know how, but by God, he'd do it. He'd do *anything*, anything at all. "Any more ideas, Miss Jacquard?" Jeremy inquired.

Berangère finished off what was left in her glass and set the crystal goblet down again. "*Oui.* You might propose to her. A girl like *Marguerethe*, I am sure, would appreciate a marriage proposal, particularly after having made love for the first time." Berangère eyed him knowingly. "They are very old-fashioned, English girls."

Jeremy raised a single dark eyebrow. So Maggie had revealed to this Frenchwoman that she had made love with him already? Good God. He'd had no idea women revealed these kinds of things to one another.

And hadn't he asked Maggie to marry him that morning? After reflecting, he thought perhaps he hadn't. It was so hard to remember. They had made love half a dozen times, and then . . .

No. He hadn't asked. How rude! No wonder she was so

put out with him. He glanced at the Frenchwoman. "Done," he said. "Now may I ask *you* something, Miss Jacquard?"

"Of course," Berangère said, with a regal inclination of her head.

"What's the *real* reason you're helping me?" He eyed her interestedly. "Is it so that you'll be able to tell everyone you know that you're friends with the Duchess of Rawlings?"

Berangère smiled widely. "But of course!"

Jeremy smiled back at her. "I suppose," he said, "that being a duke does have its advantages, then."

"Oh, indeed it does, *Jerry*," Berangère agreed gravely. "Indeed it does."

Chapter 28

*M*aggie felt headachy and tired by the time she returned to the house on Park Lane. It was a relief to slip into her own room and close the door—though she'd been a bit surprised at not encountering the duke on the stairs. She hadn't dared to ask Evers if Jeremy was at home. She did not want to draw further attention to the fact that she was once again spending the night in the house alone with him—or at least, she assumed so.

Unless, after that unpleasant scene in her studio, Jeremy had found somewhere else to sleep. With the princess, for instance.

Maggie tried to keep such thoughts resolutely out of her mind. It wasn't anything to *her* where Jeremy slept. He could sleep at the foot of Princess Usha's bed for all she cared. All Maggie wanted to do was brush out her hair—Hill had stuck so many pins in her head in an attempt to hold up the heavy dark mass of curls that her scalp was beginning to throb—and go to bed.

Alone.

"Hill?" she called, as she stepped into her bedroom. The fire had been lit, and her bedcovers turned down, but there wasn't a sign of her maid. Jerry the dog appeared instead, leaping up from the bed pillows and bounding toward Maggie, yapping enthusiastically.

"*Bon soir*, Jerry," Maggie said, stooping to lift the dog and give his ears a good scratching. "*Ça va?* Has Hill walked you already?'' It was clear from the appreciative way the dog had thrown back his head while she petted him that going for a walk was the last thing on his mind. ''I see that she has. So where is she, eh? Gossiping belowstairs, I'll wager.''

Maggie went to the bell pull at the side of her bed and yanked on it once. Then she sat down at her dressing table, placing Jerry on her lap, and began to remove her elbow-length gloves. She supposed she ought to be grateful Hill wasn't about. She did not need another lecture about how inappropriate it was for her to remain in the town house without Lord and Lady Edward's presence. For Evers had assured her, as soon as she'd asked—which she had, the moment he'd greeted her at the front door—that the duke's aunt and uncle were apparently still in Yorkshire. The butler's disapproval, though it went unuttered, had been evident in his averted gaze as he took Maggie's cloak. Evers was no more pleased about the current living situation in the town house than Hill was.

Another night, Maggie reflected grimly, unchaperoned. Another black mark against her otherwise good name. A fitting end to a perfectly horrid day.

Maggie frowned as she pulled off her gloves and then started removing her jewelry. Lord, what a dreadful evening she'd had! What had started out as excruciatingly embarrassing had ended up being merely excruciating. Augustin, determined to show her that while the duke may have broken his nose, he could never break his spirit, had insisted upon dragging her from one nightspot to another after dinner, in defiance of both his cotton-packed nostrils and her weariness. Maggie hadn't even bothered to *pretend* to be enjoying herself. It was clear it did not matter to Augustin how *she* felt about the matter. He had made plans to wine and dine her, and he intended to carry them out. He was like a man possessed by the devil. . . .

And that devil, Maggie knew very well, was Jeremy Rawlings.

Not that Maggie blamed Augustin for trying. She quite understood what he was feeling . . . or at least, she thought she did. It was a humiliating thing, surely, for a man to be struck by another in front of his fiancée. And Augustin hadn't even been able to fight back, since that single blow had felled him. And then Jeremy had apologized, so Augustin couldn't even call him out—not that Augustin would have survived a duel with the Duke of Rawlings. No matter what weapon he chose—pistols, blades, or fists—Jeremy was master of them all, and would have made short work of the Frenchman in a fight of any sort.

Poor, poor Augustin. He had no way of knowing that Jeremy had bested him in another arena as well . . . and there hadn't been a single moment all evening when Maggie might have told him about it, either. Well, maybe that wasn't strictly true. There hadn't been a single moment when Maggie felt it *right* to tell him . . . if there ever was a right time to tell the man to whom one was engaged that one had lost one's virginity to another.

And Augustin had seemed to be in such high spirits, speaking excitedly of Maggie's exhibition on Saturday and his future plans for her career. While this kept Maggie from having to answer any embarrassing questions Augustin might have asked concerning Jeremy's parting remark earlier in the evening—she was fully prepared to assure him, regardless of the fact that it was untrue, that the duke's aunt was back from Yorkshire, making it perfectly all right for the two of them to remain in the same house—on the other hand, his blind inattention to what was going on under his very own, albeit broken, nose was a little bit odd. Was it possible that Augustin did not care as much for Maggie as she had allowed herself to believe? Was there a chance that, close friends that they were, that might be all there was to the relationship?

But no, that would be too much to ask. For Maggie to have been able to part company with Augustin without hurting his feelings at all. . . . No. Things like that simply did not happen. Twenty-four-carat sapphires did not fall from the sky, handsome young dukes did not forsake princesses for painters, and young women could not break off engagements without causing hurt feelings. . . .

That was where Jeremy was. With the princess. It had to

be. Jeremy was hardly the kind of man who'd spend a night alone. And since he wasn't with her, where else could he be? Why, after she'd so been rude to him at her studio, would he even consider spending the night with her, anyway? Maggie certainly hadn't done anything to make him think he might be welcome in her bed. . . .

Which he most definitely was *not*. She'd prove it, too. Tomorrow, she'd ask Augustin to loan her some money— she'd pay him back from the sales from her exhibition—and she'd move to a hotel. Not the Dorchester, of course. A different hotel. She'd ask Augustin for the name of a decent one. And then she needn't worry about chaperons or princesses or anything. She'd be on her own, completely on her own, just like in Paris. She'd tell Jeremy he could have his precious princess, for all she cared. It was better that way, she thought. Much better.

Though she would miss him. Maggie smiled softly to herself, recalling what a shock she'd had that morning, waking in Jeremy's arms—more than that, waking with Jeremy *inside* of her! Shocking it had been, but wonderful, too. What would it be like, she wondered, to wake up that way every morning, cocooned in Jeremy's arms, feeling his sweet breath in her hair? Would it be worth it? she wondered, as she pushed down the pink satin bodice of her gown. Would putting up with all the rigmarole of being a duchess be worth it if she could look forward to waking up every morning in Jeremy's arms?

She wasn't sure.

Maggie laid her ear bobs on the glass surface of her dressing table and stood up. After reaching behind her to undo the hooks to her evening gown, she stepped out of it, leaving the dress in a puddle on the floor while she went to work on the ties to her bustle. Maybe Jeremy was right. Maybe she really could have been a duchess and still managed to paint. After all, the queen painted, a little. Oh, she didn't have shows, but she still managed to find time to paint. . . .

Not, Maggie reminded herself, that it made any difference now. Jeremy had not asked her to marry him. In all of their conversations, both before and after having made love, he had never mentioned marriage. Oh, he'd said he wasn't marrying the Star of Jaipur. But he hadn't said he was marrying Maggie, either.

Dressed only in pantaloons and a corset, Maggie sat back down at the dressing table and regarded her reflection as she began to pull pins from her hair. How could she have been so wrong about him? She, who knew what he was! Had she been swayed by his looks? Certainly he was astonishingly good-looking—even with his malaria-sallowed complexion and crooked nose, Maggie thought him even handsomer than he'd been five years earlier. Of course, five years earlier, she hadn't had the privilege of seeing him naked. Since having done so, her estimation of his physical person had risen to even more dizzying heights. Even when sleeping, the swell of his biceps had been impressive, the ridges that lined his flat stomach clearly definable. Just thinking of that trail of dark hair that led down to the thick nest between his legs brought a flush to Maggie's cheeks. No, there was no doubt about it. Physically, Jeremy was as close to perfect as any man could be.

Intellectually, he was close to perfect, as well. What Jeremy lacked in the way of formal education, he more than made up for with his quick, native intelligence. He was, without a doubt, amusing. He had often made her laugh, even when she was on the verge of tears, with his quick sarcasm and dry wit. And there wasn't any question as to his bravery. One might almost accuse him of foolhardiness, he was so cavalier about his own personal safety. Why, he'd been stabbed in the shoulder, and had thought so little of the wound—and the incident—that he'd been making ardent love not an hour later. . . .

No, if there was such a thing as a perfect man, Jeremy, despite his tendency toward violence, was it. Maggie could hardly blame the princess for having fallen in love with him. After all, Maggie herself loved him.

When the last pin had been pulled from Maggie's coiffure, the thick, shining mass spilled down her shoulders. Sighing, she lifted her horsehair brush and went to work, trying to smooth the tangles away. It was not an easy job, and her arms quickly tired. She had been painting for stretches of up to ten hours a day all week, in order to finish up the works that would be shown on Saturday. Sometimes her wrists felt so sore, she could barely lift them. Now was one of those times. She'd had too little rest in the past twenty-four hours to tackle her hair. She'd leave it for Hill to wrestle with in the morning.

Laying aside the brush, Maggie sat slumped at the dressing table, staring into her lap. Hopefully, the exhibition on Saturday would be a success. Then, at least, worries over her immediate financial future would be over.

What she was going to do about her romantic future was another matter entirely.

As she sat with her head bent, Maggie became aware that someone had come into the room, and, assuming it was her maid, she said, without lifting her gaze from her lap, "Oh, Hill. Would you see what you can do about my hair? I'm afraid it's beyond me tonight."

She felt the heavy weight of her hair lifted, and she let out a little sigh of relief. But instead of the bite of horsehair bristles against the back of her neck, Maggie felt the warm pressure of a pair of lips. Gasping, she lifted her eyes to the mirror before her and saw Jeremy's reflection grinning back at her.

Chapter 29

You!'' she cried, twisting on the velvet stool to glare up at him. "What are *you* doing here?"

Jeremy shrugged, the grin broadening to a smile. "I live here, remember?"

Jeremy, standing behind her with a half-empty glass of what looked like whisky in his hand, his cravat, waistcoat, and jacket gone, and the first three or four buttons of his shirt undone, looked supremely unconcerned by her outrage. And supremely attractive. The shadowy light from the fire on the hearth cast half his face in darkness, but she could still see the silver glow of his eyes as he stared down at her, making her overly conscious of the fact that all she had on were her underthings. Through the opening in his shirt, she caught a glimpse of the rich mat of hair that carpeted his chest.

"Now," he said. "What was that about your hair?"

"Oh!" Maggie stood up, her fingers balled into fists at her side. "I thought you were Hill! What have you done with her?"

"With your maid?" Jeremy quirked up a dark eyebrow at her. "Not a thing. Are you always so suspicious, Mags? It isn't a very attractive quality—"

"When it comes to you, yes, I'm suspicious," Maggie snapped. "Now, where is Hill?"

Jeremy looked somber. "She had a little accident."

Maggie gasped. "What sort of accident? If you've hurt her, you callous—"

"Not that kind of accident," Jeremy said, rolling his silver eyes. "She accidentally drank some tea meant for me, and now she's sleeping it off down the hall."

"Oh, yes, I see. She *accidentally* drank some tea meant for you," Maggie sneered. "And just what was in this tea, may I ask?"

"Well, nothing that will cause any permanent damage," Jeremy assured her. "Just a little opium."

"Opium!" Maggie stared at him, slack-jawed, hardly daring to believe her ears. "*You drugged my maid*?"

Jeremy winced, flashing a hasty glance at the bedroom door. "It won't hurt her," he said. "And keep your voice down, will you? I didn't drug the rest of the household, you know, just her. Unless you want Evers beating down the door, I suggest you—"

"You *admit* it?" Maggie clapped both her hands to her cheeks. "You *admit* that you drugged her?"

"Well, of course I did," Jeremy replied casually, as if it were the most obvious course of action in the world. "After the fuss you made this morning, about how shocked she was that you and I were spending the night under the same roof without a chaperon, I deemed it best. How else was I going to get to be alone with you tonight?"

"Get to be . . ." Maggie's voice trailed off as she ogled him in astonishment. The man had to be insane. The malaria must have affected his brain. She was alone in her bedroom with a lunatic. A lunatic who had drugged her maid. "Jeremy," she cried at last. "You can't go around drugging people!"

"Why not?" Jeremy was beginning to grow tired of the discussion. While it was entertaining to watch Maggie hop about the room in outrage, considering that all she had on was a corset and pair of pantaloons, through which he could see some interesting dark patches, he decided it was time to steer the conversation in a more profitable direction. "I got what I wanted, didn't I? You and I are alone together again."

And to insure that it stayed that way, Jeremy crossed the

room in three long strides, stopping only when he reached the door. Carefully setting the empty whisky glass aside, he bent down, and turned the key neatly in the lock. Maggie heard the bolt slide into place, making the room inaccessible from the hallway. Then, casting a challenging glance at Maggie over his shoulder, Jeremy deliberately withdrew the key, and dropped it into his trouser pocket. Only then did he straighten. A smile, which Maggie could only have described as diabolical, spread over his handsome face.

Un duc diabolique. Berangère had not been wrong.

Maggie continued to stare at him as if he had taken leave of his senses. A part of her wanted to burst out laughing at the very idea of the Duke of Rawlings locking himself into a bedroom with the youngest daughter of his steward. But another part of her failed to see the humor in the situation. In fact, her heart had begun to thud rather irregularly inside her chest. *She was locked inside a bedroom with the Duke of Rawlings.*

She didn't have to be a genius to figure out what was going to happen next.

But that didn't mean she had to go along with it. On the contrary. Just who did he think he was? He couldn't go around drugging women's maids and then locking himself into their bedrooms. What sort of behavior was that for a military hero? And if it really was another seduction he had planned, then he was going to be in for a sorry surprise. Maggie hadn't the slightest intention of ever making love with him again, on this or any other night.

"Well," she said, folding her arms over her breasts, hoping to hide the evidence of her wildly beating heart. "I hope you're proud of yourself. In the past twenty-four hours, you managed to break the nose of an unarmed man, nearly get yourself killed—"

"Twice," Jeremy pointed out.

"Twice?" She couldn't help looking at him in astonishment.

"Right. Somebody tried to run me down outside *The Times* this morning."

"Oh," Maggie said. "So. After you'd seduced another

man's fiancée, you had your engagement to an Indian princess announced in *The Times*, then you drugged a maid, and locked yourself into the bedroom of a woman who despises you. Congratulations. I'm sure the queen would be delighted to hear that this is how her officers comport themselves while they're off duty.''

"You don't despise me," Jeremy said confidently.

"No?" It was Maggie's turn to raise a skeptical eyebrow. "Really? You ignored me for five years, got yourself engaged to an Indian princess, assaulted my fiancé, took my virginity, and drugged my maid. Yes, Jeremy, I think it would be safe to say I despise you."

"I didn't take your virginity," he pointed out. "You gave it to me."

Maggie glared at him. "You could have said no."

"Me?" He laughed outright. "Refuse the offer of a beautiful woman?"

Maggie pointed angrily at the door. "Get out. Now," she said, accompanying each word with a stamp of her stockinged foot upon the carpet.

"Why, Miss Herbert," he cried delightedly, ignoring her command to leave. "You're jealous!"

"Ha!" Maggie sniffed at the outrageous suggestion. "Not very likely!"

"No," Jeremy said, shaking his head. His white teeth gleamed in the firelight as he approached her, grinning. When he stood just a foot away, he reached out to tuck a finger under her chin, forcibly bringing her face up toward his when she refused to look at him. "No," he said, gazing down at her happily. "You are definitely, positively jealous. But why, Mags? Surely you couldn't think anything would happen between your friend Miss Jacquard and I. After all, I think I've made it very clear to you that you're the only woman I've ever cared about in my life."

Maggie flinched, jerking her head from his grasp. His closeness was making breathing, which was difficult enough in her tight corset, an impossibility. "*That's* where you were? With *Berangère*? Then . . . then you and the princess didn't—'' She broke off, unable to finish a sentence to which she already knew the answer.

He shook his head, the smile gone. There was a touch of sadness now in his silver eyes. ''Sweet Jesus, Mags, what do you take me for? Haven't you heard a word I've been saying? There's only one girl for me, and that's you, even if you're too mule-headed to see it. If you must know, I spent the entire evening listening to your friend Berangère talk about you.'' He smoothed some of her wayward curls from her cheek. ''She's a better friend to you than you are to yourself, Mags.''

Oh, Lord. What had Berangère been telling him? Berangère was a born talker, liked nothing better than a good gossip. You could no sooner trust her with a secret than you could the corner fishmonger. God only knew what she'd been telling Jeremy.

''What do you mean?'' Maggie inquired defensively.

''Only that Miss Jacquard agrees with me,'' he said. His hand had lingered on her cheek after brushing the loose hair away, and now he dragged it down, tracing the smooth arc from her jawline to her shoulder with his callused index finger.

Maggie tried to ignore the shiver that coursed up and down her spine as he did this. More difficult to ignore was the fact that the shiver sent both peaks of her breasts hardening in the lace cups of her corset. She prayed Jeremy wouldn't notice. ''Agrees with you about what?'' she demanded, hoping to distract him.

''That you're a fool,'' he said, in the softest voice imaginable, as he calmly followed the ivory shelf of her collarbone with his finger, ''if you marry Augustin.''

''And is Berangère aware,'' Maggie asked, though her mouth had gone dry as sand at the thought of what he'd do if he noticed the way her nipples had responded to his touch, ''that you disappeared out of my life five years ago? Was I supposed to just sit and wait until you made up your mind to come home? I wasn't supposed to live any sort of life in the meantime?''

''All you needed to do was send me a line, Mags.'' The

finger slid down to press against the beginning swell of her right breast, just where her heart was drumming hardest. "A single line, and I'd have been home in an instant."

"Oh, really?" Maggie drawled, her unease making her seek refuge in sarcasm.

"Yes, really," Jeremy replied. He was standing so close to her that she could smell the scent of clean man emanating from his open shirtfront. Had she reached out her hand, she could have combed her fingers through his chest hair. "For five years I waited for some word from you, some hint as to whether or not there was any hope for me, only to learn from my aunt that you had become engaged to another man—"

"Your aunt?" Maggie blinked up at him, confused. "Lady Edward . . . ?"

"She wrote to me a few months ago, warning me about the announcement of your engagement," Jeremy admitted, watching, not without some satisfaction, as Maggie's mouth fell open. "I asked her, before I left, to keep me informed of all your activities while I was in India. Whatever she heard from your mother or sisters, she related in her correspondence to me. When she found out about your engagement, she wrote me. I boarded the first ship for England I could find."

"You . . ." Maggie was aware that she kept opening and then closing her mouth, like a goldfish that had suddenly thrown itself out of its bowl and onto the carpet, but she couldn't help herself. The realization of what he had said was only just sinking in. He had come all the way back to England because his aunt had written to him that Maggie was getting married? He had left a sickbed—a malarial sickbed—in order to stop her from marrying someone else?

He had known all along that she was engaged, had feigned ignorance of the fact at the cotillion, just for the malicious pleasure of watching her stammer out an explanation?

"You!" she burst out furiously, slapping his hand away from her heart. "You knew all along! The night you came home, when you sat on my bed . . . and then at the cotillion, you pretended—" She sucked in a lungful of air, feeling as if she were going to explode. "And I was in agony the whole time, wondering how I was going to tell you, when it turns out you knew all along! You were planning on hitting him from the beginning, weren't you? You came to the cotillion with the express purpose of hitting Augustin, and mortifying me in front of all those people!''

"Now, Mags," Jeremy said, holding up a warning finger. His gray eyes, however, glinted with amusement. "Watch that temper of yours—''

Maggie let out a strangled scream, her fingers balling into fists.

And before Jeremy could say another word in his own defense, Maggie launched herself at him, fists first. It was only thanks to his well-honed military training that Jeremy ducked in time to avoid receiving one of those fists in his mouth. To his very great astonishment, however, Maggie spun around at the last moment and sank her fist into his midriff instead. The blow didn't hurt—she didn't have enough upper body strength to really do him any damage, and besides, his stomach muscles were tough as iron—but it surprised him a good deal, especially since the move was one he had taught her himself, back when they'd been children.

"I say," he declared, straightening up with a smile. "Good show, Mags! You've been working on that right cross of yours, I see."

"You," was all Maggie could say, through teeth gritted against the pain in her right hand. Who'd have thought a man's stomach could be so hard? She felt as if she had punched a wall. "Get out of my room!"

"Now, Mags, really," Jeremy said, eyeing her as she circled him, obviously looking for another opening through which to strike at him again. "This is ridiculous. You're going to hurt yourself. Why don't we try to discuss this like adults, shall we? After all, we aren't children anymore—''

With a cry of sheer rage, Maggie went for him again, this time with both fists raised, apparently with the intention of pummeling his face to pulp. Jeremy, alarmed more by the strange sound she'd made than by the fact that she was trying to hit him again, threw up both his hands, and neatly caught her by the wrists, which he hauled into the air, causing her corset to gap rather fetchingly in the front. Not willing to be subdued without a fight, Maggie swung a stockinged foot at his shin, succeeding only in stubbing her toes against impossibly hard bone, which caused her to wince and let out a yelp of pain.

That was when Jeremy finally lost his patience.

"You see," he chided, as she twisted and thrashed in his arms, trying to break his iron-hard grip around her wrists. "I told you you were going to hurt yourself. And look what happened."

"Let . . . go . . . of . . . me!" Maggie snarled.

"Not until you've calmed down," Jeremy informed her. "You're a menace to your own—Ah!" This last was uttered as a set of small, but very sharp, teeth sank into the fingers he'd wrapped round Maggie's wrists. A quick glance showed him that while she hadn't drawn any blood, it was not for lack of trying. Jeremy stared down at her, a stunned expression on his face.

"Why, you little—"

Maggie didn't hear what he ended up calling her after *little*, because on the second syllable of that word, his shoulder suddenly heaved into her abdomen, sending her corset stays prodding painfully into her ribs, and consequently knocking the breath out of her. A second later, her feet were in the air, and her head was dangling down Jeremy's broad back. All the blood in her body immediately began rushing down toward the roots of her hair.

"What," Maggie gasped, when she could summon up enough breath to speak, "do you think you're doing?"

"Something I've been wanting to do all day," Jeremy growled, wrapping one arm loosely around her rear end, while with his free hand he seized one of her flailing ankles, to keep her from kicking him in the face as he strode forward.

"Put me down, you barbarian," Maggie sputtered. All she could see, besides the seat of Jeremy's trousers, was the floor moving rapidly above her head. She was dizzy enough that she'd lost all sense of direction, and could not imagine where

Jeremy was headed. Feeling suddenly sure that he was going to take her out into the hallway, or even possibly parade her up and down Park Lane, she began to struggle even more desperately. "Put me—"

"Gladly."

As if she were no heavier than a sack of flour, he flung her from his shoulder. Maggie let out a terrified shriek as the room spun wildly about her, then abruptly quieted when her back sank into the soft mattress of her own bed. Struggling up to her elbows, conscious of her throbbing knuckles, toes, and now, ribs, Maggie swept some of her tangled hair from her face and eyed him where he stood glaring down at her from the side of the bed.

"Are you going to behave rationally now?" he inquired politely, though there was nothing polite in the way his silver eyes, already flashing with ire, swept her body, laid out before him like a trussed ham.

Maggie looked at him, his own dark hair mussed from where she'd grabbed at it, his thickly haired chest rising and falling as rapidly as her own. As sullenly as she'd used to when they'd been children, and Jeremy, always the elder, the self-declared "more mature" of the pair, had posed the self-same question, Maggie snapped, "No!"

The silver eyes flared. "No?" His lips curled upward with delight, and Maggie felt her heart lurch. "You can't imagine how happy I am to hear you say that."

Chapter 30

*C*onsidering how loudly Maggie screeched when Jeremy launched himself at her, it was probably a good thing that he had drugged her maid. Maggie didn't realize, of course, that he intended to brace his fall with his hands. All she knew was that suddenly, two hundred and some pounds of un-adulterated male was flying toward her. She was convinced that he was trying to kill her, and attempted to protect her head with her hands, just in case.

But killing Maggie wasn't what Jeremy had had in mind at all. Far from it, as a matter of fact.

He still managed to pin her to the bed, though most of his body weight was supported by his arms; he had thrust a hand out on either side of her. Maggie didn't dare peek out from between her fingers until nearly a minute had passed, and the bed had stopped bouncing. Risking a brief, upward glance, she saw that Jeremy was smiling down at her dev-ilishly.

Her heart hammering against her corset stays, Maggie said, "All right, you've made your point. Now get out."

"Actually," Jeremy said, his grin widening, "I haven't even *begun* to make my point. . . ."

And then she felt one of his thighs, which had settled between hers, press against the gusset of her pantaloons. Startled, Maggie started to protest, but Jeremy lowered him-self to his elbows, and silenced her with his lips.

Oh, no, she groaned to herself, her heart drumming erratically inside her chest. *Not again.*

But it was happening again, and just like before, she felt powerless to stop it—didn't *want* to stop it. Once again, he was assailing all of her senses, until it seemed as if the only thing that existed in her world was Jeremy. Not just her sense of sight—though her entire field of vision was filled with him, the bronzed planes of his face, the cleft in his chin, the sharp curve of his Adam's apple. Not just her sense of touch, either—though she was more than a little conscious of the way his day's growth of beard felt against the soft skin of her face, and of the heat that seemed to radiate from his open shirtfront as he kept himself suspended just inches from her.

No, it was her other senses, the ones of which she was hardly aware until he walked into a room, that seemed to become hypersensitive to his presence. His uneven breathing sounded harsh to her ears, but thrilling, too, when she realized that *she* was the reason for that unsteadiness. What was it about the guttural—but appreciative—noises that Jeremy made when he was kissing her that made her feel so weak and melting? It was as if the very idea that he could not control these noises—as if he himself was out of control—appealed to her on some sort of animal level.

But that wasn't the only thing animalistic about their attraction to one another. Were she blindfolded and put in a room with a hundred men, Maggie would have been able to pick Jeremy out by his scent alone, it was that distinctive to her. Distinctive . . . and arousing. Maggie's nipples never failed to harden from the scent of him alone, though what could be so erotic about the mingled odors of soap, whisky, tobacco, and, very faintly, horse, she was certainly at a loss to explain. Still, whenever his peculiarly masculine scent filled her nostrils, she was nearly overwhelmed by a feeling of contentment, as if . . .

As if she were smelling home.

He even *tasted* like something from her past, something good, something she'd had for dessert once and had liked immensely. Something not quite sweet, but not at all sour. Bitter . . . but not unpleasant. Not unpleasant at all. . . .

Why, *why* did it have to be this way? *Why* did it have to be so hard to keep herself from loving him? Why couldn't he have smelled of garlic, as Augustin inevitably did, thanks to his Parisian cook? Why did he have to taste so good, to *sound* so good? Why was he so appealing to her?

Why hadn't she thought to lock her bedroom door the minute she'd come home?

Then his lips moved to her neck, and Maggie was incapable of thinking anymore. Instead, she arched her throat, which thrust her breasts, her nipples hard as pebbles in the cups of her camisole, against Jeremy's furred chest, eliciting a groan from him. A second later, his hands were inside those lace cups, lifting her breasts and bringing them—first one, and then the other—to his lips. Now the razor stubble around his mouth was grazing her sensitive aureoles as he suckled her, and Maggie sunk her fingers into his broad shoulders in reaction, a soft moan escaping her own lips.

This only seemed to encourage him, however, to acts of an even more intimate nature. Before Maggie knew what he was about, Jeremy was untying the bow that held her pantaloons in place and stealthily lowering her drawers over her hips. It was only then that Maggie realized that the cotton had become drenched with her own desire for him. Lord, and she'd been trying so hard to make him think she didn't care for him a bit! Tearing her hands from his shoulders, she tried to fling them protectively over what he had revealed to the lamplight, but he only chuckled softly at her sudden modesty.

And then he plucked her fingers aside, and inserted his own into the moist down, his eyes hooded in the half-light, the lids appearing to be drooping a little drowsily.

But Jeremy was far from feeling drowsy. He was watching Maggie's reactions to his touch intently, glorying in every undulation of her hips, every sigh that escaped her. With her waist so tightly corseted, her breath was coming in shorter and shorter bursts, but he could not bring himself to undo the laces, since she looked so incredibly feminine, with her heavy breasts and creamy hips bared, and that narrow band of pink satin cinching her middle, sloping to an em-

phatic V just below her navel, as if the garment were pointing to that part of Maggie which already drew his gaze so
hypnotically.

It wasn't just his gaze that black triangle drew, either. His
lips had already begun burning a trail along the inside of one
shapely thigh. Maggie, her head thrown back and her eyes
closed, her long hair streaming out across the white pillows,
very kindly accommodated him by parting her legs just a
little farther. . . .

And Jeremy bent, his unruly hair falling forward to brush
against her thighs, to explore that damp tangle of curls, not
with his fingers this time, but with his lips and tongue.

Maggie nearly bucked him off the bed. Instinctively, she
clamped her thighs shut, effectively trapping Jeremy in a grip
that, while highly erotic, was somewhat restrictive.

"What . . ." she gasped astonishedly, "are you *doing*?"

His voice sounding slightly strangled, Jeremy replied, "If
you'd let go of my head, I'd show you."

"But it isn't . . . you mustn't. . . ." Even as she spoke,
however, Maggie was relaxing, sinking back against the pillows. Jeremy used the opportunity to slip his hands between
her thighs and pry them gently apart.

"Jeremy, it isn't *right*. . . ."

But the words ended on a sigh of pure bliss as Jeremy's
tongue delved into her velvet furrow. Now *this* was something Maggie had certainly never heard any of the girls back
at Madame Bonheur's discuss . . . but it was the most delightful sensation she'd ever experienced—well, second to
actually having Jeremy inside of her, anyway. Reaching
down, she sank her fingers into Jeremy's thick hair, guiding
his head as he laved her, marveling at the ripples of pleasure
he was evoking within her.

And then, sooner than she would have thought possible,
those ripples turned to waves. Instead of coursing gently over
her, they began to slam into her, each one harder than the
last. And yet none of them managed to put out the flame that
was licking inside her, growing steadily hotter as he continued his ruthless assault. Her breathing, which had been uneven, turned into short, erratic gasps. The fingers in his hair

fisted, as if she were clutching the reins to a fractious horse.

Then, as he cupped her buttocks in his hands to bring her closer to his mouth, she bucked again . . . but this time with joy. Because suddenly, it seemed to Maggie as if she'd finally been swept up by one of those waves . . . higher and higher, until this time, it crested with her upon it. It doused the flame, drenching it completely. She cried out hoarsely at the immense satisfaction of it, her limbs trembling all over with the intensity of the experience, as if she really *had* been plunged into an icy sea of turquoise and foam. And when it was all over, she certainly felt as depleted and drowsy as she'd used to as a child, climbing out of the pond on the grounds of Rawlings Manor on a hot summer day, dripping wet. . . .

But she was only allowed to luxuriate in her lethargy for a second or two, however, before Jeremy's face reappeared in her line of vision. He wore an expression she recognized, one of extreme self-satisfaction, though at the same time, there was a glimmer of something else in his gray eyes. Maggie didn't recognize what it was until he'd reared up onto his knees. Then, his gaze hard upon her, his fingers began to work the buttons to his trousers. When his erection sprang free of the clinging fabric, Maggie's own eyes widened. Why, of course. That undefinable something in his face was *need*.

Need for *her*.

Which was why Maggie didn't question it when he reached over her head and grabbed one of the down-filled pillows, then tucked it, determinedly, under her hips. She didn't say a word when, without even bothering to take off his shirt, having shoved his trousers down only far enough for them to be out of his way, Jeremy positioned himself between her legs, his arms braced on either side of her. She gave the engorged organ hovering just inches from her a single, trepidatious look—it still seemed technically impossible to her that something so large could fit into a space so small, even though she'd witnessed the marvel for herself more than once in the past twenty-four hours—then lifted her gaze to meet Jeremy's. . . .

And quickly realized, as he plunged into her, what the pillow was for: It lifted and tilted her hips to just such an angle that he could practically embed himself within her. It almost seemed as if he managed to touch the back of her spine with the tip of his penis, a not unpleasurable sensation. But that wasn't all the pillow did. It drove the folds of skin just below her pubic bone into his abdomen, working as effectively as his tongue had at stimulating what was hidden there. Suddenly, the satiated feeling left her, and she found herself being swept into yet another glittering eddy of desire . . . only this time, Jeremy was there with her, riding the same incredible waves.

How long it was before the crystalline sea tossed them both back to shore, Maggie wasn't sure. Time seemed to stand still . . . and then, as she fought to catch her breath, wasted from yet another bone-wracking orgasm, Jeremy let out a thunderous yell. Startled, Maggie glanced up at his face, and saw that it was contorted with something very much like pain . . . then, a second later, the anguished expression turned to one of beatific contentment. Jeremy collapsed unceremoniously on top of her, his bare chest slick against hers, his breath hot in her ear.

"Now," he whispered, in a voice that was so full of lethargy, it was almost a purr, "d'you see why I drugged your maid?"

"I'm beginning"—though Maggie's words were pert, her tone matched his in laziness "—to get the idea."

"*Beginning* to get it?" Jeremy sighed. "I can see it's going to be a long night. . . ."

Chapter 31

When Maggie woke next, it was because Jerry, her dog, was breathing hotly into her face. Shoving him away did no good. He sat right back down in front of her, and panted some more.

Finally Maggie lifted her head to squint at the clock on her bedside table. Surely, if it was time for Jerry to be walked, it was time for Hill to come in and prepare her bath. Where was Hill?

But Maggie found that she could not see the clock on her bedside table, primarily because a massive bare shoulder blocked it from view. Staring at the shoulder, her sleep-blurred eyes coming sharply into focus all at once, Maggie was struck with the horrible realization that there was a *man* in her bed.

A *man*. In *her* bed.

Then memory came flooding back, and with it, a sense of mortification that sent hot color rushing into her cheeks. Good God. She had spent the night with Jeremy Rawlings. *Again.*

More than just spent the night with him, too. When Maggie thought of all the things they'd done during the night, her blush deepened to a fiery red. Oh, God, how could she have allowed it to happen? Once was pardonable. Twice, though reprehensible, was understandable, having liked it so much the first time. But three . . . no, four . . . Lord, how many was it now? She could hardly keep track. But plenty. Plenty of times.

And still no proposal. No explanation—that she could believe—of the Princess Usha's claims. Not even a single "I love you."

And she had fallen into bed with him like a dockside doxy.

Again.

How could she have allowed it to happen again? *How*?

But another glance at Jeremy, sleeping soundly beside her, revealed the answer to that question only too readily. Lying on his side, naked to the waist, his tanned skin startlingly dark against the blinding whiteness of the sheets, he reminded her of a slumbering god. Which god, though? He was far too large to be Pan, though he definitely had Pan's mischievous personality. He was too dark to be Apollo, though even in repose, his well-formed muscles were evident. Perhaps he was Vulcan. There was something extremely diabolical about his thick black eyebrows, which, when he was awake, he was always lifting skeptically. Yes, Vulcan it was going to have to be. . . .

Maggie roused herself. Good Lord, what was the matter with her? She was slipping off into one of her painting dream worlds, when she had problems right here, in the real world! What was she going to do about this sleeping man in her bed?

She could tell by the gray light drifting in through the sheer white curtains that it was morning, nine o'clock at least. Any minute, Hill would be walking in . . . or at least she'd try to walk in. When she found the door locked, Hill was bound to panic, since in the course of her service to the Herberts, not a one of them had ever locked a door. And then Hill, in her fright, would rouse Evers, and Evers would undoubtedly call the footmen, and then Jeremy would have to unlock the door just in order to keep it from being smashed down. And then the entire household would know that Maggie and Jeremy had . . .

Maggie leaned over and shook Jeremy's broad shoulder. "Jeremy," she whispered urgently. "Jeremy, wake up!"

Jeremy sighed in his sleep and rolled over, so that his face was just inches from hers.

"Jeremy," Maggie whispered again. "I mean it. You have to get up."

Jeremy, without opening his eyes, reached out and snaked an arm around her naked waist. Even half-asleep, his strength was impressive. He pulled her against him as easily as if she were a ragdoll. "Morning, Mags," he murmured into her hair.

"Don't you 'good morning' me," she hissed. "You've got to get out of here, before the servants get wind of it."

"Hmmm," Jeremy said, burying his face into the clouds of her hair, to nuzzle her neck, just below her left ear. "You're always so pleasant in the morning, Mags. It's one of the things I love about you. You're terribly consistent."

"I mean it, Jeremy," Maggie said. She tried to ignore the shivering sensation he was creating as he nibbled at her earlobe. "Hill could knock at any second—"

"Oh, Hill won't be knocking," Jeremy informed her, lazily stroking her left breast. He watched in fascination as her responsive nipple immediately hardened beneath his touch.

"What do you mean, Hill won't be knocking?" Maggie narrowed her eyes suspiciously at him. "You said you drugged her. Surely . . ." She gasped. "Jeremy, you didn't *kill* her, did you?"

Jeremy raised an eyebrow. "Of *course* not. What do you take me for, Mags? I only meant that the opium I slipped her last night has a rather, er, debilitating effect on the uninitiated the following morning—"

"You mean—"

"She'll probably sleep through most of today," Jeremy said, with badly feigned regret. "If she hasn't vomited it all up, of course."

"Jerry!" Maggie was so horrified, she didn't even notice that the dog leapt excitedly to his feet at her cry, and began leaping about the bed pillows, yapping. "How *could* you?"

"Stop fussing over the woman," Jeremy said, annoyed that she kept moving out of his reach. "I'll give her a raise when she comes to. She'll be fine."

"A *raise*? Jerry, I haven't been able to pay her regular wages in six months!"

Jeremy blinked at her. "Oh, well, then. I'll give her her back wages, a raise, and a bonus for her loyalty."

Maggie leaned back against the pillows, flicking an annoyed glance at him. "I think," she said, "that the person who drugged the maid should have to walk the dog."

One of Jeremy's dark eyebrows lifted. He looked as if he were trying very hard to frown, but one corner of his mouth kept curling upward, betraying his amusement at her declaration. "Oh, you think so, do you?"

"I do," Maggie said with a nod, leaning back against the pillows primly.

Jeremy gave up trying to frown, and smiled instead, all of his white, even teeth showing. "All right, then," he said with a shrug. "Come on, Jerry. Papa's taking you for a walk."

The little white dog shook itself happily, and waddled to the end of the bed, where it leapt down upon an ottoman Maggie had put there for that very purpose, and from the ottoman to the floor. Jeremy threw back the bedclothes and rose, stretching until his joints popped audibly. Maggie, in the bed, knew she ought not to look at his naked backside, but she was completely incapable of tearing her eyes away. Jeremy's buttocks were perfectly rounded, with concave indentations on either side of them, and not a hint of the coarse black hair that covered the rest of his body. He was, as Maggie had already determined, a perfect specimen of the human male, both frontward and back. How Madame Bonheur would have adored him as a model for their anatomy class! His inguinal ligament was really quite pronounced.

"Jerry's lead," Maggie said, clearing her throat a little as she watched Jeremy struggle into the trousers he'd abandoned the night before at some point during their lovemaking, "is hanging on a hook in back of the door to the dressing room."

Growling to himself, Jeremy padded barefoot to the door, and found the collar and lead. "Right," he said. "I'll just pop back down to my own room for something more suitable to wear. I do think the neighbors will talk if I appear walking down Park Lane in my evening wear at nine in the morning.''

''Whatever you like,'' Maggie said airily.

Jeremy bent to fasten the dog's collar, but the bichon frise twisted and cavorted so excitedly, it took him nearly a minute to find the tiny gold clasp. Maggie watched from the bed, bemused. When Jeremy finally succeeded in securing the dog, he straightened, and looked at her.

Sitting up in the white bed, with her dark hair tumbled wildly about her shoulders and a sheet tucked modestly up beneath her arms, Maggie looked exactly as he'd imagined she would after a night of torrid lovemaking. Her lips bore a slightly bruised appearance, from all the kissing they'd done, and there was a shine in her eyes he'd never seen before. More than anything, he wanted to crawl right back into bed with her. Damn the stupid dog, anyway.

''At your peril,'' he said warningly, ''do you move out of that bed before I return. Do you understand me, Mags? We have some things to discuss, you and I.''

Maggie, observing the challenge in his silver eyes, nodded mutely. She did not think arguing was worth the risk of delaying Jerry's much-needed trip outdoors.

Jeremy, apparently satisfied with her response, put his hand on the doorknob. When it would not turn, he reached into his trouser pocket, ignoring Maggie's derisive snort from the bed, and pulled out the key, remembering, albeit belatedly, that he'd locked it the night before to insure no interruptions. After casting a final warning glance at Maggie, he opened the door, peered out to make sure no one was watching, then slipped into the hallway, the dog bounding excitedly behind him.

Maggie, in the bed, smiled to herself. Jeremy had left behind his shirt, his socks, and his shoes, all strewn across the floor and jumbled with her own clothing from the night before. He was not, she noted, the world's tidiest person, but then, neither was she. That was probably why they got along so well. Augustin was incredibly tidy, and was forever harping at her for balling her gloves into her pockets and leaving her brushes soaking overnight. . . .

Then, as if someone had poured a pitcher of cold water down her back, Maggie bolted upright. Good God. Augustin. The exhibition. The exhibition was opening tomorrow night. The men were arriving to transport Maggie's paintings at eleven. That was in—Maggie glanced at the clock on her bedside table—an hour and a half!

In a flash, Maggie was out of bed, and tugging on the bell pull.

Down the hall, Jeremy threw open the door to his own bedroom and strode across it, Maggie's dog leaping up against his legs, his little claws sinking in deeper and deeper each time.

"I *know*," Jeremy snapped at the dog crossly. "I'm going as fast as I can."

He banged open the door to his dressing room, waking Peters, who'd taken to sleeping on a cot beneath Jeremy's many coats, despite an offer of his own room in the servants' quarters upstairs. The valet apparently felt such a move might keep him from being readily available, should his colonel need him quickly.

"Colonel," he cried happily, sitting up and wiping sleep from his eyes. "Bless me, is it morning already? Where 'ave you been? I waited up as long as I could, sir—"

"Yes, yes," Jeremy said sourly. He dragged Jerry forward on his lead. "Walk this, will you?"

Peters looked down at the excited little dog, and the smile on his face faded. "Colonel! You can't be serious. *Me?* Walk *that?* I'll be the laughingstock of the—"

"Just do it," Jeremy cut him off succinctly. "Now. What did you discover last night, tailing the frog-eater?"

Peters's scowl grew even darker. "That if 'e's the one what tried to kill you, 'e musta 'ired somebody else to do it. The Frenchie don't 'ave it in 'im, colonel. 'Is light was out by midnight. I never saw a man less likely to stab somebody else wi' a knife, much less run 'em over with a chaise-and-four."

Jeremy, flicking through the many garments hanging from

rods above his head, asked irritably, "Where's my dressing gown? The silk one?"

Peters reached beneath the cot for his wooden leg, which he hastened to fasten on beneath the trousers he'd fallen asleep in. "Right there to your left, Colonel. You want me to keep tailin' 'im then, sir?"

"Yes, of course." Jeremy thrust his arms through the wide sleeves of a dressing gown made from Indian silk, embroidered all over with images of peacocks and tigers. "What other suspects do we have? It's *got* to be the frog-eater."

Peters looked skeptical. "If you say so, sir."

Jeremy reached around his valet for the Star of Jaipur, which rested in its velvet sack on top of a chest of dresser drawers. Jeremy lifted the small bag, and opened it. The heavy sapphire rolled out into his palm, winking even in the dim light of the dressing room He tossed the sapphire into the air, then caught it, and dropped it into the deep pocket of his dressing gown. "Anything else, Peters?"

"Just this, sir." Peters removed a folded square of paper from his trouser pocket. With a sinking heart, Jeremy recognized his aunt's neat cursive, though the address looked as if it had been written in haste. Obviously hand-delivered, since it bore no postmark, its bearer had undoubtedly traveled all night to bring it from Rawlings Manor. "Looks like you've been found out, sir."

"Damned newspaper article," Jeremy growled.

Tearing the letter open, he scanned its contents briefly. He'd been found out, all right. Pegeen was furious. Apparently some complications—minor, but serious enough to have alarmed the surgeon—had kept her from making the trip back to London after the funeral, and Edward had stayed with her. But the fact that Pegeen was bedridden had not kept news of Jeremy's return to England from creeping back to her. She had an uncanny knack, he remembered, too late, for ferreting out all sorts of information from the servants . . . even servants over a hundred miles away.

She demanded that he return to Rawlings Manor at once with an explanation for both the engagement announcement and the fact that he'd remained in the town house with Maggie, unchaperoned, for so long. Or, the note threatened, she'd sic Edward on him.

And if Edward should happen to miss the birth of our seventh child, she wrote, *because he had to go all the way to London to fetch you, Jeremy, I shall personally never, ever forgive you. Your aunt Peggy.*

"Christ," Jeremy said. "From bad to worse."

Peters, still ignoring the barking dog, said expressionlessly, "I've already packed your overnight kit, sir. I suspected there might 'ave been some sort of emergency."

"Thank you, Peters." Jeremy stuffed the letter into his pocket, though the Star of Jaipur didn't leave a lot of room for it. Well, he thought to himself. Perhaps a trip back to Yorkshire wasn't *entirely* a bad idea. He wanted to do things properly. In cases like this, he knew, fathers were generally appealed to first. He didn't relish the idea of asking Sir Arthur for his daughter's hand, but it would probably be best, under the circumstances. And, as Berangère had pointed out, it might not be a bad idea to try to patch things up between Maggie and her family while he was there.

Moving to shove his feet into a pair of Indian slippers, the toes of which curled upward, Jeremy began to issue commands, suddenly becoming very much the military leader. "Take that animal to the park, Peters, and make sure you don't lose him. I wouldn't let him off the lead, if I were you—"

"Right." Peters nodded. "Little rat like 'im might get eaten by a bigger dog."

"Exactly. And my chances of actually marrying the woman I want would be significantly decreased should my manservant allow her dog to perish on his morning walk."

"Certainly, Colonel." Peters saluted smartly. "You can count on me." When Jerry, eager for his walk, struck both his front paws against Peters's wooden leg, the valet only laughed, instead of flinching in pain, as Jeremy had. "Eh, there, tiger," he said, bending down to scratch the dog's ears with actual affection. "Easy, now. We'll be off as soon as I can get me a shirt on."

Jeremy, tying the robe's sash around his waist, rallied in-

ternally for his return to the White Room. He did not believe
for a second that Maggie had stayed abed, as ordered. When
had she ever done a single thing he'd asked her to? That was
certainly part of her charm. How often were dukes disobeyed? About as often as colonels, which was to say, not
often.

But the degree to which she'd managed to disobey him
in this particular instance was surprising. Jeremy, returning
to Maggie's bedroom, gaped at the changes wrought in the
room during the course of his brief absence. Gone was all
evidence of his ever having been there . . . including his
clothing. The bed was stripped and the dressing room door
agape. From that room drifted the sounds of vigorous splashing and the nervous chatter of one of the parlormaids. A
second later, Maggie herself appeared, in the tartan dressing
gown he'd disparaged just the day before, her hair caught up
damply in some kind of braid.

Her eyes widened upon seeing him at the threshold of her
room, and with a hasty glance over her shoulder, to insure
the maid was otherwise occupied, she hissed, "What are you
doing back so soon? Where's Jerry? And what have you got
on?"

Jeremy looked down at himself. "My dressing gown," he
replied, in an injured tone.

Maggie snorted. "I'll say." She stalked over to her dressing table.

"Well," Jeremy said. "You're one to talk. Where'd you
get the one you have on? The ragpicker's bin?"

"Very funny," Maggie observed, as she dipped her fingers into a pot of cream, which she began liberally applying
to her face. "Where is my dog?"

"Peters took him to the park," Jeremy said. He glanced
crossly at the dressing room door. "I thought I told you—"

"I cannot believe," Maggie declared, her eyes very wide
and dark as they peered out at him from all the white stuff
on her face, "that you have the gall to ask a one-legged man
to walk my dog. *Really*, Jeremy."

Behind her, the dressing room door swung open, and
Pamela, a fresh-faced girl who'd been imported to London

from the family of one of Rawlings Manor's tenant farmers, came bustling into the room, carrying an armful of clothing. "Is this the dress you wanted, miss?" she asked, directly before colliding into Jeremy.

"Oh!" Her blue eyes round as saucers, the maid dropped all of Maggie's clothes and dipped a shame-faced curtsy. "Your Grace! I beg your pardon, Your Grace! I didn't see you!"

"Never mind that, Pamela," Maggie said. She wiped the cream from her face before rising calmly to help the girl retrieve the items she'd dropped. "His Grace was just leaving. Weren't you, Your Grace?"

"In a moment, Pamela," Jeremy said, and he bent down and seized Maggie by the arm. "I just need a word in private with Miss Herbert." So saying, he dragged Maggie into the dressing room, where he saw traces of a hastily drawn bath. Closing the dressing room door behind them, he turned and looked down at Maggie rebukingly. "I thought I told you not to get out of that bed."

"I thought I told you to walk my dog," Maggie retorted.

"Your dog is being walked," Jeremy pointed out. "*I* did not renege on *my* part of the bargain."

"Well, I wouldn't have reneged on mine," Maggie assured him, reaching up to adjust the lapels of his dressing gown, one of which was flipped the wrong way, "if I hadn't remembered that I have movers arriving at my studio at eleven o'clock, and that I've got to be there to meet them."

"Movers?"

"Yes, Jeremy. The exhibition, tomorrow night. Remember? They've got to transport the paintings to Augustin's gallery—"

At the mention of the Frenchman's name, a glower spread across Jeremy's face. "Look," he said urgently. "I've got to talk to you."

"Jeremy, honestly, I haven't time. I'm running very late. And you've already managed to shock Pamela to the core. We'll talk later. . . ."

She started moving toward the door, but Jeremy caught her by the sash of the hideous plaid dressing gown. When

Maggie turned a questioning—and somewhat annoyed—glance toward him, he said only, "Here. I've got to go away for a while. Watch this for me while I'm gone, all right?"

And, desperate to show her, since he could not seem to tell her, how he felt about her, he took the Star of Jaipur from his own dressing gown's pocket and dropped it into hers.

Shocked, Maggie stared not at the enormous sapphire—she seemed hardly to have noticed it—but at Jeremy's departing back. "Away?" she echoed lamely. "Where, Jerry? Where are you going? When are you coming back?"

But the only reply to her question was the click of her bedroom door as he closed it behind him.

Chapter 32

No painter, Maggie knew, liked to see her creations handled by anyone save herself. Who else but the artist can know the toil and sweat that goes into a certain work? And then to see that work hefted by a burly man who commented that they were "pretty enough pitchers" and looked as if he hadn't seen a bath in years . . . well, what artist wouldn't experience a sense of unease?

But for Maggie, unease over the handling of her works was the least of her worries. She also had that awkward scene with Jeremy earlier that morning to mull over. By the time she'd gathered her senses enough to go looking for him, she'd found that he hadn't been joking . . . he really had gone away! His valet was nowhere to be found, either. Oh, he'd returned her dog, but then, according to a very indignant Evers, he'd disappeared out the door mere seconds later!

Maggie supposed she hadn't handled Jeremy and his request to "talk" very tactfully. She needn't have been so short with him. But her mind had been full of her upcoming exhibition! Surely a woman—a *business* woman—could be excused for having a more pressing engagement. . . .

Engagement! The very word made her want to smack her hand to her forehead. *What was she going to do about Augustin?* She had to find a way today to break off their engagement. She simply couldn't go on letting him think that . . . well, that she could ever do what she'd been doing for two days now with Jeremy with *him*. It simply wasn't in the realm of the possible. Whatever happened with Jeremy—and she was far from convinced that the two of them would ever work out a mutually amicable arrangement, except perhaps, where the bedroom was concerned; they never seemed to have any problems when they were in bed together. It was only when they got *out* of bed that all sorts of disasters occurred—there would never be anyone else for her. However grateful she might be to Augustin for all his kindnesses to her, she knew she could *never* let him . . . Oh, dear, she blushed to even think about it!

It was because of these worries that what ought to have been quite simple, really, turned into a nightmare. Maggie could not seem to keep her mind on the task at hand . . . as Augustin, already put out with her over the fact that she arrived half an hour late to begin with, causing him to have to pay the moving men for a half hour of loitering about in the hallway, pointed out, several times.

"It just isn't like you, *Marguerethe*," he kept saying. "From any of the other artists I represent, I might have expected such behavior, but from you, *Marguerethe*? Perhaps there is something wrong?"

Maggie, holding her breath as one of the movers hefted the portrait of the marquis and his brother—upside down—could only murmur, "No, there's nothing wrong."

"I don't mean to criticize, only if you had known you were going to be late, you might have lent me your key, so we could have started without you—"

"I didn't know I was going to be late. Oh, do watch"—Maggie winced as the wooden frame supporting a canvas split in half under the clumsy handling of one of the men—"that stretcher."

The mover blinked at her, the painting having come apart in his hands. "It warn't my fault!" he exclaimed, as Augustin began to curse exasperatedly in French.

"Oh, dear." Maggie hurried over to examine the limp canvas. Fortunately, the painting hadn't completely dried, so the oil on it didn't split. "Perhaps I can mend it. Go—" She waved at the mover. "Go fetch those landscapes over there, if you will. Leave this one to me."

But of course, it turned out "those landscapes over there" weren't quite dry, either, a fact Augustin pointed out too late, so that they ended up with four paintings that had great, dirty thumb prints marring the edges. Knowing full well they were unsalable in such condition, Maggie set them up onto easels for some quick patchwork, only to find that she was perfectly incapable of remembering how to mix the correct shades to camouflage the damage. Meanwhile, the movers, confused by her flustered directions and annoyed by Augustin's French expletives, left half the works behind that they were supposed to have taken. Maggie and Augustin were forced to chase after them, down six flights of stairs, causing no end of delight to the other artists in the building, all of whom leaned out their studio doors to shout encouragement to them as they raced by.

It was one o'clock before the movers finally left, and then they were in a bad humor, since apparently they had expected Augustin to pay them then and there, an idea at which he scoffed heartily.

"Oh, no, *mes garçons*," he said. "Payment upon delivery."

This generated a good deal of dark muttering on the part of the moving men concerning the dire fates that awaited Maggie's paintings on the muddy roads back to Bond Street. Hearing this, Maggie sank down upon the divan by the window, her knees having given out beneath her.

"Oh, Augustin," she whispered. "Go with them. Please. Go with them."

Augustin, noticing her pale face, was only just able to stifle another stream of curses. Finally, he seized his hat and said, with as much grace as he could muster, "Very well then. I shall go with them, to insure your works are not thrown in the mud. You will stay here and repair the damaged landscapes?"

Maggie, completely dazed, nodded.

"And then you will join me at the gallery this evening, after they've been fitted into their frames, so that we may hang them according to your specifications?"

Again, Maggie nodded, although she felt about as enthusiastic about hanging her paintings as she had about moving them.

Augustin nodded and left, clearly as unhappy as she was, though for far different reasons. He, of course, still had the pain of a broken nose to deal with, on top of the strain and worry over opening an exhibition featuring a new artist the following day. And the artist wasn't helping matters any, she knew, by being so moody. Really, she ought to be falling over herself in gratitude to Augustin . . . he was doing so many wonderful things for her, and he had been so patient and tolerant.

Why couldn't she love him? Things would be so much simpler if she could just love Augustin!

But that, she knew, would never, never happen. She'd tell him tonight. She *had* to tell him tonight.

It took Maggie most of the rest of the day to repair her damaged works. It was five o'clock by the time she arrived at the gallery on Bond Street. She was freezing from her uncomfortable carriage ride, crushed in as she'd been with her canvases, and thirsty, besides, from having consumed every last drop of wine from her sideboard. She had thought the wine might help give her the courage to say to Augustin the words she'd been rehearsing all day. *Augustin,* she'd say. *I'm really very sorry, but I cannot marry you. You see, I'm in love with someone else, and it wouldn't be fair to you if I . . .*

Yes, that was good. Make no mention, Maggie, of the fact that you'd already tumbled into bed with that someone else. . . .

But the minute she stepped through the doors, she saw at once she would not be given an opportunity to make her confession. Augustin was shouting furiously at one of his assistants, who'd apparently managed to put a hammerhead straight through the wall, and into a display of kid leather gloves belonging to the shop next door. Other assistants were scurrying about, her paintings under their arms, too frightened to engender the wrath of their employer by attempting to hang anything during his tirade at one of their peers.

Wincing, Maggie crept past them, determined to deliver

her not-yet-dry canvases to the frame maker, who'd set up shop in the back, where works not yet on display were stored. But the frame maker, an Italian craftsman who apparently thought her a shopgirl of some sort, took the paintings and then waved her impatiently away when she tried to dawdle long enough to catch a glimpse of his work. Without Augustin to translate, there was no way Maggie could convey to the frame maker that she was the artist, and had every right to see how her paintings had been framed. Though she pointed at herself, and then at the canvases, and mimed painting, the Italian glared at her, and let loose a stream of threatening-sounding foreign words, so she ducked back into the gallery.

There she happened to witness Augustin cuffing the unfortunate assistant about the ears. This was more than Maggie could bear, and so she slipped out the front doors again, unnoticed by anyone, most particularly the gallery's owner.

Miserable, Maggie hesitated on the icy street, where she was jostled by fashionably attired Londoners doing their Friday-night shopping on stylish, expensive Bond Street. Really, she thought to herself. How cowardly was *that*? All that wine, and she hadn't even had the courage to go through with it. She was a horrid, horrid girl.

She supposed she had no choice but to go back to the house on Park Lane. The thought caused her to sigh heavily, her breath fogging in front of her. Jeremy would be there. She wasn't at all sure she had the strength to face him. It seemed as if every time they got together, they ended up in bed, which really didn't resolve anything. She had so many questions, so many worries concerning their relationship. For instance, why, she wondered, and not for the first time that day, had Jeremy thrust the Star of Jaipur into her pocket? She could feel its weight even now, in the bottom of her reticule. She'd had reservations about carting the heavy stone around with her all day, but she couldn't very well have left it at the house. Lord only knew where it might have disappeared to! She trusted Hill implicitly, and Evers, too, but the other servants . . .

No, it was better that the stone remained with her. But

why had Jeremy entrusted it to her? It was a curious thing to give to a girl with whom one had spent the night. Almost like . . . well, a token of his affection. Other men gave engagement rings. Jeremy Rawlings gave sapphires the size of a plum.

Unless . . . the thought occurred to her as she jounced along on the seat of the omnibus . . . unless giving her the Star of Jaipur had been Jeremy's way of proposing. But no. That was preposterous. He had proposed once, and been rejected. He would not do so again—would he? Besides, he hadn't *given* her the stone. He'd merely asked her to look after it for him. After all, someone *was* trying to kill him. It was a thing of great beauty—Maggie had removed it from her reticule just once, as the afternoon sun had peeked into her skylight, and gazed at the way its many facets glowed. It was certainly worth killing for. Not, she imagined, that *that* was why someone had been trying to kill Jeremy. He'd hardly have given *her* the stone if he thought *that* were the case. . . .

Well, she would ask him, that was all. Yes, she would ask him, as soon as she saw him, why he'd given her the stone. And that wasn't all she'd ask him, either. She'd be certain to ask him where he'd disappeared to, and just what it was he'd been so eager to discuss with her that morning.

And just where, exactly, he thought this relationship was headed. . . .

But when she returned to the house on Park Lane, Evers calmly informed her, while taking her wraps, that His Grace was not in. He had not come home for luncheon, and had left word that he would not be in for supper. This struck Maggie as more than a little suspicious. Where, in heaven's name, could he be? With the princess?

But no, that wasn't possible. Because the princess was looking for him, as well.

Maggie didn't hear this, however, until she stepped into her own room, and found her maid, Hill, who had just returned from taking Jerry for a walk. Maggie was so surprised to see them that she nearly choked.

"Hill," she cried, ashamed that, in her distress, she had

forgotten both her maid and her dog. "Are you well? I was very worried about you."

The maid certainly did not look well, but she was, at least, alive. "Oh, miss," she began, untying the strings to her cloak, as Jerry raced over and laid his paws upon Maggie's knees. "Such a night I passed! You could not imagine. Evers insists it musta been somethin' I et, only Cook denies it, since nobody else took ill, but oh! Such a night!" Hill puttered about the room as she spoke. "I don't think I ever retched so much in all my born days. Though I'll tell you, I never had such dreams in me life. Beautiful dreams, I tell you. I wish I could remember 'em properly."

Maggie, racked with guilt over having been the direct cause of her maid's illness, begged her to sit down and rest more, but Hill would have none of it. She was as full of chat and gossip as Maggie was depressed.

"And what do you think, Miss Margaret," Hill demanded, as she fluffed up Maggie's pillows, "about the duke now, eh?"

"W-what?" Maggie asked nervously.

Hill shot her young mistress a disapproving look. "You mean you didn't see it?"

"See what?"

"This morning's *Times*!"

"Oh," Maggie said, a good deal less tremulously. "No. Why?"

"Right there, on page two, it was. Mr. Evers, he showed it to me. Otherwise, I never would've believed it." Hill paused dramatically. "A retraction!"

"A retraction?" Maggie echoed weakly.

"Yes, miss. A retraction of the article the day before, sayin' he was goin' to marry that pert heathen princess."

Good God! He'd meant it! Every word he'd said. He truly hadn't intended to marry the Princess Usha after all! Why, even though it was dark outside, did Maggie suddenly feel as if the sun were shining?

"Oh, I didn't like the look of her, I didn't," Hill was saying. "Not the minute she walked in the door. *Darting eyes*, she had. You can't trust a heathen with darting eyes. . . .''

"Hill," Maggie asked curiously, "when did *you* see the princess?"

"Why, not half an hour ago, when she and that interpreter of 'er's came callin' in the house."

Maggie sprang up from her seat beside the fire, dislodging Jerry, who'd curled up into her lap. "What?" she cried. "The princess was *here*? Princess Usha was *here*?"

"Heavens, yes," Hill replied, looking more than a little surprised. "What are you shouting for? Do you want them to hear you all the way to Newcastle?"

"Does Jeremy know?" Maggie demanded. "Has anyone told Jeremy?"

"How could anyone tell the duke, when the duke boarded a train bound for Yorkshire hours ago?"

"*Yorkshire*?" Maggie cried. "Jerry went to *Yorkshire*? Are you quite certain, Hill?"

"Yes, of course I'm certain," Hill said irritably.

"But *why*?" Maggie exclaimed. "Did Jer—I mean, His Grace—say why he was going to Yorkshire? Did he . . . have some bad news from Rawlings Manor during the day, or something?"

"Well, Mr. Evers said the duke got a hand-delivered message this mornin'. I reckon it was from the Lady Edward. I wouldn't doubt she finally got wind of you and him bein' here at the town house all alone together—"

Maggie glared at her maid. "And I wonder how she would have got wind of *that*," she said angrily.

Hill looked innocent. "*I* certainly wouldn't know. That Mr. Evers, though. I wouldn't put it past *him*. . . . But why *shouldn't* His Grace pay a call on his aunt and uncle, I'd like to know?" Hill stomped over to the chair Maggie had just vacated and began to plump up its cushions. "It's high time he did, if you ask me. If *my* nephew joined the army and went away to India for five years, then got himself engaged to a heathen who was all set to bring her seven-headed Buddhas back to the vicarage—"

"Hill," Maggie interrupted. "Please. She isn't a heathen.

She simply worships in a different manner than you and I—"

"I saw her!" Hill declared emphatically. "She's a heathen! And all I'm saying is, if I were Lord and Lady Edward, I'd be right put out if my nephew didn't stop to see me first thing on his return to England."

"Yes," Maggie murmured. "Yes, I suppose so. Only it's just so strange! I saw him this morning, and he didn't say a word. . . ." Her voice trailed off. Perhaps his decision to go to Yorkshire had been *because* of their conversation this morning. After all, Maggie hadn't been exactly warm toward him.

But she'd certainly been *more* than warm to him during the night . . . surely that had to count for something! But maybe he didn't see it that way. Maybe he'd misinterpreted her sarcastic remarks and teasing, mistook them for genuine when really, she'd only been trying to disguise her own unease and embarrassment. Maybe he'd left for Yorkshire convinced that she didn't care for him. She was engaged to another man, was she not? And yet she'd given herself to *him*. . . .

Oh, Lord. She shuddered. What kind of man would want to marry a woman who'd do something like *that*? Oh, he had seemed to enjoy their lovemaking well enough. She'd heard the cry he'd let out the night before, when he'd climaxed. That had not been the shout of a bored man. That had been the cry of a man who had found release after a period of interminable imprisonment.

But then he'd left.

Oh, what was the use? She wanted him. She might as well admit it. And if she had to become a duchess, and give up her painting, in order to have him, well, she would. Oh, Lord, what was happening to her? She had never in her life wanted anything more than her painting, and now . . .

Well, now she wanted Jeremy.

Right when he didn't seem the least interested in her. Blinking sadly at the bed in which she'd enjoyed so much bliss the night before, Maggie started to sniffle. Just a little, but Hill, unfortunately, heard.

"Now, then!" she cried, coming out of Maggie's dressing room, where she'd gone to run her mistress a hot bath. "What's this? *I'm* the one with the head what's pounding fit to bust. What are *you* crying about?"

"Nothing," Maggie murmured, from behind her hands.

"*Something*'s the matter. What is it? You didn't get a note from that Frenchman of yours, I'll wager. Now, I've told you before, miss, just because a man doesn't call *one* day, doesn't mean the engagement's off. Even *two* days isn't enough to cause worry. Now, *three* days, if he's not out of the country, then I'd say, yes, there's reason for concern. But *one* day—"

"It isn't that, Hill," Maggie said, sniffling. Then she raised her head. What was she doing? *What was she doing?* Weeping, because the man she'd made love with the night before had fled to Yorkshire? Was she insane? She was no lovelorn governess, no simpering milkmaid. She was an artist! She would probably make love to dozens of men throughout her lifetime! She couldn't burst into tears every time one of them decided to take a train to see his family the next day. Look at Berangère. Maggie had never seen Berangère cry, not ever, and Berangère had scores of lovers, some of whom she could not even remember a week later. Maggie was just going to have to harden herself to be more like Berangère, that was all.

But deep inside, Maggie knew that no matter how she tried, she'd never be like Berangère. She didn't *want* scores of lovers. She couldn't imagine making love with any man but Jeremy. Even the *thought* of doing so physically repulsed her. She wanted only one man, and he was on a train headed for Yorkshire. He might as well have gone back to India again.

A tap sounded at the door. Hill, muttering to herself, went to answer it. Maggie, still trying to rally her own spirits, heard only murmurs until Hill closed the door again and rejoined her by the bed.

"Well," the older woman said, in her warmest voice. "*You* are quite popular tonight, Miss Margaret. You might be interested to know that, according to Evers, Mr. de Vey-goux is waiting downstairs to see you!''

Maggie suddenly felt sick to her stomach. "Oh, Hill, could you please send Mr. de Veygoux away? I'm really not feeling up to seeing him this evening."

Hill sniffed. "I shall do no such thing. The man is your fiancé. You can't send him away as if he were an unwanted suitor."

"Oh, Hill," Maggie said, and suddenly she was sobbing.

Hill took one look at her mistress and hurried away. When she came back, it was only a few moments later, and Maggie, ashamed of her tears, was trying to dry them on the back of her wrists. Hill would have none of that. She applied her own handkerchief to her mistress's streaming eyes and cooed, "There, there, Miss Maggie, don't you worry now, he's gone away. Right doleful he looked too when I told 'im you were ill. And with his nose all swollen up, and his eyes so bruised it's a wonder to me he can see a'tall. Poor man. He brought you more roses." Hill pointed to a bouquet she'd left on the bed. "Shall I put 'em in with the others?"

Maggie looked at the already overladen vase on her bed-side table. "I suppose so," she said miserably. "I do wish he'd stop. He must have spent a fortune on flowers already."

"He said for me to tell you that these were for missing you at the gallery this afternoon. He's right sorry about it, says he doesn't know how it could have happened, and he hopes you'll forgive him if he did anythin' to upset you." Hill began tucking the long-stemmed flowers in with the ones from the day before. "And that the repairs you did on the . . . landscapes, were they? Yes, the landscapes . . . were perfect, and that he'll see you at ten sharp tomorrow to start hanging them. Now, speakin' of tomorrow, I thought you might want to wear the white satin for your exhibition, so I'll press it first thing in the morning. The problem is, there's a button missing from the gloves that match it—how you can be so careless, I don't know—so I'll have to take a trip to Trumps to see if I can find one that matches. There." Hill stood back and gazed at her arrangement. "That's quite nice, don't you think? And they smell heavenly! So lovely to see a bit of color in winter, I always think.''

Maggie looked at the half-blown blossoms. ''Yes,'' she said, but she wasn't thinking about flowers. She was thinking about Jeremy. ''Isn't it?''

Chapter 33

$\mathscr{J}$eremy, throwing open the heavy double doors to the manor house, cursed irritably beneath his breath. The wind off the moor was biting and, what's more, had garnered gale-like force in the two hours—*two hours*—it had taken him to get from the train station to his own front door. He'd conveniently forgotten, of course, what Yorkshire could be like in the dead of winter, particularly along the moors. He had had to hire a coach at three times the usual amount and then the damned thing had nearly blown over on the Post Road. The snow was so blinding that the coachman had almost refused to go on. Jeremy had to offer him another five pounds and half the contents of his whisky flask in order to convince him to drive on.

And now, standing in the Great Hall, snow dripping from his boots and shoulders, Jeremy cursed again, this time at having arrived too late to be welcomed by anyone. It had to be past ten o'clock, a time by which, in the country, everyone had either retired or passed out from too much drink, one of the few distractions available of a winter's evening. Lord, he couldn't even find someone to relieve him of his cloak!

Stomping across the flagstone floor, noting with disapproval that most of the candles in the chandeliers overhead had already been doused, Jeremy found a chair, upon which he promptly began to heap his sodden outer wraps. He was shivering uncontrollably by this time, and longed to find a fire, but he rather doubted any had been left going on the main floor. He'd have to find Evers—*John* Evers, he reminded himself—and get him to send someone to his chamber to build up a good blaze. Lord, what a homecoming. He ought to have brought Peters with him. He ought to have gone straight to Herbert Park, and had it out with Sir Arthur then and there. He was certainly in a foul enough mood for it.

But, no. He was in just such a temper to have shot the old man, and that would never do. He'd never be able to convince Maggie to marry him after murdering her father.

It wasn't until he'd begun unraveling his muffler that he noticed the flicker of a candle flame approaching him through the gloom of the massive Great Hall, and then he called out, gruffly, to its bearer. When the flame came close enough to illuminate the identity of the person carrying it, Jeremy saw that it was someone he didn't recognize, a girl of about fourteen or fifteen, with a riotous halo of blond curls framing a pretty, only vaguely familiar face. Her dressing gown was remarkably rich for that of a servant, of ice-blue satin brocade, and there appeared to be rabbit-fur trim on her slippers. Jeremy made a mental note to speak with his uncle about how much they were paying the parlormaids these days. Surely not enough to purchase satin brocade dressing gowns.

Then the girl spoke, and Jeremy realized she couldn't possibly be a parlormaid. His aunt would never hire anyone that rude.

"Who are *you*?" she demanded, in a voice dripping with suspicion.

Jeremy squinted at her. Her eyes were as frosty blue as her dressing gown. "I was just about to ask you the same question," he said.

"*I'm* Elizabeth Rawlings," the girl replied primly. "I *live* here."

"Well, I'm your cousin Jerry," he said, after overcoming a momentary shock. The last time he'd seen Lizzie Rawlings, she'd stood no higher than his hip. Now the top of her curly-haired head reached almost to his shoulder. "And I live here, too. In fact, I *own* this house."

She blinked at him. "You're lying," she said rudely. "My cousin Jerry's in India."

"No he isn't," Jeremy said. "He's standing right in front of you. What are you doing out of bed, anyway? Does your mother know you still make a habit of wandering about the house in the dark? I thought she weaned you of that ten years ago, when they caught you after midnight in the kitchens, stuffing your face with the remains of your brother's birthday cake."

Lizzie's bow-shaped mouth popped open, and her eyes went round as eggs. "Cousin Jerry?" she breathed. "It really *is* you!"

"Of course it is." Jeremy threw his muffler down onto the chair. "Where is everybody, anyway? This place is like a tomb."

Lizzie couldn't stop staring at him. "Mamma is in bed. Mr. Parks told her she has to stay there until the baby is born, although she keeps getting up anyway. Papa is probably reading in his library. My sisters are all in bed, and I don't know where my brothers are. Why is your skin such a funny color?"

Jeremy glared at her. "I am tan. It tends to happen near the equator. Why are you out of bed?"

"You needn't speak to me," Lizzie said indignantly, "as if I were a child. I happen to be fifteen years old. I can get out of bed if I want to."

Jeremy snorted at that. "In order to meet some young swain, no doubt. Who is it? One of the footmen? I'll have him sacked on the morrow." He seized her by the arm and began steering her toward the curved double staircase that led up to an open gallery overlooking the Great Hall on three sides. "And don't think I'm not going to tell your father."

Lizzie pulled on her arm with surprising strength for a girl so slender. "Let go of me, you conceited buffoon," she commanded. "I came down here in search of the book I'm reading."

"Oh, certainly," Jeremy sneered. "What's it called? *The Young Girl's Guide to Foolish Love Affairs*?"

"I happen," Lizzie said, through gritted teeth, "to be

reading *Letters on Education*, a treatise on women's rights by Catharine McCauley, a contemporary of Mary Wollstonecraft who was much admired in her day for her eight-volume history of England.'' On the word *England*, Lizzie managed to successfully rip her arm from his grasp, but only because Jeremy was too shocked to hold on any longer.

''Good God,'' he exclaimed. ''What are you reading *that* for?''

Lizzie primly tugged on the sleeves of her dressing gown, with all the fastidiousness of a cat. ''Because, you ignoramus,'' she said contemptuously, ''I'm interested in the subject.''

Jeremy groaned. She was her mother's daughter, all right, despite the blond hair. He couldn't remember a time when his aunt hadn't had her nose buried between the pages of some piece of similarly dry reading material. He wondered what on earth it must be like to be Lizzie Rawlings, clearly a bluestocking trapped in the body of a chorus girl, and felt vaguely sorry for all the men who were going to have the misfortune of falling in love with her.

''What,'' thundered a deep voice, from the gallery overhead, ''the devil is going on down there?''

Jeremy looked up, and saw the tall, dark figure of his uncle at the top of the stairs. ''Oh, hello, Uncle Edward,'' he said casually. ''Sorry, were we disturbing you?''

''Jeremy?'' He saw his uncle reach up and remove a pair of spectacles from the bridge of his nose. Good Lord! Jeremy nearly exclaimed. Edward Rawlings, farsighted? What other calamities had taken place in Jeremy's absence?

''Yes, Uncle,'' Jeremy called cheerfully. ''It's me. I was just attempting to discipline your eldest daughter, but apparently she thinks *I'm* the one in need of direction.''

''Jeremy!'' However much Edward had aged in his nephew's absence, he'd still managed to retain his customary athleticism, as exemplified by the alacrity with which he descended the stairs in order to wrap Jeremy in an enormous bear hug.

''Good Lord,'' Jeremy cried, thoroughly embarrassed. His voice was muffled by the velvet of his uncle's smoking jacket. "If I'd known this was the kind of reception I'd receive, I'd never have left New Delhi."

Edward, looking a bit surprised at his own emotional display over seeing his nephew again, abruptly released him, but retained a fond hand on Jeremy's shoulder. "Welcome home, my boy," he said gruffly. "We missed you." Then, squinting, he added, "You look terrible. How about a whisky?"

"That sounds like an excellent idea," Jeremy promptly replied. Then, as the two men started toward the staircase, Edward paused, and turned to pierce his daughter with a stern look as she crept toward the dining room doors, located in the center of the split between the twin curving staircases.

"Where do you think *you're* going?" he demanded.

Lizzie tossed him an aggrieved glance over her shoulder, but didn't break her stride. "To fetch my book, of course," she said. "I left it at my place at dinner."

"Well." Edward cleared his throat disapprovingly. "Go and get it, and then get back to bed. And don't let your mother hear about my letting you read at the dinner table, or she'll have my hide."

"Yes, Papa," Lizzie said with a long-suffering sigh.

Turning back to Jeremy, Edward offered an apologetic smile. "They run a bit wild whenever their mother goes into her confinement. Pegeen's been upstairs for only a day or two now, but I don't think I've seen any of them since."

"So number seven's being a bit reticent?" Jeremy inquired with a grin.

"A bit, but I don't imagine it will be long now." Edward grinned back at his nephew as they began climbing the stairs to the second floor. "One look at you ought to be enough to shock your aunt into labor straightaway."

"That bad, eh?" Jeremy reached up to stroke his jaw, which was covered with dark razor stubble. "Lizzie didn't recognize me, though I can't say I knew who she was, either."

Edward studied him. "It's the tan," he said finally. "Not to mention the nose. You finally managed to goad somebody into breaking it for you, eh? Good job. I know how badly you wanted to rid yourself of that straight one you inherited. Too bad, though.'' They had reached the top of the stairs, and were just turning toward the library when Edward paused to quirk an eyebrow at him. ''I was thinking of breaking it myself, as soon as you got the courage to show your face around here.''

Jeremy took a cautious step backward, remembering the mean fist his uncle swung. ''If it's about the Star of Jaipur, I can explain.''

''Can you?'' Edward looked only mildly amused. ''This ought to be interesting. I saw the retraction in this morning's *Times*. So I take it there *isn't* going to be a new Duchess of Rawlings any time soon?''

''I didn't say *that*,'' Jeremy said. ''She just isn't from India. She's from considerably closer to home, actually.''

Edward Rawlings had been accused of being many things, but slow was not one of them.

''So *that's* how it is,'' he said shaking his head. ''Pegeen told me you'd come home as soon as you heard about Maggie's engagement, but I didn't believe her.''

Jeremy grinned at him. ''Hope you didn't place any wagers on it.''

''As a matter of fact, I think I did. Damn me! I believe I owe the Rawlings Foundling Home a hundred pounds now.'' Shaking his head with disgust, Edward started toward the library door. ''Good God, Jerry. It's been five years. Can't you let the poor girl alone?''

Jeremy's grin instantly vanished. ''No, I can't,'' he said stiffly. ''Any more than *you* can let my aunt alone, apparently.''

It was Edward's turn to smile. ''Touché,'' he said, and turned the knob. Inside the library, Jeremy was relieved to see a roaring fire and a whisky decanter, already unstopped, set out on a sideboard. He immediately went to the fire and began to warm his hands, while Edward closed the door and poured out two generous drinks.

''Here you are,'' he said, handing one of the glasses to Jeremy. ''To your homecoming.''

''Thank you.'' Jeremy tossed back most of the whisky in

a single gulp, feeling the fiery liquid immediately begin to warm his frozen extremities. He was not yet well enough that a night spent in torrid lovemaking, and a day spent on various modes of transportation, did not completely exhaust him. And now, knowing that he still had the difficult task of dealing with his aunt—not to mention winning over Maggie's family—ahead of him, tiredness crept in, like the cold, to permeate his very bones.

His uncle very obligingly took his empty glass and refilled it.

"Well," Edward said with a sigh, sinking down onto his green leather couch, where he'd apparently been reading the newspaper just minutes before, since a hastily folded *Times* lay on the floor beside his feet. "Let me see if I have this straight. You joined the Horse Guards, got shipped off to India, killed a lot of rebellious Bengals, got promoted, saved the queen's ambassador to Bombay from an assassin's bullet, got promoted, prevented the Palace of the Winds in Jaipur from being destroyed by marauding rebels, got awarded the Star of Jaipur—do stop me if I've left anything out. . . ."

"On the contrary," Jeremy said, impressed in spite of himself. "You seem to have followed my military career to the minutest detail. Except for one minor point. The Star of Jaipur is actually a sapphire, not a princess."

Edward seemed to accept this easily enough. "Ah. And that article in yesterday's *Times*?"

"The princess seems to be having some trouble accepting my decision to take the sapphire instead of her." He shrugged, as if to say *What's a poor fellow to do?*

Edward cleared his throat. "I see. Well, I must say, you managed to impress quite a lot of my peers with your daring, Jerry. There's even been talk of siccing you on the Zulus, in Isandhlwana, to nip this rumored uprising in the bud. I did my best to try to talk them out of that idea. It's my opinion you might be best utilized right here in England, consulting at Whitehall—"

Jeremy sat down on the hearth, to better warm his thawing bones. "Whitehall?" He shook his head. "Really, Uncle, I don't think I should like that at all. Isn't that sort of thing for old retired admirals, the better to relive their glory days?''

"It most certainly is not," Edward said indignantly. "Whitehall is the headquarters of Her Majesty's armed forces. You'd jolly well better say yes if they ask you to Whitehall, Jerry. There isn't an officer alive who wouldn't jump at the chance."

Jeremy shrugged. "Well, I suppose Whitehall is better than New Delhi. I'm damned tired of India. No whisky to speak of, and mosquitoes the size of your hand."

"And no women, apparently," Edward said dryly. "Aside from this princess, I mean."

Jeremy scissored a glance at him. "What are you talking about? There were plenty of women."

Edward looked skeptical. "And yet it's still Maggie?"

"Of course it's still Maggie," Jeremy said, a bit defensively. "I think I've finally earned her, you know."

Edward raised his eyebrows. "*Earned* her? What are you talking about?"

"Yes, you remember, don't you? Our conversation in the stables after you, er, walked in on us. You accused me of being a ne'er-do-well. You said I hadn't earned a girl like Maggie, since I hadn't done anything with my life." Jeremy leaned forward until his elbows rested on his knees, his whisky cradled in his hands. "Well, I think you'll agree with me that I've done quite a lot with my life. I've risked it a hundred times over in service to my country."

"You're not saying—" Edward set his own whisky, which he'd barely touched, aside. "Jerry, are you telling me that you did all this—the Horse Guards, and Jaipur—to prove yourself worthy of *Maggie*?"

"You don't think she's worth it?" Jeremy demanded, instantly on the defensive.

Edward blinked. "Think she's . . . Good God, Jeremy, that has nothing to do with it. I'm simply surprised, that's all. I would have thought you'd have forgotten all about Maggie Herbert by now."

"Why?" Jeremy asked sharply. "You said five years ago that you thought she'd make an excellent duchess. Have you changed your mind? Or maybe Sir Arthur's changed it for you. Maybe you agree with him that painting portraits isn't a proper pursuit for a woman—''

"That's not it at all, Jeremy," Edward scoffed. "All I meant is that five years is a relatively long time for a young man of your, er, lusty nature to remain . . . ahem . . . faithful to one woman. Particularly to a woman who, if I understand correctly, has recently announced her engagement to someone else."

"Well, why the hell else do you think I came back?" Jeremy demanded, standing up suddenly, and taking a quick turn across the room and back.

"Good Lord," Edward said, watching his nephew as he paced. "I never realized it before, but you're even worse than Pegeen. When you get an idea into that head of yours, you stick with it, don't you, come hell or high water?"

Jeremy snapped, "Is that so wrong?"

"Nothing wrong about it. Just amusing, is all. So. Have you killed her fiancé yet?"

"No," Jeremy said. "Though I've considered it. I thought I'd try a different approach. That's why I'm here, actually."

"Really?" Edward looked interested. "Don't tell that to Pegeen. She's going to think you actually followed her instructions for a change."

Jeremy smiled. "Well, I did get her note. And I am glad to know that you're all well. . . ."

"Hrmph." Edward looked skeptical. "You never were much of a bootlicker, were you, Jerry? How did you get so far in the military? All right then, out with it. What is it that *really* brings you to Yorkshire when the love of your life— not to mention her fiancé—are back in London?"

"Her family," Jeremy replied succinctly.

"Her *family*?" Edward looked confused. "What has her *family* to do with anything?"

"Everything. I mean to reason them out of their ludicrous disapproval of Maggie's portrait paintings, and get them to approve her marrying me instead of that frog-eater she's engaged to." Jeremy stopped pacing, and faced his uncle squarely. "Do you have any objection to that?"

Edward lifted the whisky glass he'd abandoned. "And if I did?" he queried with a grin.

Jeremy smiled, but there was no humor in the gesture. "Then I should have no choice but to strike you, Uncle."

"In that case," Edward said with mock gravity, "I haven't any objections at all."

Jeremy relaxed his fists, looking surprised. "Really, Uncle Edward? You really haven't?"

"None," Edward said with a shrug. "I quite like Maggie Herbert. She doesn't suffer fools gladly, including her own family, for which one can't help but admire her. But I do wonder how you're going to fare against her sister Anne. Your aunt says that since Mrs. Cartwright's most recent miscarriage, she hasn't been at all well. I don't mean in the physical sense, either. She's apparently developed a notion that women who are of child-bearing age, but aren't busying themselves having children, are somehow flying in the face of nature. I suppose because Anne is a woman who'd like to have more babies very badly, but hasn't been able to, it hurts her to see women who can have babies not doing so."

Jeremy, having no particular love for babies, whom he invariably found sticky-fingered and shrill, nodded to show he understood, even though he didn't, not really.

Edward went on. "Anne was never very supportive of her parents' decision to let Maggie go away to school, but I suppose, since it was *Maggie*, art school seemed the lesser of . . ." He glanced sternly at Jeremy. "Well. Several evils, anyway."

Jeremy quirked up an eyebrow at being referred to as an evil, but since his uncle had called him far worse in the past, he said nothing.

"But when Maggie announced she intended to actually *be* an artist," Edward continued, "according to Pegeen, Anne went right out of her head. Not only was one of her own sisters defying the natural order of things, but she was ruining the good Herbert name, as well."

"I see," Jeremy said. "So that's what I'm up against, is it?"

"Oh, that's not all," Edward assured him cheerfully.

"You're forgetting Sir Arthur. Anne's got him whipped up into a fine frenzy over Maggie. I've never seen him so adamant about anything. He wants her keeping to home and hearth, not gallivanting about London, painting the heads of the rich and idle. He won't be at all pleased, either by your interference with his family troubles, or your marrying his daughter. He's got quite firm ideas about both topics, you know."

"I know," Jeremy said grimly. "That's why I brought my pistol along with me."

Edward raised an eyebrow. "Oh," he said. "I see. Well, that changes things, doesn't it?"

It was Jeremy's turn to smile. "I certainly hope so."

Chapter 34

$\mathcal{M}$aggie stood in the middle of the Gallery de Veygoux and chewed her lower lip. It was nearly eleven o'clock in the morning, and Augustin still hadn't appeared. It wasn't like him to be late. Not like him at all.

Not that Maggie minded. She was not particularly looking forward to seeing him. She knew that today, there could be no more excuses. No throbbing headaches, no unhappy movers, no ham-handed assistants, and, perhaps most importantly of all, no Jeremy.

Today, she was going to break off the engagement.

Fortunately, Augustin's assistants had been at the gallery in his absence to open the doors for Maggie when she arrived. Thank goodness, or she'd have frozen to death waiting out on Bond Street for him. The weather was typical for London in February—cold and windy, with a fine curtain of sleet coating everything with ice. A lovely day for an exhibition to open, Maggie thought dryly. People would be very foolish indeed to venture out in weather like this merely to come look at a lot of "pretty pitchers," when they could stay by their fires and be comfortable, instead. Maggie knew perfectly well no one was going to come to the opening day of her exhibition.

Which was just fine by her.

Augustin would be disappointed, of course. But, secretly, Maggie would be relieved. The last thing she felt ready to do, what with the emotional upheaval she'd been through the last few days, was smile and listen to people compliment her work—or criticize it, as the case might very well be. For the first time in her life, she genuinely didn't care what anybody thought of her paintings. What did a silly bunch of canvases signify, when her heart was breaking? Yes, it really was. She was convinced of it. Her heart was breaking, and deservedly so, since she was the wickedest girl who had ever walked the face of the earth. A girl who made love with one man while engaged to another . . . why, she not only deserved a broken heart; she deserved terrible, awful reviews of her exhibition in the Sunday paper. That was what Maggie felt she deserved. And she quite hoped *The Times* would not disappoint her.

Augustin's assistant—the same one whose ears he'd boxed the day before—seemed a little concerned about her, probably because she was standing stupidly in the center of the gallery, her umbrella dripping onto the shiny wood floor. The young man timidly approached her, bearing a steaming cup of tea. Startled, Maggie accepted the tea, and hardly noticed when the clerk slipped her umbrella out from beneath her arm, and secreted it away somewhere. Then, apologizing for his employer's lateness, he asked Maggie if she wouldn't like to take a quick stroll around the gallery, to see if she approved of the way her paintings had been hung.

Maggie couldn't hide her surprise. She thought the very reason she'd been asked to be at the gallery that morning was in order to supervise the hanging of her works.

The young man flushed guiltily. Yes, he said, that was quite right. Only he and his "mates" had gone ahead and done the hanging themselves the night before. Maggie, reading through his words, saw that the fellow had been so thoroughly mortified by his blunder with the hammer the day before that he'd worked all through the night in order to impress his employer with his dependability and initiative.

And now his employer hadn't even had the courtesy to show up.

Which wasn't like Augustin. It wasn't like Augustin at all.

Maggie, touched by the gallery clerk's nervous solicitude,

and beginning to feel a bit annoyed with her fiancé for his thoughtlessness, replied that she'd very much like a tour, and Mr. Corman—which was the young man's name—eagerly began to show her about.

Her paintings had been beautifully framed—in some cases Maggie thought the frames more attractive than the actual works themselves—and hung with obvious care, so that the larger works did not overwhelm those on smaller canvases, and landscapes were carefully interspersed between the portraits, so that the eye was not tired by too much green or blue.

Maggie, sipping her tea as they walked, showered Mr. Corman and his associates with praise, though of course she could hardly keep her mind on the tour. Where, she couldn't help wondering, was Augustin? He was *never* late.

Then a hideous thought occurred to her. Supposing Jeremy was right, and it was *Augustin* who'd tried to kill him outside Twenty-two Park Lane, and then again, outside the *Times*? Supposing Augustin had followed him to Yorkshire, and even now, was trying to finish off the job?

Oh, Lord! And here she was in London, helpless to do anything to stop him!

But no, that was ridiculous. Augustin would never try to kill anyone. There wasn't a violent bone in his body. He was late, that was all. Just late. Jeremy was perfectly safe. He had used and abandoned her, apparently, but he was safe.

It was just as she was thinking this that Mr. Corman steered her round a corner, and there, in a place of honor beneath an oil lamp, hung a great painting of Jeremy himself. Maggie, so surprised she nearly dropped her teacup and saucer, froze, her eyes widening in horror.

"Where," she managed to rasp out, "did you get *that*?"

Mr. Corman looked heartily confused at her question, as well he might, considering, as he quickly pointed out, that she had sent the painting herself, along with all the others from her studio.

"Oh, no," Maggie cried. "Oh, there must be some mistake. I never meant—this painting was never meant to be displayed. The men Aug—I mean, *Monsieur* de Veygoux—

hired must have taken it by mistake. I never meant for it to be shown! Not to . . . anyone!''

Mr. Corman, his pale face pinched with concern, said, ''Oh, but—pardon me for saying so, miss—but this is one of the finest works in your collection. You surely can't mean you want us to take it down. We've made it the focal point of the show.''

At that point, Maggie *had* to put the teacup down, or let it smash to the floor. Setting it onto a small pedestal, Maggie sank down onto a blue velvet settee that had been placed in front of Jeremy's portrait, as if in anticipation of the likeness causing women to swoon.

Maggie would not actually have been surprised if some hapless woman *did* swoon from just looking it at. Painted some years ago, the portrait featured Jeremy looking exactly as he had that night on the terrace, when she'd asked him where he was going, and he'd replied, ''To the devil.'' He wore the exact same expression, half wry, half angry, one of his dark eyebrows lifted skeptically, his mouth quirked up on one side. Standing with one booted foot on her terrace's balustrade, Jeremy was pictured half turned toward the viewer. In one hand, he carried his hat. The other hand was empty, the fist clenched and resting across his raised thigh. In the background loomed Rawlings Manor, pictured exactly the way Maggie remembered seeing it, all those years ago. Jeremy was casually garbed in riding clothes that did nothing to hide the muscularity of the male body beneath them. Maggie blushed just to look at it. What could she have been *thinking*?

Well, it was all too clear what she'd been thinking.

The entire painting had been completed from memory, though to look at it, one would never have guessed. Every line, every detail, was as precise as a daguerreotype. And yet unlike a daguerreotype, the painting captured *all* of Jeremy, not just his looks, but his essence, his biting humor, his shrewd intelligence . . . and most of all, his raw sensuality, which was so evident in this painting that Maggie felt he might almost walk off the canvas, step toward her, scoop her up, and start kissing her then and there.

Thank God for the couch. For her knees had gone so weak, there was no possible way she could have remained standing.

She'd done the painting nearly two years earlier, over a course of four days. Four days of feverish painting, during which she'd allowed no one, not even Berangère or Madame Bonheur, to look at what she was doing. It had been just after she'd met Augustin, and Maggie had decided that possibly, if she painted a portrait of Jeremy, it would get him out of her system, and out of her life.

It hadn't worked. She hadn't been able to look at the finished painting without feeling an inexplicable tightness in her chest. She had put the painting away, resolving never to look at it again. And she hadn't.

Until now.

"We've got to take it down," Maggie said, but weakly.

Mr. Corman had apparently worked with enough temperamental artists to know how to handle them, since he said soothingly, "I know you're nervous about this evening, Miss Herbert, but really, this painting is your best work. It would be downright criminal not to include it in the exhibition. And look how nicely we've fit it in with those landscapes on either side of it. You don't have any similarly sized works to put in its place."

"You don't understand, Mr. Corman," Maggie said. "We've *got* to take it down. This work is part of my, um, *personal* collection. It isn't for sale, and it was never meant to be shown. To anyone. Not even the, uh, sitter. Who . . . well, there's a slight chance he . . . might come tonight."

It was a hope Maggie had hardly dared entertain. She didn't know why Jeremy had suddenly removed himself to Yorkshire. But she hoped—foolishly, she knew—that he might reappear in London for this most important night of her life. . . .

For the first time, comprehension dawned on the young man's face. "Ah," he said. "I see the difficulty, then. But still, Miss Herbert, you can't think that the gentleman pictured here would be *insulted* by this work. Surely you've rendered him in a highly complimentary style." Here his pale eyes flicked toward the painting. "No man could object to being perceived as so very . . . masculine."

Maggie, with a groan, dropped her face into her hands. She was still in this position when a new voice, behind them, startled her.

"*Marguerethe?*"

Maggie's back straightened as quickly as if someone had pulled a string attached to the top of her head. Horrified, she swung around, to see Augustin hurrying into the gallery, shedding his greatcoat even as he was calling her name.

So. He had not gone to Yorkshire to kill Jeremy. Not at all.

"Oh, dear," she murmured, with a last glance at the painting. Fortunately, Mr. Corman seemed to understand her distress, since he quickly stepped in front of the portrait, blocking most of it from view.

"*Marguerethe?*" Augustin called again. There was something in his voice Maggie didn't quite recognize. For the life of her, she could not pinpoint what it was.

Still, she rose from the settee and managed to cross the gallery with surprising composure for one who'd been so discomposed just moments before. But she'd hardly gotten within three yards of Augustin before she saw that he was far more discomposed than she. In fact, he looked quite terrible. Not his bruises—they appeared to be healing nicely, the purple smudges beneath his eyes fading to a satisfactory yellow, the swelling in his nose nowhere near as bad as it had been. No, there was something else wrong with him. Maggie couldn't put her finger on what exactly it was, but there was something different, something . . . odd.

"Oh, *Marguerethe*," Augustin said, when he saw her. The smile he gave her was a nervous one. Bending down, he kissed her quickly on either cheek. "I am so sorry I am late, *chérie*. I do not know what happened. I have never slept so late in my life—"

Maggie frowned up at him. "You *overslept*?" She found that hard to believe. Augustin, in all the time she'd known him, had always been an early riser. But she saw evidence to the truth of his claim in the corners of his eyes—they were still lightly crusted with sleep. Her frown turned to a smile. "Augustin," she said, in a chastising tone. "For shame! Did you go out last night, after you left me those beautiful roses?"

He turned away to hand his coat to one of his assistants. "Not at all, not at all," he said.

He spoke so heartily that Maggie knew he was lying. She wondered what on earth he could be trying to hide.

"I suppose," he went on, "it is merely a cold that has been coming on."

"Oh, of course," Maggie said. "A cold. I hope you have not been neglecting your health."

"No, no, nothing like that." Augustin was speaking to her, yet his mind seemed a good distance away. "What's this?" he asked, his pale gaze darting all about the gallery. "You have done all this, already? You have been busy, *chérie*! Busy, indeed!"

Maggie eyed him. Something was wrong with Augustin. She was quite certain of it. But *what*, exactly? She could not put her finger on it. "Not me," she replied, honestly enough. "Mr. Corman and his associates. They went to the trouble of hanging all the paintings last night, so they'd be quite ready when I got here, and I must say, I'm very pleased with the results." She bit her lip. Hopefully, Augustin would not notice the portrait of Jeremy . . . though how he could miss it, she did not know. The painting seemed to draw gazes to it very much in the manner that the sitter drew gazes, everywhere he went.

As she spoke, she'd noticed Augustin's employees shifting uneasily, nervous about how their employer would take the news that they had acted on their own initiative. She could tell by their astonished expressions a second later, when Augustin announced how pleased he was at the results of their labor, that praise from their employer was hard won, but worth it, on the rare occasions it was bestowed.

"*Superbe*," Augustin declared, as his gaze flicked over the mounted paintings. "I am quite pleased. And you, *Marguerethe*? You are pleased?"

Maggie agreed that she was quite pleased, and only then

did it hit her, that thing about Augustin that had been bothering her. Why, he was not looking her in the eye. That was it! He was not making eye contact with her at all. How odd, Maggie thought. Augustin is acting almost as if he feels guilty about something. How very strange. *I'm* the one who should be feeling guilty, and yet I am quite capable of meeting his gaze. She wondered what he could possibly have done to engender so much guilt. Was it possible that he *had* done something to Jeremy, after all? But no, that couldn't be! If some harm had come to Jeremy, she'd surely have heard about it by now. Wouldn't she?

Well, wouldn't she?

But even as she was wondering, Augustin began speaking again, in the same falsely hearty manner, still not looking her in the face.

"Now, *chérie*, I hope you are prepared for some very great news," he said, adjusting his cravat. "Very great news, indeed. I did not quite believe it myself when I heard it, but it was confirmed this morning by a note I received from the Lord Chancellor himself. Are you ready, *Marguerethe*?"

Maggie felt up to anything . . . except facing that painting of Jeremy again. She said, quite truthfully, "Yes, Augustin. I believe so."

"His Royal Highness the Prince of Wales himself will be attending your exhibition tonight." Augustin pronounced this with so much pleasure that Maggie could not help smiling, not at the prospect of beholding the Prince of Wales, but at Augustin's obvious delight at the news. Truth be told, she was a trifle disappointed. She had hoped he was going to say something quite different . . . that he had learned that her father was coming, or something along those lines.

But she supposed it was a fine thing to be visited by the Prince of Wales, so she said, "Oh, how very nice."

"*Vraiment*, but you are cool about it, *Marguerethe*!" Augustin cried. "Perhaps you did not hear what I said. The Prince of—"

"Yes, I heard you," Maggie said with a forced smile. "And I think it's quite nice."

"*Marguerethe*—" And now, it appeared, she had earned

his full attention. "Don't you understand? The queen has been looking to engage a portrait painter for her grandchildren. Her sending the Prince of Wales to your exhibition must mean she's considering commissioning you for the job—"

Maggie could not help but be impressed, in spite of her gloom. A commission from the queen? An artist could not ask for a greater honor.

Augustin attempted a smile, and though the result was rather hideous, what with his broken nose and complete insincerity, at least it was a smile. "What say you, mademoiselle, to sharing luncheon with me, in the café across the street, to celebrate? There we can discuss our strategy for dealing with the Prince of Wales."

That was not the only thing they needed to discuss. A tea shop was not the ideal place to break off an engagement, but Maggie supposed it would have to suffice. She would have agreed to anything, anything at all, to keep him from seeing that painting.

Then again, maybe she was being silly. What harm, after all, could one little painting do?

Chapter 35

"*How could you?*"

Jeremy opened one eye. This pronouncement, uttered as it was so near his ear, seemed to be coming from directly beside him. For a moment, quite forgetting where he was, Jeremy reached for Maggie, thinking to find her curled next to him.

Instead, his hand encountered a very round, but very firm object. Opening his other eye, Jeremy saw, to his horror, that he was touching his aunt's extremely prominent belly.

Jeremy jerked his hand away and sat up fast, his expression horrified. "Aunt Pegeen!"

Pegeen did not seem to notice her nephew's shock. "*How could you?*" she demanded again, from where she stood at the side of the bed. "For shame, Jerry!"

Jeremy eyed his aunt apprehensively. Though very pregnant, indeed, she did not look a jot different than when he'd last seen her five years earlier, with the exception of some fine laugh lines at the corners of her mouth and green eyes, and an occasional glint of gray among the dark threads of her hair, which fell loosely about her shoulders. She had clearly only just risen from bed herself, and was dressed in a voluminous green velvet robe, tied just under her breasts with a gold cord.

For the life of him, Jeremy did not know what she was referring to. Did she mean, How could he have gotten himself engaged to an Indian princess? Or was it, How could he have been away so long and not written? Hoping to distract his aunt from pursuing either topic, he said, carefully, "I thought that Parks told you to stay in bed."

"Stay in bed!" Pegeen all but shouted at him. "How am I supposed to stay in bed when I learn that my nephew has just come home after five years' absence? And that he's malarial, besides? Jeremy." Here she shook her head at him rebukingly. "How could you? How could you not have written? I'd never have told you about Maggie if I'd known you were ill!"

"Which is precisely why I didn't tell you," Jeremy muttered.

"But malaria, Jeremy!" She shook her head some more. "You look terrible."

"So I've been informed." Jeremy thought about getting out of bed, but realized he was naked beneath the sheets. He couldn't very well throw back the bedclothes and reveal himself to his aunt. Instead, he complained, "Who let you in here, anyway? Hasn't your water broken by now?"

"No, it hasn't," Pegeen said, and to his dismay she sat down on the side of the bed. "And don't be smart. Just because you're a lieutenant colonel now doesn't mean you have license to be rude to your elders."

Jeremy snorted at that. "Does Uncle Edward know you're out of bed? He's going to be extremely put out with you when he finds out about this. . . ."

Pegeen waved a hand dismissively at that. "He can't even keep track of his own children, let alone a wife. Now, tell me about you and Maggie. It was quite wicked of you, you know, Jerry, to stay in the house on Park Lane with her, without anyone there with you. Poor Evers nearly had an apoplexy over it. It was all I could do to convince him not to quit on the spot. We had to offer him quite a raise to stay, you know, *and* assure him that you had every intention of marrying her. Now, what did she say?"

Uncertain which question to answer first, Jeremy tried, "What did who say?"

"Why, Maggie, of course, when you proposed!"

"If you must know, Maggie didn't say anything when I

proposed to her, because I haven't gotten around to it just yet—" At his aunt's sharp intake of breath, Jeremy rolled his eyes. "Look, Aunt Pegeen, I'm happier than I can say to see you, and when all of this is over, you and I will have a nice little visit. But right now, I've got things to do. As, I understand, you do, as well."

"I'll be in labor for hours yet," Pegeen said, with yet another dismissive hand wave. "What exactly do you mean, you haven't gotten around to it just yet? You haven't left that poor girl hanging, without any idea of your intentions, have you, Jerry? I thought Edward warned you—"

"You're *in labor*?" Jeremy interrupted, when her words finally sunk in. "You're actually in labor *right now*?"

She blinked down at him. "Well, only since dawn. It ought to be at least two more hours before I—"

"Pegeen!" The thunderous bellow was accompanied by a great crashing sound. Pegeen jumped, and turned to see what had caused all the commotion. Glaring murderously from the door he'd just kicked open, Edward said, with enough barely restrained fury to make the hairs on the back of Jeremy's neck rise warningly, "It was my impression that you were going to stay in bed."

Pegeen tossed her head. "That was an impression held entirely by yourself and Mr. Parks. It was never shared by me."

"Pegeen." Edward seemed to be trying very hard not to smash something. "Come back to bed. Now."

"*Now?* You can't be serious. Jeremy." She turned toward her nephew. "Alistair and Anne Cartwright are downstairs in the Gold Drawing Room, along with Sir Arthur. According to Edward, you wanted to have a word with them. I do hope you're going to try to talk some sense into them. They've been just horrid to Maggie ever since—Oh!"

This last exclamation was uttered as Edward strode forward, leaned down, and lifted his wife bodily from Jeremy's bed, without apparent effort.

"Edward!" Pegeen cried, outraged. "Put me down this instant! Have you gone mad?"

"No," was her husband's terse reply, as he headed toward the door. "But evidently you have."

"I resent that. Throughout history, men have alternately ignored or condescended to women who happen to be with child"—Pegeen's voice began to grow distant, as Edward carried her out into the hallway—"just because a woman with child is considered an irrational being. Well, I'd like to inform you that there is nothing wrong with my intellect."

"That," Edward said firmly, "is an impression held entirely by yourself."

Jeremy winced, imagining how his strong-willed aunt would react at hearing her own words thrown back at her. Unfortunately, Pegeen was by then too far out of his earshot for him to hear her response to her husband's taunt. Which was just as well. Jeremy had far more important things to do than listen to his aunt and uncle bicker. Throwing back the bedclothes, he dressed hastily, though with care—after all, it wasn't just anyone waiting belowstairs: It was his future in-laws. He wanted to make a good impression.

Ten minutes later, shaved and dressed, Jeremy bounded down one of the curved staircases to the Great Hall, still struggling with the flying ends of his cravat. Damned if he shouldn't have brought Peters along. So intent was Jeremy on knotting his cravat that he very nearly collided with a manservant who was gliding toward the drawing room doors with a tray of sherry glasses in his hands. At the last possible second, the butler noticed the younger man, and abruptly halted.

"I beg your pardon, Your Grace," he said in startled tones, and Jeremy looked up.

"Evers?" Squinting, Jeremy asked suspiciously, "It *is* Evers, isn't it?"

"Indeed it is, Your Grace. My son has the pleasure of serving in your London house, while my father had the honor of buttling here for many years. . . ."

Jeremy could detect no noticeable difference between this man and the one back in London, except for the fact that the one in London had slightly more hair combed across his balding head.

"Well, it's jolly good to see you again, Evers," Jeremy said. "How's this knot look?"

Evers examined the duke's cravat. "Very nice indeed, Your Grace."

"Excellent." He nodded at the tray the butler held. "Bit early for sherry, don't you think?"

"Indeed I do, Your Grace. However, Sir Arthur became quite chilled on the ride over from Herbert Park, and I thought—"

Jeremy snorted. "I see. Well, hand it over, Evers." At the butler's startled glance, Jeremy elaborated, "Go on, give it to me. My aunt's having a baby right now. I'm sure your services are needed elsewhere. Go boil some water, or something."

Evers looked offended. "That would fall under Cook's jurisdiction, Your Grace."

"Then go and decant some brandy for my uncle. I have a feeling he's going to need it soon."

Evers inclined his head, but appeared to disapprove heartily of Jeremy and his resolve to serve his own guests. "As you wish, Your Grace," he murmured. He had already heard from his son, of course, that the new duke was difficult, but he'd had no idea things had come to *this*. He was going to have to have a word with Lord Edward. This kind of thing simply could not go on at Rawlings Manor. The duchy had, after all, a reputation to uphold.

Pausing before the Gold Drawing Room doors, Jeremy used his free hand to give the points of his waistcoat a tug. He could hear the murmur of voices coming from within the room, Alistair's easygoing baritone in direct contrast to his wife's nervous soprano, but her father's irritable bass overpowering both.

"All I would like to know is why I was forced to leave my comfortable hearth"—Sir Arthur appeared to be maintaining an air of injury—"in order to travel to the home of a man who is not even able to receive us properly."

"Really," Jeremy heard Anne say. "I must agree. I can hardly imagine we're welcome here at Rawlings, with the mistress of the house indisposed, and Lord Edward so distracted—"

How her father might have replied, Jeremy didn't wait to hear. Instead, he flung open the double doors and inquired casually, "Sherry, anyone?"

Sir Arthur, who'd been sitting on a velveteen settee of tawny gold, his pudgy hands extended toward the fire, leapt to his feet with surprising speed for a man so portly. "Good Lord," he cried, his pink jowls quivering. "Is that . . . Could it be . . . ?"

"It most certainly is," Jeremy assured him. He set the sherry tray down on an ivory-topped end table, just to the right of Sir Arthur's stunned eldest daughter, who was staring up at him with as much astonishment as if he had risen from the dead. "How do you do, Mrs. Cartwright?" Jeremy asked her, gallantly lifting one of her gloved hands and raising it in the general direction of his lips. "It's been quite a long time, hasn't it? Too long, I'd say. You look pale. May I help you to some sherry?"

Anne, an attractive woman who, Jeremy noted, was dressed in mourning—not for her mother, surely, who'd been dead for a year; could it be for the infant Edward had said she'd lost?—had changed little since he'd last seen her: Except, perhaps, for her complexion, which had always lacked brilliance, and now was devoid of any color whatsoever. He wasn't sure if the change was due merely to her shock at seeing him, or to her recent disappointments.

"I—I—" Anne licked her pale lips. "Oh, dear," she said faintly. "I wasn't aware that you had returned, Jeremy."

"*Your Grace*, my dear," Sir Arthur corrected his daughter hastily. "You must address the duke as *Your Grace*. He has come of age, after all." Leaving the comfort of the fire, Sir Arthur hurried toward Jeremy, his right hand extended. "But we were not told you were expected, Your Grace! This is a surprise, a surprise, indeed!"

"A welcome one, I hope." Jeremy grinned, shaking Maggie's father's hand.

"Oh, indeed, indeed!" Sir Arthur, though he expressed delight at seeing the Duke of Rawlings, still managed to look nervous. "And you . . . are well? You have not come home because of an illness, I hope?"

"A trifling one," Jeremy said dismissively. "But that's nothing compared with what you've gone through this past year."

Sir Arthur dropped his gaze to the emerald and gold pile of the carpet. "Ah," he said glumly. "Then you've heard of our sad loss."

"A very great loss," Jeremy said, placing what he hoped would be perceived as a comforting hand on the portly solicitor's shoulder. He wasn't ready to start strangling the old man. Not yet, anyway. "I was grieved to hear of Lady Herbert's death, very grieved, indeed. I don't believe it would be an exaggeration to say that your wife, Sir Arthur, was universally beloved."

"How kind of Your Grace to say so," Sir Arthur managed to wheeze. To Jeremy's alarm, he saw tears gathering at the corners of the old man's eyes.

Raising his eyebrows, Jeremy looked for help from Alistair, who, though he'd risen upon Jeremy's entrance, had sunk back down again in a plush armchair, some of his blond hair spilling over his forehead. The yellow, Jeremy saw, was intermingled with gray now, but otherwise, Alistair Cartwright looked exactly as he always had. Unlike Jeremy's uncle, Alistair held no seat in the House of Lords, not being titled. His wealth had been made through shrewd business dealings alone, not inheritance. Consequently, Alistair had aged a good deal less than the man he referred to as his "reform-happy friend" Edward Rawlings.

Meeting Jeremy's gaze, Alistair shrugged and looked heavenward. Although he clearly loved his wife, he had never had much patience for her father. He was not, Jeremy saw at once, going to be much help, under the present circumstances.

Jeremy dropped his hand from Sir Arthur's shoulder and said, with forced heartiness, "But I understand there is happy news in your family, as well, Sir Arthur. Isn't your youngest daughter engaged to be married?"

It was Anne who reacted first. She let out a low cry and

stood up rather abruptly, then, as if surprised at finding herself on her feet, she moved quickly over to one of the window casements. She tried to make it look as if she'd gone there apurpose to check the view, but Jeremy knew better: The view from the Gold Drawing Room was a particularly uninspiring one in winter, revealing only the snow-covered moor along which Rawlings Manor was situated.

"Uh, yes," Sir Arthur said uncertainly, his eyes on his daughter's slim back. "Yes, Margaret *is* engaged. But . . ."

Jeremy sank down onto the chaise longue Anne had vacated, his eyes never leaving Sir Arthur. "Yes?" he asked, with a smile that, had Sir Arthur happened to notice it, might have given the older man pause.

"Well," Sir Arthur said, with forced heartiness. "As you know only too well, Your Grace, Margaret has always been . . . headstrong. I think there are far pleasanter topics to discuss. Your adventures abroad, for instance. We've heard all about your brave heroics in India. And you simply *must* tell us about this, er, young woman, this Star of India—"

"Jaipur," Jeremy corrected him. He stretched out his legs along the green velvet cushion and crossed his booted ankles, folding his fingers beneath his head. "And there really isn't anything to say about her. There was some talk that she and I would marry, but that's all it was. Talk. Right now, I'd like to discuss your daughter Maggie, if I might."

"You—" Sir Arthur stared down at the duke confusedly. "Oh, dear. I really . . . I really must protest, Your Grace. That is a subject . . . that is a subject—"

"That is a subject," Jeremy drawled to the domed ceiling, "in which I have a keen interest. One might almost say a *vested* interest."

Sir Arthur's eyes, which were quite small, hidden as they were beneath the folds of his fleshy face, widened to their limits. Jeremy, if he hadn't been harboring so much resentment toward him, might almost have felt sorry for the man. "But Your Grace," he cried. "Perhaps you are not aware . . . no, I'm certain you cannot be aware . . . but Margaret has turned out to be rather a . . . disappointment. . . ."

"What?" Jeremy couldn't help but laugh at the knight's

embarrassment. "What could Maggie have possibly done to make you stammer so, Sir Arthur? Is there something the matter with this fellow she's marrying? Is he a hurdy-gurdy man?"

"No, no," Sir Arthur said. Reaching into his waistcoat pocket, the old man withdrew a handkerchief, which he then used to wipe his glistening forehead. For a man who moments before had been complaining of the cold, he seemed to have grown quite warm. "Nothing like that. You see, Your Grace, Maggie has chosen to make a mockery of all of us by parading herself about London as a . . . a . . ."

Jeremy widened his eyes in mock horror. "Good God! She's joined the chorus line at the Vauxhall!"

"Stop it. Stop it this instant!"

Jeremy looked up, surprised. Anne Cartwright still stood by the window casement, but now she was facing him. Only she didn't look like the Anne Cartwright he had known since his childhood, or even like the Anne Cartwright he'd seen just moments before. This Anne Cartwright was not pale. No, twin spots of color burned in her cheeks. And her eyes, which were not at all like her sister's eyes, not a bit warm, not a bit good-humored, were cold . . . though Jeremy did not think he mistook the fact that tears glistened within them.

"You know very well what Maggie's done," Anne said in a trembling voice. "I should have known the minute you walked through the door, Jerry. I thought you might be up to something. But never in a million years would I have guessed it had something to do with Maggie."

Her father, still confused, murmured, "Anne, dear, please! Do not shout so. Remember to whom you speak."

"Oh, I know very well to whom I speak, Papa," Anne said. "I am speaking to Jeremy Rawlings. Jeremy Rawlings, the hard-drinking, hard-fighting, hard-loving Duke of Rawlings, who cares for nothing but gratifying his own lascivious desires—"

"Now see here." Jeremy sat up and swung his feet back to the floor. "I'm not saying all of those things weren't true at one time, but it's a bit unfair to judge me by the way I was five years ago. I've changed, you know. I've worked bloody hard at it, too, and I think I deserve a second chance.''

Anne went on as if she hadn't even heard him. ''Jeremy Rawlings, because of whom my parents were forced to send my youngest sister away to another *country*, in order to protect her from his wanton lust—''

''Now that's quite enough.'' Jeremy stood up, his jaw set. ''First of all, my lust, wanton or otherwise, is none of your business, Mrs. Cartwright. And secondly, I proposed to your sister five years ago, and she turned me down, so I don't care to hear any more about parents being forced to send their daughters to other countries because of me, when, frankly, *I'm* the one who was taken advantage of.''

''You *what*?'' Anne cried breathlessly. Her father looked equally stunned. In fact, he was forced to sit down, quite heavily, on a tapestry-covered stool that creaked ominously beneath his weight.

''You heard me,'' Jeremy said, as he stalked back and forth before the fire. ''Now, you can despise me all you like. I don't really give a damn. What I care about is how Maggie's come out in all of this. Why, you people are treating her as if she were some kind of criminal, or something, when all she's doing is what she loves.''

Anne blinked a few times. ''You proposed to Maggie,'' she said, appearing still to be in some need of clarification. ''And she turned you down?''

''That's right.'' He stopped pacing and turned to face them. ''Might I ask why that is so hard for you to believe?''

''But . . .'' Anne had gone pale again. ''*Maggie?* Duchess of *Rawlings*? No, sir. No. I cannot credit it.''

Jeremy set his jaw. ''Well, you're going to have to begin crediting it. Because I intend to marry her, as soon as I convince her to have me.''

Anne didn't appear to have heard him. ''If you two were to marry, I can assure you, Jeremy, she won't stop painting. . . .''

''Nor would I ask her to,'' Jeremy said. ''Why should she? She loves to do it, and she's good at it. Have you seen any of the paintings she's done recently, Mrs. Cartwright? They're jolly good. . . .''

Sir Arthur cleared his throat. ''It would be most unseemly,'' he said. ''Most unseemly. Disgraceful, even. Quite a bit more disgraceful than had you married the Hindu girl. I'm quite sure the queen would not approve.''

''What's disgraceful,'' Jeremy said firmly, ''and what *I'm* quite sure the queen wouldn't approve of, is the way you two are carrying on about it. I'm damned tired of hearing it, and I'm putting an end to it here and now.'' Jeremy reached into his waistcoat and pulled out his pocket watch. ''There's a train leaving for London in exactly two hours. If there's anything you need to pack for a night away from home, Mrs. Cartwright, I suggest you send one of my servants to fetch it now. The brougham will be leaving in half an hour.''

Anne stared at him. ''What . . . what are you talking about?''

''We're taking a trip to London, Mrs. Cartwright,'' Jeremy explained patiently. ''Your sister's exhibition is opening tonight at her fiancé's gallery on Bond Street. It would mean a lot to her if you and your father could be there, and so I'm going to see to it that you are.''

''This . . .'' Anne exchanged astonished glances with her father. ''This is insane! I am not going anywhere!''

''Yes,'' Jeremy said quietly, putting away his watch. ''You are.''

''I'm not!'' Anne nudged her father. ''Papa, tell him!''

''Well, Anne,'' Sir Arthur said uncertainly. ''He is the, uh, duke.''

''But he can't do this!'' Anne whirled toward her husband, who had sat up a little straighter in his armchair, but otherwise appeared to be doing nothing more than observing the proceedings with a look of keen interest on his face. ''Alistair, tell him! Tell him he can't do this!''

Alistair met Jeremy's gaze, and must have seen the entreaty there, since his next words were, ''I'm sorry if it pains you, love, but I'm afraid I agree with him. It's high time you exercised some sisterly charity toward your youngest sibling.''

"Oh!" Anne blinked at him tearfully. "How could you, Alistair? How *could* you?" Flinging a hand over her mouth to stifle a sob, Anne lifted her hem and ran from the room. Her father looked after her in alarm.

"Oh, dear," he said. "I suppose I should . . . I suppose I should . . ."

"Yes," Jeremy said with a sigh. "Go after her, Sir Arthur. Just make sure she's ready to go at half past the hour."

"As you wish, Your Grace." Sir Arthur hurried from the room, but not before he'd mumbled a number of incoherent apologies.

As soon as the door had closed behind the old man, Alistair, in the armchair, began to applaud slowly. "Well done, young man," he declared, his voice dripping with sarcasm. "Well done! Couldn't have done it better myself had I tried. You ought to follow your uncle's example, and take up a seat in the House, with *your* diplomatic skills."

Sensing he was being mocked, albeit gently, Jeremy shrugged. "Well," he said. "At least I didn't have to use the pistol."

Chapter 36

After Augustin, who did not take sugar in his coffee, stirred a third cube into his cup, Maggie finally burst out with, "Won't you tell me what's wrong?"

Augustin looked up from the tablecloth, startled. "*Pardon, chérie?*"

"It can't be good for our digestion," Maggie said, a little more gently than she'd spoken before. "Eating under this cloud of gloom you seem to have brought with you. Can't you tell me what's wrong?"

"Nothing is wrong, *chérie*," Augustin said, with so much syrupy condescension that he actually reached out and patted Maggie's hand, which was resting on the table beside her cup and saucer. "Nothing is wrong at all."

But he was lying. Maggie knew good and well that he was lying. He had been speaking to her in that same patronizing tone all afternoon, first at the gallery and now at the tea shop. He still couldn't look her in the eye, and he hadn't chastised her when she'd ordered a slice of cake with her tea, as he normally would have, since Augustin felt strongly that dessert ought only be consumed after a meal, not in place of one.

This man, Maggie thought, cannot possibly be a murderer. What was it then, that was upsetting him so? Could he, Maggie wondered, have found out about Jeremy? But how? She knew perfectly well that the fact that she'd lost her virginity didn't show . . . well, except maybe to Berangère. So how could Augustin know? Jeremy surely hadn't told him. Maggie knew Jeremy too well to suspect that he might have bragged to Augustin. To do so would have been beneath Jeremy's dignity. Shooting Augustin would have been preferable to Jeremy than admitting to him that he'd deflowered his fiancée. . . .

Was it possible that *Berangère* had told him? Maggie swallowed a mouthful of cake and nodded distractedly at the waitress who asked if the young lady would like more tea. Maggie had told no one else, so if anyone had spilled the truth to Augustin, it could only have been Berangère. But why would Berangère have done such a thing? For what possible gain?

Because she wanted to help. That had to be it. Berangère, in an attempt to help Maggie make the right decision about her future, had told Augustin the truth about Maggie and Jeremy. Of course. Hadn't Berangère said *"Leave Augustin to me?"*

The more she thought about it, the more convinced Maggie became that this was the reason behind Augustin's strange behavior. Berangère had told him about Maggie's night of passion with Jeremy. And as Augustin was much too polite to bring up the subject, Maggie thought it only fitting that she should do so herself.

"Did you," she began hesitantly, "happen to run into Berangère last evening after you left me?"

Augustin dropped his coffee cup.

Fortunately, it landed in its own saucer, and didn't break, though its contents did slosh over the side and spill onto the white tablecloth. A number of other patrons glanced their way, distracted by the noise, and Maggie, who'd observed Augustin's reaction with openmouthed astonishment, thought to herself, *Oh, no! She told him! I'll kill her. I'll just kill her. Why couldn't she have left it to me?*

Augustin dabbed at the wet spot on the tablecloth with his napkin, then lifted the square of linen to his lips and dabbed nervously at the corners of his mouth, as well. "How . . . how did you know?"

Maggie smiled sadly. "Just a guess."

"I . . . I just don't know how it happened," Augustin was saying, to his lap. He was still perfectly incapable of looking Maggie in the eye.

Maggie reached across the table to pat his hand, as he'd patted hers just moments before. The gesture was pathetically inadequate, but what else could she do? She said the first thing that came into her head. It was not part of the speech she'd rehearsed. "Augustin, I'm so very, very sorry. . . ."

Augustin did lift his head then. He fastened a grateful gaze on Maggie's face and murmured, "*Vous êtes vraiment angélique.* . . ."

Maggie blinked at him. "Augustin, really," she whispered. "I'm anything *but* angelic."

"But you are!" He seized her hand and held it in a desperate grip in both his own. "What other woman would be so forgiving, so magnanimous? I am truly the luckiest man alive!"

"Forgiving?" Maggie echoed. "What have *I* to forgive? *I* should be the one asking *your* forgiveness."

"No," Augustin cried, lifting her hand to his lips and showering it with kisses. "No, I am the one who sinned. Sinned against my love! And she said you would not understand. But you do understand! And you forgive! Oh, my *Marguerethe*! Truly, I do not deserve you, dog that I am. . . ."

Maggie, startled, yanked her hand out of his grip and stared at him across the table. "What are you talking about? *Who* said I wouldn't understand?"

"Why, Berangère, of course." Augustin smiled at her tremulously. "She told me not to tell you, that you wouldn't understand, but I told her she was wrong. There is no woman in the world like my *Marguerethe*. None so forgiving, none so understanding. . . ."

Maggie stared at him. "Just for the purpose of clarification, Augustin," she said, "precisely *what* is it I am being so understanding about?"

"Why, my indiscretion, *chérie*." Augustin blinked at her. "Last night."

Maggie slumped back in her chair, stunned, though not

unpleasantly so. *Berangère*? *Augustin* had slept with *Berangère*?

"You do understand, don't you, *chérie*?" Augustin spoke rapidly and in an urgent undertone that she could only just hear above the clink of spoons in teacups, the low murmur of the other patrons' conversations, and the click-clack of the waitress's high-heeled boots. "After I left you so sadly indisposed last evening, I felt in need of a bite to eat, and so I went to the Vauxhall . . . a bit loud for my tastes, but I was feeling, I admit, a bit glum. Well, who should I run into there but Berangère, who was also alone. I invited her to dine with me, *naturellement*—"

"Oh," Maggie said, with a nod, since it seemed as if he'd paused for her approval. "*Naturellement.*"

"Well, we had a lovely meal, and with it some champagne, and then a little more champagne . . . I suppose we had a little too much champagne, because the next thing I knew, Berangère said she had broken the lace to her slipper, and would I mind escorting her back to her flat so that she could replace it. I, of course, as a gentleman, could not allow her to travel so far alone, not so late at night, and so I said yes, and then when we arrived at her flat, she opened another bottle of champagne she happened to have, and—"

"Oh," Maggie said. She felt something she could not exactly describe. It was as if an enormous weight had been lifted, not from her shoulders, as she'd sometimes heard people say, but from her heart. "I see."

The corners of Augustin's mouth were twitching, but evidently not with humor, since his next words were as impassioned as any he'd ever uttered.

"But it didn't *mean* anything, *Marguerethe*! I was a fool. I had had too much to drink, and you know Berangère, she's a lovely, vivacious woman—"

"Oh, yes," Maggie said. She was having trouble controlling the corners of her own mouth, but for entirely different reasons. "I know Berangère."

So *this* is what Berangère had meant by *taking care* of Augustin! Good Lord! Maggie ought to have known, of course. Berangère had seduced Augustin! And if Maggie wasn't mistaken, Augustin looked as if he'd enjoyed every minute of it. Surely that was part of this great guilt he was feeling. He had betrayed his bride-to-be, and he had *enjoyed* it!

Well, Maggie would help convince him that perhaps this wasn't quite the end of the world . . . on the contrary, it might be the start of something much more agreeable than his relationship with Maggie.

"Are you telling me, Augustin," Maggie inquired gravely, "that you made love to Berangère, but that you felt nothing for her?"

"No," Augustin said quickly. "No, I did not mean . . . not *nothing*. I only meant that . . . Perhaps, if you and I had not met, Berangère and I—" Augustin shook his head, as if trying to wake himself from a particularly delectable dream. "But that cannot be."

"Really?" Maggie placed her elbow on the table and rested her chin in her hand. "Why?"

Augustin stared at her as if she were demented. "Because I have pledged myself to you, *Marguerethe*!"

"You would still marry me," Maggie asked, "though you are in love with another?"

Color, quite an extraordinary amount of it, rushed into Augustin's cheeks. "I did not say . . . I did not mean . . ."

Maggie, feeling a sudden flood of warm feelings toward him, reached out and took Augustin's hand with a gentle laugh. "I am teasing you, Augustin. I'm sorry. I couldn't resist. We are such good friends, you and I, that teasing you . . . well, it comes naturally. More naturally, I'm afraid, than . . ." She lowered her eyelids. "Than other feelings."

"Ah," he said. "So that is the way it is." When she felt brave enough to lift her gaze, Maggie saw that Augustin did not look particularly crushed, only a little dispirited. "We are to be only friends, then, you and I?"

She tightened her grip on his hand. "Don't you think it would be best, Augustin? I don't think it's enough, really, for a husband and wife to simply be . . . fond of one another. Like brother and sister."

"My feelings toward you were hardly brotherly, *Mar-*

guerethe,'' Augustin said, with a rueful sigh. When Maggie, embarrassed, attempted to draw her hand from his, however, he seized it, and held on tightly. ''But I cannot fault you for admitting that for you, it was not the same. You were always very honest with me, *Marguerethe*. You told me from the beginning that you were not in love with me. I had thought that with time . . . but now I see such a thing would never have been possible. A woman like you could never love a man like me—''

''Now you're simply being ridiculous,'' Maggie said sternly. ''You know very well you have a great deal to offer the *right* woman. I just didn't happen to be she.''

''Perhaps not.'' Augustin looked wistful. ''But . . .''

''But . . . ?'' Maggie gazed curiously at him from across the table. ''But what?''

He shook his head, as if trying to rid himself of an unwanted thought, and abruptly released her hand. ''It is nothing,'' he said. ''It is only that . . . Do you think . . . Is it possible that Berangère . . . ?''

Maggie had to bite the inside of her lip to keep from smiling too broadly. ''That's a difficult question,'' she said, trying to sound thoughtful. ''It would take a good deal of manipulation on your part, Augustin, to win over Berangère. Still, she isn't a foolish girl. I'm quite certain, with the right incentives, she might come around to the idea.''

''Incentives, *Marguerethe*?''

Maggie smiled. ''She's very fond of money, Augustin.''

''Ah, I see!'' Augustin brightened considerably. ''And I have a good deal of it.''

Maggie laughed. ''Yes, you do. Perhaps if you throw enough of it in her direction . . .''

''I shall shower her with gifts,'' Augustin declared. ''Jewels and furs and flowers!''

''I think,'' Maggie said with a grin, ''that you have determined exactly the way to Berangère's heart.''

''As you say. Still, I wonder . . .'' He looked at her fondly. ''What of *your* heart, *chère Marguerethe*? I know it has not been broken by this foolish confession of mine. But I would like to see you happy. This duke of yours . . . for I

know that it is he, and not I, that you have always loved . . .
can he make you happy?''

Maggie, startled, uttered something flippant by way of
reply. But later, in the hansom cab Augustin hired to take
her home, she repeated Augustin's words to herself. What
about this duke of hers? *Could* he make her happy? Remembering the night they'd passed together, she believed he
could . . . very easily. And not just in bed, either.

But could *she* make *him* happy?

Chapter 37

*F*our hours later, she was still wondering.

Maggie's feet, in high-heeled satin slippers, were beginning to hurt. Her cheeks were definitely sore from the smile she'd forced herself to wear throughout the evening, and her right hand ached from having been squeezed by so many eager arts enthusiasts. While on the one hand, it was very pleasant to stand there and hear how talented everyone thought her, Maggie really only cared what one person thought, and he had yet to show his face.

Was he really not coming? She had been so crushed at his sudden departure from London. Her only comfort had been the information Hill had provided, about the note from Rawlings Manor. Surely a visit to his family was called for, even necessary. But to be gone from her so long . . .

But he had left only the day before! What was the matter with her? She was like a lovelorn schoolgirl, mooning after her first beau. So what if he didn't return in time for the opening of her exhibition? So what if he didn't return at all? There would be other men, surely. . . .

But an inner voice had been whispering to her all night, and that inner voice said, No. There would be only one man. Only Jeremy.

It turned out she'd been wrong when she'd told herself that no one would venture from their warm hearths in order to look at a bunch of "pretty pitchers." Her exhibition had attracted dozens—maybe even scores—of art patrons, none of whom seemed to mind the inclement weather. A pretty hired girl took their wraps as they entered the gallery, and gave them each a numbered disc with which their cloaks could later be retrieved. But since Augustin had seen to it that champagne flowed freely, and baked oysters and mushroom tarts were passed around on silver trays, not many who entered seemed eager to leave. Less than an hour after the reception began, red velvet ribbons had been pinned to the wall beside more than half of Maggie's uncommissioned works, indicating that they'd been sold.

But though toward eight o'clock, Maggie had shaken hands with over a hundred people, none of them the person for whom she'd been waiting. Supposing he didn't come? The gallery closed in an hour, and then she was being whisked off somewhere for a celebratory supper with Augustin and his friends. Not that she'd be able to eat, when all she could think about was Jeremy. How was he going to react to the news that she was no longer engaged? Would he propose to her a second time? Was it presumptuous of her to think that he would? Ought *she* to propose to *him* this time? She supposed that would only be fair. After all, she'd already turned him down once. . . .

But was she *that* sure? Was she truly convinced that she could make him happy? What did it matter? He wasn't coming. Something had happened. Maggie was certain something had happened. Maybe the train to Yorkshire had crashed. Or his curricle had overturned. Maybe this man, this mysterious killer who had been stalking him since his return from India, had finally managed to injure him seriously, and even now Jeremy was tossing about in some hospital bed, feverishly calling her name. Maggie, seizing a glass of champagne from a passing tray, downed it in a single gulp at the thought.

Then an even worse idea occurred to her. What if, she wondered, accepting another glass of champagne from a portly man with a monocle, who was effusively comparing her painting style to that of the Impressionists, once at Rawlings, Jeremy came to his senses, and realized that Maggie really would make a dreadful duchess? What if he was, right this very moment, reuniting with the Princess Usha, who was too beautiful to do anything *but* act as hostess in such a gracious dwelling as Rawlings Manor?

Maggie finished off her second champagne. No, that wouldn't happen. He loved *her*. She was sure of it. Five years, *five years*, he'd waited for her. Well, she could wait for him for one night. One night wouldn't kill her.

Except . . .

Except that now that she was free, she wanted to tell him. She wanted to tell everyone. This haughty-looking woman, shaking her hand. Maggie wanted to say to her, "Thank you very much, ma'am, for admiring my paintings, and did you know that I'm in love with the seventeenth Duke of Rawlings? You didn't? Well, it's true."

But with an effort, she managed to restrain herself. Even when people complimented her on the exhibition and then asked, curiously, as nearly everyone did, "And the portrait of that dark-haired young man. Who is he?"

At first Maggie had been horrified. She had specifically asked Mr. Corman to remove that painting. She caught his arm as he rushed about, drawing up sales slips and, her heart in her throat, begged him to take it down. But the young man had very gently extricated himself, plucking at her gloved fingers while saying, in a soothing voice, "But honestly, miss, it's the best of the lot. I listed it as not for sale, but I simply couldn't take it down. It really is a wonderful painting."

It seemed as if Mr. Corman wasn't the only one who thought so, either. Nearly everyone, including the art critic from *The Times*, commented upon it. And when Maggie wouldn't tell anyone the name of the subject, the buzz about it only grew. Only the Mitchells, with whom Maggie had attended the Althorpe cotillion, recognized the portrait, much to Maggie's chagrin.

"But isn't that—" Lady Mitchell had gasped, and even her yawning husband had raised an eyebrow.

"I say, de Veygòux," he drawled. "That's the fellow who squashed your nose t'other night. What are you about, letting a portrait of him hang in your place?"

To his credit, Augustin, who had been too busy to notice

the portrait before the opening began, laughed off Lord
Mitchell's teasing. And later, during a brief lull in the stream
of well-wishers, Augustin was able to take Maggie by the
arm and rebuke her, good-humoredly, for never having
shown him the painting before.

"Though it's probably a good thing you didn't," he admitted, in French. "For one look at it, and I'd have known
right away there was never any hope for me."

Maggie, blushing profusely, tried to apologize, but Augustin shushed her.

"Nonsense," he said. "It's a wonderful painting. If you
ever do consent to sell it, please consider allowing me the
honor of purchasing it. It might be restful to look upon of
an evening, when I get to feeling too full of myself."

Maggie had been far too embarrassed to reply. It was bad
enough to have all of her works on display for public perusal.
She did not need to have her emotions on display, as well.
But the two seemed to go hand in hand. Unlike Berangère,
Maggie had never been able to keep from putting a little of
herself into each painting she completed, so that her relationship with her work was highly personal. Each painting
was almost like a child to her, and she could not see any one
of them sold without suffering a little pang of remorse.

She was watching with regret as Mr. Corman pinned a
red velvet ribbon to one of her landscapes when a familiar
voice purred, "*Bon soir, princesse,*" behind her. Maggie
turned her head, and smiled at Berangère, who, as usual, was
looking breathtakingly elegant, this time in a low-cut evening
gown of purple velvet.

"Quite a crowd your Monsieur de Veygoux has managed
to draw up for you, *princesse,*" Berangère observed, from
behind an ostrich-plumed fan. "And they're buying, too!
You must be pleased."

Maggie accepted a third glass of champagne, this one offered to her by one of the hired waiters. "Oh, I'm very
pleased," she said, sipping the effervescent liquid, but hardly
tasting it. "But he isn't my Monsieur de Veygoux anymore."

Berangère lowered the fan in what Maggie knew very
well was feigned surprise. "*Non? Mon Dieu!* But how did

that come about, *princesse*? Did he find out about you and *le duc diabolique*?''

''No, he did not,'' Maggie said. Noticing that the Mitchells were quite close by, she took Berangère's arm and steered her toward a less populated area of the gallery, inclining her head so that she could speak into the Frenchwoman's shell-like ear. ''You know very well what happened, Berangère. There's no use playing the innocent with me. You deliberately seduced Augustin last night!''

Berangère didn't even attempt to deny it. She only lifted her clear blue eyes and asked, meekly, ''Are you very angry with me, *princesse*?''

''I will be,'' Maggie said severely, ''if you hurt him.''

''Hurt him?'' Berangère tossed her head so that some of her golden curls bounced. ''*Pfui!* I like that! I have performed the most intimate service imaginable for you, and you have the nerve to accuse me of—''

''I mean it, Berangère,'' Maggie said sternly. ''Augustin is smitten with you. You must be gentle with him. He isn't like the other men you play with. He's sensitive.''

Berangère raised her expressive eyes to the ceiling. ''*Pfui!*'' she said again. ''Sensitive! And what am I, I ask you?''

''Insensitive,'' Maggie replied, without hesitation. ''And you're wrong. I'm very grateful to you.''

''Are you?'' Berangère beamed. ''I am glad, *princesse*. I knew you would not approve of my methods—you never do—but I was so tired of seeing *ma pauvre princesse* looking sad. I had to do something. And you know, I quite like your Augustin. Did you know he is red-haired *all over*?'' Berangère raised her eyebrows meaningfully, and Maggie, embarrassed, let out a nervous laugh. Fortunately, Berangère quickly changed the subject. ''Now, where is your Jerry? How did he take the news that you are free, eh?''

Maggie frowned. She was beginning to regret the third glass of champagne. Perhaps she ought to try a baked oyster. ''He, um, doesn't know yet.''

''Doesn't know?'' Berangère snapped her fan shut and pointed it at Maggie's nose. ''Now who is playing with whom? *Marguerethe*, you must tell him. Now that there is no more fiancé, it is time for you decide. Do you want the duke, or do you not?''

Maggie's mouth dropped open. "Oh, Berangère, of course I want him! Only—"

"Don't." Berangère held up a slim hand, palm facing outward. "Do *not* tell me how undeserving you are, and what a *duchesse terrible* you'd make. I am tired of hearing it. *He* thinks you would be a good duchess, and that is all that matters."

Maggie didn't agree with her high-spirited friend, but that was beside the point. Miserably, she looked for a place to sit down. Only every chair was occupied, as were all of the velvet-cushioned benches scattered about the gallery. "Berangère, I haven't had a chance to tell him because I haven't seen him. He went back to Yorkshire for some reason, and he hasn't yet returned. And the truth is . . . well, I don't know if he ever will."

"Hasn't yet returned?" Berangère's slender eyebrows raised to their limit. "Ah. He must have met with some resistance, then. . . ."

Maggie, giving up her search for a seat, turned her head to stare down at the Frenchwoman. "Resistance?" she echoed. "What do you mean, he must have met with some resistance?"

Berangère snapped open her fan and began to wave it energetically, looking everywhere but up at Maggie. "Where is that boy with the champagne? I am parched! It is too warm in here, do you not think so?"

"Berangère," Maggie said warningly, but she didn't have a chance to continue, since Augustin suddenly seized her arm.

"*Marguerethe*," he cried, not even noticing Berangère in his excitement. "*Marguerethe*, he is here! He is here at last!"

Maggie's heart seemed to roll over in her chest. She caught her breath, and slowly turned her head in the direction that Augustin was pointing. She really *had* had too much to drink. She felt the pressure of his fingers encircling her bare arm, and was conscious that beside her, Berangère had frozen, her fan in mid-sweep, and yet for a moment, it was as if she stood alone in the room. The noisy crowd, which was thick with bustles and black coattails, fell silent all at once, and then seemed to part, as if by some unseen hand. And then a man was approaching her, a tall man, his head held high, a knowing smile on his face. . . .

But it wasn't Jeremy. It was a man Maggie had seen somewhere before, but it wasn't Jeremy. Maggie's heart, which had stuttered, suddenly began its normal rhythm again. She exhaled and, feeling a little sick, tried to wrench her arm from Augustin's grasp. His fingers were cutting off the blood circulation to her hand.

"*Nom de Dieu*," she heard Berangère breathe. "It is the Prince of Wales!"

Maggie glanced at the man once more, and realized that Berangère was right. It *was* the Prince of Wales. A large man, with a sizable belly swelling behind a white satin waistcoat, he was dressed as if to go to the theater, but had condescended to make a stop along his way. Hanging on to his arm was a woman Maggie also recognized, although she was not, by any stretch of the imagination, the Princess of Wales. Not unless the Princess of Wales had suddenly developed an affinity for face paint and marabou feathers, both of which this woman wore in profusion.

"I *knew* he would come," Maggie heard Augustin hiss triumphantly beside her. "I *knew* it! The queen is looking for a portrait artist to render her grandchildren. *Marguerethe*, it could only be you. In all of England, no one paints portraits as you do! Oh, this is the best day of my life. The best!"

Maggie could not say the same. Her disappointment, coupled with her nausea, was profound. She had been quite certain, when Augustin had called, "He's here!" that the *he* in question had been Jeremy. Where *was* he? And what had Berangère been talking about, when she'd said—

"Ah, Mr. dee Vaygoo." The prince stopped in front of Augustin, still smiling benignly. "What a delightful gallery you have, sir. And such a delightful exhibition."

Augustin stood with his mouth hanging open for a second

or two, and then, when a sly pinch from Berangère brought him round again, hastily bowed at the waist.

"T-thank you, Your Royal Highness," he stammered. "Thank you very much. I can't tell you what an honor—"

"And is this Miss Herbert?" The prince grinned down at Berangère. "I have heard much about your talent, my dear, but may I say, your beauty exceeds your skill with a paintbrush."

Without so much as blinking, Berangère dropped into the prettiest curtsy imaginable and said, her long eyelashes lowered coquettishly, "*Merci beaucoup*, Your Highness. But you flatter me. I am not the artist." Berangère straightened and, seeing that Maggie had been trying to slink behind her, hoping no one would notice her, stepped quickly out of the way and said, giving Maggie a firm push forward, "*This* is Mademoiselle Herbert, Your Highness."

Maggie staggered a step or two forward, then, completely mortified, dipped her knees perfunctorily, hoping they would not give out entirely beneath her. "Your Royal Highness," she said, to the floor. Her cheeks, she could tell, were blazing with embarrassment.

"Ah!" Smiling broadly, the Prince of Wales extended a dimpled hand, and Maggie, looking up, saw that he expected her to place hers in it. She did so, marveling at the softness of the fingers of the heir to the throne. "My dear, you are as pretty as any of your pictures."

Maggie, wishing very much that the floor would open and swallow her into it, murmured, "Thank you, sir."

"Tell me now," the prince went on, still grasping her hand. "Who is this young man with the flashing eyes that you've rendered so admirably?"

Confused, Maggie lifted her eyes and was horrified to see that they were standing beneath the portrait of Jeremy. Her throat suddenly dry as sand, Maggie croaked, "Oh. That's . . . that's the seventeenth Duke of Rawlings."

The Prince of Wales raised his eyebrows. "Is it now?" To his lady companion, he said, "That'd be Edward Rawlings's nephew, Bella, the one who caused all that commotion in Jaipur."

"Ah," said Bella, parting her heavily made-up lips to reveal a set of startlingly yellow, and not very straight, teeth. "He's very good-looking."

The prince wasn't paying any attention to her, though. "Tell me," he said to Maggie, though he was squinting at the canvas before him. "These horses here, in the background. Are they supposed to be grays?"

Maggie leaned forward to squint with him. "Yes, sir," she said, after a minute. "They are."

"Damn!" The prince abruptly straightened, dropping her hand as if she'd singed him. "Those are the grays old Edward Rawlings won from me, Bella! The matched geldings!"

"Are they?" Bella asked, without interest.

"I loved those horses," the prince said mournfully. Then, looking as if something had just occurred to him, he said to Maggie, "Tell me something, my dear. Do you ever paint pictures of animals? You know, dogs and things?"

Maggie, most of her nausea having dissipated with the prince's interest in Jeremy's portrait, couldn't help smiling. She knew exactly what was coming. "Yes, sir," she said. "Quite often, as a matter of fact."

"Splendid!" The prince clapped his hands together. "Then do you think you could paint a portrait of this truly exquisite mare I purchased last week? Such a beauty, she is, black all over. Named her Midnight, as a matter of fact. Do you think you could do that for me, Miss Herbert?"

"I would be honored, sir," Maggie said, gravely bowing her head, though her bare shoulders twitched a little with merriment.

"Excellent!" Beaming, the prince winked at Augustin. "Quite a girl you have there, dee Vaygoo. Quite a girl. Send her round on Monday morning, would you? Might even introduce 'er to Mother." Turning, the Prince of Wales extended his arm toward his companion. "I am exceedingly glad we took the trouble to stop by, aren't you, Bella?"

Bella smiled her terrible smile again, and then the prince led her away, as gently as if she were as light as the feathers with which her gown was trimmed, and might blow away at any moment.

No sooner was the Prince of Wales out of earshot than Augustin threw his arms around Maggie and, to her very great surprise, lifted her into the air, spinning her around as if she too were made from nothing but marabou down.

"*Marguerethe*!" he cried excitedly. "*Marguerethe*, do you know what this means?"

Maggie, dizzy, seized Augustin's shoulders and cried, "Put me down! Oh, God, Augustin, put me down, before I'm sick."

Augustin obliged her, but did not release his hold on her waist. "*Marguerethe*, this is the best day of my life! Do you realize what this means? It means that finally, after years of trying, the de Veygoux family can claim to be purveyors of art to the queen of England herself! Have you any idea how much that is going to mean to the business, to my family back in Paris? *Mon Dieu*, I've got to cable them right away!"

"Fine, Augustin," Maggie said, laughing good-naturedly. "But let go of me first. I drank too much champagne, and if you keep spinning me around like that, it all just might come back up—"

Unable to staunch his enthusiasm, Augustin pulled Maggie forward and planted a firm kiss on her lips. No sooner did he release her than the crowd parted once again, this time to reveal someone she recognized at once.

"Jeremy!" Maggie cried delightedly.

Then all of the laughter that had been bubbling up inside of her died. Because behind Jeremy were two other people she recognized. The *last* two people she would have ever expected to see at her exhibition.

Maggie felt all the champagne she'd consumed throughout the evening suddenly rise up into her throat.

Chapter 38

*J*eremy had expected Maggie to react strongly upon his arriving at her exhibition with her estranged family in tow. He'd expected tears, maybe even words of reproach: Maggie had never been one to keep her feelings to herself.

But he never thought that he'd find her in the arms of someone else.

His surprise at having done so was so great that he didn't even notice the look of total and complete shock that registered upon her face the moment her gaze flicked to the couple behind him. Instead, he began striding toward the fiancé, who'd gone ashen faced at seeing him. Well, and why not? Jeremy was certain it was perfectly obvious from his livid expression what he intended to do, which was, of course, call the bastard out. Really, this had gone on long enough. If *Maggie* would not give the fellow the mitten, well, *he* jolly well would. . . .

Then a soft, and all too familiar voice sounded behind him.

"Colonel-Duke?"

Jeremy froze, mid-step. No. It couldn't be. It simply . . . couldn't . . . be. . . .

But it was. Pivoting around slowly, on one foot, he saw that what Maggie and her fiancé had been staring at was *not* Sir Arthur and his eldest daughter. No, it was the Princess Usha, glitteringly attired in a white evening gown dripping with pearls, and accompanied by her translator, Sanjay.

Oh, Sir Arthur was there, all right. He hadn't managed to slip away into the crowd, or anything. A man that large couldn't very well slip anywhere. But his presence was overshadowed by the radiant glow of the princess, who was gazing at Jeremy with her black eyes limpid with love—or greed. Jeremy could never be too certain with Usha.

Good God! No wonder everyone was staring!

And no wonder Maggie had looked as stunned as *he* undoubtedly had, finding her in the arms of another.

Stalking back in the direction from which he'd come, Jeremy seized the princess by the arm, ignoring her inquisitive "Colonel-Duke?" and hauled her off through the crowd, who parted hastily when they saw him coming. Maybe it was the extraordinarily attractive creature he held in tow. Or maybe it was the coldness in his gray eyes. Whichever the case, the gathered intelligentsia and arts patrons moved out of his way, and with alacrity.

"*What,*" Jeremy hissed, beneath his breath, when he'd finally gotten Usha off into a relatively secluded corner of the gallery, "*are you doing here?*"

Sanjay had scurried after them, and now, bowing slightly, he said, "Many apologies, Your Grace. We followed Miss Herbert here, on the assumption that where she goes, you tend to follow."

Jeremy could hardly believe his ears. His plan, his lovely plan to reunite Maggie with her family, spoiled by this obnoxious, empty-headed little princess! Out of the corner of his eye, Jeremy saw that the reunion, which he himself engineered, was taking place without him. Maggie had extended a gracious hand to her father, who for the first time all evening seemed to have been stricken dumb. His daughter Anne had been the silent one during the long train ride to London, sitting beside her husband with her back ramrod straight and her mouth firmly shut. Jeremy had found himself wishing fervently that Sir Arthur would follow his daughter's example. Maggie's father had done nothing but complain during the entire course of the journey, alternately bleating about the discomfort of the trip and the ludicrousness of its purpose. Jeremy had almost drawn the pistol on him, in the hopes that it might shut him up.

Alistair, however, seeing that the duke's patience was wearing thin, had lectured the old man on parenting, quoting at length from the Old Testament about a father's duty to love his children, despite their faults. Jeremy had listened in surprise, having been previously unaware that Alistair Cartwright was so familiar with the Good Book. It was only when his wife dryly pointed out that nowhere in the Bible was it written that "Fathers should suffer their little daughters to become artists" that Jeremy realized Alistair had been playing fast and loose with Scripture.

No, the only thing that Jeremy had seen silence Sir Arthur was the sight of the Prince of Wales shaking his youngest daughter's hand. That and the promise the prince had elicited from Maggie that she'd call at Kensington Palace on Monday had nearly caused the old man an apoplexy . . . of joy. His knees buckling, Sir Arthur had had to be guided to a low couch by his son-in-law, where he sat murmuring, "His Royal Highness, the Prince of Wales. His Royal Highness, the Prince of Wales. Requested the pleasure of the company of my daughter Monday morning. Did you hear that, Mr. Cartwright? Did you hear?"

"I heard, old bean," Alistair assured his father-in-law, patting him on the shoulder. "I heard."

Even Anne had seemed unnerved by the scene. Her trepidation upon entering the gallery had been considerable—it was obvious she'd expected it to be filled with half-naked opium-eaters. Instead, they'd seen only respectably garbed Londoners, many of whom she'd recognized as living in her own elegant neighborhood. And the paintings! Here there were no obscene pictures of fully clothed men playing at cards on the grass, while nude women cavorted in the background. There were no long-legged ballerinas, or sleeping prostitutes—shocking images portrayed by many of the modern artists Anne had read about. Instead, Maggie's paintings were simple pastoral scenes, gentle depictions of children at play, or portraits of quite everyday-looking people. Anne had blinked at them in astonishment. Why, there was nothing the least bit shocking about them. They were, in fact, rather sweet. Had Anne been wrong, perhaps, about Maggie's decision to become an artist? Had Anne been wrong about the art world in general?

Jeremy had watched the mother of four struggle with her own conscience. Like Maggie, Anne was incapable of hiding her feelings. And the wonder, the admiration she'd felt, upon discovering her little sister in the company of the queen's own son, had been almost as palpable as Sir Arthur's.

Only Jeremy, it seemed, had been more unnerved by what followed the prince's compliment—the exuberant embrace Maggie and her fiancé had shared—than by the compliment itself. True, Maggie had looked like an unwilling participant. Certainly she'd commanded de Veygoux to set her down. But it had been hard to tell just *how* unwilling Maggie had been.

Now, Anne had moved forward, and was speaking to her youngest sister in a soft voice. Jeremy supposed it was soft. He could not hear a blessed thing, except the bleating of Sanjay, as he tried to explain why the princess had found it necessary to follow him here, of all places. It was a poor explanation. It was quite clear that Usha's only intent had been to embarrass him, and engender sympathy for herself. And she did look a pathetic creature—well, an exquisitely beautiful one, but pathetic, just the same. She was staring up at him with those bewitching eyes, round as shillings, her pulse fluttering visibly in her long throat. Any number of artsy-looking men—Jeremy thought he recognized them from the building in which Maggie had her studio—were eyeing her, nudging one another, and whispering furtively, undoubtedly trying to figure out how much they'd have to pay *this* young woman to pose for them.

And meanwhile, across the room, Maggie and her sister had sunk down onto a bench with one another, while Berangère Jacquard smugly looked on, basking in all the glory that should have been Jeremy's. . . .

"Sanjay," Jeremy said with a heavy sigh. "This is *really* not a good time."

"This I understand," the translator said apologetically.

"However, it is necessary that I ask you, one last time, if you are *quite* sure you do not want the princess."

Jeremy stared at him in astonishment. "Of *course* I'm sure. I've been telling you both that for nearly a year now. Nothing's changed."

"That," Sanjay replied, with a brisk nod, "was what I thought. I wanted only to be absolutely certain, however—"

Jeremy glanced at him hopefully. "Because you're going back to India now?"

"Oh, yes," Sanjay said. "We are going back to India now. But not before . . ."

His voice trailed off as Jeremy narrowed his silver-eyed gaze. But it wasn't the translator that the duke was sizing up. Not at all. It was the painting which Sanjay had been blocking from view all this time. Jeremy had not seen which work it was that had so impressed the heir to the throne, and his shock at suddenly being faced with a nearly life-size replica of himself showed in his incredulous expression.

He didn't know why he was so shocked. Perhaps because suddenly, he was face-to-face with a moment in time he'd thought he'd shared with only one other person. But that person, it seemed, had thought little enough of it to be willing to share it with hundreds of other people. He knew precisely what the portrait depicted—it was the moment when, five years earlier, Jeremy had been leaving Maggie's bedroom, and she'd asked him where he was going. To the devil, he'd replied. And then Maggie had uttered the words that had stayed with him, night and day, during the entire time he'd been away: Give him my regards.

A curiously Maggie-like statement. How many other girls would have been so calm, under the circumstances? Instead of rebuking him, or being shocked at his blasé attitude, she had merely smiled, and asked that he give the devil her regards.

And hadn't that been what Jeremy had been doing, all those years in India? Giving the devil her regards?

And she'd immortalized the moment, in vivid color, for all to see. Every detail, from his cynical, detached expression, to the way the moonlight had played over the moor that night, delineating his uncle's grazing Thoroughbreds, had been rendered with uncanny accuracy. There was emotion there, too, but just what that emotion was, Jeremy couldn't tell. Regret? Maybe. Longing? Possibly. But there was one thing that was very evidently missing. And that was trust. The man depicted in this painting was haughtily good-looking, self-assured, and cynical. But he clearly wasn't trustworthy. That was evident in the cruel twist Maggie had given his full lips. It was obvious in the sardonic glint she'd managed to capture in his silver eyes. She might as well have simply painted the words at the bottom of the canvas:

Portrait of a ne'er-do-well.

It was then that Jeremy realized what a fool he'd been. All of these years, he'd treasured the memory of that bitter-sweet evening in his mind, playing it over and over again while he waited for some word from her, never doubting for a moment that it would come. And all the time, *this* was how she'd thought of him: a lecherous, conniving ne'er-do-well.

No wonder she'd never written. No wonder she'd gone and gotten herself engaged to someone else. She'd never trusted him, never believed in him. And this painting was proof positive that she never would. He could seduce her every night of the week, drag her family from here to New Delhi and back again, and she still wouldn't agree to marry him. When she'd admitted, all those years ago, that she couldn't marry him because she didn't trust herself, it wasn't herself she was talking about at all.

It was him. The painting proved it. She didn't trust him. And she never would.

Blindly, numbly, Jeremy turned to go. He had no conscious thought, other than a sudden urge to head for the door.

He never made it that far.

Jeremy felt the bullet graze his ear well before he heard the shot. It was deafeningly loud in the stuffy gallery. So loud, in fact, that any number of waiters dropped their trays of champagne glasses, adding to the general hysteria which broke out immediately afterward.

Chapter 39

*M*aggie hadn't seen Anne in nearly a year, and she did not think her sister looked particularly well. Then again, Maggie didn't suppose she looked all that fit herself. The shock of seeing the Princess Usha at her exhibition had been a hard one. Hadn't she just been standing there, entertaining the thought that Jeremy might have decided Usha was right for him after all? Then, to see him striding toward her with that grim expression on his face, with the princess just a few feet behind . . .

Well, Maggie had never felt faint in her life, but at that moment, her knees went weak.

Fortunately, Augustin had noticed, and had swiftly steered her toward a vacant bench. Sinking down onto the soft cushion, Maggie barely had time to gather her wits about her before Alistair Cartwright, of all people, was dancing nervously in front of her.

"Sorry we're late, Maggie," he said, in his usual jovial manner. "His Grace hustled us out of Yorkshire so fast, we felt sure we'd make it by seven. Only the damned roads were coated in ice, and it ended up taking forever to get from the train station. . . ."

Even then, Maggie didn't really understand. Anne had actually had to step into her line of vision before she began to understand. Her thoughts seemed to be coming so slowly, as if one by one, they were squeezing through some narrow door in her mind. When Anne sat down on the bench beside her, and lifted her hand, Maggie still didn't quite understand what was going on.

"Oh, Maggie." Anne's gloved fingers nervously plucked at hers. "Are you . . . May I . . . speak to you?"

Maggie, a little surprised at her sister's hesitant manner— Anne, though shy around strangers, was generally quite forthright when it came to family members—said vaguely, "Why, yes. Of course."

Anne, with a nervous glance at her husband, licked her pale lips and said, "What I've come to say will only take a minute. I don't . . . I don't want to keep you from your party—"

Maggie was starting to come around now. She was beginning to notice things again. She saw, for instance, that her father was perched on a bench very like her own, and that Mr. Corman was fanning him and waving a snifter of brandy under his nose. And that Augustin was talking to the critic from *The Times*, moving his arms enthusiastically as he described something. And that, across the room, Jeremy was talking to the princess's interpreter.

"I don't expect you to forgive me for the way I've treated you, Maggie," Anne was saying, in a soft voice. "I realize I was wrong now, and that excuses are only that . . . excuses. I've never been like you, Maggie. I've never been very confident or outspoken. The only brave thing I ever did was marry Alistair, and I only did that because he made it so easy for me. He pursued me . . . it was so simple to say yes. And since that was the only courageous act I'd ever undertaken, it . . . hurt me to have failed so miserably at it—"

"Failed at it?" That caught Maggie's attention. "What are you talking about? You're the perfect wife, Anne, and the perfect mother. It's a wonder to me my nieces and nephews aren't completely spoiled, the way you coddle them."

Anne said, in a voice so low Maggie could barely hear it, "But I managed to lose so many of their brothers and sisters. How could I not treat the ones that lived so preciously?"

Maggie felt a pang of pity for her sister that was so sharp, it was almost physical. "Is *that* why you think of yourself as a failure? Because you miscarried? Anne, that's ridiculous.

You can't blame yourself for that. And you know Alistair would never—"

"Yes." Anne held up a gloved hand, as if to ward off the onslaught of Maggie's words. "I know. I suppose I always knew, deep down inside. But it's only today that I realized how much Alistair cares. Enough to let the Duke of Rawlings transport us to London, practically at gunpoint, in an effort to reunite us with you."

"Gunpoint." Maggie did not laugh. "Do you hate me that much, Anne, that you'd only come to see me on pain of death?"

"I believe I did, once," Anne said honestly. "After all, you did what I was never brave enough to do: You followed the desires of your own heart. I'm not saying there's anything I'd rather be than Alistair Cartwright's wife, and mother to his children. Only that . . . I lacked the courage to find out. Mother knew it. That's why out of all of us, she liked you best. You were the only brave one. Nothing frightened you, not the dark, not mice, not heights, nothing—"

"Anne," Maggie interrupted, thinking of that day, five years earlier, in the Rawlings Manor stables. "That isn't true."

"It is. Of course it is. And I suppose I've always resented you for it. It was only natural for Mamma to admire you the most, since you were always so forthright about your desires, for all we tried to warn you to try to curb them. What galled me was that you wanted all of these extraordinary things: you wanted to paint. You wanted to go to Paris. You wanted the Duke of Rawlings—and you always got them. You *always* got what you wanted, Maggie. And it was hard for someone like me, who never even had the courage to admit to having a heart's desire, to watch a sister not only admitting to having one, but then attaining it, time after time—"

Maggie said woodenly, "The letter."

"I beg your pardon?"

"The letter Jeremy sent to Herbert Park, after Mamma died." Maggie spoke with a certainty she did not really feel. "It didn't go astray, did it? You took it."

For the first time, Anne looked close to tears. "Yes," she said, with a sob. "I did."

Maggie shook her head. "Oh, Anne," she sighed. "How *could* you? I can understand your being upset with me about the way I'd behaved with him, but that letter. . . . How *could* you?"

"I didn't . . . I just didn't think it was fair." Anne's tear-stained face, framed by her beaver-trimmed bonnet, looked pathetically small. "You'd always had everything, everything you ever wanted. And to have a duke, too . . . it didn't seem fair."

Maggie, more hurt than she was willing to admit, looked down at the tops of her slippers.

"I know it was wrong of me, Maggie. I didn't realize how wrong until this morning, when Jeremy admitted he'd asked you to marry him all those years ago. . . . I had no idea that your feelings for him were . . . returned. I mean, I always knew that you loved him, but that he . . . well, Maggie, you can imagine how very badly I felt. I know you won't believe me, but when I destroyed that letter of his, I really did think I was doing you a favor. Never in a million years would I have dreamt that he'd proposed to you. Why on earth did you say no?"

Maggie just shook her head. "I'm not as brave as you credit me with being, Anne. I said no out of fear, pure and simple."

Anne's eyes widened, just a little. "I never would have thought it possible. You, who never feared anything."

"I was afraid of a lot of things, Anne," Maggie said. Suddenly, she felt very tired. "I just never let on."

"Well. Then you ought to have become an actress, not a painter. Can you ever forgive me, Maggie?"

Maggie was about to do so, without hesitation, when a gunshot tore through the gallery, causing a plump arts patron, who'd been busily pretending not to hear the interesting conversation taking place between the lady artist and her sister, to squeal with alarm. Anne started, and cried, "Good God! What was *that*?"

But Maggie knew. It was Jeremy's assassin. He had found him. Found him vulnerable at last.

She was up and on her feet in a split second. While the rest of the crowd was stampeding for the exits, frantically trying to get away from the flying bullets, Maggie was hurling herself *toward* the corner of the room from which the smell of charred gunpowder was wafting. She had to employ her knees and elbows against the well-dressed Londoners struggling for the doors, in order to make known her desire to get past. Finally, with her breathing erratic and her heart in her throat, she stumbled across the last velvet train, and found herself facing an extraordinary scene.

Jeremy, one hand flung to the side of his head, had whirled around to face his assailant, in whose hand the pistol was still smoking. Mercifully, the bullet seemed only to have nicked the duke's ear—the amount of blood that had already soaked into the collar of his shirt was horrifying—and gone on to embed itself into the painting behind him—the portrait, Maggie realized, of Jeremy. There was now a rather large hole in the chest of the portrait of Jeremy, just below the last ruffle of his cravat, right where his heart would have been. . . .

But the most shocking thing of all, to Maggie, at least, was not the wound Jeremy had sustained, or the damage the bullet had done, but the identity of Jeremy's would-be assassin. For it was not Augustin, as Jeremy's valet had insisted, though Augustin was standing there, seemingly transfixed with terror, a round-eyed Berangère clinging to his arm.

No, it was *Sanjay*. Sanjay, the princess's polite, even-tempered translator, who even now looked quite apologetic as he trained the still-smoking derringer at Jeremy's chest.

"I am so sorry," Sanjay said, sounding as if he meant it. "I do not have the world's best aim. I was trying to kill you—you are a very difficult man to kill, Your Grace—and succeeded only in causing you pain. Never fear, however. This next bullet should put an end to all your misery—"

Next bullet? Maggie inhaled to scream in horror, ready to throw herself at the tall man's arm, when Jeremy brought his hand away from his ear, revealing a goodly amount of blood and a V-shaped nick in the lobe, and demanded, in a furious voice, "*Me? Me?* What the devil do you want to kill *me* for? What did I ever do to *you*?"

Sanjay smiled, and Maggie noticed for the first time how white his teeth looked against his brown skin. "Why, I would have thought that was perfectly obvious. You dishonored the Star of Jaipur."

Maggie swung her terrified gaze to Usha, and was amazed to see that the Indian girl looked every bit as stunned as anyone else in the room. She was staring at her translator with wide, fearful eyes, both of her gloved hands pressed to her cheeks.

"Dishonored the—" Jeremy rolled his eyes. "Now, really, I've had just about as much of this as a man can take. I haven't dishonored anybody. If anybody dishonored anybody around here, the princess dishonored herself, following me around and making such a nuisance of herself. She isn't in love with me. She doesn't even want *me*. It's just my title she wants, and my money. *I'm* the one who's been dishonored, really, if you think about it."

"How *dare* you?" Sanjay, though he'd seemed almost eerily calm before, now began to shake with anger. Maggie saw the pistol begin to waver a little from side to side. "How *dare* you speak so of the woman I love?"

This was a development that no one, most especially the princess, who had lowered her hands from her face and was now gazing at Sanjay as if he were a newly unwrapped gift, seemed to have expected.

"*You love me?*" the princess squeaked, in English that was every bit as clipped and unaccented as Maggie's.

Sanjay tossed her an impatient look. "Of course I love you. Why do you think—" Then he froze, his mouth forming a little *O* of surprise that, had the situation not been so dire, might have been comical. "You speak *English*?"

"Of course I speak English." The princess looked disgusted. "I'm not *stupid*."

Sanjay seemed to go quite pale beneath his deep tan. "But . . . if you speak English, Your Highness, then why . . .

why have you pretended so long that you cannot?''

The princess rolled her eyes. "Really, Denish," she said. "Are you so dense that you cannot figure that out for yourself?''

Apparently he was that dense, since he stammered, "But . . . but . . .''

Princess Usha looked thoroughly annoyed. "Put that pistol away," she said sharply. "Who gave you permission to murder the colonel? *I* certainly did not.''

Sanjay hesitated, though only for a second. Still, it was a second too long for Jeremy's valet, Peters, who stepped suddenly from behind a pillar, his own pistol trained upon the other man's heart.

"You 'eard the princess, fella," Peters said. "Put the piece away.''

To Maggie's very great relief, the translator dropped the gun into the valet's outstretched hand. Looking satisfied, Peters lowered his own weapon, then said casually to Jeremy, "Sorry, Colonel. I was watchin' the frog-eater, like you asked. Never thought fer a minute the translator might've been the one behind it all.''

"Quite all right," Jeremy said, waving a hand dismissively.

But it wasn't all right with Sanjay. "I only did it for you, my princess," he exclaimed with heartfelt emotion. "You cannot know how long I have loved you, and how much I wished to kill this cocky fellow here for so callously failing to return your love!''

Princess Usha snorted. Maggie stared, but there really was no other way to describe the sound that came out of the Star of Jaipur's mouth. She had actually snorted, as any English girl might have done, when confronted by such tripe.

"*I?* Love *him?*" she sneered, nodding toward Jeremy, who by now had wrenched a handkerchief out of his waistcoat pocket, and was holding it to his ear. "You must be joking. I could never love *him*.''

Sanjay looked as bewildered as Maggie felt. "Then why did you insist on following him all this way, Your Highness?''

"It wasn't *him* I wanted," Usha declared. "It was the Star, of course."

"Star?" Sanjay stammered. "Which star?"

"*My* star, of course. The Star of Jaipur." Usha glared daggers at Jeremy. "My uncle gave it to him for saving the Palace of the Winds, which he hadn't any right to do. It was my mother's. It was to be passed on to me."

A single glance at Jeremy told Maggie he was completely unimpressed by this story. His ear had stopped bleeding, but his collar and cravat were now stained vermilion.

"I pleaded with my uncle not to give away the Star," Usha continued matter-of-factly, "but he insisted that since the colonel would not take *me*, he must be rewarded somehow. And so he took what ought to have been my dower, and awarded it to a man who cared so little for it, he kept it in his pocket, instead of on a pedestal, as it deserves."

Jeremy was frowning. He said thoughtfully, "I didn't know the sapphire belonged to you. I thought it belonged to the maharajah."

Usha raised her gaze to the ceiling. "God forbid my uncle should have paid anyone out of his *own* coffers! How much easier for him to pay from someone else's, and still receive the credit for possessing so magnanimous a spirit."

"So you came to England," Jeremy said, speaking slowly, "with the intention of stealing the stone back?"

"Stealing?" Usha echoed, as if the word were somehow distasteful to her. "I said nothing of stealing."

"Well, I never exactly heard you ask for it," Jeremy pointed out. "So I can only assume you meant to—"

"I meant to *persuade* you to give it back to me," the princess said. "But I must say, you are the most unpersuadable man I have ever met. No one has ever been as resistant to my charms as you." This she announced with a good deal of indignation. "It was most frustrating."

"Well," Jeremy replied, "forgive me, but I find you much more persuasive this way than you were before, pretending you couldn't speak English—"

Usha raised an ebony brow. "Truly? How interesting. Most men find ignorance in a woman absolutely irresistible."

She nodded at Sanjay. "Denish, for instance."

Sanjay, hearing his name, perked up alertly. "There is nothing I would not do for you, Princess," he said. "Nothing!"

For a woman who ought to have been used to men falling over themselves to do her bidding, Usha looked quite pleased by this exclamation. Still, she was not finished upbraiding him for acting on his own initiative. "But to try to kill the colonel," she chastised him. "And this is not the first time, I take it?"

"No." Sanjay had the goodness to look ashamed of himself. "I was the man who stabbed you outside of your home, Your Grace."

"And did you try to run me down in the street one day?" Jeremy asked curiously.

"Indeed, that was I." Sanjay hung his head. "Undoubtedly you will wish to send for the authorities. I am willing to go to jail, knowing that all I have done, I did in service to the one true Star of Jaipur."

Usha, looking more beautiful than ever—an expression of heartfelt delight had spread across her lovely features—reached out and touched the translator's shoulder. "This you would do for me? Go to jail forever in this cold place?" she asked. "*You*, who have been so severe upon me, all my life?"

Sanjay snatched up the hand she'd laid upon him, and began raining kisses upon it. Between kisses, he murmured, "Anything. I would do anything for you, my beautiful, beautiful Usha. If I have ever been severe upon you it is because I, like other men, am not blind to your imperfections . . . they only make me love you more."

Instead of being insulted by any hint that she might possess flaws, as Maggie would have expected a woman like Usha would be, she let out a soft cry of delight. Then she sobered. "But you know, Denish, that love between you and I can never be. I must return to India to marry the man my uncle has chosen for me—"

"No!" Sanjay pressed her hand to his heart, as if she had

wounded him there. "No, never. We will stay here. I will find work. There is much I can do—"

Maggie was so touched by the tender scene before her that she actually felt tears stinging her own eyes. A glance around the room showed her that she was not the only one who felt this way. Both Bérangère and Augustin seemed deeply moved, as did Anne and Alistair, who had not, to Maggie's surprise, fled the gallery with the others. Even Peters looked less cocky than usual.

Only Jeremy seemed immune to the moment's poignancy, but that did not keep Maggie from abruptly stepping forward. Before she knew what she was about, she had shaken the Star of Jaipur out of her reticule, and placed it into the hand of an astonished Usha.

"Here," she said, in a hoarse voice as she folded the princess's fingers around the heavy jewel. "This might help. I believe it belongs to you, anyway."

Chapter 40

*T*he immensity of what she'd just done didn't even occur to Maggie until she stepped away from the young couple and glanced, with tear-filled eyes, at Jeremy. What she saw in his face brought her back to reality in a hurry.

Jeremy looked shocked. More than just shocked: About as horrified as she'd undoubtedly looked when she'd first heard the shot from Sanjay's gun ring out. And he was looking at *her*, those silver eyes were boring into *her*, inscrutable as ever. . . .

Oh, Lord! Maggie froze in mid-step, her consternated gaze locked on his. What had she done?

She had just given away a twenty-four-carat sapphire, that's what! How much was a twenty-four-carat sapphire worth? Obviously quite a lot, if the way Usha and Sanjay were hopping about so enthusiastically behind her was any indication. Berangère looked as if someone had just slapped her, a sure sign that what Maggie had done had been foolish in the extreme, and Peters's mouth was agape, while Augustin and Maggie's family merely looked confused.

Dear God! What had she done?

But even as she stood there, twisting her fingers in confusion, the princess and her former translator were rushing forward to thank her, taking her hands and supplicating themselves over them. Then, when her cheeks had turned crimson and she thought she might die on the spot, they turned their attention to Jeremy. . . .

But Jeremy shrugged out of their reach without a word, turned, and left the gallery, followed quickly by his valet, who ran after his master, calling, "Colonel? Colonel, wait!"

Dumbstruck, Maggie stared after them. What had happened? Why was Jeremy so angry? Good Lord, what had she done?

It wasn't until someone gave her quite a hard push in the back that she roused herself. Turning, Maggie was surprised to see her sister Anne standing behind her, her face pale as alabaster.

"Don't just stand there," Anne said, pointing toward the doors through which Jeremy had just disappeared. "Go after him, Maggie!"

"Oh, dear," Maggie said. She chewed her lower lip nervously. "I oughtn't to—I suppose I shouldn't have given them the sapphire. After all, it was Jeremy's—"

Both of Anne's eyebrows came down in a rush. "Don't be stupid," she hissed. "It's got nothing to do with *that*. Just *go!*"

Maggie needed no further urging. A second later, she was headed for the doors through which Jeremy had just stormed. Her father, however, had risen from the couch upon which he'd sunk earlier in the evening, not moving from it even when he heard gunfire. Now, he caught her by the arm.

"Margaret," he said eagerly. "Where are you going? We have so much to talk about, you and I. I understand that you'll be going to see the Prince of Wales on Monday. As it happens, I have nothing to do on Monday. Might I recommend myself as an escort? It really isn't seemly for young women to be traipsing about London unescorted—"

Maggie's only response was a snarl, with which she jerked her arm from her father's grasp, and rushed out onto Bond Street. The weather was no better than it had been during the day, and Maggie, in her sleeveless gown and delicate slippers, immediately began to shiver. Pellets of ice rained down on her from the sky, which, though it was close to nine o'clock in the evening, glowed pinkly, the low cloud cover reflecting the lights of London. She was just in time to see the Rawlings curricle, pulled by a pair of matched chestnuts, clatter away from the curb.

Maggie swore beneath her breath and raised an arm. Hansom cab after hansom cab rattled past her, spraying her white satin skirt with dirty slush, but it never even occurred to her to return inside for her wrap. Dodging pedestrian traffic as well as horse-drawn vehicles, Maggie waded out into the street, one bare white arm raised, her satin shoes soon soaked through with icy water. Miraculously, a vacant hansom finally noticed her, and the driver, alarmed by her state of undress, started to hop down from his seat to help her into the carriage. Maggie, however, gathered up her skirts and was inside before he could even tip his hat.

"Twenty-two Park Lane," she cried, praying she had enough coins in her reticule to pay the fare. "And please hurry."

The driver sat back down and hastily chirruped his single steed, a tired-looking bay whose breath rose through the London fog in smoky tendrils. "Yes, miss. Beggin' your pardon, miss, but oughtn't you be wearin' a coat?"

Maggie, realizing only then that she was freezing, dove to reach for the lap blanket, which she wrapped about her shoulders, despite the fact it was made of very scratchy wool, and smelled rather fetid. "Yes," she said. "Please hurry."

To his credit, the driver tried. But it was Saturday night. Though the theaters had not yet let out, there was a good deal of traffic in the streets, which were icy, besides. Congestion clogged many of the thoroughfares, and where there was congestion, there were beggars and women of questionable virtue, the former pleading for pennies, the latter scanning each vehicle for gentlemen with whom they might pass an hour or two going round the park, snug beneath a lap blanket. Lord knew how many lice-ridden ladies of the evening the blanket round her shoulders had sheltered. Then there were the flower and orange sellers hawking their wares in the middle of the street, further stalling traffic. It was nearly an hour, by Maggie's estimates, before the hansom cab pulled up in front of the Rawlings town house, and by that time, her teeth were chattering with the cold, and she was wishing she'd been just a little less hasty, and had waited for her hat and muff before bursting out of the gallery.

Mercifully, she had enough money to pay the driver. She thanked him, and hurried up the steps to the house. One of the footmen, hearing the clatter of a carriage pulling up, opened the door before she'd even had time to pull the key from her bag, and cried, in tones of astonishment, "Miss Herbert? Is that you, then?"

Maggie, hurrying past him into the house, soon saw what had shocked him so. A glance at the wall-sized mirror to one side of the marble foyer revealed a tall girl with her hair mostly falling down, a once-white dress now flecked all over with wet gray soot and brown mud, her skin very nearly blue with cold, except where it was bright red with frostbite. She couldn't feel her toes anymore, and the beading on her train was torn where she'd snagged it on the hansom cab's rear wheel as she'd descended.

"Never mind that now," she said, mostly to herself. "Has His Grace returned, Freddie?"

The footman looked surprised. "Yes, miss. Been home this past half hour. Retired straightaway to 'is room. Let me call for your maid, Miss Margaret. You must be needin' somethin' warm to drink—"

"No, no, don't bother." Maggie had already started up the stairs, hiking up her skirt nearly to her knees. "I'm quite all right."

"But miss—"

"I'm all right!" Maggie hurried up to the door to the Green Room just as Evers was emerging from it, an empty crystal decanter in his hands. If she'd thought the footman looked startled from her blowzy appearance, his astonishment was nothing compared to that of the butler's, whose eyes very nearly popped out of his head at the sight of her.

"Miss Margaret!" Evers cried. "Are you unwell?"

Panting, Maggie said, between gulps of breath, "I am perfectly well, thank you, Evers. But I must see His Grace right away."

Evers raised his eyebrows. "But Miss Margaret, I'm afraid that's quite impossible. His Grace has retired for the evening. He had a terrible accident, you know. One of his ears was torn quite painfully. . . .''

Maggie noticed that Evers's gaze had strayed toward her chest, which was rising and falling as she tried to catch her breath. She couldn't exactly blame him. She was aware that in her haste to climb the stairs, she might have disarranged a few things that, until then, had been adequately covered. "Evers," she said breathlessly. "I must see His Grace on a matter of utmost urgency."

"It will have to wait until morning," the butler said firmly, his eyes back on her face. "Really, Miss Margaret, but you look extraordinarily pale. Are you quite well? Might I offer you some sort of restorative—"

Maggie's patience snapped. "You might offer to get out of my way," she shouted, so loudly that the butler very nearly dropped the decanter he held. "I'm going to see the duke, and I don't care what you or anybody else has to say about it!"

And with that, Maggie pushed past him, laid her hand upon the door latch, and flung open the duke's bedroom door.

Chapter 41

*T*he last thing Maggie expected to see, on the other side of the doorway, was Jeremy, naked, in a portable brass bathtub. But that's exactly the sight that met her eyes as she stumbled into the master bedroom. That, and a very surprised-looking Peters, shaking out his colonel's coat.

The last thing Jeremy expected to see, at that point, was a breathless and clearly disheveled Maggie. But that's exactly what he did see stagger through his bedroom door.

"Good God, Mags," Jeremy said mildly, from the tub. "What happened to you? You look as if you'd been to hell and back."

Before Maggie had a chance to reply, Evers insinuated his way through the doorway, crying, "I *am* sorry, Your Grace. She insisted upon being admitted to see you. I told her that you had retired for the evening, but she simply would *not* take no for an answer." To Maggie, the butler said, as he wrapped a firm hand around her upper arm, "Now, Miss Margaret, that is quite enough. His Grace is thoroughly indisposed, as you can see. I'm sure whatever it is you have to tell him can wait until morning—"

Maggie wrenched her arm from Evers's grasp. "No, it cannot," she snapped. "And if you touch me again, I shall stick my thumb in your eye."

Evers blinked indignantly, and Maggie felt a moment's guilt. After all, the butler had only been doing his job. But he didn't, she told herself, have to do it so well.

"Really, Miss Margaret!" cried the butler. "I shall be forwarding information about your behavior this evening to your father!"

In the brass bathtub that had been set up a few feet from the hearth, Jeremy rolled his eyes. "Really, Mags," he drawled. "I quite agree with Evers. There isn't any need for dramatics. Just say what you have to say, and then get back to your fiancé, like a good girl."

"He is no longer," Maggie said loftily, "my fiancé, a fact you might have discovered for yourself if you had bothered to ask questions tonight before storming out so rudely. But far be it from *me* to suggest that the Duke of Rawlings might possibly be wrong about something." Tossing her head, Maggie turned to go.

"Wait!"

The booming command was so loud, the decanter Evers carried tinkled a little as he jiggled it with surprise. Maggie, however, only glanced casually back over one bare shoulder.

"Are you addressing *me* in that uncivil manner, Your Grace?" she inquired.

Jeremy was leaning forward in his bath, his hands gripping the brass sides so tightly that she could clearly see that his knuckles had gone white. "What do you mean, he's no longer your fiancé?" Jeremy demanded, in a deadly serious voice.

"What I said." Maggie started toward the door again. "But what do you care? You told me to get out. And so I am. Gladly."

"Maggie!"

This time the voice was so loud that Evers let out a squeak and darted from the room, nearly shoving Maggie out of the way in his haste to escape the duke's wrath. Peters dropped the coat he was brushing, then bent hastily to pick it up, hoping his colonel hadn't noticed. Only Maggie remained where she was, just inside the room, but one hand on the door latch.

"What?" she asked coldly, again speaking over her shoulder.

Scissoring a glance at his valet, Jeremy said, in tones of impatience, "Peters. Leave us."

The valet didn't waste any time. For a one-legged man, Peters could move with alacrity when instructed. He didn't disappear into the dressing room, either, but limped toward the door through which the butler had disappeared. He did pause, however, long enough to give Maggie a slow wink. Maggie, taken aback by this comradely gesture, blinked in astonishment as the door clicked shut behind him.

"Now," Jeremy said, releasing the sides of the tub and leaning back. The steam from the hot water rose up in wispy tendrils around him. When he spoke again, it was with measured calm. "What's this about de Veygoux no longer being your fiancé?"

Maggie felt something cold pressing against her bare back. Reaching behind her, she found an ivory hairpin dangling from the elaborate coiffure that Hill had arranged on top of her head earlier in the evening. She pulled the pin from her limp and tangled hair. "What I said," she informed him, more coolly than she felt, "is that I am no longer engaged to Mr. de Veygoux."

"I see." Jeremy, raising his arms until they balanced along the sides of the tub, studied her. It was dark in the Green Room. The only light was that which came from the roaring fire in the fireplace, and from the oil lamp at the side of the duke's enormous bed. The firelight, striking the brass tub, reflected against the high ceiling, and the bright gold patches overhead danced crazily whenever Jeremy caused the water to slosh inside the tub.

Still, in spite of the dim lighting, Maggie could easily make out the satin-skinned swell of his biceps, as he draped his heavily muscled arms along the tub's rims. The thick patches of dark hair that nested beneath those arms matched the inky mat that carpeted his broad chest, tapering down until it disappeared below the water's surface. The opaqueness of the soapy water kept her from seeing much more than that, but Maggie already knew what lay below those murky depths. His ear, she saw, was no longer bleeding at all. Even his wounded shoulder seemed better. For a man with malaria, he healed very quickly.

Jeremy, for his part, could see Maggie quite well, for all she stood silhouetted against the fire. And what a silhouette it was. Her gown, plastered damply to her body, fit her like a second skin. It was all Jeremy could do to keep himself from leaping from the tub and throwing her back against the bed.

Only the memory of that damned painting kept him where he was. It wasn't enough, he told himself, for her to want him. She had to trust him, too.

Still, it was with a slightly trembling hand that Jeremy reached out and lifted a bell-shaped glass from a small collapsible table his valet had set up beside the tub. The *ballon* contained an amber liquid that Jeremy neatly downed. Ah. Better.

"And how," he asked, after he'd swallowed, "did that come about? The disintegration of your engagement, I mean. Because when I saw you earlier this evening, you were in his arms. You hardly looked like a couple that had gone their separate ways."

"Well, we're still friends," Maggie replied. She couldn't help but gaze a little longingly at what was left in Jeremy's glass. Her chill was only just beginning to dissipate. If only, she thought, she'd accepted the footman's offer of a toddy. She really believed she might never be warm again. "We'll probably always be friends," she went on. "Augustin was just happy because the Prince of Wales commissioned me to do a portrait for him, that's all. But he's not in love with me anymore. He's in love with Berangère now."

"Really?" Jeremy put the glass, not quite empty, back on the tabletop. "And how do you suppose that came about?"

"Oh," Maggie said, with a shrug. What did it matter? Why were they wasting time talking, when they could be in one another's arms? "Berangère seduced him."

Jeremy raised his dark, sardonic eyebrows. That had not, he noted, been part of the scheme he had worked out with Berangère. And yet it was a brilliant bit of improvisation on her part. He'd have to see that she was amply rewarded for it. "Interesting turn of events," he commented dryly.

"I thought so." Maggie looked down, fingering the hairpin she held. "Much like . . . well, many of the things that happened tonight."

Jeremy did not comment on that. Did he know what she was referring to? He had to! He *had* to know she was referring to the princess. But he wasn't saying anything. What was *wrong* with him? she wondered. She'd have thought that upon hearing her engagement had been broken off, he'd have leapt right out of that tub and thrown his arms around her. But it looked as if ravishing her—or having anything to do with her—was the last thing on his mind. He seemed perfectly content to stay where he was. A brief glance showed that he wasn't even looking in her direction. He was gazing into the fire, his face expressionless. Good Lord, Maggie thought. Was he *that* upset about the sapphire?

Or was it something else? Was it that now that she was free, he wasn't sure he wanted her anymore? Maggie's heart, the only part of her that didn't feel chilled, went cold at the thought. Maybe he'd only wanted her when he thought he couldn't have her. But no, that couldn't be. He'd gone to all that trouble to bring her family to her! Why would he do that for someone he wasn't in love with, for someone he didn't want to marry?

So why wasn't he asking now, when she was finally prepared to say yes?

Maybe because he'd finally realized she was the stupidest, least courageous girl in the world. Oh, she was willing to take risks, all right—she'd hung a lot of her paintings on a wall and let people look at them and make comments about them—but when it came to something that really mattered— her heart—she'd use any excuse she could to keep from exposing it. And why would a man like Jeremy, who was braver than anyone she'd ever known, want to marry a stupid coward like herself?

He wouldn't. Not unless she proved to him she wasn't the coward he thought her.

Taking a deep breath, Maggie crossed the room, not stopping until she reached the table where he'd placed his glass.

Leaning down, she reached for the *ballon*. Jeremy's gaze, which had been fastened on the fire, immediately dipped to her décolletage. This, at least, was encouraging.

"May I?" she asked, indicating the glass.

Jeremy nodded wordlessly, then licked his lips, which seemed to have gone suddenly dry.

"Thank you." Maggie lifted the glass to her own blood-less lips. Tilting back the *ballon*, she allowed the fiery liquid to slide down her throat. The brandy began to warm her at once, all the way down to her frozen toes, in a way fire couldn't.

Jeremy, she noticed, seemed to be suffering from a similar sensation, only it wasn't his toes that were affected. He twisted a little, enough to send the steaming water sloshing over the sides of the brass tub. He did not, however, appear to notice.

"That's better," Maggie said. She lowered the now empty glass, taking careful note of the way Jeremy's eyes followed her every movement. The silver-flecked gaze didn't leave her as she sank down onto a leather-covered ottoman a few feet away from the tub. Nor did it stray when she reached up and began pulling the rest of the ivory pins from her thick, dark hair.

Jeremy licked his lips. "So," he said. "If you're so full of explanations, how do you explain that"—He cleared his throat—"painting?"

It took Maggie a second before she realized what he was talking about. Painting? What painting? Then, suddenly, his anger—all of that white-hot rage—seemed to make sense. The painting! The painting of Jeremy! She hadn't been aware that he'd seen it. Well, no wonder, then. . . .

"That painting," she began carefully. "It wasn't sup-posed to be in the show."

Jeremy's expression did not change, nor did he look away from her. "Wasn't it?"

"No." Maggie set a handful of pins down upon the floor. "Those moving men Augustin sent over to my studio picked it up by mistake. Then one of the gallery assistants hung it, without checking with me first, and wouldn't take it down when I asked. I don't think it's a very good example of my work. I did it a long time ago.''

Jeremy watched as she gave the knot in her hair a tug, bringing the thick mass cascading down over her bare shoulders. "Did you?" he asked tonelessly.

"Yes. I had some idiotic idea that if I painted a portrait of you, I'd be able to . . . I don't know. Get you out of my bloodstream.'' She began to work on the pearl buttons to her gloves.

"I see.'' Jeremy was very still inside the bath. "It worked, apparently.''

She flicked a glance at him. "Don't be stupid. You know it didn't work. If it had, would I be here?''

"I don't know,'' Jeremy replied truthfully. "I don't know what you're doing here.''

Maggie, finished peeling off her gloves, reached down and began slipping out of her wet shoes. "You *are* stupid, then,'' was all she said.

Jeremy bristled, sitting up straight in the tub. "You know, for once, Mags, I agree with you. I *am* stupid. I thought that you and I had something special. I really did. But it became clear to me when I saw that portrait—''

"Would you please,'' Maggie said disgustedly, lifting her skirt to undo her garters, "forget about that damned painting?''

"You made me look like some kind of criminal,'' he accused her. "Like a gambler, or a horse thief, or something.''

"Oh, for God's sake,'' Maggie snapped. She'd propped one foot on the side of the brass tub, and was rolling down a damp silk stocking. "I was seventeen years old! To me, you *were* a criminal. You'd stolen my heart. And need I remind you that to this day, I haven't yet gotten it back?''

"What about you?'' Jeremy demanded. "For five years, I waited for you, only to find out you'd gone and gotten yourself engaged to somebody else!''

"I know,'' Maggie said, going to work on the stocking on her left leg. "I'm guilty, too. Although allow me to remind you that at the time, I thought you'd just gotten your-self awarded your very own princess. . . .''

Jeremy snorted. ''Well. You saw for yourself how well *that* turned out.''

''I did,'' Maggie admitted. ''And I'm sorry I ever doubted you. And I'm . . .'' She swallowed, thinking, Well, I had bet-ter get this over with, and finished, in a rush, ''And I'm sorry I gave away your sapphire.''

Jeremy waved a hand dismissively. It was clear that she'd been wrong, back in the gallery. He hadn't been angry about the loss of the Star of Jaipur. He hadn't even seemed to give the matter a second thought. It was *Maggie* who concerned him. That realization sent a thrill of pleasure racing up and down her spine.

''And even now that the damned frog-eater's out of the picture,'' he complained bitterly, ''the fact remains that if you marry me, you're still going to have to be a duchess. I can't change that.''

Maggie, bare-legged, went to work on the buttons that fastened her gown at the side. ''I know,'' she said. She felt giddy, almost weak with relief.

''So what are you doing here?'' Jeremy bellowed in frus-tration.

Maggie stood up, allowing the stained satin gown to col-lapse around her feet. Standing in only her corset and pan-taloons, she said, far more calmly than she felt, ''Looking for someone to scrub my back.''

Jeremy stared at her. She resembled nothing short of a street courtesan, in her obscenely tight-fitting underclothes, with all her dark hair spilling down her back. It seemed com-pletely out of character for her to be throwing herself at him in this fashion, and for a second or two, he could only look at her, completely stunned. But then he saw that despite the saucy thrust of her considerable chest, her breath was coming in quick, shallow bursts, as if she'd just run a very great distance, and there was trepidation in her velvet brown eyes. She wasn't at all sure of his reception.

And that, more than anything else that evening, was what caused him to lean forward and seize bodily hold of her.

"Jeremy," she cried gladly, as his wet arms closed around her. Then she added, "Wait—" when he started to pull her from the ottoman. And then, "What are you doing?" when he dragged her back into the tub with him.

"Oh!" The water threatening to spill over the sides of the tub from the combined weight of both their bodies, Maggie floundered in his lap, her pantaloons now plastered wetly to her body. "Jeremy!" she cried. The warm water soaked the ends of her hair, and crept into the crevice between her breasts. Beneath her, she felt Jeremy's thighs, slick and hard, as he struggled to keep her from scrambling away. "My God, I was only joking!"

"Were you?" Jeremy pushed some of her long hair aside and nuzzled her neck, just below her earlobe. "Well, I'm not."

Maggie, in spite of her indignation, could not ignore the tingling sensations his lips produced upon her skin. They seemed to make every part of her body come alive, most especially her nipples, which tightened at the mere touch of his mouth along her neck. She threw out a hand to keep him at bay, not ready for this passionate assault, but it was too late. She might as well have tried to keep a tree from falling. Jeremy pressed forward, his lips seeking hers, while his fingers worked busily at the now sodden stays to her corset. It seemed as if he had the soaking-wet garment off her body and over the side of the tub in about the same amount of time it took him to break down Maggie's token resistance. She moaned her surrender as he reached up with both hands to palm the hardened peaks of her breasts.

That moan was all the invitation he needed. Suddenly, she felt his tongue thrust past her softly parted lips. While one hand stayed to caress a heavy breast, the other dipped below the water's surface to pluck at the string that kept her pantaloons closed. Her protest when he finally snapped the ribbon in two was lost against his mouth. What did it matter? she thought muzzily. He could afford to buy her new underwear, every day, if necessary.

Maggie had a feeling it was going to be necessary.

Tossing the lace-trimmed pantaloons over his shoulder,

Jeremy gathered her to him once more, until she was straddling his lap, his coarse chest hair grazing her breasts as he crushed her in his strong embrace. Beneath the water, she could feel his excitement pressing rigidly against the swollen crevice between her thighs. All she had to do, she realized, was lower herself onto that rock-hard shaft. . . .

She did so, moving so slowly that it wasn't until she'd actually captured the tip of his penis inside her that Jeremy realized what she was doing. His eyelids, which had been lowered, flew open. Maggie, giving him an impish grin, sank down a little more, delighting in his sharp intake of breath as the tightness of her hot sheath closed around him. His hands moved to cup her buttocks, his fingers sinking into her soft flesh with bold urgency. Maggie lowered herself another inch, and then Jeremy, apparently unable to stand this sweet torture a second more, thrust himself into her, pressing down on her buttocks at the same time, so that their bodies met so explosively that a wave of bathwater cascaded over the opposite end of the tub.

Not that either of them noticed. Locked with Jeremy at last, Maggie began to move against him, slowly at first, and then with more and more imperativeness, as Jeremy rocked beneath her, until, gripping the sides of the brass tub, she threw her head back, and gave a shudder that seemed to begin at her scalp and tingle all the way down to the arches of her feet. She could have sworn at that moment that all the golden light reflected across the ceiling suddenly came showering down upon her, kissing her bare skin all over, and carpeting the room in tiny shards of gold leaf.

It was only when Jeremy, equally spent beneath her, complained, without sounding at all displeased, "Good God, Mags. What were you trying to do, drown me?" that she came to her senses, and realized there was no gold leaf anywhere, just a goodly amount of water on the floor.

"Oh, dear," Maggie said, a little breathlessly, as she looked around the room.

"I'll say." Jeremy sat up, but kept her firmly clasped to him. "Now. What were you saying about needing someone to scrub your back?"

She looked away from him, feeling suddenly shy. "Oh, yes. Would you be willing?"

"I don't know," he said cautiously. "It depends. Is this a one-time offer, or a lifetime commitment?"

"I was hoping for the lifetime commitment," she said, unable to meet his gaze.

Jeremy watched her closely. "A lifetime commitment to scrubbing your back. In exchange for what?"

"Um." Maggie bit her lower lip. "Well . . . I'll be your wife."

Jeremy froze. "But what about the duchess thing?"

"I was thinking," Maggie said slowly, "that it might not be so bad. I mean, if you wouldn't mind spending time in London—"

"Oh, I'll have to," Jeremy interrupted. "I'm to be a consultant at Whitehall, or something. We'd have to spend most of the year here in London, I'm afraid. I'm sure Uncle Edward and Aunt Pegeen won't mind."

"Oh, yes," Maggie said eagerly. "I think it might be best if we just let them have the manor house."

"Certainly," Jeremy said. "With all those children—"

"They really ought to stay in the country."

"Right. And it might be a little uncomfortable, living so close to your father. . . ."

"Yes," Maggie agreed. "Herbert Park *is* a bit close to Rawlings Manor—"

"But we could always go visit him," Jeremy said. "I mean, if you wanted to."

"That might be nice," Maggie said carefully. "As long as it wasn't too often. . . ."

After a moment or two of silence, during which Jeremy stared at the ceiling, he finally asked, "Do you really mean it, Mags? Are you sure?"

Maggie, lying in his arms, nodded. "Yes. I'm sure."

"I had a stone for a ring for you, you know," Jeremy said. "Quite a nice one, actually. A sapphire."

Maggie wrinkled her nose. "I don't really like sapphires, actually."

"Oh, well, that's good." His silver eyes twinkled warmly. "Because I lost it, you know."

"What a shame." Maggie smiled. And then she kissed him again, and it was a long, long while before they said anything more.

Chapter 42

Edward, not bothering to knock, threw open the door to the Green Room and shouted, "Jerry!"

An assortment of mounds lying within the confines of the enormous four-poster bed stirred, and Jeremy raised a bleary-eyed head. "What? Who is that?"

"It's me," Edward said. Observing with disgust that his nephew had left his bath things, including the bath itself, strewn across the room, he went to the windows and pulled back the dark green portieres, letting in the strong rays from the morning sun. "I've come to report that your aunt was safely delivered of another son yesterday. She has, I'm sorry to say, decided to call him Jeremy. Despite my assertions to the contrary, she's convinced that you've finally shown maturity enough to handle the role of godfather. She demanded that I haul myself all the way to London to inform you that the christening's in three weeks. Do you think you'll be able to tumble out of that bed long enough to attend?"

Beside Jeremy, another set of mounds moved. Then, to Edward's very great astonishment, Maggie Herbert's head appeared above the bedclothes. "What?" she asked, groggily echoing Jeremy. "Who's there?"

Edward, standing beside the window seat, folded his arms across his chest. "All right," he said sternly. "That's it.

"Tongues are wagging. It is Rescue River."

"Gossip central," he agreed.

"And speaking of wagging tongues," she said, "imagine what people will assume if you come and live in the guesthouse. They'll think we're a couple. I'm not comfortable with that."

"I understand." He looked down at his hands, traced a scar that peeked out from his shirt cuff. "I'm not exactly a blue-ribbon bronco."

"Vito!" She sounded exasperated. "You haven't changed a bit since you had to try on six different shirts for the homecoming dance."

"That was a long time ago. And the truth is, I have changed."

She rolled her eyes. "You're still good-looking, okay? Women don't mind scars." Then she pressed her lips together as her cheeks grew pink.

His heart rate accelerated just a little. Why was she blushing? Did she think he was good-looking?

But of course, she hadn't seen the worst of his scars.

And even if there was a little spark between them, it couldn't go anywhere. Because he was living with a secret he couldn't let her discover.

Lee Tobin McClain read *Gone with the Wind* in the third grade and has been a hopeless romantic ever since. When she's not writing angst-filled love stories with happy endings, she's getting inspiration from her church singles group, her gymnastics-obsessed teenage daughter and her rescue dog and cat. In her day job, Lee gets to encourage aspiring romance writers in Seton Hill University's low-residency MFA program. Visit her at leetobinmcclain.com.

Books by Lee Tobin McClain

Love Inspired

Rescue River

Engaged to the Single Mom
His Secret Child
Small-Town Nanny
The Soldier and the Single Mom
The Soldier's Secret Child

Lone Star Cowboy League: Boys Ranch

The Nanny's Texas Christmas

The Soldier's Secret Child

Lee Tobin McClain

HARLEQUIN® LOVE INSPIRED®

Recycling programs
for this product may
not exist in your area.

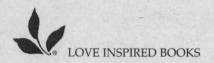

LOVE INSPIRED BOOKS

ISBN-13: 978-0-373-62292-4

The Soldier's Secret Child

Copyright © 2017 by Lee Tobin McClain

www.Harlequin.com

Printed in U.S.A.

I will give you a new heart and put a new spirit in you; I will remove from you your heart of stone and give you a heart of flesh.
—*Ezekiel* 36:26

To my daughter, Grace, who shows me
every day that families aren't about bloodlines;
they're about heart.

Chapter One

Lacey McPherson leaned back, propped her hands on the low white picket fence and surveyed the wedding reception before her with satisfaction. She'd pulled it off.

She'd given her beloved brother and his bride a wedding reception to remember, not letting her own anti-romance attitude show. But she had to admit she'd be glad when her half-remodeled guesthouse stopped being a nest for lovebirds.

"Nothing like a spring wedding, eh, Lacey?"

She jumped, startled at the sound of the gruff, familiar voice right behind her. She spun around. "Vito D'Angelo, you scared me!" And then her eyes widened and she gasped. "What happened?"

His warm brown eyes took her back to her teen years. She'd been such a dreamer then, not good at navigating high school drama, and her brother's friend had stepped in more than once to defend her from girls who wanted to gossip or boys who tried to take advantage. She and her brother had welcomed invitations to the D'Angelo family's big, loud Italian dinners.

But now the most noticeable thing about his face

wasn't his eyes, but the double scar that ran from his forehead to his jawline. A smaller scar slashed from his lower lip to his chin.

Instinctively she reached out toward his face.

He caught her hand, held it. "I know. I look bad. But you should see the other guy."

His attempt at a joke made her hurt more than it made her laugh. "You don't look bad. It's just...wow, they barely missed your eye." Awkwardly, she tried to hug him with the fence in between.

He broke away and came inside through the open gate. "How're you doing, Lace? At least *you're* still gorgeous, huh? But you're too thin."

"You sound just like your grandma. And you're late for the wedding." Her heart was still racing from the surprise, both of seeing him and of how he looked.

She wanted to find out what had happened. But this wasn't the time or the place.

"Buck won't mind my being late. He looks busy." Vito looked past the wedding guests toward Lacey's brother, laughing and talking in the summer sun, his arm slung around his new bride. "Looks happy, too. Glad he found someone."

A slightly wistful quality in Vito's words made Lacey study her old friend. She hadn't seen him in almost ten years, not since he'd brought his army buddy home on a furlough and Lacey had fallen hard for the handsome stranger who'd quickly become her husband. Back then, after one very stormy conversation, Vito had faded into the background. He'd been in the firestorm that had killed Gerry, had tried to save him and had written to Lacey after Gerry's death. But he'd continued on with another Iraq tour and then another. She'd heard he'd been injured, had undergone a lot of surgery and rehab.

Looking at him now, she saw that he'd filled out from slim to brawny, and his hair curled over his ears, odd for a career military man. "How long are you home?"

"For good. I'm out of the army."

"Out?" She stared. "Why? That was all you ever wanted to do!" She paused. "Just like Gerry."

"I felt awful I didn't make his funeral." He put an arm around her shoulders and tugged her to his side. "Aw, Lace, I'm sorry about all of it."

Her throat tightened and she nodded. Gerry had been dead for a year and a half, but the loss still ached.

A shout went up from the crowd and something came hurtling toward her. Instinctively she put her hands up, but Vito stepped in front of her, catching the missile.

Immediately, he turned and handed it to her.

A bouquet of flowers? Why would someone…

Oh. *The* bouquet. Gina's.

She looked across the crowd at her friend, glowing in her pearl-colored gown. Gina kept encouraging Lacey to date again. Happily in love, she wanted everyone to share in the same kind of joy.

The crowd's noise had quieted, and some of the guests frowned and murmured. Probably because Gina had obviously targeted Lacey, who'd been widowed less than two years ago. One of the older guests shook her head. "Completely inappropriate," she said, loud enough for most of those nearby to hear.

Well, that wouldn't do. Gina was a Californian, relatively new to Ohio and still finding her way through the unspoken rules and rituals of the Midwest. She hadn't meant to do anything wrong.

Lacey forced a laugh and shook the bouquet threateningly at Gina. "You're not going to get away with this, you know," she said, keeping her tone light. "I'm passing it on to..." She looked around. "To my friend Daisy."

"Too late." Daisy waved a finger in front of her face and backed away. "You caught it."

"Actually, Vito caught it," old Gramps Camden said. "Not sure what happens when a man catches the bouquet."

As the crowd went back to general talk, Lacey tried to hand off the bouquet to all the females near her, but they all laughingly refused.

Curious about Vito's reaction, she turned to joke with him, but he was gone.

Later, after Gina and Buck had run out to Buck's shaving-cream-decorated truck, heads down against a hail of birdseed, Lacey gave cleanup instructions to the two high school girls who were helping her with the reception. Then, after making sure that the remaining guests were well fed and happy, she went into the guesthouse. She needed to check on Nonna D'Angelo.

Having Nonna stay here was working out great. The light nursing care she needed was right up Lacey's alley, and she enjoyed the older woman's company. And the extra bit of income Nonna insisted on paying had enabled Lacey to quit her job at the regional hospital. Now that the wedding was over, she could dive into the final stages of readying the guesthouse for its fall opening.

Nonna D'Angelo had mingled during the early part of the reception, but she'd gone inside to rest more than an hour ago. Now Lacey heard the older woman crying and hastened her step, but then a reassuring male voice rumbled and the crying stopped.

Vito.

Of course, he'd come in to see his grandma first thing. He hadn't been home in over a year, and they'd always been close.

She'd just take a quick peek to make sure Nonna wasn't getting overexcited, and then leave them to their reunion.

Slowly, she strolled down the hall to the room she'd made up for Nonna D, keeping her ears open, giving them time. She surveyed the glossy wood floors with satisfaction. The place was coming along. She'd redo this wallpaper sometime, but the faded roses weren't half-bad for now. Gave the place its historical character.

She ran her hand along the long, thin table she'd just bought for the entryway, straightened her favorite, goofy ceramic rooster and a vase of flowers. Mr. Whiskers jumped up onto the table, and Lacey stopped to rub his face and ears, evoking a purr. "Where's the Missus, huh?" she cooed quietly. "Is she hiding?"

Hearing another weepy sniffle from Nonna D, Lacey quickened her step and stopped in the doorway of Nonna's room.

"My beautiful boy," Nonna was saying with a catch in her voice. "You were always the good-looking one."

Vito sat on the edge of the bed, looking distinctly uncomfortable as Nonna sat up in bed to inspect his cheek and brush his hair back behind his ears.

She felt a quick defensiveness on Vito's behalf. Sure, the scars were noticeable. But to Lacey, they added to his rugged appeal.

Nonna saw her and her weathered face broke into a

smile, her eyes sparkling behind large glasses. "There's my sweet girl. Come in and see my boy Vito."

"We talked already, Nonna." Vito was rubbing the back of his neck. "Lacey, I didn't realize you were taking care of my grandma to this extent. I'll take her home tomorrow."

"Oh, no!" Lacey said. "I'm so happy to do it!"

"I can't go home!" Nonna said at the same time.

"Why not?" Vito looked from Nonna to Lacey and back again.

"I need my nursing help," Nonna explained. "Lacey, here, is a wonderful nurse. She's practically saved my life!"

Lacey's cheeks burned. "I'm really a Certified Nursing Assistant, not a nurse," she explained. "And I haven't done anything special, just helped with medications and such." In truth, she knew she'd helped Nonna D'Angelo with the mental side as well as the physical, calming her anxiety and making sure she ate well, arranging some outings and visits so the woman didn't sink into the depression so common among people with her health issues.

"Medications? What's wrong?"

"It's my heart," Nonna started to explain.

Vito had the nerve to chuckle. "Oh, now, Nonna. You've been talking about your heart for twenty years, and you never needed a nurse before."

"Things are different now." The older woman's chin quivered.

He reached out and patted her arm. "You'll be fine."

Lacey drew in a breath. Should she intervene? Families were sometimes in denial about the seriousness of a beloved relative's health problems, and patients sometimes shielded their families from the truth.

"If you want to move your grandma, that's fine," she said, "but I'd recommend waiting a couple more weeks."

"That's right." Nonna looked relieved. "Lacey needs the money and I need the help."

Vito frowned. "Can we afford this?" He looked down at his grandma and seemed to realize that the woman was getting distressed. "Tell you what, Grandma, Lacey and I will talk about this and figure some things out. I won't leave without saying goodbye."

"All right, dear." She shot a concerned glance at Lacey.

She leaned down in the guise of straightening a pillow for Nonna. "I'll explain everything," she reassured her.

She led the way to the front room, out of earshot from Nonna D'Angelo. Then she turned to Vito, frowning. "You don't think I'm taking advantage of your grandma, do you?"

"No!" He reached for her, but when she took a step back, he crossed his arms instead. "I would never think that, Lacey. I know you. I just don't know if you've thought this through."

She restrained an eye roll. "You always did like to interfere when your help wasn't needed."

"Look, if this is about that talk we had years back…" He waved a dismissive hand. "Let's just forget that."

She knew exactly what he meant. As soon as Vito had found out Gerry had proposed, he'd come storming over to her house and pulled her out onto the front porch to try and talk her out of it. "You were wrong," she said now.

"I wasn't wrong." When she opened her mouth to protest, he held up a hand. "But I was wrong to interfere."

That wasn't exactly what she'd said, but whatever.

"But back to my grandma. I don't know what her insurance is like, but I know it hardly ever covers in-home nursing care. I'm living on limited means and until I get back on my feet—"

"It's handled. It's fine."

He ran a hand through his thick, dark hair. "She's always tended to be a hypochondriac—"

"A heart attack is nothing to take lightly."

"A *heart attack*?" Vito's jaw dropped. "Nonna had a heart attack?"

His surprise was so genuine that her annoyance about what she'd thought was neglect faded away. "About two weeks ago. She didn't tell you?"

"No, she didn't tell me. Do you think I'd have stayed away if I'd known?" His square jaw tightened. "Not a word. How bad was it?"

Lacey spread her hands. "Look, I'm just a CNA. You should definitely talk to her doctor."

"But from what you've seen, give me a guess."

Outside, she could hear people talking quietly. Dishes rattled in the kitchen, the girls cleaning up. She blew out a breath. "It was moderate severity. She had some damage, and there are some restrictions on what she can do. Changes she needs to make."

"What kind of changes?" He thrust his hands in his pockets and paced. "I can't believe she had a heart attack and I didn't know. Why didn't you call me?"

"It's her business what she tells people."

His mouth twisted to one side. "C'mon, Lace."

"I'm serious. Patients have the right to confidentiality. I couldn't breach that. In fact," she said, stricken, "I probably shouldn't have told you even now."

"You're my friend. You can tell me as a friend. Now,

what kind of changes? What does she need to do to get back on her feet?"

She perched on the arm of an overstuffed chair. "You can probably guess. It's a lot about diet. She needs to start a gentle exercise program. I have her walking around the block twice a day."

He stared. "Nonna's walking? Like, for exercise?"

"I know, right?" She smiled a little. "It wasn't easy to talk her into it. I make sure we have an interesting destination."

"How did you get so involved?"

She let her forehead sink down into her hand for just a second, then looked back up. Vito. He'd never take her seriously. He'd always been a big brother to her, and he always would be.

He held up a hand. "I'm not questioning it, Lacey. I'm grateful. And I feel awful having been out of the loop, not helping her. I've had lots of personal stuff going on, but that's no excuse."

His words flicked on a switch of interest in her, but she ignored it. "I worked her hall at the hospital, and since she knew me, we talked. She was worried about coming home alone, but she didn't want to bother you, and your brother's far away. I was looking to make a change, anyway, moving toward freelance home care so I could have time to finish renovating this place." She waved an arm toward the unfinished breakfast area, currently walled off with sheets of plastic.

"So you made a deal with her." He still sounded a little skeptical.

"Yes, if that's what you want to call it." She stood, full of restless energy, and paced over to the fireplace, rearranging the collection of colored glass bottles on the mantel. "She's had a lot of anxiety, which is common in people recovering from a heart attack. She's on several new medications, and one of them causes fatigue and dizziness. The social worker was going to insist on having her go to a nursing home for proper care, which she couldn't afford, so this was a good arrangement." She looked over at him, mentally daring him to question her.

He rubbed a hand over the back of his neck. "A nursing home. Wow."

"It wouldn't have suited her."

"For how long? How long do you think she'll need the extra care?"

Lacey shrugged, moved an amber bottle to better catch the sun. "I don't know. Usually people take a couple of months to get back up to speed. And your brother's happy to pay for as long as we need."

Vito's dark eyebrows shot up. "She told him and not me?"

"She said you'd find out soon enough, when you came back home."

"And he's paying for everything?"

"He felt bad, being so far away, and apparently he begged her to let him help. Look, if you want to make a change in her care, I totally understand." It would mess up her own plans, of course; she'd given notice at the hospital only when she had this job to see her through, so if Nonna left, she'd have to apply for a part-time job right away. But Nonna was improving daily. If she had Vito with her, and he could focus on her needs, she'd probably be fine. A lot of her anxiety and depression stemmed from loneliness and fear.

Truth was, Lacey had found the older woman a hedge

against her own loneliness, as her brother had gotten more and more involved in his wedding plans.

Now Buck and Gina and their dogs would be living in a little cottage on the other side of town. She'd see them a lot, but it wouldn't be the same as having Buck living here. "Whatever you decide," she said. "For now, we'd better go reassure your grandma, and then I need to attend to the rest of my guests."

Vito followed Lacey back into his grandmother's room, his mind reeling. Nonna had mostly raised him and his brother, Eugene, after their parents' accident, and she was one of the few family members he had left. More to the point, he was one of *her* only family members, and he should have been here for her.

Everyone treated him like he was made of glass, but the fact was, he was perfectly healthy on the inside. His surgeries had been a success, and his hearing loss was corrected with state-of-the-art hearing aids, courtesy of the VA.

He just *looked* bad.

And while the scars that slashed across his face, the worse ones on his chest, made it even more unlikely that he'd achieve his dream of marriage and a large family, he couldn't blame his bachelorhood entirely on the war. Women had always liked him, yes—as a friend. And nothing but a friend. He lacked the cool charisma that most women seemed to want in a boyfriend or husband.

Entering his grandmother's room, he pulled up a chair for Lacey, and then sat down on the edge of Nonna's bed, carefully, trying not to jolt her out of her light doze. He was newly conscious that she was pale, and thinner than she'd been. A glance around the attractive bedroom revealed a stash of pill bottles he hadn't noticed before.

Nonna's eyes fluttered open and she reached out.

He caught her hand in his. "Hey, how're you feeling?"

She pursed her lips and glared at Lacey. "You told him about my heart."

"Yes, I told him! Of course I told him!" Lacey's voice had a fond but scolding tone. "You should have let him know yourself, Nonna. I thought you had."

He squeezed his grandmother's hand. "Don't you know I would've dropped everything and come?"

Nonna made a disgusted noise. "That's exactly why I didn't tell you. You and your brother have your own lives to lead. And I was able to find a very good arrangement on my own." She smiled at Lacey.

"It *is* a good arrangement, and I'm glad for it." Vito glanced over at Lacey, who had gotten up to pour water into a small vase of flowers.

With its blue-patterned wallpaper, lamp-lit bedside table and a handmade quilt on the bed, the room was cozy. Through the door of the small private bathroom, he glimpsed handicapped-accessible rails and a shower seat.

Yes, this was a good situation for her. "Look, I want to take you back to the house, but we'll wait until you're a little better."

Nonna started to say something, and then broke off, picking restlessly at the blanket.

"I haven't even been over to see the place yet," he continued, making plans as he thought it through. "I just got into town. But I'll check it out, make sure you've got everything you need."

"About that, dear..." Nonna's voice sounded uncharacteristically subdued.

"I hope you don't mind, but I'm planning to live there with you for a while." He smiled. It was true comfort, knowing he could come back to Rescue River anytime and find a welcome, a place to stay and a home-cooked meal.

Lacey nodded approvingly, and for some reason it warmed Vito to see it.

"Neither one of us will be able to live there," Nonna said, her voice small.

Lacey's eyebrows rose in surprise, and he could feel the same expression on his own face. "What do you mean?"

"Now, don't be angry, either of you," she said, grasping his hand, "but I rented out the house."

"You *what?*"

"When did you do that?" Lacey sounded bewildered.

"We signed the papers yesterday when you were out grocery shopping," Nonna said, looking everywhere but at Vito and Lacey.

"Who'd you rent it to?" If it had just been finalized yesterday, surely everything could be revoked once the situation was explained. Lacey hadn't said anything about cognitive problems, but Nonna *was* in her early eighties. Maybe she wasn't thinking clearly.

Nonna smiled and clasped her hands together. "The most lovely migrant family," she said. "Three children and another on the way, and they're hoping to find a way to settle here. I gave them a good price, and they're going to keep the place up and do some repairs for me."

"Nonna..." Vito didn't know where to begin. He knew that this was the way things worked in his hometown—a lot of bartering, a lot of helping out those in need. "You aren't planning to stay here at the guesthouse indefinitely, right? How long of a lease did you sign?"

"Just a year." She folded her hands on top of her blanket and smiled.

"A year?" Not wanting to yell at his aged grandma, Vito stood and ran his hands through his hair. "Either you're going to have to revoke it, or I'm going to have to find another place for you and me to live." Never mind how he'd afford the rent. Or the fact that he'd named Nonna's house as his permanent residence in all the social services paperwork.

"No, dear. I have it all figured out." She took Lacey's hand in hers, and then reached toward him with her other hand. Once she had ahold of each of them, she smiled from one to the other. "Vito, if Lacey agrees, you can stay here."

No. She wasn't thinking clearly. "Nonna, that's not going to work. Lacey made this arrangement with you, not with me." And certainly not with the other guest he had in tow. No way could Lacey find out the truth about Charlie.

"But Lacey was thinking of getting another boarder for this period while she's remodeling. It's hard to find the right one, because of all the noise." Lacey started to speak, but Nonna held up a hand. "The noise doesn't bother me. I can just turn down my hearing aid."

Vito knew what was coming and he felt his face heat. "Nonna…"

"Vito's perfect," she said, looking at Lacey, "because he can do the same thing."

Lacey's eyebrows lifted as she looked at him.

No point in trying to hide his less visible disability now. "It's true," he said, brushing back his hair to show his behind-the-ear hearing aids. "But that doesn't mean you have to take us in." In fact, staying here was the last thing that would work for him.

He'd promised Gerry he'd take care of his son, conceived during the affair Gerry had while married to Lacey. And he'd promised to keep Charlie's parentage a secret from Lacey.

He was glad he could help his friend, sinner though Gerry had been. Charlie needed a reliable father figure, and Lacey needed to maintain her illusions about her husband. It would serve no purpose for her to find out the truth now; it would only hurt her.

Lacey frowned. "I *was* looking to take in another boarder. I was thinking of maybe somebody who worked the three-to-eleven shift at the pretzel factory. They could come home and sleep, and they wouldn't be bothered by my working on the house at all hours."

"That makes sense," he said, relieved. "That would be better."

"But the thing is," she said slowly, "I haven't found anyone, even though I've been advertising for a couple of weeks. If you wanted to…"

Anxiety clawed at him from inside. How was he supposed to handle this? He could throttle Gerry for putting him into this situation. "I… There are some complications. I need to give this some thought." He knew he was being cryptic, but he needed time to figure it all out.

Unfortunately, Nonna wasn't one to accept anything cryptic from her grandchildren. "What complications? What's going on?"

Vito stood, then sat back down again. Nonna was going to have to know about Charlie soon enough. Lacey, too, along with everyone else in town. It would seem weirder if he tried to hide it now. "The thing is," he said, "I'm not alone. I have someone with me."

"Girlfriend? Wife?" Lacey sounded extremely curious.

Nonna, on the other hand, looked disappointed. "You would never get married without letting your *nonna* know," she said, reaching up to pinch his cheek, and then pulling her hand back, looking apologetic. It took him a minute to realize that she'd hesitated because of his scars.

"One of my finished rooms is a double," Lacey said thoughtfully. "But I don't know what your…friend… would think of the mess and the noise."

This was going off the rails. "It's not a girlfriend or wife," he said.

"Then who?" Nonna smacked his arm in a way that reminded him of when he'd been small and misbehaving. "If not a woman, then who?"

Vito drew in a breath. "Actually," he said, "I've recently become certified as a foster parent."

Both women stared at him with wide, surprised eyes.

"So I'd be bringing along my eight-year-old foster son."

He was saved from further explanation by a crash, followed by the sound of shattering glass and running feet.

Chapter Two

Lacey raced out of Nonna's bedroom, leaving Vito to reassure the older woman. A quick scan of the hall revealed the breakage: her ceramic rooster lay in pieces on the floor.

One of the kids, probably; they were all sugared up on wedding cake and running around. She hurried to get a broom and dustpan, not wanting any of the remaining wedding guests to injure themselves. As she dropped the colorful pieces into the trash, she felt a moment's regret.

More important than the untimely demise of her admittedly tacky rooster, she wondered about Vito fostering a child. That, she hadn't expected.

"Miss Lacey!" It was little Mindy, Sam Hinton's daughter. "I saw who did that!"

"Did you? Stay back," she warned as she checked the area for any remaining ceramic pieces.

"Yes," Mindy said, "and he's hiding under the front porch right now!"

Behind her, Lacey heard Vito coming out of Nonna's bedroom, then pausing to talk some more, and a suspicion of who the young criminal might be came over her. "I'll go talk to him," she said. "It wasn't Xavier, was it?"

"No. It was a kid I don't know. Is he going to get in trouble?"

"I don't think so, honey. Not too much trouble, anyway. Why don't you go tell your dad what happened?"

"Yeah! He's gotta know!" As Mindy rushed off to her important task, Lacey walked out of the house and stood on the porch, looking around. The remaining guests were in the side yard, talking and laughing, so no one seemed to notice her.

She went down the steps and around to the side of the house where there was an opening in the latticework; she knew because she'd had to crawl under there when she'd first found Mrs. Whiskers, hiding with a couple of kittens. When she squatted down, she heard a little sniffling sound that touched her heart. Moving aside the branches of a lilac bush, breathing in the sweet fragrance of the fading purple flowers, she spoke into the darkness. "It's okay. I didn't like that rooster much, anyway."

There was silence, and then a stirring, but no voice. From the other side of the yard, she could hear conversations and laughter. But this shaded spot felt private.

"I remember one time I broke my grandma's favorite lamp," she said conversationally, settling into a sitting position on the cool grass. "I ran and hid in an apple tree."

"Did they find you?" a boy's voice asked. Not a familiar voice. Since she knew every kid at the wedding, her suspicion that the culprit was Vito's new foster son increased. "Yes, they found me. My brother told them where I was."

"Did you get in trouble?"

"I sure did." She remembered her grandma's reprimand, her father chiming in, her own teary apology.

"Did they hit you?" the boy asked, his voice low.

The plaintive question squeezed Lacey's heart. "No, I just got scolded a lot. And I had to give my grandma my allowance to help pay for a new lamp."

"I don't get an allowance. Did you..." There was a pause, a sniffle. "Did you have to go live somewhere else after that?"

Lacey's eyes widened as she put it all together. Vito had said he'd *recently* become certified as a foster parent. So this must be a new arrangement. It would make all the sense in the world that a boy who'd just been placed with a new foster father would feel insecure about whether he'd be allowed to stay.

But why had Vito, a single man with issues of his own, taken on this new challenge? "No, I didn't have to go live somewhere else," she said firmly, "and what's more, no kind adult would send a kid away for breaking a silly old lamp. Or a silly old rooster, either."

Branches rustled behind her, and then Vito came around the edge of the bushes. "There you are! What happened? Is everything okay?"

She pointed toward the latticed area where the boy was hiding, giving Vito a meaningful look. "I think the person who *accidentally*—" she emphasized the word "—broke the rooster is worried he'll get sent away."

"What?" Vito's thick dark eyebrows came down as understanding dawned in his eyes. He squatted beside her. "Charlie, is that you? Kids don't get sent away for stuff like that."

There was another shuffling under the porch, and then a head came into view. Messy, light brown hair, a sprinkling of freckles, worried-looking eyes. "But they might get sent away if they were keeping their dad from having a place to live."

Oh. The boy must have heard Vito say he couldn't live here because of having a foster son.

"We'll find a place to live," Vito said. "Come on out."

The boy looked at him steadily and didn't move.

"Charlie! I mean it!"

Lacey put a hand on Vito's arm. "Hey, Charlie," she said softly. "I grew up next door to this guy. I was three years younger and a lot smaller, and I did some annoying things. And he never, ever hit me." She felt Vito's arm tense beneath hers and squeezed. "And he wouldn't hurt you, either. Right, Vito?" She looked over at him.

His mouth twisted. "That's right." He went forward on one knee and held out a hand to the boy. "Come on out. We talked about this. Remember, I look meaner than I really am."

The boy hesitated, then crawled out without taking Vito's hand. Instead, he scuttled over to the other side of Lacey and crouched.

Vito drew in a breath and blew it out. His brow furrowed. "You're going to need to apologize to Miss Lacey, here, and then we'll find out how you can make up for what you did."

The boy wrapped his arms around upraised knees. A tear leaked out and he backhanded it away. "I can't make it up. Don't have any money."

"I might have some chores you could do," Lacey said, easing backward so she wasn't directly between Charlie and Vito. "Especially if you and your foster dad are going to be living here." As soon as she said it, she regretted the words. "Or living nearby," she amended hastily.

She liked Vito, always had. And she adored his grandmother, who clearly wanted her family gathered around her. But Lacey had been planning to have the next few months as a quiet, calm oasis before opening her guesthouse. She still had healing to do.

Having Vito and this boy here wasn't conducive to quiet serenity. On the other hand, young Charlie seemed to have thrown himself on her for protection, and that touched her.

"Can we live here? Really?" The boy jumped up and started hopping from one foot to the next. "'Cause this place is cool! You have a tire swing! And there's a basketball hoop right across the street!"

Vito stood, looking at her quizzically. "The grownups will be doing some talking," he said firmly. "For tonight, we're staying out at the motel like we planned. But before we go back there, I want you to apologize."

The boy looked at Lacey, then away, digging the toe of a well-worn sneaker into the dirt. "I'm real sorry I broke your rooster. It was an accident."

She nodded, getting to her feet. "That's all right. I think I can find another one kind of like it."

Her own soft feelings surprised her. Generally, she avoided little ones, especially babies; they were a reminder of all she couldn't have.

But this boy touched her heart. Maybe it was because his reaction to breaking the rooster was so similar to her own reaction when she'd broken the lamp. *Hide. Don't let the grown-ups know, because you never know what disaster will happen when grown-ups get upset.* She'd been fortunate, found by her grandma and father instead of her mom. Come to think of it, her brother had probably gone to them on purpose. He'd wanted her to get in trouble, but not from their volatile mother.

Lacey was beyond all that now, at least she thought so, but she still identified with the feeling of accidentally causing disasters and facing out-of-proportion consequences.

"And the other question you have to answer," Vito said, putting an arm around Charlie's shoulders lightly, ignoring the boy's automatic wince, "is how you got down here when you were supposed to be staying with Valencia."

Lacey moved to stand by Charlie, and her presence seemed to relax him.

"I asked her if we could take a walk," Charlie explained, a defensive tone coming into his voice. "When we came by here, she started talking to the people and I came inside. I just wanted to look around."

"You're not to do things like that without permission." Vito pinched the bridge of his nose. "You have another apology to make, to Valencia. And no dessert after dinner tonight."

The boy's lower lip came out, and Lacey felt the absurd impulse to slip him an extra piece of wedding cake.

An accented voice called from the other side of the yard. "Charlie! Charlie!"

"You run and tell Miss Valencia you're sorry you didn't stay close to her. And then wait for me on the porch."

As the boy ran toward the babysitter's anxious voice, Lacey looked up at Vito. "In over your head?"

"Totally." He blew out a breath. "What do I know about raising kids?"

"How'd you get into it, anyway?"

"It's complicated." He looked away, then back at her. "Listen, don't feel pressured into having us stay at your guesthouse. I don't expect that, no matter what Nonna says. And you can see that we'd be a handful."

She looked into his warm brown eyes. "I *can* see that. And I honestly don't know if it would work. But what are you going to do if you can't stay here?"

"That's the million-dollar question." He rubbed his chin. "We'll figure something out."

"Let me sleep on it. It's been a crazy day."

"Of course it has, and I'm sorry to add to that." They headed toward the rest of the guests, and he put an arm around her shoulders and squeezed. It was an innocent gesture, a friendly gesture, the same thing he'd done with Charlie.

But for some reason, it disconcerted her now, and she stepped away.

Something flashed in Vito's eyes and he cleared his throat. "Look, tomorrow Charlie has a visit with his birth mom up in Raystown. Let me take you to lunch. We can talk about Nonna and the possibility of Charlie and me staying here. Or more likely, how to break it to Nonna that we *won't* be staying here."

She'd planned to spend the next afternoon cleaning up and recovering from the wedding. "That'll work."

"The Chatterbox? Noon?" His voice was strictly businesslike.

"Where else?" She wondered why he'd gone chilly on her. "I'm looking forward to catching up."

And she was. Sort of.

* * *

The next morning, Vito pulled his truck into the parking lot at the Supervised Visitation Center and glanced into the backseat of the extended cab. Yes, a storm was brewing.

"Why do I have to do this?" Charlie mumbled. "Am I going back to live with her?"

"No." He twisted farther around to get more comfortable. "We talked about this. Your mom loves you, but she can't do a good job taking care of you, and you need to have a forever home." He'd practically memorized the words from the foster parenting handbook, and it was a good thing. Because apparently, Charlie needed to hear them a bunch of times.

"Then why do I have to visit? I wanted to play basketball with Xavier, that kid from the wedding yesterday. He said maybe I could come over."

Vito pulled up another memorized phrase and forced cheer into his voice. "It's important for you to have a relationship with your mom. Important for you and for her."

The whole situation was awful for a kid, and Krystal, Charlie's mother, wasn't easy to deal with. She'd neglected Charlie, and worse, exposed him to danger—mostly from her poorly chosen boyfriends—way too many times.

Someone who hurt a kid ought to be in prison, in Vito's mind, at the very least. But he had to keep reminding himself that Krystal was sick.

"You'll have fun with your mom," he said. "I think you guys are going to go out for lunch in a little while and maybe over to the lake afterward."

"That doesn't sound fun." Charlie crossed his arms

and looked out the window, making no move to get out of the car.

Vito looked that way, too, and saw Krystal getting out of the passenger side of a late-model SUV. Maybe things were looking up for her. He'd only met her a few times, but she'd been driving a car noticeably on its last legs.

The SUV roared off, passing them, with a balding, bearded, forty-something guy at the wheel. Vito looked back at Charlie in time to see the boy cringe. "What's wrong, buddy?" he asked. "Do you know that guy?"

Charlie nodded but didn't say anything.

Krystal strolled over to the back stoop of the Center, smoking a cigarette. Vito wished for a similarly easy way to calm his nerves.

He wished he knew how to be a father. He'd only had Charlie full-time for a month, most of which they'd spent in Cleveland, closing down Vito's previous life, getting ready to move home. Charlie had been well and truly welcomed by the Cleveland branch of Vito's family, though everyone had agreed on waiting to tell Nonna about Charlie until the foster care situation was definite. If everything went well, he'd be able to adopt Charlie after another six months and be the boy's permanent, real father.

Learning how to parent well would take a lifetime.

Vito got out of the car. The small, wire-supported trees around the brand-new building were trying their best, sporting a few green leaves. A robin hopped along the bare ground, poking for worms, and more birds chirped overhead. It was a nice summer day, and Vito was half tempted to get back in the truck and drive away, take Charlie to the lake himself.

But that wasn't the agreement he'd made. He opened

the passenger door and Charlie got out. His glance in his mother's direction was urgent and hungry.

Of course. This visit was important. No matter what parents did, kids always wanted to love them.

Vito forced a spring into his step as they approached the building and Krystal. "Hey," he greeted her, and tried the door.

"It's locked, genius." Krystal drew harder on her cigarette. She hadn't glanced at or touched Charlie, who'd stopped a few steps short of the little porch.

Looking at the two of them, Vito's heart about broke. He considered his big, extended family up in Cleveland, the hugs, the cheek pinches, the loud greetings. He had it good, always had. He squatted beside Charlie and cast about for conversation. "Charlie's been doing great," he said to Krystal, not that she'd asked. "Going to sign him up for summer softball."

"Nice for you. I never could afford it." She looked at Charlie then, and her face softened. "Hey, kid. You got tall in the past couple months."

Vito was so close to Charlie that he could sense the boy's urge to run to his mom as well as the fear that pinned him to Vito's side.

The fear worried him.

But Charlie would be safe. This was a supervised visit, if the caseworker ever got here.

"You were Gerry's buddy," Krystal said suddenly. "Did you know about me, or did he just talk about *her*?"

What was Vito supposed to say to that, especially in front of Charlie? The boy needed to think highly of his father, to remember that he'd died a hero's death, not that he'd lived a terribly flawed life. "It's better we focus on now," he said to Krystal, nodding his head sideways, subtly, at Charlie.

She snorted, but dropped the subject, turning away to respond to her buzzing phone.

Focus on now. He needed to take his own advice. Except he had to think about the future and make plans, to consider the possibility of him and Charlie staying with the *her*—Lacey—that Krystal was mad about. Which would be a really rotten idea, now that the ramifications of it all came to him.

He wasn't sure how much Krystal knew about Lacey and Gerry, what kind of promises Gerry might have made to her. From what he'd been able to figure out, Krystal hadn't known that Gerry was married, at least not at first. No wonder she was angry. Problem was, she'd likely pass that anger on to Charlie. She didn't seem like a person who had a very good filter.

And if she talked to Charlie about Lacey, and Charlie was living at Lacey's boardinghouse, the boy could get all mixed up inside.

If Gerry were still alive, Vito would strangle him. The jerk hadn't been married to Lacey for a year before he'd started stepping out on her.

Krystal put her phone away, lit another cigarette and sat down on the edge of the stoop. She beckoned to Charlie. "Come on, sit by me. You scared?"

Charlie hesitated, then walked over and sat gingerly beside her. When she put her arm around him, though, he turned into her and hugged her suddenly and hard, and grief tightened her face.

Vito stepped back to give them some space and covertly studied Krystal. He didn't understand Gerry. The man had had Lacey as a wife—gorgeous, sweet Lacey—

and he'd cheated on her with Krystal. Who, admittedly, had a stellar figure and long black hair. She'd probably been beautiful back then. But now the hair was disheveled. Her eyes were heavy-lidded, her skin pitted with some kind of scars. Vito wasn't sure what all she was addicted to, but the drugs had obviously taken their toll.

It looked like she'd stayed sober to visit with Charlie today, knowing she'd have to submit to a drug test. Maybe she'd had to stay clean a couple of days. That would put any addict into a bad mood.

Even before she'd been an addict, Krystal couldn't have compared to Lacey.

A battered subcompact pulled into the parking lot and jolted to a halt, its muffler obviously failing. The driver-side door flew open and the short, curly-haired caseworker got out. After pulling an overstuffed briefcase and a couple of bags from her car, she bustled over to them.

"Sorry I'm late! These Sunday visits are crazy. Maybe we can switch to Mondays or Tuesdays?" She was fumbling for the key as she spoke. "Come on in, guys! Thanks so much, Vito!"

"Charlie." Vito got the boy's attention, held his eyes. "I'll be back at three, okay?"

Relief shone on Charlie's face. He ran to Vito, gave him a short hug and whispered into his ear: "Come back for sure, okay?"

"You got it, buddy." Vito's voice choked up a little bit.

Charlie let go and looked at Vito. Then his eyes narrowed and he grinned purposefully. "And can we stay at that place instead of the motel?" he whispered. "With the cat and the nice lady?"

Vito knew manipulation when he saw it, but he also knew the boy needed both security and honesty.

"What's he begging for now?" Krystal grinned as she flicked her cigarette butt into the bare soil beside the building. "I recognize that look."

"I'm starting to recognize it, too," Vito said, meeting Krystal's eyes. Some kind of understanding arced between them, and he felt a moment of kinship and sorrow for the woman who'd given birth to Charlie but wouldn't get to raise him.

"Well, can we?" Charlie asked.

"We'll see. No promises." Vito squeezed the boy's shoulder. "You be good, and I'll see you right here at three o'clock."

In reality, he wished he could just sweep the boy up and take him home, and not just to protect him from an awkward day with his mom. Vito wasn't looking forward to the lunch date—no, *not* a date—he was facing in only a few hours. Whatever he and Lacey decided, it was going to make someone unhappy.

Chapter Three

"They left the two of us in charge of the nursery? Are they crazy?" Lacey's friend Susan put her purse up on a shelf and came over to where Lacey stood beside a crib, trying to coax a baby to sleep.

"I'm just glad it's you working with me." Lacey picked up the baby, who'd started to fuss, and swayed gently. "You won't freak out if I freak out."

Working in the church nursery was Lacey's counselor's idea, a way to help Lacey deal with her miscarriage and subsequent infertility. She needed to desensitize herself, find ways to be around babies without getting upset by them, especially if she was going to open a family-friendly guesthouse and make a success of it.

The desensitization had started accidentally, when Gina Patterson had showed up in town earlier this year with her son, Bobby, just ten months old at the time. With nowhere else to turn, she'd spent the early spring at the guesthouse, in the process falling in love with Lacey's brother, Buck. Being around little Bobby had made Lacey miserable at first, but she was learning. More than that, she was motivated; she wanted to serve others and get out of her own pain, build a well-rounded life for herself.

Which included being around babies. "I'm here to work through my issues," she told Susan, "but why are *you* here?"

Susan's tawny skin went pink. "Sam and I decided it would be a good idea for me to get comfortable with babies. I used to be terrified of even touching them, but… I guess I'd better learn."

Something in Susan's tone made Lacey take notice, and she mentally reviewed what Susan had just said. Then she stared at her friend. "Wait a minute. Are you expecting? Already?"

Susan looked down at the floor, and then met Lacey's eyes. "Yeah. We just found out."

Selfish tears sprang to Lacey's eyes as she looked down at the infant she held, feeling its weight in her arms. Something she'd never experience for herself, with her own child. A joy that Susan and many of Lacey's other friends would find effortlessly.

Susan would be a part of the circle of happy young mothers in town. Lacey wouldn't, not ever.

"I'm so sorry to cause you pain. News like this must be hard for you to hear."

Susan's kind words jolted Lacey out of her own self-centered heartache. Finding out you were having a baby was one of the most joyous times of a woman's life. She remembered when the two pink lines had shown up on her own pregnancy test. Remembered her video call to Gerry. She'd shown the test to him, and they'd both cried tears of joy.

Susan deserved to have that joy, too. She shouldn't have to focus on her friend's losses.

Lacey lifted the baby to her shoulder so she could reach out and put an arm around Susan. "It does hurt a little—I'm not going to lie. But what kind of friend would I be not to celebrate with you? I'm thrilled!"

"You're the best, Lace." Susan wrapped her arms around Lacey, the baby in between them, and Lacey let herself cry just a little more. Susan understood. She'd stayed a year at Lacey's guesthouse before the remodeling, the horrible year when Lacey had lost both Gerry and the baby. Susan had been an incredible comfort.

"Anyway," Susan added, "I'm going to need your help to fit in with the perfect mothers of Rescue River. You know I have a knack for saying the wrong thing."

"You'll be fine." And it was true. Susan was outspoken and blunt, but she gave everything she had to the kids she taught at the local elementary school, and people here loved her for it. "How's Sam handling the news?"

"Making a million plans and bossing me around, of course." But Susan smiled as she said it, and for just a moment, Lacey felt even more jealous of the happy-married-woman smile on Susan's face than of the tiny, growing baby in her belly.

"Hey, guys, can I leave Bobby here for a little while?" Lou Ann Miller, who was taking care of Gina's baby while she and Buck enjoyed a honeymoon at the shore, stood at the half door. "I want to go to adult Sunday school, but there's no way he'll sit through our book discussion."

"Sure." Lacey thrust the infant she'd been holding into Susan's arms. "Just hold her head steady. Yeah, like that." She walked over to the door and opened it. "Come on in, Bobby!"

"Laaasss," he said, walking right into her leg and hugging it. "Laaasss."

Lacey's heart warmed, and she reached down to pick Bobby up. "He'll be fine. Take your time," she said to Lou Ann. "Wave bye-bye to Miss Lou Ann, okay?"

Two more toddlers got dropped off, and then a diaper needed changing. Little Emmie Farmingham, who was almost three, twirled to show Lacey and Susan her new summer dress, patterned with garden vegetables and sporting a carrot for a pocket. Then she proceeded to pull the dress off.

Once they'd gotten Emmie dressed again, the infant sleeping and the other two toddlers playing side by side with plastic blocks, Susan and Lacey settled down into the tiny chairs around the low table. "Babies are great, I guess," Susan said doubtfully, "but I have to say, I like bigger kids better. I wish one could just land in my lap at age five, like Mindy did."

"Not me." Lacey looked over at the toddlers, another surge of regret piercing her heart. "I've always loved the little ones."

"I know you have." Susan's voice was gentle. "Hey, want to come over and have lunch with us after this? I think Sam's grilling. You could bring your swimsuit."

"You're sweet." The thought of lounging by Sam and Susan's pool was appealing. And Susan was a great friend; she'd stand by Lacey even as she was going through this huge transition of having a child. She wouldn't abandon Lacey, and that mattered.

Lacey shook her head with real disappointment. "Can't. I'm meeting Vito for lunch."

"Oh, *Vito*." Susan punched her arm, gently. "Is this a date?"

"It's not like that. We're old friends."

Susan ignored her words. "You should see where it leads. He seems like a great guy, from what I saw of him at the end of the reception. Good-looking, too. Even with the scars." Susan's hand flew to her mouth. "I shouldn't say things like that, should I?"

"Probably not." Lacey rolled her eyes at her friend, pretending exasperation. "But it's okay. You can't help but notice his scars. Anyway, we're just going to talk about this crazy idea his grandma dreamed up." She explained how Nonna had unexpectedly rented out her own house, and how Vito was newly a foster father. "Apparently, Vito had no idea that was her plan. He was counting on bringing his foster son, Charlie, to live in Nonna's big house out in the country. I actually got the feeling Nonna had kept it a secret on purpose, to make sure Vito ended up staying at the guesthouse."

"But that would be perfect!" Susan clapped her hands. "Vito could be with his *nonna*, and Charlie could get a sense of family, and they'd be right in town to get, like, reintegrated into the community."

"Yes, but—"

"And you wanted someone else to room in, right? He'd pay rent, which would help with your expenses. He and Charlie could have separate rooms, or those two connecting ones upstairs."

Lacey's response was cut off by the sound of crashing blocks and a wail, and they got busy playing with the babies. The subject of Vito moving into the guesthouse didn't come up again, but Lacey couldn't stop thinking about it.

Susan seemed to think it was a great idea, and Nonna had talked to Lacey over breakfast about how wonderful it would be to have Vito there and to get to know the newest member of the family. Her eyes had sparkled when she said that, and few enough things had brought a sparkle to Nonna's eyes since the heart attack.

There were all kinds of reasons to embrace the idea of Vito and Charlie moving in, but Lacey still felt uneasy about it.

She couldn't begin to articulate why, even to herself.

At lunchtime, Vito stood outside the Chatterbox Café, looking up at the town's outdoor clock, which clearly showed it was only eleven forty-five. He was early. Why had he come so early?

He loosened the itchy collar of his new button-down shirt. He shouldn't have worn a brand-new shirt today, should have at least washed it first, except that he was living out of a suitcase and he'd been rushing to get Charlie ready to go and there hadn't been the chance.

He could have just worn an old, comfortable shirt, but the fact was, he was trying to look good. Which was obviously a losing battle.

It wasn't about Lacey. It was about the fact that he'd probably see other people he knew here at the Chatterbox, and he needed to present a professional image. He had good benefits from the VA—they were paying for his online degree—but a man needed to work, and Vito would be looking for a part-time job just as soon as he'd found a place to live and gotten Charlie settled. Maybe something with kids, since he was looking to become a teacher.

No, it wasn't about Lacey. He'd had some feelings for her once, but he'd turned those off when she'd married, of course. He'd been over her for years.

"Vito!" Lacey approached, a summery yellow dress swirling around her legs, the wind blowing her short hair into messiness.

She looked so beautiful that, for a moment, he couldn't breathe.

He crooked his arm for her to take it, an automatic gesture he'd learned at his *nonna*'s knee. The way a gentleman treated a lady. And then he remembered how she'd stepped away when he'd done the Italian thing and thrown an arm around her yesterday. He put his arm back at his side.

People are disgusted by your scars, he reminded himself. *And she hasn't seen the half of them.*

As they turned toward the café—Vito carefully *not* touching her—he caught a whiff of something lemony and wondered if it was her shampoo, or if she'd worn perfume.

Inside, everything was familiar: the smell of meat loaf and fries, the red vinyl booths and vintage tables trimmed with aluminum, the sight of people he'd known since childhood. Even the counter waitress, Nora Jean, had been here since he was a kid and called a greeting.

"Sit anywhere, you two. Lindy'll wait on you, but I'm coming over to say hello just as soon as these guys give me a break." She waved at her full counter.

Dion Coleman, the police chief, swiveled in his chair and stood to pound Vito on the back. "I'm glad to see your ugly mug," he joked. Which didn't feel awkward, because it was the exact same thing Dion had always said when Vito came home, even before his injuries. "Police business has been slow these past months, but with you home, it's sure to pick up."

Vito shook the man's hand with genuine pleasure. "I'll

see what I can do about knocking down some mailboxes and shooting up signs, just to give you something to do. You're getting soft." He nodded down at Dion's flat belly and then at the grilled chicken salad on the counter in front of him. "Eating too much. Just like a cop."

"You never change." Dion was laughing as he sat back down. "Give me a call, you hear? We have some catching up to do."

Lacey had headed toward one of the few empty booths at the back of the café, and as he followed her it seemed to Vito that conversation stopped, then rose again when he'd passed. He rubbed a hand across his face, feeling the uneven ridges of his scars.

As soon as they sat down, they were mobbed. The young waitress could barely squeeze in to take their order. Everyone, friend or acquaintance, stopped by to say hello. They wanted to know where he was staying, how long he'd be in town, where he was stationed. Explaining that he wasn't in the army anymore felt embarrassing, since he'd always intended it to be his life's work. More embarrassing were the sympathetic nods and arm pats. People felt sorry for him.

But he kept it upbeat and answered questions patiently. Once people knew his story, they'd settle down some. And maybe someone would think of him when a job opening came up, so he made sure to let everyone know he was looking.

After people had drifted back to their tables and they'd managed to eat some of their lunch, Lacey wiped her mouth and smiled at him. "That got a little crazy. Are you wishing we'd gone somewhere else?"

He swallowed his massive bite of cheeseburger and

shook his head. "Best to get it over fast. Let people get a good look."

She took a sip of soda. "You think they all came over to look at your scars?"

"That, and find out the latest news. But mostly to see how bad the damage is, up close and personal." His support group at the VA had warned him about people's reactions, how they might not be able to see anything but his scars at first.

"They're not looking at your scars in a bad way," Lacey said, frowning. "They're grateful for your service."

Of course, that was what most of the people who'd greeted them had said. And they weren't lying. It was just that initial cringe that got to him. He wasn't used to scaring people just by the way he looked.

His friend with severe facial burns had told Vito that you never really got used to it. "Older people do better, but young people like pretty," he'd said. "Makes it a challenge to get a date."

The waitress refilled his coffee cup and headed to a booth across the way. Vito gestured toward her. "You can't tell me someone like that, someone who doesn't know me, isn't disgusted when she first sees me."

Lacey looked at him for a long moment, her brown eyes steady. "Look over there," she said, pointing to a twenty-something man in an up-to-date wheelchair, sitting at a table with an older woman. "That's our waitress's brother," she said. "He served, too."

Vito blinked and looked more closely, seeing how the man's head lolled to one side, held up by a special support. He wore a hoodie and sweats, and as Vito watched, the older woman put a bite of something into his mouth.

"Wounded in service?"

Lacey nodded. "I think he was a Marine."

"Is a Marine," Vito corrected. "And I'm sorry. You're right. I need to get out of my own head. I'm more fortunate than a lot of guys." He met her eyes. "Gerry included, and I'm a jerk to focus on myself."

She shrugged. "We all do that sometimes."

Had Lacey always had this steady maturity? He couldn't help but remember her as a younger girl, pestering him and her brother when they'd wanted to go out and do something fun. And he remembered how flightily she'd fallen for Gerry, swept away by love and unable to listen to anyone's warnings.

Now though, there was real thoughtfulness to her. She was quieter than she'd been, and more assertive.

He liked that. Liked a woman who'd call him on his dumb mistakes.

And he didn't need to be thinking about how much he liked the new Lacey. Best to get to the real reason for their lunch. "So, I was looking into options for Charlie and me," he said. "I talked to the family Nonna rented her house to."

"And? Did you ask if they'd let her out of the contract?"

"I couldn't even bring it up." He lifted his hands, shrugging. "They're thrilled with the house and the price Nonna gave them, and they need the space. And she's pregnant out to here." He held a hand in front of his stomach.

"Well, look who's back in town!" Old Mr. Love from the hardware store, who had to be in his eighties, stopped by their table and patted his shoulder. "I'd recognize that voice anywhere!"

Vito stood and greeted the man, and then looked at the gray-haired woman with him. "Miss Minnie Falcon? Is that you?"

"That's right, young man. You'd better not forget your old Sunday school teacher."

"I couldn't ever forget." He took her hand, gently. Unlike some of the other kids in Sunday school, he'd actually appreciated Miss Minnie's knowledge of the Old and New Testament, and the way she brought the stories to life, infusing them with a sense of biblical history.

Mr. Love was leaning toward Lacey. "I was hoping you'd find romance." His voice, meant to be low, carried clearly to Vito and Miss Minnie. "Now that Buck's out of your hair, it's your turn, young lady." He nodded toward Vito, raising an eyebrow.

"Harold!" Miss Minnie scolded. "Don't make assumptions. Come on. Let's get that corner table before someone else takes it." She patted Vito's arm. "It was nice to see you. Don't be a stranger. We like visitors over at the Senior Towers." She turned and headed across the restaurant at a brisk pace, pushing her wheeled walker.

"When a lady talks, you listen." Mr. Love gave Vito an apologetic shrug as he turned and followed Miss Minnie, putting a hand on her shoulder.

After they were out of earshot, Vito lifted an eyebrow at Lacey. "They're a couple?"

"It's anybody's guess. They both say they're just friends, but tongues are wagging. It *is* Rescue River."

"Gossip central," he agreed, sipping coffee.

"And speaking of wagging tongues," she said, "imagine what people will assume about us if you come and live in the guesthouse. Just like Mr. Love assumed when he saw us together here. They'll think *we're* a couple. And I'm not comfortable with that."

"I understand." He looked down at his hands, traced a scar that peeked out from his shirt cuff. "I'm not exactly a blue-ribbon bronco."

"Vito!" She sounded exasperated. "You haven't changed a bit since you had to try on six different shirts for the homecoming dance."

The memory made him chuckle. He'd gotten her to sit on the porch and judge while he tried on shirt after shirt, running back to his room to change each time she'd nixed his selection.

Little did she know that Buck had begged him to keep her busy while he tried to steal a few kisses from cheerleader Tiffany Townsend, ostensibly at their house for help with homework.

"That was a long time ago," he said now. "And the truth is, I *have* changed."

She rolled her eyes. "You're still good-looking, okay? Women don't mind scars." Then she pressed her lips together as her cheeks grew pink.

His heart rate accelerated, just a little. Why was she blushing? Did *she* think he was good-looking?

But of course, she hadn't seen the worst of his scars.

And even if there *was* a little spark between them, it couldn't go anywhere. Because he was living with a secret he couldn't let her discover.

"Look," she said, and then took a big gulp of soda. "Getting back to the idea of you and Charlie staying at the guesthouse. I'd be willing to consider it, for Nonna's sake, but…I'm trying to build a rich, full life as a single person, see, and I don't want everyone asking me questions or trying to match us up. I'm just getting over being

Lacey, the pitiful widow. And now, if I have this good-looking man living in my guesthouse…" A flush crept up her cheeks again and she dropped her head, propping her forehead on her hand. "I'm just digging myself in deeper here, huh?"

She *did* think he was good-looking. All of a sudden, other people's curious stares didn't bother him half as much.

"Can I get you anything else?" The perky waitress was back, looking at Lacey with curiosity. "You okay, Lacey?"

"I need something chocolate," she said, looking up at the waitress but avoiding Vito's eyes.

"Right away! I totally understand!"

Vito didn't get women's obsession with chocolate, but he respected it. He waited until the server had brought Lacey a big slice of chocolate cream pie before blundering forward with their meeting's purpose. "I have an appointment tonight to talk to a woman who might want to rent me a couple of rooms in her farmhouse, out past the dog rescue. And there's the top floor of a house available over in Eastley."

"That's good, I guess." She toyed with the whipped cream on her pie. "But Nonna won't like having you so far away. And Charlie could make more friends in town, right?"

"He really took a shine to the place and to you, it's true."

"And Nonna wants you to live there. She pulled out all the stops at breakfast, trying to talk me into it again."

"She phoned me, too."

Lacey was absently fingering the chain around her

neck, and when he looked more closely, he saw what hung on it.

A man's wedding ring. Undoubtedly Gerry's.

He wasn't worth it, Lace.

A shapely blonde in a tight-fitting dress approached their table. Tiffany Townsend. "Well, Vito D'Angelo. Aren't *you* a sight for sore eyes."

He snorted. "No." And then he thought about what Lacey had said: *Women don't mind scars*. And nobody, even a less-than-favorite classmate like Tiffany, deserved a rude response. He pasted on a smile. "Hey, Tiffany. It's been a long time."

"Where are you hiding yourself these days?" She bent over the table, and Vito leaned back in the booth, trying to look anywhere but down her low-cut dress. "We should get together sometime!" she gushed, putting a hand on his arm.

This was where a suave man would smile and flirt and make a date. But Vito had never been suave. He'd always been the one to console the girls whose boyfriends got caught on Tiffany's well-baited line. Always the friend, happy to take them out for coffee or a milk shake and to listen to them.

Unfortunately for his love life, it hadn't usually gone further than that.

Tiffany was looking at him expectantly. "Where did you say you're staying?"

"I'm not really..." He broke off. Did he really want to get into his personal business with Tiffany?

Lacey cleared her throat, grasped Vito's scarred hand and smiled up at Tiffany. "He's staying at my guesthouse," she said sweetly. "With me."

"Oh." There was a world of meaning in that word,

backed up by Tiffany's raised eyebrows. "Well, then. It was good to see you." She spun on her high heels and walked over to the counter, where she leaned toward Nora Jean and started talking fast and hard.

Vito turned his hand over, palm to palm with Lacey. "Thanks," he said, "but you didn't have to do that."

"Tiffany hasn't changed a bit since high school," Lacey said. "She'd break your heart."

"It's not in the market."

"Mine, either."

They looked at each other and some electrical-like current materialized between them, running from their locked eyes to their intertwined hands.

No, Vito's heart wasn't in the market. He had enough to do to rebuild a life and raise a boy and keep a secret.

But if it *had* been in the market, it would run more toward someone like Lacey than toward someone like Tiffany.

Lacey glanced toward the counter. "Don't look now," she said, "but Tiffany and Nora Jean are staring at us."

"This is how rumors get started." He squeezed her hand a little, then could have kicked himself. Was he flirting? With the one woman he could never, ever get involved with?

"That's true," Lacey said briskly, looking away. "And we've obviously done a good job of starting a rumor today. So…"

"So what?" He squeezed her hand again, let go and thought of living at the guesthouse with Nonna and Charlie.

Charlie could walk to the park, or better yet, ride a bike. Vito was pretty sure there was one in Nonna's garage that he could fix up.

Vito could see Nonna every day. Do something good for the woman who'd done so much for him.

And he could get back on his feet, start his online classes. Maybe Nonna, as she got better, would watch Charlie for him some, giving him a chance to go out and find a decent job.

Soon enough, Nonna would be well and Charlie would be settled in school and Vito would have some money to spare. At which point he could find them another place to live.

He'd only have to keep his secret for the summer. After that, he and Charlie would live elsewhere and would drift naturally out of Lacey's circle of friends. At that point, it was doubtful that she'd learn about Charlie's parentage; there'd be no reason for it to come up.

How likely was it that Lacey would find out the truth over the summer?

"Maybe you could stay for a while," she said. "I'm opening the guesthouse this fall, officially, but until then, having a long-term guest who didn't mind noise would help out."

"How about a guest who makes noise? Charlie's not a quiet kid."

"I liked him."

"Well, then," Vito said, trying to ignore the feeling that he was making a huge mistake, "if you're seriously making the offer, it looks like you've got yourself a couple of tenants for the summer."

Chapter Four

The next Wednesday afternoon, Lacey looked out the kitchen window as Charlie and Vito brought a last load of boxes in from Vito's pickup. Pop music played loudly—Charlie's choice. She'd heard their good-natured argument earlier. The bang of the front screen door sent Mr. Whiskers flying from his favorite sunning spot on the floor. He disappeared into the basement, where his companion, Mrs. Whiskers, had already retreated.

Some part of Lacey liked the noise and life, but part of her worried. There went her peaceful summer—and Nonna's, too. This might be a really bad idea.

She glanced over at the older woman, relaxing in the rocking chair Lacey had put in a warm, sunny corner beside the stove. Maybe she'd leave the chair there. It gave the room a cozy feel. And Nonna didn't look any too disturbed by the ruckus Vito and Charlie were creating. Her eyes sparkled with more interest than she'd shown in the previous couple of weeks.

"I'd better get busy with dinner." Lacey opened the refrigerator door and studied the contents.

"I used to be such a good cook," Nonna commented. "Nowadays, I just don't have the energy."

"You will again." Lacey pulled mushrooms, sweet peppers and broccoli from the fridge. "You'd better. I don't think I could face the future without your lasagna in it."

"I could teach you to make it."

Lacey chuckled. "I'm really not much of a cook. And besides, we need to work on healthy meals. Maybe we can figure out a way to make some heart-healthy lasagna one of these days."

As she measured out brown rice and started it cooking, she looked over to see Nonna's frown. "What's wrong?"

"What are you making?"

"Stir-fried veggies on brown rice. It'll be good." Truthfully, it was one of Lacey's few staples, a quick, healthy meal she often whipped up for herself after work.

"No meat?" Nonna sounded scandalized. "You can't serve a meal to men without meat. At least a little, for flavor."

Lacey stopped in the middle of chopping the broccoli into small florets. "I'm cooking for men?"

"Aren't you fixing dinner for Vito and Charlie, too?" Nonna's eyebrows lifted.

"We didn't talk about sharing meals." Out the window, she saw Vito close the truck cab and wipe his forehead with the back of his hand before picking up one of the street side boxes to carry in. "They *are* working up a sweat out there, but where would I put them?" She nodded toward the small wooden table against the wall, where she and Nonna had been taking their meals. Once again, she sensed their quiet, relaxing summer dissolving away.

At the same time, Nonna was an extrovert, so maybe having more people around would suit her. As for Lacey, she needed to get used to having people in the house, to ease into hosting a bed-and-breakfast gradually, rather than waiting until she had a houseful of paying guests to feed in her big dining room. And who better than good old Vito?

"There's always room for more around a happy home's table," Nonna said, rocking.

"I guess we *could* move it out from the wall."

Vito walked by carrying a double stack of boxes, and Lacey hurried to the kitchen door. "Are you okay with that? Do you need help?" Though from the way his biceps stretched the sleeves of his white T-shirt, he was most definitely okay.

"There's nothing wrong with me below the neck." He sounded uncharacteristically irritable. "I can carry a couple of boxes."

Where had *that* come from? She lifted her hands and took a step back. "Fine with me," she said sharply.

From above them on the stairs, Charlie crowed, "Ooo-eee, a fight!"

Vito ignored him and stomped up the stairs, still carrying both boxes.

"You come in here, son." Nonna stood behind Lacey, beckoning to Charlie.

Lacey bit her lip. She didn't want Nonna to overexert herself. And being from an earlier generation, she might have unreasonable expectations of how a kid like Charlie would behave.

But Nonna was whispering to Charlie, and they both

laughed, and then he helped her back to her rocking chair. That was good.

Lacey went back to her cutting board, looked at the stack of veggies and reluctantly acknowledged to herself that Nonna was probably right. If she could even get a red-blooded man and an eight-year-old boy to eat stir-fry, the least she could do was put some beef in it. She rummaged through her refrigerator and found a pack of round steak, already cut into strips. Lazy woman's meat. She drizzled oil into the wok, let it heat a minute, and then dumped in the beef strips.

"Hey, Lace." It was Vito's deep voice, coming from the kitchen doorway. "C'mere a minute."

She glanced around. The rice was cooking, Nonna and Charlie were still talking quietly and the beef was barely starting to brown. She wiped her hands on a kitchen towel. "What's up?" she asked as she crossed the kitchen toward him. "You're not going to bite my head off again, are you?"

"No." He beckoned her toward the front room, where they could talk without the others hearing. "Look, I'm sorry I snapped. Charlie's been a handful and..." He trailed off and rubbed the back of his neck.

"And what?"

"And...I hate being treated like there's something wrong with me. I'm still plenty strong."

"I noticed." But she remembered a similar feeling herself, after her miscarriage; people had tiptoed around her, offering to carry her groceries and help her to a seat in church. When really, she'd been just fine physically. "I'm sorry, too, then. I know how annoying it is to be treated like an invalid."

"So we're good?" He put an arm around her.

It was a gesture as natural as breathing to Vito as well as to the rest of his Italian family. She'd always liked that about them.

But now, something felt different about Vito's warm arm around her shoulders. Maybe it was that he was so much bigger and brawnier than he'd been as a younger man.

Disconcerted, she hunched her shoulders and stepped away.

Some emotion flickered in his eyes and was gone, so quickly she wasn't sure she'd seen it.

"Hi!" Charlie came out of the kitchen, smiling innocently. He sidestepped toward Nonna's room.

"Where you headed, buddy?" Vito asked.

"Lacey, dear," Nonna called from the kitchen. "I'd like to rest up a little before dinner."

"I'm glad she called me." Lacey heard herself talking a little faster than usual, heard a breathless sound in her own voice. "I try to walk with her, because I have so many area rugs and the house can be a bit of an obstacle course. But of course, she likes to be independent." Why was she blathering like she was nervous, around Vito?

"I'll help her." Vito went into the kitchen and Lacey trailed behind. "Come on, Nonna, I'll walk with you. Smells good," he added, glancing over to where the beef sizzled on the stove.

It *did* smell good, and the praise from Vito warmed her. She added in sliced mushrooms and onions.

For a moment, all she could hear was the slight sizzle of the food on the stove and the tick of the big kitchen clock on the wall. Peace and quiet. Maybe this was going to work out okay.

The quiet didn't last long. From Nonna's room, she

could hear Charlie talking, telling some story. Vito's deeper voice chimed in. His comfortable, familiar laugh tickled her nerve endings in a most peculiar way. Then she heard his heavy step on the stairs. No doubt he was going up to do a little more unpacking while Charlie was occupied. Vito was a hard worker.

And just why was she so conscious of him? What was wrong with her?

She walked over to the sink and picked up the photo she kept on a built-in wooden shelf beside it. Gerry, in uniform, arriving home on one of his furloughs. Someone had snapped a photo of her hugging him, her hair, longer then, flying out behind her, joy in every muscle of her body.

She clasped the picture close to her chest. *That* was reality.

Reassured, she moved out the table and located some chairs for Charlie and Vito, almost wishing Buck hadn't taken her bigger kitchen table with him when he'd moved. She checked on the dinner. Just about done. She found grapes and peaches to put in a nice bowl, both a centerpiece and a healthy dessert.

"What's going on here?" She heard Vito's voice from Nonna's room a little later. He must have come back downstairs. She hadn't even noticed. Good.

Charlie's voice rose, then Nonna's. It sounded like an argument, and Lacey's patient shouldn't be arguing. She wiped her hands and hurried to check on Nonna.

When she looked into the room, both Nonna and Charlie had identical guilty expressions. And identical white smudges on their faces. Beside Nonna was a box from the bakery that someone had brought over yesterday. Cannoli.

"Dessert before dinner, Charlie?" Vito was shaking his head. "You know that's not allowed."

"Nonna!" Lacey scolded. "Rich, heavy pastries aren't on your diet. You know the doctor's worried about your blood sugar."

"She told me where they were and asked me to get them for her," Charlie protested. "And you told me I was supposed to treat older people with respect."

Vito blew out a sigh. "You just need to check with me first, buddy. And Nonna, you've got to stick to your eating plan. It's for your health!"

"What's life without cannoli?" Nonna said plaintively. "Do I have to give up all my treats?"

Vito knelt beside his grandmother. "I think you can have a few planned treats. But sneaking cannoli before dinner means you won't have an appetite for the healthy stuff."

"I didn't anyway," Nonna muttered.

"Me, either." Charlie went to stand beside Nonna on the other side. Obviously, he'd made a new friend in Nonna, and that was all to the good for both of them—as long as it didn't lead to Nonna falling off the diet bandwagon.

It was up to Lacey to be firm, so she marched over and picked up the bakery box. "Whatever you men don't eat for dessert is getting donated tonight," she said firmly. "Obviously, it's too much of a temptation to have things like this in the house."

An acrid smell tickled her nose.

"What's that burning?" Vito asked at the same moment.

"Dinner!" Lacey wailed and rushed into the kitchen, where smoke poured from the rice pan. In the wok, the beef and vegetables had shrunk down and appeared to be permanently attached to the wok's surface.

All her work to make dinner nice and healthy, gone to waste.

She turned off the burners and stared at the ruined food, tears gathering in her eyes. In her head she could hear her mother's criticism of the cookies she'd baked: *you'll never be much of a chef, will you?*

She remembered Gerry shoving away his dinner plate the first night they'd come back from their honeymoon, saying he wasn't hungry.

Nonna was calling questions from her room and Charlie shouted back: "Lacey burned up dinner!"

The acrid smoke stung her eyes, and then the smoke detector went off with an earsplitting series of beeps.

This was not the serene life she had been looking for. She was a failure as a cook.

She burst into tears.

Vito coughed from the smoke and winced from the alarm's relentless beeping. He turned down the volume on his hearing aids and moved toward Lacey, his arms lifting automatically to comfort her with a hug.

She clung on to him for one precious second, then let go and looked around like she didn't know what to do next.

He needed to take charge. He shut off the smoke detectors, one after the other. Then he opened all the windows in the kitchen, gulping in big breaths of fresh air.

Lacey flopped down at the kitchen table, wiping tears. He beckoned to Charlie. "Run and tell Nonna everything's fine, but dinner will be a little late." As Charlie left the room, Vito scraped the ruined food into the garbage and filled the two pans halfway with soapy water. They'd need some serious scrubbing later.

Lacey was sniffling now, blowing her nose and wiping her eyes.

He leaned back against the counter and studied her. "How come this got you so upset? You're not a crier."

She laughed. "I am, these days. And I'm also a loser in the kitchen, in case you didn't notice. My mom always told me that, and Gerry concurred."

"Gerry?" That was a surprise. The man had eaten enough MREs in the military that he should have been grateful for any home cooking, however simple.

She pushed herself to her feet. "What'll we eat now? Nonna needs dinner. We all do. I guess, maybe, pizza? But that's not the healthiest choice for your grandma."

"Do you have canned tomatoes?" Vito asked her. "Onions? Garlic? Pasta?"

She nodded and blew her nose again. "I think so."

"Great. You sit down and I'll give you stuff to chop. I'm going to make a spaghetti sauce." He might not know what words to say to comfort her, but he could definitely cook her a meal.

"Spaghetti!" Charlie yelled, pumping his fist as he ran into the kitchen.

"That's right." Vito stepped in front of the racing boy. "And you, young man, are going to do some chores. Starting with taking out this garbage."

Charlie started to protest, but Vito just pointed at the garbage can. Charlie yanked out the bag and stomped out of the house with it.

Lacey chopped and Vito opened cans of tomatoes and set the sauce to cooking. As the onions sizzled in olive oil, the day's tension rolled off him. When Charlie came back in, he had Gramps Camden, a weathered-looking, gray-haired man, with him.

Lacey gave the older man a hug, then turned to Vito. "You remember Gramps Camden, don't you?"

Vito stood and greeted the older man, who'd been a part of the community as long as he could remember.

"Wanted to pay a visit," he said in his trademark grouchy way. "See what you've got going on over here."

"You'll stay for dinner, won't you?" Lacey asked.

"Twist my arm," the old man said. "Cooking's good over at the Senior Towers, but nothing beats homemade."

Lacey asked Charlie to take a couple of bills out to the mailbox, and he went happily enough.

A knock came on the back screen door, and there was Gina, the woman Lacey's brother, Buck, had married, holding a toddler by the hand. "Hey, Lace, are you in there?"

"C'mon in." Lacey got up and opened the door for the woman, a rueful smile on her face. "Welcome to the zoo."

"Hey," Gina greeted Vito and Gramps Camden, and then turned to Lacey, holding the little boy by his shoulders as he attempted to toddle away. "Can you watch Bobby for ten or fifteen minutes? I have to run over to the Senior Towers to check out a few facts."

Vito's curiosity must have shown on his face, because she explained. "I'm doing some research on the town and the guesthouse. This place was a stop on the Underground Railroad and has a really amazing history."

"Laaaaas," the little boy said, walking into Lacey's outstretched arms.

"Hey, how's my sweet boy?" Lacey wrapped the child in a giant hug, and then stood, lifting him to perch on her hip. Her bad mood was apparently gone. "Look, Bobby, this is Vito. And this is Mr. Camden. Can you say hi?"

Bobby buried his face in Lacey's neck.

"Taking off," Gina said, and hurried out the back door.

Lacey cuddled the little boy close, nuzzling his neck, and then brought him to the window. "Look at the birdies," she said, pointing toward a feeder outside the window where a couple of goldfinches fluttered.

"Birdie," Bobby agreed.

"You're a natural," Vito said, meaning it. Lacey looked right at home with a child in her arms, and the picture made a longing rise in him. He wanted a baby. More than one.

And Lacey probably needed to have another baby. It would help her get over the pain of her devastating miscarriage.

Lacey set the table, having Bobby bring napkins along to help, letting him place them haphazardly on the table and chairs.

Vito tasted the sauce and frowned. "It needs something."

"I have basil growing outside. At least, I *think* it's still alive. Want some?"

"Fresh basil? For sure."

"Come on, Bobby." She helped the little boy maneuver across the kitchen and through the back door.

Could Vito be blamed for looking out the window to see where her herbs were planted? After all, he might do more cooking here. He was enjoying it.

And once he looked, and saw her kneeling in the golden late-afternoon sunlight, pointing and talking with Bobby, he found it hard to look away.

"Take a picture, it lasts longer," Gramps muttered. "Do I have to chaperone everyone around here?"

Vito blinked and went back to his cooking, but the image of Lacey, the curve of her neck, soft hair blowing in the breeze, stayed with him.

Who was he to think romantically about someone so beautiful, so perfect?

Half an hour later, they were about to sit down to a not-bad-looking dinner when Gina tapped on the back door.

"Mama!" Bobby cried and toddled toward the door.

She opened the door, scooped up her son and gave him a big loud kiss.

"You'll stay for dinner, won't you?" Lacey asked Gina.

"Oh…no. I would but…I need to get home." Her cheeks went pink and Vito put it together. She was a new bride, must have just gotten back from a brief honeymoon. She wanted to get home to her new husband.

Envy tugged at Vito's heart. Would he ever have a wife who was eager to return to him, or would he always remain just the best friend?

Dinner was fun. Nonna insisted they put on some Italian opera music—"the most romantic music on earth!"—and then got into a good-natured argument with Gramps Camden, who insisted that Frank Sinatra sang the best love songs. Her eyes sparkled with pleasure as everyone talked and joked and ate. Charlie enjoyed the company, too. Both of them would benefit from being part of a bigger family, Vito realized. He would, as well.

He just didn't know how to make it happen. But at least for the summer, it was something they could enjoy here at Lacey's. He would talk to her about having meals together as often as possible, splitting grocery bills and sharing cooking duties.

When he stood to clear the dishes, Lacey put a hand on his arm. "It's okay, Vito. You cooked, so I'll clean up."

"It's a lot," he protested, trying not to notice the delicate feel of her hand.

"I have an excellent helper," she said, letting go of Vito and patting Charlie's arm. "Right?"

"Sure," the boy said with surprising good cheer.

Of course. Lacey had that effect on every male of the species. Her charm wasn't meant specially for him.

"You can walk me back over to the Towers," Gramps said unexpectedly to Vito, so after a few minutes of parting conversation, the two of them headed down to the street. The Towers were almost next door to Lacey's guesthouse, and Gramps seemed plenty strong to get there on his own, but maybe he just wanted the company. Fine with Vito. He needed to get away from pretty Lacey, get some fresh air.

"How you handling those scars?" Gramps asked abruptly.

Vito felt the heat rise up his neck and was glad for the darkness and the cool breeze. "Apart from terrifying women and children, no big deal."

Gramps chuckled. "It's what's on the inside that counts. Any woman worth her salt will know that. The kid over there seems like he gets it, too."

It was true; the few occasions Charlie still cringed away from Vito had more to do with leftover fears related to his mother's boyfriends than with Vito's looks.

They were almost to the front door of the Towers now, and Vito was ready to say goodbye when Gramps stopped and turned toward him. "Just what are your intentions toward Lacey?"

Vito pulled back to stare at the older man. "Intentions?"

"That's right. Some of us over at the Towers got to talking. Wondered whether you and she had more than a landlord-tenant friendship."

"Hey, hey now." Vito held up a hand. "Nobody needs to be gossiping about Lacey. She's had enough trouble in her life already."

Gramps propped a hand on the railing beside the door. "Don't you think we know that? For that matter, you have, too. The both of you have— What is it young folks call it?"

"Baggage," Vito said. "And we may be young compared to…some people, but we're not so young we need to be told what to do."

Gramps snorted. "Think you know everything, do you?"

"No. Not everything. Not much. But I do know my love life's my business, just as Lacey's love life is hers."

"Give it some thought before you mingle them together, that's all. I'd hate to see either Lacey or that boy hurt."

"I'd hate to see that, too." Vito lifted an eyebrow. "We done here?"

"We're done," Gramps said, "but have a care how you spend the rest of your evening over there."

And even though he found the warning annoying, Vito figured it was probably a wise one.

Chapter Five

When Vito walked back into the guesthouse, he heard dishes clattering in the kitchen. Lacey. Like a magnet, she drew him.

And maybe Gramps knew just what he was talking about. Being careful was the goal Vito needed to shoot for. A vulnerable woman and a vulnerable child were both somewhat under his protection, and Gramps didn't know the half of how any relationship between Lacey and Vito could cause damage to both of them.

He'd expected to see Charlie in the kitchen, but when he got there Lacey was alone, squatting to put away a pan.

"Hey," he said softly, not wanting to startle her. "Where's Charlie?"

She stood and turned toward him. "I told him he could watch TV. He was a good helper, but apparently, it's time for one of his favorite shows."

"Oh, right." Vito should go. He should go right upstairs, right now.

But in the soft lamplight, he couldn't look away from her.

She was looking at him, too, her eyes wide and confused.

He took a step toward her.

Leaning against the counter with one hip, she picked up a framed photo from the counter, studied it for a few seconds, and then placed it carefully on the shelf beside the sink.

"What's that?" He walked over but stopped a good three feet away from her. A safe distance.

She picked it back up and held it out for him to see. "It was Gerry's second time home on furlough. I'd missed him so much that when he came off the plane, I broke away from the other wives and ran screaming to hug him. Somebody caught it on film."

Vito studied the picture of Lacey and his friend, and his heart hurt. They *did* look happy, thrilled to see each other. "Could've been in the newspaper. Good picture."

"It was in the *Plain Dealer*," she said, smiling shyly. "That embarrassed Gerry. Me, too, a little. Everyone kept coming up to us to say they'd seen it."

"Gerry didn't like that, huh?" Vito felt sick inside, because he knew why.

Gerry had already been involved with Krystal at that point. Maybe she'd even been pregnant with Charlie. He thought about asking Lacey the year, and then didn't. He didn't even want to know.

How awkward for Gerry that his girlfriend might see his loving wife hugging on him.

Gerry had been such a jerk.

"He was everything I ever wanted," Lacey said dreamily, studying the picture. "Sometimes I don't think I'll ever get over him."

"Right. Look, I'd better go check on Charlie and catch

some sleep myself." He turned and walked out of the room. An abrupt departure might be a little rude, but it was better than staying there, listening to her express her adoration of a man who'd not been worth one ounce of it. Better than blurting out something that would destroy that idealized image she had of Gerry.

Don't speak ill of the dead. It was a common maxim, and valid.

Was he making a huge mistake to stay here, even though that was what Nonna and Charlie both wanted?

He scrubbed a hand across his face and headed up the stairs. He needed to focus on his professional goals and forget about his personal desire to have a wife and a large family. He needed to make sure that personal desire didn't settle on Lacey, like Gramps seemed to worry it would.

He and Charlie were living in the home of the one woman he could never, ever be involved with. He'd promised Gerry at the moment of his death, and that meant something. It meant a lot. The sooner he got that straight in his head, the better.

On Friday, Lacey strolled along the sidewalk with Vito and Charlie and tried to shake the odd feeling that they were a family, doing errands together. It was a strange thought, especially given that her goal was to get her guesthouse up and running so that she could dive into her self-sufficient, single-woman life and make it good.

She just needed to keep in mind the purpose of this trip: to create a cozy room at the guesthouse for any child who came to stay for a night or a weekend.

It was only midafternoon, but with the arrival of summer, a lot of people seemed to be taking off work early on Fridays. A group of women clustered outside of the Chatterbox Café, talking. A young couple pushed their baby in a stroller. Several people she knew vaguely from the Senior Towers were taking their afternoon walk, and outside Chez la Ferme, Rescue River's only fancy restaurant, Sam Hinton stood with sleeves rolled up, talking to another man in a suit, smiling like he'd just tied up a deal.

"You're sure you don't mind focusing on Charlie's room right now?" Vito asked as Charlie ran ahead to examine a heavily chromed motorcycle in front of the Chatterbox. "It's not the project you were planning on, I'm sure."

"It's not, but it's a good change of plans. Having a room or two decorated for kids will only add to the guesthouse's appeal. And that little room off the big one is perfect for that."

"And you're being kind. Charlie's been in a mood, so maybe this will help." They reached Love's Hardware, and Vito held the door for her, then called for Charlie to come join them.

The front of the store was crowded with summer merchandise, garden tools and stacked bags of mulch and grass seed. A faint, pungent smell attested to the fertilizer and weed killer in stock. Farther back, bins of nails and screws and bolts occupied one wall while pipes and sinks and bathtubs dominated the other. Overhead, modern light fixtures, price tags hanging, intermixed with old-fashioned signs advertising long-gone brands of household appliances. The soft sound of R & B played in the background.

A string of small bells chimed on the door as it closed

behind them, and the store's owner, Mr. Love, came forward immediately, one weathered brown hand extended, subtly guiding him through the store aisle. His vision wasn't the best, but he still managed his hardware store almost entirely on his own.

"Hey, Mr. Love, it's Lacey. And you remember Vito D'Angelo, right?"

"I sure do, sure do. Glad to see you folks on such a fine day." Mr. Love fumbled for their hands, and then clasped each in a friendly greeting.

"And this is his foster son, Charlie."

"Say hello," Vito prompted the boy, urging him forward.

Charlie scowled as if he might refuse. But as he looked up at Mr. Love, he seemed impressed by the man's age and courtly dignity. "Hi, it's nice to meet you," he said, holding out his hand to shake in a surprising display of good manners.

After Lacey had explained their mission, Mr. Love led them over to the paint section, where Charlie's momentary sweetness vanished. "I want this blue," he said, selecting a bold cobalt paint chip and holding it out as if the decision was made.

Lacey bit her lip. She'd told Charlie he could help pick out the color, but she and her future guests were the ones who'd have to live with it. "How about something a little lighter, Charlie? It's an old-fashioned house, and this is a pretty modern color." She offered up a sample card featuring various shades of blue. "I was thinking of something in this range."

"That's boring. I want this one."

"It's Lacey's decision, buddy," Vito said, putting a

firm hand on Charlie's shoulder. "We're guests in her house, and she's nice to let you choose the color blue."

Charlie's lower lip stuck out a mile.

"Let's look at the cobalt in shades," Lacey suggested. "We could have that color, just a little lighter. Do you like this one?" She pointed at a shade halfway down the sample card.

"That one's okay." Charlie pointed at one toward the end, almost as bright as his original pick.

"Charlie. Lacey has the last word."

Lacey bent to see Charlie's downcast face. "I promise I'll take your ideas into consideration."

"Fine." Charlie gave Lacey a dirty look.

"Come on, let's go see the power tools," Vito suggested. "Guy stuff," he added, winking at Lacey.

Immediately, her distress about Charlie's attitude faded as her heart gave a funny little twist.

"I have to let my granddaughter mix the paint or she gets mad at me," Mr. Love said to Lacey. In a lower voice, he added, "I can't see the colors too well, but if you'd like, I can ask her to add in a little more white to whatever shade the boy picked."

"That would be fantastic," Lacey said gratefully. "Thank you."

"Don't you worry about young Charlie," Mr. Love said, patting her arm. "Kids usually come around."

That was true, and besides, Charlie wasn't her problem to worry about. But there was no point in explaining that to Mr. Love, so she let it go.

On the way home, they walked by a group of slightly older boys playing basketball in the park, and Charlie wanted to join in.

"No, buddy," Vito said. "We're painting today."

"I don't wanna paint! I wanna play outside!"

That made sense to Lacey, but Vito shook his head. "You can run ahead and play basketball outside the guesthouse for a while."

"That's no fun, playing by myself." But Charlie took off ahead of them, staying in sight, but kicking stones in an obvious display of bad temper.

Vito blew out a sigh. "Sure wish there was a manual on how to parent," he said.

"I think you're doing great," she said, reassuring him. "What's Charlie's background, anyway? Was it difficult?"

Vito looked away, then back at her. "Yeah. His mom's an addict. She loves him, but not as much as she loves to get high."

Poor Charlie. "What about his dad?"

Vito looked away again and didn't answer.

A sudden, surprising thought came into Lacey's head: was Charlie *Vito's* biological son?

But no. If Vito had fathered a child, he wouldn't deny it and pretend to just be the foster dad.

"His dad's passed," Vito said finally. "And Mom keeps getting involved with men who rough her up. It happened to Charlie a few times, too, which is why he originally went into foster care. His mom wasn't able to make a change, so Charlie's free for adoption. I hope we'll have that finalized within a few months."

"That's great, Vito." Even as she said it, she wondered how and why he'd gotten involved in foster care. It was so good of him, but not something most single men in their early thirties would consider. "Why did—"

"Charlie learned a rough style of play in some of his old neighborhoods," Vito interrupted quickly, almost as if he wanted to avoid her questions. "And he doesn't have the best social skills. If he's going to play basketball in the park, I need to be there to supervise."

"You could stay with him now. You don't have to help me paint his room."

"Thanks, but no. It's only right that we help. And besides," he said, flashing her a smile, "it's what I want to do."

So they spent the afternoon painting as a team. Sun poured through the open windows, and birds sang outside. Stroking the brush, and then the roller, across the walls, soothed Lacey's heart. Again, more strongly this time, she got that weird feeling of being a family with Vito.

He was good around the house. He could fix things, he could paint, he could cook. And he liked to do those things with her.

Unlike Gerry, who'd always begged off family chores.

Charlie burst into the room, planted his feet wide and crossed his arms. He looked around the half-painted room, his lip curling. "That's not the color I wanted."

Something about his stance and his expression looked oddly familiar to Lacey, but she couldn't put her finger on what it was.

"The second coat'll make it brighter, buddy," Vito said. "Why don't you stay in here and I'll teach you to paint with the roller?"

"No way. That's boring." Charlie turned to stomp out and landed a foot directly in the tray of paint. When he saw what he'd done, he ran out of the room, tracking paint the whole way.

Vito leaped up and hurried after him, while Lacey raced to wipe up the paint before it dried on the hardwood floors, chuckling a little to herself. With Vito and Charlie around, there would never be a dull moment.

"Oh, man, I'm sorry," Vito said as he returned to see her scrubbing at a last footprint. "Charlie's in time-out in the kitchen, since I can't exactly send him to his room, and he'll be back up in a few minutes to help. Neatly. To make up for this mess."

"It's okay. It's part of having a kid."

Vito sighed. "I guess it is, but I wasn't ready for it. I never know if I'm doing the right thing or not."

"You're doing a good job. Really good." She smiled up at him.

"Thanks. I don't feel so sure."

Just like the other night, their eyes caught and held for a beat too long.

Charlie burst into the room in sock feet and stood, hands on hips. "I'm here, but I ain't apologizing and I ain't helping." He lifted his chin and glared at Vito as if daring him to exert his authority as a father.

Vito opened his mouth to speak, but Lacey's heart went out to the hurting little boy, and she held up a hand. "Let me talk to him," she said, and walked over to Charlie. "It's been a rough day, hasn't it? But that paint came right off and it won't be a problem."

"So?"

In every stiff line of his body she read a need for a mother's comfort. "Hey," she said, putting an arm around him, "I'm glad you're here and I think this is going to be a great room for you. You can help decorate it."

For a second Charlie relaxed against her, but then he went stiff again and stepped away, his face red. "That's what you said about the paint, and then I got this baby color!" He waved a hand at the nearest wall.

"Oh, honey—"

"Don't call me that! Only my real mom can call me that!"

"Charlie…" Vito said in a warning voice, approaching the two of them.

"She doesn't have any kids! She's not a mom, so why is she acting like one?"

The words rang in Lacey's ears.

It was true. She wasn't a mom, and Charlie, with a child's insight, had seen right into the dream inside her head. On some barely conscious level she'd been pretending that Charlie was her child and Vito was her husband, and it had to stop.

Slowly, she backed away from Charlie just as Vito reached him.

"I want you to apologize to Miss Lacey," Vito said firmly.

"I'm not apologizing!" Tears ran down Charlie's reddened face, but he ignored them, frowning fiercely and thrusting his chest out.

"Charlie." Vito put a hand on the boy's shoulder.

"Don't you touch me! You're not my real dad. And you're ugly, too!" Charlie ran from the room.

Vito's hand went to his scarred face for just a moment, and then he followed Charlie.

Even in the middle of her own hurt feelings, Lacey wanted to comfort him, to tell him he *wasn't* ugly.

But that was exactly the problem. She wasn't the mom of the family. She wasn't the wife.

She never would play that role, and she needed to stop pretending and accept the truth.

Chapter Six

"Let's see if we can scare up a basketball game at the park," Vito said to Charlie the next day after lunch.

"Yeah!" Charlie dropped his handheld game and jumped up.

Vito laughed. He was still getting used to the time frame of an eight-year-old. "In ten minutes, okay? I have to clean up our dishes and make a phone call."

Vito had planned to spend Saturday setting up Charlie's room and looking for jobs online. But Charlie's behavior the previous day had changed his mind. Vito was no expert, but it seemed to him that Charlie needed structure, and chores, and attention. So they'd spent the morning weeding the gardens around the guesthouse, and with a little prodding Charlie had worked hard. He'd even taken a glass of lemonade to Lacey, who was sanding woodwork in the breakfast room, and Vito had heard her talk cheerfully to Charlie, which was a relief. Apparently, she wasn't holding a grudge against Charlie for yesterday's behavior.

So, amends made, Vito and Charlie half walked, half jogged to the park together, bouncing a basketball.

Lawn mowers and weed eaters roared, filling the air with the pungent fragrance of vegetation, and several people called greetings from flower beds and front yards. Things weren't much different than when Vito himself had been eight, growing up here.

The call he'd made had been to Troy Hinton, an old acquaintance whose son, Xavier, was just Charlie's age. Troy and Xavier met them by the basketball courts at the park, and immediately, the boys ran out onto the blacktop to play. Vito and Troy sat down on a bench to watch.

Xavier played well for an eight-year-old, making a few baskets, dribbling without too much traveling. Charlie, though, was on fire, making well more than half of the shots he took. Paternal pride warmed Vito's chest. He'd make sure Charlie tried out for the school team as soon as he got to sixth grade.

"That's a good thing you're doing, fostering him," Troy said, nodding toward Charlie. "He seems like he's settling in fine."

That reminded Vito of yesterday, and he shook his head. "A few bumps in the road."

"Yeah?" Troy bent down to flick a piece of dirt off his leg.

"I think he misses his mom. He sees her once a week, but that's hard on a kid."

"Any chance of her getting him back?"

Vito shook his head. "No. Supervised visits is all."

"Gotcha." Troy was watching the two boys play.

Even at eight, Charlie used his elbows and threw a few too many shoves.

"Charlie!" Vito called.

When Charlie looked over, Vito just shook his head. Charlie's mouth twisted, and then he nodded.

"We talked about sportsmanship this morning. I don't know why he thinks he can play street ball here, in the park."

Troy chuckled. "It's a process. And Xavier's holding his own." Indeed, the boy did some fancy footwork and stole the ball from Charlie.

Which was impressive, considering Xavier's background. "How's his health?"

"Almost two years cancer-free."

"That's great." Although Vito had been overseas, he'd heard from Nonna about the careworn single mom who'd come to town to work at Troy's dog rescue, bringing her son who was struggling with leukemia. Now Troy and Angelica were married, with another child, and it was great to know that Xavier was healthy and strong.

"He's doing so well that we can't keep up with him in the summer. So we've got him in a weekday program here at the park. Six hours a day, lots of activity. Charlie should join."

"Well…" Vito thought about it. "That's tempting, but Charlie has a few issues."

"People who run it are good with issues. And you should also bring him to the Kennel Kids." Troy explained the program for at-risk boys, helping once a week at the dog rescue farm Troy operated.

Vito had to thank God for how things were working out here in Rescue River. It was a great place to raise kids. "Sounds perfect, if you've got a space for him."

"Might have one for you, too. I could use a little help."

"Oh, so that's how it is," Vito joked, but truthfully, he was glad to be asked. Vito liked dogs, and Troy. And most of all, he wanted to do positive things for Charlie, and with him. "Sure thing. I can help out."

The boys came running over, panting, and grabbed water bottles to chug.

"You guys should come play!" Charlie said, looking from Vito to Troy.

"Aw, Dad's too tired." Xavier bounced the basketball hard so it went back up higher than his head.

"Who says?" Troy got to his feet and grinned at Vito. "Hintons against D'Angelos, what do you say?"

"I'm not a D'Angelo," Charlie protested.

"But you're going to be, pretty soon." Vito stood, too, and ruffled Charlie's hair. "Meanwhile, let's show these Hintons how it's done."

After an hour of play that left them all breathless and sweating, Troy and Xavier invited Charlie to come out to the farm for a few hours, and Vito agreed. It was good for Charlie to make friends.

But that left Vito with a hole in his day. He'd finished the preliminary work for his online courses, and the term didn't start for another week. Nonna was spending the day visiting at the Senior Towers.

He thought of Troy Hinton, married, raising two kids, the town veterinarian and dog rescue owner, volunteering with the Kennel Kids. What was Vito contributing by comparison? And Troy had a big property to handle, a place for kids to run, while Vito was living in two rooms.

He walked through the park, feeling uncharacteristically blue. There was a soccer game going on, a coed team of kids a little younger than Charlie, and Vito stopped to watch. The game wasn't too serious. Parents chatted with each other in the bleachers while coaches hollered instructions, mostly encouraging rather than overly competitive. Nearby, a family with a new baby

sat on a blanket, cheering on their kids who were playing while cuddling with toddlers who looked like twins.

Vito wanted that. Wanted a family, a large family. It
was in his blood.

Suddenly, someone tapped his shoulder, and he
turned to see Lacey and another woman, pretty, dark-
haired, with Asian features.

"Hi!" the dark-haired woman said, holding out a hand.
"I'm Susan Hinton. I've heard a lot about you."

What did that mean? He shook Susan's hand and shot
a glance at Lacey. Her cheeks were pink. What had she
been telling Susan?

"Vito D'Angelo," he supplied, since Lacey seemed to
be tongue-tied. "It's a pleasure. Are you related to Troy?"

"Sure am. I'm married to his brother, Sam."

"I know Sam. Sorry to have missed the wedding."
He'd been invited, but he'd been in the thick of his surgery at that point.

"Mindy could score," Lacey said, gesturing toward
the soccer game. She looked like a teenager, dressed in
cutoffs and a soft blue T-shirt. Her short blond hair lifted
and tossed in the breeze, and Vito liked that she didn't
glue it down with hair spray.

He felt an urge to brush back a strand that had fallen
into her eyes, but that would be completely inappropriate. They weren't that kind of friends.

"C'mon, Mindy, go for it!" Susan yelled, and the little girl in question kicked the ball hard, making a goal.
"Good job!"

"Susan's a teacher," Lacey said when the hubbub had
died down. "She might have some good ideas about your
career change."

"You're switching over to teaching?" Susan asked. "What age of kids?"

"I like the little ones," Vito admitted. "Seems like elementary teachers make a big difference."

"And we need more men in the profession," Susan said promptly. "Are you planning to stay local?"

"If I can find work."

Susan opened her mouth as if she were going to ask another question, but a shout interrupted her. Mindy, the child who'd scored a goal, ran over, accompanied by two little girls about the same age. "Did you see, Mama, did you see?"

"I saw." Susan hugged the little girl close. "You're getting better every day."

Vito was watching the pair, so it took a minute for him to become aware that the other two girls were staring up at him.

"What happened to the side of your face?" one of them asked.

"He looks *mean*," said the other little girl.

The remarks shouldn't have stung—he'd known that was how kids would feel, hadn't he?—but they did, anyway.

"Cheyenne! Shelby!" Susan spun and squatted right in front of the other two girls. "You know it's not polite to make personal remarks about someone's appearance."

"I'm sorry, Miss Hayashi," one of them said right away.

"It's Mrs. Hinton, dummy," the other said. "Don't you know she got married?"

Susan put a hand on each girl's shoulder. "First of all, it's more important to be... Do you remember what?"

"More important to be polite than right," the two and little Mindy chorused.

"And furthermore, Shelby," Susan said sternly, "this gentleman got those injuries serving our country, and you *will* show him the respect he deserves."

Vito didn't know which felt worse: being told how bad he looked by a second-gradeish little girl, or being defended by a woman approximately half his size. "Hey, it's okay," he said, squatting down, too, making sure his better half was turned toward the girls. "It can be a surprise to see somebody who looks different."

Mindy shoved in front of him. "I'm *glad* he looks different. Different is cool." She reached up and unhooked something from her back and then started fumbling with her arm.

"Don't take it off! Don't take it off!" the other two girls screamed, sounding more excited than upset.

At which point Vito realized that Mindy had a prosthetic arm, which she seemed set on removing.

Other kids ran in their direction, no doubt attracted by the screams. Vito stood and glanced at Lacey, who gave him a palms up that clearly said she had no idea how to handle the situation.

"Mindy!" Susan's voice was stern, all teacher. "Don't you dare take off that arm. You know the rules."

Mindy's forehead wrinkled, and she and Susan glared at each other. Then, slowly, Mindy twisted something back into place and let go of her prosthetic. "I just wanted to show them that everybody's different, and that's okay," she said sulkily.

Susan knelt and hugged her. "That was a very kind impulse. Now, why don't you girls get back on the field? I think the second half is starting."

Vito took a step back. "Hey, it was nice meeting you," he said to Susan.

"Vito—" Lacey sounded worried.

"Got to go. See you later." What he really needed to do was to be alone. Today's little scene had hammered the truth home to him: he couldn't work with kids in person. His appearance would create a ruckus that would interfere with their learning.

The trouble was he liked kids. And interacting with them through a computer screen just didn't have the same appeal.

Lacey looked from where Susan was ushering the little girls back into the soccer game, toward the path where Vito was walking away, shoulders slumped.

"I'm headed home," she called to Susan, and then took off after Vito. She couldn't stand what she'd just seen.

He was walking fast enough that she was out of breath by the time she got within earshot. "Vito, wait!"

He turned around to wait for her.

"Where are you going? Are you okay?" she asked breathlessly.

"I'm going for a walk, and I'm fine." His words were uncharacteristically clipped.

"Mind if I come?" She started walking beside him, sure of her welcome. After all, this was Vito. He was always glad to see her.

"Actually…" He walked slowly, glanced over at her. "Look, I'm not fit company. Go on back and hang out with Susan."

She gave him a mock glare. "No way! You hung out

with me plenty when I wasn't fit company. I'm just returning the favor to an old friend."

He started to say something, then closed his mouth,
and mortification sent heat up Lacey's neck. She was
being intrusive. It was one of her flaws, according to
Gerry, and she half expected Vito to bite her head off.

But he didn't speak and his face wasn't angry. They
walked quietly for a few minutes, past the high school.
The fragrance of new-mown grass tickled Lacey's nose.
From somewhere, she smelled meat grilling, a summer
barbecue.

"Where are you headed?" she repeated, because he
hadn't answered. "Can I tag along?" Then she worried
she'd pushed too far.

"I'm going to the river. To think." He gave her shoulders a quick squeeze. "And sure, you can come. Sorry
to be such a bear."

So she followed him down a little path between the
grasses and trees and they emerged on the riverbank.
As if by agreement, they both stopped, looking at the
sunlight glinting off the water, hearing the wind rustle
through the weeping willow trees overhead.

"I'm sorry that happened back there," she said. "That
must be hard to deal with, especially…" She trailed off.

"Especially what?"

"Especially when you were always so handsome."

He laughed, shaking his head at the same time. "Oh,
Lace. My biggest fan."

She had been, too. In fact, as a younger teen, she'd
dreamed of a day when she'd be older, with clear skin
and actual curves, and Vito would ask her out. A visceral
memory flashed into her mind: lying on the floor of her
bedroom, feet propped up on a footstool and CD player

blasting out a sad love song, which in her fourteen-year-old brain she'd applied to herself and Vito's lost love.

"You were the best looking of all the guys in your class," she said. "Everyone said so."

He didn't deny it, exactly, but he waved a dismissive hand. "A lot of good it did me. I could barely get a date."

That had to be an exaggeration; she remembered plenty of girls noticing him. But it was true, he hadn't dated as much as you'd expect of a boy with his looks. "You were too nice. You weren't a player."

He laughed. "That's true, I never got that down." They turned and strolled along the river's grassy bank. "Now I look mean, like the little girl said. Maybe I should cultivate a mean persona to match. I'd get all the girls."

"As if that's going to happen." Lacey couldn't imagine Vito being mean. It just wasn't in his nature. "Is that what you want, Vito? All the girls?"

He gave her a look she couldn't read. "Not all. But I'd like to get married, start a family, and I'm not getting any younger."

"Is that why you're adopting Charlie?"

He lifted a shoulder and looked away. "That's part of it."

"As far as getting married," she said, "you could have any woman you wanted."

A muscle contracted in his scarred cheek. "Don't, Lace."

"Don't what?" She stumbled on a root and he automatically caught her arm, steadied her.

"Don't lie to me. If I couldn't get the girls before, I'm not going to get them now."

"I'm not lying. You have a…" She paused, considering how to say it. "You have a rugged appeal."

"Is that so?" He looked over at her, his expression skeptical.

For some reason, her face heated, and she lifted it to cool in the breeze from the river. She focused on the birdcalls and blue sky, visible through a network of green leaves, while she tried to get her bearings.

When she looked back at him, he was still watching her. "Think of Tiffany Townsend," she said, trying to sound offhand. "She was all over you."

He rolled his eyes, just a little, making her remember him as a teen. "Tiffany Townsend isn't what I want."

"What do you want?"

Instead of answering, he walked a few paces to the right and lifted a streamer of honeysuckle growing against a thick strand of trees. Beyond it was a cave-like depression in a natural rock wall. "Wonder if kids are still carving their names in here?"

She laughed. "Lover's Cave. I'd forgotten about it." She followed him inside, the temperature dropping a good few degrees, making a chill rise up on her arms.

Vito pinched off a vine of honeysuckle flowers, inhaled their scent, and then tucked them into Laccy's hair. "For a lovely lady."

Wow. Why wasn't Vito married by now? He was chivalrous, a natural romantic. Who *wouldn't* want to be with a man like that?

Inside the small enclosure, she turned to him, then stepped back, feeling overwhelmed by the closeness. *Make conversation; this is awkward.* "Did you ever kiss a girl in here?"

He laughed outright. "My *nonna* taught me better than to kiss and tell. Why? Were you kissed in here?"

"No." She remembered bringing Gerry down to the

river, showing him the sights of her younger days. She'd hoped to finally get a kiss in Lover's Cave, but he hadn't wanted to follow her inside. Romantic gestures weren't his thing, but that was okay. He'd loved her; she was sure of that.

"What was wrong with the boys in your grade? Why didn't you get kissed here?"

"Guys didn't like my type." She turned away, catching a whiff of honeysuckle.

He touched her face, making her look at him. "What type is that?"

"Shy. Backward."

"Are you still?"

Lacey's heart was pounding. "I…I might be."

His fingers still rested on her cheek, featherlight. "Don't be nervous. It's just me."

A hysterical giggle bubbled up inside her, along with a warm, melty breathlessness. She couldn't look away from him.

He cupped her face with both hands. Oh, wow, was he really going to kiss her? Her heart was about to fly out of her chest and she blurted out the first nervous thought she had. "You never answered my question."

"What was it? I'm getting distracted." He smiled a little, but his eyes were intense, serious.

He was *incredibly* attractive, scars and all.

"I asked you," she said breathlessly, "what *do* you want, if you don't want someone like Tiffany?"

"I want…" He paused, looked out through the veil of honeysuckle vines and let his hands fall away from her face. Breathed in, breathed out, audibly, and then eased out of the cave, holding the honeysuckle curtain for her, but careful not to touch her. "I want what I can't have."

Suddenly chilled, Lacey rubbed her bare arms, looking away from him. Whatever Vito wanted, it was obviously not her.

Chapter Seven

"Come on, Nonna, let's go sit on the porch." Vito was walking his grandmother out of the kitchen after dinner. Nonna hadn't eaten much of it despite his and Charlie's cajoling. Vito wished Lacey had stayed to eat with them, but she'd had something else urgent to do.

Most likely, urgently avoiding *him*. And rightly so. He was avoiding her, too, and kicking himself for that little romantic interlude in Lover's Cave.

"I'm a little tired for the porch, dear." Nonna held tightly on to his arm.

She sounded depressed, something Lacey had mentioned was common in patients recovering from a heart attack. Activity and socializing were part of the solution, so Vito pressed on. "But you've been in your room all day. A talk and a little air will do you good."

"Well…" She paused. "Will you sit with me?"

"Nothing I'd rather do." He kissed her soft cheek, noticing the fragrance of lavender that always clung to her, and his heart tightened with love.

He and Nonna walked slowly down the guesthouse hall. She still clung to his arm, and when they got to the bench beside the door, she stopped. "I'll just...rest here a minute. Could you get me another glass of that iced tea? I'm so thirsty."

"Sure." He settled her on the bench and went back to the kitchen to pour iced tea, looking out into the driveway to see if, by chance, Lacey had come in without his noticing. He'd feel better if she were here. Only because Nonna wasn't feeling well.

When he reached the guesthouse door with the tea, he saw that Nonna was already out on the porch. "Charlie helped me out," she said, gesturing to where the boy was shooting hoops across the street. "He's a good boy."

He set their tea on the table between the rocking chairs and sat down. The evening air was warm, but the humidity was down and the light breeze made for comfortable porch-sitting. In fact, several people were outside down the block, in front of the Senior Towers. A young couple walked by pushing a stroller, talking rapidly in Spanish. Marilyn Smith strolled past the basketball hoop with her Saint Bernard, and Charlie and his friend stopped playing to pet it and ask her excited questions.

Evening in a small town. He loved it here.

"Tell me about your course work, dear," Nonna said. "Is it going well?"

"Just finished a couple of modules today. It's interesting material."

"And you like taking a class on the computer?"

He shrugged. "Honestly, I'd rather be in a classroom where I could talk and listen, but we don't have a college here, and this is the easiest, cheapest option."

"That's just what Lou Ann Miller says. She's almost done with her degree. At her age!"

They chatted on about Vito's courses and Lou Ann and other people they knew in common, greeted a few neighbors walking by.

After a while, Vito noticed that Nonna had gotten quiet, and he looked over to see her eyes blinking closed. In the slanting evening sunlight, her skin looked wrinkled like thin cloth, and her coloring wasn't as robust as he'd have liked to see.

Lacey's little car drove into the driveway. She pulled behind the guesthouse, and moments later the back screen door slammed. Normally, she'd have come in by the front porch, stopping to pull a couple of weeds from the flower bed and say hello to Nonna. So she was still avoiding him, obviously, but at least she was home in case Nonna needed her.

Nonna started awake and looked around as if she was confused. "Tell me about your courses, dear," she said.

"We just talked about that." Vito studied her. "Are you feeling okay? Do you want to go inside?"

"I'm fine. I meant your job hunt. Tell me about your job hunt." She smiled reassuringly, looking like her old self.

"I keep seeing jobs that look interesting, but they're all in person." He paused, then added, "I want an on-line job."

As usual, Nonna read his mind. "You can't hide forever," she said, patting his hand.

"You're right, and I'm a coward for wanting to hide behind the computer. Except…would you want your kids to have a scary teacher?"

"I'd want them to have a smart, caring teacher. And besides, once people get to know you, they forget about those little scars. I have."

It was what Lacey had said, too. It was what Troy had said. It was even what his friends in the VA support group said. He didn't know why he was having such a hard time getting over his scarred face.

And okay, he was bummed for a number of reasons. If things had been different, if Charlie hadn't needed a home and if he hadn't been so scarred, then maybe he and Lacey could have made a go of things. She'd seemed a little interested, for a minute there.

But things weren't different, and he needed to focus on the here and now, and on those who needed him. He glanced over at Nonna.

She was slumped over in her chair at an odd angle, her eyes closed.

"Nonna!" He leaped up and tried a gentle shake of her shoulders that failed to wake her. "Charlie, come here!" he called over his shoulder.

He lifted his grandmother from the chair and carried her to the door just as Charlie arrived and opened it for him. "Is she okay?" Charlie asked.

"Not yet. Get Lacey, now!" Vito carried Nonna into her bedroom and set her gently on the bed. He should never have encouraged her to go out on the porch. On the other hand, what if she'd fainted in her room, alone? What had brought this on? Up until tonight she'd seemed to be improving daily.

Lacey burst into the room, stethoscope in hand, and bent over the bed, studying Nonna. "What happened?"

"She wasn't feeling well, and then she passed out."

Lacey took her pulse and listened. "It's rapid but…" She stopped, listened again. "It's settling a bit." She opened Nonna's bedside drawer and pulled out a pen-like device, a test strip, and some kind of a meter. "I'm going to test her blood sugar."

Charlie hovered in the door of the room as Lacey pricked Nonna's finger, and Vito debated sending him away. But he and Nonna were developing a nice friendship, and Charlie deserved to be included in what was going on.

Nonna's eyes fluttered open. She was breathing fast, like she'd run a race.

Vito's throat constricted, looking at her. She was fragile. Why hadn't he realized how fragile she was?

Lacey frowned at the test strip, left the room and returned with a hypodermic needle. "Little pinch," she said to Nonna as she extracted clear liquid from a small bottle and injected her arm. "Your blood sugar is through the roof. What happened? It hasn't been this high in weeks!"

There was a snuffling sound from the doorway; Charlie was crying. Vito held out an arm, and Charlie ran and pressed beside him, looking at Nonna with open worry.

Lacey propped Nonna up and sat on the bed, holding her hand. "Are you feeling better? You passed out."

"Was it the cake?" Charlie blurted out.

Vito's head spun to look at the boy at the same time Lacey's did. "What cake?" they asked in unison.

Charlie pressed his lips together and looked at Nonna, whose expression was guilty.

"I...I gave him money..." Nonna broke off and leaned back against the pillow, her eyes closing.

"What happened?" Vito set Charlie in front of him, put his hands on the boy's shoulders and studied him sternly. "Tell the truth."

"She gave me money and asked me to get her cake from the bakery. I didn't know what to do! I wanted her to have a treat. She said it would be our secret. And she gave me the rest of the money so I could get something, too." Charlie was crying openly now. "I'm sorry! I didn't know it would hurt her.'"

Vito shook his head and patted the boy's shoulder, not sure whether to comfort or punish him. "Remember, you're supposed to come ask me, not just go do something another adult tells you to do. Even if it's Nonna."

"Is she going to be okay?"

"She'll be okay." Lacey gave Charlie's hand a quick squeeze. "But your dad's right. Don't ever bring her something to eat again without asking one of us."

Even in the midst of his worries, Vito noticed that Lacey had automatically called him Charlie's dad. He liked the sound of that.

But he was second-guessing himself for bringing Charlie to live here at all. The kid was eight. He didn't know how to properly assist in the care of a very sick elderly woman, and he didn't have an idea of consequences.

Nonna said something, her voice weak, and Lacey put a hand on Charlie's arm. "Let's listen to Nonna."

"I...told him...to do it. Not his fault." She offered up a guilty smile that was a shadow of her usual bright one.

"Nonna! This is serious. We're going to have to take you to the emergency room to get you checked out."

"Oh, no," Nonna said as Charlie broke into fresh tears. "I just want to rest."

Lacey bit her lip and looked at Vito. "I might be able to talk Dr. Griffin into coming over to take a look at her," she said. "It would be exhausting for her to go to the ER, and I *think* she's going to be okay once her sugar comes down, but I'm not qualified to judge."

"If you could do that, I'd be very grateful." He knew that old Dr. Griffin lived right down the street.

"Okay. Charlie, would you like to come help me get the doctor?"

Charlie nodded, sniffling.

"Could you run upstairs and get my purse out of my bedroom?"

"Sure!" Charlie ran.

Vito was grateful. Lacey had every reason to be angry at the boy, but she was instead helping him to feel better by giving him a job. But that was how she was: forgiving, mature, wise beyond her years.

"Doc owes me a favor," Lacey said quietly to Vito. "I'm sure he'll come, if he's home. Just sit with her until we get back. It'll only be five minutes."

He nodded, gently stroking Nonna's arm, and Lacey and Charlie went out the door.

Beside Nonna's bed was a photo of him and his brother as children. She'd taken them in and raised them after their parents' accident, putting aside her bridge games and bus trips to rejoin the world of PTA meetings and kids' sporting events. And she'd done it with such good cheer that he'd never, until recently, understood the burden it must have been to her.

Now it was time for him to return the favor. To make sure that she was getting the very best care she could.

Which meant that later tonight if, God willing, Nonna was okay, Vito needed to have a very serious talk with Lacey.

After ushering Doc Griffin out the door with profuse thanks, Lacey walked back into the guesthouse as

Vito emerged from Nonna's room, gently closing her door behind him.

"She's already asleep," he said. "She's exhausted, but she said to tell you again that she's sorry."

Lacey shook her head and paced the hall. "I'm the one who should be sorry. I should have been keeping closer track of her food."

"She's an adult," Vito said. "She made a choice." But something in his voice told her he didn't completely believe what he was saying, and what he said next confirmed it. "If you have a minute, could we talk?"

"Of course." She gestured for him to come into the front sitting room as her heart sank.

She'd been avoiding him hard all week, since that crazy moment in Lover's Cave. She'd thought he was going to kiss her, and she was sure that expectation had shone on her face. But instead of doing it, he'd gently pushed her away from him.

He was too kind to give her a real rejection, but even his careful one had made her feel like a loser.

He stood in the middle of the room, looking more masculine than ever amidst the delicate Victorian furnishings, and she realized he was waiting for her to sit down first. Who had those kind of manners these days?

Vito, that was who. And she was starting to care for him more than she should. Even though he didn't return the feelings, and nothing would come of it, she felt guilty. What would Gerry think if he knew that she was looking at his best friend in a way she'd once reserved for him?

Or, if the truth be told, in a different way but with the same end game? Because there weren't two men in the world more different than Vito and Gerry. And while

Gerry's confidence and swagger had swept her away when she was young, Vito's warm and caring style appealed to her now.

He was still standing, waiting, so she sank down onto the chesterfield and pulled her feet up under her, leaving Vito to take the matching chair. It was a little small for him. Good. Maybe this conversation would be brief.

He cleared his throat. "I was wondering if you've been avoiding me."

Lacey felt her eyebrows shoot up, and against her will, heat rose into her cheeks. "Avoiding you?"

He nodded patiently. "After what happened last weekend. You know, at Lover's Cave."

She blew out a breath. She'd hoped to avoid that topic, but here he was bringing it out into the open to deal with. "I, um..." She wanted to lie, but couldn't bring herself to do it. "Maybe a little," she admitted.

"I thought so." He leaned forward, elbows on knees, and held her gaze. "You don't have to worry about a repeat. And you don't have to stay away from your own house to keep me at bay."

Keep *him* at bay? But of course, chivalrous to the core, Vito would put it like that. Make it seem like she was the one rejecting him, when in point of fact, it had been the other way around.

She swallowed and tore her eyes away from his. And for the life of her, she couldn't think of what to say.

How could she respond when she didn't even know what she felt, herself? When these feelings about Vito tugged at her loyalty to Gerry, even making her question some of her husband's behaviors? When Vito didn't seem to share her attraction at all?

"The thing is," he said, "I'm worried about Nonna's

care. If Charlie and I are keeping you from focusing on that, then we should move out."

"She wouldn't like that."

"But if you hadn't come home tonight, and known just what to do, and given her that injection, something much worse could have happened, right?"

Miserably, Lacey twisted her hands together, staring at the floor. "I'm really sorry. I can see why you think I've been neglectful."

"That's not it. I don't think you and she ever had an arrangement where you had to be here with her 24/7. Did you?"

"No." Honesty compelled her to add, "But part of the appeal of living here was that she'd have me around a lot while I remodeled. Which I usually am. It's just been a week of running errands instead of remodeling."

He nodded. "I've been too focused on my own stuff, too, and apparently, it's given Nonna and Charlie too much time to get into trouble together."

"Does Charlie understand that he's not to do that anymore?"

"Yes. He was pretty upset when he saw Nonna passed out. He's grown very fond of her." He looked into her eyes again. "And of you. You've been very kind to him."

"He's a good kid."

He nodded. "So, this arrangement is working out well for Nonna, and well for Charlie. It's just you and me who need to manage our…interactions."

If he could be up front and honest, so could she. "I won't need to avoid you if you're serious about no repeat of that. I…I'm not over Gerry, you see." She fingered the necklace where she wore his wedding ring. "I know it's been over a year, which some people say is enough time, but it's not. He was everything to me."

A shadow crossed Vito's face, and for the first time she realized that he didn't talk much about Gerry. She wondered why. They'd been close comrades, right? Close enough for Gerry to come home with Vito on leave from the army. "You know what he was like," she persisted. "What a great guy he was."

Vito nodded once. "I know what he was like."

"So you can see why…well, why it's hard to get over him. He'll always be my hero."

A muscle worked in Vito's scarred face. "I understand. And believe me, the last thing I want is to displace that feeling in you. So please, stay and care for Nonna and don't worry about Charlie and me."

He stood and walked quickly out of the room.

And Lacey stared after him, wondering why it seemed that he was leaving a lot unsaid.

Chapter Eight

Vito was deep into finishing a research paper on the educator John Dewey when Charlie barged into his room. "Nonna's bored," he announced.

"Bored?" Vito came slowly back to twenty-first-century Ohio. "You're bored?"

"Well, yeah," Charlie said thoughtfully, "a little. But I came to tell you that *Nonna* is bored."

That brought Vito to full attention. "Did she ask you to get her sweets again?"

"No." Charlie shook his head vigorously. "She wouldn't. But she wants me to play a card game called Briscola, and it's too hard. And she wants me to watch TV with her, only I don't like her shows."

"I'll go spend some time with her." Vito ruffled Charlie's hair. "You probably want to go outside and ride that bike, don't you?" He'd fixed up an old one for Charlie over the weekend.

"Yeah," Charlie said, looking relieved that Vito understood. "Can I?"

"Let's see who's outside. If you stay on this block and be careful of cars, it's okay."

After he'd walked out with Charlie and made sure there were several parents in yards up and down the street, keeping an eye on the kids, Vito went back inside and headed toward Nonna's room. He'd stayed up late working on his research paper and spent most of the day on it, as well, and he felt like the letters on the computer monitor were still bouncing in front of his eyes. But it was all good. He was finding all the teaching theories extraordinarily interesting and it made him certain he'd done the right thing, enrolling in school.

Distracted, he tapped on the edge of Nonna's open door and walked in before realizing that Lacey was there, sitting beside Nonna, both of them engrossed in a television show.

A week had passed since Nonna's health scare and their talk, and they were settling into a routine in which Lacey spent more time at home. A routine that most emphatically did *not* include strolls to Lover's Cave. In fact, it barely included being in the same room together.

Lacey glanced up, saw him and looked away.

Nonna clicked off the television. "I can't believe he picked the blonde. I'm very disappointed in that young man."

"Well, she *was* the prettiest," Lacey said, laughing. "But you're right. I don't see the relationship lasting very long."

"Hey, Nonna." Vito bent over to kiss his grandmother's cheek, conscious that it was the first time he'd seen her that day. He'd been neglectful, working on this paper. He'd do better tomorrow.

The silver lining was that Lacey was spending more time with Nonna, staying home more. He'd heard her up at all hours, working on the renovations. Now, he realized guiltily that one reason she might be staying up late was that Nonna was needing her companionship during the day. Which was partly her job, but also partly his responsibility.

Lacey stood up. "I should go get some stuff done." It was clearly an excuse to get away from Vito.

Perversely, that made him want her to stay.

Apparently, Nonna felt the same. "Could you wait just a minute, dear? There's something I want to talk to you two about."

"O-kaaay." She sat down again with obvious reluctance.

Vito focused on his grandmother. "Charlie says you're bored, Nonna."

"Oh, my, bored doesn't begin to describe it." She patted Lacey's hand. "Although it's not for this one's lack of trying."

"I can't hang out as much as I'd like," Lacey said apologetically. "I've got to finish the renovations before the end of the summer, and there's so much to do. But I was thinking, maybe you're well enough to do more of the activities over at the Senior Towers."

"That's a great idea," Vito said, relieved. "Don't they have a bridge group?"

"Yes, and a drop-in lunch program, as well." Lacey smiled at Nonna. "You'd definitely get more exciting lunch choices over there than you get when I fix lunch. And it would get you walking more, which would be great for your health."

"How does that sound, Nonna?"

She shrugged. "Good, I guess," she said. "But..." She trailed off, plucking at the edge of her blanket.

"But what?"

She looked up. "I need a project."

"Like what, a craft project?"

"No, I want to start something new. With people."

That made sense; Nonna wasn't a sit-home-and-knit type of person, or at least, she hadn't been. "Like when you started your baking club that burned everything? Or that barbershop quartet, back when we were kids?" Vito smiled, remembering the off-key singing that had emanated from the big old house's front room when the ladies came to practice. Both groups had been disasters, but entertaining for all involved. Everyone wanted to join in Nonna's projects because she was so much fun as a person.

It made all the sense in the world that she would want to do something like that again.

"Do you have any ideas of what you might want to do?" Lacey asked her.

"Well…" She smiled winningly.

Vito shook his head. "Nonna, when you get that look on your face, I get very afraid."

"What's the idea?" Lacey sounded amused.

Nonna pushed herself up, looking livelier than she'd been the past week. "All right, I'll tell you. You know the show we were just watching?"

"*Bachelor Matches*, sure," Lacey said. "But what's that got to do with you having a project?"

Nonna clasped her hands together and swung her legs to the side of her bed. "I want to start a new matchmaker service in Rescue River."

"What?" Vito's jaw about dropped. "Why?"

"I don't think—" Lacey began.

"You remember the stories from the old country," Nonna interrupted, gripping Vito's hand. "My Tia Bianca, she was a *paraninfo*. Known for matchmaking throughout our village and beyond. She continued until she died at ninety-seven, and the whole region came to her funeral."

Vito nodded, frowning. He did remember the stories, but he wondered what was behind this.

"I need to start with some test clients," she continued, "and because of all you two have done for me, you can have the honor. For free!"

"Oh, Nonna, no," Lacey said. "I don't think this is a good idea. I don't want you to overexert yourself."

"She's right." Vito moved to sit beside his grandmother. The last thing he needed was Nonna trying to match him up with some unsuspecting woman who would be horrified by his scars.

"If I don't do this, then what do I have to live for?" Nonna's chin trembled. "Why do I even get up in the morning? Of what use am I to the world?" She buried her face in thin, blue-veined hands, her shoulders shaking.

Vito looked over at Lacey and saw his own concern mirrored on her face.

"Nonna, you have so much to live for!" she said.

"So many people who love you," Vito added, putting an arm around her shoulders.

"But none of it *means* anything!" she said, her face still buried in her hands.

Tears. Vito couldn't handle a woman's tears. "Oh, well, Nonna, if it's that important to you…"

"I could maybe see it if you get someone else involved to help you," Lacey said. "Someone sensible like Lou Ann Miller or Miss Minnie Falcon."

Nonna lifted her head, her teary face transformed by a huge smile. "Yes, they can help, both of them!"

"Good," Lacey said. "And not too much at once. Don't get carried away."

"It'll be just the two of you to start. Now, Vito. What do you want in a woman?"

Vito blinked. How had she recovered from her tears so quickly? Had he missed something?

Or had Nonna been hoodwinking them?

"Could you get me a tablet of paper, dear?" Nonna said to Lacey. "I don't want to miss a word."

"Here you go," Lacey said, handing Nonna a legal pad and a pencil. "And now I've got to get to sanding woodwork."

"Oh, stay, dear. I want to talk to you, too."

Lacey laughed. "Don't you think these interviews should be private?" She spun and walked toward the door.

Vito watched her go, thinking of Nonna's question. The truth was, he wanted someone like Lacey. But because of the secret he had promised to keep, he could never, ever have her.

The next Saturday, Lacey climbed out of her car at A Dog's Last Chance, Troy Hinton's animal rescue farm. As she stretched her arms high, she felt like a weight was gone from her shoulders.

Grasses blew in the soft breeze and looking off to the fenced area by the barn, she could see one dog's shiny black fur, another's mottled brown and white coat. Beside her, the creek rushed, a soothing sound, and red-winged blackbirds perched on the fence.

It was good to get away from the guesthouse. Good to do something for others.

Good to get away from Vito and the constant tension of trying to avoid him.

He'd been in her thoughts so much lately, and in a confusing way. He was so hardworking—up late most nights at his computer, making steady progress toward finishing his degree. He spent time with Charlie every evening, getting involved in the life of the town, even lending a hand with the youth soccer team when one of the coaches had a family emergency.

And he was so patient with Nonna, whose matchmaking service was going full speed ahead, obviously giving the woman something fun to do, but in the process, making Lacey uncomfortable.

A shiny new SUV pulled up beside her car, and Lacey was surprised to see her friend Susan getting out. "Nice car!" she said, remembering the rusty subcompact that Susan had driven when she'd lived for a year at the unrenovated guesthouse.

Susan made a face. "Sam. Just because we're expecting, he thinks we need to have a huge vehicle. I had to talk him down from a full-size van."

"How are you feeling?" Lacey could now ask the question without even a twinge of pain, and that told her she was moving forward, getting over her miscarriage and ready to celebrate other people's happiness.

"I'm feeling great, but Sam treats me like I'm made of glass." Susan rolled her eyes. "He didn't want me to come today. He's afraid one of the big dogs will knock me down. Like I haven't done this eighty thousand times before. And like a stumble would hurt the baby!"

"He loves you."

"He does." Susan's eyes softened. "And he's a control freak. But speaking of men…how's Vito?"

Lacey shrugged. "He's fine. Seems busy."

"You don't see much of him?"

"Well, since he's staying at the guesthouse, of course I see him. But we keep to ourselves."

"By choice, or would you like to see more of him?"

Lacey met her friend's perceptive eyes and looked away. "It's by choice. He makes me nervous."

"Nervous? Why?"

Lacey shrugged. "I don't know. He's so…"

"Big? Manly?"

Lacey laughed and shook her head a little. "Something like that. Come on, you've got to show me the ropes before all the kids arrive."

Susan was a longtime volunteer at the Kennel Kids, and she'd talked Lacey into getting involved. Lacey's therapist thought it was a good idea, too—a way to be involved with others and kids, not necessarily babies but with people. Making a difference.

"Speaking of Vito…" Susan said as they approached the barn where the sound of dogs barking was more audible.

Or at least, that was what Lacey thought her friend had said. "What?" she called over a new wave of barking.

"He's here. Vito." Susan gestured toward the barn, where Vito and Charlie stood talking to Troy Hinton, who ran the place and the Kennel Kids.

Lacey swallowed. What was he doing here?

Just then, he turned around and saw her. "What are you doing here?" he asked, sounding surprised.

"My question, too." They both looked at each other, and Lacey saw in Vito's eyes the same ambivalence she felt herself.

Susan nudged her. "I'm gonna go get set up. Come over when you're ready. No rush."

"Charlie's doing Kennel Kids," Vito explained.

Relief washed over Lacey, along with something like disappointment. "Oh. So you're just dropping him off?"

"I'm…actually staying to help. Unless that's a problem?"

She lifted her hands, palms out. "No! No, it's fine."

Across the barn, Troy Hinton was hoisting a dog crate to his shoulder. "If anyone has a free hand, we could use your help here," he called.

Lacey moved forward at the same time Vito did, and they jostled each other. And then bounced apart like two rubber balls. "Sorry!" they both said simultaneously, and Vito stepped back to let her go ahead.

Lacey blushed as she hurried toward Troy. She started to lift a crate.

"Vito, could you help her with that?" Troy nodded her direction. "It's a heavy one."

So she and Vito took ends of the crate and followed Troy.

"Put it down there. We like to have a few crates out here for the dogs to get away from the kids. It's a tough gig for them. Could you two bring one more so I can get started with these kids?"

"Sure." Vito headed back, and then turned to see if she was coming.

She followed reluctantly. Why had she and Vito ended up together? Why wasn't it Susan over here with her?

"Hey, look, why don't you go ahead and help Susan?" Vito said, apparently reading her mind. "I can get that last crate."

"No, it's okay. I'll help you. It's too heavy."

Vito gave her a look. "I'm every bit as strong as I used to be, even if I do have a few injuries."

"I know that!" Then, ashamed of her exasperated tone, she followed him into the barn and took the bull by the horns. "I'm sorry if this is awkward, Vito. I wish it wasn't."

"You don't want to be around me?"

"It's not that. I just…" More seriously, she was worried he didn't want to be around her.

"Hey, D'Angelo, c'mon! We don't have all day here!" Troy sounded impatient.

Lacey flinched and stole a glance at Vito. That kind of thing had always made Gerry livid; he'd hated to be corrected. It was a guy thing.

Except, to her surprise, Vito laughed. "That's rich, coming from you, Hinton." And then he hustled over to the crate. "Guess we'd better get a move on."

She hurried to help him, wondering as she did what it meant that Vito hadn't gotten angry.

Had Gerry been unusually touchy?

She went to the crate and lifted the other side, breathing in the good smells—hay and animals. And maybe it was the thought of hay, but her necklace felt itchy on her neck.

"Dad!" Charlie ran over, his whole face lit up in a smile. "Can I get a dog? Mr. Hinton said they need homes." He jogged alongside them as they carried out the large crate.

Vito went still, looking at Charlie, then at Lacey. "It's the first time he called me 'Dad,'" he whispered.

Lacey wanted to hug both of them, but her hands were full, so she settled for a *"Wow"* mouthed across the crate as they continued carrying it out.

"Hey, Lacey," Charlie added, coming up beside her, obviously unaware of the emotions he'd evoked. "Want me to help with that? That's no job for a girl."

Lacey chuckled. "Girls can do a lot of jobs, including moving things. But yes, if you'd like to, you can take that corner." She winked meaningfully at Vito, warning him to slow down.

He gave a subtle nod, and something arced between them. It was nice to be able to communicate without words sometimes.

After they'd put the crate down, Charlie grinned at her. "*You* wouldn't mind having a dog around, would you, Miss Lacey?"

He was way too cute with that grin. She couldn't resist ruffling his hair. "I won't answer that on the grounds that it might incriminate me with your dad," she said, "but confidentially...I do like dogs."

"See, Dad?"

"Way to throw me under the bus," Vito complained, but there was a smile in his voice.

"Can we get one?"

Vito held up a hand. "That's not a decision we're going to make today."

Charlie looked like he wanted to whine, but shouts from a couple of newly arrived boys distracted him and he ran off. Vito watched him go, shaking his head. "It's hard for me to deny him anything."

A man Lacey knew vaguely emerged from the barn with two pit bulls on leads. As he approached the boys, Charlie took several steps back in obvious fear.

The man clearly noticed. "Hey, Troy," he called, "we have some new Kennel Kids here today. You want to give the bully breeds talk?"

She and Vito drifted over and listened while Troy explained that it was all in how the pit bull was raised, how some were taught to fight while others were raised in a gentle environment, how one always had to be careful in approaching a dog like this.

Troy's words triggered a thought. Charlie had apparently been raised in a rough environment, and he, too, acted out sometimes; he needed to be approached with care. But with love—the kind of love that Vito was so unselfishly offering him—he was starting, even now, to grow into his potential and to become the person God had made him to be.

She watched as one of the smaller pit bulls, a white female named Gracie, was brought out and went from boy to boy. The group started dissolving, some of the boys playing with puppies, others learning to clean kennels, others helping to leash and train dogs. Charlie knelt, and the white pit bull approached him slowly, cautiously.

"Hold out your hand so she can sniff it," Vito encouraged, and after a moment's hesitation, Charlie did.

Watching Vito, she saw someone so much more than the handsome older boy who'd protected her from school bullies when she was younger. He was fatherly now, a man, a hero. He accepted what had happened to him and ran with it, growing into a person of value.

But then again, the seed of the man he'd become had been present in the kind, handsome boy next door.

"Lacey!" Susan gave her a light punch on the shoulder, and she started and turned to her friend. "I've been trying to get your attention forever." She looked where Lacey was looking, and then a slow smile broke out across her face. "Are you *sure* you don't have feelings?"

"No! It's just Vito."

"Somehow, I'm not convinced."

"No way! The truth is, I keep thinking about Gerry."

One of the other volunteers turned. "Gerry McPherson? Boy, that guy was a piece of work."

Lacey cocked her head to one side, feeling her smile slip a little.

"What does *that* mean?" Susan asked, her voice protective.

Lacey looked at the other volunteer, and suddenly, she didn't want to hear what he was going to say.

And then Vito stepped up beside her. "Gerry McPherson was my friend and Lacey's husband." He put an arm around her, a tense arm. "And he died serving our country." His chin lifted a little and he gave the man a level stare.

The other guy raised his hands. "Hey, didn't mean anything." He turned and walked rapidly away.

Susan gave Lacey a curious look and went over to help one of the younger Kennel Kids, who was having trouble unhooking a black Lab's leash.

"Thanks." Lacey sidestepped away from Vito so she could see him better, and immediately he let his arm drop from her shoulders.

A chill ran over her where his arm had been.

What had the man meant, that Gerry was a piece of work?

She didn't want to face the tiny sliver of doubt that had pierced her.

A couple of hours later, Vito stood up from repairing a broken crate and was startled to find himself surrounded: Susan on one side and Troy's wife, Angelica, on the other.

"So, Vito," Angelica said, "what's going on between you and Lacey?"

"Not one thing. Why?"

"Oh, just wondering." The two women sat down beside him, each working on one of the broken crates.

He wasn't lying about nothing going on, at least not in a guy sense; there wasn't anything of the dating variety going on, that was for sure. On the other hand, there was a lot going on emotionally, every time he saw Lacey.

Man, that had been a close one with that stupid guy almost revealing something bad about Gerry. Lacey had looked so shocked and stricken that he hadn't been able to handle it.

She for sure still believed the best about Gerry. And that was good. He'd always remain a hero in her eyes.

And Gerry *had* definitely had a heroic side. In battle, there wasn't another man in the world Vito would've trusted more. They'd saved each other's skins more than once.

But the home front—specifically, women—had been Gerry's downfall. Something rotten in the way he was raised, or maybe the fact that he'd been so handsome and suave. Too many women had flocked to him, and Gerry hadn't ever been taught how to treat women with respect. To him, a woman who threw herself at him was fair game.

Any woman was fair game. Lacey definitely hadn't thrown herself at him; she wouldn't have known how. But she'd gotten swept away and before Vito could turn around and warn her, she'd gone and fallen for Gerry.

Vito had tried to talk her out of it, but that had been a miserable failure. Once someone was that far gone, you couldn't bring her back.

At that point, the only thing he could do was to insist that if Gerry wanted Lacey, he needed to marry her, not just use her and throw her away.

It had just about killed him to do it, because by that time, he'd thought Lacey was something pretty special himself. Talking his friend into marrying her was like cutting off his own arm. He'd had to admit, just to himself, that he'd been waiting for Lacey to get old enough that he could honorably ask her out.

Gerry had beaten him to it, had gotten in there and stolen her heart.

And he'd treated her despicably.

And now Vito was in a position of hiding Gerry's wrongdoing from the woman he still, if the truth be told, carried a torch for.

"Earth to Vito," Angelica teased, and he snapped back into the here and now. "You *sure* there's nothing going on?"

"I'm sure," he said heavily. "And there never will be anything going on."

Chapter Nine

The next Friday, Vito heard a high-pitched shout from Nonna's room. "Vito! Lacey!"

He scrambled up from the computer and down the stairs on Lacey's heels. "What's wrong, Nonna?" she was asking as they both entered Nonna's room.

"Are you okay?" he asked his grandmother, who was sitting at the small writing desk looking perfectly fine. In fact, her color was better than he'd ever seen it.

Lacey put a hand on Nonna's shoulder. "You scared us. What's going on?"

"It's my first success," the older woman said. "I found you both dates for tonight!"

Vito had to restrain himself from rolling his eyes. Just what he needed, a blind date.

"Tonight?" Lacey sounded just as distressed as Vito felt. "I...I have plans."

Nonna's eyes sparkled behind her glasses. "The same plans you've had for the past three Friday nights, young lady? A date with a paint can?"

Lacey smiled ruefully. "Actually...yes."

Nonna rubbed her hands together. "I hope you both

have some dressy clothes. You'll need to be ready at six o'clock."

Vito groaned inwardly. The last thing he wanted was to put on a suit. "Why dressy? This is Rescue River."

"You both have reservations with your dates at Chez la Ferme."

"No way!" Vito said.

"That's not how you do a blind date, Nonna." Lacey's forehead creased. "For one thing, it's really expensive."

"You get coffee first," Vito added. And then he processed what Lacey had said and looked over at her. How would she know? Was she doing online dating?

He found her looking back at him with a similar question in her eyes, and he felt himself flushing. The truth was, he *had* put his profile up on a Christian dating site a couple of times. And he'd gotten no results worth pursuing, which he attributed to women being turned off by his ugly mug. Or his lack of wealth.

"What if we don't like them, Nonna? Then we're stuck spending hours together." Lacey sank down onto the edge of Nonna's bed, facing them both.

"Whereas with coffee," Vito added, "you can escape after half an hour."

"You're taking a negative attitude," Nonna said. "Why do you think you'll want to escape?"

Vito looked at Lacey, and she looked back at him, and they both laughed. And then he narrowed his eyes at her. So she *had* online dated. But when?

Nonna steepled her hands and stared down at the floor. "I'm sorry," she said. "Do you want me to cancel the whole thing?" Her tone was desolate.

Vito looked at her bowed head and slumped shoulders

and his heart melted. "No, Nonna, it's okay. I'm game. But just this once."

"Me, too," Lacey said with a sigh. "Who's my date?"

Nonna smiled gleefully up at them. "It's a surprise! You won't know until you get to the restaurant."

"Wait," Vito said. "We're *both* at Chez la Ferme tonight? Why there?"

"It's the only nice place in town. I'm so excited for you. You're going to have a wonderful time."

There was no trace of her former sadness, and Vito studied her narrowly. He had the feeling he'd just been manipulated.

"Be ready at six. You're meeting your dates at six thirty."

As they walked out, Vito couldn't help shaking his head. That Nonna. She really was a matchmaker, and she was also someone to whom he, at least, couldn't say no.

At five minutes before six, Vito came out of his room at the guesthouse. He'd driven Charlie over to a new friend's house, and as a result, he'd had to get ready quickly. Not that it mattered. Less time to spend in this necktie that felt like it was strangling him.

He needed to work on his attitude, he knew that. Maybe Nonna's matchmaking was God's way of finding him a partner, someone who'd help him fulfill his dream of building a loving family. Lacey wasn't the only woman in the world, despite what his heart said.

Halfway down the stairs, he caught his breath.

There was Lacey in a sleeveless blue dress that highlighted her figure and her coloring. She stood in front of an ornamental mirror, attempting to fasten a necklace.

Breathe. She's not for you.

He walked slowly the rest of the way down the stairs, watching her struggle with the small clasp. "Need some help?"

"Oh! Um, sure." She held out the ends of the necklace, her back to him, bowing her head.

Her neck looked slender and vulnerable. Her short hair brushed his fingers, soft and light as bird feathers.

He could smell her sweet, spicy perfume.

Breathe.

He fumbled a little with the tiny clasp, dropped one end, had to start over. "Sorry. Big fingers." But that wasn't really the problem. He knew how to fasten a necklace; he'd been doing it for his women friends forever.

Why did it feel so different with Lacey?

Why was he going slowly on purpose, trying to extend the moment, to stay close to her?

He finished and stepped back quickly, forbidding his hands to linger on her shoulders. "Whoever you're meeting tonight is going to be very happy."

She turned toward him, a smile curving her lips as she gave him an undisguised once-over. "Your date will be, too."

He laughed a little, shook his head. "My date is going to be in for a surprise, but not such a pleasant one."

"You look good, Vito." She reached up and, with one finger, touched his face. The bad side of it. "Except that there's a little shaving cream…right…here."

Their eyes met and her touch lingered on his face.

That soft, small finger, touching a place no one had ever touched, except in a medical capacity, made him suck in a breath. "It's hard to shave with…this." He gestured toward the ridged, scarred side of his face.

She let her hand open to cup his cheek. "I'm sure."

The moment lingered. He felt like he couldn't look away from Lacey's steady, light brown eyes.

Until Nonna opened her door and clapped her hands. From her room came strains of opera music. "Don't you both look gorgeous!"

Vito took a step backward and Lacey let her hand fall to her side.

"We clean up okay," he said, clearing his throat, trying to keep his cool. "How are we going to know our dates?"

"It's all set up at the restaurant."

Vito bit back a sigh and slid his hands into his pockets. "You're not going to tell us who, are you?"

"And spoil the anticipation? Of course not. That's just one of the things that will be unique about my matchmaking service. Now, you two had better get going."

That brought up another angle he hadn't considered. "Would it be awkward if we walked together to dates with other people?" he asked Lacey. "Or would you rather drive, with those heels?" *Which look spectacular*, he thought but didn't say.

"They're wedges—they're fine." Her cheeks were a little pinker than usual. "Um, sure, we can walk."

So they strolled together through the downtown of Rescue River, all dressed up. The evening air was warm, and shouts from the park indicated that families were enjoying the evening. Vito leaned just a little closer to Lacey to catch another whiff of her perfume, wishing with all his heart that he could spend this evening with her, as her date.

His thoughts toward his old friend Gerry, who'd made him promise to keep Charlie's parentage a secret, were becoming more uncharitable by the minute. The man had been a hero and a friend, and Vito mourned the loss of him, but he couldn't deny resenting the promise that stood like a wall between him and the woman he was coming to care for more each day.

"Who do you think our dates are?" she asked, looking up at him with laughter in her eyes. "Will it be people we know or complete strangers?"

"Bound to be people we know. It's Rescue River. And Nonna knows the same people we do." He actually hoped it was someone who knew what he looked like, just to spare himself the awkward moment that often happened when people met him for the first time.

They approached Chez la Ferme to discover a small crowd of people waiting outside. "Looks like they're backed up. Hope Nonna really did make a reservation."

"Or not." Lacey made a wry face. "I do have that paint can waiting for me at home."

He chuckled. She wasn't any more into this whole game than he was. "Look, there's Daisy."

"And Dion." Vito lifted an eyebrow. Were the police chief and the social worker officially admitting they were a couple? Because being together at Chez la Ferme pretty much guaranteed that they'd be perceived that way.

"Hey!" Lacey hugged both of them, first Daisy, then Dion. "Long wait?"

"Not if you let them know you're here." Dion punched Vito's arm lightly. "Get with the program, my brother."

So Vito walked in to the hostess stand and gave his name.

"Oh, yes, Mr. D'Angelo. We've been expecting you." The hostess gave him a broad smile. "Your table will be ready in just a few minutes."

Obviously, she was in on Nonna's secret.

Almost as soon as he'd exited the restaurant, while he was still walking toward his friends, the hostess came behind him. "Dion Coleman?" she called. "And Lacey McPherson?"

A slow smile crossed Dion's face. "Oh, your grandma," he said to Vito, shaking his head. And then he crooked his arm for Lacey. "Shall we?"

Lacey's eyebrows lifted as she looked up at the police chief. "Well, okay, then." She took his arm and the two of them turned toward the restaurant.

Vito's stomach seemed to drop to his toes as he watched the pair. He couldn't help noticing the details: the large squared-off college ring that glinted against Dion's dark skin, the expensive cut of his suit, the suave way he put a hand on the small of Lacey's back to guide her inside.

They were good-looking enough that several people in the crowd turned to watch. Or maybe the raised eyebrows were because Dion was linked with Daisy in the town's collective, gossipy mind.

Vito had known he couldn't be with Lacey himself, on account of Charlie. He'd almost—not quite, but almost—accepted that.

What he hadn't anticipated was how seeing Lacey with someone else would feel like a punch in the stomach.

And he should have known, because it had happened before, with Gerry. This exact same feeling: *You're not going to get her. She's going to choose someone else. And you're going to have to stand there and be a man about it. Do the right thing.*

Speaking of doing the right thing, he was being rude

to Daisy, standing there watching Lacey and Dion disappear inside the restaurant like a hungry dog, tongue hanging out.

He schooled his expression before he turned to Daisy. Was that a similar look on her face?

That brought him out of himself. He couldn't have Lacey, and it was wrong to think she should save herself for him, that she shouldn't find happiness with someone else. Dion was a good man, respected by everyone in town.

And now, he needed to go through with the evening's plans as if he didn't feel gutshot. He didn't know Daisy well, but he assumed that if Dion was set up with Lacey, Daisy was probably set up with him. He turned to her. "Any chance you're here for a blind date, too? Set up by my grandma?"

"Yeah." She nodded. She didn't look enthusiastic.

He soldiered on, as he'd been trained to do. "Well, you didn't get the prize," he said, "but you'll get a good dinner. I think I'm your date."

"Oh. Okay." She didn't sound thrilled, but not horrified, either. "What do you mean, not the prize?"

He gestured vaguely toward the scarred side of his face. "Only a doting grandma could love this mug."

She didn't deny the ugliness of his scars, but she shrugged them away. "Most women care more about what's inside. Whereas men…" She trailed off, and then glanced down at her own curvy body. "I'm not the prize, either, compared to her." She gestured toward the door through which Dion and Lacey had disappeared.

It was true. Vito didn't find Daisy as attractive as he found Lacey. But then, he didn't find *any* woman that attractive. For better or worse, his heart had attached itself to Lacey, and he was realizing more every minute that his wasn't the kind of heart that could easily change directions. Still, Daisy—blonde, vivacious and with a killer smile—was something of a showstopper herself. And he wasn't going to be rude to her. "You *are* a prize. Anyone with any sense would wonder how someone like me got to go out with a knockout like you. I'm honored to be your date."

The crowd by the door was thinning out, and a bench opened up. "Want to sit down?"

So they sat, and talked about her work in social services, and his desire to become a teacher. She was a good conversationalist, easy to talk to. He found himself confessing his worries about scaring kids, his desire to work with them in person, and his pretty-sure decision to go with online teaching. When the hostess called them to go inside, she had to do it several times, apparently, from her expression when she came out to get them.

As they followed her into the restaurant, replete with stained glass and low lighting and good smells of bread and prime rib, they kept talking.

"Don't do online teaching if your heart is in the real classroom," she urged him as they crossed the restaurant behind the maître d'. "Kids respond to the whole person, not just how you look. I used to worry about them teasing me about my weight, but they're completely fine with it."

"As are most men," he assured her. "Women think we all like stick-skinny women, but that's not the case. You're beautiful."

"Your table, sir." The maître d' gestured, and Vito held Daisy's chair for her.

Only then did he realize that Dion and Lacey were

just around a small corner from them, probably within earshot of most things they would say.

Not only that, but the two of them were leaning toward each other, sharing an appetizer and appearing to have a marvelous time.

Chapter Ten

Lacey looked at the handsome man across the table from her and tried to ignore Vito and Daisy being seated practically right behind them.

Unfortunately, she couldn't ignore what she'd heard. "You're a beautiful woman," Vito had said to Daisy.

Which was true, and she didn't begrudge Daisy the praise, but the way it stung alerted her to something she hadn't quite realized before: she wanted Vito for herself.

"Hey," Dion said. "What's going on?"

She shrugged and toyed with her water glass.

"All of a sudden you're not comfortable," he said. "Is it something I said?"

"No! No, you're fine. What were we talking about?" She laughed nervously. "I'm sorry, I'm a little intimidated."

His forehead creased. "Intimidated? Why?"

"You're kind of known for your wisdom," she said, "not to mention that you're the police chief."

"Which is all a nice way of saying I'm an old man," he said, "who's fortunate to be out with a fine-looking young woman."

The words were gallant, but Lacey could tell Dion wasn't interested in her in *that* way. Rather than feeling insulted, she felt relieved and suddenly more comfortable. This was a little awkward, especially with Vito and Daisy so close, but at least she knew she wasn't misleading Dion.

"I'm the fortunate one," she said. "I might pick your brain about some Bible stuff. You're said to know everything there is to know."

"Who says that?"

"Angelica's husband, Troy. He thinks you're the font of all wisdom. And my brother's a fan, too."

"Don't you be thinking I'm perfect," he warned. "Nobody's perfect. Nobody's even close, right? That's what the good book says."

"See, you're making my point for me, quoting scripture at the drop of a hat." She frowned. "Anyway, of course, you're right. But I've spent my whole life trying to be good. Trying to be perfect."

"We all try," he said, "and that's not bad."

She did her best to ignore the rumble of Vito's voice behind her, but it played along her nerve endings like an instrument. She forced it away, forced herself to talk with Dion about her brother, with whom he'd had a good deal of official contact until Buck had dried out and they'd become friends. She forced herself to rave over the delicious, beautifully presented food: Dion's prime rib, her own organic grilled salmon.

"That was great," she said when they'd pushed away their plates.

"Yes, it was," he said, "but let me ask you something. Are you in this matchmaking thing for real?"

She looked at him and slowly shook her head. "Not

really. I'm just doing it for Nonna. You?" She only asked the question to be polite, because she was pretty sure of the answer. "I always heard you were with Daisy."

"Everyone thinks that," he said, smoothly changing the subject. "You're a newish widow. It makes sense you're not ready to do a lot of dating."

"Yeah. I...I really loved my husband."

Dion didn't say, "He was a good guy." That would normally be the remark you made, wouldn't it? But instead, he said, "That's obvious. Gerry was blessed to have you. But—" he raised a finger and pinned her with a steady gaze "—at some point, you're going to have to move on. You're too young of a woman to give up on life."

She wasn't going to tell him about her infertility. Instead, she turned the tables. "Do you take your own advice?"

Dion cocked his head to one side, smiling at her. "Touché. I've been on my own a lot longer than you have, and I should probably be letting go of some baggage by now."

She wanted to ask him about his past, but the way his face closed when he mentioned it told her she shouldn't. "Moving on isn't as easy as it sounds, is it?"

"No," he said. "But let your feelings lead and you'll be fine. Your feelings and your heart. And most of all, the Lord."

Well, if she were to let her feelings lead... Involuntarily, she glanced over at Vito and then back at Dion. "I'm ashamed to say that I haven't spent much time consulting the Lord about this," she admitted.

The server took their plates away and promised to be

right back with the dessert tray. "There's no time like the present," Dion said, "to take it to the Lord. Want to?"

So she let him take her hand in his, closed her eyes, listened to Dion's quiet words and said a few herself. Asked for forgiveness that she'd neglected to seek God's guidance in her feelings. Asked Him to lead her in the right direction.

When they were finished, she felt cleansed.

"And now," Dion said, "if we can get their attention, do you think we should move our table together with our friends for dessert?"

"I, um, I don't know if Nonna would approve."

"Nonna's not here, is she? Hey, Vito." Dion caught his attention and made the suggestion, and the servers rushed to help, assuring them it was no problem.

Once they were all sitting together, there was a slightly awkward silence, broken by the approach of the dessert tray. The waiter began to describe the offerings.

Lacey looked over at Daisy. "I need chocolate. Now. You?"

"I agree."

After a restless night, Vito woke Charlie up early, figuring they'd grab breakfast and go burn off some energy on the basketball court. But even before they reached the main floor of the guesthouse, delicious smells of cinnamon and bread wafted toward them.

Could Lacey be up baking cinnamon rolls?

But when they walked into the kitchen, there was Nonna in her Kiss the Cook apron, bending over to check on something in the oven and looking like her old self.

At the table was Miss Minnie Falcon, matriarch of the Senior Towers and former Sunday school teacher to almost every child in Rescue River. Next to her was Lou Ann Miller, stirring sugar into a cup of coffee.

"You're looking good, Nonna," he said, walking over to the stove and giving his grandmother a kiss.

"And that smells good!" Charlie came over as Nonna removed the pan from the oven. "Can I have some?"

"Five minutes, *cùcciolo*." She patted Charlie's shoulder, smiling.

Vito felt a great weight lifting off him, a weight he hadn't known he was carrying. Nonna was going to be okay. Suddenly he could see it and feel it and believe it. Not only that, but she'd called Charlie by the same affectionate name she used to use on Vito and his brother. That, more than anything, meant Charlie was becoming part of their family. He swallowed against a sudden tightness in his throat and walked over to greet the ladies at the table.

As good as her word, Nonna brought a steaming loaf of cinnamon bread, along with small cups of butter and jam, and placed them in the middle of the table.

"Italian breakfast like the old days." Vito put an arm around Nonna, still feeling a little misty-eyed.

Charlie's hand froze in the act of grabbing a piece of the bread. "Why is it brown?" he asked.

"Because I used the healthy flour. It tastes just as good, so eat up."

Charlie grabbed a piece, slathered it with butter and jam and took a huge bite before anyone else had even secured a piece. "It's good, Nonna," he said, his mouth full of food.

Vito leaned close to Charlie's ear. "Good table manners will get you more food," he whispered.

Charlie raised his eyebrows. "What'd I do?"

"Don't talk with your mouth full." They'd cover the grabby behavior later. First things first.

Miss Minnie put a clawlike hand on Vito's arm. "I understand you were our first matchmaking client," she said.

"Yes, tell us all about it." Lou Ann Miller raised a slice of bread to her nose and inhaled, closing her eyes. "Fabulous, dear. You've outdone yourself."

As Nonna beamed, the door from the backyard opened and Lacey breezed in. She wore a red-and-white-checkered shirt and cutoff shorts and she looked as carefree as she had at twelve.

And he was a goner.

"That smells amazing, Nonna D'Angelo," she said, approaching the table. "And look, whole grains! I'm impressed."

"Hey, Miss Lacey, you're not wearing your necklace."

Lacey's hand flew to her throat. "Oh, wow, I'll run up and get it before I eat."

"Want me to get it for you?" The words were out of Vito's mouth before he realized that he didn't, in fact, want to get her the necklace. Didn't want her to wear Gerry's wedding ring around her neck anymore.

"Oh, it's okay. I'll get it." She half walked, half skipped out of the kitchen.

"My Vito." Nonna pinched his cheek—the second time someone had touched his scars in the past two days. "Always too nice for your own good."

"That's right," Miss Minnie said unexpectedly. "Being kind isn't all there is to life. Take a stand!"

"What are you ladies talking about?"

Lou Ann Miller glanced over at Charlie, who'd grabbed his handheld game and was immersed in it, still chewing on a huge mouthful of bread. She turned back to Vito. "Your love life is what we're talking about."

Vito looked from Lou Ann to his grandmother to Miss Minnie. "Seriously? Is that what I'm doing wrong? Being kind and nice?" But of course, they didn't know about his Charlie deception, which wasn't nice at all.

"Tell us about last night," Nonna said instead of answering his question. She removed her apron and sat down at the table and looked up at him expectantly.

"It was…fine. Daisy is great."

"And you don't want to date her."

"Well, of course he doesn't. For one thing, she's attached to Dion Coleman at the hip."

"And then there's the fact that Vito's affections are elsewhere."

"That's obvious. The question is what can we do about it?"

The three women's conversation was spinning out of control. "Nobody needs to do anything about it," he protested. "I can handle my own life."

The only good thing was that Charlie wasn't listening; he was just eating bread and playing with his game.

Lacey came back into the room and Vito didn't know whether to be glad or sorry. He got busy cleaning up the breakfast dishes and washing mixing bowls and bread pans.

"How was your date with Dion?" Lou Ann asked her.

Vito couldn't help tuning his ears to hear what she would say. They'd all ended the evening together, on a friendly note and laughing about various people's efforts to play matchmaker over the years, but Vito still had a sinking feeling he couldn't compete with Dion, suave and good-looking and successful.

And he *couldn't* compete, he reminded himself. He couldn't have Lacey, because telling her the truth would destroy her world. Destroy her image of the husband whose ring she wore around her neck.

"It was great," she said easily. "He's a lot less intimidating on a date than when he's being the police chief. Mmmm, this bread is good."

Vito glanced over to see three gray heads turn toward Lacey. "So," Nonna said, "do you like Dion?"

"She means *like* like," Charlie supplied, his mouth full. "Like a boyfriend."

It seemed like everyone in the room—except Charlie—was holding their breath.

"No, I don't think so." Lacey seemed unconscious of how much interest her words were generating. "And I don't think he likes me that way, either, but I'm glad to get to know him better as a friend. He's a good guy and a wonderful Christian."

Vito let out a breath and his tight shoulders relaxed. He grabbed a dish towel and started drying cutlery with great energy.

"I'm not really ready to date," she continued, fingering her necklace. "I'm afraid you're going to have to find some other clients."

There was a little commotion outside the door, and then it opened, framing Buck, Gina and little Bobby, who toddled across the room toward Lacey. "Laasss," he crowed reverently, crashing into her leg and hanging on.

"Hi, honey!" She lifted him onto her lap and tickled his stomach, making him laugh.

She looked beautiful with a baby.

She would look beautiful with *his* baby.

Man, he had it bad and he had to stop.

"Mind if the dogs come in, Lace?" Buck asked.

She glanced down at Mr. Whiskers. "Run while you can, buddy," she said, and then beckoned for Gina to let the dogs in.

Immediately, Crater, a large black mutt with a deep scar on his back, galloped in. At his heels was a small white mop of a dog, barking joyously.

Charlie threw himself out of the chair and started rolling and roughhousing with them.

Vito looked at the ladies to see if they found the ruckus disturbing, but they were watching and laughing. Bobby struggled out of Lacey's lap and toddled fearlessly into the fray.

Buck and Gina came over to the table and talked above the kids and dogs, and all the noise created a dull roar Vito couldn't really follow, given his hearing loss. His aids worked well with individual conversations, but big noisy groups were still a challenge.

He was wiping down counters when Charlie came over and tugged at his arm. He bent down to hear what the boy had to say.

"Can we get a dog now, Dad?"

That had been predictable. "Of these two, which kind do you like?"

"Can we get two?"

"No!"

"Then, I like the big one. Can we get one like that? With cool scars?"

The phrasing made Vito lift an eyebrow. Cool scars, huh? That scars could be cool was a new concept to him. "We'll start thinking about it more seriously," he promised.

Given how strong his feelings for Lacey had become, he had some serious thinking of his own to do, as well.

When there was a knock on the front door, Lacey hurried to answer it, relieved to escape the busy kitchen and the probing questions of Nonna D'Angelo, Miss Minnie and Lou Ann. Not to mention Vito's thoughtful eyes.

It was Daisy. "Hey, I was walking by, and I thought I'd take the chance that you were here. Do you have a minute?"

"Um, sure." She and Daisy knew each other, but they weren't drop-in friends. She came out on the porch and gestured toward a rocking chair, tucking her feet under herself in the porch swing. "What's up?"

"I just wanted to make sure we're okay about last night."

Lacey forced a laugh. "We were clearly all victims of the grandma matchmaking brigade. What happened isn't your fault or mine, or any of ours."

"And it was fun in the end, right?"

"Sure." As she thought back, she realized that it *had* been fun, sitting and laughing with Vito and Daisy and Dion. Except for that nagging anxiety at the pit of her stomach.

Daisy was watching her, eyes narrowed. "But…" she prompted.

Lacey shrugged. "Nothing."

"It's not nothing. I *knew* something was bugging you last night. What's going on?"

"Nothing's going on." She paused. "If you're worried about whether I like Dion, I do, but not as a boyfriend."

Daisy waved a hand. "I know. I could tell. And it's not my business, anyway. I *wish* Dion would meet someone."

Lacey lifted an eyebrow, but didn't comment. She couldn't tell if Daisy meant it or not.

"And I'm not interested in Vito that way, either."

Lacey tried to school her facial expression, but she couldn't help feeling happy. "I…wasn't sure."

"I mean, he's great," Daisy said, "but I'm pretty sure he only has eyes for you."

Lacey had thought she couldn't get any more joyous, but an extra wave of it washed over her at Daisy's words. "You really think so?"

Daisy nodded. "I sat and had dinner with him, and he was great, he really was. So nice and flattering and kind. But he couldn't stop himself from looking over at you guys every time you and Dion laughed."

A breathless feeling took Lacey over then. Maybe this—her and Vito—could really happen. Maybe it would. "Do you think it's wrong for me to think about another man, so soon after losing Gerry? As a social worker, I mean?"

Daisy studied her thoughtfully. "It's been over a year, right?"

She nodded.

"And what have you done to get over the loss?"

"Well…" Lacey thought about it. "I've had counseling, with a psychologist and with Pastor Ricky. And with some of my friends, too, unofficially. I'm doing desensitizing things about kids, because…did you know I lost a baby, too?" She was amazed that she could say the words openly now, with only an ache instead of a sharp, horrific pain.

Daisy nodded. "I heard, and I'm sorry for your loss. That must have been terribly hard to deal with."

"Well…yeah. The worst. And I never thought I'd heal,

but Buck, and little Bobby, and the church… Lots of people have helped me, and life goes on."

The door flew open and Charlie emerged. He threw his arms around Lacey and said into her ear: "I think Dad's getting me a dog!" Then he ran down the stairs and across the street to the basketball hoop where a couple of neighborhood kids were playing.

Lacey looked after him and blinked. "That came out of nowhere. I thought he didn't like me."

"If you seem to pose a threat to his relationship with Vito, he may act out. On the other hand, he might very well need a mother figure." Daisy leaned back in the chair, rocking gently.

"A mother figure?" Lacey laughed. "Why would he think of me that way? I'm not even dating his dad."

"Yet. Charlie may see something that the two of you won't yet acknowledge."

Heat suffused Lacey's cheeks and she didn't know how to respond. Because the truth was, she was interested in dating Vito. After last night, watching him with Daisy, she was sure of it.

There was a fumbling sound at the door and Miss Minnie Falcon made her way out, struggling a little with her rolling walker. Both Lacey and Daisy jumped up to help her.

"Would you like to sit a spell on your old porch?" Lacey asked. She'd bought the house from Miss Minnie two years ago when it had become too much for her to handle, and she tried to encourage the older woman to maintain her connection. It made Miss Minnie happy, and as her brother's wife, Gina, had discovered, Miss Minnie and the house itself were full of stories. Besides, Lacey enjoyed the sharp-tongued woman's company.

"Thank you, dear. I wouldn't mind."

Lacey made sure Miss Minnie was settled comfortably while Daisy folded her walker and put it against the porch railing.

"It got a little too noisy in that kitchen. I like children, but in controlled circumstances."

"I hear you," Daisy said. "It's probably just as well I don't have children." Then Daisy's eyes went round and she looked at Lacey apologetically. "I'm sorry. I guess this is a sensitive topic for you."

"Kind of," Lacey said. Then, to her own surprise, she added, "Especially since I can't have kids."

"Never?" Daisy's eyes widened, and she reached out to give Lacey's hand a quick squeeze.

"That's what they say." She lowered her head, and then looked from one woman to the other. "Please don't tell anyone, okay? I…I'm still getting used to it. And it's not common knowledge."

"It shouldn't be," Miss Minnie said, her voice a little sharp. "Young people share far too much about themselves these days. Some things are simply private."

Daisy laughed. "I take it you're not baring your soul on social media, Miss Minnie?"

"My, no." The older woman turned back toward Lacey. "There are other ways to nurture children, besides bearing them."

Lacey opened her mouth to disagree, and then realized she was wrong. Miss Minnie knew what she was talking about from personal experience. "You taught Sunday school for almost all the kids in Rescue River, so I guess you're right. That's one way."

"And you're sure getting close with Charlie, from the looks of things," Daisy said. "Kids need all kinds of people in their lives to grow up right. Not just their parents." She turned to Miss Minnie. "Did you ever regret not having kids?"

Lacey flinched a little. That was definitely a personal question. Daisy was the type to ask them, but Miss Minnie was the type to offer a sharp reply.

"Not that it's commonly known, but of course I did," the older woman said. "That's the reason I taught Sunday school all those years. If you don't have a family, you have to do a little more figuring to build a good life for yourself."

"You may not have much family, but I hear you do have a boyfriend," Daisy said slyly.

Lacey smiled, remembering what she'd seen at the Chatterbox. "Mr. Love, right?"

"You young people and your gossip tire me out. I need to get back home." But a faint blush colored Miss Minnie's cheeks.

"We're sorry." Lacey stood to help the woman to her feet. "We don't mean to tease. It's just nice to see…" She paused to clarify her own thoughts. "It's nice to see a single person having a fun, active social life."

"That's right," Daisy contributed, picking up Miss Minnie's walker. "We single ladies have to stick together. And what's more, it's crazy that any time you're friends with a man, people start linking you up romantically."

Lacey and Miss Minnie glanced at each other as they made their way down the steps. Was Daisy talking about Dion? Was she or wasn't she involved with him?

After they'd walked Miss Minnie back to the Senior Towers, they stopped on the sidewalk to talk before parting ways.

"You going to the fireworks tonight?" Lacey asked.

"Yeah, I love the Fourth of July. You?"

Lacey shrugged. "I'll probably watch them from the front porch, with Nonna."

"And Vito?"

"Stop trying to match-make," Lacey scolded. "You heard what Miss Minnie said. We all share too much about our personal lives." But even saying that felt hypocritical, because the thought of Vito, of watching fireworks under the stars together, made a delicious excitement fill her chest. "I'm sure he and Charlie will watch the fireworks, one way or another."

"Then I'm sure you'll enjoy plenty of fireworks," Daisy teased.

"Hey, now!" She watched the woman—who was maybe going to become a closer friend—wave and stroll down the street.

A fluttery excitement filled her. Maybe it *would* be a night to remember.

Or maybe not. She herself was starting to feel like a relationship with Vito might be possible. But she wasn't sure how he felt. With Vito, it always seemed to be one step forward, one step back.

Chapter Eleven

On Monday afternoon, Vito was tempted to turn down his hearing aids as he drove home from the dog rescue with Charlie and his new dog going crazy in the back. Had he just made a big mistake? What was Lacey going to think of this new, and very loud, guest?

At a stop sign, he looked back to check on them. Wolfie, the new white husky mix, stood eager in the giant crate Troy had lent them, bungee-corded in place in the bed of the pickup. Charlie was turned around as far as his seat belt would allow, poking at the dog through the open back window, talking nonsense to it, turning back toward Vito to shout "look at him, *look* at him." The disbelieving thrill in his voice and his eyes melted Vito's heart.

Whatever the challenges, he thanked God that he could do this for Charlie.

When they pulled into the guesthouse driveway, Lacey was outside on her knees, weeding the narrow flower garden that fronted the house. Dressed in old jeans and gardening gloves, she looked up and smiled, brushing blond bangs out of her eyes with the back of her hand.

Vito felt an unbelievable warmth just looking at her.

They'd finally relaxed around each other, watching the fireworks together, eating Nonna's new, healthy concoctions, hanging around the house. Homey, domestic stuff. It was dangerous territory, but he couldn't resist reveling in it for a little while, at least.

He stopped the truck, and Charlie jumped out. "Miss Lacey, Miss Lacey, come see my new dog!"

She stood easily and pressed her hands to the small of her back, smiling, then headed toward the vehicle where Vito was opening the back hatch. "I can't wait to meet him!"

Vito opened the hatch and the crate, and Wolfie bounded out. He leaped up on Lacey, his paws almost to her shoulders, nearly knocking her down. Then he ran through the yard in circles, barking, his big feet tearing at Lacey's flowers. Finally, he approached Charlie in a play bow, his blue eyes dancing, his mouth open in a laughing pant.

"Sorry, sorry!" Vito ran to hook the new leash on to Wolfie's collar, but the dog darted away.

Charlie tackled the dog, and the two of them rolled on the ground together like a couple of puppies, while Vito struggled to find the ring on the dog's collar to hook on the leash.

Finally, he attached the leash and put the looped end in Charlie's hand. "Hold on to him!" he told Charlie, and then stepped back beside Lacey to watch the pair. "I'm sorry about your garden. I'll fix it. He's a little excited."

"So what happened to the concept of a small dog?" she asked drily.

Vito inhaled the scent of wild roses that seemed to come from Lacey's hair. "I know. I'm sorry. I should have called to make sure a bigger dog was okay. It's just… We were playing with a bunch of the dogs, and it was as if they chose each other."

"He was the one, Lacey! Isn't he cool?" Charlie rose to his knees as the dog bounded around him in circles, barking.

A smile tugged at the corner of Lacey's mouth, and in that moment, Vito saw her tenderness for Charlie and fell a little bit more in love with her.

"Well…we did have Crater here, and he was as big as…what's this guy's name?"

"Wolfie!" Charlie shouted, pouncing on the dog again.

"Hold tight to that leash while I get his stuff out," Vito warned, and then turned back to the truck and started unloading dog food and dishes. Rather than an expensive dog bed, they'd stopped by the Goodwill store; a big blanket would do for the dog to sleep on.

He was carrying it all up to the porch when Nonna came out.

"What have we here?" she asked, smiling.

"It's Charlie's new dog." Vito looked over in time to see the dog pull out of Charlie's grip and head for the porch.

Before Vito could do anything, Lacey dived for the leash and held on. The dog actually pulled her for a couple of feet before she was able to stop it. "Sit, Wolfie!" she commanded, but the dog just cocked his head at her, his mouth open in what looked like a laugh.

Lacey sat up cross-legged and held the leash firmly. "Nonna, this dog's a little crazy. Make sure you're sit-

ting down when he's around, and wear long pants until
he settles down." To Vito she added, "He's strong and
he's got big claws. He could knock Nonna down in a second, and those claws could scratch her up pretty bad."

"He knocked me down," Charlie said, almost proudly.
"And he scratched me, too." He held up an arm. Even
from this distance, Vito could see the thin line of blood.

They'd definitely start training Wolfie today.

"Why was Wolfie at the shelter?" he heard Lacey
ask Charlie. "He looks like a purebred, and he acts like
a puppy."

"He's two years old, and the people who had him said
he was un, un…" He looked up at Vito.

"Unmanageable?" Lacey asked drily.

"That's it!"

Lacey rolled her eyes at Vito, looking exactly like
she had as a teenager.

He put down the supplies and spread his hands. "I
know. I know, and I'm sorry. It was just something in
his eyes."

"Wolfie's, or Charlie's?"

"Both. Charlie fell in love with Wolfie as soon as he
saw him, for whatever reason." He noticed the "I found a
home" placard they'd gotten at the shelter. "Supposedly,
we have two weeks to test everything out. If he doesn't
work for us, we can choose another dog."

"And two other families tried him and he didn't work
out, so he was really sad," Charlie said. "I hope we can
keep him. We can keep him, can't we, Dad?"

Vito blew out a breath. "We're going to do our best
to give him a good home. With love and attention and
discipline, he should settle down."

"Like me," Charlie said offhandedly, and went to hug Wolfie. "Don't worry, guy. Dad let *me* stay."

Lacey's hand flew to her mouth and Vito felt his throat tighten. They glanced at each other, and it was as if they agreed without words: this *had* to work.

His phone buzzed in his pocket, and seeing that the dog was safely under Lacey's control, he pulled it out for a quick look.

He didn't recognize the number, but it was local. "Hey, I'd better take this just in case it's about a job," he said to Lacey. "Can you…" He waved a hand at Charlie, the new dog and Nonna.

"Got it," she said instantly. "Come on, Charlie. Let's see if we can teach him how to walk nicely on a leash."

The fact that she had his back so readily and without complaint made Vito's heart swell with gratitude. He clicked on the call.

"Vito D'Angelo? This is Sandra Sutherland, head of the school district's summer programs. You interviewed with one of my people last week."

"That's right." He sank down onto the porch step to focus. "What's up?"

"I'd like to talk to you about a job opening for this summer, with a possibility of extending into fall. How are you with special needs boys? Older, say from eight to sixteen?"

Without even thinking about it, he laughed. "That's getting to be my specialty." He looked down the street at Charlie.

She went on to detail the job of Vito's dreams: part-time for now, sports centered, mentoring and counseling a small group four mornings per week. "We thought you'd be perfect for it."

"Can I ask why?"

She spoke slowly, thoughtfully. "Your background as a veteran, your leadership experience and the fact that you're familiar with the foster care system all play into it. And..." She hesitated.

Why would she sound so uncomfortable? Even as he thought of the question, Vito's hand went to his face and he knew the answer. "Do some of the kids have physical disabilities? Visible ones?"

"That's it," she said, sounding relieved. "We actually have two boys, siblings, who were in a terrible house fire. They lost their mother, and they have some disfiguring burns. They've been acting out, even within the small group, so when Marnie came to me and said she had a good interview with you, and she mentioned your scars..."

Vito blew out a breath and looked skyward. Was this what God was doing? He'd never thought his scarred face would be an asset.

"Look, if you're interested and available, we could set up a time to talk. Sooner rather than later, though. Their current group leader just quit."

He couldn't help chuckling again. Between Charlie, and Wolfie the dog, and these boys, it looked like he was headed toward a career in rehab. "I'm free later today," he said, and they set up a time.

He clicked his phone off and just sat a minute, thinking.

He wanted a career in education, with children. But with his looks, he'd figured he couldn't do anything but online teaching. Now, come to find out, there was a perfect job within reach—partly *because* of how he looked.

Special ed. Physical limitations. He hadn't thought

about it before, but he was definitely strong enough to lift kids in and out of wheelchairs. At the VA, he'd gotten to know guys with all kinds of disabilities. And with his own very visible scars, the students would know instantly that he understood.

Father God, You work in mysterious ways.

His heart beating faster, he looked down the street and saw Lacey and Charlie coming back toward the house, laughing, trying to manage the unruly Wolfie. He stood up and headed toward them. He wanted nothing more than to tell Lacey the good news.

A job, Charlie, and maybe Lacey. Everything he wanted was within reach. Under one condition: he had to figure out a way to tell Lacey the truth about Charlie.

Lacey looked up from trying to contain Wolfie's enthusiasm and saw Vito walking toward them, face alight with some kind of excitement. The call he'd gotten must have been good news.

"Dad! Dad!" Charlie bounced toward Vito, leaving Lacey to try to hold Wolfie back with both hands as he lunged after the boy he seemed to know already was his.

Vito ruffled Charlie's hair. "How's it going? We better help Lacey, huh?"

They came toward her and Vito took hold of the out-of-control dog's leash. "We need to figure out how to work off some of his energy," he said.

"That's what me and Lacey were trying to do! Only, he's so crazy and he doesn't know how to walk on a leash and he ran after a squirrel and we almost couldn't hold on!"

"He's excited, buddy. We'd better let him run in the yard at the guesthouse, if that's okay with Lacey."

"Good idea," she said. "He was about to yank my arm off!"

Once they'd gotten him inside the fence, they all ran and played with him. It didn't take long to discover that the fence had a broken section; Charlie and Lacey ran after the dog and brought him back while Vito did a makeshift fix. After Wolfie's energy finally started to calm, Vito and Lacey sat down on a bench together while Charlie lay beside the dog, holding tightly to his leash.

"So, finally I can ask. What had you looking so excited after that phone call?"

Vito's face lit up. "I might have a job."

As he told her about the offer, Lacey nodded. It sounded perfect for someone as nurturing—and strong—as Vito.

"I'm going to have to set up some doggie day care for Wolfie, I think, and Charlie has his park program, so we'll be out of your hair a little more if this all works out."

She tilted her head to one side, studying him. "You're the least self-centered guy I know."

He looked blank. "What do you mean?"

"Most men would be crowing and bragging about getting a job, but you're all about how to take care of your responsibilities and how it'll affect other people. That's...refreshing."

His eyes narrowed. "You sound like you've had some experience with another type of guy."

She looked at the ground, nodding, feeling guilty. Lately she'd been having some realizations that were altering her view of her marriage, and it wasn't at all comfortable.

"Gerry?"

She hesitated a moment. But she could tell Vito, couldn't she? "Yes. I hate to say it, but he tended to think of himself first. When the time came to reenlist, he didn't even ask me—he just did it and bragged about it. And I was pregnant!"

"You're kidding. That wasn't right. You deserved better." He touched her chin, forcing her to look at him. "You deserve the very best."

She met his warm brown eyes and her heart beat faster. She didn't know about deserving the very best, but she had the feeling that being with Vito would *be* the very best. Maybe even, in some ways, better than being with Gerry. It was a disloyal thought that made her look away from Vito, but that lingered in her mind long into the night.

Two days later, Vito set out lawn chairs at the lake and pulled a picnic lunch—courtesy of the Chatterbox Café—out of the back of the pickup.

It was his way of making it up to Lacey for all the hassles of having a giant new dog in her guesthouse. He'd talked her into taking the day off with them—his last day off for a while, as his new job started tomorrow.

"I wish we could've brought Wolfie," Charlie said, his face pouty as he reluctantly helped unload the picnic basket. Since Monday, he and the dog had been inseparable.

"This is a good way to test out the doggie day care where he's going to spend mornings. And Lacey needs a break."

Charlie made a face, and Vito sighed. The boy and Lacey had been getting along great, but when he was in a bad mood, he tended to take it out on everyone. He hadn't wanted to come to the lake because it meant being separated from Wolfie. And probably because Vito's new job started tomorrow. Even though it wouldn't mean much of an adjustment for Charlie, even though he liked his summer parks program, anything new was tough on a kid who'd had too many changes and losses in his young life.

"I'll take over if you want to check out the water," Lacey said to Charlie, coming over to the table. "Man, it's hot! I'm coming in as soon as we get our stuff set up."

She was wearing a perfectly modest black one-piece and cutoff denim shorts. With her blond hair and sun-kissed, rosy face, the combination was striking.

Very striking.

"Hey, Charlie!" came a boy's shout from the beach area.

"Xavier's here!" Charlie's bad mood dissipated instantly. "Cool!" Without asking permission, he ran down toward the water.

"Stay in the shallow part," Vito called after him. He waved to Xavier's mom, Angelica, who was sitting with several other women right at the dividing line between grass and sand. He pointed at Charlie and she nodded, indicating she'd keep an eye on him.

"Can he swim?" Lacey asked.

"Not real well. His old life wasn't conducive to swimming lessons."

She spread a red-and-white plastic tablecloth on the splintery picnic table and anchored it with mustard, ketchup and pickle bottles. "Speaking of his other life, how are his visits with his mom going?"

"Okay, when she shows up sober." She and Charlie had had two supervised visits since the first Sunday one. One of the other planned visits she'd canceled, and once, she'd shown up high, causing the social worker to nix her seeing Charlie. "Whether the visit works out or not, he gets upset. Tuesdays are rough."

"Well, let's make his Wednesday better." She flashed a brilliant smile at him as she set out a big container of lemonade. "Man, I'm hot. I'm going to go say hi to Angelica and dip in the water."

"I'll probably be down." Vito wiped his forehead on his T-shirt sleeve.

Before Iraq, he'd have whipped off his shirt and jumped in the water in a heartbeat. Now, though, he hesitated.

For one thing, he'd have to take out his hearing aids. And while he could still hear some, especially if a person spoke clearly and was close by, he couldn't keep up with conversations, especially when there was a lot of background noise.

Add to that the dark, raised scars that slashed across his chest and back, ugly reminders of the plate glass window that had exploded beside him that last violent day in Kabul. He'd taken the brunt of the glass in his chest, with a few choice gashes in his face and back.

Outside of a hospital, the only person who'd ever seen the scars on his torso was Charlie, and he'd recoiled the first time Vito had taken off his shirt in his presence.

To have a whole beach full of people do the same might be more than Vito could handle.

It wasn't that he was vain, but he hadn't yet gotten used to turning people off, scaring kids. And mostly, he couldn't stand for perfect, gorgeous Lacey to see how he looked without his shirt.

Hearing young, angry voices shouting down at the water, Vito abandoned his load of beach towels and headed toward where Charlie and Xavier seemed to be in a standoff.

"It's not *fair*." Charlie clenched a fist and got into fighting position.

"Charlie!" Vito shouted, speeding up to a run.

"Take that!" Xavier let out a banshee scream and brought his foot up in an ineffectual martial arts kick, at the same moment that Charlie tried to punch him.

Somehow, both boys ended up on the ground, which seemed to end the disagreement.

Vito reached the boys. "Hey, Charlie, you know hitting doesn't solve any problems."

Angelica came over, not looking too concerned. "Xavier. You know you're not to practice karate on your friends. You need to apologize."

"You, too, Charlie."

Identical sulky lower lips came out.

Identical mumbles of "Sorry."

Then Xavier's face brightened. "C'mon, let's get in the lake!" he yelled, and both boys scrambled to their feet and ran to the water as if nothing had happened between them.

Getting in the lake sounded really refreshing. "Sorry about that," Vito said to Angelica. "I didn't see how it started, but I'll speak to Charlie."

"Don't worry about it. These things happen with boys, and they don't last but a minute." She smiled at him. "How's Wolfie working out?"

"He's a handful," Vito said, chuckling. "Bet Troy's glad to have him off his hands."

"There's a sucker born every minute," she teased. "Actually, he's a great dog. He just needed to find the right home." She nodded toward the other women. "Come on over and say hi."

The sight of Lacey, hair slicked back, perched on the end of someone's beach chair, was all the magnet he needed. He went over and greeted Gina and a woman named Sidney. They had their chairs circled around three babies, and as he watched, little Bobby held out his arms to Lacey and she lifted him up. "Such a big boy!" she said, nuzzling his bare stomach and blowing a raspberry on it, making the toddler laugh wildly.

Vito's heart seemed to pause, then pound. Lacey looked incredible with little Bobby, like she was born to be a mother. And suddenly, Vito wished with all his heart that she could be the mother of all the children he wanted to have.

If only he could tell her the truth about Charlie, cutting away the huge secret between them, he could let her know how he felt and see if there was any chance she'd be interested in him. But telling the truth would destroy her happy illusions about her husband and her marriage. Not to mention the impact the truth would have on Charlie, if he could even understand it.

And Vito didn't take promises lightly, especially deathbed promises.

The trouble was, he was having a hard time imagining a future without Lacey in it. Somehow, in these weeks of living at the guesthouse, she'd become integral to his life and his happiness.

"Dad! Come in the water!" Charlie and Xavier were throwing a beach ball back and forth.

"You should get in." Lacey smiled up at him. "The water feels great."

The sun beat down and he was sweating hard now,

partly from the heat of the day and partly from the warmth he felt inside, being here with Lacey.

"Let's take the babies down to dip their feet in the water," Angelica suggested. The other women agreed, and soon they were all at the water's edge, wading.

"You're not worried about getting burned, are you?" Lacey asked him. "You're dark skinned. But I have some sunscreen back at the car if you need it."

"Why d'you have your shirt on, Dad?" Charlie asked, crashing into Vito as he leaped to catch the ball.

Vito's face heated, and to avoid answering, he splashed Charlie. That led to a huge splash fight and Vito was able to cool off some, even though he didn't dunk to get his shirt entirely wet. It was white, and his scars would show through.

When they got hungry, they headed back up to the picnic tables and Vito grilled hot dogs. The women and babies had declined to join them, but Xavier had come over to get a hot dog. It was fun and relaxing, just the kind of day he'd hoped they could have, a gift to Charlie and to Lacey, too.

"You nervous about starting your job tomorrow?" Lacey asked as they ate.

"A little," he admitted. "It's definitely going to be a challenge. I expect some testing."

"You'll handle it well," she reassured him. "You're great with kids."

Charlie grabbed the ketchup and squirted it on his hot dog. The bottle made a raspberry sound which Charlie immediately imitated, laughing.

"Let me do it!" Xavier cried, grabbing for the ketchup. As he tried to tug it from Charlie's hand, he accidentally squeezed the bottle. Ketchup sprayed around the table, painting a line across Charlie, Lacey and Vito's chests.

"That's enough!" Vito plucked the squirt bottle from Xavier's hand and set it at the other end of the table, away from the boys.

"I'm sorry," Xavier said, looking serious and a little frightened as he surveyed the damage.

"It looks like blood!" Charlie said. He and Xavier looked at each other. Charlie made another raspberry sound, and both boys burst out laughing.

Vito rolled his eyes. "Sorry," he said as he handed napkins to Lacey, and dabbed at the mess on his own shirt.

She shrugged and met his eyes, her own twinkling, and he was struck again with how great she was. She didn't get bent out of shape about boys and their antics. What a partner she'd be.

"This isn't coming off, and it stinks," she announced, gesturing to the ketchup on her shirt. "I'm getting in the water. And I bet I can beat you two boys." She jumped up from the picnic table and took off.

Immediately, the boys followed her, laughing and yelling.

Vito watched from the picnic table, alone and sweating in a now-even-smellier T-shirt. More than one male head turned to watch Lacey's progress. With her short hair and petite figure, laughing with the boys, she looked like a kid. But if you took a second look—as several guys were doing—she was all woman.

He dearly wanted to take his shirt off and follow her into the water. To be an easy, relaxed part of things. A partner she could be proud of.

He let his head drop into his hands, closed his eyes

and prayed for insight and help. Insight to understand what to do, and help to do the right thing. Not just now, in regards to his ultimately silly shirt dilemma, but overall, in regards to his promise.

The smell of warm ketchup got to him, though, and he lifted his head again without any answers.

Except a memory from his time rehabbing at the VA: had *he* ever lost esteem for someone because they had scars?

And the answer was glaringly obvious: of course not. He respected the way they'd gotten them, and he looked beyond.

Charlie and the other kids might not be mature enough to do that, but Lacey? Of all people, she was one of the least superficial he knew.

On the other hand, he wasn't just interested in gaining her respect. He wanted more. He wanted her to be drawn to him physically, as he was to her.

And why was he so obsessed with what Lacey thought of him, when their relationship couldn't go anywhere?

Like a slap in the face, it hit him: he was in love with her.

Not just a crush, a remnant of high school attraction.

Full-fledged, grown-up *love*.

Wow.

He just sat and tried to wrap his mind around that concept for a while, until the boys got out of the water and started throwing a football and Lacey came back toward the table.

"Hey, lazy," she said, grabbing his hand and tugging it. "The water feels great. Come get in!"

He let her pull him up and she laughed and let go of

his hand, walking toward the water with a flirtatious smile over her shoulder.

All of a sudden, he didn't want to be the good friend anymore. For once, he wanted to follow his instincts and desires, to be the main man. To try and see whether his scars were really the turnoff he feared they'd be.

He pulled off his T-shirt, removed his hearing aids and located their case, all the while psyching himself up for an encounter in some ways more terrifying than heading into battle.

Chapter Twelve

Lacey's cheeks heated as she headed down toward the lake. Had she been too forward? What was she thinking, insisting that Vito come swimming?

She glanced over her shoulder to see if he was following her. When she saw him fiddling with his ear, her hand flew to her mouth.

She usually didn't even remember that he wore hearing aids. But of course, he couldn't wear them into the water.

Was that why he'd been reluctant to come in?

She glanced again. Or was it the scar that slashed across his back, dark and very visible?

Pushing him had been a mistake. He was such a good sport he'd come if begged, but she hoped she hadn't caused him to do something he didn't want to do.

Kids shouted as they ran and splashed in the shallow part of the lake. As she walked by a group of teen girls, she inhaled the fragrance of coconut oil, something every dermatologist in the world would blanch at. Some things never changed.

She just hoped the kids and teens would be tactful about Vito's scars.

She waded into the lake, waist deep, then looked back to see whether he was following. And sucked in her breath.

The front of his chest, which she hadn't seen before, was crisscrossed with scars. Long ones and short ones, visible even with his dark Italian skin.

Their eyes met, and Vito's steps faltered a little.

Should she say something? Walk back toward him? Tell him his battle scars didn't affect her feelings toward him, except maybe to warm her heart that he'd sacrificed for his country?

But instinct told her to treat him just as she always had. Meaning, how they'd all acted at the lake as kids, since they hadn't been here together since.

He'd reached the water's edge now, and she grinned in invitation and flicked water at him with her hand. "Scared?" she taunted.

"A little." There seemed to be a double meaning in his words. "But I can play scared." He took a few steps toward her. Suddenly, he dived underwater. A few seconds later, she felt a hand wrap around her ankle, and then she was under, giggling into the green water.

She surfaced, shaking her wet hair out of her eyes. Hooked a toe around Vito's ankle and pushed hard.

He toppled backward and came up, grinning and holding up his hands. "Truce! Peace!"

Their playfulness attracted Xavier and Charlie, who came splashing toward them. "Dad, gross—put a shirt on!" Charlie yelled loud enough for the whole beach to hear.

And apparently, despite his hearing impairment, Vito could make out the words, too.

Around them, a few kids and teens stared openly at Vito. One boy, a little older than Charlie and Xavier, said something that made the nearby kids laugh.

A flush crawled up Vito's face. "I never claimed to be a beauty queen," he said to Charlie with a half smile.

He was handling it well, but she ached for him. He'd earned those scars defending his country, and she honored him for it.

Xavier studied him thoughtfully. "Kids used to tease me for being bald, when I had cancer. Mom said to ignore them."

Vito didn't respond.

Charlie went up and tugged his arm. "Hey! Are your hearing aids out?"

Vito looked down at Charlie. "What?"

"Can't he hear?" Xavier asked.

This was getting to be a little much, and Lacey decided to intervene. "Have you boys ever heard of chicken fights?"

Neither had, so she knelt in the water and told Xavier to climb up on her shoulders. "Get on your dad's shoulders, Charlie," she said, deliberately speaking loudly. "The game is, try to knock each other off."

"Get down, Dad!" Charlie yelled into Vito's ear.

Vito grinned at her, kneeled and took Charlie onto his powerful shoulders. When he stood, he and Charlie towered over Xavier and Lacey.

"Come on, Xavier. We may be short, but we're fast," she said, and went in low.

They splashed and played for a while, with both boys getting thoroughly and repeatedly dunked. Lacey's shoulders ached from carrying a heavy, wiggling boy, but she didn't mind. The water was cool and she hadn't laughed so hard in a long time.

Most of the rest of the swimmers drifted away, except for a few kids who talked their parents into participating.

Best of all, nobody was talking about hearing problems or scars.

Finally, Angelica called the boys to come and rest, and when she offered up watermelon as an enticement, they splashed their way to shore.

"Do you want to go get some?" Vito asked.

She shook her head. "I'm not hungry."

"Swim out to the dock?"

"Sure, and I'll beat you!" Lacey plunged her face into the water and started swimming fast.

It felt good. She seemed to have some extra energy saved up, a shaky excitement that made her want to move.

She was starting to feel such a mix of things for Vito. Admiration. Desire to protect. Caring.

Maybe even love.

She shoved that thought away and swam faster. She couldn't be falling in love with Vito, could she? Vito, her old friend and high school crush. Vito, the guy who'd always been around, always ready to lend an ear or a smile or a hand with whatever you were working on, be it figuring out algebra problems or speaking up against bullies or healing a broken heart.

Was he spending time with her now just to help her get over Gerry? It seemed like, in his eyes, she'd been seeing something more.

She reached the dock at the same moment he did, but touched it first. "I won!" she crowed into his ear.

"You did." He grinned at her as he hoisted himself out onto the wooden platform.

She found the ladder and climbed up, narrowing her eyes at him. "Wait a minute. Did you try your hardest?"

"Let's just say the D'Angelos are swimmers. And gentlemen."

"You *did* let me win!"

He didn't admit to it, but he flashed a grin that took her breath away. Standing above her dripping wet, his teeth flashing against dark skin, his eyes laughing, he looked like a hero from some ancient, epic tale.

She couldn't seem to move. She just knelt there transfixed, halfway up the ladder, staring up at him.

He extended his hand toward her. "Come aboard, milady," he said, and helped her to the dock.

She needed the help. She couldn't seem to catch her breath.

They lay side by side, faces toward the blue sky, the sun warming their wet bodies. Beside them, a little railing shielded them from those on the beach, though their shouts were still audible. Lacey was exquisitely conscious of Vito, the warmth of his arm close to hers, the even sound of his breathing.

She couldn't understand what was going on inside her. This was Vito, her old neighbor, comfortable and safe. Vito, who'd always seemed out of reach because he was older.

Yet he was someone else, too, someone new. The things he'd been through had forged him into a man of strength and valor, a man she couldn't help but admire. It was starting to seem like she both wanted and needed him in her life.

"Do you remember coming out here as kids?" he asked unexpectedly.

"Sure." She watched a cloud laze across the sky, and then turned so she could speak into his ear. "Buck and I came with Dad pretty often when we were little."

"How come your mom never came? Was she...sick, even back then?"

"I don't know. She never wanted to do family things. Always busy with her dreams and plans, I guess."

Vito didn't answer, but he reached over and patted her hand, warm on the dock beside her.

"I don't know when she started with the pills." Lacey followed the swooping path of a dark bird, thinking about it. "I think she was okay when I was real small, but then she just started going in her bedroom and shutting the door." As she said it, she got a visceral memory of standing outside the closed door, hand raised to knock. She'd tried not to do it, knowing that Mom didn't like to be disturbed, but she hadn't been able to stop herself from knocking, then pounding on the door.

Where had Buck and her father been? Why had she been there alone for so long, with just her mother?

"If I had a kid," she said, still speaking into his ear to help him hear her, "I just hope I'd have more sense than to leave her to fend for herself like Mom did to me."

"You would. You're great with Charlie."

His automatic, assured response touched her. "Thanks, Vito."

"It's not about having the sense, it's about heart," he said with a shrug. "And heart, you've got."

His words surprised tears into her eyes. "I appreciate that."

He propped himself on one elbow to look at her, shading the sun. He was all she could see. "I can't say enough about you, Lacey. You were always sweet, and likable, and cute…"

She snorted. "Cute like a little brat, you mean."

He cocked his head to one side. "No, not exactly. I found you…appealing, as you grew up."

"You *did*?"

"Uh-huh." He reached out and brushed back a strand of her hair.

"Why didn't you ever, you know, ask me out?"

His eyebrows drew together. "You were three years younger! That wouldn't have been right."

She laughed up at him. "You're such a Boy Scout."

His eyes narrowed. "If you could read my mind, you'd know that's far from true."

"Then, or now?"

"What do you mean?"

"Are you talking about what was in your mind then, or now?" Something, some magnetic force field, drew her to reach toward his chest, the thick, luxuriant mat of hair sliced through by scars.

He caught her hand, held it still. "Don't."

"Why not?"

Shaking his head, he continued to hold her gaze.

"Because of this?" She tugged her hand away from him and traced the air above one of the multiple fault lines on his chest. Almost, but not quite, touching it.

He sucked in a breath, his eyes still pinning her. "Do you have any idea of what you're doing?"

"What am I doing?"

He caught her chin in his hand and let his thumb brush across her lower lip.

She drew in a sharp breath, staring at him. Every nerve felt alive, every sense awake.

"You have no idea how long I've wanted to do this." He leaned closer, studying her face as if trying to read her thoughts, her mood, her feelings.

"Do what?" she asked, hearing the breathy sound of her voice.

"This." He slid his hand to the back of her head and pressed his lips to hers.

The next Saturday, Vito's head was still spinning.

Kissing Lacey had been the sweetest and most promising moment of his life. Now he just had to figure out what was next.

He'd been busy with his new job for the past couple of days, and Lacey had been taking up the slack, spending extra time with Nonna and Charlie. She hadn't said anything about their kiss, but she'd given him some secret smiles that burned right into his soul.

He had to talk to her, and soon. But this morning, to give her privacy and time to get some detailed renovation work done, he'd taken Nonna and Charlie out for breakfast at the Chatterbox.

Now, seeing Charlie wave to a friend, hearing Nonna's happy conversation with a woman at a neighboring table, he felt full to the brim. His new life in Rescue River was working out, and he had a lot to be thankful for.

"Hey, Dad," Charlie said. "Am I still seeing Mom on Tuesday, now that you're working?"

"Yes. I'll drive you, and then we're going to see if the social worker can bring you home. If she can't, I can take off early." He'd explained his commitment to Charlie's schedule during his job interview, and his new employer was willing to be flexible.

"Mom said maybe she could drive me, only there's a lady she doesn't like in Rescue River."

"That's nice of her to offer, but your mom isn't allowed to transport…" All of a sudden Vito processed what Charlie had said and his heart skipped a beat. "Did she say anything about the lady?" he asked, carefully keeping his voice even.

"I think it was because of my dad. My other dad," Charlie clarified around a mouthful of pancakes. "Hey, Rafael asked if I could go to the park and play basketball, and they're leaving now. Can I?"

"Um, let me talk to his mom." His thoughts spinning, Vito slid out of the booth and made arrangements with Rafael's mother, forcing himself to focus. Charlie's social skills were improving rapidly enough that he felt okay about letting the boy go play some ball without him—after a stern warning about sportsmanship and manners.

Once that was settled, he paid the check and escorted Nonna out of the restaurant.

As they walked slowly toward the guesthouse, Vito wondered what Krystal had said to Charlie. If she was talking that openly about the past—what did it mean?

He took Nonna's arm when the sidewalk got bumpy. Quite possibly, it meant the whole truth could come out soon.

The woman in Rescue River whom Krystal had told Charlie she didn't like—and who was connected to Charlie's other dad—could be no one else but Lacey.

But Krystal didn't know Lacey, did she? Was there

a chance she'd say enough that Charlie would put it all together?

He looked over at Nonna. "What if there were something you needed to tell the truth about, only you'd made a promise not to?"

"Ah, difficult," she said, looking at him with sharp, curious brown eyes.

Clearly she was waiting for him to say more, but he didn't. If he was going to tell the truth, it had to start with Lacey. So he focused on watching a couple strapping twin babies into a double stroller.

A pang of envy swept through him. He wanted what they seemed to have. A happy, uncomplicated relationship of raising children together.

"Have you prayed about this problem?" Nonna asked.

Had he prayed? He nodded slowly. He'd sent up some urgent, brief pleas to God, for sure.

"And listened to the response?"

He blew out a breath. "Not really. I guess I need to."

They reached the guesthouse in time to see Lacey hauling a big load of trash to the curb, struggling a little. Vito jogged over and took the boxes out of her hands, earning a smile.

Lacey went to Nonna. "Are you going around the block another time? I can walk with you if Vito's got things to do." Lacey didn't look at him, but her cheeks were pink and he didn't think it was just the exertion. There had been a tentative, sweet promise in their interactions since their kiss earlier this week.

Nonna put a hand on Lacey's arm and another on Vito's. "I've had enough for now. Why don't you two walk?" She gave Vito a meaningful look, and when Lacey turned away, she mouthed *"Tell her!"*

How had Nonna guessed that his secret had to do with Lacey?

Was he supposed to tell her *now*?

As soon as they'd gotten Nonna settled on the porch with her latest large-print library book, Vito and Lacey headed out, strolling toward the park. Behind them, Wolfie barked a request to go along.

"Should we go back and get him?" Lacey asked, clearly unaware of Vito's inner turmoil. "He's about to break through the fence again."

"Not this time. I put another nail in it yesterday."

"Thanks. I'll have to get somebody to do a real repair soon." Lacey lifted her face to the sun. "I've been inside all morning, painting woodwork. The fresh air smells good."

"I'm glad you could come." He wanted to put his arm around her. He wanted to build a family with her! But the wretched secret stood between them.

Should loyalty outweigh love? He pondered the question, watching a jogger and his golden Lab loping across the park.

"We haven't had a chance to talk since you started your new job," Lacey said. "How'd it go, really? Did the kids give you a hard time?"

The cowardly side of him was grateful for the distraction. This was territory he could handle. "It went well. The kids are a challenge, for sure, but I liked working with them."

"And your scars didn't make one bit of difference, did they?" She was smiling smugly, obviously sure she was right.

And she *was* right. "The kids made a couple of comments, but it was no big deal. I didn't overreact and the whole discussion just went away." He hesitated, then added, "You've helped me feel okay with how I look, especially because of...of how you responded to me the other day, at the lake."

She stared down at the sidewalk, but the corner of her mouth curved up in a smile.

He needed to tell her the truth about Charlie. He was going to tell her.

"I admire your being able to handle a big group of kids like that," she murmured, so quietly he had to lean down to hear her.

Thinking about how he could break the truth gently, he gave a distracted answer to her comment. "I like big groups of kids. In fact, that's my dream—to have enough kids of my own to form a baseball team."

He was about to add "with you" when she stopped still. The smile was gone from her face.

"You know what," she said, "I just realized I left something cooking on the stove. I need to run back and get it. You keep walking, okay? I don't want to interrupt your morning exercise."

She turned and hurried back toward the guesthouse.

Vito looked after her, puzzled by her abrupt departure. His *morning exercise*? And he was surprised to learn she had something cooking when she'd been painting woodwork.

He'd been about to tell her the truth. Was that God, letting him know it wasn't the right time yet?

And if so, why had Lacey suddenly started acting so weird?

Chapter Thirteen

Numb from Vito's comment about wanting a large family, Lacey stirred canned soup on the stove and tried not to think.

If she didn't think, maybe it wouldn't hurt so much that she could never, ever give Vito what he wanted.

"Miss Lacey! Miss Lacey!" Charlie barged through the screen door, letting it bang behind him. He threw his arms around her. "Guess how many baskets I made today in one-on-one?"

She clung to him for a minute, relishing the feel of sweaty boy, and then resolutely untangled herself from his arms and stepped back. Charlie was getting way too close to her, given that she'd just learned she and Vito should never, *could* never, be a couple.

"Maybe you and Dad can come watch me play," he continued, unaware of her turmoil. "And Dad said sometime we could go see a real live Cavaliers game, all three of us!"

There is no "us."

She needed to be truthful. That was kinder in the long run.

Wolfie whined at the back door and Lacey let him in, figuring the dog could comfort Charlie in the face of what she was about to say. "I don't think that's going to happen," she said, crossing her arms, deliberately keeping her distance. "You and your dad are going to move out soon, and then we won't all see so much of each other."

Charlie visibly deflated, sinking down to put his arms around Wolfie's neck. "But I don't want to move."

How quickly he accepted the truth of what she said, and her heart broke for this child who'd seen too much change and loss. She didn't know much about Charlie's background, but she knew his mom wasn't reliable enough to raise him. That had to hurt him right at the core.

And it meant he shouldn't get overly close to Lacey, because she was just going to be another loss. "You and your dad are going to be a forever family," she said, resisting the urge to hug him. "But that's not going to happen here." She forced herself to add, "It's not going to happen with me."

He looked at her with wide, sad eyes and she felt like she'd kicked a puppy. And even if her words had been for Charlie's own good, she hated that she was hurting him.

"Later," he said, then turned and straightened his shoulders. "Come on, Wolfie." And then both dog and boy ran up the stairs.

Tears rose in Lacey's eyes, and one spilled over and ran down her cheek. She wanted to call him back, to hug him and tell him that yes, they'd still be close, and yes, they could do things together in the future.

But that would just prolong the pain. Vito needed

someone who could give him and Charlie a family, and he *would* find someone.

And that someone wouldn't be her.

Automatically, for comfort, she felt for her necklace. But she wasn't wearing it. After kissing Vito, she'd decided that it was time to remove it. Time to stop focusing on Gerry, and start focusing on life ahead.

She'd been wrong.

She turned off the soup, for which she had no appetite, and trudged up the stairs. Went into her room, opened her old jewelry box and pulled the chain back out.

She'd thought she was going to make new memories with Vito and Charlie, but she was going to have to stick with the old memories. Of Gerry and the child she'd lost. Memories that didn't seem like nearly enough to build a life on now that she'd tasted what love and family could mean at Vito's side.

But Vito wanted a big family. He'd be wonderful with a big family, and she wasn't going to deny him that.

The chain and ring settling around her neck felt heavy in a way they never had before.

Suddenly bereft of energy, she closed her bedroom door, pulled the shades and lay down in the semidarkness, too tired and miserable even to pray.

Saturday afternoon, Vito arrived at the church food distribution late and out of sorts.

Lacey had been scheduled to volunteer, too, he was sure of it; she'd come out onto the porch, car keys in hand.

But when she'd realized that he and Charlie were planning to go, she'd turned abruptly and gone back inside, shutting her door with a decisive click.

Not only that, but Charlie was on his worst behavior. After Lacey's defection he'd refused to go and, when Vito had insisted, he'd let loose with a tantrum that had surely roused the neighborhood. Now he wore a sneer better befitting a teenage delinquent than an eight-year-old boy.

"Hey, Charlie's here!" Angelica waved from where she and Troy were sorting out boxes of doughnuts and pastries. "C'mon, the Kennel Kids scored the best place on the line. We get to give out the desserts, and eat whatever's left over!"

Charlie scowled, but he walked down to the end of the line where several other boys from the group stood joking and roughhousing. Troy and Angelica seemed to have them under control, though, and Xavier greeted Charlie enthusiastically.

Relieved, Vito scouted around for a role that didn't involve a lot of chitchat. He wasn't in the mood today. As the line of food bank patrons entered the church's fellowship hall and picked up boxes to fill, Vito started carrying crates of produce from the loading dock at the back of the building to resupply those on the front lines.

He tried to distract himself from his gloomy thoughts by focusing on the scent of sun-ripened tomatoes and bundles of green onions, but it didn't work. He kept going back to Lacey's pale, strained face, to the definitive click of her door closing.

Had their new connectedness been an illusion? Had she had second thoughts about pursuing a relationship with someone who had disabilities and a challenging child to raise?

Was there some way she could have found out the truth about Charlie?

But they'd walked together this morning, and she'd been perfectly fine, seeming interested in him, his job, their conversation.

"Hey, Vito!" The father of the migrant family who was renting Nonna's house—was his name Vasquez?—took the empty crate Vito handed him and started filling it with bundles of kale. "Thanks for working today."

"Thank *you*." Vito tried for a good humor he didn't feel. "I'm impressed that you're helping, as busy as you must be with the new baby."

"The bambino has not arrived yet, and my wife, she is very uncomfortable." The man worked deftly as he spoke, lining up the bundles for maximum space in the box. "She cannot work now, so I will have to join the food line this month. But at least I can help others, too."

"Good plan." Vito took the crate from Mr. Vasquez and reminded himself that his weren't the worst problems in the world. Some families struggled to scrape together enough food to eat.

He walked back toward the line, focusing on the friendly chatter between helpers and recipients. Interesting that the line between the two sometimes blurred, as with Mr. Vasquez.

He'd just put the crate down when a highly irate voice sounded behind him. "Vito! I need to talk to you!"

It was Susan Hinton, and she tugged him over toward a quiet corner of the fellowship hall. "What did you say to Lacey?"

"What do you mean?"

Susan's hands were on her hips. "She's been doing so well, but when I stopped by the guesthouse to pick her up for volunteering, she looked awful. Said she couldn't come, and when I asked her if she was sick, if she needed anything, she said no and went back in her room. She *never* misses."

Vito lifted his hands, palms up. "I could ask you the same question. She's backed off from me, just today, and I don't know why."

Susan's eyes narrowed. "Since when? What went on?"

"I have no idea."

She actually smacked him on the arm. "Come on. Don't be a typical guy. What did you say to her?"

"I don't know." He leaned against a stack of boxes, trying to recreate the scene of their walk this morning in his mind. "I was talking about my new job. And not just because I was going on and on about myself. She wanted to know. She was fine one minute, and then boom, she lit out of there like I'd insulted her best friend."

"What, exactly, did you say?" Susan leaned back, crossing her arms over her chest. "And I'm not just being nosy. Lacey's had a lot happen to her, and she went through a pretty bad depression. I'd hate to see her sink back into that."

"Me, too." He frowned, thinking. "I was talking about working with the kids, and she said she didn't know how I could handle working with that many. I told her I love kids, want to have a passel of them myself someday, and it was about then that she seemed to back off. Was that… do you think I somehow offended her?"

Susan threw her hands up and snorted with disgust. "Vito!" Several people turned to look at them, and she tugged him closer and lowered her voice. "Look, I don't know that it's my place to tell you this, but Lacey *can't* have kids."

That hit him like a blow to deflect, news that had to be wrong. "But…she got pregnant with Gerry, right?"

She looked from one side to the other, making sure they weren't overheard. "When she miscarried, there was some damage. She's infertile now, and that's been really, really hard for her to deal with."

Pain sliced through him just as if it were he, himself, who couldn't have kids. Lacey would be such a great mom. Sometimes, life just wasn't fair.

"And so when you said..." Susan trailed off.

Understanding broke through. "Did she back off because I said I wanted a lot of kids?"

"I don't know. She's the type who'd sacrifice her own desires so other people would get what they wanted."

"Wait a minute, I'm confused. What *are* her own desires?"

"She really likes you, Vito, if you haven't wrecked it. Talk to her. That is, unless her infertility means you aren't interested in her, like some ancient king who only likes women so he can get a son."

Vito lifted his hands, palms up. "Whoa. That's not me. Not at all." His mind was reeling, but this was something he could maybe fix. "Look, I have to go. Can you tell them... Do you think they can handle the rest without..."

"Go." Susan actually shoved him toward the door. "The line's short today and it's almost done."

"Thanks. Thanks, Susan. Let me get Charlie, and I'm outta here."

Despite the sad news he'd learned about Lacey, hope was rising in him. If she cared for him so much that she'd sacrifice her own desires so he could have kids... But didn't she see that what he wanted was her? Kids came into families in all kinds of ways. Just look at Charlie.

The boy wasn't with the rest of the Kennel Kids. "He

said he needed to talk to you," Angelica said. "Didn't he come over?"

"No…" Vito turned and scanned the room. "I'll find him. Thanks."

Alongside his excitement about possibly working things out with Lacey, self-blame pushed at him. He'd been paying so much attention to Susan's story that he'd forgotten to keep an eye on Charlie.

Finally, he thought to talk to the other Kennel Kids. "He said he was outta here, going home," one of the younger ones finally volunteered.

"Thanks." Vito blew out a breath, quickly left the church and walked the three blocks to the guesthouse at record speed. He'd told Charlie he had to stay and help the whole time. What did this new wave of defiance mean?

Nonna was at the front gate, headed out for lunch with Lou Ann Miller. "Did you see Charlie come in?" Vito asked.

"No, but I've been getting ready. I wouldn't have heard him if he went right upstairs. Is anything wrong?"

"Everything's fine. He's just in trouble."

"Don't be too hard on him, dear." Nonna patted Vito's arm, and then the two women headed down the sidewalk.

He trotted up the stairs. Noticed the door to Lacey's room was still closed. Was she in there?

He *really* wanted to talk to her, but he had to deal with Charlie's disobedience first. He pounded on the door to Charlie's room, and when there was no answer, flung it open.

The lecture he'd been about to give died on his lips.

The room was empty. Not just empty of people, but empty of stuff. Charlie's stuff.

He opened the closet door. There was a hamper of dirty clothes, but the clean ones were gone. As was Charlie's suitcase.

His heart pounding, he ran out onto the landing. "Charlie! Charlie!"

No answer, but Lacey's door opened. "What's wrong?"

He looked from window to window, searching the yard on both sides of the guesthouse, but they were quiet, empty.

"Vito? What's going on?"

"Have you seen Charlie?"

"Not since you guys left for the church. Where is he?"

"That," Vito said grimly, "is the million-dollar question. I think he's run away."

Chapter Fourteen

Vito continued searching even as he explained the situation to Lacey, trying to stay calm.

"I just can't believe he'd run away. He's so happy here, and with you." Lacey walked into Charlie's room. She opened the closet door, and then squatted to look under the bed—all places Vito had already checked.

Vito strode into his adjoining room. He flung open the closet door and checked it top to bottom. "I never thought of him running, either, but he's not here. And his suitcase is gone." Quickly and methodically, he searched the rest of his room. News stories of all the bad things that could happen to kids played through his head, one after another.

A thought struck him and he went back to the window, lifted the screen and leaned out. He gave a whistle, and Wolfie trotted over to that side of the yard, panting, looking up expectantly.

"It's okay, boy," he said, and shut the window. Surely Charlie wouldn't have left without his beloved dog.

When he looked back into the room, Lacey was at

Charlie's little desk, rifling through papers and maga-
zines and empty potato chip bags.

"I'd better call Dion." He had his phone out to punch
in the police chief's number when Lacey cried out softly.

"Look at this. Is this his handwriting?"

Vito took the torn piece of notebook paper from her
and scanned it quickly, his heart sinking with every
word he read.

I thot I cud have a mom and dad. I need a mom.
Take care of Wofie.

And he'd signed it, "Love, Charlie."

Vito's heart seemed to stop in his chest.

"What does it mean?" Lacey clutched her arms
around herself. "'I need a mom.' And who did he think
would be his mom? Was it…was it me?"

"Maybe." He caught Lacey's eye, held it. "Believe me
when I say I didn't try to plant that idea. But right now
I'm more worried about where he's headed."

"Could he have gone to his mom?"

"That's what I'm afraid of." He turned toward the
door. "I can't even imagine how upset he was, to leave
without Wolfie."

"But you said she's an addict…"

"She is, and she isn't very selective about her boyfriends. I've got to find him." He headed down the stairs.

She followed behind. "Where does she live? Where
has he been meeting her?"

"He's been meeting her at a center in Raystown. But
she actually lives in Barnsdale. Way too far to walk,
and he knows that."

Lacey grabbed his arm, stopping him. "There's a bus

that goes to Barnsdale. We were talking one day, Charlie and Nonna and me, and we looked over the bus route together. He was sounding out the words, and when he came to Barnsdale, he said that's where he used to live."

Vito groaned. "I have a feeling that's exactly what he did. Is the bus stop still at the front of Cramer's Drugstore?"

She nodded. "Let's go. Maybe we can catch him before he gets the bus. I don't even know the schedule anymore, but the bus can't run very often."

They each grabbed phones, wallets and keys and rushed out to Vito's car. As they climbed in, Wolfie howled his distress at being left behind.

"Let's drive slow and watch. He could be headed back home. I doubt a bus driver would even take a kid as young as Charlie."

"I don't know. He can be pretty smart about figuring out ways to do things and making up stories."

They were at the drugstore in minutes, and Lacey got out of the car and rushed in before Vito even had a chance to park. By the time he got inside, seconds later, she was in heated conversation with a teenage clerk.

"Why didn't anyone stop him?" she was lamenting. "A little boy, alone?"

"Kids eight and over can ride unaccompanied." The young woman shrugged. "He had the right paperwork, looked like. The driver always checks."

Vito's heart sank. Charlie was perfectly capable of talking an adult into filling out a form for him. "How long ago did the bus leave?"

The teenager looked at the wall behind her, taking what seemed like an extremely long time to skim over a schedule. "Must've been about…an hour ago?"

He and Lacey looked at each other. "Let's go," she said.

As they reached the truck, the ramifications of what might be in front of them rushed into Vito's mind. Krystal, Lacey, Charlie. All together. "Lace...you might not want to go along. Someone should stay back at the guesthouse, in case he comes back."

"I'll call Lou Ann on the way and ask her and Nonna to go back."

"It's not safe—"

"*Charlie's* not safe. And you need backup."

He pulled out of the parking lot and headed toward Barnsdale. "I need backup I don't have to worry about. You can only come if you stay in the truck and be ready to call the police if needed. That's it, Lacey. I don't want you tangling with Krystal and her boyfriends, or whoever else is crashing at her place."

"Fine."

As they drove in silence, Vito's mind hopscotched from topic to topic. How would Charlie get from the bus stop to his house on the poorer side of town? Should he explain the whole situation about Charlie and Krystal and Gerry so that Lacey could be prepared? Why had Charlie run away, really?

He heard a small sound from the seat beside him. When he glanced over, he saw Lacey brushing her forefinger under her eye. "What's wrong?"

"I think I know why Charlie ran away," she said with a hitch in her voice. "I think it's my fault."

"How could it be your fault?" He kept his eyes on the rural road before him, pushing the speed limit.

"Because I told him we couldn't keep doing things together." She fumbled in her purse, found a tissue and blew her nose. "I told him we couldn't be a family."

Whoa. "How did you get into that conversation? When?"

"Just this morning." She paused, took a breath. "He came in from basketball, talking about all the things we three were going to do together, and I thought...I thought he'd better not expect that. So I just...told him it wasn't happening."

"Why?"

"Because it can't." He could barely hear her voice, low and hoarse.

He risked taking a hand off the steering wheel and gave her arm a quick squeeze. "We have to talk. Susan told me some stuff."

"What stuff?" She shifted to face him, sounding uneasy.

A passing road sign told Vito they were halfway to Barnsdale. "Look, I'm sorry if this is none of my business, but apparently Susan thought I should know about your infertility."

She drew in a little gasp, her hand rising to her mouth.

There was probably a tactful way to have this conversation, but he didn't know it, not now. "I'm sorry, hon. That's got to be tough, maybe the toughest thing for a woman."

She didn't say anything, and when he glanced over, her lips were pressed tightly together and her body rigid.

"But there are all kinds of ways to be a parent. It's not just biological. I mean, look at me and Charlie."

She didn't answer, and they rode without talking into Barnsdale, passing the automobile factory on one side of the road and a couple of small machine shops on the other.

He tried again. "When all this is over, when we find

Charlie and get him home safe, I want to have more of a conversation about this. Okay?"

She nodded, reached over and squeezed his arm. "We'll find him."

Vito pulled onto the street where Krystal had been renting a place, the last address he had for her. Dingy cottages and overgrown yards lined both sides of the street. "This isn't going to be pleasant. Remember, I want you to stay in the car."

"I know. I'm ready to call the cops." She looked around uneasily.

He stopped the truck in front of Krystal's place. "And Lace…"

"What?"

He hooked an arm around her neck, pulled her to him and gave her a fast, hard kiss. Then he pulled back to look into her eyes. "Remember, whatever happens, I want this with you." He got out of the truck before he could say too much.

There was a bang as the screen door flew open and back on broken hinges, slamming into the front of the house.

"Hey, what's going on, my man Vito!" Krystal came out on the front stoop, started down the concrete steps, and then grabbed the railing and sat down abruptly.

A man appeared in the doorway behind her, the same one Vito had seen driving the SUV. The balding, bearded one who'd made Charlie cringe.

Vito strode up the narrow walkway. "Is Charlie here?"

"Yeah, he's here." Krystal held up a can of beer like she was making a toast. "Decided he'd rather live with his good old mom after all."

Relief that he'd found Charlie warred with worry

about the situation the boy had gotten himself into. "I'd like to talk to him."

The bearded man came out onto the stoop, his face unfriendly. "What's your business here?"

"Just looking for my son." Vito visually searched the place, glancing around the weedy yard, up at the little house's windows.

A curtain moved in one. Was it Charlie?

"You been stepping out on me?" The man nudged Krystal with his knee, none too gently.

"Aw, cut it out, Manny."

"You've got it wrong." Vito kept his voice calm, because he could tell that the man was volatile. "I'm just an acquaintance of Krystal's. Taking care of her son."

"You the daddy?" Manny asked.

Behind him, Vito heard the window of his truck being lowered. Lacey.

"I'm not his dad yet, but I'm going to adopt him. Let's just get him down here and I'll be on my way."

"Maybe I don't like the way you look." Manny shoved past Krystal and came down the steps. "Maybe I want you to leave right now."

Vito automatically straightened up, his fists clenching. He wanted to punch the jerk, but for Charlie's sake he couldn't. He needed to stay calm and keep things peaceful. "I'd be glad to leave you people to your own business as soon as I have Charlie."

Then everything happened at once.

Manny drew back a fist, but Krystal rushed up and grabbed it. Manny shook her off and shoved her back, roughly, causing her to fall back onto the steps. At the same moment Charlie came running out of the house.

He crashed into his mother, who reached out reflexively to grab him.

Manny, unaware what was going on behind him, threw a punch that Vito dodged, but landed a second one on Vito's shoulder, knocking him back.

Behind him, the truck door opened. "Charlie!" Lacey cried. "Over here!"

Manny advanced on Vito, and with no time to regret the violence, Vito threw a one-two punch, connecting with Manny's ribs and then the side of his throat. Manny fell to the ground, gasping for air.

Vito spun to help Charlie just in time to see the boy extract himself from his mother's grip and run to Lacey. She was turning to usher him into the truck when Krystal spoke up.

"Hey!" she called, her voice slurred but plenty loud. "Wait a minute. I know who you are!"

Vito's heart skipped a beat and he ran toward Lacey and Charlie, intent on getting them into the truck so they didn't find out the truth this way.

Her heart pumping, her adrenaline high, Lacey ushered Charlie into the backseat. Then she turned to see where Vito was. She'd drive Charlie away herself if she needed to, even if it meant temporarily leaving Vito behind. He could fend for himself better than Charlie could.

Vito was approaching the truck at a run, so Lacey went around to get in the passenger's seat.

The dark-haired woman, Charlie's mother, reached the truck just as Lacey opened the passenger door. "I know who you are," she said, her tone angry.

Vito came back around from the driver's side. "Come on, Krystal, we'll talk another time. When you're sober."

"I'm sober enough to recognize *her*."

Lacey studied the woman. "How do you know me? I don't think I've met you."

"Krystal—" Vito started.

She held up a hand and interrupted him, still glaring at Lacey. "*You're* the woman who stole my man away."

That was so far from anything Lacey expected that she could only stare at Krystal.

"Hey, now," Vito said, "this can wait. Charlie doesn't need to hear this."

Lacey stepped away from the truck door. Before she could close it in an effort to block Charlie's hearing them, Krystal slammed it shut.

Someone clicked the locks. Vito.

She looked past Vito to Krystal, filled with a sinking feeling she didn't understand. "How do you know me?"

"Guy named Gerry McPherson sound familiar?"

"Ye-e-e-s," Lacey said slowly. "He was my husband."

"Well, he was *my* fiancé. And the father of my child."

"The father of your…"

"Him." Krystal pointed toward the backseat. "Charlie."

Lacey looked at Vito, who should be denying what this madwoman said, but Vito's face was a stone.

The edges of her world started to crumble. "Gerry was Charlie's father?"

"That's right. I gave him more than you ever did."

The words stabbed her, but she ignored the pain. She had to explain to the woman how wrong she was. "But Charlie's eight. I was married to Gerry when…" She stared at Krystal.

Krystal threw up her hands. "You didn't even know, did you?"

Slowly Lacey shook her head. What she was hearing couldn't possibly be right.

"Yeah, he was seeing me on the side. At first, I didn't know about you, either." The anger was draining out of the woman's voice. "When I figured out that he was married, I tried to break it off, but he said your marriage was on the rocks and he was leaving. It was only when I saw that photo in the paper that I realized he'd been lying. You two were hugging each other like lovebirds, all happy." She shook her head, her expression bitter. "He wasn't worth the time I put into him."

"At least you got…Charlie." She heard the choked sound of her own voice as if from a distance.

Gerry had been cheating on her?

Could it be true?

She cleared her throat. "How long were you seeing him?"

"Couple of years. He didn't come around as much after Charlie was born. To be fair, he was overseas a lot after that."

"Don't be fair to him!" Lacey snapped. "Did he see you when he came home, too?"

"Yeah. Some. Not much." Something like compassion had crept into Krystal's voice. "Charlie doesn't remember him."

Lacey sagged back against the truck, unable to process what she was hearing.

Gerry had been unfaithful during the whole course of their marriage.

He'd conceived a son with this woman in front of her.

He'd met the son and seen the woman when he came home on leave.

And she'd known none of it.

She put her hands over her face, trying to block it out, trying to preserve the memory of the husband she'd adored, of the happy marriage she'd thought she had.

Vito cleared his throat.

The sound brought a whole new betrayal into focus, and she dropped her hands away from her eyes and turned to stare at him. "You knew."

Slowly, he nodded.

"You knew, and you stayed in my house, brought Gerry's son into my house, and you didn't tell me."

"Cold, Vito," Krystal said.

"Lacey, I wanted to tell you. Started to, so many times. But I promised Gerry I wouldn't."

Krystal snorted. "Yeah, well, we all made promises, didn't we? And look how much good that did."

Lacey stared from Krystal to Vito, trying to process it all.

Vito was still talking. "I promised that I'd take care of Charlie and look out for you, too. He knew how much it would hurt you…"

"Oh, that's rich," Krystal said.

Lacey just stared and shook her head. He'd kept the truth from her so as not to *hurt* her? At Gerry's behest?

There was a sound from inside the truck, and she turned to see Charlie knocking on the window and mouthing words, his face anxious.

Lacey just stared at him, the boy she'd come to care for so much. The boy whose eyebrows arched high and dark, just like Gerry's had.

He was Gerry's son.

Gerry *had* a son. She herself had had so much trouble conceiving, and when she'd finally gotten pregnant, it had been too late: Gerry had been killed, and she had lost the baby.

Charlie was rattling the truck door now, and Vito and Krystal were arguing about something, but the words blurred into a mishmash she couldn't understand.

It was all too much. She had to get out of here.

She spun away and started walking down the road, faster and faster until she was nearly at a run.

Chapter Fifteen

For a few seconds, Vito was paralyzed, watching Lacey disappear down the street.

Charlie's rattling of the door and the sounds of Krystal's voice speaking to Manny, who was waking up, snapped him out of it.

He needed to go after Lacey. He needed to reassure and help Charlie. And he probably needed to make sure Krystal was okay, too.

The confusion of prioritizing made his military training kick in. *Secure those closest and most vulnerable.*

He opened the truck door and leaned in toward Charlie. "Listen, we're going to talk this through and figure it all out."

Charlie slumped. "Am I in trouble?"

"Yes, you're in trouble, but everyone gets in trouble. It's okay." He knew what Charlie would ask next, and he held up a hand to forestall it. "You're not getting sent away. You're still going to be my son and you can still see your mom every week."

"What about Miss Lacey?"

Vito blew out a breath. No dishonesty. That was what

had gotten him in trouble in the first place. "I just don't know, Charlie. She's pretty mad at me right now."

"How come?"

"Grown-up business. We'll talk about it later." He stood, patted Charlie's shoulder, and then reached in and gave the boy a hug. "Sit tight. I've got to check on your mom and then we'll go make sure Lacey is safe."

He shut Charlie's door gently, and then walked a few steps toward Krystal. "You going to be okay?" he asked, nodding toward Manny. "I can call the cops for you."

"I got this," she said. "Go after her."

He took her word for it and drove out in the direction Lacey had gone, scanning the road. It was late afternoon and clouds were rolling in, thick and ominous. He had to get her before this storm started—or, given the neighborhood, something worse happened. "Help me watch for Lacey," he told Charlie.

A moment later, Charlie leaned forward in the seat and pointed. "Is that her?"

He could see her yellow shirt. She was desperately waving down a truck. No. She wouldn't get in a stranger's vehicle. Would she?

Did she want to avoid him that badly?

The truck stopped. The passenger door opened, and Lacey climbed in.

Vito hit the gas. "Do you know anyone who drives a blue pickup?" It seemed to have writing on the side, but Vito couldn't read it.

His stomach was lurching. If something happened to Lacey...

He got behind the truck, which was traveling at a normal rate of speed, and was relieved to see it was headed toward Rescue River, rather than away. Maybe she'd known the person and was getting a safe ride. But he still followed, just to be sure.

His head was still spinning from the way it had all gone down. Lacey had found out the truth about Gerry in the worst possible way.

Why hadn't he told her before? The betrayal in her eyes had just about killed him.

How awful for her to find out about her adored, war hero husband from his lover, screaming jealously at her.

And normally, she'd have turned to him for comfort. But instead, she'd looked at him as the betrayer, and rightly so.

Except he'd promised Gerry he wouldn't tell.

He tried to think of how it could've worked out differently. What all he'd done wrong. He shouldn't have made the promise. He shouldn't have moved in with Lacey. But that had been for Nonna...

There was a sniffle from the seat behind him, and Vito pulled his attention away from his thoughts and to Charlie. "Hey, buddy. What's the matter?"

"I thought Mom would want me," Charlie said in a subdued voice. "But when I got to her house, she told me to go away because Manny would get mad. And then Manny saw me."

"Did he hurt you?" Vito would kill the man if he had.

"No, but he made Mom shut me in the bedroom. And they said I couldn't come out. And they were gonna call you, but then they started fighting and kind of forgot about me."

"You can't do that, buddy. You can't run away. And you can't live with your mom." As he spoke, he was watching the truck in front of him, relieved to see it taking the exit that led to the guesthouse.

"I know." Charlie's voice was subdued.

"We're gonna figure this out, talk about it." Vito reached over and ruffled Charlie's hair. "Right now, though, we've got to check on Lacey."

He followed the truck, and when it pulled up in front of Lacey's place, he pulled up behind it.

"Do I have to stay in the truck again?" Charlie's voice was quiet.

"No, buddy, but you have to let me talk a little bit to Lacey. Grown-up business. Go see Wolfie. Okay? Take him out and walk him down the street, but stay where you can see me. We'll go inside in just a minute."

"Good, because I'm hungry."

They both got out of the truck, and Vito watched to make sure Charlie was safely out of earshot. He turned in time to see a dark-haired man walking beside Lacey toward the front door.

Jealousy burned inside him. He didn't want anyone else walking with Lacey. Especially not some tall, buff, thirty-ish guy with no scars and, probably, no baggage.

He followed them up the steps. "Lacey, I need to talk to you."

She ignored him and turned to the dark-haired man. "Thank you for the ride."

"Would you like me to stay?" the man asked in a courteous voice with just a trace of a Spanish accent.

She glanced toward Vito without meeting his eyes. "Maybe for a few minutes, if you don't mind. I just need to talk to…my other boarder, without him bothering me, and make a couple of arrangements."

"It's no problem." He sat down in the porch chair Vito had begun to consider his own.

Lacey turned to go inside.

Vito started to follow. "Lacey—"

"The lady prefers that you don't come in," the other man said, standing up to block Vito as Lacey continued on inside.

Vito stopped, lifted an eyebrow, wondered if he was going to have to fight again that day.

"She's an old friend, and she told me on the way home that she doesn't want you around. Not my business why." The man shrugged. "Sorry, man."

Vito sat down heavily on the front steps. He could smell someone barbecuing for Saturday dinner. He and Lacey had done the same just last week.

Before everything had fallen apart.

Charlie came back into the yard, tugging Wolfie. He started up the steps. "Let's go in. I'm starving."

"Can't. Not yet."

"Why not?"

"Lacey is… She doesn't want us to come in just yet, but we can in a little while."

Charlie's lower lip began to stick out. "I want to go to my own room."

Except it wasn't his own room. "Just a little while, buddy."

The dark-haired man stood and went down to his truck. He came back with a sandwich encased in plastic wrap and an apple. "Here," he said to Charlie. "It's good. Turkey and cheese."

"Thanks!" Charlie grabbed the sandwich and started unwrapping it.

"That's your lunch, man," Vito protested.

"I have kids. I understand." He sat back down in the same porch chair.

"Hey, you don't have to wait around. I won't bother her."

"I said I'd wait," the man said quietly. "No offense."

So they sat in silence while Charlie scarfed down the sandwich, and then played in the yard with Wolfie. It was another forty-five minutes before Lacey came out the door.

"Thanks, Eduardo," she said, still not looking at Vito. "I'm sorry to keep you from your work. I'm fine now."

"You're sure?"

"I'm sure."

They both watched as Eduardo trotted down the steps and swung into his truck. Charlie came over, holding Wolfie tight on his leash, in control for once. "Hi, Miss Lacey," he said uncertainly.

She knelt in front of him, giving Wolfie a quick head rub, and then turning her full attention to Charlie. "I need to talk to you about something serious," she said. "Can you listen?"

He nodded, eyes wide.

"I like you a lot," she said. "I'm really sorry it didn't work out for me and your dad, but that's not your fault."

Charlie swallowed hard, and Vito did the same.

"You always have a safe home with your dad. That isn't changing. You don't run away from him anymore, okay?"

"Okay." Charlie's voice was low.

"And because I really like you, this is hard, but…you and your dad are going to need to move out."

Charlie looked down at the floor, nodded and turned away, nuzzling his face in Wolfie's fur. Wolfie, seeming to understand the boy's sadness, whined a little and licked Charlie's face.

Vito felt like he'd been punched in the stomach, hard.

Lacey stood and faced him. "Vito, I've made arrangements for Nonna to stay at the Senior Towers. They have a room open for her for however long she needs, and they can help her move in tomorrow. I have a call in to a friend of mine, a nurse, who'll check on her every day."

"You didn't have to—"

"Let me finish." She held up a hand. "You're going to have to find another place for you and Charlie to stay. I'm going away for a few days, and I want you out when I get back." Her voice was cold and distant.

She didn't wait for an answer, but turned and walked into the house, letting the door bang behind her.

Vito's shoulders slumped and he felt like collapsing down onto the porch and burying his head in his hands.

She was really, truly rejecting him. He loved her, and he'd lost her. Despair clutched his stomach with strong, cold fingers.

But he had a son to care for.

He swallowed the lump in his throat and straightened his shoulders. Looked out across the lawn.

There was Charlie's basketball. They couldn't forget that.

He walked down the steps, heavily, to pick it up.

"We gonna play, Dad?" Charlie asked eagerly.

"No, son." Vito carried the basketball up the stairs, not even bouncing it. "We're going to have to start packing, and I have to start looking for a new place for us to live."

He went to the front door, held it open for Charlie, and then followed the boy inside.

He felt utterly broken. And the only reason he was

standing upright, trying to be strong, was because Nonna and Charlie depended on him.

It was Lacey's fifth day at the Ohio Rural Retreat Center, and she was finding some small measure of peace.

She'd cried so much that her eyes felt permanently swollen. She'd prayed almost continually. She'd sought counsel with the center's spiritual advisors.

She knew now that she needed to put her faith in God, not men.

She knew she wasn't healed yet, not even close.

The thought of Fiona Farmingham coming to visit with her today was terrifying. It wasn't that she didn't like Fiona; she barely knew her. And she had Fiona to thank for the idea of coming here. When she'd blurted out a piece of an explanation to Eduardo in that horrible truck ride home—"my husband wasn't who I thought he was"—Eduardo had urged her to get in touch with Fiona, who'd had something similar happen to her. And then he'd gone further and called Fiona, who'd texted her the address of the retreat center where she'd stayed when her world had fallen apart.

There was a knock on the door of her small, monk-like cell. "Your visitor is here," came the quiet, soothing voice of the retreat receptionist.

Trying not to show her reluctance, Lacey went out to the reception area and greeted Fiona with a handshake, then an awkward hug.

"Would you like to walk?" Fiona asked. "When I was here, I always liked the trail around the pond."

"Um, sure." She hoped Fiona didn't plan to stay long,

that she wouldn't say anything to burst the fragile, peaceful bubble Lacey had built around herself.

But it couldn't last forever, of course. She was going to have to get back to renovating the guesthouse. To rebuilding her life in Rescue River as a strong single woman.

That had been her goal all along. When and why had she let that fade? But she knew the answer: it was when Vito and Charlie had come. Ever so gradually, they'd slipped into her heart so that now, having lost them, she didn't feel strong. She felt weak and vulnerable and raw.

"Thanks for agreeing to a visit," Fiona said as they walked toward the center's small pond, separated from the main building by a stand of trees. "I just felt really led to talk to you. And if your nights have been anything like mine were, you're not sleeping well, so I figured an early morning visit would be okay."

"I appreciate it," Lacey lied politely. "Where are your kids?"

"With the nanny," Fiona said, sounding apologetic. It was no secret that she was quite wealthy after her scandalous divorce settlement, but she didn't flaunt her money; in fact, people said she didn't like mentioning it.

A red-winged blackbird, perched on a cattail at the pond's edge, let out its trademark "okalee, okalee" before taking flight, bright red and yellow wing patches flashing in the early morning sun. "This is an amazing place," Lacey said, meaning it. "Thank you for telling me about it."

"Of course. How are you doing?" The question wasn't a surface platitude, but a real inquiry.

"I'm…managing, but barely," Lacey admitted.

"That's normal," Fiona said matter-of-factly. "When I

found out my husband had a whole other family, it took a year to even start to feel normal again."

Her blunt words reached Lacey in a way the retreat counselors' soothing tones hadn't. Fiona had been there, had experienced the loss and humiliation Lacey was going through. "Did you ever feel like it might have been a dream, like you were going to wake up any minute and none of it would be true?"

Fiona nodded. "All the time. And then you keep on realizing, no, it's true, my life wasn't at all like what it seemed to be."

"Exactly. It's like my memories were stolen. The happiness I had with Gerry was all a huge lie."

"Well." Fiona reached out to run her fingers alongside the reeds that rimmed the pond. "I don't know if it was all a lie. My therapist said that men who lead double lives can really believe they love both women. Or in my case, both families."

Lacey inhaled the rich, damp-earth fragrance of the wetlands. "I don't know how you stood it, with four kids to watch out for. I'm barely managing with just myself."

"You do what you have to do. For me, the betrayal was the worst part. It messed with my whole image of myself as a woman, like I wasn't enough."

Lacey looked over at Fiona, tall, with long, wavy red hair and an hourglass figure. *She* had felt like she wasn't enough? "Did you get over that?"

Fiona shook her head. "You will, I'm sure, but I didn't. I've got my hands full with my kids and starting a business. Even if I felt like I could trust a man again— which I don't—I wouldn't have time for it."

"I hear you. My guesthouse is yelling for me to get back to renovations."

They walked in companionable silence for a few minutes. Green-headed mallards flew down and landed on the pond, skidding along. Overhead, the sky turned a brighter blue.

"I just wonder if everyone in town knew but me," Lacey burst out finally.

"I wondered the same thing, and I found out as soon as the truth started getting publicized. People *did* know, and they rushed to tell me how they'd suspected, or what they'd heard." She sighed. "That was bad enough, but when my kids started getting teased and bullied, I'd had it. I had to leave. It's why I moved to Rescue River."

"Oh, how awful for you *and* your kids!" Lacey felt almost ashamed for being upset about her own situation. Fiona, with her four kids suffering, had it so much worse.

"It was awful, but things are better now. Much better. What happened with your husband? How did you find out?"

So Lacey explained the whole situation. "And then Vito, he brought Gerry's child into my home! He was living there all along, knowing that secret."

"Ouch."

The sun was rising higher, and Lacey slipped off her sweatshirt and tied it around her waist. "He was an old friend, but he lied to me."

"Did he actively lie? He seems like a really nice guy, but you never know."

Lacey thought back. "No, he never actively lied. I think the subject of Charlie's dad might have come up once, but he told me Charlie's father had died. And that he was Vito's war buddy. All of which was technically true. But—" she lifted her hands, palms up "—why did he come to live in the guesthouse—with my husband's son—when he had to know how much the truth would hurt me? And then we…" Tears rose to her eyes and she blinked them back. "We started getting close. I thought he cared for me." She almost choked on her words.

Fiona put an arm around her, giving her a quick shoulder-hug. "That sounds so hurtful. But do you think he did it on purpose, to be mean?"

Unbidden, an image of Vito's kind face swam before Lacey's teary eyes. She thought back over the time when he'd decided to stay at the guesthouse. "Nooooo," she said slowly. "He was actually reluctant to stay, and only agreed because his grandma was so keen on it."

"So he didn't exactly come knocking on your door, looking for a place to live."

"No. But he should have told me the truth!"

"He should have." Fiona hesitated. "That's a pretty hard thing to tell."

"I guess." Lacey didn't want to look at Vito's side, not yet. She was still too angry at him.

"And the thing is, were you perfect? That's what my counselor made me look at, in my situation. Were there any mistakes you made, in your marriage?"

"I was stupid," Lacey said bitterly.

"Well…yeah. You kind of were."

Lacey blinked, surprised. Not many people would speak that bluntly to someone who wasn't an old friend.

"We weren't wise as serpents, were we?" Fiona stared off into the distance. "Neither of us. And people suffered because of it."

Lacey had never thought of it that way. She'd focused on how she was an innocent victim, not on how she'd had a responsibility to be wise as well as gentle and kind.

And yes, people had suffered. She thought of Charlie's hurt face when she'd told him she wouldn't be doing things with Vito anymore. It was a big part of why he'd run away.

Kicking him and Vito out on the street... Making Nonna move to the Towers... Yeah. "I've made a lot of people miserable, dragged them down with me."

They were coming to the end of the loop around the pond. "Don't beat yourself up. That's not what I mean at all. I'm really sorry for what happened to you. It's just... we're all a mix, right? Nobody's perfect. Not your husband, not you. And not Vito, either."

"True."

They walked quietly for a few more minutes, and when they reached the parking lot, Fiona stopped. "I've got to get back to the kids. But I just want you to know, there's life after this. You can come back, live well. Keep on praying, and I'll pray for you, too."

They hugged, for real this time. "Thanks for coming to see me," Lacey said. "It helped. A lot."

And as she waved, and then headed back inside, she felt better. Not healed, but better. And it was a good thing, because tomorrow she had to go back to town, hold her head high and probably encounter Vito and Charlie.

Chapter Sixteen

A week later, Vito parked in front of the Senior Towers and headed inside. He'd been so busy with Charlie and his job that he hadn't visited his grandmother for the past couple of days, and he felt guilty.

That wasn't the reason for the heaviness in his soul, though. *That* came from his unresolved issues with Lacey. Even now, if he looked down the street, he could see her on the porch of her guesthouse, talking and laughing with a couple of visitors.

He hoped to catch her eye, but she didn't even glance his way.

He trudged inside the Senior Towers, trying to look at the bright side. Charlie was doing well; Vito had explained the whole situation to his social worker, and a couple of sessions with her, Vito, and Charlie had helped the boy to understand as much of the truth as an eight-year-old needed to know. They'd talked over running away, and Charlie had promised to make a phone call to his social worker if he ever felt like doing it again.

They'd found half of a double to rent on the edge of town, with a huge fenced yard and a dog-friendly neighbor in the other half of the house. So that was another good thing.

His course work was going well, and his new job even better. He loved working with the at-risk boys, and already his supervisor had talked with him about a possible full-time opening once he had his degree.

The scars weren't really an issue, in the job or otherwise. In fact, he felt almost foolish about how much he'd let them get in his way when he'd first returned to Rescue River. Now if a newcomer stared or a kid made a comment, he could let it roll off him, knowing that to most people, it was what was inside that mattered.

Lacey had helped him see that first. He owed her a debt of gratitude, but it was one he couldn't pay. To approach her again, after what he'd done, would be an insult to her.

He straightened his shoulders and ordered himself to focus on what he could do, not on what he couldn't. He'd go spend time with Nonna, help her feel better and recover from the move.

He walked into the Senior Towers and crossed the lobby. He was about to push the button on the elevator when he distinguished Nonna's voice, and he turned to see her emerging from the exercise room in the midst of a crowd of women. She wore hot pink sweats and a T-shirt that said… He squinted and read the words, Vintage Workout Queen.

She walked to him and gave him a strong hug. "My Vito! Come on. Sit down here in the lobby. I can spare a few minutes before I meet with my business partners."

Vito blinked. "Business partners?"

"Yes, Lou Ann and Minnie. The matchmaking business is taking off. Now, tell me what's new with you, and you know what I mean."

He tried to deflect the conversation to his work, and to Charlie, but Nonna saw right through it.

"I'm glad those things are going well, but what about Lacey? Have you mended that fence yet?"

He shook his head. "No, and I don't think it's going to get mended. Some things just can't be fixed." Nonna didn't know the details of what had happened between them, didn't know about Charlie's parentage, but she knew something serious had split them apart.

"Bella? Are you ready?" It was Lou Ann Miller, and it took Vito a minute to realize she was talking to Nonna. He'd almost forgotten his grandmother had a first name. "Oh, hello, Vito."

"Go rouse Minnie," Nonna instructed the other woman. "We have to do a quick consultation with our first client, Vito, here, before we start working on our business plan."

That was the *last* thing he needed. "Nonna... I was really just coming to check on you, not to talk about my own troubles. How are you feeling?"

She waved a hand. "I'm fine. Better every day, and these ladies—" she waved toward Lou Ann and Minnie, now both coming down the hall, talking busily "—they keep me in the loop. Lou Ann knows about all the news outside the Towers, and Minnie knows what's going on inside. I love it here!"

Vito felt a pang. He wasn't really needed by his grandma, not anymore. Nonna was making a new life for herself.

The other two women reached the cozy corner where Nonna and Vito sat, and Lou Ann pulled up chairs for both of them, leaving Vito surrounded and without an escape route.

Immediately, Nonna launched an explanation. "Vito, here, is estranged from the woman he most loves, because of some kind of fight. He thinks the relationship is doomed."

"Do you still have feelings for her?" Lou Ann demanded.

He was torn between telling the three interfering woman to go jump in the lake and embracing them for taking his troubles seriously. He chose the latter. "I still have feelings. But I did something that hurt her terribly."

"Did you apologize?" Miss Minnie asked.

"Yes, of course. But she kicked me out of the guest-house, and she isn't speaking to me."

"Why did you do it?" Lou Ann asked.

He shrugged helplessly. "Loyalty, I guess. Loyalty to an old friend."

"Loyalty is an important value," Miss Minnie said. "But love...remember your Bible, Vito. The greatest of these is Love."

It was true. He saw that now, too late.

"So he's just backing away. Out of politeness!" Nonna leaned forward and pinched his cheek. "My Vito. Always the best friend. Always so nice."

"Too nice," Miss Minnie declared.

Lou Ann Miller looked thoughtful. "If you give up on her, maybe you just don't care enough. Why, I know a couple right here in Rescue River who had to keep huge secrets from each other. But they pushed through their problems. Now they're happily married."

Happily married. If there was any possibility at all of that for him and Lacey...

"The choice is yours," Nonna said. *"Coraggio, ragazzo mio."*

Lacey was what he wanted most in the world. Could he risk another try, a heartfelt apology, a grand gesture that might sway her back in his direction?

What did he have to lose?

Nonna seemed to see the decision on his face. "If you need any help," she said, "we're here for you."

He stood and kissed her cheek. "I will most definitely take you up on that."

From a high-backed chair that faced away from their corner, Gramps Camden stood and pointed a finger at Vito. "For once, the ladies are right. Being polite doesn't get a man much of anything."

As the ladies scolded Gramps for eavesdropping, Vito waved and headed for the door, feeling more energy with each step he took.

He had some serious planning to do.

A week later, Lacey hugged Nonna at the door to the Senior Towers, glad to feel that the older woman was gaining weight and strength. "Don't worry," she said. "I'll take you to the party next week. Are you sure you don't want me to walk you upstairs?"

"I'm fine. And I'm sorry I got the date wrong. Maybe I'm losing my marbles." Nonna shrugged.

"It's all right. I enjoyed spending some time with you." Truthfully, the excursion had filled a gap in Lacey's week. Even though she'd tried to rebuild her life, to spend time with girlfriends and focus on her work, she still found herself lonely.

Still found herself missing Vito and Charlie.

Nonna reached up and straightened Lacey's collar,

plucked a stray hair off her shoulders. "Do you know what we always said in Italy? *Si apra all'amore.* Be open to love."

"Um, sure." Maybe Nonna *was* getting a little confused, because that remark had been apropos of nothing.

She drove the half block to the guesthouse and parked in the driveway, taking her time. She didn't want to go inside an empty house. Without Charlie roughhousing and Wolfie barking, without Vito's deep voice, the place felt empty.

But delaying wouldn't solve her problem. She clasped the cross she'd hung around her neck, in place of the wedding ring she'd worn before. It was a reminder: she could do all things through Christ.

Including survive loneliness.

She climbed out of the car and walked slowly toward the front entrance, checking her flower beds, which were doing great. Looked reflexively at the broken fence. She really needed to...

She stopped. Looked again.

The makeshift fix they'd done weeks ago, when Wolfie had escaped, wasn't there. Instead, the fence was repaired.

She knelt down, awkward in her dress and heels, and examined it. The two broken pickets had been replaced with new ones, painted white. Only when you were very close could you see that the paint was a little brighter on the new pickets.

She frowned. Who would have repaired her fence?

Wondering, she walked toward the front of the house. As she rounded the corner, she heard music.

Opera music. *Italian* opera music.

What had Nonna called it? *The most romantic music on earth.*

What in the world?

The wonderful smell of Italian food—lasagna?—wafted through the air.

As she climbed the front steps, she saw something pink.

Her heart pounding, she reached the top of the steps. A trail of rose petals led her across the porch to a table set for two, topped with a white tablecloth.

She stared at the centerpiece, and tears rose to her eyes.

A ceramic rooster, exactly like the one Charlie had broken the day she'd met him.

No longer could she doubt who was responsible for what she was seeing.

She turned toward the front door. At the same moment, Vito emerged through it, a bowl of salad in one hand and a tray of pasta in the other. He wore dress trousers, a white dress shirt and an apron. Focused on balancing both dishes, he didn't notice her at first, but when he did, a strange expression crossed his face.

"Lacey," he said his voice intent. "Wait." He turned and carefully put down the two items on a side table.

Then he undid his apron and took it off, his eyes never leaving hers.

"How did you…" She broke off.

Walking slowly across the porch, he stood before her, not touching her. "I trespassed. Nonna gave me her key."

"Nonna…" She cocked her head to one side and reviewed the afternoon. Nonna's sudden invitation to a party, her insisting that Lacey dress up, the realization that it was the wrong date… "She was in on this. And you fixed my fence."

"For a good cause."

"What do you mean?"

He walked around her and pulled out a chair. "Explaining will take a minute. Would you like to sit down?"

She hesitated, feeling a little railroaded, but curious, too. "Oka-a-a-ay."

He poured iced tea, the raspberry flavor she always ordered at the Chatterbox, looking for all the world like a handsome Italian waiter. But then he pulled a chair to face her and sat down, close enough that their knees almost touched. Almost, but not quite. "The good cause is…an apology. Lacey, I am so sorry for what I did to you. There's no excuse for dishonesty."

She wanted to forgive him instantly. The music, the tea, the rose petals, the mended fence, the ceramic rooster—all of it created a romantic little world. But she couldn't just succumb to it. She needed to be as wise as a serpent, not just gentle as a dove. Not just go with her heart. "I would like to hear why you did what you did. I wasn't in a condition to listen before."

He drew in a breath and nodded. "Of course. You deserve that." Still, he seemed reluctant to speak.

"I can take it, Vito! Whatever happened, it's probably better than what I've been imagining!"

"Right." He reached for her, then pulled his hand back. "It was only in the last couple of months of Gerry's life that I found out he'd been unfaithful to you."

The word stung, even though she knew it was true. "How did you find out?"

"He was burning letters," he explained. "Building a fire was dangerous over there, so I went to stop him. He said he had just a few more to burn, and he was turning over a new leaf. I still had to stop him—I was his commanding officer by then—and I happened to see a…suggestive card. It didn't look like something you'd send, so I asked him about it."

The thought of another woman sending racy cards to her husband made Lacey's face hot with anger and humiliation. Was that what Gerry had wanted in a woman? Hadn't her tame, loving letters been enough?

Vito was watching her face, and he reached out and wrapped his hand around her clenched fist. "He was *burning* it, Lace. He'd had a couple of risky encounters that had made him think about his life, and he wanted to get a fresh start."

"Either that, or he was afraid of getting caught."

"No, I think he was sincere. He really did love you. He just wasn't used to…" Vito seemed to cast about for the right word. "To monogamy, I guess. That's why I regret introducing you two."

"That's why you tried to warn me about him. You knew what he was like."

Vito nodded. "But you were in love, and I hoped marriage would change him. And it did. It just took a while. When you let him know you were expecting a baby, it made him want to change his ways, be a better husband and father."

"He already had a child!"

"Yeah." Vito sighed. "I found out about that at the very end. You sure you want to hear?"

"Tell me."

"Okay." He looked out toward the street, his shoulders unconsciously straightening into military posture. "Three of us were cut off from the others, and both

Gerry and Luiz were hit and bleeding pretty bad. When Luiz died and Gerry realized the medics might not get there in time for him, either, he told me about Charlie. He asked me to take care of Charlie if Krystal couldn't. And he asked me to look out for you, and to keep you in the dark about who Charlie was, because he thought it would kill you to know. Before I could make him see it wasn't possible to do all those things together, he was gone."

Lacey just sat, trying to process what Vito was saying.

"I tried to save him, Lace. And I tried to do what he asked, though I didn't succeed very well." He sighed. "I thought things were okay for Charlie and Krystal. I thought it might be best for you if I stayed away. But then I got injured, and there was the rehab, and then everything hit the fan with Krystal and I found out Charlie was about to be put into the system... Well, first things first, I thought. Charlie is a kid."

"Of course." Lacey stared down at the porch floor. "It was my own fault I was so foolish, marrying Gerry. I was vulnerable to anyone."

"I was foolish, too, but I've learned. I've learned that honesty and...and *love*...trump loyalty to a bad cause."

She froze, not daring to look at him. "Love?"

He squeezed her hand, then reached up to brush a finger across her cheek. When he spoke, his voice was serious. "I love you, Lacey. I... Maybe I always have, kind of, but now it's grown-up and serious and forever."

Cautiously she looked at him through her eyelashes, not wanting to let her joy and terror show. She drew in a breath. "I have an apology to make, too. I was wrong to kick you and Charlie out. I was angry at Gerry, really, and at myself, and I took it out on you."

"Understandable."

"Is Charlie okay?"

He nodded. "We've had a few sessions with his social worker to talk it all through. She helped me understand how much to tell Charlie. Right now, he knows that his dad was a hero, but made some mistakes. That he felt ashamed he wasn't married to Charlie's mom. And that none of it is Charlie's fault. That seems like about as much as he can take in, right now."

"That's good." She bit her lip. "I shouldn't have taken out my hurt on you, and especially on an innocent child."

"For whatever you did wrong, I forgive you."

"And I forgive you."

They looked at each other. "Are we good?" he asked.

"We're good." She felt a strange breathlessness as he stood and pulled her gently to her feet.

And into his arms.

Being held by him, seeing and believing how much he cared, soothed some deep place inside her that wanted to be cared for and loved.

His hand rubbed slow circles on her back. "I hated being at odds," he said, and she felt the rumble of his voice against her cheek. "I want to be your friend. At *least* your friend. I want to be more."

She pulled away enough that she could look up at his face. "What kind of more?" she murmured in a husky tone that didn't even sound like her.

"This kind." He leaned down and pressed his lips to hers.

After a long while he lifted his head, sniffing the air, and then pulled away.

Lacey smelled it at the same time he did. "Something's burning!"

They ran inside and Vito pulled a scorched cake from the oven. "Oh, man, it was chocolate, too!"

She burst out laughing.

And then they were both laughing, and crying, and hugging each other, and kissing a little more. "It was so awful being apart from you. I never want that to happen again," he said.

"I don't, either." She pulled back. "But Vito. That nice meal is getting cold."

He laughed. "It'll warm up just fine. Come here."

He was right, of course. She stepped forward into his arms. "I love you," she said.

Epilogue

"I predicted this as soon as I saw you catch that bouquet," Susan Hinton said, looking around the guesthouse lawn with satisfaction.

"You couldn't have!" Lacey laughed. "Vito wasn't even back yet."

"I saw him come up behind you and I knew."

Gina, Lacey's sister-in-law, came over to where Lacey and Susan sat, under the party tent they'd put up against a summer shower. "Vito and Buck are exchanging fatherhood tips with Sam."

Lacey craned her neck and saw Sam Hinton, holding three-month-old Sam Jr. as if he were made of glass. Buck squatted to wipe the cake from little Bobby's face. And Vito was bending down to speak to Charlie, who looked adorably grown-up in his junior tux.

Lacey felt fully recovered from the devastating news about Gerry being Charlie's father. There even seemed to be a strange rightness in her helping Vito to raise Gerry's child.

Nonna approached Vito and took his arm, pulling him toward Lacey. She seemed years younger than she had after her heart attack; indeed, she was helping to teach heart attack recovery classes at the Senior Towers and was so happily enmeshed in the social circles there that she'd decided to live at the towers full-time.

"I need to talk to the bride and groom," Nonna said as she reached Lacey and her friends. "Alone."

Vito lifted an eyebrow and reached to pull Lacey from her reclining position. The very touch of his hand gave her goose bumps. They'd spent glorious time together during the past year, getting to know each other as the adults they were now. Vito had finished his online studies and student teaching, and had the offer of a job for the fall. Meanwhile, he'd been working with Lacey at the guesthouse, which had become so successful that she'd had to hire help—help that would now manage the place while she and Vito honeymooned.

The thought of their honeymoon on a South Carolina beach made Lacey's skin warm. She couldn't even regret that they could only manage a long weekend, with the guesthouse to run and Charlie to parent. She was so, so ready to begin married life with Vito.

"I'm afraid I've been interfering again," Nonna said, a twinkle in her eye.

"Nonna! What now?" Vito's tone was indulgent.

"You have that look on your face," Lacey added. "What have you been up to?"

Nonna looked from Vito to Lacey and bit her lip. "First, I have a confession to make." She hesitated, then added, "My interfering has been going on for a while."

"What do you mean? The matchmaking date?" Lacey had suspected for some time that Nonna had arranged for her and Vito to go out with Daisy and Dion, knowing it would push them into acknowledging their feelings for each other.

Nonna patted Lacey's arm as if she were a bright student. "Yes, the whole matchmaking service was a scheme to get the two of you together. Of course, it's grown beyond that." Lou Ann and Miss Minnie had become Nonna's first lieutenants, matching up the singles of Rescue River.

"I'm just wondering when you three ladies will do some matchmaking on each other," Vito said. He didn't sound particularly surprised about Nonna's interference, either.

"Oh, no!" Nonna looked shocked. "We're having far too much fun to weigh ourselves down with cranky old men."

That made Lacey burst out laughing. "You're incorrigible."

"Well, and it didn't begin with the matchmaking service, either."

"What else?" Vito put on a mock-serious tone. "Tell us everything."

"I…well, I may have arranged for Lacey to take care of me, and my home to be unavailable, when I found out you were coming home, dear." She looked up through her glasses at Vito, her face tender. "You're going to be a wonderful husband, but I was afraid you'd be my age before you figured it out. When I ended up on Lacey's floor at the hospital, and heard about her history, and saw how lovely she'd grown up to be…well, I may have done a little scheming."

"Nonna D'Angelo!" Indignation warred with laughter in Lacey's heart. Laughter won on this glorious day.

"I have a way to make it up to you," Nonna said hastily. "You both know I came into a small inheritance when my cousin Paolo died last year."

Vito nodded, and Lacey just looked at Nonna, wondering where this was going. What would Nonna think of next?

"I've been trying to decide what use to make of it. What can I do, at my age? I have a few plans, but the first one is I want to give you this." She reached into her handbag and pulled out a small, gift wrapped box. She handed it to Lacey. "Open it."

The box was featherlight, and inside, there was nothing but paper. "I think you forgot to put the gift in—"

"Nonna!" Vito had pulled out the papers and was scanning them. "You can't do this!"

"I can, and I've already done it. You're booked for a week at a villa in Tuscany, and then a week in Rome and Venice. You leave tomorrow." She crossed her arms and smiled with satisfaction.

"But…our reservations in South Carolina…"

"Canceled. That was the interfering part." Nonna looked only slightly abashed. "You'll still get a wonderful honeymoon. It's just the destination that'll be different."

Lacey stared at Nonna and then at Vito. "Italy?" she asked faintly. "I've never been out of the country."

"And that's why your brother had to check into whether you had a passport. You do. Some trip to Canada that didn't materialize?" Nonna waved her hand as if the details didn't matter.

Lacey looked at Vito. "Italy."

"Together." A smile spread across his face. "I've never been, either."

"And that's why you need two weeks," Nonna said firmly. "Everything's all arranged. The guesthouse, Charlie, reservations in *Italia*."

Lacey looked up to see Buck, Charlie, Susan and Sam all crowded together, looking at them, coming over to congratulate them on their changed honeymoon schedule and destination. It looked like everyone had been in on the surprise. Even Charlie knew that he and Wolfie would get to spend a little longer at the dog rescue farm with Xavier.

A regular clinking and ringing sound came, the traditional instruction to kiss. Vito pulled Lacey into his arms and kissed her tenderly, then held her against his chest.

"Is this what it's going to be like to be married to you?" he rumbled into her ear. "Surprises and adventures?"

"Enough to keep you on your toes." She laughed up at him as he pulled her closer, and then looked beyond, to the clear blue sky. Vito was amazing, and life with him and Charlie was going to be an adventure.

But she knew deep inside that none of this was a surprise to her heavenly father, who'd orchestrated all of it and would guide them through the rest of their days.

* * * * *

Dear Reader,

Thank you for coming with me on another visit to Rescue River! Lacey has been a part of the Rescue River community from the beginning. Most recently, she was part of Buck and Gina's story, when she reluctantly provided shelter to the struggling single mom. Once everyone else found happiness, it was only fair that Lacey should find love, too…and Vito, the romantic Italian, seemed like just the right man to bring out Lacey's tender side.

Both Vito and Lacey carry scars and baggage from the past. Don't we all? Fortunately, our heavenly father forgives our mistakes and leads us to be new creations in Christ. He can even soften a heart of stone.

Visit my website, *www.leetobinmcclain.com*, and sign up for my newsletter to keep track of all the news from Rescue River.

Wishing you a happy summer filled with many books!

Lee

Get 2 Free Books,
Plus 2 Free Gifts—
just for trying the Reader Service!

Love Inspired®

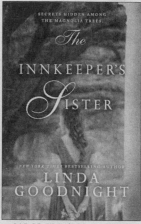